BETWEEN DESPAIR & HOPE

JESS WISECUP

Copyright © 2022 by Jess Wisecup.

All rights reserved. Printed in the United States of America. No part of this book may be used or reproduced in any manner whatsoever without written permission except in the case of brief quotations embodied in critical articles or reviews.

This book is a work of fiction. Names, characters, businesses, organizations, places, events and incidents either are the product of the author's imagination or are used fictitiously. Any resemblance to actual persons, living or dead, events, or locales is entirely coincidental.

For information contact:
hello@jesswisecupbooks.com

Cover design by AMDesignstudios
Internal art by Eternal Geekery
Editing by A.E. Mann Editing
Sensitivity Reading by Ruthie Bowles

First Edition: August 2022

ISBN: 9798846010666

For those who continue to search for their light.
And those who *are* the light.

Also by Jess Wisecup

The Divine Between Series
Between Wrath and Mercy
Between Despair and Hope
Between Book 3 – 2023
Between Book 4 – To Be Determined

AUTHOR'S NOTE

This book took quite a bit out of me to write for a few different reasons. The first being, I had no idea what I was doing with all of this *authoring*, but here I am, doing the thing. The heavier subject matter of this book was also a struggle. If Between Wrath and Mercy was my heart, Between Despair and Hope is my soul. It is important for me to note that there are many different ways to respond to various types of trauma, and it is imperative to understand that all reactions and coping strategies are not universal. In this book, a lot of the experiences are my own. With that said, check the link below to protect your heart.

The Divine Between series should only be read by mature readers (18+) and contains scenes that may make some readers uncomfortable. For a full list, please visit my website.

www.jesswisecupbooks.com

Please remember you are not alone. If you are in the United States and are in distress, prevention and crisis options are available if you dial 988 or 1-800-273-TALK.

PRONUNCIATION GUIDE

Names:
Emmeline Highclere – Em-muh-leen High-clear
Lucia Highclere – Lou-see-uh High-clear
Elora Calvert – El-or-uh Cal-vair
Rainier Vestana – Rain-ier (like "tier") Vest-ah-nuh
Lavenia Vestana – Luh-vin-ee-uh Vest-ah-nuh
Soren Vestana – Sore-in Vest-ah-nuh
Shivani Vestana – Shiv-on-ee Vest-ah-nuh
Dewalt Holata – Duh-walt Hole-ate-uh
Mairin – My-reen
Thyra – Tier-uh
Cyran Umbroth – Sigh-run Um-broth
Nor – Nor (like "ignore")
Vondi – V-on-dee
Ciarden – Kier (like "tier")-den
Aonara – Eye-uh-nar-uh
Rhia – Ree-uh
Hanwen – Han-when

Places:
Vesta – Vest-uh
Mira – Meer-uh
Ardian – Are-dee-un
Ravemont – Rav (like "ravioli")-mont
Olistos – Ol-is-toes

Cinturon Pass – Cent-er-on Pass
Astana – Ah-stahn-uh
Lamera – Luh-meer-uh
Nara's Cove – Nar-uh 's Cove
Folterra – Fol (like "fold")-tair-uh
Mindengar – Min-din-gar
Evenmoor – Ev-un-moor
Nythyr – Nith-ier (like "tier")
Kieża – Key-ay-ż (like the "g" in mirage)-uh
Pelmuzu – Pel-moo-zoo
Seyma's Gulf – Say-muh's Gulf

Creatures:
Onaán – Oh-nah (like the "a" in "cat")-on
Tírrúil – Tier-rue-il
Itzki – Its-key
Itzkim – Its–kim
Irses – Er-seas
Traekka – Tray-kuh
Lux – Lucks
Shika – She-kuh
Ifash – Ee-fash (like "fashion")
Hyše – He-shuh
Ryo – Ree-oh

Phrases:
Tak du – Tok doo
Min viltasma – Meen vil-tas-muh

The Beloved and the Accursed:
two sides of one coin,
Blessed by the gods,
lives forever adjoined.
Both touched by
the light and the dark,
With wrath's caress
and fecundity's mark;
Bloom, blood, and bone
are the ties which bind
The betrayer, body, and bane
to their future descried.
One will wrest peace
from the grips of such blight,
While the other will do
naught but turn from the light;
In each hand, they hold
the death of another
And the fate of the kingdoms
bound by lovers.

CHAPTER 1

Dewalt

In the midst of battle, time flowed differently. It sped up and slowed down as hearts raced and blood soaked the earth. I had always compared it to the space between breath. Quick gasps between a lunge and a defensive block—time moved faster when I didn't have a spare moment to think. It was after the battle, time changed. When blood stopped rushing through my veins, the sound deafening, when all I could hear were moans of the dying and shouts of my remaining men chasing after the adversary, that was when time slowed down. When I could hear the last bloody gurgle of a man's existence. That was when time was cruelest.

Soldiers lay dead on the ground around me, their blood slowly seeping into the earth. The Folterrans were retreating, and it didn't make any gods damned sense. They still outnumbered us—though barely. Rainier was gone, and I hadn't seen Emma since she'd rifted out, trying to find her daughter. An hour ago at most, I felt the ground shake and saw a flash of light, but it wasn't as if I could go explore it. I had hoped my people were alright, but I was busy. Now, though, with all the soldiers dead or pulling back, I had the time.

My divinity was tapped, and the headache behind my eyes was there in force—the bond between Lavenia and me had grown taut, telling me I needed her to share the load. But she was probably elbow deep in gore, and I needed to find someone, *anyone*, who might know why the retreat was called, the horns issuing some sort of message. I picked my way through the corpses as I walked back toward the fortress. Good men—*my* men—lay dead before me, scattered amongst the mercenaries. Mercenaries were the worst type of soldiers, ones without conviction, and I was glad to see them dead. But for my men, Vestian men—some I'd even trained myself—I would return, and Rainier and I would bury them. We'd always done things this way. He would open the earth, creating graves, and then between the two of us, Raj, and Brenna, we would lay our soldiers to rest. Rainier and Raj had made the agreement over a decade ago. We did it to show our soldiers that leadership weighed their lives in high regard. It was how we did things.

I needed to find my people. Rainier, Emma, Raj—I didn't know where they were. I threw a hand up to block the sun as I searched for anyone I knew. I thought I saw Brenna near the fort, her slight frame crouched down close to the ground. Perhaps whispering the sacred words to the gods, sending one of our soldiers on their final journey. She was a captain as I was, and yet she always made the time when one of our soldiers needed guidance. When my boot kicked a body and it moaned, I glanced down to make sure it wasn't one of my own. But then I saw the Folterran soldier—not a mercenary—open his eyes. I crouched beside him while I refastened my hair at my nape.

"Tell me why you're retreating." Unsure if I had enough in me, I didn't bother using my divinity to compel the truth out of the dying man and was surprised when he answered.

"The king is dead."

My breath caught in my throat, hoping he meant his own king. Rainier hadn't been crowned yet. The Folterrans might not even know Soren was dead, so the odds were good he spoke of the Bone King. Even so, I asked, "Dryul is dead?"

The man licked his lips as he wheezed. Because of a wound to his gut, he was bleeding out slowly. I didn't care. "Yes, Dryul is dead. Water?"

Ignoring his request, I stood and left, heading toward the fortress at a quick jog. Maybe I'd find more information there.

Who killed the King of Bones? Was it Rainier? Emma? Where the fuck was everyone?

The mercenaries I had dispatched moments before hadn't realized their brethren were retreating, and I had weaved a vision causing the dozen men to turn on one another, thinking they were Vestian forces. By the time I finished, the battlefield was empty of Folterrans, and my remaining men were handling whatever mercenaries lingered. Now, as I approached the missing gate, I didn't see any living opposing forces. Eventually, I spotted someone who could give me answers.

She stood high above me on the battlement, shoving a severed head onto a spike above the gate. Always one for barbaric theatrics, Thyra. I didn't realize whose head I was looking at until I stood just below them. Stopping and holding one hand above my eyes as I looked up, I squinted at the display. I'd seen him putting on a hell of a fight against some of my better soldiers. She'd killed her fucking father. I felt a grin spread across my face as I called up to her.

"Did you make it long, drawn-out, and painful?"

She looked down at me, a surprising expression of boredom on her face. That wasn't what I expected. She nodded toward the stairwell, and I met her at the base of the steps a moment later. "He wanted warrior death. I made sure not to give it to him. He woke from the queen putting him to sleep like baby, and he died right after, shitting himself. Also like baby." Her smile was tired, but I knew she felt relieved the bastard was dead. I clasped her on the shoulder and nodded, our friendship requiring little in the way of words.

A rift opened nearby, and I spun to face it. I wasn't prepared for what I saw.

Emma was on the ground, wailing and covered in blood. So much blood. And there was a body beside her.

Oh, fuck.

Thyra and I ran, closing the distance as fast as we could to get to her. Cursing myself, I hadn't even realized Emmeline's Second wasn't with her. But I wasn't with Rainier either. Those fools were too similar. I watched in horror as Emma pulled the body—the body of a girl—into her lap, and she screamed, an endless hoarse moan I knew would haunt my dreams. I slowed as I approached, not sure what to do. We needed Rainier. I was uncertain, not knowing if sending an impulse would endanger him, but I did it anyway, doing my best to summon my friend.

"Take her to Mairin. Now!" Her voice was a croak, and I was afraid to question her. She had to know Mairin couldn't do anything more than what she'd done herself. I knelt down next to her and put a hand on her knee, trying to calm her before I took the body from her arms. I couldn't even see what the girl looked like, there was so much blood. "She's not dead, you fuck!" Emma's voice was a shrill cry as she pushed the body toward me, and I cradled it. She was still warm, and I saw the imperceptible rise of her chest.

"Shit!"

I ran.

Soldiers cleared out of my way; two even ran ahead to hold the doors of the keep open. I started shouting for Mairin the moment I crossed the threshold, and she was running toward me by the time I reached the dining hall. Somehow, the woman paled to an even lighter shade as she pointed toward a pallet on the ground. It was filthy, and I tried not to think about why it was abandoned. After I gently lowered the girl—Elora, I reminded myself—I took a step back and looked at her.

It was hard to tell with all the blood, but she looked so much like Lucia. Still, there were minor differences, just enough to set them apart. Her hair was curly, and her skin was the color of warm sand from the northern coast. But the similarities were enough. Though her eyes were closed, I knew they belonged to her mother and aunt. The white hair caused a striking resemblance. With her eyes shut and face slack, barely alive, she looked hauntingly familiar. I backed up, unable to handle the memory colliding with reality. Headed for the door, I paused when Lavenia called out behind me.

"Where's the blood even coming from?" I stopped to watch as the two women assessed her body. The blood was the worst under her neck, and I could see the slightest line starting below her ear. "Divine hell, her throat was slit! Emma must've healed it."

I spun and strode off toward the courtyard. If Emma had healed an injury like that, gods, her own daughter's throat, she would have been depleted, especially if she'd had to fight off Dryul too. As I came out into the courtyard, I saw Thyra through the rift, half-dragging, half-supporting Raj, while Emma kept it open. By the time I got there, the captain had collapsed on the ground next to Emma. When she didn't make any move to assess him, still holding the rift open, I looked at her in confusion.

"Dryul and Cyran's bodies are out there. Probably outside the thorns, I don't know. Bring them to me," she said, hollow and without emotion. Her eyes were bloodshot, thin lines of red filling the whites, and her face was wan. I hurried through, knowing she couldn't have much divinity left.

When I had glanced through the rift before, I hadn't understood what I saw. But now, on the other side of it, I realized she had somehow built an orb around her and Elora. Thorny branches rose from the ground, tall, before they curved inward. I'd never seen anything like it. I picked the spot that looked thinnest and started hacking away with my sword, Thyra joining me with her ax. We didn't speak as we worked, and my mind went to Rainier. Where was he? Had Emma faced Dryul alone? Did that mean Rainier was with Declan? If that little shit was dead—I couldn't bear the thought of it. My best friend was many things, but he wasn't weak. If his divinity was tapped though—I wouldn't let myself think about the possibility.

Finally, Thyra and I burst through the thorns, working our way around the orb in opposite directions. I hadn't gone more than ten paces when I heard a quiet moaning. I saw nothing until I turned inward, towards the branches thrusting up from the ground. There, amongst the thorns, lay Cyran. Alive.

"Shit, Thyra! Help!" I went to work cutting him free. He had a branch thrust through his shoulder and another through his leg. It took us a long time, and a surprising amount of stoicism from Cyran, before we could get him out. I was relieved he'd survived whatever they had faced from Dryul. I knew Emma suspected the prince held love for her daughter, and as long as Mairin found a way to help Elora, both children were safe and whole. Thyra had found the Bone King—properly dead—so when I finally cut Cyran free, I hoisted him into my arms as Thyra dragged the king's body.

It was when I was walking back through the rift that Emma surprised me more than anything.

"No, don't bring him a step closer. Cut his head off, and bring it to me."

The little prince was in a cell—only alive because Mairin convinced Emma to keep him for questioning and torture, unknowingly volunteering me for the job. I was fine with it though; he deserved it well enough. Mairin and Ven had cleaned Elora of blood, carefully replacing her clothing with something Raj's daughter supplied. I avoided looking at her for too long, her position and slack expression unsettling. Emma hadn't left the girl's side as she slept.

To make matters worse, none of our scouts found any information about Rainier. A whole day had passed without a single whisper. I knew something was very wrong, but I held out hope. We would know if Declan had killed him—he wouldn't have been able to keep quiet about it. And Emma hadn't felt the crippling pain which occurred after a bond was broken by death, but instead, she couldn't feel him on the other end of it. She still had access to his gifts, could feel the bond itself, just not him. I had the distinct notion he'd been captured, but I couldn't bring myself to discuss it with her. Not yet.

I was keeping myself busy, making right the ruined fort so many called home, when Shivani arrived—a shock, considering she would have needed to find someone who could rift her ass this far, and they'd have to be familiar with the rift points. Thoughts of her travel here left me as she thundered toward the fortress itself, moving past me through the courtyard, a look on her face which spoke of destruction.

Shit.

I followed behind her as she slammed into the dining hall, full of the wounded and dying, screeching about Rainier. Raj handled her, fully healed thanks to Emma, and pulled her off to his quarters within the fortress. I figured I should let Emma know sooner rather than later what hell we were about to contend with and made my way to the set of private quarters where we'd settled her and her daughter. Mairin and Lavenia were already there when I arrived. Elora was in the bed, still sleeping, Emma's body curled around her. She rolled over, blue depths still bloodshot, and I could tell she hadn't had a single moment of sleep. Mairin and Lavenia sat on a sofa together, the merrow leaning against Ven's shoulder and snoring softly. She'd barely gotten any rest either.

I spoke quietly, not eager to upset anyone more than I had to. "Shivani is here, and she is out for blood."

Emma slowly lifted her head, careful not to disturb the daughter she lay with. "I think I know what it's about. Wake up Mairin. She should hear this too." Emma pulled herself up, moving to the edge of the bed, arms braced on either side of her, shoulders high. She looked small and exhausted. Frail and without emotion. It was abnormal for her, and, while I knew the circumstances were also abnormal, it was worrisome. When Mairin leaned forward, rubbing her face as she woke, Emma began.

"Before the battle yesterday, Rain sent a message to his mother. In case—" She took a deep, shaky breath, and I saw her hands clench in the sheets. "In the event of Rain's death, he wanted his mother to know his proper heir." Mairin and I both glanced at Lavenia before looking back to Emma, who remained expressionless. "Elora is Rain's daughter. By blood."

I heard Ven gasp as my eyes shot to the small form in the bed. It would explain the complexion and curly hair, and she was around the right age. But that would have meant Rainier had a daughter and didn't know it.

"Did you keep her from him?" The accusation left my mouth before I could stop it.

"Dewalt, I will say this only once. I did not know. I am goddess-blessed, and Elora was Rhia's gift to me. Her conception was unlikely, and yet it happened all the same. We planned to tell you three once we told Elora, but—" She gestured to her daughter and hung her head. I'd never seen her look more defeated.

"You're sure, Emma?" Quiet, Lavenia's voice was soft—kind. She sounded hopeful.

Emma's head dipped. "Yes, I'm sure. That was why Faxon sold her—to punish me." She paused and looked at the girl on the bed, her eyes soft. "She has Rain's smile." Emma gave us a small one of her own before exhaling harshly. "I suppose Shivani is here to, I don't know, call me a whore, probably. And I just cannot—"

The door burst open, and the bitch in question stood on the threshold.

"There you are." Her hawkish gaze rested on Emma, who barely lifted her chin in response. The woman was broken. "Explain. Explain why Rainier is not here, and explain this foolishness about your daughter being his blood."

Emma took a deep breath, but I cut her off.

"Rainier rifted away with Prince Declan—well, I suppose King Declan, now—and we haven't seen him since. Our scouts have found nothing. Your guess is as good as ours. And as for Elora being his blood, well, Shivani, when two people love each other, sometimes—"

Emma cut me off at the sight of the queen mother's face. Probably a good idea.

"Shivani, I am the Beloved, not Elora. I am blessed by all four of the gods. Rhia, as her blessing, saw to it I had a child. Elora is his, surely as she is mine."

"What do you mean 'saw to it'?" The sneer she wore was so much like the ones she reserved for me. It was strange to see her look upon someone else with the same disdain.

"Do you really want the details, Mama?" Lavenia's attempt at deterring Shivani was sound, but the woman was not one to shy away. She turned towards Emma, squaring her shoulders, and raised a single brow. Emma sighed, but didn't back down either.

"We had sex the night Lucia died, and Elora was born nine months later."

"And you conveniently didn't tell him about her until now? Until it suited you because you needed his help?" Shivani's stare darted toward Lavenia first, and then, to my surprise, her eyes met mine. "You don't seriously believe her, do you? Why keep this a secret for so long?" Hostile tension filled the room, and when Emma didn't bite back, merely shaking her head, I further realized just how bad-off my friend was. I felt a bit selfish, realizing I'd been hoping for Emma to tear Shivani apart. She would have deserved it.

"I didn't tell him because I didn't know. I didn't think it was possible for her to be his." Emma looked down at her hands.

"Why wouldn't you think it was possible?" Shivani's eyes narrowed. "We're all adults here. Explain. If he didn't finish, then the girl isn't his." Straight to the point, Shivani crossed her arms as she glowered down at Emma. The queen mother dominated the room, and I remembered she was who Rainier learned it from. I wasn't sure if I should intervene, but Lavenia caught my eye and shook her head—so I maintained my silence. Emma heaved a sigh as she slid over on the bed, turning toward her daughter and brushing her hair off her face. I averted my eyes. I still wasn't used to it.

"He didn't finish, no, but Rhia does as Rhia wants. She was born on the Spring Equinox. Would you like to—"

"But you married right after your sister died, did you not? The babe would be his, especially if—"

I saw fire in Emma's eyes then as her head snapped toward Shivani. "She is not Faxon's child, which is the very reason he sold her to Declan. I will allow you one more question before I ask you to leave, because I am exhausted, and I've been through hell, Shivani."

"Oh, I have no more questions, but if you think you can just set up your child as heir to the throne, and then—"

"That's enough, Shivani. You need to go," I muttered and grabbed her by the arm, tugging her toward the door. Since she wasn't the queen anymore, it wasn't as if she could punish me too severely. The queen mother looked down at my hand on her bicep in outrage, planting her feet. Emma stared at the floor, broken and dejected, so I didn't hesitate. Rainier wouldn't let his mother speak to his wife this way. "*Go back to the palace and stay there.*" I had never compelled royalty before. I wasn't even sure I was strong enough to do it to Shivani. But when she turned to the door and Mairin let out a snort, we all exhaled a breath and watched her go.

CHAPTER 2

Emmeline

Three Weeks Later

As I slammed my fist down on the table, I noticed the blood on my knuckles with vague displeasure, uncertain if it belonged to me or not. I was about to wipe it away when I saw Shivani's gaze land on my hand, and I watched her mouth tighten.

Let her see it.

Let her see what her inaction had wrought.

I stared at her, making every bit of my disgust visible, before turning toward the rest of the council. "What more do you want from me? Declan has him at Darkhold. Soldiers saw your king push Declan through the rift. At what point will you act? I am but one person, how am—"

"One person who claims to be the Beloved," the councilor, Lord Kress, sneered. I saw Dewalt lean forward in his seat out of the corner of my eye.

"I make no such claim."

"The soldiers from the battle—"

"*The soldiers from the battle* saw your king disappear through a rift with Declan. Focus on that," I retorted.

"The manner of his disappearance is strange. Declan has not uttered a word or made a demand since Dryul died. It is not in—"

"Since *your queen* rid us of Dryul." Dewalt's chair made a loud screeching sound as he shot out of it. "You should be thanking her," he growled. I gave him a tempering glance. We were both on the verge of unhelpful aggression, and I felt the dark tingle of shadows at my fingertips. Shivani had been suspicious about what happened to Rain, all but accusing me of attempting to put Elora on the throne. It was clear she was hesitant to believe my version of events. Though, I found it interesting she hadn't been so bold as to say those things in front of the council. Perhaps she knew in the back of her mind I spoke the truth. Or, more likely, she feared Rain's reaction to her treatment when he returned.

"Emmeline, we are gathering information," Shivani said. "Our spies have not caught sight of him in Darkhold. The general does not want to make a move until we know for sure he's there. It is unlike Declan not to flaunt."

"It has been three weeks. If Declan doesn't have him in Darkhold, it shouldn't stop us from sending a message. Give me a thousand men. That's it. Please." It was the closest I'd come to begging. I couldn't do this alone. I was powerful, but I needed more than that. Pride and power wouldn't save Rain. I wasn't sure a thousand men would be enough, but I'd make it work to get him back.

"And if he doesn't have him in Darkhold and we start a war, then what? He could be anywhere—from Evenmoor to the countless other strongholds in Folterra. We attack the capital, and they slit his throat in Glenharbor." Her face was tight, voice clipped. "We have to know his location."

"I brought you the hands of the man who helped Declan carry him to his ship. I brought you the eyes of the soldier who tied him up. Both men claimed the ship was headed to Darkhold. Why would Declan leave them behind if not to give proof he'd taken Rainier? Short of us laying siege and seeing him in person, what else is there? Give me the men."

"For now, this kingdom and how it chooses to react is entrusted to me. I am deferring to General Ashmont, and until our spies see my son or hear word, we will wait. Rainier would want me to ensure bringing war to Vesta was the last possible resort."

Lavenia reached up from her seat next to me and grabbed my hand as it started twitching.

"Does the rest of the council defer to Ashmont?" Dewalt looked around the room, and I watched as almost every set of eyes averted to the ground.

Cowards.

"Cowards," Dewalt murmured under his breath. I was reminded of how grateful I was for my friends. Dewalt and the others had been with me every step of this. I squeezed Lavenia's hand as I watched my friend slam back into his seat, defeated. The councilor on his other side stared at him, almost scared. I had to admit, he looked rather fearsome. Once we returned to the palace, he and Thyra had shaved the sides of their heads. Dewalt had long held the beliefs of the old gods in high regard, but Thyra had seen his interest once they freed her and took it upon herself to help foster the beliefs she'd been raised with. So, when they shaved the sides of their heads, it sent a message to those familiar with the practice.

War.

It was clear this wasn't the first time they'd done it after their tattoos were exposed. They both kept their hair pulled back, putting the illustrations on full display. On one side of his head, Dewalt had a wyvern ingesting its own tail, and the other held a design with words in a language I couldn't read. I hadn't yet asked him what they meant. Thyra had twin wolves on either side, both with heads tilted back in a howl. I had found myself staring at them on more than one occasion, letting my mind focus on the intricacies of the ink rather than anger and fear which consumed me.

Thyra had noticed my gaze one night. I'd been lying in bed with Elora while my Second sat by the fire, keeping me company. Keeping guard—of me. Making sure I didn't try once again to leave for Darkhold by myself. It was difficult to be grateful for someone while resenting them. She'd stopped me on more than one occasion from leaving. In that moment, she'd moved to sit beside me on the bed, quietly telling me about the Mother and her wolves, a story about the old gods I'd never heard before. Elora had smiled in her sleep for the first time as the woman told the tale, and Thyra embraced me in a hug so fierce, I knew she had accepted Elora as part of her little handmade family just as quickly as she'd accepted me. Thyra had been watchful since Rain had been captured, taking my protection as seriously as he would want her to. Dewalt had been just as attentive, if not more so. He tried to get me out of my head but hadn't been successful.

The door to the council chambers slammed open, drawing me out of my thoughts, and a servant walked in with a small package. He paused, waiting for Shivani to wave him over before he set it down on the table in front of her. He murmured something, gave a quick bow, and left.

"It seems we have a letter from Declan."

I caught my breath for a second before I ran straight to Shivani. I expected her to pull the letter out of my line of sight, but instead, I noted her swallow as she held it between us, allowing me to read what she'd already started.

Declan held Rain in Darkhold, and he was alive.

The price of his ransom? Me.

Taking one last look at my sleeping daughter, sadly convinced she wouldn't wake, I put on Rain's robe and slipped out onto the balcony. The faint smell of his soap lingered on my skin, the only comfort I could give myself. Barefoot, I stepped onto the grass I had grown over the past few weeks. It was sparse in most places, bare in others, but I was proud of what I'd done. Rain had moved the earth and set gardeners to cultivate and transplant all the vegetation, creating a perfect garden in the middle of a third story balcony. In one of my frenzied states, I'd requested a gardener to seed it. And then, using my divinity like I had with the branches on the field, I coaxed the seeds to take root. I assumed it was part of Rain's earth manipulation, something he hadn't shown me or perhaps wasn't very good at. I struggled to move the dirt itself, so maybe we each had our specialty.

It was well after midnight, the stars doing little to illuminate my surroundings as the new moon approached once again. It had been nearly a month since I got Elora back and lost Rain. With him gone, I felt adrift. It was strikingly similar to how I felt after Lucia died. I didn't have either of the two people I cared about most. Not in the way I needed. Sometimes, the pain was almost too much to bear.

I walked the length of a path between lilac bushes, eyeing the wisteria crossing the trellis above me. Only branches were left of the plant, the gardener having pruned and trimmed it for the winter. It felt appropriate the garden Rain had created for us in beautiful moments of hope was frozen, dead for now. When I finally approached the railing, I spread my hands out over it and exhaled, watching the steam from my breath dissipate in the crisp air. I didn't mind the cold; it helped me think. And since I was wide awake and thinking was all I'd likely do until dawn, I wanted the brisk clarity the winter air brought me. In the morning, I would meet with the council once again, and I knew what I needed to do. Since I had not been crowned as queen, I had little say in anything. But the moment I saw the message, I knew what had to be done. Vesta needed him. Elora deserved him.

I'd make the trade.

Dewalt had crowded me after the meeting, probably suspecting what I was thinking. He claimed I would have followers between Rain's personal guard and the soldiers under Raj's control at the Cascade. But why risk them? Not now, not after Declan's letter. During the attack on the Cascade, Raj and Dewalt's men suffered losses I didn't want to think about. They were as fractured as I was. I'd helped Dewalt bury every single one of their soldiers, taking on the role Rain usually held. It was a struggle, learning how to move the earth while mourning their loss. No one had commented on my sloppy efforts, for which I was grateful. What men remained at the Cascade worked to remove the mercenaries and soldiers left behind in Clearhill, pushing them out so they could rebuild. Those men were already spread thin, and it was clear Ashmont had no intentions of attacking Darkhold. What options did I have? Ignore Declan's demands and let them kill Rain? No. Vesta needed Rain more than it needed me. Lavenia had been helping Shivani keep things running properly, but Vesta would suffer without him.

I'd had those few sweet days with him, and they'd have to be enough.

The gods had brought Rain and me together again, ignoring his prayers to forget me and planting me in front of him instead. And they were nothing if not cruel to tear us apart so quickly. I shuddered when I remembered Ciarden and the way the God of Dark had appeared to me, blessing me. The sharp glint from his elongated teeth. The menacing smile. He appeared gleeful as he waited for the destruction I brought down because of Elora's death.

Gods, she had died that day. In the truest sense of the word, she died. Her heart had stopped, and blood had spilled from her body. Afterwards, I remembered Faxon's addled words and cursed him once more. You will be covered in her blood, and it will stink of your curse. I wasn't sure if Faxon even knew what he'd been saying. Every time his voice broke through my thoughts, I wondered if he knew and hated him for it anew.

There had been so much blood.

When the prince slit her throat, he did it deep. There was no mistaking his intentions. Mairin had convinced me to spare him, claiming his aura knew no evil. Too exhausted to continue arguing with her, I had allowed it, permitting Dewalt to question him with force only until Rain returned. Until Elora woke or Rain came back, the prince could rot in the dungeon. Dewalt wanted me to accompany him, to read Cyran's heart while he questioned him to help break the verit oath he was working against, to see what questions might lead him in the right direction. I couldn't. I would beat the boy to the point of death and heal him, over and over. I knew my limits, and I would be cruel if given the opportunity.

But no merrow stood between me and the men who hurt Rain, I showed no mercy, and they had information I wanted.

Feeling the itch of Ciarden's blessing beneath my skin made me fearful of what I would do to the boy. I didn't think I should give into the temptation—the vile dark power coiling deep in my stomach. Ciarden had never been portrayed as evil, and, in fact, was the patron god of many good things. He was the caretaker of sleep, of dreams, of storms which made our lands flourish. He was the hunt and passion—often attributed as the god of pleasure and desire. None of these things were evil, and yet what I felt within me reeked of it.

Ciarden clearly wasn't a conduit or a human, and it unsettled me to think about every time I imagined him. The fangs protruding from the corners of a wicked smile were especially unsettling. I would have thought he was elvish because of the teeth, but couldn't remember if the tips of his ears were pointed. He had eyes the color of frost; I saw them too often in my dreams and nightmares alike. Dryul haunted me too—his body on top of mine, fingers scratching at my throat. The moment I'd told Cyran to take her, and he'd split her skin instead, a curtain of blood raining down. In that instant, I had felt the world stop. And then just behind them, Ciarden—the moonlit skin and dark hair and the way he licked his lips when he watched me. The way his shadows became mine and touched me, ensnared me, their caress a wicked pleasure.

And then I killed Dryul, and something else overcame me. Something predatory and vicious. Something which wasn't quite me. Maybe it was the divine light meshing with the golden part of my soul. But it took over, and I couldn't remember anything after that. Not until I woke with Elora in my lap, her wound healed and her heart beating again. I barely had enough divinity left to form the rift, let alone hold it open as I had for Thyra and Dewalt.

I made my way back inside, pulling Rain's robe closer to me. I was careful when I opened the door, wanting the bedroom to stay warm and comfortable for Elora. Though, part of me wondered if a shock to her system would do her good. If dumping ice water on her would wake her, I'd do it with no remorse. I'd wake her and take my time telling her how much I loved her, saying my goodbyes. To say it while she slept was painful.

She had been dead, and I brought her back. But was this living?

The next morning, everyone gathered in the council room, and all hell broke loose. It had been an hour of arguments and bickering which grated my nerves. Shivani and I sat on opposite ends of the table, the only silent people in the room. I had tuned out the individual voices of the council, only staring at the shell sitting on the table in front of me, a low buzz of sound registering in my ears. Declan had sent it, claiming it had been in Rain's pocket. The shell was tiny, no larger than a coin, with white and red coloration on its scalloped edges. I wondered how long he had carried it, waiting to give it to me. The shell was proof he had Rain, and Shivani had eyed me cautiously when she handed it over, waiting for me to confirm the truth. I didn't have to say it because she saw it in my eyes. Gods, it hurt. In his letter, Declan spoke of sending us bloodier gifts if we hesitated. The thought of Rain being hurt pushed me to speak. I'd decided the moment I read the letter, and I'd allowed them to debate for too long already.

"I'll go."

Dewalt was the only one who heard me, his mouth clamping shut mid-argument, and he whipped around to face me, eyes ablaze. "Shut up, Emma. Shut the fuck up."

I ignored him, standing up and speaking louder. "I'll go. Maybe I can kill him, but if I can't, you'll have your king. I will go."

The council members quieted. Shivani's gaze remained on the table in front of her, hands clasped in her lap as they had been for the last hour.

"Your Majesty, that is unwise. Perhaps Folterra does not know we have one of their princes in our dungeon. We can try to negotiate." Sad and placating, Lord Durand's argument was weak, and I didn't want to hear it. He'd been one of the few councilors who gave vocal support to me, however limited it might've been.

"Durand, I appreciate it, but is it not more unwise to let Declan send back pieces of your king? I will not allow it." Voices rang out around the room as I sat down. Arrangements were already in place with Thyra to ensure Elora would be well-cared for. I still needed to write a letter, to put in words what my heart ached to say. Was there a simple way to explain I was sorry, that Rain was her father, that I had tried, and I loved her? Gods, how I loved her. I would have gone through this hell over again for her. I was grateful for the time I'd had with Rain, but it was time for me to take care of Vesta. And Vesta needed its king. I barely noticed when Dewalt knelt beside me.

"Emmeline, what the hell are you thinking? If you go to Declan, he'll kill you which is as good as killing you both." He had his hands on my knees, turning my body toward him, forcing me to look at him. He and Thyra had been the only two to really look at me these past weeks. While Thyra was there, providing comfort in her presence, Dewalt was the one who saw my grief and anger, who understood and was unafraid. I had barely spoken to anyone outside of these council meetings and for good reason. What was there to say?

"Dewalt, if I don't do it, he'll kill him. Which is also as good as killing us both. The difference in my plan is that one of us will survive, and Vesta needs Rain, not me."

"What about Elora?"

"What about her?"

"He wouldn't want you to leave her. He did what he did specifically to protect you. Elora is his heir, and—"

"Do you think Shivani will legitimize her without Rain? She hasn't even woken up yet, Dewalt. It's me. You and I both know it has to be me. I have to go."

My friend shook his head, and his braid slipped over his shoulder. "Emma, we will figure something out. You both are such self-sacrificing fucks. Gods, this is the twin flame thing, isn't it? You're both doomed to the same sort of stupidity." He shook his head. "I'm not letting you do this, even if I have to throw you in the dungeon myself." He must have been speaking louder than I realized, because Shivani's voice rose over the din.

"While I hope the dungeon won't be necessary, the duke is right, Emmeline. You're not going. We will attempt to negotiate, let them know we have Prince Cyran. Based on what you told me of Dryul's death, they likely assumed Cyran was also dead. Let us correct their notion and see what comes from it."

I bristled. The one time she seemed to be considerate of me, she was still against me. I palmed the shell, rubbing my thumb across the grooves, frustration coursing through my veins. Declan demanded my presence in Folterra by the full moon, a little over three weeks away. I wouldn't let him kill Rain, but I supposed it wouldn't hurt to attempt negotiations.

"I will go if you can't come up with a better solution, but I'm only going to give you a week to find it."

To my shock, Shivani nodded. I tilted my chin down in respect and did my best not to run from the room—hoping to keep my rising nausea at bay. I felt Dewalt following behind me, and for the first time in three weeks, I decided I would listen to him. There was a certain little princeling I desired to speak to.

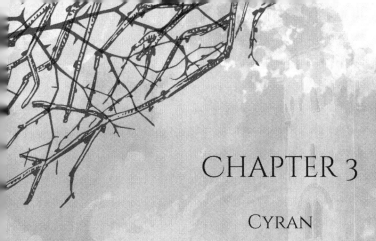

CHAPTER 3

CYRAN

"Thank you, truly. I appreciate it." I held the cloth to my ear and pulled it away to find more blood. The wound kept opening up in my sleep, and it was quite a nuisance. The long-haired bastard had ripped out my earring weeks ago, and it still hadn't healed. It was one of the first things he did when he brought me to the dungeon in Astana. The captain, Dewalt was his name, placed me in a cell and told me it had special meaning to the queen. After he put me in the obsidian chains, I may have mouthed off to him, and he definitely ripped my earring straight out in response. To be fair, I probably deserved it. I had killed Elora, and I deserved every bad thing which had happened to me since.

But now, I knew that wasn't exactly true, was it? I'd killed her, but she wasn't dead—or so I'd heard. The guard who brought me a cloth for my ear was rather talkative if I was kind to him. His name was Oak, and he towered over me—an apt name. I thought he was lonely, and as fate would have it, so was I. So what if a polite word or two got him talking? Was it manipulative? Maybe. Did that stop me? Not at all.

Emmeline had brought Elora back to life. Or something like it, at least. When he told me, I had to send him away. I wouldn't let him witness my vulnerability. I'd never felt so relieved in all my life. A weight had lifted from me, and I didn't even care that I was still in the bloody dungeon. If my worst inconvenience was my earlobe wanting to open and bleed, I didn't care. I hadn't killed her. If I was stuck here for the rest of my life, at least I knew her light hadn't gone out because of me. But Oak knew nothing else.

Why hadn't she come to me? To yell at me? To call me an imbecile? To tell me how she loathed me?

As always, I asked Oak, "Still no sight of the queen's daughter?"

And as always, he said, "No, Cyran."

Though my first thought upon finding out she was alive was relief, fear chased it. Did that mean I failed? I saw my father die, but still. Was all of it for nothing?

Declan still lived. I saw Emmeline gain control of the shadows. Had I done what I was supposed to? Had it worked?

I had to hope what I did was worth it because the toll on my mind was heavy. I shouldn't have cared as much as I did. Obviously, I didn't want to kill Elora. She had been my friend, so of course I was relieved when I found out I hadn't been successful. But why did I care about the girl so much? She was funny and wild, kind and undeniably beautiful, but why did I continue asking about her every day? Why did I dream about her? I had enjoyed her company during the month she was in my care, and I'd felt a bit lost when Declan took her from me. But that was only because I knew then what he might do to her since she wasn't the Beloved. He didn't need her anymore. No one deserved his anger, but even less did anyone deserve his indifference.

Was it pity which drew me to her? The father she knew was a worm, and mine, well, I had experience with terrible fathers. But after Mother died, I was raised by tutors and Magdalena in a gods damn palace. It's not as if we had anything in common. Her father had been adequate until he wasn't. Mine had pawned me off on Declan. My brother wasn't exactly a nurturing father; he beat me regularly when I was younger, especially once Ismene came to stay with us. Every time she earned a beating, I took it, so I was getting them almost every day for a while. When I finally left Darkhold, I made Evenmoor my sanctuary. And I wondered if it helped heal Elora as it had me. She was just learning that her parents were imperfect. Emmeline seemed reasonable and intelligent, and yet she'd failed her daughter by keeping secrets from her. Not to even mention Faxon's betrayal.

I smiled, remembering the day she arrived at Evenmoor. Faxon, the piece of waste, was already in the city, drinking, and they had brought Elora into her chambers cuffed in obsidian and full of rage. Rage which, I learned later, had led her to bite off a mercenary's ear; I had to compensate him more for the inconvenience. I didn't make her stay in the dungeon, knowing she was to eventually be married to my brother—the poor thing—so her chambers were comfortable. There was a small bookcase with an assortment of novels to soothe her inevitable boredom, a soft bed, a few beautiful gowns to choose from, all things I'd thought to include in her chambers. Ismene had helped me, hating as I did what we had to do for Declan. I thought I was being rather benevolent, and yet when I walked in, Elora chucked the thickest tome she could find straight at my head. I wasn't as adept with the shadows as Declan, but I had some control. With short notice, I could only send out a tiny wisp to protect my forehead; the book merely fell to the ground without making contact.

"Let me go, you bastard!" She had a mouth on her, and she rushed toward me, proving she had courage to go along with it. I'd easily grabbed her and backed her up against the bed, forcing her to sit. And then I introduced myself. When she kicked me in the balls, I vowed to never underestimate her again.

While I could have been around her significantly less than I was, I felt this pull toward her, and I didn't understand it. Even now, I felt it. Felt *her*, my wild one. I knew she was somewhere in the palace, and I wanted to find her. I wanted to explain everything to her. Not that it excused it, not at all. Especially when I thought...but I had to. I had to do it. I had to pay the price. But now, the longer I had to think about it, I knew if I was given the choice once more, I wouldn't have paid it. No, if I could go back, I wouldn't have done what I did.

"Afternoon, shit stain. Did you miss me?"

I groaned when I heard the captain's voice and didn't stop as the flickering light from the hallway illuminated his tall silhouette in the doorway of my cell. He'd been to visit just yesterday, and I had hoped to avoid two days of his mental torture in a row. But when I had felt the harsh pain radiating up my elbow from one of his impulses, I knew the odds were not in my favor.

"We have a guest with us today. Hurry." He stepped back out into the hall and waited as I pulled myself off the pallet. The obsidian chains were long and didn't hold my wrists too tightly. If I was a better fighter, I might have made a move. I could have jumped at the man and pulled the chains around his neck and killed him. Or at least tried to. But I barely knew how to use a sword. To be fair, it made me feel decent about myself, knowing it scared Declan to let me learn too much, afraid I would attempt to overthrow him one day. The thought wasn't so amusing now though, considering the odds were even lower than before. I didn't think many kings were overthrown from the dungeon of an enemy kingdom. Shuddering, I remembered Declan was King of Folterra. I wondered how Ismene was doing. Was she still in Evenmoor or had he moved her to Darkhold?

I followed the captain out of my cell, eager for the marginally fresher air outside it. "Someone wants to see me? I'm flattered." Sometimes I wondered what possessed me to say the things I did. The captain had proven he didn't have any qualms with injuring me, though he balked when he saw the bruises across my back. Funny, he couldn't appreciate my brother's handiwork.

"'Want' isn't quite the word, little boy. I'd watch your tongue if I were you. She's not in the best of moods today." She. My damn heart leapt at the idea Elora might be the one who wanted to see me. I just wanted to see the glare on her face, to replace the memory of the shocked horror she wore as the light faded from her eyes. The image haunted me, and I wanted nothing more than to rid myself of it. Even if the expression was full of loathing and hatred, it was better than what I had. Besides, I was used to hatred and loathing. It was something I could handle.

I followed the captain up the stairs into the upper level of cells. They were bigger and lighter—less rancid, too. I wondered if one day I might get transferred to them, if I behaved. Dewalt always took me to these cells to question me. He preferred the one at the end of the hall because, rather than bars, it had a door; he didn't like an audience. Sure enough, I saw the door was open, light from the barred window shining bright. My heart began a steady gallop, hoping it was Elora who waited for me. Elora, who would smack me the minute I walked in.

At first, I didn't notice her, pushed back into the corner of the room like she was. Her arms were crossed with her hands tucked firmly into her armpits, as if she was fighting against herself to keep them off me. The sinking sensation of disappointment filled me when I realized it wasn't Elora.

I'd never seen Emmeline look so small. The ferocity she held for her daughter had always made her seem so much more. She was the daughter of a minor lord, and yet she had looked at me, a prince, with a countenance dripping of derision so potent, I thought it might kill her. When she'd accused me of sending mercenaries to rape her, when she stood in front of me in nothing but a man's shirt—that woman could have killed me without a second thought. But the woman I saw now? The only word which came to mind was broken. She didn't look like a woman who had brought her daughter back from death. My stomach felt rock hard, and I froze, rooted to the spot. Had Oak been wrong? Was Elora actually dead?

She didn't even look at me as Dewalt chained me to the bracket in the center of the floor. I was on my knees, my hands between my legs and attached to the bracket. Emmeline actually turned away from me at one point, staring pointedly at the barred window.

"You know what I'm going to ask you, right?" Dewalt's voice was kinder than normal. If I didn't know any better, I would have thought he felt bad for me. He had been asking me the same question for weeks, and I didn't know what he'd hoped to get out of it. But maybe it would go somewhere this time. Maybe the oath would let me speak.

"I do. Perhaps I can answer now." I nodded toward Emmeline in the corner, hopeful.

"*Why did you slit Elora's throat?*" I felt his compulsion and my words warring with the oath I'd sworn. My throat was working, swallowing, and I tried so hard to get out what I needed to say. I wanted to tell them. I *needed* to tell them. But I'd sworn a verit oath, and that power was stronger. Nourished by the same earth magick those with elvish blood drew from, it mixed with my own divinity, making it nearly impossible to break. I felt closer to success this time though, with Emmeline here. I wanted to tell her, to help her understand why I did it. To explain why Elora was the price I had to pay.

"Seer." The word slipped out past my gritted teeth. Dewalt's face matched my own, eyebrows high and shock written across it. My throat promptly closed when I said it, and I couldn't breathe. This happened every time I fought the verit oath, and Dewalt noticed it, giving the quiet order releasing me from his compulsion. I was gasping for breath as they spoke to one another.

"That's the most I've ever been able to get from him," he said to Emmeline as she took a step forward. She unfolded her arms and put one hand over the other. It took me a moment to realize she was healing busted knuckles.

"And he says it's because of the verit oath?"

"Yes. He can answer some questions about the oath, but not enough. He says if certain conditions are fulfilled, he can speak, but it won't let him tell me what those conditions are. See why I wanted your help?" She nodded, taking a few steps toward me. When she got close, I could see the dark circles under her eyes—she hadn't been sleeping. When I finally caught my breath, I decided to ask what Dewalt wouldn't answer.

"Is Elora alive?" I asked, voice ruined.

"She is not dead." Her eyes narrowed on me, and I remembered her abilities as a harrower. She didn't have a weapon on her; she *was* the weapon. Thank the gods Ismene's ability never went as far as stopping hearts. But perhaps it could, with Emmeline to teach her.

"She is alright?"

"No. She is not. Answer the gods damn question. Why did you do it?"

"What do you mean? Is she—weren't you able to heal her?"

The sharp crack of her palm against my cheek took me by surprise, and I fell backwards onto the ground. Shadows danced around her hands, dangerous. I'd seen it before with my brother. His shadows always made an appearance every time he punished me. I closed my eyes, pushing the memories away.

"Why did you do what you did?" Voice quiet and precise, she took a step back, and I watched her shadows disappear, a pained look on her face as she wrested control of them.

When it was her asking, rather than the captain, I didn't feel the verit oath clamp down.

Finally.

"A seer foretold it. I had to." Emmeline and the captain exchanged a glance. "I swore a verit oath that I could only tell you after—afterwards. Because otherwise you'd stop me." Gods, I wished she had stopped me.

"Well, out with it, princeling." Her jaw jutted out, and it reminded me so much of Elora.

"I was in the village outside Evenmoor, hunting down Faxon to bring him back to the estate. Declan didn't want me to harm the man, but I'd had enough. He was drinking himself stupid on my credit, and I already disliked him. I didn't know the details about the transaction, just that he'd sold Elora, and she called him Papa. I didn't know about..." Emmeline inclined her head, wanting me to press forward. "An elfling stopped me in the street. She was only a child—twelve at most. She begged me to follow her, that her mother needed help."

"You, a prince of Folterra, followed a little elvish girl on the street because she wanted you to?" the captain asked. He sounded dubious, and, truly, I didn't blame him.

"The gods only know why, because I don't. Maybe it was her magick. The elf-blood was strong; her teeth were sharp, and her ears were quite pointy." I paused, taking a breath. I was rambling. "Anyway, her mother was a seer, not a drop of elf-blood I could see, and I would've left if she hadn't told me the name of my mother's cat. But she made me swear a bloody verit oath before she showed me anything. The little girl and I exchanged the words, forged the oath. I swore to only tell you—after. After I did what I did. I tried to tell Elora. I tried to tell her but the oath wouldn't let me—shit, that's not important." I rubbed my face. "The seer showed a vision of war at my brother's hand, of cities burned to ash. Dead children, dead animals, everyone dead. Everything was dark, and the sun hid behind shadows. And then the vision changed—everything was fine again. Cities flourished, people were happy and healthy, night wasn't a depthless impenetrable hell. And Elora's death was the only thing that could stop it. The seer showed me exactly what would happen that day with you and my father, and how it had to happen. Elora's death was the only thing which could prevent the endless night."

Emmeline was motionless as she stared at me. The captain gripped her elbow after a few moments when her shoulders rolled forward, her posture slackening.

"Elora's death caused Ciarden to bless me—to...to complete—" She cursed as she fled the room, and the captain followed closely behind, leaving me chained on the ground.

Oak had been lingering outside the cell when I told my tale to Emmeline and the captain. He came in and unhooked me from the ground, but instead of taking me back to that dank hole a floor below, he allowed us to linger a bit longer. Bless the man; I could have kissed him. I moved closer to the barred window, trying to stand in the sun. It wasn't warm by any means, but it was light. I soaked it up like a cat.

What had Emmeline meant when she said Elora wasn't alright? The woman clearly hadn't been sleeping, and she was a shell of a person. The girl wasn't dead, so what could it have meant? If only I could get the gods forsaken chains off of me. I would build an illusion and break into her dreams if I could, just to see her. When I had my arm around her, my dagger to her throat, I'd told her I was sorry. I told her I could...Had I meant it?

"They're both staying in the king's quarters, and I spoke to that pretty laundress I told you about? Ofie? She said she'd come find me if there was a chance..." I stared at him, uncertain why he was telling me this. "Why aren't you excited?"

"Why would I be excited about that, Oak?"

"Don't pretend you don't want to see her. She doesn't leave the rooms. I think—Ofie said she's stuck, that all she does is sleep. She can't wake, and the healers don't know what to do."

I stopped breathing. She was trapped, stuck sleeping. And it was my fault. Was she dreaming? Was she having nightmares? Considering the horror of what I'd done to her was her last memory, it was probable. Gods, I was a fool. I stilled, realizing what Oak had said.

"You'll take me to see her?"

He nodded, and I felt my chest tighten. I had told him I hadn't wanted to do what I did, just that I had to and had regretted it. It seemed he believed me. But how had I instilled any sort of loyalty in the man? I didn't deserve it. I didn't deserve a bit of it. Despite that, I would take him up on it. I knew it would risk his standing as a guard; I knew I was risking my own life in doing it. But it didn't matter. I needed to see her, to fix her. Who better to accompany a girl who couldn't wake than a boy who dallied in dreams?

CHAPTER 4

Emmeline

After the revelation with Cyran, I immediately ran to the library, poring over everything I could find to understand more about the promises he had made: one to the seer and one to Faxon. I assumed he made the one to Faxon first, because it was in direct contradiction with what the seer had told him to do. That first oath had been a promise of safety while Elora was under his protection, and he had gotten around it to slice her throat. I had made choices based on that verit oath. I had made choices based on my judgment of his character in the illusions. I had thought Elora was relatively safe. We'd had a plan with the Cascade, and then it all went to shit.

I couldn't help but blame myself.

I had let us get distracted by our past. I didn't deserve happiness while Elora wasn't by my side. It was what I deserved—her being killed, trapped in an unending slumber, and Rain being taken. Every bad thing that happened was because I'd chosen myself. Foolish woman. I'd accepted Lucia's sacrifice, accepted she had died for me to have this life, and I had nothing but audacity to think I could actually keep it.

I must have dozed off at the table because I woke to Mairin and Thyra chatting quietly beside me. The merrow slid a steaming mug across the table.

"Coffee?"

The library was empty, and, looking out the window, I realized it was long past sunset. I warmed my hands against the mug, feeling chilled because of a draft in the room. Since there had been a group of people at the table by the fire when I had arrived—members of the court who gawked at me often—I had found a spot in the corner, putting as much distance between them and myself as possible. Thankfully, none of them felt brave enough to approach their new queen. Especially not with Thyra beside me.

While useful in keeping me away from prying eyes, the corner did nothing in terms of warmth. Noticing the table by the recently tended fire now sat empty,

I began gathering the books in my arms to move when a thought struck me. I concentrated, looking at the crackling flames, before using my divinity to pull some of the heated air across the room to where we sat. It was an odd sensation, almost like inhaling in my subconscious, which brought the warmth over to us. Mairin made a purring sound as I twined the warm air around her ankles and whipped it up her body, sending her hair above and behind her, giving her a surprised look. Thyra laughed, deep and full, as her braid whipped over her shoulder. I chuckled, and the sound surprised me; I hadn't laughed in weeks. Not since Rain. His radiant smile appeared in my mind, and all humor left me.

"Why didn't you wake me?" I asked my Second.

"Because you sleep like shit. You needed it."

"Your aura is fucked too. What were you thinking about before you fell asleep?" I felt the heat of Mairin's scrutiny on the side of my face.

"The better question would be what wasn't I thinking about," I replied.

"Explain."

I sighed. "Hell, Mairin. All of it, alright?"

"Her Majesty feels guilty," Thyra supplied. I hadn't realized my feelings and emotions had projected so clearly.

"What do I have to do to get you to stop calling me that? You sleep in my chambers every night, Thyra." I darted my eyes over to my traitorous friend. "And yes, I feel guilty."

With sad eyes, Mairin asked, "Why?"

I didn't want to have this conversation, but I knew between the two of them they'd pry it out of me.

"Because I'm an idiot. I trusted Cyran. I made stupid decisions because I was distracted with Rain. Because," I whispered, voice low. I didn't even want to say the words. "While my daughter was abducted, I let myself think she was safe. I let myself relax. It was selfish. I am not a good mother."

"We all thought she was safe," Thyra offered.

Snapping, I raised my voice. "I am her mother. I should have known better. I never should have allowed myself even a moment of respite while she was gone. Distracted by a man, my gods." My laugh was cold. "No matter how much I love him, no matter how much he means to me, there's no excuse."

"Not just a man. Her *father*." Mairin nodded to my ring finger as she spoke. "You said Aonara blessed you on your wedding night, right?"

"Yes."

"Your Maj—Emmeline, the light, your fire, saved people at the Cascade. Saved me," Thyra said, voice gentle.

Thinking about my friend with that gods forsaken blade pressed to her neck sent a chill through me. I'd been ready to slit my own throat to save her, but I had trusted my instincts at the last moment and had thrown my dagger and divinity toward them.

"She knows she saved people, Thyra; she's just looking for someone to blame, and why change how she's treated herself the last sixteen years."

"But I *am* to blame. I—That happiness we had is tainted because I should have been—"

Mairin cut me off.

"Should have been what? Weeping? Where would that have gotten you?" She started ticking her fingers one by one as if making a list. "You didn't know where Elora was being held; you met with Soren to ask for aid, and he threw you in the dungeons—don't start; he deserved it. If you would have bypassed Soren, his assassins might have killed her first." She continued ticking her fingers. "You thought she was safe and cared for. And frankly, it seems like she was. Dewalt told me what the boy said, and I saw his aura."

I scowled at her.

"I know you're going to do it anyway, but you can't beat yourself up over choosing yourself for once in your life. I've known you long enough; I know your heart."

Thyra nodded emphatically next to her.

"If I had my head on straight, I'd have thought about the situation with Cyran more clearly. I wouldn't have let Rain fall in love with me again, and he wouldn't be in Darkhold now."

At that, Thyra's laugh filled the room. I didn't find it particularly funny, but she had her head tilted back completely, her hand resting on her stomach. "Little dyrr, you have lost your mind," she said between gasping breaths. Even Mairin wore a smile and chuckled along with her.

"It's true. I hurt us both by entertaining the idea," I argued.

"*Emma,*" she stressed, the weight of my name on Thyra's lips meant to send a message. "If you think the king would act any other way, you need to check your head." Mairin smiled, reaching over to grasp my hand as Thyra continued. "I have known King Rainier for many years. I did not know your name but I knew you. He did not fall in love with you *again*. Always, that man has loved you."

My chest tightened as Mairin interjected her own thoughts on the matter.

"You entertaining his affections changed nothing. Just because you trusted someone you shouldn't, just because you trusted a plan that went to shit, just because you were following through in action instead of tears, doesn't mean you were wrong. And, I know I'm not one, so maybe this isn't my place to say, but you aren't only a mother. Your identity isn't your daughter. It isn't your dead sister. Hell, your identity isn't the Beloved either. You are a woman who did her best in an impossible situation, and just because you stole some happiness for yourself does not mean you are a bad mother."

"Agree," Thyra nodded before adding softly, "I think it would be lucky if more mothers were like you."

Tears came to my eyes, and I brushed them away as I sniffled. "Careful, Thyra, you'll have me thinking too highly of myself."

Thyra smiled before yawning, and I glanced over at the clock on the mantel.

"Go to bed, get some rest." Thyra's stare was dubious. "Mairin won't let me get into any trouble. Promise."

My shadow, as she often felt like, looked over at Mairin, who nodded, confirming she'd mind me. I knew their intentions were to take care of me, to stop me from doing something reckless and endangering myself. But I still didn't like feeling like such an inconvenience to them. Thyra stood, reaching upward into a stretch before heading toward the door. As she passed me, I reached out and grabbed her hand.

"Thank you, Thyra. I don't know what I'd do without you." She dipped her head, a flush creeping up her cheeks.

"You're welcome, Emma."

I squeezed her hand before letting go and sending her on her way.

After a moment, Mairin asked, "What are we researching about the Beloved?"

"I don't know. Everything?"

I wanted to know how the gifts from the gods were *supposed* to work. I didn't care as much about the supposed conflict between the Beloved and the Accursed. Not now, at least—I'd think about that later. What I was more concerned about was how the various blessings worked within me. The prophecy as I'd known it, hell as the rest of Vesta had known it, only involved Aonara's blessing. But all four of the gods had blessed me. I still wasn't sure if I agreed with the term. Was it a blessing? Was having this power colliding and meshing within me—light and dark—anything other than a curse?

Rhia had blessed me with Elora, anchoring me to this life, and Hanwen had blessed me with abundance, the hum of my almost endless divinity reverberating within me. But Aonara and Ciarden, their abilities were total and complete. And Ciarden's felt...tainted. I wanted to know if they were supposed to feel like that. Already, I'd been tempted to use the shadows in ways I didn't want. When I was in the dungeon with Dewalt, questioning Cyran, I had to look away for long moments. The power itching beneath my skin had begged to be used on the boy.

When Cyran told me the reason for what he'd done, I had to leave the room. Even though I'd gone into the cell of the man who'd bound Rain, using my fists to take some of the edge off, I still didn't trust myself. But the moment he said it, the shadows danced over the surface of my skin, aching to break free. I wasn't sure which direction to aim the rage either. If Cyran spoke true, he did it for the good of the Three Kingdoms. Not that it mattered; I'd rather see the world burn than my child dead. But I could understand. I could understand why a prince raised by a monster might think her death was worth it.

But her death being the reason Ciarden blessed me? The fourth god had watched me suffer, watched fury and horror fill me, before he blessed me with his dark power. Cursed me with it.

Lucia had died for me, protected me, so I could live. Elora had died for me, been sacrificed for me, so I could become the Beloved. And for what? I didn't want this. I didn't want to be part of that gods forsaken prophecy. But I had to be, didn't I? Though I had healed her wounds and started her heart, she had died because of me. Cyran had been forced to kill her because of me.

I needed to make what Cyran had done to her worth it—not just for the world but for the prince too. What he'd done to her had clearly taken a toll on him, but he thought he was doing it for the greater good. Could I believe him? I supposed I could find a mindbreaker to infiltrate his memories, but I'd heard his heart. It was a sure and steady beat when he had explained what he'd seen. I needed to ensure that his vision of peace, the reward for his vile actions, would some day come to pass.

While I'd slept, I'd dreamed of that day. Cyran had gently lowered her to the ground and held her as tears ran down his face. I'd seen it that day but dismissed it. For the first time, I wondered if he might deserve my forgiveness.

I was back in my private quarters before dawn. They were nearly as big as the lower level of Rain's estate, with a sitting and dining area attached to the balcony garden and our private room. The sitting room bore comfortable furniture, the divan and matching armchairs made from cherry wood and upholstered with a deep red velvet matching the rug in the bedroom. The dining table was round, small enough it only held four chairs, and I ached at its waiting potential. Would the three of us ever sit there?

Standing in front of the recently tended fire, grateful a servant had done it, I struggled with the buttons of my gown as I undressed. I tried not to think about how Rain should be with me, helping me with nimble fingers. Thyra had brought a good portion of my wardrobe to the palace, and I hadn't yet repeated a single item he'd ordered for me. Gripping Rain's robe which I'd left draped across the armchair, pulling it around my body, I inhaled his scent deeply. It was fading, and I hoped he'd be back in it, letting me breathe him in, before the scent was gone completely. I felt a surge of guilt, being here safe inside the palace, not in Folterra. I should have been in Darkhold trying to free him. I certainly wasn't helpless, but I didn't know what I could do by myself, especially after the promise I had made to him when he'd ordered me to stay in the fortress. He wanted me to stay safe for Elora because one of us had to. I knew what he would want me to do now, but I simply couldn't.

If Shivani didn't come up with an alternate plan, I'd turn myself over to Declan. I'd do my best to kill him, but I wouldn't jeopardize Rain any further. The line between my brows deepened as I sunk down into the chair, thinking about how angry I was that Shivani hadn't yet acted. I only sat for a moment before I heard a distinctly male snore coming from the other room, and I froze.

What the hell?

Someone was in my bedroom with Elora.

I jumped up, tying Rain's robe tight around my waist, and drew dive fire into my hands, white light cracking through my skin as if I was made of it. I'd been practicing over the weeks, remembering how Soren had held his crimson and purple flame. I'd improved drastically. Since the door to the bedroom was cracked, I could nudge it open with my hip, holding the fire sparking in my hands. My jaw dropped when I realized what I was looking at.

There was a guard—the big one I'd sent sprawling to the ground on my trip to the dungeon not so long ago—asleep in the chair next to the fire. He was the one I heard snoring. I looked over at Elora and stilled, noticing an arm draped over her, someone lying beside her. My heart dropped into my stomach as I approached. The hand was pale, and there were red marks on his wrists. I knew exactly who was in my bed with his arm wrapped around my daughter, and I wasn't sure how to react. How the hell had he gotten in? It was clear someone had reported my whereabouts, and, obviously, the giant in the chair had something to do with it. My bare feet were quiet on the floor, and I barely breathed. I let the fire dwindle in one of my hands and grabbed the boy's shoulder, rolling him over onto his back.

He looked younger in sleep, his hazelnut hair hanging down over his forehead, face slack and peaceful. I almost felt bad for waking him. But not quite.

"Cyran, what in the gods' names are you doing here?"

His eyes snapped open, and his facial expression morphed into horror as he sat up, kicking and shoving his way back into the bed, away from Elora and away from me. "I'm sorry, I—I thought I could help. I didn't do anything, I'm sor—" His voice gave way to raucous sobs which tore through his body. "Please, I'm sorry. I'm so sorry." He caught his head in his hands, grasping his hair with his fingers and tugging hard. "She won't—I can't get her to—I just want her to wake up." He curled into himself, gasping for breath, looking as if he might snap in two. It was that vision of him, the broken boy curling into himself, which caused me to move. I let my fire drop away completely, and I sat down next to him, his toes touching the side of my leg. He gaped at me, arms wrapped around his knees, and he flinched as I reached out. Recognizing the action, I pulled my hand back. In Brambleton, there'd been a few children who reacted that way before, often the ones whose fathers were the worst drunks. I immediately regretted slapping him. But how could I regret that? He'd hurt my baby, and he deserved it. I was confused on a few different levels, and all I knew was instinct told me to be kind to him.

"Can I?" I wasn't sure what I was asking, but he nodded, and I instantly knew what he needed. Reaching over and pulling him toward me, I put both arms around him. He was stiff and frozen for only a moment. When he sank into my body, limbs loose, and let out sobs I understood more than I cared to, I couldn't help but stroke his back, providing the comfort I wished for myself. I turned a bit, so I could still see Elora, while I held him. She rolled over, as if the sound of his crying disturbed her, and her face wore a frown.

"I tried...to wake her. I was trying. She—She's having nightmares. Because of me." I stiffened, not wanting to hear that. There was only so much I could stand, so much I could tolerate. I'd been ready to kill this boy until just a few hours ago. And I still didn't forgive him. I still felt the call for his blood, the desire to end him, from the dark within me. But he was just a boy. A boy who had obviously been beaten by the men he'd seen destroy and burn and kill in a vision. I remembered the mistakes my friends and I had made in the past when I was his age. The mistakes Rain had made, Dewalt and Lucia too. The world was unfair at that age. Not quite a child, not quite an adult, everything learned the hardest way. Holding this boy in my arms, it reminded me of Rain—a broken man who had thought he'd done the right thing, fulfilling a responsibility he'd never asked for, but a duty he felt beholden to. And how he and I both paid for it. For years. It was with that in mind I let Cyran continue.

"I don't even know if she recognized me before you woke me. I'm sorry. I shouldn't have come in here. I just wanted to help." He sat up, sliding away from me as he wiped his nose. Elora stirred. Though she was frowning, she wasn't whimpering in her sleep as she sometimes did. I reached over and tucked her back under the blanket, gently tracing my fingertips across her cheeks, and her face softened. When I turned back toward Cyran, the guard in my chair gave a loud snore and roused himself awake. I'd forgotten he was there; I was so involved with the young prince.

"Oh gods, Your Majesty!" When he slammed down onto the floor in front of me, I could have sworn it shook.

"Get out." The order was sharp, and to his credit, he only paused for a moment to look at the boy on the bed beside me, a question in his eyes as he stood. "No, I'll deal with him. Find Thyra and send her to me." I had things I needed to discuss with my Second.

CHAPTER 5

Elora

He was gone. He was there, and then he was gone. He had been crying, and he never cried. He'd only whispered in my ear and then hurt me. That's all he ever did. He said sweet things to me, and then he hurt me. Ever since the beginning.

But this time he cried. He stood facing me, but was still holding me at the same time. How? Mama was on the ground with that evil, evil man on top of her. And then the prince was standing there on the other side of her, watching me and crying. Why was he crying? What was wrong? Why did I care? All he did was hurt me. That was all he ever did.

He wasn't wearing his jewelry or his arrogance. He was just Cyran, stripped down. Was he here to hurt me or comfort me? I was always bad at telling the difference.

"Elora! Wake up!" He was shouting. What did he mean? I was awake. But maybe I wasn't? He put his hand on my head, pulling me back against his chest as he leaned in, whispering in my ear.

And then came the pain. Every time, I remembered he did this to me. Cyran. The Folterran prince was the reason I dreamed, the reason I hurt, the reason I cried. He betrayed me. He betrayed me just like...

I was cold—so, so cold. And then I woke up.

I was in the meadow near Ravemont. Mama took me all the time when I was little. But then I stopped wanting to visit, and she stopped taking me. However, when I woke up on the ground among the wildflowers, the sun beating down and warming me, I felt relief.

I watched the clouds above me, fluffy cats giving way to fighting dragons, and a wolf howling. My head was in Mama's lap, and she ran her fingers through my curls. I looked up to find her face, but the sun was behind her head, and I couldn't make it out. She sang an old rhyme to me, her voice raspy and quiet, the familiar comfort lulling me to sleep.

Brave girl of mine, blessing divine, brought to me under the two twin skies.

I was falling.

My head slammed against the ground, the orange leaves of fall swaying above me. Papa leaned over me. "Are you alright?" And then he was yelling at someone, angry. I tasted blood on my lips, but I felt no wound. It must have belonged to the man. I'd told him to let go, hadn't I? Why didn't he let go?

"Papa?"

He leaned over me again, but it wasn't him anymore. A man smiled down at me, but I couldn't make out anything else with the sun shining behind him. But that wasn't why I couldn't make his features out. He had no features at all anymore. I screamed, but the only thing that came out was blood.

I was choking. I was choking on so much blood.

And then I was standing, Cyran holding me. I relaxed when I breathed in his soft cedar scent. I was angry with him, but I couldn't remember why. He was warm and sturdy. His hands were on my arms, and I felt his lips against my ear. I shuddered. I didn't know if I wanted to kiss him or hit him.

And then it hurt. This was his fault. This was all his fault.

Was I dead?

I fell. The ground was soft, and his hands caught me. "Elora, I'm sorry."

No, you're not. I screamed it, but he couldn't hear me. I cried for my mother, but she didn't hear me either. No one could hear me. Everything went black, and I was weightless. I floated, but I could feel their hands. Someone's hands. Mama's hands? They couldn't be Cyran's hands; his hands would only burn.

He was my ruin.

I saw a pinprick of light on the horizon and moved toward it. Was I floating or swimming? Was I running? I wasn't sure—but I was moving, and it was growing. It was getting brighter, bigger.

"Elora, please wake up. It's me. Please wake up and yell at me. I deserve it. I deserve your hatred. I deserve everything you want to throw at me. Just wake up. Just wake up and hate me. You can kill me if you want to; I won't even move. I'll hand you the knife."

Cyran.

He was crying again. He stood in the light. No, he was the light. I stayed back, safe in the dark. Safe from him. Part of me wanted to run to him, to run and hit him. To kill him. But that wouldn't help, would it? I'd still be dead. Did I want to kill him, anyway? Would he be stuck here with me? Part of me wanted that. Why did I want that?

"Elora? I'm here too, honey. You're sleeping. I miss you so much, baby girl. Can you try to wake up, Elora? We're waiting for you."

Was Mama the light, too? Was it a trick? Would she disappear? Would I see her face?

I stopped and sat just on the edge of the light. I could see them, as if looking through water. Mama looked tired. Her hair was a tangly mess. Had she even brushed it? She had circles under her eyes, and she was wringing her hands. Cy looked tired too.

Not Cy. Cyran.

He wasn't Cy anymore. Cy was my friend. Cy was kind and sad. He held me when I cried about Papa. My friend had made illusions out of my nightmares and used his shadows to protect me in my dreams. I knew they weren't real, but he did it to make me feel better. But he wasn't Cy anymore. He was Prince Cyran, the monster his brother had made him into.

I turned and ran.

I fell down, skinning my knees, and cried. Papa came running, like always. He looked mad until he saw my tears, and his face softened, his brown eyes holding patience for his little girl.

"Elora, you're alright. Go see your mama; she'll fix it right up." When I stood though, he smacked me. "You are her daughter, never mine." I stood there with my hand on my cheek and tears streaming down my face. "You are nothing, just like her."

I wanted to tell Cy. He'd know what to do. But then I remembered I couldn't trust him, though I couldn't remember why.

I was walking down the stairs, heading into a cozy dining room. Recognizing it from Evenmoor, I slowed my steps.

"Good morning, *min viltasma*."

"What does that mean?"

"It's something my mother used to say."

Wait, that's not right.

He never told me before. I asked him every time he called me that, but he never answered. Looking at him, I tried to understand. He sat at the table, calm, his hands clasped in front of him on the table. He didn't wear any of his jewelry. I'd only seen him without it once before, when I crawled into his bed. It was the night Papa said what he did, and I didn't want to be alone. Cy had held me when I cried. But he looked so different. Older. His rich brown hair hung down into his eyes, not pushed back away from his face like he normally had it, and his hazel eyes were bloodshot. It looked as if he'd been crying.

"Is this real?" I stopped at the bottom of the stairs and watched him, wary.

"It is in your mind, but it is real, all the same. I'm using my divinity. Would you like some tea?" He nodded toward the table in front of him, where two teacups now sat.

I hesitated. Everything else had felt so familiar, but this was different. It felt more...real.

"We can talk from this distance, if you'd like." He nodded toward the sideboard on the wall next to me, and I found a full teacup sitting there. I grabbed it before sitting on the bottom step behind me. He watched me, and I noticed a slight frown before he shook his head, wiping his face of expression. "What do you want to talk about, Elora?"

I stared at him. Why would I want to talk to him? I didn't trust him. But he looked so sad, and it made my chest hurt.

"Am I dreaming? Why are you using an illusion?"

"I know I asked what you want to talk about, but usually talking about that upsets you, and I can't hold the illusion." He wiped his face, long fingers pushing his hair back. He had red rashes around his wrists like I had when I first arrived in Evenmoor.

"What happened to your wrists?"

He sighed, tilting his head up while his fingers were still in his hair. "Another touchy subject, *viltasma*."

"Well, what can we talk about then? How about that? Viltasma—what does it mean?"

He put his hands down in his lap and lifted his eyes to meet my gaze.

"Yes, that's fine. We can talk about that." He gave me a soft smile, just enough to see the hint of a dimple. "My mother died when I was nine years old. She was very sick—the wasting sickness. After my father, she swore off conduits. She refused to see a healer to help her. But before all of that, when I was little, she'd always called me '*vilta*.' It means 'wild thing.'"

I tilted my head to the side as I said, "You do not strike me as wild, Cy." I stiffened, realizing a second too late I called him by my nickname for him. He noticed too, and his eyes met mine, unreadable.

"I used to be when I was little, but when she got sick, I had to be calm for her. And then after she died, I couldn't be wild, not anymore. I had to be the perfect, little prince."

"But you call me *viltasma*. That's not the same word."

"No, it's not." There was that smile again. "The 'sma' changes the meaning. It means beautiful."

"Beautiful, wild thing? That's what you call me?" He nodded, eyes glinting almost amber in this light, full of caution. "Why?" I asked.

"Why wouldn't I?" I rolled my eyes, but felt my face flush. He continued. "You're beautiful. I don't need to explain that, do I? I know you grew up poor, but surely you had a mirror?" He waited for me to answer. He was serious.

"Of course I had a mirror! Gods, Cyran, why are you such a pain?"

He grinned, a full one this time, and he looked more like himself. "Well, I wasn't sure! I don't know how much mirrors cost!"

"We had a mirror, you imbecile." My smile had a mind of its own. I was still mad at him, but I couldn't quite remember it now. "I don't think I'm wild, though. And what does 'min' mean? You say that with it sometimes."

He flushed, rubbing the back of his neck. "It means 'my.' When I call you that, it means 'my beautiful, wild thing.'" He blew out a breath before giving me a sheepish smile, and I felt lightheaded. "And you bit someone's ear off, Elora. How are you not wild?"

"Are you never going to let that go? Your thugs grabbed me in the woods and slapped those chains on me. What was I supposed to do?" My mood soured in an instant. "You have the marks on your wrists. Why have you been in chains, Cy?"

"I told you that was a touchy subject, darling."

"I don't care. Are you alright? Where are we?"

"Elora—"

"No! Does Declan have you? Does he have both of us?"

He sighed. "We are both in Astana."

"Then who put you in chains? You helped us. You helped! Why would Mama or..." I hesitated, not sure if I wanted to talk about him. "The Crown Prince wouldn't put you in chains if you helped us. What happened Cy? Why—why am I asleep?"

"If you come sit with me, I'll explain." He looked at me, pleading, before pulling out the chair next to him. Crossing the room, I looked down and noticed I wasn't wearing shoes. I wore a nightgown, one I had never seen before, but it was fine—soft, white silk embroidered with tiny peonies grazed the floor as I walked. When I sat down, he held out his hand, wanting me to take it. Looking up at him, I let him see my fear, let him know this was a sacrifice for me to trust him, as I slid my hand into his.

"Elora, we've had this conversation a few times, and you never remember it. Every time, you get extremely upset. Rightfully so, but still. I want to tell you, but you have to promise to keep calm. Do you think you can stay calm?"

My stomach plummeted. What would make me that upset? Why had he been in chains? Why was I sleeping? I tasted copper, and breathing became difficult.

Then it came to me.

"Did you—Cyran, did you—?" I felt like I was choking, and I reached up to grab my neck before whispering the accusation. "You killed me?"

"Yes, and I'm so sorry, Elora. But you're not dead. Your mother brought you back."

"But I was dead? Before Mama...brought me back?" I struggled to understand. If I wasn't dead, then Cyran couldn't have done what he said—what I remembered.

"Yes, you were dead, but now you're not. You won't wake, and I'm trying to fix it."

"But you were the one who killed me?"

"Yes."

Tears streamed down his face.

"Why?" My heart was breaking in two. How could he do that to me? He took a deep breath and closed his eyes. His hand tightened around mine, even as I felt him behind me. His hand on my forehead pulled me back into his chest, his warm breath on my ear.

"I think I could have truly loved you, min viltasma. If only we'd had the time."

CHAPTER 6

Rainier

It was the tenth day in a row I woke to ice-cold water being dumped over my body, and, gods damn, it did not piss me off any less. Declan had asked if I was cold, and I had stupidly told him no. I'd imprisoned my fair share of people; I'd known to expect what Declan would do to me, but I thought the water was a bit much. He insisted on speaking with me, or speaking at me rather, every single day, and that was torture in its own right.

One good thing about the water was the fact whoever was tasked to dump it rarely emptied it completely, leaving me something to drink. Otherwise, I remained thirsty. After those first days of not having any, the small amount I got from the bucket was enough it almost made the discomfort worth it. Barely. I wished he'd just kill me. What did I have to live for, anyway?

Elora was dead. I had felt it through the bond—from Emma. Her pain. I felt her die inside. I felt a piece of me shatter, knowing the only thing which would have caused that agony.

Our daughter was dead.

And her mother might be too. My Em.

Though I hadn't felt that soul-splitting pain, the agony associated with a bond torn by death, I hadn't felt her at all. I'd tugged on it before Declan knocked me out, and she wasn't there. Ever since then, I'd been stuck in this basalt dungeon, divinity blocked by the lava rock. Would the pain be waiting for me the moment I got out? I'd rather be dead than feel it.

I didn't have hope anymore. At first, in those early days when he'd had me beaten so severely I couldn't see, I held onto that fierce dying ember. The inkling that Emma had lived. I'd seen that light on the field of tents and hoped whatever she did had killed and maimed and destroyed. It had to have been Dryul, the cause of those shadows and the cause of her pain. I'd been listening to anyone who might address Declan, hoping for the genuflection given to a king, but I hadn't heard it. I supposed Declan might not expect those formalities, though it truly didn't seem like him. It made me accept the real possibility that Dryul had not only lived, but he'd killed Emma too. He'd done something to disrupt our bond and killed her while I was unconscious. Had my soul gone through the bond with her? I'd been numb ever since I pulled on those golden threads and didn't find her on the other end.

I was trying to protect her, to keep her safe. Declan seemed to think he was the Accursed, and I'd kept him away from her. When he revealed what he thought about himself and his plan to kill her, I rifted us away, relieved, even if it might have brought about my death. But had she died anyway? The gods were fucking bastards to bring her back to me like this, then rip her away from me. And to take my daughter too?

I had nothing left.

If I got out, what would I go back to? Two graves to water with my tears? That was if Shivani even attempted a rescue. I didn't want her to. I wanted to keep my soldiers far away from Darkhold, wanted Declan to just end this torment. But that skinny fuck would not oblige me. When I heard two sets of feet walking down the hall, I sat upright. I knew how it worked by now. He'd send the ogre in to either beat me or pin me, and I was far too weak anymore to fight back. Without my divinity and the proper energy to do anything, the beatings rarely lasted long. Before, when I had attempted to fight, Declan's lackey had thrown me so hard against the walls of my cell, I'd been dizzy with a headache for a week. I didn't bother anymore. When he opened my cell, Declan's face split into a toothy grin, unnaturally white and straight.

If I ever had any doubt, Declan Umbroth, King of Folterra, had proven to me that I could never be like him or his forefathers, and I had little hope for the future of our kingdoms.

"Good morning, Your Majesty. Did you sleep well?" He eyed the floor and the intentional lack of any sort of bedding, knowing full well I could barely sleep. The lava rock gave me a perpetual throbbing behind my eyes, and it made it hard to find comfort. The draíbea made it hard to focus though, so I was perpetually staring at a wall—unable to think or sleep.

I thought perhaps I'd take a different approach today with him. Normally, I didn't talk, merely grunted, hoping it would discourage him from speaking as much as he did. But so far, he never seemed to tire of hearing his own voice. That was what made me decide to answer him today. Perhaps if I spoke to him, I'd get something out of it. Maybe if I pissed him off enough, he'd just snap my neck in a rage. The idea of luck being on my side in such a way brought a smile to my face.

"Fuck you." I spat at him and was impressed by how close I got to his feet.

"My, my, Rainy. Is that how we're feeling today?" It wasn't the first time he called me Rainy, and it wasn't the first time I vividly imagined disemboweling him.

"I'm feeling like you should just fucking kill me, and get it over with already." Perhaps I should have attempted subtlety.

Oh well.

"And miss out on the fun? Your little shell arrived in Astana within the past few days. They've offered me a deal, and I'm deciding whether to take it. Do you think sending parts of you back to them will sweeten the pot for me?"

My stomach dropped, knowing what that would do to Emma if she'd made it out alive.

"I don't know, Declan. What I do know is you're a stupid fuck if you think Shivani is going to do much for you. What did you even ask for?" My mother might negotiate for me, but there was a limit to what she would do. She was ruthless, as my father had taught her to be, and she wouldn't enter a war she couldn't win. Not over me—not with Lavenia still alive. If Declan had Nythyr backing him too? Vesta wouldn't stand a chance.

"I think it may surprise you what she will do. I have my eyes in your little palace, and something tells me Shivani may be more than willing to give me what I asked for." He shut the cell door and leaned against it, crossing his legs and arms casually.

"Are you going to tell me, or is this just another excuse to hear yourself speak?"

"Well, since she cannot bring my father back to life, I asked for the next best thing."

So, Em had killed Dryul. I felt a surge of pride despite the situation. My girl had done what she'd wanted to do, what I'd wanted to do for her for years. She'd done it. Of course she did. Something cold gripped my heart, squeezing tight. She'd done it; had she died for it too? Declan continued. "I'm not going to tell you what it is. It will be a pleasant surprise for you when it arrives."

That was ominous. "Lucky me. And when will that be?"

"Oh, I gave them until the full moon. Three weeks from now, in case you've lost count."

"I'll write it on my schedule." Hopefully, I'd be dead before then, and Shivani would cease negotiations. Though, if she made whatever deal he spoke of, it wouldn't be too hard to fake my presence, Declan continuing to make demands with nothing to trade but my corpse. The corpse of an uncrowned king. I supposed it was even, one king's death for another. "Will I be invited to your coronation as well?"

He laughed, head tilted back against the wall. "I admit I might have cocked that one up, lad. It already happened. If I'd have known you'd wanted to attend, I would have made sure of it. Given you a place of honor at the dinner afterwards. Do you suppose they'll call me the Death King? Death Prince was rather dreadful. I want something original. Ooh, I wonder if Bloody King will still suit you if you never draw blood as the king." He tilted his head to the side as he moved closer to me. "Did you know you have nightmares, Rainy?"

Of course I fucking knew I had nightmares. The past week I'd been finding Em in the caves, but I was too late. Her body would be bloated and floating, her eyes open and milky. Every time. Sometimes her corpse spoke to me, sometimes it didn't. Now and then, I had a nightmare about Lucia or Elora; I could never tell which. I knew Elora looked like her, so my mind struggled to figure out an image for her. Half the time it was Lucia with curly hair and no face, her skin smooth across her skull. The worst part about the nightmares was the fact I'd never have Elora's actual face to replace that image with.

He nudged my foot with his boot.

"Do you want to talk about it, son?" He put on a gruff voice and moved his hands to his hips. Fuck, I hated him. I spat at him again, this time making contact with his shin. He made a sound of disgust but otherwise didn't react. "You sure have quite the temper. I guess you are young yet." He crossed his arms, tilting his head as he softened his voice. "You cry out for her, you know. It is rather sweet, if you pretend she isn't filth. I can't quite get past the fact she allowed herself to be impregnated by the man her sister was engaged to." All I did was glare at him. "And to think, you never got to meet the girl. My little sister was quite fond of her. She was a rather pretty girl, if coarse. I suppose that's what happens when a child is raised by a whore in a shack, though."

"Don't fucking call her that." He merely raised a brow, nonplussed. "No, you bastard, I didn't get to meet Elora. And now they're both dead, so just kill me already, alright? There can't be anything you want more than my death." He tsked at me and backed up to the wall, casually leaning against it and studying me.

"Ah, that's where you're wrong, my friend. On more than one account." I just stared at him as I mentally reviewed my words. The only other thing which could have been wrong—I stopped the line of thought, not wanting to believe what he was seeming to insinuate. I couldn't take it if I was wrong. "The two inaccuracies are related, funny enough. Vesta has something I want more than your death. And it's your woman. Though, Shivani made me a different offer I must consider."

I stopped breathing for just a moment. Em had made it? My eyes watered, and I pinched myself, hoping the pain would bring me back from that weakness. I couldn't let Declan see it. I watched him, waiting for him to go on.

"Don't get too excited. Your wife is alive, but your child is quite dead. One of my soldiers was close enough to see, and he told me there was more blood than you could have imagined."

I gritted my teeth. "She killed your father for doing it. She'll kill you too."

"Ah, another point in which you are mistaken."

He left without another word.

"Rainier, wake up." The voice was a whisper, hot in my ear. The fog was dense in the room, and it was hard for me to open my eyes, that sensation of feeling both heavy and light all at once. I felt groggy, like I was in a cloud, and I could smell draíbea, the thick mint and cherry scent sliding down the back of my throat. I was leaning against a wall, but there was a weight on me as I opened my eyes. "Good morning, sweetheart."

Emma was sitting in my lap, eyes close to me as she looked into mine. The same perfect shade of blue, just a bit more aquamarine than the Mahowin Sea. She leaned in and kissed my jaw, moving down my neck. I put my hands on her hips even though I knew this was a hallucination from the smoke. There was no way I wasn't still in the hell of a dungeon at Darkhold, and there was no way she was here with me. She pulled herself from my neck, cupping my face as she kissed me.

I was so tired and slow. How much draíbea had they burned in the room? If I felt like this—weak to the point of barely able to move—it had to have been a lot. I was hallucinating, but since I missed her, I let it play out. Lately, I'd been trying to rouse myself from dreams of her, knowing they often turned into nightmares. They all started with me going through a rift to find her, nearly drowning over and over. I'd never seen her alive in my dreams. Perhaps I was having this hallucination because of the relief I felt, knowing she was alive. I immediately felt guilty thinking about it. There should have been no relief at all in my grief—not with my daughter dead. I'd never felt more at odds with myself.

She rolled her body against mine, and I felt myself harden beneath her. Fuck, how was this fake Emma just as mesmerizing? I traced my hands over her arms, up her neck, and grasped the back of her head and kissed her. Gods, I missed her mouth. I slid my tongue to the seam of her lips, bartering for entrance, when an ice cold hand gripped me by the top of the head and slammed it back against the wall. A surprisingly warm hand pressed against my forehead, smaller compared to the one which still held my head.

"What the fuck?"

"Hold still, Rainier. It hurts less that way. You haven't had a memory taken before?" The face which spoke belonged to Emma, but the voice did not match. I felt something sharp against my stomach and attempted to look down. A cool, sharp touch of metal hit my neck, and I knew she wielded a knife in each hand. "No, no, Rainier. The mindbreaker is taking a memory for me to use later. The lava stone blocks her, so we had to move you out here." I looked out of the corner of my eye to see a different corridor of the dungeons, one without basalt. The blade pressed against my neck. "Don't even think about it. I'll slice your throat before you can even move. And then I'll let Zen do what he wants with you."

Out of the corner of my eye, I saw a massive body attached to the hand on my head. I couldn't make out much, but I noticed an odd smell. Almost like dirt or decaying vegetation. Next to the great oaf, I saw another woman, nondescript with mouse brown hair and eyes. She was the one with her hand on my forehead while Emmeline, or the shifter who stole her form, straddled me with her knife pressed against my artery. I didn't dare call her bluff. Just yesterday, I would have, hoping she'd go through with it, but now I knew Em had survived, and I couldn't let that happen.

"What is your biggest regret as the Bloody Prince?" The mindbreaker asked.

I couldn't help it as my mind flickered to thoughts of skirmishes on Varmeer, memories rushing to the forefront of my mind, unbidden. I had pushed those thoughts so far away, but they were being pulled to the surface, harsh and quick. The worst one froze in my mind, allowing me to see the broken and bloodied body. No, I would not think about that. I stared at my wife's eyes, a stunningly accurate impersonation, willing my mind to go blank.

"What is your biggest regret as the Bloody Prince?"

Honey-brown eyes flashed into my mind. A boy.

"Fuck you." I turned my head toward the woman asking, and I felt the shifter in my lap press down hard.

"Who was that boy? Did you kill him?"

Unseeing eyes and a small, limp body.

"Fuck. You."

"Did you do that to him?"

The grin he threw me over his shoulder the last time I saw him. His name was Vondi.

"I'm going to fucking kill you."

"I got it; I got the memory. That's enough."

The small woman skittered out of the room, as if in fear. I inhaled, quelling my rage as I glared at the woman in my lap, even though I could barely keep my eyes open. I let them shut as the shifter climbed off of me, blade still pressed against my neck. That was when I felt it.

The bond.

For a brief, shining second, I felt it. Until Zen slammed my head against the wall, knocking me out.

This time I didn't wake to water but to the sound of my cell door creaking open, and I pushed myself into a sitting position. It must have been the middle of the night because it didn't feel like I'd slept for long. Someone walked around the door, and I couldn't see their face for the brightness of the lantern they carried, walking toward me as I adjusted to the light. They were small, and I was confused. As the person approached, I could finally pick out features in the flicker of light. I inhaled when I saw white hair.

"Hello, Papa."

She sat down on the floor, a ways away from me, and crossed her legs. Blood saturated the long white dress she wore. The sound of wet fabric flopping onto the floor reached my ears as she situated her gown around her. Was this another fucking nightmare? I looked up, finding a face, and knew it wasn't quite like all the rest of the images my subconscious had given me. She studied me carefully, not giving away any emotion. This made no sense. She couldn't be here. Elora was dead. Unless this was her spirit here to haunt me. I shuddered as I took in the blood covering her small form. This sweet girl was mine, and she was dead. And she had died so horribly, her blood spilling down her body. I wanted to hold her, even while being nauseated by this ghastly apparition. It wasn't her, it wasn't her, it wasn't her. But she was mine. And she was beautiful. She had her mother's eyes, and her hair was Lucia's—but curly. A mass of tight spirals spreading out from her head. It reminded me of Ven's hair when she didn't braid it.

"Aren't you going to say hello to me?"

She gave me a shy smile, and her voice was quiet, almost timid—not at all what I imagined. Clearly this was a nightmare, but I couldn't help but take in her presence, this girl who I'd imagined a thousand different times. I had mostly pictured Lucia, but now that I saw her, I realized it was wrong. Her features were a bit off, not quite Em's, and I noticed her smile quirked up at the side. And her nose—the tip pointed upwards, just like mine did. Her skin was more of an olive color, somewhere between me and Em. She was more than I ever thought to dream about, to wish for, this girl who changed my life. She made me a father, and I didn't know if she ever knew that. This version of her did, this nightmare version covered in blood—she knew. But the real Elora, she might never have known.

"Mama was tricked, and she got my throat slit open." She tilted her head back and showed me the laceration. I nearly vomited, the thought of my flesh and blood, something like that happening to her. The vision would be forever embedded in my mind, haunting me for years to come. "There was blood everywhere, Papa."

I blinked a few times, eyes focusing in the dim lighting, when I realized this wasn't a nightmare, but rather Declan using his shifter to fuck with me. Since draíbea caused hallucinations on its own, it was hard to keep track. And a small part of me wanted her to be real.

The things she said hurt, making me dream and hope and wish—and mourn for a time I'd never have. When she called me Papa, my heart soared for a moment before I realized how stupid that was. It was something I'd thought about since Em realized she was mine. Faxon raised her. She knew him as Papa. Maybe one day she'd call me that, but not yet. Not now. I had eagerly looked forward to the chance to be that for her, to earn it. And I would have. I would have done everything in my power to show the depth of my love for her.

If she hadn't died.

I'd never get the chance to prove it. She would never call me Papa. That was an unexpected pain, one I hadn't thought of during these weeks. She might have died without knowing just how much I loved her and wanted to know her. And I had only just begun. I'd anticipated my love only growing deeper as I learned her, learned her heart. And now I would never have the chance.

This could be a gift, this chance to see her—even if it wasn't truly her. But this might not even be what Elora looked like, just a wild guess. A good one, though. The girl in front of me was dead. And that devastation hit me so hard, I didn't think the weight of it would ever leave me.

But Emma was alive.

Em, the other half of me—she was alive. The taste of my relief was sour, tainted because of the death of our child. Grief and relief intertwined so tightly within me, I didn't know where one started and the other began. I just wanted Emma. I wanted to hold her. To comfort her. That babe of mine she carried for me, raised and loved for me, taught and cherished for me, was dead. And we couldn't even help each other through it.

The girl, not my daughter, grew impatient, and my head snapped up as she started yelling at me. "I died because of you. Because you didn't fear Declan. Because you left Mama at the battle. Mama is going to hate you. She will never forgive you." Her hands darted out, and she dragged her nails down my face—hard. I didn't move as she turned and pranced out of the room, shutting the cell door behind her.

Did Declan really have a dynamic shifter or was I that out of my mind from the draíbea? Everything was so gods damned hazy, I couldn't trust my own eyes anymore. Nothing made sense.

I oddly wanted the girl to come back though, eager to look upon my daughter even if it was a trick from Declan. If she was dead, I'd never get to look at the real version of her. I'd never lay my eyes upon her, never hear her real voice. She died without me holding her and telling her I'd had a space for her in my heart all along, just waiting for her to fill it.

I started, remembering what Declan had said. Vesta had something he wanted. Emma was alive, and Declan wanted her. If my mother made the trade, he'd kill her, and the thoughts I'd been swarmed with for the last few weeks would come to fruition. I'd have lost them both. I didn't realize how little I trusted my mother until that instant. She loved me, but I didn't think she'd risk a war for me. But Emmeline? My mother would risk Emma. And Em would probably let her. They might even try to come up with a plan to make the trade and somehow try to kill Declan. The two had more in common than they liked to think. They both pissed me off better than anyone else, that was for sure.

With Elora dead and me locked away, there was nothing Em wouldn't do to get me back. Thinking she was dead all this time had prevented me from worrying about her as much as I now did. She was hurting, and she needed me. I needed to get out of here. I needed to get to her. I needed to get out before they could make a trade. Before my mother could destroy my gods damn soul.

CHAPTER 7

Emmeline

I knew two things: one, I was asleep; two, this wasn't exactly a dream.

I didn't remember going to sleep. I had been anxious, pacing about my quarters, hoping I'd made the right choices in the past week. Every night, I'd brought Cyran up from the dungeons and had him enter Elora's mind in an illusion, attempting to make progress. We were just two days away from the deadline I had given Shivani, and I knew the choice I was going to have to make. I had sat down, mentally writing the letter I'd have to leave for Rain and Elora, and evidently fallen asleep.

Wearing a white dress made of fabric which felt like a whisper, I realized I was at Ravemont. As I walked down the halls of the west wing, I glanced down and froze in my tracks. My belly was round, fit to burst. I hadn't even noticed it. Logically, I knew this was a dream about my pregnancy with Elora, yet it didn't have that hazy dream-like quality. I floated down the hall, tracing my fingertips across the waist-high molding, white and freshly painted, and noticed the wallpaper above it wasn't right. When I lived there, it had been blue with a white damask pattern on top of it. But this was the same wallpaper I'd seen at Ravemont months ago, a slip-printed white flower over a golden yellow background. Pressing my hand to the top of my belly, my wedding ring Rain had gifted me caught the light, glittering red in the candlelight. This didn't feel like a dream; it felt real. I continued, making my way to the room I'd once shared with my first husband, the room I'd mourned Lucia in, the room I'd nearly died in when I gave birth. My feet were cold as I padded down the hallway. Even the pregnancy waddle felt real, and my bladder already felt full.

When I turned the corner to my old room, Elora was in my bed, sprawled across it in a familiar position. Her blanket had moved, exposing her bare foot, and I went to tuck it in. It was at that moment when I realized exactly what the dream felt like. An illusion. Who else other than Cyran had that ability? Did Declan? Why would he make me pregnant? I inhaled a deep breath and felt the baby kick. Divine hell, it felt so real. More real than any illusion I'd ever been in. The constant reassurance of Elora's presence had been an anchor in those last weeks of pregnancy—the long, tiresome days before she was born. When my skin felt too tight, and everything felt itchy no matter how much I scratched. I remembered wanting to sleep all hours while simultaneously wanting to tear my room apart, cleaning and organizing, even though it didn't need it. I remembered the fear of the unknown and the longing for my sister to be there with me, for my mother to care. It was those fearful moments when Elora's tiny foot would dig into my ribs, reminding me she was there, that she wanted to meet me. I had phantom kicks for a while after she was born, always fluttering about even while I held her at my breast. It was a sensation I had never thought to feel again, and yet I could now. It soothed me. I rubbed at the little foot pushing against me, stretching my skin tight, and groaned a bit as the babe adjusted. My back was hurting, the ache of the weight I carried in my stomach clear. I'd never felt a dream so realistic.

Warm hands slid around my body, resting on my rounded stomach. I looked down, knowing those hands with every part of my soul. I took a shuddering breath as tears formed on my lashes. It wasn't him. I knew it wasn't him, but I didn't want to turn around. I couldn't. Instead, I tilted my head back and relaxed in the warmth I knew wasn't real and let the tears trickle down my face. He held me, pressing a kiss to that spot behind my ear which killed me, and I choked out a sob. Covering his hands with my own, I let myself give into the sorrow and sobbed freely before he slipped his hands out to rest atop mine, his thumbs lightly caressing the backs of my hands. How could someone know him just as well as I did? What cruel person created this illusion? Who would do this to me? I looked at Elora as she rolled over on the bed, a sleepy smile on her face, and screwed my eyes up tight. It felt so real, and I wondered if this was showing me a future I could have had but lost because Rain had been taken.

"I can't promise the king, but I could give you the babe." Her voice was pleasant and lyrical, and as Rain's arms left me, I turned to face her. He was gone, of course, and my stomach had returned to normal. Both of the losses felt monumental. She wore a dress matching the cut of mine, though it was a deep violet. She clasped her hands in front of her, and I saw countless rings on her rich, brown fingers. Her hair was long, flowing past her shoulders, and the black spirals were shining—a cloud of impossible beauty.

"Rhia."

"Are you not happy to see me again, beloved?" She cocked her head in assessment, a slight frown tilting the corners of her lips down.

"Is that my title or an endearment?" I snapped.

"Can it not be both?" Her heart-shaped mouth turned up into a small smile.

"What do you want?" What she had shown me had been cruel, and I had no desire to deal with yet another god. They'd all made me theirs to use, and the weight was heavy.

Her brows furrowed as she looked at me before she sucked her lower lip into her mouth. "Emmeline, I came to offer you a gift. The last time, I didn't exactly offer it." She nodded to my daughter on the bed behind me.

"What do you mean?"

"You were sinking back then, suffering alone, and I heard you. I heard your heart's pleas. I heard you on the cliff side and blessed you with Elora. And she saved you." She spoke of the day after the burial, the day after I sent Rain away, when I stood at the same cliff we'd fought on, and my thoughts had gone dark. I'd lost everything, and for a few moments I thought just how easy it would be to fall. I wasn't sure what changed my mind, but Rhia had heard my heart and intervened. I had known she blessed me with Elora but hadn't realized why she might have done it. "I'm offering to do it again. Your heart is hardening, and I want to help."

"With a baby? You think what I need is a baby?" My stomach was in my throat. Was she so out of touch? She truly did not know what my heart desired and craved? "I don't need another baby; I need *my* baby to wake up. I need my husband!"

"Did you know you get your harrowing from me? Do you know how many times it has saved you?"

"No. It saved Elora, not me."

"The first time was when you shared it with him. When you both were young, and he found you."

"Shared it with him? I didn't—what?"

She laughed, a dainty sound. "The bond you two started."

"We weren't bonded back then."

"Not completely, no. But you started it in that cave. How else would he have your divinity?"

"But we didn't mingle our blood. How could he?"

She sighed. "The Myriad has taken many liberties. Would you like to know how it used to be done? The first ceremony was between Aonara and Ciarden. It's supposed to be done all at once. Promises of the Mind, spilling of blood for the Body, and the mingling of it for the Soul bond. With time, it's become muddled."

"But blood didn't spill back then—with us."

"It did."

I blinked at her, confused, casting my mind back to those heated, fumbling moments. Rhia's gaze moved downward, a purposeful head tilt accompanying her pointed nod.

"Oh."

I'd barely bled. Blood had certainly not *spilled* anywhere. I remembered wondering why people spoke of bloodied sheets as proof of consummation and assumed it was a turn of phrase.

"If that's all it takes, why aren't more people bonded by mistake? Especially if the Mind doesn't require any blood."

"Most people are not twin flames. Your souls had already begun to entwine. Be grateful for what you started with him that day. More gratitude in general would be nice." She frowned at me before letting out a long-suffering sigh. "The boy will be the key to waking her, and you will be the key to your husband. As long as everything happens as it should. But in the meantime?" She glanced pointedly down at my stomach. "You haven't had your courses yet; I could give you a babe."

I'd been about to ask about our souls—twin flames—and what she meant by that, but her words stopped me. I froze, calculating just how long it had been since I'd been with Rain, and realized I hadn't bled since right after Elora left for Mira. That had been nearly two months ago. I should have bled twice since then. I deflated, apprehension taking over me. Rain had been on the tonic, and we'd only been together that way a few times, but still. It meant nothing to a goddess, I supposed. "Am I not already?"

"No, dear, you are not."

I exhaled in relief. Surely, it was the stress I had been under which caused my courses to stall. A thought occurred to me which gave me pause.

"If—are you the only…Would I have had Elora without you?"

"It is not impossible, I suppose, but highly unlikely you would have found yourself with child."

Closing my eyes, I nodded. I didn't know how to feel about that. Should I feel grateful I had no choice in the matter? I got Elora, I'd be forever thankful for that, but was I no more than a plaything? Did any of us have autonomy if the gods could do as they pleased?

"I do not want a baby, Rhia. Please. Maybe one day, but certainly not now. Do you know how I will save him? I'm running out of time."

The goddess moved, gliding across the room in the same unsettling manner as Aonara had after our bonding ceremony. She sat on the foot of the bed, narrow hips tucking between Elora's feet and the edge. "I do not know more than what Hanwen has told me, which is that he is eager to watch you. He mentioned his drakes," she said with a smile, dreamily, before she looked up at me. "He has always loved them. None of the others could ever make them."

"The drakes? What do you mean 'the others'?"

Her mouth formed a perfect O before she covered it with her fingertips. "Let us worry about the drakes. You formed them once already, and I know he is eager to see them again."

"When did I form drakes?" I frowned; I had no idea what she was talking about.

"After Ciarden blessed you. When you sent your shadows out. Ciarden's gifts manifest differently for each person he bestows them upon. You're the first in a very long time to have drakes as their manifestation. Hanwen is excited for it."

"Why would Hanwen care about how I use Ciarden's gifts?"

"The memories. He thrives in them."

"What does that mean, Rhia?" I snapped, frustrated that everyone insisted on speaking to me in riddles.

Her eyes moved to the window where the sun was setting outside, the sky a watercolor of pinks, purples, and blues. "You'll find out, but I must go. Are you sure?" She glanced down at my belly.

"I'm sure. But wait, what about—"

"It would have been a boy."

When I finally woke, I felt what I thought was perhaps an echo of our bond. My chest ached, and it was almost as if those golden threads had just been there, and I'd missed them. Hand to my chest, I attempted to catch my breath, but the memory of Rain holding me, his warm hands on my belly, rounded with his child, consumed me. His son. It hurt more than anything else I'd thought about in his absence, and I was so angry. I let out a shriek as I reached for the closest thing on my nightstand and threw it across the room, hitting the wall next to the bedroom door. When I realized what I'd done, I was out of the bed in a shot, already sobbing before I picked up the broken pieces of the conch shell on the ground. The shell Rain had gifted me that very first day with him in Mira. The body of the shell was intact, but the delicate outer flange where the shell opened had snapped off. I hadn't meant to throw it, just grabbing the first thing I found. I held the pieces of a memory in my hands as the tears fell. It was there on my knees next to the door, in only my nightgown, where Dewalt found me. He had knocked, but when I didn't answer, he came in anyway.

"I heard a—shit, Emma." He didn't know the significance of the shell. He didn't know I'd thrown it and was responsible for what I sat here mourning, and yet he was on the ground with me in a second, pulling me into his arms. "Come here."

We sat like that for a long time, Dewalt's sandalwood scent enveloping me. I was grateful for him. He didn't speak, just held me, knowing how broken and hopeless I was. My friend didn't try to make me feel better or ask any questions; he was just there. He would have talked, listened, done whatever I asked of him. But at that moment, he did exactly what I needed. The door creaked open again, and Thyra peeked her head in. I tried to hide the pain I wore on my face, and she dipped her head before walking behind me, gently pulling my hair away from my neck and braiding it as Dewalt put both of his hands on my upper arms, pushing me away from him. His expression gave me pause.

"Why are you here? What's going on?"

"Shivani is here." He said, frown clear on his face.

"What the hell does she want?" I asked as I wiped at my eyes and tried not to sniffle.

"An audience," Thyra replied tightly.

I rose, clutching the pieces of shell, and Thyra's hands left my hair. Moments later, in the bathing chamber, I opened my hands over the counter, pieces falling out of my grasp and blood dripping onto the shards. I didn't bother to clean it up.

I chose not to dress, opting to put on Rain's robe once more. Walking out of the bedchamber into the sitting area, I held my breath. Shivani sat at the dining table, waiting with clasped hands. My eyes raked over her frame, and it mildly surprised me to see she wore pants. I'd never seen her in anything but loose, flowing, elegant dresses in bright, jewel tones. But today, she wore black breeches with a simple dark blue tunic. Her hair was wrapped up in a matching scarf, and she wore no jewelry. Shivani's skin was normally smooth and plumped; she'd always had a glow and barely looked older than me, though she was well over two hundred years old. She had always looked healthy. That wasn't the case today. Today, she looked gaunt. Today, she looked tired.

Good. I was tired too.

"How is the girl?" She was quiet, lacking her usual demeanor of disgust.

"The girl? You mean your granddaughter? Elora is still sleeping." She tilted her head downwards, closing her eyes for just a moment. She still hadn't come to visit Elora, and I wondered if maybe she laid eyes on her, really studied her face, she'd see it. But I didn't know if I cared.

"I had hoped she would have woken by now." She sounded sincere, and it took me by surprise. She'd sent her healer to me a few times, and the woman had determined, much like myself and Mairin, that there wasn't much more to be done other than to wait. But I hadn't thought Rain's mother actually cared. I still wasn't sure she did.

"As had I, Shivani."

"The Supreme has offered his skills for Elora." Her words were clipped, and I saw her brow furrow as she watched me. It surprised me to know the man I'd met with in Lamera wanted to help. After everything at the Cascade, I'd honestly forgotten anything to do with the Myriad. I had forgotten about Rain stealing a text from the Supreme, the two of us learning the true prophecy under an apple tree. The Supreme had to have known we took it. And he was interested in Elora. I didn't hesitate with my answer.

"No."

"He is renowned as a healer, and you know how rare it is for him to leave the Seat. It is an honor."

"I said no. I do not want the Myriad near her. Rain does not want the Myriad near her. You may send him my thanks, but I will be declining."

Shivani's temple throbbed as she clenched her jaw shut. I walked to the other side of the room and sat in the armchair near the fireplace, leaving her at the table.

"Declan heard our offer and accepted. We will be delivering his brother to him, and he will release Rainier."

"No." The reply was out of my mouth before I could stop it. Her brows shot up.

"No?"

"He is a child who worked to betray that monster. We cannot send him back."

Shivani stared at me, expression blank. "He slit your daughter's throat. I don't understand, Emma."

"Emmeline," I corrected her. She'd shown me no kindness, no familiarity. Just suspicion and distaste. I wouldn't let her attempt to win me over with familiar pleasantry. "There is more to it than it seems. The boy is working to help wake her. Besides, I do not trust Declan. I do not put it past him to offer us a trade—"

Her fists were clenched in her lap as she interrupted me. "You'll choose that boy over Rainier?"

"Do you no longer have an army? Is this trade the best thing that General Ashmont has come up with?"

"He does not feel that the risk to our soldiers is—"

"Just say he's afraid, Shivani. Just say you both are too cowardly to come up with a plan to save your king, to save *your son*."

"Declan has—"

"Declan has an army made mostly of slaves and mercenaries. They hold no fondness for him. You have an army who is loyal to their king, or perhaps they're only loyal to the queen mother," I spat.

"General Ashmont believes to move on Folterra would cause Declan to kill Rainier anyway, Emmeline. It would be better to negotiate with the—"

"Who is to say if we give him the prince, he'll even deliver Rainier to us? He has dynamic shifters, Shivani. Prince Cyran confirmed it."

"I'd be able to tell—" she sputtered, as if offended.

"He also has a mindbreaker who could easily infiltrate Rain's memories. We would find out, probably when our bond never came back, but by then it might be too late. In all likelihood, it already *is* too late. The Rainier we are getting back…" I shook my head and took a quick breath, burying the threatening emotions and bringing forth the ones of anger instead. "You wasted so much gods damn time not believing me, questioning me. Weeks, Shivani!" I stood, throwing my arms out from my sides.

"That was my fault, and I'm sorry." For a moment, I believed her.

"Then fix it, gods damn it! You can't tell me Vesta has held Folterra at bay for centuries, only to be outsmarted now by a delusional king who thinks he's a god?"

"Emmeline, all we have to do is give him—"

"Get out, Shivani." She stood, jaw dropping as she stared at me. "Either crown me, since I have the courage you are so desperately lacking, or get the fuck out." I gritted my teeth, pushing the words past them. "Rain would not want me to send a child to his death."

"That child slit your daughter's throat, yet you sit here and—"

"Yes, and I brought her back, and I killed the fucking Folterran king while doing it! Must I kill another king? I've always had to do everything on my own. What's one more thing to add to the list? You are a gutless, spineless coward. Get out, Shivani. Get *out*!" I screamed at her, and Dewalt and Thyra launched into the room from where they'd been waiting in the corridor. Shooting a look at Thyra, my Second knew what I desired and gripped Shivani tightly by the elbow, leading her toward the door.

"I'm not letting her take Cyran. Meet back here this evening to discuss how to make the council see we need action?" I asked, and Dewalt nodded. "I'm going back to sleep."

I sent a silent prayer to the gods to leave me alone and let me rest.

CHAPTER 8

Dewalt

With Emma going back to sleep and Thyra settled in on the sofa, I headed toward Lavenia's bedchamber. Really, the chambers belonged to both of us, as I was her bonded partner, but it had never felt like mine. When I had to stay at the palace, I often preferred Rainier's chambers. My union was not one made of romantic love, and it was not a secret to those who worked within the palace. More often than not, it was frowned upon. If only they understood how much love their princess actually had for me. She'd sworn her life to me for our mutual benefit, but I suspected it was more for me than it was for her.

Thinking about Ven set the bond between us on fire. We'd been together only a few weeks prior, but it was already calling for me to be inside her again. The two of us weren't on the same page mentally. We could normally go weeks and weeks without renewing the bond of the Body. But I felt the sharp pull, and I knew she could too. I turned down the corridor to her chambers, and felt her touch on the bond, almost a gentle tickle. I was already hard, the insistence of our connection sending blood straight to my dick. When I came to her door, I didn't bother knocking, slipping off my boots in the entryway. A servant had sent for me when she heard word of Shivani's ambush, so I hadn't bothered to dress, leaving my shirt unbuttoned and hair unbound as I raced to intercept that situation. I should have known better; Emma didn't need me to stand up to her. I took my shirt off, tossing it on the ground as I walked down the hall.

"Ven? Are you busy?"

A long moan sounded from around the corner, and I felt the bond vibrate with anticipation. When I turned into the living area, my pants tightened. Ven was naked, sitting in the corner of a tufted lounger, her head tilted back and legs spread wide. A mane of wild, curly hair blocked most of my view as Mairin knelt before her. They were a rich display of color writhing in front of me, bright and alive. Lavenia's tight black curls, short after taking her braids out and cutting her hair, rested on her tawny shoulders as she lounged on the bright sapphire chaise. Mairin's vivid orange mane and warm ivory skin completed the image, and I couldn't help but stare, taking them in. Entrancing, I watched as Ven's smooth, angular body twitched and Mairin's soft, luscious ass bounced from her movements.

I watched Ven's hand snake down her chest, gently caressing Mairin's forehead as she brushed her hair out of the way, digging fingertips into her scalp. The touch was gentle, reverent almost, and I cleared my throat, afraid I was interrupting something private. Lavenia occasionally took others to bed, but it was rare. And since we'd already been with Mairin together, I expected that to be our dynamic. But they'd started without me, which generally meant something with Ven.

"What are you waiting for? I know you feel this shit just as bad as I do," Lavenia breathed. She looked at me through lowered lashes as Mairin continued with her tongue.

"I do, but I didn't want to interrupt." I shrugged, and my dick rather forcefully twitched against the fabric of my breeches in argument. The golden thread between us gave an insistent snap, and Ven let out a whimper.

"You're not. Come here." She motioned me over, and I didn't need to be told twice. Sloughing off my pants, I paused. I needed more than just Ven's consent.

"Mairin?"

The last time we'd been together, we'd barely paid attention to one another, mostly both focusing on Ven, and I assumed it would be the same this time. But still, I didn't want to insert myself into what was happening without her permission. The merrow stopped with her mouth, turning to look over her shoulder with glistening lips. Two of her fingers moved with a purpose as she pounded into Ven's pussy, and the motion distracted me.

"I suppose I'll share her," she said, a coy smile tipping up her mouth as her tongue darted out, licking Ven's arousal from her lips.

"Come here, D," Lavenia sighed. It was a good thing she did, because I wasn't sure I'd have been able to hold the bond at bay much longer. She gestured for me to climb onto the chaise next to her, and I did, resting on my knees as she grabbed me through my undershorts. Mairin was kissing up her thigh as Ven pulled at my waistband, freeing me from the restrictive clothing. I hissed as Ven's hand slid down, grip firm, before batting it away.

"I'm not going to let this go to waste," I said as I reached down, gliding my hand through the mess between her legs. She moaned as Mairin's hand moved up, tweaking those nipples as I took my hand to my cock, running her wetness up and down my hard length.

When Ven gripped me, sliding her hand down roughly, she tugged me closer, and I let out a grunt as she pulled me into her mouth. It wasn't like her to do that, usually opting for only what the bond demanded, but fuck if I was going to stop her. I groaned, tilting my head back and closing my eyes.

As Ven moaned around my cock, I opened my eyes, and looked down to see how Mairin pounded into her. Her legs shook as the merrow pushed three fingers inside her, looking up at her as she swirled her tongue on that sensitive spot. Ven gasped, and though I fell out of her mouth, she kept her grip on me firm. She writhed and whimpered as Mairin continued, the eye contact between them heavy, rife with tension.

And in Mairin's eyes, I saw the truth of the merrow's feelings as she looked up at Ven. Alongside the lust, there was awe and adoration. It gave me a moment's pause until Ven squeezed me hard enough to hurt, and I had to gently pry her fingers from my skin as I hissed through my teeth.

"Gods, Mai, I—" Ven's panting breaths cut her off a second before Mairin pulled away, kissing her inner thighs as she sat back on her heels and peered up at me, fingers still pumping.

"How does it work? Do you need to make each other come?" She tugged on Ven's nipple with her free hand, earning a low groan from the woman spread bare beside us.

"I've never thought about it." I paused, thinking about the last time the bond had been sated. "Usually, we're finishing together, yes."

Mairin nodded before gently withdrawing her fingers from Ven's heat. She gently ran her hands up the tops of Ven's thighs, up her stomach, and stopped at her breasts. Bending over, she pressed a kiss between them, and I knew that, for them, this was more. The cave had been a night of drunken fun as we renewed our bond, but this was different. I already knew where I stood. When the merrow moved up her body and kissed Lavenia tenderly on the mouth, still rubbing tight circles on Ven's clit, I averted my eyes. A throaty sound came from Ven, and I knew she was close. I felt a bit stupid on my knees next to them with my cock out while they shared this tender moment, until Mairin surprised me. Spitting on her palm, she grasped me in her hand as she forced me to sit.

"What are you doing?" I asked. I was rock-hard, and the bond was insistent, wanting me inside Ven. I didn't know how much more I could take.

"Getting you ready for her," she answered as she stroked me from base to tip. I let my head tilt back as I stretched my arms over the back of the chaise. Ven sat up beside me, pulling the merrow in for a passionate kiss.

"You tease," she said against Mairin's lips.

"I've almost got you there, sweets. I'm willing to let him steal it from me as long as you say my name when he does." The merrow's voice was a low rasp, and Ven nodded, not looking at me. Perhaps if I were a better man, I would've told Mairin to take the orgasm she earned. It was clear the merrow felt something more, and, though the three of us had been together before and her hand was on my cock, the dynamic between us was off. There was an imbalance, and I owed it to us, to Ven, to make sure it was what we all wanted. If I were a better man, I would've stopped things and talked to Lavenia about where they stood. If I were a better man, I wouldn't have felt abandoned.

There were a lot of things I'd have done differently if I were a better man.

I grabbed Ven, pulling her into my lap and turning her so her back was to my chest, my hands on her waist. Mairin's hand still gripped me, lining me up with Ven, until she lowered herself. She was so fucking wet, and she felt good wrapped around me.

Ven hovered over me, lowering herself slowly, as she gripped my wrists. After a few moments when she still hadn't taken me fully, I used my hold on her hips to pull her down as I pushed up at the same time.

"Shit, shit," she gasped. "Divine hell, D, you're too big this way."

"You can do it, princess," I teased. She resisted, so I moved my hands up her back and shoulders, rubbing soothing circles with my thumbs.

Mairin made eye contact with me over Ven's shoulder before her eyes moved in a slow caress down Ven's form, lingering where our flesh met. She surged forward, and the merrow's hand found its way to Ven's clit. I could feel her rubbing circles on that sensitive spot, and Ven relaxed incrementally. The bond vibrated, almost pushing me to finish just from being inside her. I was tempted to thrust hard a few times to be done with it, to let them explore without me, but I could tell the bond needed more from us. Ven leaned back, head against my shoulder, as she relaxed even further.

"Almost, beautiful," Mairin whispered, leaning forward to kiss her. "Just a little bit more." Placing two hands on her shoulders, Mairin pushed down as Ven gasped, and she finally took all of me.

"That's it," I whispered in her ear. "Told you you could do it."

Ven's moan was her only response as the merrow slammed to her knees and got to work.

"Fuck," I grunted as I felt a warm tongue graze where our bodies met, and Ven froze on top of me. Her pussy clenched around me, and I nearly came right then.

"Gods, Mai," Ven moaned as Mairin laved our skin—tasting, sucking, *savoring*.

When Ven collapsed back against my chest, head lolling, I wrapped my arms around her waist and slowly pushed up into her, matching Mairin's pace. One thread from the bond was tight, nearly vibrating, and I plucked at it, and Ven tightened around me even more. I ignored the other threads, not nearly as strong, and buried my nose into her neck, inhaling her. I knew what this was, and wondered if Ven did too. The last time our bond had been this weak, it was during her relationship with Brenna.

Fingertips replaced Mairin's tongue as she stood slowly, pressing her lips in a path up Ven's hips and stomach and chest before leaning in for a kiss. I shifted, moving her just so—

"Divine hell, right there. Don't stop," she gasped, a guttural moan chasing her words. Mairin's fingertips moved with frenzy as I kept my tempo. We were both close, right on the edge, and I had to ignore Mairin whispering in Ven's ear, the look in her eyes something I felt I shouldn't be seeing.

Gods, this had to be the last time. The air between them was charged with emotion, and I wanted no part in it. Lavenia had outgrown me, and I didn't want to hold her back. I cursed myself for not being able to see this at a shallower level. One beautiful woman was riding me while another kissed her. What the hell was my problem?

I closed my eyes when Ven started panting the merrow's name, and I focused on the sensation just to push me past the point of no return. And when she clenched around me, and I gave that final push into her, causing my dick and the bond to pulse, I knew I was right. Knew I'd let the threads sever, and I'd never experience that divine connection again.

Tilting my head back, I came down from it as Lavenia still sat atop me, falling forward into Mairin's hold as she caught her breath. I wasn't sure what I was feeling when I leaned in, pressing my cheek to her back. It wasn't a goodbye; neither of us were going anywhere. But all the same, I knew things between us would change from here, and I took one final moment to savor the connection with my closest friend. Lavenia had always been the person who kept me from sinking, and I'd always been someone she could rely on as a constant. We understood one another better than we understood ourselves, and she was going to have to trust me. It was time to let our bond break.

I dreaded the hours before dinner every day, and today was no exception. I was in a strange mood after things with Lavenia. Even though it made perfect sense, I had a feeling she would fight it. When I'd suggested she break it off for Brenna, she fought me before finally agreeing, but by then, it was too little, too late. I would not let her use me as a crutch anymore, never mind the fact I was just as guilty. I'd be the voice of reason for both of us.

Emma wasn't in her chambers anymore by the time I arrived. She knew she could count on me, so she was probably off with Thyra preparing for our meeting that evening. To force her to maintain her sanity, I'd insisted on making her leave. Between her healing and taking part in illusions with Cyran, I knew it was taking a toll on her. Someone was going to have to make her take breaks.

Because of this, I found myself in Emma's chambers daily, talking to an unconscious girl who wouldn't wake. I wasn't sure I understood the point of it, but Emma and the prince claimed she was more active in the illusions the more people talked to her. Honestly, it felt a bit stupid, but I'd do as I was told. I'd give both of them a much-needed break. Emma would barely talk to anyone about anything, and Cyran looked like a kicked puppy any time they brought him out of the dungeon. Between the marks I had noticed on his body and the vision he'd seen, I almost felt bad for the boy.

Almost.

He clearly had a rough life, but that didn't excuse shit. He killed my brother's child. We'd always been brothers, even before I bonded with his sister. In another life, Rainier would have been my brother in a different way, both of us married to the sisters we called our own. But fate was cruel and the gods unmoving. And yet, he was my brother all the same. Cyran killed his flesh and blood, regardless of the fact Emma had brought her back. But if she never woke, what did that count for? It didn't matter if a gods damned seer told him to do it. It was unforgivable.

I understood why Emma considered showing mercy, especially since he seemed so repentant and eager to help, but I wouldn't be offering the prince kindness any time soon. I often wondered what Rainier would think of him and how he would feel about the man his daughter supposedly loved being the one to kill her.

Gods, Rainier had a daughter.

The man was meant to be a father. He was patient as hell, something he'd proven in how he won over Emma. He was kind and intelligent, eager to provide for and teach the younger soldiers. I couldn't wait to see him be a father to this girl. A beautiful girl who shared the best features of both of her parents. She didn't look as much like Lucia as I'd imagined, so many elements not quite the same, but it was close enough that those two hours felt like a mild form of torture. I had to make sure to face her, take in the parts of her which looked like Rainier, knowing if I caught her in the corner of my eye, I'd think about her aunt. It was strange to see her and think of Lucia. Elora wasn't even sixteen years old, but she reminded me so much of the girl I loved. It made me face just how young she was when she died.

Not trusting myself to think of something appropriate to talk to a sleeping girl about for hours, I read to her. I had always loved to read, but I didn't think my choice of reading material lent well to waking a teenage girl, more likely to keep her sleeping longer. Battle strategizing wasn't particularly exciting. I asked Emma what kind of stories the girl liked, but her answer was vague. The dark circles under her eyes were only getting worse as time wore on. I knew bringing Cyran up from the dungeons was a risk, and she'd be worried about Shivani's agreement to Declan's deal. I understood Emma's concern. She was the only person protecting the boy, though I wasn't sure how much he deserved the protection. I had half a mind to hand him over to Declan myself, but I knew I'd be ball-less in an instant if I went through with it. But within the past week since she began accompanying Cyran in illusions with Elora, Emma had a certain hopefulness to her, so I kept my mouth shut.

With everything she was going through, I didn't want to harass her about what books Elora liked. I remembered Rainier reading one belonging to her while we traveled. I'd made fun of him for reading it. *You think that will win Emma over?* I'd said. In response, he used his divinity to throw a ball of mud at my head. He'd been unknowingly reading his daughter's favorite book. It hurt to think they might never get to talk about it. I'd searched for the book, but couldn't find the copy he'd read.

With no more guidance, I decided on one of the ancient epics from when the gods roamed the earth. The story of Nulo had always resonated with me, and I thought it was an apt adventure for her to hear, if she could hear it at all. Nulo was the consort of both Hanwen and Rhia, loving both gods until his eventual death at the hands of another one of Hanwen's lovers. The tale was told from the perspective of Rhia and highlighted exactly why she was the patron god of mercy.

The story began with Nulo earning Hanwen's attentions on the field of battle. Before the Three Kingdoms broke apart, all three were once one land mass and one civilization called Ishurynn. The gods ruled from the center of the massive continent, where Lamera now sat. Or so the story claimed. Nulo was from the northern part of the kingdom, where summers were hot and dry and winters were cool and wet. I thought the beginning of the story was quite interesting, how Rhia—or rather the unnamed bard who wrote from her perspective—described the political strife between different parts of the kingdom and the methods the gods used to settle their differences. Though Elora letting out a soft snore told me perhaps she didn't feel the same.

"Not quite doing it for you? Give me a moment. I'll skip ahead." I smiled as she rolled over, wondering if the girl would remember me when she woke. With her face slack with sleep, she looked so much like her mother and, in turn, her aunt. I preferred it when she frowned or smiled, the features of her father shining through. I searched for those expressions, helping to draw me from the past.

I flipped ahead to the part where Rhia finally met Nulo, thinking it might interest her more. Nulo had already won the affections of Hanwen, and the god had taken him for a lover. And yet, Nulo wanted more. One would have thought the attentions of one god would have been enough, but when Rhia showed him the slightest interest, he became intent on winning her heart. Ciarden had blessed Nulo's family line, oddly enough. Other than Aonara, Nulo had been favored by all the gods in some way. His divinity manifesting in the mind, Nulo visited Rhia in her dreams, unbeknownst to Hanwen. Now, Rhia believed the god wouldn't have cared, as they'd all shared different lovers in the past, but the idea of the secret love affair made it more alluring. Describing Rhia's dreams where she fell in love with the man, leaving out the illicit parts because Elora was a child after all, I noticed her growing agitated. She wore a frown and thrashed about on the bed.

"Fuck, alright," I muttered under my breath, flipping pages. I knew some of Cyran's visits to her mind ended in hysterics, but still. She let out a small whimper, and I watched her brow crinkle, somehow a perfect mixture of Emma and Rainier. Gods, they were lucky.

Uncertain now of my choice in literature, I tried to find a section of the story which wouldn't upset her. Considering I had forgotten about Nulo's betrayal, I thought maybe I was better served not to tell her the rest. Though the man betrayed her, portraying their relationship to Hanwen as something she had coerced him into, Rhia wept when another one of Hanwen's lovers killed Nulo. Her tears filled the font for over a year, pouring parts of her soul into the life-giving waters. And when she finished, the opportunity to kill the lover arose, and she chose mercy, not wanting to force the same feeling of grief upon Hanwen.

Though my divinity hailed from Ciarden, I had always felt a fondness for Rhia—the woman scorned who still loved and forgave. I wondered if Elora would come to rely on the goddess to get her through her trauma when she finally woke. I knew she wasn't Lucia, but I felt a fondness for her that made me fiercely protective of her. The girl had been lied to and broken, used for money and to fulfill a prophecy. When she did wake up, I expected anger, and I would teach her how to channel it and turn her into something formidable.

Though I had put the book down, I still had a short time during my shift until dinner, so I described to her all the ways I'd teach her to defend herself, to protect the ones she loved, and to arm herself with weapons past her divinity—all while using both in tandem. Demonstrating despite her inability to watch, I stood and pointed out exactly where the kidneys were. I'd truly train her when she woke; I thought getting to know her and immersing myself in her personality would take the sting of her appearance away. Maybe training Elora would help me process some of those feelings about Lucia I'd kept bottled deep within me. This girl would know how to fight. It wasn't hand-to-hand combat which had killed Lucia, but part of me always wondered if I could have helped prepare her better. I'd make sure this girl would be ready for anything.

Going into detail about the exact method of disembowelment I preferred, I jumped when Emma let the door shut behind her.

"Divine hell, Dewalt. Really?" She sounded so tired, and though she startled me at that moment, her weariness weighed heavily on me.

"Sorry." I shrugged, smiling at her. "It's not like she knows what I'm saying, anyway." It was the wrong thing to say. I hadn't meant it in a way to upset her, but as I turned toward her, I saw her shoulders drop. She made the slightest sound in the back of her throat, and it broke my gods damned heart. "I didn't mean it. She's going to—" She stopped me with her hand, a slash through the air which cut. I felt horrible. She turned away, shrugging her cloak off onto a chair. Based on her rosy cheeks and the damp fabric, I assumed she'd just been outside. I approached her, bringing the book with me to put away.

"Listen, I am not a smart man. If I could shove my foot any deeper into my mouth, it'd shoot out my ass." She snorted despite herself, glowering up at me. There she was. I rested my hand on her shoulder, proving my sincerity. "I do think she can hear me, by the way. She didn't like it when I was reading about Nulo and Rhia falling in love through dreams. She tossed and turned, moved more than I've ever seen her."

Those big, blue eyes were full of tears and hope. Fuck. She nodded and blinked hard, her lower lip quivering, before she pulled away from me. "Thank you. I'm sure dinner will be ready soon. Thanks for sitting with her. I'll see you tomorrow."

"How about I have dinner with you here?" I knew she hadn't been eating. When she gave me a noncommittal shrug and headed toward the bathing suite, I knew she didn't want me to stay.

Too damn bad.

When she shut the door behind her, I sat down at the small dining table in the other half of the suite and bided my time. I had to show her it wasn't hopeless. Elora was improving each day, and I was still optimistic the council would come up with something better than exchanging the boy. I heard Emma's outburst this morning, but I wondered if I could persuade her into seeing that trading Cyran might be our only choice. Declan's original deadline was in a week. I knew it had to be weighing heavily on Emma, and I was worried she might do something desperate. Or worse yet, do exactly as she said she would and deliver herself to Declan.

I wasn't sure when Thyra would be back. Gods, I was grateful for that woman. The friendship she and Emma seemed to share before Rainier was taken was something I found fascinating. It was rare for someone to stomach a situation such as that. But, not only did Emma stomach it, she befriended the woman. I respected the hell out of her for it; I knew I wouldn't be so understanding. I wondered if the two of them ever discussed it, or if it was just an unspoken agreement that none of it mattered. Thyra knew her place, knew she wanted nothing from her prince—now king. It had been over a decade by now. And Emma, well, Emma knew where she stood with him—even if it took her far too long to come to that conclusion. Stubborn as a mule, that woman. Thyra had been a much-needed comfort to her these past weeks while Ven and Mairin were busy. Besides that, when either of them had any free time, they were spending it together. I didn't have any extra responsibilities. Everyone else was too busy for Emma, other than Thyra, and she'd been bearing the weight of it more than me. It was my turn now.

A few moments later, the door opened. Emma froze in the doorway, carrying her hairbrush and wearing fresh clothes—comfortable pants and a thick sweater I thought belonged to Rainier.

"Are you not going to eat?" She scowled at me, and I took heart in the familiar expression.

"I'm thinking of having it brought up here. Mine and yours." I folded my hands in my lap, certain she was going to get angry.

"D, go. I'm fine." She peeked her head into the bedroom to check on Elora while she angrily pulled her brush through her long, golden-brown locks. It was often I thanked the gods her hair was that color, rather than white. I leaned back farther into the chair and crossed my ankle over my knee. I'd get her to talk to me, even if it was to tell me just how long it would take her to skin me alive. "Gods damn it, Dewalt. What do you want?"

"You're not sleeping, you're not eating, you're not talking." She stood in the doorway to the bedroom, her hand on the knob to pull it shut. I'd sit here all night if I had to. Watching her frown deepen and her skin flush, I knew I was in trouble.

"I'm not sleeping because every time I start to," she said, "she moves, she sighs, she twitches, and I'm awake. I'm not eating, because I'm not hungry. And I'm not talking because what the hell is there to possibly talk about?" Her voice grew louder with each word, and I sat patiently. "What do you want to talk about, Dewalt?" She nearly screeched the last sentence as she stomped closer to me.

"I want to talk about whatever you want to talk about, Emmeline."

She stood over me, hands on her hips. "I have nothing to speak of. My husband is locked up in Darkhold, body parts about to get chopped off and sent to me unless I give Declan a gods damned child. My daughter died. Yes, I brought her back, but she still sleeps. And I'm just sitting here with a thumb up my ass, waiting for Shivani, of all people, to do something. And she's not going to, unless it involves sending the boy. And I don't want that, so, it still has to be me." She stared down at me for a couple of seconds before her blinking became rapid. I knew what was coming next, and she wouldn't appreciate me witnessing it. She needed to talk—and I'd help it happen—but I knew she'd want to break down in private. So, I did what I do best.

"Why don't you pull your thumb out and sit down and talk to me, and we can decide together what to do next? I think you'll need your whole hand for whatever we come up with, though I'm sure Rainier will be glad to know you kept your ass ready—" When she swung out to punch me in the jaw, I grinned up at her as I caught her wrist.

Her eyes were glowing white.

Lucia's eyes did that sometimes. Fuck. I felt my smile fall before I cleared my throat. "You have to talk to someone, and I'm here. Let me listen?" I let go of her hand and watched as her eyes faded back to their normal color, and she heaved out a long sigh. She sat down on the floor in front of the fire, her body slow and tired as she did it. I needed to get some food in her.

"Fine. I don't know what you intend to get out of this. What am I supposed to do? I can't take on Darkhold, even if I'm the gods damn Beloved. Oh, and there's that! There's so much other shit, the fact that I'm the Beloved didn't even merit mentioning." I couldn't help but chuckle.

"Shivani is his mother. You know better than anybody what she's feeling. She won't let him die." She looked down at her hands in her lap. "I think we should force her hand. She'll have to move the army if we refuse to trade either of you."

"Dewalt, you know I can't risk that. He's too important."

"I sure as fuck thought he would have convinced you of the same by now. They both need you." She flinched, and I softened my voice. "You're not sitting here doing nothing, alright? You're doing your best with Elora. You're healing her every single day, keeping her as healthy as you can. You and Cyran are infiltrating her dreams. She's going to wake up eventually, and it'll be because of one of those things. Besides, I think Rainier would be furious if I got to talk to his daughter before he did. Maybe she knows it, and she's just waiting for him." She gave me a weak smile before it twisted into a frown; I swiftly continued. "You brought Shivani the proof that Rainier went to Darkhold—as much proof as we could get. And as for the rest of it...I know you don't want to, but do you think we should consider—"

"No, I'm not giving the boy to Declan. He's a child. A stupid child, but—" She took a deep breath. "If I give him Cyran, who is to say he'll even give Rain back to me? And if he doesn't, then that's just two dead men. Both of them are part of Elora's life in some way, and I'm—no, I'm not doing that. The boy is helping her, and I'll let her decide what to do with him when she wakes. What we are doing is making a difference."

"Alright, I won't ask again. But you can't go, Emma." She refused to look at me, and I knew what she was thinking. "I can't let you go. He'd fucking kill me." When she didn't answer, I tried an alternate approach. "Have you heard from Aedwyn or Aerfen yet?" The spy shifters had been gone for weeks, and I had a bad feeling about it.

"No." Her voice grew quiet. "I don't know. What do I do, Dewalt?" Elbows propped up on her knees, she dropped her head in her hands. I wasn't helping; I was making it worse.

"We take the guard to the Cascade. We can make sure we are in Darkhold next week. Fuck if I know a plan from there, but I'll send a message to Raj tonight."

"Dewalt, the guard is still recovering. Rainier wouldn't want—"

"Honestly, fuck what he wants." The words slipped out of me before I even thought them. I didn't even know I'd been thinking them. She lifted her head and stared at me, mouth parting in surprise. Shit. "I just mean—"

"No, no. You're right. Fuck what he wants." She gave me a small smile, then shook her head. "That...Gods, I don't want to say anything bad about him right now, because what if—I am just so angry with him, Dewalt."

I nodded as I watched her, the hands she clenched into fists and the set of her jaw.

"He's done this to me twice now." She took a deep breath before continuing, and though it was because of anger, I was grateful for any sort of emotion from her other than despondence. "He gets scared that something is going to happen to me, and starts rifting without thought. The first time he nearly killed me, and now?" She laughed with no humor. "I understand why he does it. I really do. But I am not helpless. I killed the gods damn King of Bones, and I brought my child back from death. Not to mention all the other shit he's witnessed. I wish he'd just...have a little more faith in me." She blew out a breath as she rubbed her hands down her face. "I can't lose him. I can't. He is everything to me, Dewalt." Her voice cracked. "We both made so many mistakes. I wasted what little time I had with him being a stubborn fool."

"We're not going to lose him. You're right about a few things though. You're both stubborn fools. Him rifting Declan away from you was his way of protecting you, even if he knew you didn't need it. It makes sense though, since you're twin flames and all. The moment you stopped being an idiot, he had to fill the void."

She huffed a laugh, and I saw a smile turn up at the corners of her mouth. I felt a small inkling of relief at the sight.

"I'm sorry I just spewed all of that at you. That wasn't fair." She rubbed at her eyes, and I wasn't sure if it was sleep or tears she was holding at bay.

"No, I wanted you to talk to me. You needed it. We have both loved the same people all our lives, just in different ways. I get it. You get it. So, let me be here for you, alright?"

She nodded, and I let out a breath. It was time for some levity and then I'd call a servant to bring us dinner before our meeting. "You know, you don't have to brag about killing Dryul all by yourself. I'm still pissed you didn't fetch me first." I was joking but I surprised myself that there was some honesty in my words. The man had murdered Lucia, and I'd have loved to be part of that kill.

"I don't remember it," she whispered as her eyes met mine. I froze, waiting. She'd never told this part of the story. "I remember hearing his heart stop, but I don't know what I did to kill him, D. Cyran had just—and I went for her, and Dryul was behind me. Ciarden blessed me, and the shadows? They just took care of it. I didn't control them at all, they just dealt with him for me. And then...I don't remember healing her, bringing her back, nothing. I woke up holding her as I was forming the rift."

Not sure what to say, I offered the only thing I could. "She'll wake up, and we'll get him back. Even *I* don't think the gods are that cruel as to keep them apart."

CHAPTER 9

CYRAN

I'D MET QUITE A few members of the queen's inner circle in the past week, and the one who unnerved me the most was the merrow. She unsettled me. They hadn't meant to tell me what she was, but I'd overheard them talking.

I knew merrows were real; I had never questioned the fact they existed, as I knew so many people did. I knew they were real because I had met one as a child. My mother had taken me to the southern shore of Folterra, just west of Mindengar, and I'd fallen asleep on the sand. It was only a couple of years before she died, but I was rather small for my age. I woke to what I came to understand was a selkie, dragging me toward the water. It was giant, and it held my arm in its mouth, sharp teeth digging in. I still bore the scars. I had fought and pushed and tried to get away from it, but it wouldn't let me go. I was screaming, but my mother was sleeping deeply and couldn't hear me. Finally, the selkie got me to the water, and I was struggling to keep my head above it, screaming all the while.

At one point, I went under, and the next thing I knew, I was being hoisted out of the water and thrown onto the sand. Sitting there a few moments later, coughing out saltwater, the selkie was gone, and in its place was a merrow. He had long yellow-green hair, ratty and tangled, hanging down in eyes with film over them, giving them a black tint. I remembered thinking he didn't have a nose, though I guessed he had slits to breathe. His skin was a pale-blue green color, and he was covered in scales so small and fine, I wouldn't have realized it wasn't skin if they hadn't cast a slight iridescent gleam in the sunlight. He opened his mouth, and countless pointed teeth filled it. Sitting in the water, I couldn't see his tail, though I was sure he had one. He had pushed backwards toward the sea with strong arms that could've instantly killed me. But they hadn't. They'd saved me. He had hissed at me, saying something I couldn't understand, and I turned and ran.

Ever since that happened, I had dreamt of merrows. I had never imagined what they might have looked like on land, but their human forms were a perfect disguise. I never would have guessed the woman I'd seen could have turned into *that*. I supposed he saved me, and I should have been grateful. But I was already so terrified from the selkie, and the hiss sounded so damn aggressive, I held fear for the creatures to this day.

I avoided almost every person who came into the queen's chambers while I was there, feeling their hatred seep from their skin. They despised me, and for good reason. When the captain had come to my cell, later than usual, I was surprised. I'd thought Emmeline wanted to take a break, but it turned out she just wanted me there at the same time she and her inner circle held a meeting.

That was why, just after rousing from a disastrous illusion with Elora, I found myself face to face with the merrow. My blood hammered through my veins, still too close to sleep to push the fear away. I pulled my fingers through my hair and straightened my clothes before sitting up. I'd fallen asleep slouched in the chair next to the bed, holding Elora's hand. It made it easier to connect with her.

"I'm here to ask you some questions, and I intend to compel the answer out of you to make both of our lives easier." My audible gulp nearly echoed through the room, and I swore I saw her lip twitch. I didn't find it very funny. "I can also compel you to forget all of this, so you don't remember, if you'd like. Compulsions aren't comfortable if you're f—"

"They're not comfortable in general."

"So, you're familiar?"

"Yes, and you don't need to make me forget. May I eat first?" The nausea had been overwhelming the last time Dewalt had questioned me on an empty stomach. The merrow nodded toward a tray on the nightstand I hadn't noticed, and I took a few moments to shove some sliced turkey down my throat, along with beans and potatoes. I probably didn't have to eat it as quickly as I did, but I was nervous, especially with her watching me. I wondered about her teeth and started choking. Mairin just stood there watching me with preternatural stillness as I frantically reached for my glass of water and gulped it down. Gods, she made me uncomfortable.

"Alright, little pig, let us begin. Look me in the eye." I glared at her, not appreciating the nickname. When she began to sing, I felt my body relax, though my heart started racing. I stared at her eyes, watching the film slide over them, reminding me of the merrow from my memory.

"Tell me any penetrable weak points within Darkhold." Her voice was terrifying. While Mairin spoke in the common tongue, her voice held that same quality of otherness the merrow from my childhood had. I wanted to run away screaming. But I focused on her question, the compulsion forcing my attention to the task at hand. It was interesting, being forced to answer a question you weren't certain of the answer, almost as if the compulsion was navigating the memories of my mind like a library. It turned me down an alcove, and I saw a sewer grate at the end.

"The sewers." My mouth opened, and the words came out without my consent, though I had no intentions of fighting it.

"The sewers within the palace itself or Darkhold as a whole?"

"Both. There is only one entrance into the palace itself, but plenty of tunnels to get to it through the capital. The cons of hygienic sophistication, I suppose. Perhaps that's why King Soren never splurged on it here. Astana smells putrid."

"Stop talking." My jaw snapped shut of its own accord, and I glared at the short woman who stood in front of me, barely taller than my seated form. She certainly didn't look that frightening, with her plush curves and kind smile, but I knew what her other form would look like. "Where is the entrance to the palace?"

"I do not know how to get in from the outside, but below the dungeons there is a pit which leads out to the river. It's where they throw the bodies. I believe all the waste from the palace meets up with it on the path out to the river."

"How deep is the pit below the dungeon? If we could get into it, swim through the shit," she made a face, and I didn't blame her. "Would someone be able to climb up from below?"

I didn't know, but I felt the compulsion move through me to verify. I had never seen it, just heard people talk about throwing bodies down into it, discussing the rats which waited below. "I do not know."

"Can you think of anything else that might help us regarding the sewers, other than the obvious?"

The divinity and I sat with the question, allowing it to tour the library inside my mind, and found I had nothing to add. When I told her no, the merrow released it, and the film over her eyes opened.

"Why was it you who came to compel me? Nearly everyone here can do it. Do you know how rare that is? I've only ever met—"

"Because I'm curious about you. I know you had a vision, and I know you have feelings for the girl." I balked, not sure if I wanted to correct her. My eyes drifted over to Elora who lay sleeping beside us, a small smile on her lips. What was the point of having feelings for someone you'd wronged—multiple times over? "Why did you do it?"

"You know about the vision, yet ask why I did it?"

"I know about the vision and the fact you clearly feel something for Elora. You saw a vision, and it was bad. Bad enough for you to kill her. You were raised by that foul prince, and yet you knew you had to do what was needed to awaken the Beloved. Who taught you that?"

I looked down at my hands, still not quite sure what she was asking. I didn't have a choice. Was Elora more important than the Three Kingdoms? Maybe to Emmeline, to the king. But to me? I didn't know. I did then, but not anymore.

"Who taught you about making hard decisions for the greater good, piglet?" Quiet, her voice coaxed a response from me.

"My mother. She—she was a good woman. I-I thought she would have been disappointed in me if I didn't do what I needed to do to stop Declan. She feared him, knew what he was capable of. But now I'm wondering if she would have been disappointed because of what I did."

The door creaked open, and I looked down at my hands. The hands that killed the only light I'd experienced since my mother died. I missed my friend.

"She wouldn't have been disappointed in your choice. She would have been sad you had to make it." The door snicked shut.

Back in my cell that night, thoughts of my illusions with Elora haunted me. I kept falling into sad dreams of hers. Memories of her and Faxon plagued her lately. I got to see her as a small child trying to maneuver a fishing pole, making the man put a worm on the end while she apologized to the bait the whole time. It hurt my heart to know the poor, innocent thing would be sold by the man who truly seemed to love her in those memories. He sold her to *me*. And then what had I done to her?

Another scene which tortured us was Declan taking her from me. The night before he took her, she had fallen asleep on the chaise in my chambers. We'd both been reading, and instead of waking her and sending her to her room, I put one of my blankets over her and laid in my own bed, watching her. Her memory began with us both waking up around the same time, realizing later that it was because of the sounds of Declan pounding through the estate. But until he got there, we laid there in sleepy silence, just watching each other wake. She had smiled at me, and the sun from the window hit her face in a way which made her blue eyes shine.

Then the door burst open, and Declan ruined everything, as he always did. She relived the way he leered at her on my chaise, the cruel spread of his smile over his face. The way his eyes slid down to the blanket which had moved down her waist and the sliver of skin showing where her shirt had lifted. She yanked it down, and, even after seeing the memory a dozen times, the anger roiled in my gut. The Cyran from her memories just lay in the bed, unmoving, until he finally sat up and faced Declan. Is that what I had done? Had my disgust for my brother not been clear on my face? The fear of what he was about to do? I supposed it must have been what she saw, because why would she remember it as such otherwise? When he hauled her away, picking her up at the waist so her back pressed against his chest as her legs kicked out, she couldn't see me. She heard me though. She heard me beg Declan not to take her. She didn't see me grab onto his belt loop and pull him toward me. She didn't see him send a shadow down my throat. She didn't see him beat me after he took her away, to the point where one of his healers took pity on me. I had pissed blood for a week.

The most common memory was her last one, and I ached every single time I saw it. I wished I could go back. I wished I could have made Emmeline only think I'd done it. The vision had been vague, but what if I would have just thought longer and harder about it? What if I could have made Emmeline believe it was real? Just enough to awaken Ciarden's power. What if I had been able to tell Elora about the vision? She could have helped me come up with something.

I had so many regrets.

Even though I was tired from the illusion with Elora, since they didn't bother putting me in chains anymore, I tried once again to contact Ismene. I was shocked when I found her. I'd conjured up her bedroom within Evenmoor, the dark earth tones of the room a comfort to me. The walls were a deep green paisley pattern, and I drew my eyes from them to my sister sitting on the bed. When she turned her head to look at me, I nearly vomited. Both of her eyes were bruised, a deep purple and greenish color. One was swollen shut, and I could only see one hazel eye which matched mine. I knew without me being there, it might be worse for her, but he'd never hit her hard enough to leave a mark before. When I could finally speak, she sat quietly with her hands in her lap.

"I'm so sorry, Ismene. Are you alright? Well, of course you're not alright, but—I've been trying to reach you. I've been trying every night, Iz, I swear." My eyes moved down to her wrists and didn't see any red marks, common with obsidian cuffs. She tracked the movement and pulled her long black hair over her shoulders to hang loose behind her back. There was a red circle around her neck.

"A necklace. He forgot to put it back on after he used me for harrowing. I can take it off, but if he finds me without it, well..." She gestured to her eyes. I walked across the space to her and knelt, taking her hands in mine.

"I should be there. I'm sorry. I should have made sure you could come with—"

"Cyran, you need me here, so I can help. Listen, before he comes and wakes me. There is a group of rebels. They can help you. Put them in contact with the Vestian queen."

I felt the pull, the tingle as the illusion fought me. Bloody hell.

"Iz, I'm sorry. Please, just be careful. Do what he says, alright? Try not to talk back to him. Do whatever you have to. I'll try to find a way to get to you."

"No, I'm not leaving here until Declan is dead. You need my eyes, you need me. Besides, who is going to take care of Magda?" The housekeeper who had raised us since our mothers died could take care of herself, and I told my sister as much. She was shaking her head as the illusion started to fade.

"I'll check in whenever I can, Iz. I promise. Midday and after sunset, I'll try every night." She was nodding when I was pushed out.

I'd thought I was being pushed out from her side of the illusion, but when I came to, it was to chains being clamped back onto my wrists, the obsidian burning my skin.

"What is happening?"

My question went unanswered as I was hauled to my feet and pushed out of my cell.

CHAPTER 10

Rainier

The room was smoky, the sickly-sweet scent clouding the air. I felt it coating my throat and my skin, making me tired. I couldn't remember a time when I didn't smell the draíbea. I didn't know how many days I'd been in the cell, but she was with me, so I didn't care. Hallucination or no, she had come for me.

"She's dead, and it's because of you!" She was shouting at me, arms clutched around her knees. I tried crawling toward her, but I couldn't. Everything felt strange, as if I was moving through a fog. I needed to hold her. She needed me.

"I'm sorry, Em. It's my fault. Come here," I said, my tongue thick as I formed the words. I reached for her, and she lifted her head. She was farther away from me than she was just a moment ago, wasn't she? Why wouldn't she just let me hold her?

I must have fallen asleep, because when I opened my eyes again, I was laying flat on my back with her hovering over my face. She shouldn't have been here, or maybe I shouldn't have been here. Something was wrong. *Everything* was wrong. Where were we?

"I saw what you did to that boy, Rainier." She laughed, a high-pitched thing that didn't sound like her. "And you thought you were better than your father? That's why our daughter died. You didn't deserve her after what you did, so the gods took her from us."

Tears threatened, and I choked on a gasp. She was right. I didn't deserve either of them. Not after Vondi. I didn't deserve my wife or the daughter she gave me. The daughter I'd never met and never would. "Please, Em."

I opened my eyes, and I blinked. I'd somehow been put on the rack. She kissed me while they did it. Her lips on mine would get me through the pain. It hurt so gods damn bad, but at least she was with me. I tried to kiss her back but couldn't. I could barely breathe.

"You're doing so good, Rainier. You're so strong for me. Look at me—open your eyes."

I obeyed, gritting my teeth, and found her watching me. She slowly unbuttoned her shirt as pain seared through my body, joints on fire. I tried to focus—she was so beautiful. But it hurt so badly. She bared her breasts, slowly rubbing her nipples as I pulled against my bindings.

"You've done well enough; maybe I'll let you fuck me." She ran her hands over herself as she looked at me, but I was only looking at her face. I didn't want that. I wanted to hold her, to fold her in my arms. If she'd just let me do that and tell her how sorry I was, everything would be alright.

I should never have left her. We were always leaving each other.

I shouted, unable to stifle my pain any longer. The harsh sound was only barely louder than the pop echoing throughout the room as fire seared through my shoulder, and I blacked out.

When I finally came to, she was gone.

In her place was Declan and a chessboard. The strange smelling man, an ogre I thought, stood next to him, fists balled at his hips.

"Come, Rainy day. Play a game with me. Maybe you won't be so sad after."

I grunted from my position on the ground and rolled over, facing the wall. My limbs ached, and the haze of the draíbea made it nearly impossible to function.

"Bring him over," Declan barked, and the footsteps I heard roused me into action. I wouldn't be manhandled any more than I already had been. Dragging myself to a seated position, I looked up at the ogre towering over me.

"Zen," Declan growled, and I was hoisted to my feet. Not bothering to fight him, I moved on unsteady legs to the chair Declan had brought in for his stupid game.

"What the fuck is wrong with you?" My words slurred.

"I have the mark," he said.

"I don't know what the hell you're talking about."

"Of the Accursed. I've always had it."

I tried to speak but couldn't get my mouth to form the words.

"You truly know nothing, do you? Father protected me over it. Killed your silly little betrothed because of it. Though, I suppose he did you a favor with that, didn't he?"

"Fuck you."

"Uniting and ruling over the Three Kingdoms is my birthright. It is owed to me. I was blessed by Aonara when I was an infant. I shouldn't have lived through my birth, but I did. Ciarden's blessing came soon after. I don't remember it, but I'd apparently been so angry at my father for taking away a toy, my shadows nearly killed him. He couldn't see the god chuckling beside him, but when I described what happened, he knew."

"And Hanwen and Rhia—get on with your story."

"Not quite. Rhia is the only blessing I still lack. But I have the mark—death's kiss."

"I don't know what that means." Was he even making sense? My head swam.

"Oh, Rainy, this is tiresome. Move your pawn."

"I'm not playing chess."

"Zen, take his thumb."

"Fuck, fine!" I shouted, knocking over three pieces in an attempt to move one.

"Sweet Ciarden, you're pathetic."

"I don't know what you want from me, Dec." His shocked repulsion from the nickname was comical, and I found myself chuckling like a fool.

"You won't be laughing once I'm done with your family."

I didn't remember anything after lunging over the table at him.

"It isn't real, Your Majesty. They're not who you think; don't listen to them." When I lifted my head, light brown eyes met mine, visible through the tiny gap in her face covering. A woman. I'd never heard a novice speak before. She had whispered, and I was lucky I even heard her. She held my face in her hands as she stared at me. I tried to focus, but it wasn't easy. "They're giving you draíbea in the gruel. Only eat the bread."

Draíbea in the gods damned food. I'd smelled it in the air, the cloying scent stinking up the room, and I'd smoked it countless times throughout my life. But I'd been taught at a young age the hallucinogenic wasn't pleasant or safe to ingest. Though, if it helped me get through this, kept me from thinking, was it truly that bad?

It didn't matter; I didn't think I could eat.

"Look at me, Rainier. You need to listen. Are you listening?" I felt my head nod, moving despite myself. "Don't eat the gruel. Push it around on your plate, but don't eat it. I can't do anything about what they burn, but do not eat it. It will help you stay lucid, so you'll know what's real." She tapped her hand against my cheek, and I blinked. My motions were slow as she shoved the bread into my hand, and I nearly dropped it.

"Eat the bread, not the gruel." The words were difficult to push past my lips, as if they didn't want to move. The woman nodded, shushing me and patting my cheek again.

"Good, yes. You heard me." She repeated her instructions as she slid a sling over my shoulder, her touch delicate. I didn't know why she bothered; I was too numb for it to hurt. "My name is Nor, and you can trust me."

"I don't know if I believe that, Nor." I chewed the bread in my mouth, narrowly avoiding biting down on my tongue. My body didn't want to cooperate. It was just as well; I surely looked insane talking to myself.

"You have little choice, do you? If you want to risk it and eat the gruel, it would be a stupid decision, but it's yours to make." The woman narrowed her eyes at me, her dark brows furrowing. "Now, don't forget to move the food around on your plate, or they'll send someone in here to force feed you—and it might not be me."

She left the room without another word. I belatedly noticed that while she wore the attire of a novice—the loose pleated pants and tunic—she didn't have the robe, and the white fabric was stained. I finished my bread and moved the gruel around as she'd told me to, the draíbea in my system more than enough to keep me disoriented. I vowed then that if I were ever to get out of Darkhold, I'd never touch it again.

My cell door burst open moments later, and Declan stood on the other side with his arms crossed. A man stepped past him through the door, carrying something in his arms. Not something—someone.

Em.

"What happened? Is she alright?" I was frantic, but my limbs wouldn't cooperate as I struggled to stand. Her head was lolling over his arm, and I saw a large bruise at her temple. "Answer me, gods damn it!" Declan merely watched me as the man laid her down on the ground. I had barely made it to my knees, and I tried to calm my breathing so I could really look at her, track the rise and fall of her chest.

"Good morning, Rainy. I've received news from my spies. Bad news. Do you know what that might be?" I shook my head as I watched her. She was breathing, thank the gods. "It involves this bitch on the ground."

I growled as I looked up at him. "Don't fucking call her that. What did you do to her?" I tried once more to stand, but my legs wouldn't cooperate. I slammed into the wall beside me, tweaking my shoulder painfully.

"Nothing too awful, as of yet. Your whore wife doesn't want to hand over my little brother. Care to tell me why?"

Of course she didn't. He was just a boy. If she were here, did that mean she'd hidden him? My nose stung; I was so gods damned proud of her. She was so strong. And she needed me to be strong. I couldn't tell Declan the truth of it. That his brother had worked to betray him.

"How would I know?" It was the wrong response. Declan took a step toward her and slammed his boot down on her hand. Though she didn't wake, she whimpered, and a frown formed on her face. I roared, diving across the floor to get to her. I didn't make it far before the ogre had me in his grasp. "Fucker! Get away from her!"

"Rainier, lad, I want you to think very, very hard. Why would your wife refuse to trade my brother for you?" He pulled Emma up by the hair. Her eyes were fluttering as if she were about to wake up.

"I don't know! You've kept me stuck here. I don't know why she would refuse." I couldn't betray the boy, not after he helped us. Even if Elora died.

How was Emma here? She'd been with me before, through the pain, but I was confused. Why was she even here? Had she come for me? And now, she was on the ground—broken and unconscious. It made no sense.

"Mmm, I think you're lying. I think you do know. And I'm going to make you watch while I beat her until you tell me the truth." And with that, he pushed her down so her body bent in half.

He ripped the back of her dress, exposing soft, perfect skin, and I launched myself at him, doing my damnedest to fight against the grip of the monster who held my arms behind my back.

"Me," I grunted, half-mad with rage. "Not her. Never her."

The bastard only laughed.

"Now, now, is that any way for a king to act? Stoicism, Rainier. That will be a lesson I can teach you. It will go easier if you bottle those emotions and just tell me what I need to know."

"I told you, I don't—" He cut me off, brandishing the switch I hadn't yet noticed. Emma was rousing, and I heard her moan as she struggled to sit up. "Don't fucking touch her." My voice was hoarse as I screamed at him. When he brought the switch down across her back, she screamed and collapsed to the ground—low, rasping sobs breaking free. My own matched hers. She wanted me to be strong for her. She'd clearly taken steps to protect Cyran, but I couldn't—*wouldn't*—watch this happen to her. I'd have to tell him something else, something he'd believe. "She was probably trying to lure you to Astana." He tsked and brought the switch down over her back again. I would kill him. I would fucking kill him.

"I won't hit her again, Rainy. I'll just fuck her mouth instead. You think you'll break and answer me before I make her swallow my seed?"

No. It was enough—he'd won.

"Fine! Fuck! Elora loved him. She's probably trying to protect him because of that." It seemed enough of a truth that he might believe me. Enough that he might spare her and still be unaware of his brother's deception against him. He stopped, turning his body to face me, and I watched his lips spread into a sickening smile.

"I knew the little whore spent the night in his bed. Like mother, like daughter, hmm?" He nudged Emma with his foot, and she flinched away from him. I would kill this man, rip him limb from fucking limb. "Do you think she was pregnant when she died?"

"Shut your gods damn mouth. I swear on fucking Hanwen himself—" He held the switch over her body, and my jaw slammed shut.

"That's what I thought. So emotional." He crouched down next to Emma and pulled her head back to look at him. The sound which crawled up my throat was inhuman as I saw the tears on her face, her skin flushed. "I think I'll have my way with you as my brother had his way with your daughter. Won't that be fun?"

He dragged her out of the room by her hair.

I wished I ate the gruel.

CHAPTER 11

Emmeline

After discussing our options late into the night with my most trusted circle, I rose with bleary eyes, stumbling as I readied myself for the council meeting which would decide my fate. I knew if Shivani had decided to sacrifice Cyran, I would offer to go in his stead. While Lavenia and Thyra had hoped she'd come up with a different plan, pushing General Ashmont into action, I had little optimism when it came to Shivani. Especially after our parting words.

Dressing quickly in breeches and a simple button-down shirt, I took a moment to look at my daughter. Still asleep, hair braided to prevent matting, she looked peaceful. The faint scar on her neck still hadn't disappeared, despite my best efforts, and I wondered how she'd feel about it upon waking. I would probably never know, as it was unlikely I'd be here to see it. I had faith she'd wake up, though. As long as Cyran was still here, working with her through illusions.

Once I got Rain back, if he used his resources to find anyone who could help, she'd be alright. I'd already entrusted my letters for them to Mairin, the merrow being the only person who I believed wouldn't act to thwart me at the meeting. The others knew my intentions but argued with me at every turn. Mairin had only nodded, understanding in her eyes. I looked down at my little girl, overwhelmed by my emotions. She'd be in good hands. Better, more capable hands. Hands that could protect her and never would have let her fall into any of this mess to begin with.

I'd never felt more guilty or questioned my abilities as a mother more than I had in the last few weeks. I was a child myself when I had her, but I was so tormented by what happened to Lucia, I didn't think. I hid her to keep her safe. Gods, if I only knew about Rain, our lives would have been so different. The guilt of it was something I wasn't sure would ever leave me. Yes, the Myriad would have possibly still been involved, but Rain would have done anything to protect us. Even if he wouldn't have been able to marry me back then, he would have moved mountains to protect his daughter. I had to trust that turning myself over to Declan would return Rain to Elora and to Vesta.

Leaning down, I brushed loose curls from her forehead and cupped her cheek, watching her white eyelashes flutter against her skin, knowing that if hope alone could wake her, it would have by now. Lips pressed to her brow, I allowed myself one moment to break down, and when a tear trickled down my cheek, I caught it so as not to disturb her.

Pocketing the small shell Declan had sent from Rain, I trudged to the door leading into the rest of our suite, just as the outer door leading to the palace slammed open.

"He's gone."

My stomach dropped as I watched Dewalt's hands fall to his knees as he bent over, breathless. Panic threaded through me. I could not bear it if—

"Who? Who is gone?"

"The boy. Cyran. Shivani sent him to Declan," Thyra supplied, jogging into view behind Dewalt, her face flushed crimson.

I hadn't stopped pacing in the hour since Dewalt and Thyra's discovery of the empty dungeon cell. I was at a loss. I didn't know what to do. Perhaps it wasn't out of any fear for his wellbeing, or, worse, it was possible I cared about the boy who slit my daughter's throat. But he was my best shot at bringing Elora back from this in-between state of life and death. She'd shown massive improvements since he'd been entering her mind, and I'd been able to go with him. To see her, to talk to her. Even if she didn't understand, even if she didn't wake, even if it was all I had with her for the rest of my days, losing Cyran was devastating.

"We can go after him. They were only rifting him to the Cascade, then riding from there," Dewalt said, eyes dark. He seemed to take the loss as a theft.

"And then what? Have Shivani throw us in a cell too and send him back to Declan anyway?"

"We won't bring him back here. We'll take him to the estate, ward it, bring Elora there too."

I pondered the idea; it wasn't a bad one.

"Do you know when exactly they left? Can we even catch up to them?"

"Early this morning, before dawn. Rivvens isn't as strong as you or Rainier. It will take him longer to rift. If we leave now..." he trailed off.

I nodded, arms crossed tightly over my body, thinking of the repercussions. If we did this, if we stole the boy, it could endanger Rain. I'd have to know Ashmont would finally act.

"Who is most senior in rank after Ashmont?" I asked.

Dewalt looked over at Lavenia, who, along with Mairin, had joined us in the last quarter hour. She ran a hand through her dark curls and sighed.

"I suppose Raj, if we work under the assumption that Rainier is king."

"Good. Thyra, send word to Raj to get here as quickly as possible. Lavenia and Raj are going to lead a coup."

Thyra nodded before leaving the room, not a single complaint from her lips. Lavenia's eyebrows rose, but she had no further reaction. Dewalt laughed, mopping a hand over his brow before resting his head in his hand.

"Care to explain your plan?" he asked.

"Rain is king; Lavenia is heir if we discount Elora. They'll listen to you," I offered, and she studied me for a moment before nodding slowly. "Listen, I—I can't have this endangering Rain. I choose him. I choose him over this boy, over everyone save Elora. But the prince can help her, even if he's just a child. If Shivani has already notified Declan, he will be angry when we don't follow through. I need the army poised. Lavenia, compel whoever the hell you need to compel to make this happen." Her face tightened at my words, but I continued. "Please, Ven. I—if I had any other idea, anything else, I'd do it. But I have nothing. When Raj gets here, the two of you can mobilize, and you probably won't have to compel anyone anymore. This is the best I've got."

My friend heaved a sigh as she leaned forward, putting her head in both hands. I let her think and turned to Mairin.

"You'll come with us and protect the boy after we fetch him? Bring him to the estate?" The merrow nodded, a curious look on her face. "I'm not coming back until I have Rain. I'm done. So, I need you to swear you'll look after them both." I cast a glance toward the shut door to the bedroom which held my daughter.

"I swear it. I'll bring them both to the estate and have it warded."

Thyra slammed back into the room, flustered more than she was before.

"The queen mother is on her way with guards. They'll be here in minutes."

"Shit!" Dewalt jumped from his seat in a panic. My hand was in my pocket, tracing my fingertips over that shell from Rain.

Deep breath in, slow exhale. I closed my eyes, imagining his fingers threading through mine after he'd stopped me from hurting myself at the inn in Mira. When he'd gripped my wrist during my fit of fury and frustration, his warm body next to mine, and calmed me with his presence. He was the other half of my soul, and it only took me a moment to find a solution when I attempted to think like him. A small smile spread across my face, and I opened my eyes.

"Dewalt, go get Elora."

He blinked at me for a moment before nodding and slipping into the bedroom.

Thyra was right—we only had a few minutes. I heard the door burst open as the rift closed behind me.

Shivani had forgotten that part of my divinity was from Rain. After my stint in the dungeon, Rain had the wards keyed to his power, and that power was *mine*.

It took a few hours, but by the time we left the freshly warded estate, Lavenia and Elora were protected by the members of Rain's guard who had returned to the capital rather than staying behind to help rebuild the Cascade. As soon as Raj arrived, he and Lavenia would do what needed to be done to ensure my success. When Shivani chose to do this, to go against what I said and what Rain would want, it was she who forced my hand instead of the other way around. I would make sure she regretted that decision. And whatever happened over the next few days would end in Rain's return to Astana. I would make sure of it, even if I had to wipe Darkhold off the gods damn map.

While we waited for the soldiers to arrive, I made sure we were prepared for a few days. My wardrobe was blessedly stocked, and I dressed appropriately, packing extra leggings to wear under my breeches, a few extra sweaters and gloves and cloaks. I turned to the other side of the closet and grabbed clothing for Rain, not even considering an outcome where I wouldn't be reunited with him in the coming days. I slipped upstairs to the room Dewalt stayed in, grateful he had some clothing there to choose from. Surreptitiously, I grabbed an extra pair of pants, figuring Thyra was better suited for Dewalt's tall and lean garments than she was for my own.

The concentration of getting us to the apple tree gave me a headache. The memory of Rain wiping juice from my chin and kissing me with sweetened lips was a painful one. It took me entirely too long to realize the version of the apple tree I was imagining wouldn't be close enough to what waited for us. There would be snow and the tree would be bare. By the time my mental image aligned closely enough to the tree itself and the four of us marched through the rift, my skull felt like it was about to burst. But my divinity bubbled like a pot boiling over, and I wondered if it was due to finally using more than the bare minimum. Following my intuition, I pulled flames into my hands, skimming some of the power off and easing the pressure.

I sent some of my healing divinity to my head, hopeful it would counteract the pain gathering at the base of my skull. Huddled around my divine fire, the others were silent. Dewalt had already made it clear he'd accompany me to the bitter end after we retrieved Cyran, doing whatever he could to help infiltrate Darkhold. But I wouldn't risk another person I loved. If I thought for a second we wouldn't succeed, I'd do what I needed to ensure his safety.

We were nearly halfway to the Cascade when I had to stop for a longer break, head aching again. No one had spoken, all four of us huddled around the small fire I'd lit from kindling Dewalt had gathered. Thinking about how I'd protect both him and Thyra, I was startled when I heard a rift open nearby, and I hadn't realized how desperately I'd wanted to hear the sound coming from someone who wasn't me.

The disappointment was a stone in my gut.

Raj, a soldier named Nix I vaguely remembered, and a woman I didn't recognize came through the rift, and I exhaled a sigh—relief and sorrow mingling. Raj's steps stuttered for a second before he was hauling Dewalt into an embrace, both men clapping each other on the back in a gesture I found far more painful than expected. Both men were tall, strong, vibrant—would I still be able to say the same about Rain once we got him back?

"Your note was quite vague," Raj said as he glanced over Dewalt's shoulder at Thyra.

"There wasn't time," Thyra grunted before deferring to me. The captain's gaze moved over to settle on me, and something flashed across his face I couldn't quite decipher. He crossed the distance between us and bowed, grasping my hand in his as he lifted it to his lips.

"Quit this, Raj, what are—"

"Your Majesty, I'm sorry it has come to this. I will do my best."

Pity. That was what his eyes contained. Not malicious, not inconceivable considering the circumstances, but unwelcome all the same.

I pulled my hand away.

"Thank you. Lavenia already has a few ideas for how to handle Shivani and this situation, and I trust the both of you to do what needs to be done." I said, crossing my arms over my body and averting my gaze. Raj was a widower, and pity from him only made me feel as if he thought my journey would soon mirror his.

The woman who had accompanied the two men pushed past them and swept down into a curtsy. It took me a moment to realize her accent was crisp like Cyran's. Folterran. "Your Majesty," she said. "My name is Aida. I'm Raj's—"

"The children's tutor," Raj butted in, and I swore I saw his cheeks darken.

Dewalt chuckled but quickly stifled it when I shot him a look. My headache had eased by then, so I decided it was time to continue on our journey.

"The prince hadn't arrived at the Cascade yet when you left, had he? Did you pass them?"

The captain shook his head. "No, but it's possible Rivvens took a different route. His family lives this way. Or they could have detoured at Nara's Cove."

I nodded, hoping we could catch them before they made it too far.

Mairin, who had been uncharacteristically quiet, pressed a hand down on my shoulder before announcing we needed to leave. We exchanged goodbyes, and I ignored Raj's cautious gaze, half-tempted to snap at him. I had never been any good at handling people looking at me as if I'd shatter. The only reason I didn't lash out was because of the last person who had looked at me like that. I remembered what I'd give to take back any harsh word I'd ever said to the man who'd not only ensured I didn't fall apart, but mended my cracks as they'd formed.

Night fell as we finally arrived in Nara's Cove, and I was exhausted. Every rift I made was more and more difficult, and my head throbbed. Dewalt and Mairin were bickering about something, and I tilted my head onto Thyra's shoulder where she sat beside me. We'd found a bench to rest upon while I recovered. It was strange, the exhaustion. My divinity was fine, too plentiful, if I were honest. Now that we were in public, I didn't want to draw attention to us by using it too blatantly. I directed my shadows underneath the bench, allowing them to swirl unnoticed, and I closed my eyes.

The rifting had to have truly tired me because I hadn't had an appetite in the last days, only eating when I remembered I needed to. Even now, my breeches had grown looser in my hips, and it wasn't a good thing. I knew I was losing muscle and what I was doing wasn't sustainable.

But when Mairin shook me awake, the smell of fried fish made my stomach growl audibly.

"Emma, you need to rift. Now. To the Cascade. Stand up!" she shouted, frantic.

"Alright, hold on. Can I have a bite of food first?"

"Fuck! No. You need to make the rift right now."

I stared at her for just a moment, not understanding her sudden desperation. Once I stood, I stretched before spreading my hands in front of me. Picturing the front gate of the Cascade, I attempted to fold and pierce as Rain had described to me, but nothing happened.

Nothing happened at all.

Before, it had taken a few tries before I was successful, but every time I tried, I had felt the glimmer of the rift, asking to be shaped and molded. But this time, there wasn't the faintest hint of it.

"Oh gods, what's wrong?" I murmured, aware of three pairs of eyes on me. I felt the shadows swirling around my ankles, unleashed from beneath the bench I'd just risen from. Mairin made a sound in the back of her throat I chose to ignore as I attempted the rift again.

Nothing.

A freezing wind swept over us, and in my attempt to shield us from the brunt of it, I realized. I froze, not needing the merrow to confirm.

"The bond has broken."

The words were a curse on my lips.

CHAPTER 12

LAVENIA

"Your Highness, all the king has left is a bitter red. I admit, I should have already placed an order, but will that do?"

I nodded, smiling up at Sterling. I'd known the butler since I was young, ever since Rainier built his estate so he wouldn't have to stay at the palace. My brother probably hadn't expected me to join him, but given my choices, I was sure he understood why I followed him.

I'd always been his little shadow.

Drinking from the glass Sterling had sat before me, I let the alcohol rest on my tongue for a moment before swallowing. Besides being bitter, the wine was dry. It wasn't my favorite, but it made sense today. I rested my elbows on the table and put my head in my hands.

A gods damn coup.

Emma was insane. She either had more faith in me than she should, or she was desperate. Probably both. I didn't have a great relationship with my mother—which was clear to anyone who paid attention—but I'd never stood up against her like this. Wearing clothing to piss her off was one thing, but using my birthright to steal an army out from underneath her was completely different.

Dewalt had pulled me aside before they left, sitting down with me in the dining room at the estate. He knew I was panicking. There were few things which set me on edge, and dealing with my mother was one of them. Dewalt took a few moments to remind me exactly who and what we were doing this for, and it helped. This wasn't real; it was only temporary. Retrieving Rainier meant I'd never have to do any of this again, and I'd have my brother back. Because if I didn't, if he didn't come back—assuming my mother wouldn't legitimize Elora—the armies would be mine anyway. And nobody wanted that.

I sure as hell didn't want to be queen, to rule Vesta. That was Rainier's burden. He was good at it. I didn't know if I could be good at it—I'd hated the idea so much.

I stared into the dark burgundy liquid in my glass, allowing my thoughts to drift to the woman they'd often been dwelling on. I wasn't worried about her; she could take care of herself. And gods, was that attractive. Mairin was strong, smart, and she didn't have to be held accountable to anyone but herself. She would never have responsibilities she didn't want, and she was confident in what she did with her life. It was intimidating.

I sighed, tossing back the rest of my wine—a mistake I rued immediately. I was moping, and I needed to stop. Finding Emma again had made me so gods damned happy, but I'd have been lying to myself if I said it had nothing to do with Rainier finally marrying, solidifying his role as future king and solidifying me as unimportant. It was selfish, but as our father had grown sicker and Rainier had grown no closer to choosing someone to bond with, I'd been quite stressed about it.

I didn't like being stressed.

With Rainier gone, it was all I'd felt. And I'd had my mother to contend with on top of it. Working with her daily was torment enough, but having to listen to her prattle on about Elora not being my brother's child wore on my spirit. She almost seemed more worried about that than she did about actually rescuing him. I'd tried to convince her not to rely on Ashmont, to give Emma some sort of hope, but if there was something Shivani Vestana did not do, it was bend.

Believe me, Lavenia. I want your brother returned more than you do, considering you stand to inherit the crown if he does not.

Sterling was back, refilling my wine before turning toward the door, footsteps soft.

"Princess?" he asked.

"Mm?"

"You've always known how to make your brother shine. Now it's your turn. You can do it." The grey at his temples had spread considerably in the past year, and I watched the corners of his eyes crinkle as he gave me a tight smile.

"I'm only the spare," I said, surprising myself by speaking the words aloud.

"I don't think you're *only* anything, Your Highness."

Sterling had left me to my thoughts, and I only allowed myself to sit and pout into my glass of wine for an hour or so before finally meandering up to bed. Though my body was tired as I dragged myself up the stairs, the moment I laid down, sleep evaded me. I tossed and turned for a long time until I was finally able to get a few hours' rest before Raj arrived.

And arrive he did.

I woke up to an earth-shaking blast, and I scrambled out of bed. It was still dark outside, long before dawn, and I tossed on my robe before stampeding down the stairs. Sterling came running down the hallway, dressed in a striped nightgown which fell to his knees. If I had time, I would have made fun of him.

"What was that?"

"I don't know, Your Highness. The wards?" He held a candlestick, the moon coming through the windows not quite enough for us to see by. Could my mother do something like that to the wards? Was she attempting to stop me before I'd even done anything? But when I looked outside, I only saw three figures halfway down the drive.

This wasn't my mother's style. She would have either come alone to guilt trip me herself, or she would've had an entourage. Though, whatever caused that blast was enough to intimidate. Glancing around, I saw a cloak tossed over a chaise and pulled it around me.

I was looking for a weapon when the house shook again, the glass in the panes rattling.

"Divine hell," I mumbled, pushing the door open.

"Oi, Venia! Get your sweet ass over here, and let us in!"

I groaned as I headed toward the three figures, pulling my cloak tight. I'd know that annoying voice anywhere. "Hanwen's ass, Nixy," I shouted back. "Knock hard enough?"

"Sorry, that was me," a feminine voice called out. I was closing in on them, recognizing Nix and Raj standing on either side of the woman. She was taller than me with long black hair, and I thought I'd heard an accent.

"Aida," she said with a wave as I neared them. "Elvish. Sorry, I'm not good at being delicate, and it was the best I could do. He told me to do it." She leaned in toward Raj, and even in the moonlight, I could see his body language change from her touch. I looked at him a beat too long but waited, deciding to tease him later.

"I don't know how to drop the wards for just the three of you, and I'm not dropping the entire thing," I said, frowning. I wasn't about to repeat the same mistake my brother made all those years ago. He'd only needed to drop it for Emma so she could leave with him, but the two of them had dropped them entirely.

"Oh, you just step outside it, and I'll redraw it. Easy."

"Easy." I stared.

A small smile lit her features. "Do you mind? It's quite cold."

I winced when my ears popped as I stepped through the wards. It only took a few moments for Aida to spill a drop of her elven-blood, calling out to her earth magick as she redrew the boundary to include the three of them.

"What are you doing here, Nixy? You got them here, so must I continue to suffer your presence?"

"Ah, Venia," he whined, drawing out the end, a lilting 'yuh' sound which made me want to smack him. "Don't tell me you didn't miss me."

"I didn't."

"You wound me, darling. I've certainly missed you."

"Stop talking," Raj barked, and I couldn't help but laugh as we walked toward the estate. "His uncle has influence, and as much as it pains me, Nix could help us convince him. When do we meet the other captains?"

"Morning."

"Good. We can get a few hours' sleep before we overthrow Shivani." He clapped his hand to my shoulder as he walked past, and I wondered if Raj knew just how sick and nervous I was over the thought.

"I wish Dewalt were here."

Raj and I were alone, riding into town in the early hours of the morning. We'd chosen a pub close to the barracks, not bothering to risk a meeting at the palace.

"Ven, I'm going to be frank with you; I think I've earned that. May I?"

I nodded, ready for one of his lectures. While Dewalt and Rainier had trained me to use a sword as a child, Raj had been the one to really take his time with me, not treating me like the annoying little sister I was. I'd always valued his opinion, even if I hated the way he sometimes gave it.

"You have relied on that boy far too long, and he has let you because of his own demons. You may look young enough to be my daughter, but the fact is you're both old enough to be your own damn person. You don't need Dewalt; you need to own your shit. Stop using him as an excuse. You both deserve better, and the people you care about deserve better too."

The last line was a thinly veiled jab about my relationship with Brenna, and it stung. He'd saved any commentary about the situation when it happened, but his admission now told me firmly what camp he was in over it.

"I am my own person. Dewalt is too. We just—"

"Use each other as a shield?"

"No," I snapped. "We're fine. It works for us, Raj. Just because you don't understand doesn't mean you get to say shit like that to me."

Hurt flashed across his features.

"I do understand, Ven. You know I don't care about any of that, how your relationship works." He shuddered before continuing. "You're telling me that if it weren't for the bond, you'd be together?" At my lack of response, he continued. "Exactly. You use each other for the bond, and you use each other as a shield to not deal with your own issues."

"And what is *my* issue, Raj? Dewalt, fine, obviously you mean Lucia. But what's my big problem?"

"Do you want me to answer that right now?" Dubious, he looked over at me.

"No," I said. "I'm already nervous enough. I don't need to be pissed off."

"You don't—you're right. But I'll tell you one of your problems because it is pertinent." He paused, waiting for my permission to continue, which I reluctantly gave. "Shivani has done a number on you. You are more than capable. Without Dewalt, without your brother, just you. Alright?"

When I didn't reply, he repeated himself, and I nodded. I wasn't quite convinced he was right, but it would do no good to argue with him. The rest of the ride was silent, and when we finally arrived at the pub, Raj insisted on helping me off the horse, knowing there were eyes on us, expecting propriety.

There were always eyes. Someone was always watching, waiting to report back to my mother, waiting to spread rumors, to write in the papers some supposed slight. Rainier had it worse than I did, but ever since I'd bonded with Dewalt, the commentary about me was more about what a disappointment I was by not bothering to secure something beneficial for the kingdom. That was one thing my mother did right for me. She didn't force me to wed and bond for some sort of alliance. Though she'd pressured him, she hadn't truly forced Rainier either. Between Lucia's death and her arrangement with our father, she didn't want that for us. And I was grateful.

Raj held open the door to the Red Lion, a pub normally closed during early morning hours, and it disappointed me to see only three of the seven captains even showed up to hear what I had to say. I masked it, allowing those who did show to genuflect and bow as was appropriate before we sat down where they'd been waiting. The table was one of the larger ones, clearly meant for more people, and I felt a tinge of embarrassment in my stomach. I'd been expecting a few more.

"Your Highness, I have to say my presence here is perhaps an unwise decision. If Queen Shiv—"

"Queen mother. She is no longer the queen, though I suspect she will latch onto whatever power is still afforded to her," I corrected.

"Right, yes. If the queen mother found out…" Captain Blane said, trailing off.

"Firstly, you were summoned for a meeting with your princess. She can't do anything to you for obeying a royal order. It would reflect poorly on her. Secondly, if we are successful, she won't be an issue. And if we are unsuccessful? It is me you have to worry about." Hoping they didn't notice my wavering tone, I gripped Raj's hand under the table. They had to see right through me. I barely spoke at council meetings when my opinion was asked for, but here I was, attempting to defy my mother.

"What exactly do you want?" The austere man to my right, Captain Louis, asked, not unkindly.

"Queen Emmeline is attempting to stop my mother from trading the Folterran prince for Rainier—for the king."

"Why?" Captain Blane cut me off before I could continue, outrage in his eyes.

"It is complicated," I sighed. I didn't want to divulge that not only did my brother have an heir, but she was in mortal danger thanks to the prince Emma now sought. "He has a use, and he is but a child. It isn't something my brother would want."

"You stand to wear his crown if he dies, so what you claim he would want doesn't matter, does it?"

"You're not wrong, but why would I come to you with the request to rally your men to my cause? I want to go to Folterra and lead an attack on Darkhold to save my brother." Captain Blane was poised to interrupt me again, but I held up my hand. "As soon as she finds the boy, Emmeline—the queen—plans to rally with us at the Cascade. The two of us together will lead the rescue of the king. We need soldiers."

"So, you attempted to procure them by undermining me, by staging a coup. I have to worry about the company you've been keeping, daughter."

I tensed, and Raj's hand squeezed tighter as we heard my mother behind me; she must have been waiting in the pub. Someone had told her.

"One of us has to have a spine, Mother."

The only captain who'd stayed quiet, Bowell, smirked at me before standing. The other two stood quickly, scrambling out of their seats. They clearly weren't in on this ambush either. Of course, my mother had to do it this way.

"I suggest everyone except my daughter leave. I'd like a word."

I felt her hand on my shoulder as Raj released mine with a squeeze.

"Your Highness, would you like me to stay?"

Looking at Raj with affection, I thanked him, but dismissed him all the same. Once it was just the two of us left, my mother sat down in a chair beside me.

And waited.

"I suppose you want to gloat. Get it over with. If you plan to stop me, you'll have to toss me in the dungeon. Otherwise, I'd like to reschedule my meeting."

"I suppose I'm confused, Lala." I stiffened at her use of the name she'd called me when I was small. The name I'd called myself because I couldn't say my real name. "I thought things between us had changed since your father."

Since we'd spent hours together keeping the man down.

"I thought so too," I said.

"Then what are you doing?" she whispered, and she finally drew my gaze. She wore a sapphire gown, more plain than her usual attire. Her hair was in twists which she'd pulled to the back of her head, and she wore no cosmetics. The bags under her eyes were apparent, and I realized she reminded me of Emma. "Baby, I did what was best."

"But you didn't. If you'd stopped being so gods damn stubborn, you'd know."

"You're telling me your brother is worth less than that little fool?"

"It is not my place to speak about someone's worth, but he was helping with Elora. They've made progress. Emma said she told you."

"She mentioned it, but I'm sure we can find other people to help with the girl."

"The girl?" I laughed. "Your granddaughter. It's been weeks, and you have found no one. The prince was helping quite a bit. Emma could go into illusions with him to see her. You'd know that if you would have listened to me and come to visit." I softened my voice, knowing taking that tone with her wouldn't get us anywhere. "Mama, she's beautiful."

Her mouth tightened, and she looked away. Gods, she was stubborn.

"The fact remains that the best thing for *Vesta* would be to trade the princeling, regardless of his abilities to help one child. You might be queen soon, and the fact you cannot see the bigger picture is astounding."

"Mama, I think what you cannot see is that if I become queen, we have to go to war. Or do you expect us to stand idly by while Folterra captures and kills our king?"

"Trading the boy avoids war altogether!" She threw up her hands in exasperation. "What does your simple mind fail to comprehend there? Lavenia, you are not that stupid. Quit play-acting as such. *Think*. You are a princess of this kingdom and cannot afford not to."

My chest tightened, and I screwed my eyes shut. An image of my mother destroying the fort I'd attempted to build out of cushions and blankets in our sitting room came to mind. *You are a princess first, before you are a child. Clean it up.*

Clenching my fists, I stood. "Even if we traded the boy, there would still be war. Do you think Rainier will return as a friend to Declan Umbroth? Perhaps you are the one who cannot afford to be so simple-minded. Emma is going to save Cyran, and then we are going to save Rainier. I hope if you stand against us, Rainier shows you mercy in the end."

I was halfway to the door when I heard my mother sigh, and her chair pushed back.

"Lavenia," she sighed my name. "Wait, please," she said as I lifted my hand to the door. I stopped moving but didn't turn to look back at her as her footsteps approached. "The pressure to run things without him is unbelievable. And you are clearly not ready, nor do I think you will ever be, to shoulder that burden." There was a pinch in my nostrils, although her disappointment wasn't new. "So, I've been doing what myself and Ashmont thought was best. But now that Emma has gone to fetch the boy, it throws everything off. If she is successful, war is imminent. Talk to the captains. Rally your soldiers."

My jaw dropped as I turned to face her. She only paused for a moment, something like uncertainty etching her features.

"I am no less of a failure than you are. Maybe you'll succeed with the approach I've been too afraid to take."

Leave it to my mother to insult me and encourage me in the same breath.

"Without the boy, the only thing we have left to lose is your brother. Get him back."

CHAPTER 13

Emmeline

It took us hours we didn't have to find someone who could rift us to the Cascade. Dewalt and Thyra made rounds to every establishment within walking distance of the docks until they finally came back to the pub where Mairin and I waited, Dewalt forcibly dragging a man behind him. Though Dewalt's face was a mask of rage, and I worried for a second when I saw a shadow of a bruise under his eye, Thyra wore a grin.

"He can get us to Clearhill," Dewalt said as he let go of the man and slammed down in a seat next to me.

"Name your price," I said. Dark, tousled hair, a half-buttoned shirt, and undone breeches told me Dewalt had roused the man from some state of undress, and though the pub was still open, the hour had grown late.

Dewalt scoffed. "His price is that I won't fucking kill him for punching me in the face."

"Gods damn, man. I already paid the libertine. You gotta pay me for that. I said I'd help you when I was done."

"And I believe *I* said we didn't have time for your two extra minutes."

Thyra chuckled to herself.

"Pay him for his libertine," I ordered. I was just grateful we'd found someone to get us there. I'd been on the verge of a breakdown since the moment I realized the bond of the Body had broken. When I closed my eyes, I swore I could see it. Two remaining golden threads stretching endlessly toward...nothing. Toward a cold, black void when it should have been him on the other end. Golden-brown skin, green eyes, rough hands and a soft touch. Mine. I'd anticipated a thread breaking, had known it could happen eventually. But gods, it hurt once it finally had. It threw off my limited plans for Rain's rescue as well. If he weren't in any shape to rift us out, would we be able to escape? I could protect us to an extent, but would that be enough?

Dewalt grumbled as he pulled out payment for the man, and within minutes we were walking through a rift into Clearhill.

The town was in a considerably better state than the last time I'd seen it. To be fair, it couldn't have been much worse. Though it had only been a few weeks, Raj had worked miracles with the funds I'd procured from the Crown. It had been one of my only successes amongst the council, and it was a battle hard-won. Since the Cascade was on Folterran soil and we had no claim on Clearhill, many of the councilors opposed doing anything to help rebuild it. Which enraged me. The town was full of women and children who had been coexisting peacefully with the Vestian forces, and the Folterran mercenaries had razed it when they attacked the Cascade. The council didn't see it as our responsibility, even though Declan had done it because of us. There had been countless arguments with the council when I'd found Lavenia's hand on my leg, squeezing under the table, urging me to calm down before Rain's divinity shook the palace any harder. It had been hard to control without him on the other end.

It had been the early days, when Elora slept like a stone, and I regularly checked to make sure she was breathing. Nights when I didn't even doze, feeling for him at the end of the bond and being met with impenetrable darkness, my thoughts swirling dangerously. That morning, Thyra had thwarted me from leaving, and I was in no mood to deal with the men and women of the council telling me it wasn't our responsibility to help the village. I coaxed the shadows to hover over my skin and took some satisfaction in seeing their discomfort. I didn't want to threaten them, knew that a good ruler shouldn't use force or violence to get what they wanted, but I struggled to maintain that ideal when what I wanted was something good.

Surprisingly, it had been Shivani who swayed them. It had made me optimistic, only for it to get thrown back in my face later. I'd stupidly hoped her siding with me in that situation signified she'd stopped suspecting Elora wasn't Rain's daughter. I'd hoped it was an olive branch of sorts and had invited her to come visit with Elora, to talk to her. Gods, I had been desperate, hoping for anything which would help rouse her. When Shivani declined, a pinched look on her face, it struck deeper than it should have. I felt pitiful for being hurt by it; I was a grown woman, for gods' sake. Though it was more hurt for Elora than it was for me. There wasn't a single gods damn adult in my baby's life who hadn't failed her. Except Rain. Rain was the only one who'd done nothing to fail her, and he was gone.

It should have been me who was taken by Declan.

Walking through the seaside village, we headed south toward the Cascade, needing to procure horses for our continued journey. When I took in my surroundings, I saw that Raj had been working methodically, moving from the coast inward. There was still much to be done, but for the first time since that awful day, I felt like I'd actually made a difference.

When we arrived at the Cascade, we found Shivani's men were only a half day's ride ahead of us. We didn't hesitate, readying horses and leaving not long after speaking with the watch commander. After a few hours' trip north up the coastal road, assuming they'd stick to it before crossing through the mountains, I noticed how tired Mairin looked. Dewalt and Thyra were used to this type of travel; they sat tall and straight in their saddle, but Mairin looked how I felt. I was also exhausted, but my mind wouldn't allow me to rest. Thinking about it for only a few moments, I sent out shadows toward Mairin, helping bolster her and support her. It took little effort, and it helped take the edge off my divinity. The immediate release of tension which had been coiling within reminded me I needed to use it more often. Mairin jumped as the shadows swept around her.

"What are you doing?"

"Helping. Lean forward if you want; I'll keep you upright if you want to rest."

"Worry about yourself," she snapped, and though I couldn't see her scowl in the dark, I could sense it.

"Actually, that's a good idea." I did myself the same favor.

"Don't you have to concentrate to keep them like that?" the merrow asked.

"Yes, and no. It's hard to explain. Like walking while talking. I need to use my divinity—let some of the extra power go. I suppose if Rain were here to share it, I might not feel it as strongly."

"He'll be sharing it soon," she replied, anticipating my thoughts going dark.

"I know," I murmured, trying to convince myself more than anything.

We fell into silence again for a while, and the shadows helped. Mairin seemed to fall asleep next to me, leaning back into the embrace of the dark I provided, and I couldn't help but smile at her. Her head was tipped toward me, and her mouth hung open. She wore her hair loose, and it tumbled down her back, swaying in the breeze. She looked so young when she slept.

I wondered how close it was to dawn when Dewalt held up his hand, a low whistle coming out as he slowed to a walk.

"Those are our soldiers," he said, as he brought his horse off the path.

Looking off into the distance toward a bend in the road, I counted over a dozen men before we ducked into the sparse trees on the mountainside. Though it was still dark, I used my shadows to shroud us, helping blend in. This close to the coast, the trees didn't provide the best coverage.

"It has to be them, right?" I asked, my voice a whisper.

"I assume. I'll go scout and see if I can spot the boy." Dewalt swung off his horse, pushing through the shadows and crouching low as he made his way through the trees. I didn't like him going alone, but I knew better than to argue with him about this. He knew what he was doing. It didn't stop me from pacing, worried about my friend. Too many people had been taken from me.

"Your—Emma, it's going to be alright." Thyra stood nearby, watching me pace. "Between the four of us, we should be fine. Shivani has surely threatened them to not hurt the boy, and they won't hurt us. It will be fine."

While I heard her words, I didn't stop pacing and wringing my hands until Dewalt returned, a sour look on his face.

"They've already made the trade. There's a village a few hours north where they passed the boy off," he reported.

"To who? Declan? Soldiers?"

"I'm not sure. They're making camp before they head back to the Cascade. If you want me to grab one of them and compel them—

"No, we don't have time. We need to go."

It was with a sigh and a nervous look thrown at me that Mairin said, "We'll have to go past them."

"I'll use my shadows to cover us or bind them, or my light to blind them. I don't care. We have to go." I was already mounting my horse, Thyra following suit, when Dewalt crossed his arms and cleared his throat.

"Emma, I don't know if this is worth it anymore. It was one thing to take on our own soldiers, but Declan's? We won't be able to get to Rainier if we die attempting to save the prince."

"Elora never wakes up if we don't save him. We can find Cyran and still save Rain. I won't let us die."

He studied me a moment longer before mounting his own horse. "On your head be it," Dewalt mumbled, but it didn't stop him from following as I set the pace with renewed purpose.

Opting to avoid Shivani's soldiers on the path, I brought us farther east, closer to the coast and nearly to the water where the sand was packed. The wind was frigid without the meager coverage from the trees, and the waves crashed with force. We were far enough away, I couldn't even make out the soldiers in the distance, although I used the shadows to protect us once again.

When we finally approached the village hours later, I knew we'd have to stop for a short time, our horses needing the rest. I considered leaving them and attempting to buy fresh steeds, but the village didn't seem big enough. Knowing our accents would give us away as hailing from Vesta, we proceeded to the pub in the village center with caution. It was early, and the only people outside were a few women stringing up laundry on a shared clothesline. One woman's toddler clung to her dress, a smudge on her face and a tremble on her lip, a wail barely kept at bay behind it. Loose strawberry blonde curls rested on her shoulders, and it caused an ache in my chest. I'd never missed those moments more than in recent days. I cursed my past self, eager for those days of clinging to skirts to end and ready for Elora to gain some independence. I'd have given anything to go back to those days. It was simpler then.

Thyra led the way, and we elected for her to do the talking as much as possible, unaware of the barkeep's loyalties, who was eyeing us warily as he cleaned out a glass with a rag.

"The missus is in the back baking some muffins, but they're not quite ready yet. No one comes in this early," he said, his voice leaving off the brittle endings of his words.

"We'd like muffins, yes," Thyra began, leaning into her accent more than usual. "We heard rumor of king's men passing through not many hours past?"

"I wouldn't know about that, ma'am. We just opened up not too long ago and heard nothing overnight."

His heart was beating out of his chest. Why did he lie? I took a step around Thyra, leaning on the bar next to her.

"What's your name, sir?"

Dark brown eyes whipped over to me, his heart still racing. "Aldric, ma'am. And yours?" He cleared his throat, looking down at the glass he still polished.

I took a chance, perhaps a stupid decision given where we were, but I had a suspicion.

"My name is Emmeline Vestana," I whispered, and the man dropped his glass. "I'm trying to find Prince Cyran before they deliver him to his brother. I know soldiers delivered him here, to this very village, only a few hours ago. Why do you lie?"

I watched his throat bob as a clamoring in the hall behind him broke out. My hand was on my sword in an instant as Thyra and Dewalt flanked me.

It wasn't until I heard her voice ring out that I realized Mairin hadn't been with us.

"You'll never guess who I found!" she sang before snorting like a pig. Pushing her way through the double doors behind Aldric, she led Prince Cyran out in front of her as he rubbed sleep from his eyes.

Twenty minutes later, I was struggling to keep my eyes open as Cyran finished explaining what had happened after Shivani's men took him.

"I was getting a bit of rest before having someone escort me back to the Cascade. I was going to ask that captain—Raj, I think his name was? To send me back to Astana."

"Declan's soldiers will be here at sunset, so he will need to be gone long before then," Aldric said, a scowl deepening on his face. "Though I have no fucking idea why he'd want to go back to Astana when we have rebel forces gathering."

I rubbed my hand over my face while Dewalt squeezed my shoulder. He'd been leading the conversation. Mairin had skipped to the door, locking any wandering villagers out, and I'd looked at the boy, dumbstruck, until Aldric offered to explain.

"You deceived Rivvens with only three men? He didn't question you at all?" Dewalt asked.

"Aye, myself and two others. We intercepted one of the letters, so we knew the terms of the trade. I thought the boy was going to ruin it all by giving us the slip."

Cyran looked up at me, a grim hint of a smile on his lips, before saying, "I split open his friend's lip with my forehead."

"You still plan to go back with them, Your Highness?" Aldric didn't like the idea, and I didn't know if I blamed him. Clearly, rebels in Folterra didn't want Cyran in his brother's hands as much as I didn't. But I supposed sending him off to an enemy continent wasn't much better. He was likely a symbol of hope to them, and though we'd be keeping him safe, I could see why the man would dislike it.

"Yes. I have...interests in Astana I must attend to." His eyes met mine before his gaze dipped to the floor. "My brother sitting on the throne is abhorrent, I know. I do not want him there either." The boy sighed, looking much older than his years, before rolling his shoulders back and lifting his head high. A royal gesture. "Once I'm finished in Astana, we can discuss what to do further. I trust we will keep in touch while I am gone."

The boy could have escaped, worked to overthrow his brother, or hell, he could have disappeared if he wanted. After listening to his heart as he spoke, I knew he was telling the truth. He wanted to finish what we started with Elora.

"Let us rest for a short while before we head back?" I suggested, and my companions all nodded in agreement. Thyra offered to take the first watch as Aldric's wife escorted us to two rooms at the top of the stairs, nestled cozily above the kitchen. Dewalt and Cyran went into one room while Mairin and I slipped into its twin across the hall.

We both laid there in silence, sunlight drifting in through the small circular window at the peak of the room. My divinity was buzzing, every part of me tense and ready to defend and attack. I'd been prepared to fight to get the boy back—not expecting Rivvens to be tricked by a rebel barkeep and his friends. It was pitiful, really, and the incompetence annoyed me, even if it had made my task easier. But that nervous energy still ran beneath my skin, and I struggled. I knew I should have been relieved, but my thoughts only turned toward what was to come.

Declan would find out, and he would act with aggression. I worried Lavenia wouldn't be successful in commandeering forces. I worried they wouldn't be at the Cascade in time to meet us. As it was, I couldn't rift. I couldn't do anything to get us to Declan faster. Was there any point of me going back to the Cascade? Nixy was the only soldier at the fortress who could rift, unless Lavenia brought more with her. It wasn't as if he could rift the whole army. Sighing, I rolled over and allowed my shadows to grow within the room, blotting out the light shining in above me. Mairin didn't react, and the soft snore I heard from her told me why she didn't notice.

I knew it was pointless to go to Darkhold on my own—it would take far too long, and it was possible the Folterrans sent to fetch Cyran could rift, delivering news of what had happened before we arrived. The only responsible route forward was to go to the Cascade and pray to the gods the soldiers who could rift would get us there before Declan reacted rashly. Dark thoughts swirled, twisting and twining in my mind. Perhaps it was reckless to not trade Cyran. Declan wouldn't have immediately executed his own brother—it was unlikely he knew of his deception—but the risk to Rain was monumental. What if I'd allowed it, and I'd been wrong? If I'd allowed the trade and Declan executed his brother along with the hope of my daughter one day waking?

I was damned no matter which choice I made. I didn't know what the hell I was doing. I wasn't made for this. I wasn't cut out to develop strategies, to make difficult decisions about people I loved. I held so many lives in my hands with my choices, and I'd never asked for that. Not once. Stifling a sob so as not to wake Mairin, I cursed the gods for putting me in this position. For making me choose a path when all were uncertain.

I loved Rain desperately, but a small part of me couldn't help but resent him for making this my reality. He'd put me in this position by not having faith in my ability to protect myself, even though it was something he'd promised to work on. That night in the tent, after we'd traversed the Cinturon Pass and before he traversed my body with gentle caresses and a wicked tongue, he'd told me he wouldn't forget. But not even a moon's turn later, he'd forgotten, risking himself without a thought. He hadn't known the full extent of my power when he'd done it. He hadn't known that Hanwen blessed me and cursed me with more divinity than I knew what to do with. Rain couldn't have known what would happen with Ciarden when our daughter's blood spilled on the wildflowers beneath her feet. He couldn't have known what would have happened.

Even though he'd acted in my best interests, it hurt that this was happening because he thought I was incapable. I'd make sure once we got him back, Rain would see just how capable I was—how capable he'd forced me to become in his absence. And then I'd torment him with my own soft touches and wicked tongue, ensuring he would never forget again. It was thoughts of his future punishment which finally calmed me to sleep. Closing my eyes, I could hear his sighs, feel his calloused touch on my sensitive skin. I could hear his filthy words and his loving ones, the way he whispered my name before kissing that soft spot behind my ear. I longed for him, and I let myself drift off, hoping to meet him in my dreams.

CHAPTER 14

Rainier

ONE MORNING I WOKE and looked across my cell to find Emma sitting against the wall. She had a cloak drawn tight around her, her head leaning back against the stone. Her cheeks were flushed that beautiful rosy pink I loved, and her eyes were closed. Had Declan let her come back to me?

"Are you alright, Em? Did he—do you feel alright?" I whispered, not wanting to wake her from sleep. Her eyes snapped open, and she looked angry.

"You're awake. I have something I need to tell you, but you have to be strong for me." She rose from the ground and approached on steady legs. Her long hair fell in beautiful waves down her chest, and she tugged on her cloak as if she were cold.

"Of course, yes. Please tell me."

"He said if you can last twenty minutes without a sound, I'm allowed to tell you." She crouched down in front of me and tilted my chin up with a bent forefinger. She smelled...off. Not herself. But I supposed that was because we were stuck in Darkhold. The scent was almost like juniper; I didn't like it. "Do you think you can handle that, darling?"

I nodded.

I'd been in the contraption for longer; twenty minutes wasn't bad. I was worried though, as I'd been eating the gruel again. The draíbea helped my nightmares, and I'd had plenty since he took her from me. I was afraid I wouldn't remember what she needed to tell me. Perhaps it was about us getting out of here. I wanted to go home—with her.

I tried not to move my arm too much as I stood, the dislocated shoulder aching, and I followed her to the table at the side of the room. I hated that he made her do this to me, knew it probably killed her inside to inflict pain. But she kept a strong demeanor, trying to shield me from it. She was so strong for me, so I'd be strong for her. Quiet.

The cell door opened, and the footsteps I'd come to dread followed. For the first time, I really looked at the man who helped strap me into the device of my agony. The ogre who'd been a part of much of my torture appeared to be a creature of few words, and I caught a whiff of him as he went past. He smelled like rot—inhuman. I adjusted, bringing my eyes back to Emma. Those blue depths would get me through this.

She leaned over, cupping my face in her hands as he started his torment. It hurt worse than it ever had before, making my vow of silence much more difficult. Perhaps my body couldn't withstand it. Eventually, my injured shoulder moved in such a way it went numb, and I was grateful for it. He was going faster, pulling tighter. It had taken nearly an hour for my shoulder to dislocate the last time, and I wouldn't be surprised if my other ended up dislocated this time. My body tensed, and I felt my abdomen tightening. I thought she could sense my struggle as she leaned forward to kiss me, her lips meeting mine as I let out a sharp breath. I frowned as my lips met hers; she didn't feel right. There had always been a sort of pull between us, but I didn't feel it. Perhaps the draíbea haze or the lava rock was dampening it, but I was confused. I screwed my eyes tight and closed my lips, trying to get through the last few moments without a sound. I was strong for her. For us. She would tell me of a plan she had come up with—perhaps a deal she'd made with Declan to get us out.

I was certain it had been twenty minutes when I heard my wrist pop. Thankfully, the entire arm was deprived of sensation, so I didn't feel it. I saw her grimace as she looked at it, and I felt hot and weak all over to see her sickened face. The rest of my body ached, but the cold air in the room licked up my spine, numbing the pain. I sighed when the man started unstrapping my bindings, and I attempted to keep my face passive. She couldn't heal me now, not with the basalt in the dungeon, and I didn't want to remind her of it, knowing it would pain her. I only opened my eyes once the footsteps of my tormentor left the room.

"Can you tell me now?" I asked, shifting my hip to turn to the side, not ready to sit up. I watched her with misguided hope. She cocked her head as she stared down at me. Had her mannerisms always been so crisp?

"It's easier if I just show you."

She opened her cloak, letting it fall off her shoulders. My gaze tracked down her body, not sure what she was showing me, as she unbuttoned the loose shirt she wore. I barely breathed, watching her face. Was she about to show me some sort of branding from Declan? She didn't look upset as I watched her. In fact, I was shocked to see a small smile on her lips.

She unbuttoned the last button and dropped the thin shirt on top of her cloak. Her face softened, and I let my eyes move downwards, taking in the beautiful swell of her breasts, until my gaze rested on her stomach. Without the loose shirt to disguise it, I was taken aback. It was—no. Could she—?

"Em?" Voice strangled—fear and adoration warring in my tone.

"Yes, I am." Her smile was faint as she looked at me, a single brow arched. I brought my good hand up to my face. I couldn't believe it. Her belly was slightly more rounded; she couldn't have been very far along. I didn't know if I should laugh or cry. She'd been adamant about not having any more children—she could never give me an heir. This was a gift. But that wasn't what mattered, and my mind turned dark.

"Will you survive it? I—Em, will you be alright?"

"Why wouldn't I be?" Her nose wrinkled as she looked at me with confusion. She would know better than I would, I supposed, but I couldn't stand the thought of losing her, even if it meant a babe. I hoped her divinity would protect her again, as it had with Elora. I stoppered a sob as it climbed up my throat. Our daughter—our blood—was dead. But with this babe, perhaps I could do better. Maybe I could keep this one safe.

"Do you know how to get us out of here? We can't stay here, not with..." I glanced pointedly down at her stomach, the round swell of life that grew there. "Come here."

I wanted to kiss her, to touch her. I sat up, leaning against the wall. When she climbed upon the table, settling into my lap, I was overcome with emotion. Using my good hand to rub up her spine, I pulled her in by the neck to kiss her. My love, my life. She was growing a tiny body inside of her, just for the two of us to love and care for. I'd make the most of every single minute.

I had tears in my eyes as I kissed her, pulling her lower lip into my mouth, ignoring the wrongness I still felt. It was just the lava rock or the draíbea. I reached up, smoothing her hair down as I looked her in the eyes. Her smile widened, turning into a sickening grin, and it made me nervous.

"It isn't yours."

"What?" I looked at her in horror, the reality of her words sinking in. Questions flooded my mind. How long had we been here? Was it Faxon's? She'd said that she hadn't been with him, so it couldn't be his. She *felt* like she hadn't. I was the first person who had touched her in years; I knew it in my soul. That could only mean—

"Declan?"

She nodded, and I saw red. The man had taken something from her he had no right to take, but he'd taken something from me too. My eyes tracked over her body as she leaned forward, taking my face in her hands. I was panicking, and I knew if we hadn't been in the dampening cell, the earth below us would have been shaking.

"He was stronger than you," she whispered, and my stomach tightened with nausea and rage. I was staring at her collarbone, the same spot I'd traced with my tongue countless times, and that was when I realized.

The Damia constellation. A formation of stars which mirrored the freckles above her collarbone—they were missing. The woman in my lap didn't have that pattern of stars I'd memorized, that I could picture when I closed my eyes. I checked her other side, just to make sure. To ensure I hadn't lost my gods damned mind. I slowed my panicked breaths and tried to think logically.

I wondered why I hadn't realized it before this moment. The novice's words came back to me, cutting through the haze. She'd told me as much. Told me not to trust them. I hadn't understood at the time. I'd been so gods damned inundated with draíbea, things hadn't made any sense. But the more I thought, the more wrong it felt. She didn't smell like her, and her eyes didn't have that light. The electricity between us wasn't right.

How could I have thought this was her? Oh gods, how could I have—fuck.

As if in reminder, my shoulder pulsed as I moved it. Emma wouldn't have let Declan force her to do this to me, not without a fight.

"What are you going to name it?" I asked, voice quiet. I wouldn't look her in the eyes, not yet.

"That's what you want to know? What am I going to name it?" I could hear the frown, but even her voice sounded wrong to me now.

"What was the name of the stable-cat you and Lucia snuck in that one winter? The one Nana nearly beat you for? Charlie, wasn't it?" The cat's name had been Hanny, named after the god he most would have bonded with. The twins had told the story so many times, the cat lived in infamy.

"Yes, Charlie. He was a good cat."

I already knew, but her answer confirmed it. This wasn't my wife.

I slid my arm up, shoulder aching, and cupped her face. "I love you, Emmeline. I'm sorry I wasn't strong enough."

Carefully, I used my bad arm to hold her head steady as I reared my good one back, and I punched her as hard as I could in the temple. She fell down on the table beside me, and I rotated, pinning her thigh under my knee. I punched her in the eye as hard as I could as she screamed.

"Rainier, stop, you're hurting me!" I ignored her and punched her again. With my strong arm unusable, I wasn't able to hit her as hard as I wanted. I hoped if I hit her enough, the blows would kill the shifter bitch. She was unconscious when the brute came in to pull me off her.

Unfortunately, her chest still rose with a breath.

CHAPTER 15

EMMELINE

WE MADE IT BACK to the Cascade in record time. Cyran rode with Mairin, and I couldn't help but find some amusement in his expression. Mairin had told me he was especially skittish around her, and I assumed it was because she was a merrow. Every time we stopped, he was quick to dismount and put distance between the two of them. I wasn't sure if it heartened the others to have the prince back or if it was because we got a few hours' rest, but spirits were high on the ride back to the fortress.

It did not last.

I knew it had only been a day, but the lack of additional soldiers and no word from Raj or Lavenia worried me. I couldn't expect her to overthrow her mother in a day, but I wasn't sure how long we could wait for reinforcements before we left for Darkhold. As night fell, I knew Declan's men, those who had been sent to retrieve the prince, wouldn't find him there, and they would report back to him with haste.

"She'll be here. They'll come," Dewalt said, stopping me from my incessant pacing. He had taken it upon himself to escort me to the same room Elora and I had stayed in the last time I was at the Cascade, while Thyra retrieved food which I would surely only pick at. I closed my eyes, trying to calm my thunderous heart. Dewalt and Thyra realized I was on the verge of something dangerous, and I didn't blame them for their reaction.

"And what if she doesn't? I'm leaving in the morning. I think you and Thyra should wait for Lavenia and follow behind with—"

"Do you think I'm stupid?" Dewalt's scowl aged him, his features going harsh. "No, Emma. We will go together—in the morning," he added before I could interrupt. "Lavenia and Raj are more than capable of commanding an army. They'll know where we are headed."

Staring out the window, arms crossed over my body, I stopped myself from arguing with him. "You're a good friend, D. I haven't said it enough."

"Don't start."

"Don't start what? I mean it. You've been—between you and Thyra—" I shook my head, lost for words.

"Don't start these half-assed conversations that are little more than goodbyes. You're not going to trade yourself, or whatever other half-cocked scheme you have brewing up there, and neither of us is going to die. So cut the shit."

A smile tugged at my lips as I turned toward him, stifling a snort as I looked at his lanky body stretched out on the ratty chaise—entirely too small for him. He looked down, picking at his nails, and the flickering candlelight painted his face in moving shadows. His head was turned, so the wyvern pointed toward me. The ink was black, but so intricately done, I had to marvel at it. How long had he sat still while someone took a needle to his skull?

"What?" he asked, noticing my gaze.

"How long did that take?" I glanced at the side of his head and sat on the edge of the bed across from him.

"A couple hours. The one on my back took all day. I know a woman in the capital who does it. Elvish." At my confused expression, he continued his explanation. "She is more of an artist than anything. She paints the image with magicked pigments. It hurts like hell when she does the incantation, but it's better than sitting through hours of needle-tapping."

"You have one on your back?" Though I'd briefly seen him naked at the lake all those weeks ago, I hadn't seen a tattoo, likely covered by his hair.

"My Shika tattoo." His eyes grew dark, and he adjusted on the chaise. I remembered him mentioning it when I'd overheard him talking to Lavenia about Rain and Keeva's betrothal. I shuddered, too aware of the fact the Nythyrians would find out soon that their princess was missing. Too many of my decisions were bouncing back at once, and I forced the thoughts out of my mind.

"For Lucia?" I asked softly, not wanting to upset him.

"I got it a year after she died. I was so angry at the gods—still am." He shrugged. "I can relate to the tale."

The Shika constellation was named after the woman whose husband had fought and raged against the gods after Hanwen killed her, angry that the most beautiful woman he'd ever seen was loyal to her spouse. The man had somehow stripped Hanwen and Rhia's child of immortality in retribution. I'd only half-believed in the gods until they meddled in my life only a few weeks ago, and I wondered if the story was true. Had Rhia and Hanwen been forced to continue living their immortal existence after their child aged and died?

"Do you think you'll always be this angry?"

"Do birds sing?" Dewalt snorted before lifting a hand to his face and sighing. "Fuck, Emma. I don't know. I'm...tired. I don't know if I have it in me to be angry anymore. Don't say shit. Don't make me regret telling you this, but seeing Rainier happy again gave me hope."

He sat up from where he'd been lounging, smoothing his large hands down his thighs, not looking at me. I didn't move, just waiting, unsure of what to say and certain he had more to get off his chest. He rewarded my patience when he cleared his throat, still looking down.

"She's dead—I saw her body, know she's dead. I *know* this. I also know that I haven't been able to emotionally tie myself to someone like that ever since. Rainier knew you were gone, married, had no fucking hopes of ever seeing you again. And you came back, and he suddenly had this life, this whole gods damned family, that he'd only ever dreamed of. If he can get that—fuck, is it wrong to think I might deserve something more too? Not to have her back—I know that's impossible, and I'm not delusional, but being in love might be...Hell, even if she were terrible, a fraction of the joy you two have would be nice."

"Dewalt..." It was the first time I'd gleaned he *wanted* to move on. Before now, he'd seemed perfectly content in his anger. Words failed me.

"Don't. There's nothing to say." He crouched in front of the fireplace, adding a log and using the poker to distract himself. "I'm going to let the bond with Ven break."

"What?" Shock froze me.

"Yeah," he grunted. "You've seen her and Mairin. I won't ruin her relationships just because I'm a fucking mess."

"I'm sure that's not how she—"

"Oh, it's definitely not how she sees it. But we're just using each other. I love her, but we're holding each other back. You weren't here for it, but things with Brenna..." He shook his head. "She's never going to be the one to do it, so it has to be me."

I stared at the back of his head, traced the curve of the braid going down the center of his back. His broad shoulders sloped forward, dejected.

"I thought you—with Mairin—"

"We did, but that doesn't matter. She wants Ven in a way I don't think I'm capable of. It's not like I haven't tried, Emma. Do you know how much easier it would be if I could? Sometimes I think I might not be...It doesn't matter; Ven doesn't see me that way either. She's the only person who has always had my back, but *because* she's my person, I have to do right by her. Maybe one day, the feelings we have for each other could have been something more, but I really don't think so. I mean, it's been a decade of being her bonded partner, and our feelings haven't changed."

I reached down to take my boots off, leaning forward to unlace them as Dewalt poked at the logs in the grate.

"It seems like you've thought about this for a while," I offered. I didn't know the inner workings of his relationship with Ven, and I didn't think it was my place to tell him if I agreed or disagreed. I wished for Rain's presence once more, knowing he'd have the words for his best friend and brother.

"Since you walked into Ravemont, honestly. If Rainier can have a second chance, why can't I? For a while, I thought it could be Ven, *wanted* it to be Ven. But it's not happening, and now Ven has a chance with someone else." He tilted his head. "Can merrows perform the ritual?"

He peered at me over his shoulder with a furrowed brow, and I chuckled.

"You know, I don't know. I didn't know merrows were real until recently."

"Well, the Myriad doesn't allow anyone with elf-blood to perform it. I imagine it's the same with merrows. Only those with divinity from the gods. Fuck, now I don't know if this is the right decision. Can't have you and Rainier running things for centuries without us." He smiled, but it didn't reach his eyes.

"It isn't as if you can't perform it with someone else. You have plenty of time."

"You just want me to look older, so I don't outshine you with my beauty. Your age is nothing to be ashamed of. I've only noticed a few grey hairs."

"You're older than me, you ass," I laughed.

"Oh, but I don't look it." He stood, preening. I threw my shoe at him, grinning as he yelped, catching my boot just before it hit his most prized appendage.

"If you want Elora to have cousins one day, you'd better watch where you throw things, Your Majesty."

I sobered at the mention of Elora. I was eager for Mairin and the prince to return to the estate, hopeful she'd continue to improve in my absence. Dewalt approached me where I sat on the end of the bed, and patted me roughly on top of my head. I glared up at him.

"Don't worry, mouse. She'll be fine. I'll be training her in no time."

We said little before he left, closing the door behind him.

Near midnight, finally on the verge of sleep after it had evaded me well into the night, there was a loud banging on my door. I grabbed my dagger from the nightstand beside me and jumped to my feet. The moon barely lit the room, and the fire had burned down to embers.

"Who is it?" I rasped, voice hoarse from near-sleep.

"Cyran. Let me in," he panted. He'd been running.

I slipped my pants back on, pulling them up from the puddle on the floor I'd made of them, and was across the room and swinging the door open before he had time to catch his breath.

"The king. Rainier. Declan already knows about me. He is going to execute him dawn after next."

I blinked at him.

The moment Cyran's words registered, the message from his sister making sense, a part of me died. That hope I'd been feeling in recent days was no more, and I lost control of my divinity. I could feel the heat in my eyes, knowing they were responsible for the glow cast about the room, and felt the shadows swirling from my hands up my arms to nestle around my neck. When the shadows spread, whipping around the room, the princeling bravely took my hands. He spoke, but I couldn't hear it, the tremendous rocketing of my heart drowning out his words. The thoughts of Rain, the other half of me dying alone, executed at Declan's hands, rushed through my mind. I saw lifeless green eyes, the echoes of his laughter in the lines on his face, his warm hands now cold, all the things that made him—gone.

Moments later—I didn't know how long—Dewalt was there, grabbing my face in his hands. I didn't care to hear what he had to say. I didn't know what I was doing, what I could do. But I wasn't finished. I couldn't give up; I *wouldn't*. I pushed away from Dewalt, not trusting my harrowing to not hurt him, dimly noticing Thyra and Mairin on the threshold and Cyran standing nearby. Dropping to the floor, I curled into myself, my knees and arms tucked beneath me, and willed my shadows to encircle me—protecting myself, but more than that—protecting my family from me.

I needed to focus on something else, something real, something living. That horrifying image of Rain couldn't take over my thoughts. I needed to think of a moment which embodied him—life and joy, vibrancy and power—or I'd give up. His intense grin as he chased after me at the lake came to mind. When I'd pushed him off the cliff into the water and he ran after me, picking me up and throwing me in. He was strong and happy and carefree. That was the Rain I would think about, the Rain I would remember. The Rain who would get me through this, who would help me focus on the ever-damned task of rescuing him. I felt my shadows recede, and the surrounding heartbeats quieted, no longer a raging stampede through my mind. Taking a deep, shuddering breath, I felt something nudge me beneath my body. I sat up abruptly, trying to understand. There, at my knees, was a tiny creature, made more of shadow than anything else.

The rest of the room fell away as I looked down. It was no bigger than a kitten, and I wasn't even sure I'd be able to pick it up or if my hand would go right through it. I held my finger out to it, bent at the knuckle, and it nipped at me. It had sharp little teeth, and it was more corporeal than I originally thought, the shadows around it shifting. Was this a drake? The stone drakes flanking the doors of the Myriad Seat were huge compared to this, but the resemblance was striking. Lizard-like in appearance, with larger, armored bodies, this seemed like a smaller version of the stone depictions. Had I somehow formed this creature? How had I done it?

The memories. He thrives in them.

Rhia's words came back to me, unbidden. I'd been thinking about that beautiful moment with Rain at the lake, and while it calmed me, replacing the nasty image which had made its way into my mind, it also helped me form this tiny monster. I glanced up, my eyes meeting Cyran's and then Dewalt's. Mairin and Thyra stared in silence behind them. They all looked at me with slack jaws before Dewalt crouched on the ground, keeping a bit of distance from me.

"Did you—what is that, Emma?" His voice drew the attention of the drake, and it bounded towards him before it latched onto his arm by the teeth. "Ow, fuck!" He tried to grab the creature by the back of the neck, and it reared back and bit that hand instead. I suppressed a chuckle as I got up to my knees and reached for the baby. That's what I thought it was, at least. As cute as it was, I wasn't sure how useful an army of tiny drakes would be.

"Come here, sweetheart." I grabbed it by the back of its neck and cradled it in my lap. It had four perfectly formed feet with four sharp claws each—its size not the only thing it had in common with a kitten. It was a silver color, reminding me of the eastern cliffs of the Alsors, and I suspected that was exactly the reason for it, considering the memory which had helped form it. The shadows had dissipated, and I was able to see the details on its skin. It was covered in tiny scales, no bigger than my pinky fingernail, and they shimmered in the moonlight. I couldn't tell if it was male or female, but it nipped gently at my fingertips as I held it there, flicking its tail lazily. The tail was the same length as its body, tiny spikes running down the center of its spine. They were sharp and painful as they dug into my legs. Two green eyes peeked out beneath a defined ridge on its triangular face, and it hurt. They were the same pine-green shade Rain's eyes sometimes turned. I felt a tear sneak past my lashes as I looked at the tiny creature made of one of my best memories. I watched with joy and fascination as it used a long tongue to lick one of the two horns at the top of its head. Wiggling my fingers over its face,

I smiled as it lunged, nipping and licking a second later to soften the hurt. The action reminded me of the herding dog we'd had when Elora was young.

"I'm not sure what I'm doing, but I'm going to try to make it bigger. We're going to need all the help we can get. We are leaving for Darkhold within the hour."

I was calm as I stood, a grim determination taking over my actions and mind. Cradling the drake to my chest, I made my way out into the halls of the fortress, passing curious stares from a handful of soldiers out into the courtyard. Continuing onward, I waved to the watch commander who opened the gate and allowed me to pass. The little bugger had started gnawing on my fingers, and it became less cute by the moment.

"Alright, little one. Let's see what I can do with you."

An hour later I stood beside the drake I'd created from a memory. His name was Irses, one of the first constellations Rain had ever taught me when we were young, bonding beneath the night sky. Irses told the story of the gods' hope-bearer, and it seemed fitting. It hadn't taken the full hour to help the creature grow, and I wasn't sure if there was a limit. I wanted to mount the beast, though, and as it was, this height would cause me to struggle. The drake now stood tall, shoulders level with the top of Dewalt's head. The scales had darkened as the creature grew but still maintained their shimmer. Dewalt and I stood far outside the fortress, halfway to Clearhill, the light of the moon keeping us company. Thyra was on her way with the soldiers we'd found suitable for the task, and all I could do was wait. I was pacing, nervous. Irses tail twitched as he watched me, making me think he was agitated. Dewalt was worried, but what was there to do about it? We only had until nightfall to get there, and I was terrified we'd be too late. We needed to leave.

"They ought to be back by now with someone to rift us." Dewalt turned his wary gaze away from the drake, cautious since Irses bit him, and looked toward the path leading to the fortress.

I heard Thyra before I saw her. My divinity had cast a wide net from where we stood, my swell of power more vast and thorough since Hanwen's blessing, and I could hear quite a few heartbeats approaching in the dark. I thrummed with anticipation and fear. We'd rift, force the horses through and wear them out until whoever could rift us was ready to form another. It was a trip we'd planned the other night with the help of the few spies we had, but Dewalt and Cyran had spent some time speaking to Aldric before we left the village, incorporating the rebels into our plans. But that was when we thought we had longer, and I worried we wouldn't make it in time or those set to help us wouldn't be ready.

Thyra and the others rode up on horseback, and her horse stalled, rearing back when it saw Irses. I ran forward stupidly, not paying attention to the hooves which could have killed me, and pressed my hand to the steed, calming its racing heart. I somehow avoided injury as the horse calmed down. Thyra had fallen off, unprepared for what happened. She shouted a curse in her language as she backed away, putting distance between her and the drake, who merely looked at her curiously. He was considerably bigger than the last time she saw him, only an hour prior.

I heard the grumbles of the other soldiers; one woman and three men whom I recognized from our travels together this past autumn but could only remember the name of the tiny girl off to the right. She was from a kingdom farther east than Skos, a warrior who had been imprisoned with Thyra, and she didn't speak a single word of the common tongue. But she fought so quickly and fiercely it didn't matter, especially since she spoke Thyra's language. Though I doubted it was even her real name, Shade had earned it, moving with a quiet efficiency which often went unnoticed.

"Your Majesty, what in the—" the tallest soldier began.

"We don't have time for more than this basic explanation. This is Irses, a drake that I created, and it's going to help us get the king back. Try to keep your horses calm; it won't bite."

"Your Majesty, the rifter here can't take you to Darkhold. She's never been," Thyra said as she stood and dusted her pants off. "I wanted to bring you soldiers. I can have someone rift me to Nara's Cove? I find someone else who knows way?" Her accent was thicker than usual, stress accenting her words.

My heart dropped to my stomach. I should have expected that, but considering I'd been able to rift myself only a day ago, it wasn't something I'd even considered. We couldn't wait for Lavenia to arrive with reinforcements, with more soldiers who might be able to rift, and the hope I'd experienced after creating Irses was dashed. I folded into myself. I barely had time to get us to Darkhold, to stop the other half of me from being executed. I hadn't even mourned the breaking of the bond, hadn't had a moment to think about what it meant.

I sank down to my knees. Holding my face in my hands, I let out a scream. I'd been so full of determination and hope, I hadn't even realized in recent days how much his abilities had dwindled within me. I felt my divinity slipping out of my control for the second time that evening. Thyra reached out her hand and knelt beside me.

"Get back. I could hurt you." My words were a begging plea, choked.

I couldn't do it. I was going to fail him, fail Elora. Fail the gods damn kingdom. I curled in on myself again, assuming the same position I had before, protecting them from me with my shadows. I counted my breaths, attempting to gain control, wondering if I'd accidentally create another drake. The thought came to me, and I felt almost mad. Could I purposefully do that? What if—could I give it wings?

My mind raced, searching for a memory.

The fall.

The awful moment when Declan made me jump off the parapet at the Cascade.

For a brief moment, it had felt like flying instead of falling—until the fear took over. I sat up, amassing the shadows in my hand, focusing on the memory and imagining a tiny Irses but with wings. I gasped when the small creature formed in my palm. Closing my eyes, I imagined the fall, envisioning wings unfolding from my back, strong enough to take flight, membranous and large. I imagined the tan color of the walls of the fortress, the deep blue of the sea below me. I kept my eyes closed as the creature grew in my hand, and I moved it to rest in my arms, an adorable snarl escaping it. After a few moments, when the drake was almost too heavy for me to hold, I inspected it. Light brown eyes looked back at me, the same color as the fortress, set in the scaled body of a beautiful, azure drake. Though, based on the delicate furled wings protruding from its back, it wasn't a drake at all.

"Divine hell." One soldier, Bly, I thought his name was, approached slowly. "Is that a *dragon*? Did you make a fucking dragon?" He paused before he remembered himself as he knelt down. "Shit! Did you make a...dragon, Your Majesty?"

I couldn't help but snort. Thyra was still close, even though I'd told her to get back, and I could hear her awed whisper.

"*Traekka*." Her eyes were wide, and she tenderly touched one of the shimmering scales with a fingertip.

"What did you say?" I whispered, wonder-struck. My divinity hummed, hope and reverence clashing and causing it to respond in a way it hadn't since Rain had been gone.

"Dragon. It's beautiful, Emma." I beamed at her, thrilled that my friend had finally called me by my name without stumbling over it.

"She's yours." I wasn't sure if the dragon I held was a she, but the features seemed more delicate. "Let me...finish growing her." My words sounded so strange, but I still needed to bring the dragon in my hands to a useful and ferocious size.

I'd done it. I'd found a way to get us to Darkhold.

I realized it was the first time Ciarden's powers hadn't felt tainted in my hands. Was it because I had mixed it with my memories? My very essence? I had my work cut out for me; I had to make more drakes—dragons—and fast. They were large enough two people could ride on each, and I hoped I could add wings to Irses. I closed my eyes, searching for the golden bond, wanting to pluck it, to send him a message we were coming. I knew he couldn't feel it, and inflexible darkness waited at the other end, but I still gently traced those remaining golden threads.

I looked north, toward the mountain range we'd have to fly over, protecting Darkhold from the sea. We were all clothed appropriately for the weather, but I worried about finding a pass to cut through the frosty peaks. I decided in that moment, I'd be stopping to retrieve Aldric, forcing him to help us with the rebels, since our plans hadn't had time to solidify. I hoped they were ready.

I'm coming for you, Rain.

CHAPTER 16

RAINIER

"Good morning, lad." I looked at the bastard with one eye, my other having swollen shut, and wished I could go back to sleep. They weren't even bothering to give me the gruel, just pouring water down my throat with a draíbea mixture for good measure. I wasn't hungry anymore, the gnawing pain in my gut having subsided within the last day. I was weak and tired, and I could barely remember the reason for this treatment. I vaguely remembered being beaten for something I said to Emma. Did to Emma. Not Emma.

Not Emma. Not Emma. Not Emma.

The mantra in my head I kept struggling to repeat. I couldn't quite remember why, but it echoed there, incessant. I swallowed, throat dry as if I'd gulped down sand, and glared up at Declan.

"More's the pity you caught on—I was having such fun. But I suppose all children outgrow their toys, and I guess now's the time I retire you. Do you have a message you'd like to leave for your wife? I won't bring her in here since you weren't too eager to see her last time." His thin lips twisted up into a wicked smile.

Not Emma. Not Emma. Not Emma.

I grunted at him, not sure if I could form words. My jaw felt broken, and I knew for a fact a few teeth were loose. I kept my mouth shut.

"My men arrived to fetch my brother, and they found your soldiers had been outsmarted. Between rebel traitors and your whore wife, the fool is on his way back to Astana. It would seem I'm going to have to go fetch the boy myself. But that means I can't leave you here."

I fought a smile. She'd protected the boy. She was smart and stubborn, my wife. But she came here and endangered herself anyway.

No, that wasn't right. She wasn't here. That wasn't Emma.

The memory of punching her in the head came to mind. A pang went through my gut, remembering the cry she gave, but I reminded myself once again—it wasn't her. A shifter. It was a shifter.

Not Emma. Not Emma. Not Emma.

"Do you not understand what I'm getting at, Rainy?" That fucking nickname.

"I tend not to pay attention when you speak." The words were slurred. My jaw was definitely broken.

"Well, that won't be a problem for you much longer, King Rainier. Maybe they'll still call you the Bloody King after all, though for a different reason. Perhaps the Headless King? Which do you think sounds better?"

Ah, I was going to be executed. I wondered if it should have unnerved me that my only thought was relief.

"Do you ever tire of hearing yourself?" I asked, words still difficult. My tongue almost felt too big for my mouth. The man's eyes narrowed as he tapped his foot. He played at nonchalance as he leaned against the stone wall of my cell, but his body language gave him away. He fidgeted nervously as his eyes roamed over me. "Tell me, Declan, do you think there are no Vestian spies here in Darkhold?" I asked, smiling as I saw a muscle in his cheek twitch. Though, to be fair, my vision was currently lacking depth.

"I'm not so sure how many you have left. My archers shot a hawk out of the sky weeks ago. I was told it turned into a woman before she landed. She made quite a mess." His lips pursed as my gut twisted. Aerfen. Emma must have sent them. If Declan shot her down—fuck. I wondered if they had caught Aedwyn. "I'm not sure how this is relevant, Rainier."

"How long do you think you will have left in this world once she knows I have left it?" He snorted, kicking up his heel behind him. I continued anyway. "She's going to kill you, you know, and I'm quite upset I won't be here to see it. But I'm sure she'll make it interesting." I knew I spoke truth. Emma would be hell-bent on avenging me.

Gods, would she be alright? With Elora dead, and me too? I'd find her again—in the next life. We both knew it to be true, but how much would she suffer before then? How long would she be here alone? When we met again, we wouldn't remember each other, wouldn't know what we'd been through. Our souls would remember, just as they did now. That unstoppable pull between us would be the same, but this life would be ash before it happened. And Elora—we'd never have her again. Was there any point in the pattern of twin flames? To the repetitive madness which ruled and ruined?

I was drawn from my thoughts when Declan's shiny boots moved into my field of vision. He crouched in front of me, keeping his distance despite the fact I could barely see straight, let alone injure him. I lifted my head, a smirk on my face as I watched his lips twist in a sneer.

"You surely know she threw a dagger at my father. But do you know the only reason she missed was because of me? Your shifter doesn't know how deadly the woman she pretends to be is," I said.

"You remember then, don't you? When Arietta showed your wife pregnant with my child, she was only showing you a vision of the future. You'll be dead, and I'll fuck her until she forgets your name, until I erase every trace of you." He laughed as I stared at him. "I imagine Rhia wouldn't overlook me if I gave the Beloved a babe. Oh, it could be fun if I made the shifter fuck her as you, I suppose, to get her wet and ready for me." He clapped as he stood. "Do you suppose Arietta can get your size right for your little wench? Perhaps I'll send her in for a peek. Anyway, none of this is important. You'll be dead in the morning, I'll fetch my brother, and I'll fuck your wife while I'm in Astana. Does that sound good to you, Rainy?" He scoffed as I spat at him, ignoring the pain in my jaw. He didn't flinch when it hit the floor at his feet.

"I will take what is owed to me, mark my word," he growled.

I sat in my cell for hours, lost in my thoughts. The draíbea made it difficult, but every time I fell into that stupor, I would pull on my arm, jolting my shoulder. The pain would pull me out of it. Surprisingly, the relief of my impending death was accompanied by intense gratitude. I should have been angry or perhaps frightened, but I wasn't—I knew what waited for me. I'd be able to see my daughter, the shining light I'd never gotten to meet. And then, I'd wait for Em. The next life I'd have would connect me to the beautiful soul I got to call mine for so brief a time.

Perhaps I'd get it right sooner in the next life.

I thought about her smile, the laugh which accompanied it, and I felt my lips lift. I thought about the eyes I could read without a word, the way her skin wrinkled between her brows when she gave me that adorable scowl, and I was grateful. I would fill my last moments with images of her. Appreciative of the new memories, the beautiful month I had with her would live in my mind the final moments before Declan killed me. I briefly wondered how he'd do it. Hadn't he said something about a headless king? Gods, I hoped I was right. I would've expected much worse from him; a clean decapitation would be a blessing.

I slept off and on, not sure if I was dreaming or living in my memories, and I felt a sense of peace settle over my bones. I thought of praying to one of the gods, but wasn't sure which one to choose. It didn't feel right to pray to Ciarden, hoping to ease my death, though I was sure he might provide some sense of clarity for me. Ultimately, I chose Rhia. Her authority over travel was the reason for choosing her. The more I thought about it, the more connected I felt to that aspect of her divine being. My body would surely die, yet my soul would only travel, journeying on to the next life.

I implored Rhia to make my path simple, to ease my fears and worries, and then I turned my thoughts to Emma. This would set her on a new path as well, and I begged Rhia to watch over her, as it would likely lead her down a road of vengeance and violence. I didn't want that for her. Vesta needed her. My mother, damn her, would probably try to maintain control. But, gods, with Elora dead, Lavenia would ascend. Emma could help her. The two of them would be a force to be reckoned with if they could implement all the good I knew they'd dream up. I wanted her to make a difference, but I worried she'd be so focused on avenging me she wouldn't have the chance.

And what if she was the Beloved? I hoped, for her sake, our suspicions weren't correct. To have that responsibility on top of losing the two people most important to her? Gods, she would break. And I wouldn't be there to put her back together. Fuck, that was the worst part. I didn't care about dying. I knew I'd be with her again. The *real* her. There'd be new freckles to memorize, new eyes to get lost in, but I'd be with her again. The worst part was my absence in the meantime and her solitude.

Would the piece of our soul which belonged to me somehow attach to her and be with her? No one knew how it worked; the soul which twin flames shared was a mystery yet to be solved. The last recorded pair were from a millennium ago. I'd done research the day we performed the ritual. While she got ready with my sister and the merrow, I spent time in the palace library researching. I had found little, and I wasn't sure what I found was accurate. It didn't matter though; we would have figured it all out together—if only we had the time.

I remembered what she said to me the day I took her into the cavern by the lake, when she'd asked me what it was we were doing. When she called me her friend and told me I wasted so much time looking for her. She was right, I had wasted time, but it wasn't time wasted in looking for her.

It was time I wasted on fear.

We could have had sixteen amazing years, and I'd wasted my time being a coward. It might have always come to this; my death had always been on the horizon. Royals amongst the Three Kingdoms were never far from eternal sleep. But we would've had a life, a family. Maybe my soul would wait in the afterlife until Em was ready for me. Maybe I'd be with Elora. I could meet her, hold her, tell her I loved her—all the things I was robbed of in this life. None of it was fair, but perhaps I'd meet my girl, spend time with her while I waited for her mother.

I'd fallen asleep again after another session on the table when cool hands pressed on either side of my face. I opened my eyes and couldn't make out a thing. There was no torch, nothing to illuminate the room.

"Wake up. Zen will be in here soon, and I need you to hear me."

Nor. I took a deep breath, trying to focus my attention on what she was whispering with hushed words.

"They're coming, Rainier. The rebels are planning to get you out of here. I don't know much more, but I know something is happening. I'm going to give you something to get the draíbea out of your system, but you have to promise to help us if you can."

"Help who? Give me something?" I shook my head, sloshing around the words in my mind to make them make sense. I spoke quietly—she clearly didn't want to be overheard.

"Declan—he's trying to impress the goddess, to get her blessing. And to do that, he rapes the novices, tries to get them with child. We're locked in a barracks outside like cattle. We're freezing and starving, and so many carry a babe. Please help us as I've helped you."

My cell door slammed open, a torch illuminating the room, and I heard those footsteps I dreaded as my mind struggled to understand what she'd said.

"You were supposed to wait for me, *chanbi*."

Finally able to see, I watched as she tensed. Reaching into the depths of my hazy mind, I struggled to define the word he'd said. I'd heard it before but couldn't quite place it. It was derogatory, I knew that, and it lent truth to what she'd just told me.

"I wanted to see if he truly needed to be shaved. I don't know why the king insists on it if he's just going to kill him." When she turned, I saw the evidence of a black eye and wondered how she got it. It was in the stage of healing where it looked almost green and yellow, a murky contrast to her olive skin.

"Without a torch? Do you think I'm stupid, *chanbi*? Or is it you who is stupid?" He approached her, and that scent of rot, like an overripe mushroom, filled the air. He lifted a hand toward her, and she flinched before clearing her throat. He closed his hand into a fist and let it drop to his side, but the threat still registered.

"I couldn't find a torch, and my hands work just fine, thank you, Zen." She raised her head to look at him, and the motion reminded me so much of the defiant chin Emma liked to give me. This girl didn't stutter as she lied so blatantly. I had respect for her. She'd clearly been through some trauma. And at the hands of Declan, no less. Fuck, what was it she had just said? A barrack full of novices—female, if they were pregnant—exposed to the winter air and assault by Declan. But what did she expect me to do? I was set to die soon. Squaring her shoulders, she addressed him. "Now, are you going to give me the razor or not? Did you bring the clothing Declan requested?"

The man, or ogre as I suspected, tossed a bundle he held in his free hand, hitting the novice in the face with the clothing intended for me. I heard metal hit the stone floor below, the razor she was to use on my beard falling to the ground. She'd have her work cut out for her. I didn't think I'd gone this long without shaving before. I realized, with an internal groan, she was probably going to be forced to shave it with no water or oil. Fuck. I was in for pain. Declan must have wanted my face to look a certain way for the spike he planned to place it on. I cringed as the novice—Nor, I reminded myself—gently pulled my skin taut.

I raised my eyes to hers, trying not to move as she pressed the blade to my skin and watched me tentatively. I screwed my eyes shut, hoping she'd understand what I meant. She was pressing too hard; I knew I was going to get cut up, but I hoped I could avoid the worst of it. Thank the gods she understood and relieved some of the pressure, and I opened my eyes again. She began, and it felt about as bad as I expected. I could feel her tearing the skin and knew it would be red and raw, even if she didn't cut me. And she didn't. To her credit, the nicks were minimal, but I still felt them.

I found it difficult to get my hopes up over what she'd said. What were the chances they'd succeed? And what did the Folterran rebels have to gain by helping me escape? It made little sense. They wouldn't risk themselves for the Vestian king. Besides, Darkhold was impenetrable—surrounded by mountains. I inhaled sharply as the blade snagged on my skin. I saw her expression change, though I could only see that thin strip of her eyes because of the veil she wore, and it was a clear grimace of apology.

She clearly had things she needed to say as she finished shaving my face, and fuck if I wasn't doing everything I could to focus on anything else. Gods, there might have been some value in adding it to my list of torture methods. Perhaps if I ever captured Declan, I'd make someone do this to his whole gods damn body. And with a dull blade too. As it was, this blade was too sharp, and I knew I'd have cuts and blood all over my face. When she was finally done, Zen grunted impatiently. I'd forgotten he was there.

"Give him more of the draíbea before we put the shirt on him."

Nor pulled something out of the pocket of those strange loose-fitting pants, and I recognized it as the vials they'd been using to pour the noxious plant down my throat. She unstopped it as she lifted it to my mouth. Her eyes were wide as she glanced at the bottle before glancing back at me. It took a moment for the warning to register.

"Come on, *chanbi*, hurry up."

I remembered the word a while later as I vomited like she had said I would.

Chanbi.

No one.

CHAPTER 17

Emmeline

We landed in the mountains east of Darkhold in the afternoon but had to wait until night fell before we made any moves. Thyra and Shade made their way on foot into the small village at the base of the mountains, intending to procure horses and contact the rebel forces. Our plans involved the sewers, and Aldric had mentioned a man named Nigel, whose riverside property seemed to be the perfect location to begin that part of the journey. When we'd stopped to get Aldric, the tavern where we'd met him was burned to the ground, and the rest of the town stood empty. But Dewalt had remembered his words well enough, and I hoped Thyra would have more information for us when she came back. I worried, unsure we'd be able to make our way there without being seen. If anyone saw the dragons before we were ready, we'd have a hard time.

Sweet hell, I had made *dragons*. When I attempted to add wings to Irses, the beast had not been pleased. What was it with my ability to find the most stubborn animal and call it mine? He had shuddered away from my touch, and part of me wondered if the wings hurt as they erupted from his back. While I grew them, focusing on the memory of Rain and I at the cliff, I thought it might be wise to soften the spines on his back, knowing I'd have to climb onto him to ride. It had been easier than I thought, the shadows and divinity working together to form him like clay. When I was done, he huffed a hot breath on the top of my head, and the moist air smelled like the forest between Brambleton and the Alsors. Before I knew it, he had launched himself into the sky, spreading those massive wings and blocking out the stars above us. It was a sight to behold. It was common knowledge that drakes had truly existed when the gods walked the earth, but dragons had only ever been myth and legend. The fact I'd created one with my hands and divinity had caused a reverent silence to fall over the soldiers on the ground with me.

Now, the beast was curled up to sleep, keeping distance from the other dragons save the small one, made from the last dregs of my gifts and who I hadn't yet named. It was a relief to feel my divinity taper off, the churning power muddling underneath my skin finally finding an outlet. The dragon was still large enough for Shade to ride upon, though no bigger than a pony, and, other than the face she made, I didn't once hear her complain. Not that I would've known what she said unless Thyra translated.

I couldn't contain my awe as I stared at the creatures. Irses' wings were nearly translucent in the daylight, with a faint blue tint to them and four long bones which the membrane stretched between. A small claw sat at the top where the bones met. The wings were over ten meters wide, and I couldn't help the shiver up my spine as I recalled how easily his enormous body glided through the air. The little one was annoying him now, Irses clearly wanting to take a nap. I couldn't help my smile as the large dragon pinned the small, dark-green one under his wing with a huff and forced him to settle down. It was bizarre to see the five other dragons piled up nearby, with tails and long necks twining around each other.

Dewalt sat near his own dragon, his hand resting on her snout, and I felt a pang of guilt. I had been trying to remember the times we'd trained together, hoping the dragon would be more keen to obey him if the memory included Dewalt. But I had glanced over at him, the lines of a frown forming because he didn't like how much divinity I was using. Seeing how easily the sour expression sat on his face made me sad for him, which led me to think of Lucia. The memory was an innocuous one, just the five of us laying in the meadow. The resulting dragon had been white like her hair but with an opalescent gleam because of her scales, and the eyes were my own. Lucia's. Dewalt had tilted his head and sighed. I wasn't sure if it was sadness or annoyance, but I had grimaced and apologized. She had blinked up lazily at me, and then arched her head backwards to where he sat before rolling over in my lap and licking his hand. He had looked at me, bewildered almost, and chuckled.

"Lucia would be so mad if I named a pet after her. Do you think she'd forgive me in this instance because it's a gods damned dragon?" The dragon in question huffed a breath, and it had shocked me when a small spark of white came out of her mouth.

"Was that fire?" I'd asked.

"I think it was divine fire. Aonara's fucking dragon."

The tiny thing had stretched out a delicate wing and yawned before pulling herself into Dewalt's lap and curling up into a ball. She was the most precious of the dragons I'd made, and I adored her. Though the memory had been of Lucia, I could only think of Elora as I watched her.

We'd decided on the name Lux, not too close to Lucia's name, but close enough. Dewalt had used a hooked finger to rub under the dragon's chin, and I smiled at him, hopeful since she didn't bite him as Irses had.

"I'm going to have to grow her, but if she can use fire..." Clearing my throat, I'd held out my palm. "Can I hold your hand and see if you can help me? Maybe it will help you have more influence and control over her. Remember the day in the meadow when Nana eventually sent Mister Carson to fetch us? When he fell in the mud?" He nodded, and we worked together, a hand in each other's and a hand on the dragon, as I grew her with my divinity. I wasn't sure it had done anything to help, but it felt easier and less draining.

As I laid in the grass now, watching them, I noticed the breath coming from Lux's mouth was much steamier than the other dragons. There was another one I'd created after I made Lux who could breathe fire, though it wasn't divine fire. I had imagined shooting the tírrúil that killed Sam, the young soldier I'd failed a few months prior. If my flaming arrow had loosed a moment sooner, perhaps the boy wouldn't have died. Ifash, or Iffy, as Bly had been calling him, was the deepest black color with blood-red eyes. I tried not to think of why. He unsettled me, reminding me of my gods damn failure, but I knew his fire breathing would not go unappreciated.

Dewalt stood, strolling over to me as he stretched his neck. He and Thyra had braided their hair tight, multiple loops and twists which kept it tidy and out of the way. Dewalt wasn't thrilled about his role in our plan, but he'd do what I needed from him.

"With me and Shade in the sewers, what do you plan to do with our dragons?" I glanced over at Irses, who somehow had managed to get the tiny terror to sleep under his wing.

"I'm thinking that I'll ride Lux, so I can command her as I see fit. I know this is unbelievable, but I know Irses will follow. He—the memory I'd been thinking of when I made him was one of Rain. He's been so in tune with me since I made him, and I think he'd protect me."

Dewalt nodded as he glanced over at the largest dragon, the one I'd made with the memory of Rain and I falling back in love at the lake. As if feeling our eyes on him, the beast opened its own and looked at me with the green eye of the man we were trying to save. I gave a shaky exhale. I was terrified. What if this didn't work? What if Declan killed Rain the moment he knew we were there? What if we were betrayed by any number of the Folterran rebels within and outside the palace?

"Stop. Emma, it's going to be alright. This is going to work. This plan was a decent enough plan when we made it. We just had to move it up. And now we have dragons. I mean, fuck, we have tilted the odds—not we—you. *You* have tilted the odds into our favor so tremendously; it's going to be alright. I know it."

I had held it together and stayed calm ever since I created Traekka. I hadn't let my emotions get the better of me, but just waiting here for Thyra to return was proving problematic. It would be several hours before she returned, and even longer before night descended, allowing us to sneak in undetected. And all I'd been thinking about and all I *would* think about was failure. There were so many ways our plan could go wrong. Dewalt and Shade could get found out and get killed. Though we'd never heard from Aedwyn and Aerfen, our other spies confirmed Rain was in Darkhold and had given us the location of the dungeons. I'd had to check; Shivani's fear wasn't without reason. If he was being held somewhere else, an attack on Declan's stronghold could have been devastating if Rain wasn't there. Even knowing Rain *was* there didn't soothe me. Who knew what they might do to him once my presence was made known? I felt my lip quiver as I stared at Irses curled up along a rock-wall. He stared back, unblinking, but raised his head to look at me. I averted my gaze to Dewalt, not wanting to summon a dragon over to comfort me as well. The look on my friend's face made my shields break, and I couldn't stop the tears that burst forth.

"What if it's not alright, Dewalt? What if I get him killed?" I was sitting cross-legged on the ground, and I pulled my knees up and rested my forehead against them as Dewalt watched me.

"Emma, his execution is already scheduled for tomorrow. He did this to himself, and you couldn't possibly make it any worse."

"If Cyran—"

"Don't. Fuck, Cyran rescued himself. Or got rescued by the rebels, I suppose. You had little to do with it."

"But I could have taken him to—"

"Oh, for fuck's sake. You couldn't have. No matter how much you might think you'd do anything for Rainier, you'd do more for Elora."

I lifted my head to tell him what he'd just said didn't make me feel any better, but a sob broke past my lips. I tried to rein in my emotions as I noticed the other soldiers glance over in my direction. They'd been giving me space, and a small part of me wondered if they feared me. Dewalt's panicked eyes met mine.

"No, no, shit. That's not—no. You're a good fucking mother. And he'd want you to make that choice. It helps her, protects the kid. Emma, I'm sorry. Listen," he said, tugging me closer to him as he split the distance, hooking one arm around my back while his other rested on my knee. "We have to take this risk, and you are brave—so fucking brave—for taking it. But this is something we have to do. We have to do it, no matter what. So there isn't any gods damned sense in thinking in 'what ifs,' alright?"

He was right. What point was there in that line of thought? I had no choice; I would do this either way to save Rain. Dewalt rubbed my back, and I focused on the beats of the hearts surrounding us, trying to steady myself.

I sat up with a shock, my tears slowing even further, as I speared my divinity more accurately, listening to the surrounding creatures.

"What is it?"

"Their hearts beat with mine."

I tried to sleep during that brief respite before dark fell, but I was still exhausted hours later when I took Dewalt to the rebels downriver.

There was no graceful way to ride on a dragon, especially without some sort of saddle. When we got back to Astana, I was going to have to figure out something. It wasn't exactly comfortable being pressed so close to Dewalt on Irses' neck. We were flying high to avoid being noticed, and we were both shivering, despite being pressed together. We were not remotely prepared for how cold it would be that high. Irses finally brought us to the southwestern outskirts of the capital, where the Shun River branched off to smaller creeks and streams. It turned out Nigel's wife could manipulate water, and she would use those abilities to launch Dewalt and Shade upstream. The closer they got to the palace, the worse 'Shit River,' as the locals called it, would be.

Shade was waiting for us, having went straight there instead of coming back with Thyra. Dewalt's arm shot out, pinpointing the home Thyra had told us to look for. When we landed, both Nigel and Shade came outside of a small run-down shack, which I was surprised still stood. Nigel hung back for a moment, hesitating as he saw Irses.

"Holy goddess' ass. You really are the Beloved."

I snorted as Dewalt slid off Irses behind me. I didn't bother getting down; it was too much of a pain to get back up. I stared up the river where the palace was waiting for me, where Rain was waiting. It was still hours before dawn, but I was nervous as all hell. Thyra had brought back news of Declan's gathered army, waiting just northwest of Darkhold, and I convinced myself we would be gone before they became a problem. I hoped having the element of surprise would turn the tides in our favor before they brought hell down upon us. Dewalt grabbed my ankle, and I nearly jumped out of my skin.

"I won't be adding any rings to my tattoo. Don't worry," he said.

"What?"

"The bicep." He flexed the arm in question, and I rolled my eyes. "The rings, for all the people I cared about who I've lost. I suppose I need to get one removed now though." He grinned up at me for a moment, waiting for me to understand what he'd said.

"You got a tattoo for me? D, it's not like I died."

"No, but it's not like you didn't either. Anyway, neither of us should worry. One Shika tattoo is enough—I don't have room for another. Besides, something tells me you couldn't handle a tattoo."

I frowned at him, ignoring his insult, and thought of the dragon I'd named after Shika. The stars in her constellation were supposedly the pieces of her and her husband, strewn about in the skies after Rhia and Hanwen brought down vengeance upon them. A story Rain had told me when we were young. When he'd pointed out each supposed body part and told the tale in gruesome detail. The dragon I'd formed had been made with the memory of my daughter's death and her healing after. She was a deep, blood-red color, and there were shadows circling and wrapping around her, drawn to her, never dissipating as they had with the others. Her eyes were a molten black, as if made of the same shadows.

"Be safe."

"If I get some sort of disease from this, you're going to wait on me and treat me like a king, right?"

"Of course," I said, smiling despite my fear. "Rain is lucky to have you."

"We are all lucky to have *him*, and we will get him back. I'll see you on the other side, Emma."

He squeezed my ankle again before he walked off with Shade, and they headed to a dock behind the house. I tightened my legs around Irses and said the word *up* for good measure. He seemed very bright; I wasn't sure if he could understand me, but I wanted to teach him words all the same. Dewalt and I had calculated how long it would take the two of them to make their way up the river with the help of the rebel conduit, and I knew I had to hurry to provide adequate distraction to keep them safe.

Finally, after returning to the mountain where my soldiers waited, going over the plan one last time, we were off. It felt crazy to talk to the dragons, but it seemed they understood what I'd said when they flew in formation with me. I rode in the front with Lux, ready to lead the first attack on the palace. Shika and Hyše flanked me on either side, the two fierce female dragons made with memories of pain and terror. I'd chosen soldiers to ride them who were less needed for stealth than they were for their brawn. I had a feeling this would come down to hand-to-hand combat, and we wouldn't be able to bully Darkhold with the might of dragons alone. We didn't have enough of the beasts. Traekka flanked Shika on one side while Bly rode Ifash on the other. I'd instructed him to wait until after I'd attacked before using the fire-breather to bring hell down upon the soldier's barracks. Irses circled above us, watchful, while the small dragon Shade had ridden circled below us.

As we approached the palace, seat of the Umbroth reign, horns rang out. Nestled in a valley between the mountains, the castle was surrounded by natural protection. A tall central tower sat in the middle with a wing off to either side of it. The stone was a dark-grey but appeared stark black at night, giving meaning to its name. Thick fog swirled, casting an ominous look upon the grounds. To the west of the palace proper, I spotted the barracks. They were less decadent but made of the same dark-grey stone. Soldiers ran out, spreading across the grounds, small as ants swarming a picnic from my vantage point. What I needed was on the eastern side of the palace though, and I wouldn't take any chances.

They knew we were here, and we needed to be fast before they got to Rain. Thanks to the spies, I had a rough layout of the palace, and I cried out as I pushed Lux down, down, down, to the eastern wing which housed the dungeon. It was dark, the ground only lit by the light of the moon, and soldiers took cover as I dipped low. Bly on Ifash had darted west to the barracks, taking Shika and the two soldiers on her back with him. Shade's dragon followed behind. Irses tucked his wings in tight, quickly descending to cover my empty left side. His sheer intelligence and understanding astounded me.

Though I didn't give her any vocal command, Lux did what I wanted, leaving a trail of divine fire on our path toward the eastern wing, separating it from the rest of the palace. I hadn't been paying attention to how cold I was, but now I noticed how warm my thighs were, pressed tight around her neck. Hearing a roar, I glanced to the west as the barracks lit up in my periphery. Shika was on the ground, bashing her tail into the debris that Ifash had brought down with his fire. I saw the silhouettes of her riders on the ground, one with his mace out, swinging at the soldiers fleeing from the burning building. Thyra had dipped as soon as Lux attacked, landing with Traekka as they both helped kill the Folterran soldiers roused from their beds. Part of me felt a pang of guilt—they were just soldiers, after all—but I pushed it aside. There was no room for that type of thinking. This was war; there would be bloodshed and death, and Declan was to blame for it. He had to have known there would be retaliation. Had to have known the cost of what he had done and the choices he made.

I shrieked, drawn out of my thoughts by searing pain across the top of my leg, an arrow the cause of it. Lux veered sharply the moment I was hit. I winced at the sudden movement; it was difficult to hold onto her with my legs because of the pain. Looking down in a panic, I breathed a sigh of relief when I discovered the arrow hadn't sunk home into my leg, though the gouge it left behind was deep. I began to heal it, struggling to hold onto Lux while my divinity did its work. While I concentrated, Irses let out a tremendous roar and dove for the ground. I wasn't sure what he was going for but had a feeling it was the archer who wounded me. Hyše was nearby, her rust-colored body staying just in my line of sight while her rider, Lasu—a dark-haired warrior with one eye—watched me warily, clearly concerned about my ability to stay on Lux.

He wasn't alone in that.

The answer came to me as shadows skirted over my skin, and I could have kicked myself for not thinking of it sooner. Coaxing those shadows up and out, I managed to brace myself as I finished healing the wound. Secured on top of Lux, Irses caught my attention. He held a man in his mouth as he flew up, higher and higher, until they were at my height.

And then he dropped him.

I heard his screams at first, and it cut off when Irses caught him in his mouth again, and threw the man once more. He repeated the process, allowing the archer to fall before he caught him, until finally I called out to him, unsure if he could hear me.

"Don't play with your food!"

The dragon whipped his head toward me as he let the body of the soldier tumble out of his mouth and fall to the ground. I started laughing, unable to control myself. Hysterical. The surprise he heeded my directions, the annoyance in his eyes as he let the man fall, and the fact I now had dragons to feed with no idea what to feed them set me off.

I watched Hyše as Lasu set her in a dive, clearly no longer concerned about my injury. Irses joined me once again, and I wiped the sweat off my brow. I glanced down, satisfied with the red shiny skin I could see through the hole in my breeches before setting myself back on the task at hand. Turning Lux toward the center of the palace, we approached the tower said to hold Declan's suite. Perhaps I could cut off the head of the beast now. Irses stayed just behind while Lux and I circled the tower, attempting to find the Folterran king's balcony.

I found it on my second loop around the tower as the man came crashing out, naked. His hair was a disheveled mess, and the woman, who ran behind him, had a blanket wrapped around her. I dug my knee into Lux, trying to get her to bank tightly and turn toward him as Declan let out a bellow, and I felt a disturbance in the air which called to part of me. I threw out an arm just in time, my shadows reaching out to intercept his. My mount faced Declan head-on as she gave a vicious roar, and her divine fire enveloped the side of the tower. Lux stalled, back-flapping her wings and pulling up vertically, so we stayed in one place as we waited for the fire to subside. When I could finally see, I noticed the body of his companion on the balcony, but Declan had somehow made it back inside. And I watched as a man created a rift for him. He looked at me and smirked as they both stepped through.

Shit.

There were only two places he could have been heading. We were out of time. I squeezed Lux with my thighs as I pushed her forward, choosing at the last moment to divert from my path when I saw the glimmer of something pulling me toward it.

CHAPTER 18

DeWalt

Shit River was an understatement. Shade and I were in a small boat, and I was rowing us up the last stretch before we reached the grate leading into the sewer system. In our original plan, Emma was supposed to be with us, using her shadows to help protect us from sight, but there was no need. No one in their right mind got close to the river in this part of the city. Besides, the dragons would draw attention, leaving us unseen. My eyes had finally stopped watering, though the smell still burned my nose. I knew once we were underground, it would only get worse.

We finally reached the giant grate, and the rush of water and sludge was too great for us to row past. I hopped out of the small boat as near to the shore as I could bring us, cringing as I felt the water climb up my boots, and pulled it to the bank while Shade watched for any late-night walkers who preferred the smell of sewage. She clambered out, and we started walking. We'd have to climb into the river and slip through the bars and hope to the gods there was a walkway within, or we'd be trudging through shit the entire way. A flicker caught my eye, and I glanced up.

Emma had begun her assault.

I suppressed a shiver as I watched divine fire spray forth from Lux. I couldn't see the dragon from this distance, but I stopped to watch all the same, before Shade tugged on my shirt. She nodded toward the grate, and I jolted into action. If Emma had begun, we needed to hurry. I noticed a small walkway hovering right above the water level and sighed in relief. Shade picked her way across and slid between the bars easily. Worried I wouldn't fit, I held my breath as I wiggled through. I was grateful we wouldn't be leaving this way, unsure if Rainier would be able to squeeze through as he was much broader than I was. I couldn't see a thing, and Shade used a match to light the torch she carried.

"Praise the gods." I couldn't help the sigh I released when I saw how far the walkway extended up the tunnel. I recited the directions Nigel had given us as I began jogging up the walkway. The man was more integral in the rebel system than I originally thought, and I was eager to maintain contact with him once we escaped.

I dragged Shade by the hand behind me as I flew through the tunnel. We needed to hurry, and I was worried we wouldn't get there in time since the assault on the palace had already begun. Thankfully, it was a straight line until we got closer, and Shade kept pace easily, her torch bouncing as she ran. When we finally approached the bend Nigel had mentioned, I was distracted, worrying about how much time we had left. Still running as I turned the corner, I fell straight into the sewage.

"Fuck!" I shouted, as Shade watched me from above. She didn't laugh, and my appreciation for the tiny woman doubled.

"Alright, Captain?"

I looked at her in shock; I'd never heard her speak the common tongue. Though her accent was thick, I understood her, and the look of pride on her face made me smile despite the fact I stood in slow-moving sewage up to my chest. My mood soured when I realized the walkway didn't continue down this branch.

"Could be better, Shade. Thanks for asking." She tilted her head, confused. She clearly only knew a few words in the common tongue, and I was a bit flattered she used them on me. I looked between her and my chest, knowing she would be fully submerged if she got in here with me. I sighed when I realized the alternative. Turning, I offered my back to her, and she climbed onto my shoulders. She was light and still able to hold the torch this way. I grabbed her legs and trudged through the shit.

At the end of the tunnel was another grate with bars much more narrow than the last, and I knew I wouldn't be able to make it through. Nigel thought this might happen and had supplied us with something to help. I knew it would take longer than we wanted, but we didn't have a choice.

"We need the—" Shade was already pushing the glass jar into my hand as she held onto the fuse attached to it, keeping it out of the sewage below. I fastened the bottle to one bar, and once convinced it would stay, I backed up as far as we could. The fuse was too damn short. I turned us to the side to protect us as Shade used her torch to light it. I moved to run, difficult in the water, attempting to give us more distance.

It still wasn't enough.

The grate blasted open on one side, and Shade and I fell forward into the water. I surfaced, looking for any signs of her, but didn't see the woman. I reached beneath the water, trying to find her, and finally loosened a breath as I felt her hand grasp mine. But when I pulled, she wasn't coming up.

Fuck.

She had to have been stuck. Pulling my dagger out, I held my breath as I went under. She dragged my hand up to her hair, and it felt taut, so I began slicing through it with haste. The moment it was free, she pushed off the bottom, and I held her up so she could get air. Heaving for breath, I watched in horror as brown liquid trickled into her mouth. Not sure why that was where I drew the line, I started gagging as I reached out to wipe her face off, but it didn't help at all. We were covered in it. Finally, as she stopped coughing, I turned around to see our newest problem.

The grate was open, the metal bars gone on one side, but there were tiny pockets of flames burning on the surface of the water. I didn't want to think about all the different flammable things we were wading through. It was helpful to an extent, considering the torch Shade had held was long gone, but I was not looking forward to getting past it. I hoisted the woman back onto my shoulders, and she let out a tiny squeak from the surprise as I situated her. After I wiped my face once more from the shit-water that dripped down off of her onto me, she adjusted so it wouldn't continue happening.

"*Tak du*, Shade."

Thank you.

She patted my head in response, and I chuckled as I set off through the grate, weaving between patches of flames. It wasn't long before we took the last turn, the correct path marked by the extremely narrow entrance. I almost missed it, considering the flow of water coming out of it was fast enough it didn't seem like a corridor at all. I started mumbling under my breath as I realized the only way we'd be able to continue. Shade reached down and grabbed my head, pointing it towards the narrow tunnel and urging me on. She was right; we didn't have time. I held my breath as I pushed forward while I used my arms to pull us through the opening. Bracketing a hand on either side of the wall, it took all my strength to get us through. When I grunted, Shade slapped her hand over my mouth, quieting me, and I nearly puked into it. Finally through the narrow entrance, I could move to the side, not having to fight the current as much.

The end of the tunnel was dimly lit from a torch somewhere above. When Shade pointed ahead, as if there were another option, I rolled my eyes as I continued. Stumbling, I barely caught myself as I stepped over something which felt suspiciously like a body. Noticing a line which came halfway up the bricks at the end of the tunnel, I realized we were lucky. If the tunnel was at its full capacity, I wouldn't have been able to touch the bottom. As it was, the putrid water came up to my chin. I swore under my breath when I realized the ledge was much higher than I had expected. After Shade climbed up to stand on my shoulders and she still couldn't reach, I pantomimed lifting her until she caught on, and I held her at the ankles, pushing up as she gripped onto the brick the best she could.

"Close?" I wasn't sure if she'd understand me at all, but I tried anyway, whispering in case someone was at the top. I could hear shouting in the distance but couldn't make out the words. She started bouncing on my hands, and it only took me a moment to realize what she wanted from me. I was going to have to launch her and hope for the best. I bent my arms, thanking the gods for my daily training, and on my third bounce, I pushed her up as she jumped, her fingertips barely catching the edge of the drop off. She scrambled over the ledge, and I was impressed when it only took her a moment before she was ready.

The rope she tossed down was wet and slimy, and I struggled to keep my grip as I climbed. I heard a grunt from Shade and a loud thump, quickly propelling me despite the difficulty. When I reached the top, she was already there, offering me a hand despite her busted eyebrow. I looked behind her, finding a dead guard, and she met my eyes with a devilish grin.

Gods, she was terrifying.

Neither of us had any idea where Rainier might be within the dungeons, but we took off at a run to find him. I grabbed a blade from my bandolier as I ran, trying to wipe the handle so it was dry, but nothing helped. It hadn't been long when I could finally decipher the word being screamed above us.

Fire.

I heard people running, and I wondered if Emma had set the whole gods damned wing on fire. I smelled it a second later, my senses dulled by the stench of the river. Shade and I took off down opposite directions, and the empty cells gave way to occupied ones. Part of me thought I should free them, especially if there was a fire, but Rainier came first. I heard a dreadful roar from above and worried about our escape amidst the destruction. There was a woman who held onto her bars, screeching for help, and I almost ran past her until I saw the ring of keys near her door. I grabbed it, sticking in one after another until her cell unlocked.

"I'm going to let you out, but I need to know where the King of Vesta is. Do you know?"

The woman nodded but didn't speak. All she wore was a shift, blackened with filth, and I could see every bone in her body. They must have been starving her. I opened the cell, and she ran, pushing past me. I panicked, running after her, thinking she conned me.

"This way!" she called out over her shoulder as she turned down another row of cells, and I followed. She stopped when we came upon some stairs, pointing past them. "Down there," she said. And then she was gone.

I ran as I called out his name, grateful I hadn't met any more guards other than the one Shade killed.

"Dewalt?" I heard his voice, a croak of disbelief, as I ran toward the end of the corridor. Chills ran down my spine; I was so gods damned relieved.

Someone in clothes I belatedly realized belonged to a Myriad novice went sprinting past me, but they paid me no mind before turning down another corridor. I kept calling Rainier's name, but he'd stopped answering. I opened the slit in several doors, peering in for my friend and growing more nervous as he remained unresponsive, save for that first shout.

When I finally found his cell, I looked in and felt my stomach drop out of my ass. A puff of air which stank of the most pungent draíbea wafted through the small opening as I fumbled for the keys. No wonder he wasn't answering me—I'd be lucky if he was even conscious.

Rainier was lying on the ground near a pile of what I assumed was his own sick. He was thinner, features gaunt and pale—skin ashen. He had cuts all over his gods damned face like someone tried to shave him in the dark with their eyes closed. That wasn't even the worst of his appearance, his jaw and brow swollen and bruised from a recent beating. The clothes they'd put him in hung off his frame, and his pants looked loose on his hips.

"Rainier, you awake?"

He blinked at the hole in the door, blinded by the torch I held next to me, before pushing up to sit. I noticed the censer hanging from the ceiling, out of reach, as it emitted noxious fumes into the air. I was already feeling something from it, and I wasn't even in the room.

"Are you—" He cleared his throat. "Dewalt?"

"Yes, friend. It's me. I'm going to get you out of here."

He grunted, and I didn't waste another moment as I shoved each key into the lock.

"I swear to the gods..." He trailed off, mumbling something incoherent.

I dropped the ring of keys onto the ground, my slimy fingers not able to grasp them properly.

"Ciarden's crusty ass, gods damn it." I bent over to pick them up and was rewarded with a chuckle I hadn't realized I missed.

"How long has it been?" Rainier stretched as he spoke.

"Uh, Winter Solstice is in two weeks."

Finally, I found the right key and swung his cell door open.

"I missed your birthday then. Happy birthday, D."

"Leave it to you to say shit like that and somehow make me feel worse," I said.

He was still on the ground, and I worried that once he actually stood, the true toll of what he'd been through would be so clear on his body that I wouldn't be able to hold my shit together. I put the torch in a bracket just inside the room and took him in. He was thinner than me, and it wasn't right. Everything about the way he looked was wrong. The way he was wishing me happy birthday like he hadn't been in a gods damned dungeon this entire time was wrong. Fuck.

"We should have come sooner. Shivani wouldn't..." I trailed off as he shook his head, and I stepped into the cell. The weight of the lava rock bore down on me, making it hard to breathe. They'd had him in this dampening cell the entire fucking time. We'd be lucky if his divinity didn't kill us once he was free. I stilled as I noticed what sat along the far side of the cell.

"The rack? He put you in the fucking rack?"

That was why he had yet to stand. He probably couldn't. Rainier didn't reply as a voice bellowed from the hallway.

"HURRY! WE NEED TO GET THE CHILDREN OUT BEFORE IT COLLAPSES!"

We both jumped as we heard the shriek and a stampeding of feet as three novices ran past, headed toward the stairs. I was shocked they spoke, even in a situation like this, and I shrugged. Good—I was glad Emma was destroying everything.

"Fuck. Dewalt, go help."

"What? No. Can you stand?"

"No, you need to go help them. The novices are being tortured—all women. I smell fire, Dewalt. Whatever you have done—" He shook his head. "Please, I made a promise. Go help and come back for me."

"Emma would fucking kill me. No! We can go help them together."

He flinched when I said her name, and it struck me as odd.

"Dewalt, I can't fucking walk. She's here, right? Em will find me," he whispered as he closed his eyes. "*Go help them.*"

I watched him as he tried and failed to stand. He was clearly weak, and I felt my chest tighten. It took everything I had not to reach out and help him up, and I crossed the distance between us before I stopped myself. The man could be prideful to a fault, and I knew he'd be furious if I touched him.

"What is that smell?" he questioned.

"It's me; don't ask."

"Go. Go help them. That's an order from your king." His face was grim as he stretched his neck, and I knew I had no choice but to follow his order.

"You'll deal with her then?" He nodded, and I saw his throat bob. "I'll be back if she doesn't beat me here first. Try not to die in the meantime."

He chuckled, but I passed one of my knives to him anyway. When he went to pull away, I grasped his wrist and ignored just how thin he was, looking into eyes holding a tired sadness I couldn't begin to comprehend.

"I'll be back, Rainier."

Fuck the Myriad.

I didn't give a rat's ass what happened to the novices, even if they were getting tortured. Rainier knew how I felt about anyone who associated with them, after what they put Lucia through, after they failed her, yet he sent me on this gods forsaken errand. I just wanted to get my friend and go. Easily catching up to the novices who'd been running down the corridor, they led us up from the dungeon down a long, open hall—opulent to a distasteful degree. Gold-coating was on nearly everything, and the carpeted flooring looked expensive. When we finally got outside, I understood the fear.

The building they ran toward seemed to be attached to the palace itself, nestled against the eastern wing.

Divine fire had set it ablaze.

I glanced about, looking for Emma and the dragon, not finding either. But what I did see was absolute fucking mayhem. Bly sat atop his dragon, Ifash, who used his tail to slam Folterran soldiers to the ground. Scanning the chaos, I found Thyra swinging her ax over her head before relieving another soldier of their own. There was fire and roaring and smoke, and, even though we only had a handful of soldiers, we weren't overwhelmed because of the sheer power of the dragons.

I let my thoughts wander, hopeful that Emma could make a gods damned army out of them.

Darting past wreckage and ruin, I intercepted a Folterran soldier who was running toward the novices in a way I didn't trust. I didn't know what the fuck his plans were, but I would not wait to find out. I didn't give a damn about them, but I needed to help and get the fuck back to Rainier. Not only did the soldier not expect what was coming, the novices had no idea what I'd just saved them from when I sliced the man's throat, dropping his body to the ground.

Fighting the smoke, I followed the novices. I didn't know what Rainier would have me do. The whole front of the building was aflame, and if anyone were inside, they'd be lucky if they weren't dead already. The women fell to the ground, wailing and pointing upward, and it took a moment to see why.

The structure was on the verge of collapse, and the upstairs windows had all burst out. But there was a small child standing in a second-story window, reaching down and crying as smoke billowed out around him. The babe couldn't have been more than two years old.

Gods damn it. Just what I fucking need.

Jogging over to the window, I shouted up at the little one, "I want you to jump to me, alright? I'll catch you."

The crying didn't stop, and if anything, the child looked even more terrified before backing away from the window.

"No, no, come here! It'll be fun," I pleaded, trying to convince myself as much as I was the child. They backed completely out of sight, and I cursed before heading toward the front of the building.

One woman had approached the door, yanking on the metal handle despite the gods damned padlock someone had put at the top, and screeched as she drew her hand back from the heat. I ran forward to help as the ground shuddered below my feet. Glancing over my shoulder, I saw Lux slamming down, and Emma was off of her, sprinting to the dungeons.

Thank the gods, since I was clearly preoccupied here. I turned back to the building and the novice at the door faced me, screaming as if she thought I was going to attack her. She pointed over my shoulder though, and I realized what had frightened her.

"Oh. Yeah, dragons. They're—"

Two ridiculous things happened at once. First, the novice fainted, falling forward into my arms with bulging eyes. And second, the door behind her burst open, the entire frame coming with it attached by the padlock.

A woman stood in the doorway, panting and covered in soot. Her veil was torn halfway off, and the hood had fallen down, revealing a mass of dark waves. Her shirt had been ripped open, revealing her shoulder and entire arm. Staring at me, enraged as she took in the novice in my arms, she started shouting at me. "Put her down and help me now!"

And I obeyed, gently lowering the novice to the ground before lunging forward, taking the bundle the other woman shoved at me. I only realized it was an infant when it squirmed in my hold.

"What am I supposed to do with this?" I shouted back at her.

Where was I supposed to take a baby? She looked at me as if I were stupid and gestured to the other novices behind me.

I supposed that made sense.

Turning toward the one closest to me, I pushed the bundle into their arms. I gestured toward the western side of the palace, shouting about the rebels Nigel had promised me would be waiting. He'd offered his assistance just in case we needed it, knowing we had dragons to escape on. I was thankful the man had the idea.

"How many are inside?" I turned back to the woman who busted open the door and was surprised to notice she'd pulled the remaining fabric from her head. It felt like an affront to the gods, to see a novice's face, and I knew if a master saw her, they'd have her beaten. It was a shame she'd chosen that lifestyle, considering the face she'd uncovered was fucking beautiful despite the soot and disgust covering her features.

"There are two dozen of us in total, but I counted at least six dead. That leaves, what, thirteen unaccounted for?" She glanced at the novices on the ground behind me to confirm. "They might not all be here though. He uses us around the palace."

Glancing over her shoulder, I looked at the top of the staircase in horror, spotting the small child from the window.

"Fuck!" I shouted, shoving past her and taking the stairs two at a time, hoping they held up despite the supporting beams being in flames. I snatched the child with no gentleness and raced back down the stairs, shoving the little one into the woman's arms. She slammed backwards from the weight, falling back against the door behind her. By the time two novices ran past, each carrying a child on the hip, she had steadied on her feet as she cradled the babe to her chest, glaring up at me.

"Sorry," I gritted out, wincing. "Any more upstairs?"

"Shouldn't be. Mathias must have followed me up there when I ran up to check, and I didn't see him." She coughed, rubbing the boy's head.

"Which way should I go?"

"Down the hall—back right corner. I haven't seen those novices come out. Last three doors."

Turning on a heel, I held my breath and navigated the best I could through the debris, past the staircase and down the hall she'd indicated. I'd done some calculations, tallying how many women and children I'd seen, and after passing a few more novices bearing little ones, I thought there might only be one person left. Checking each room—cell, more like—I didn't find anyone until the very last room at the end of the hall. The smoke wasn't as penetrating back here, but the last door was locked from the outside, no key in sight. I kicked it open.

I nearly retched at what I saw. I was coughing anyway at that point, smoke taking its toll, and bile rose in my gorge. Holding my shirt over my face, I attempted to filter out some of the smoke in my lungs.

She wasn't alive, that much was clear. Even under the smoke, the room had clearly been visited by death, and I doubted it was the fire that killed her. Strapped to a bed, the heavily pregnant woman was covered in blood from the waist down, and with the way her legs were contorted—

She'd died in childbirth. Alone.

She even had the fucking veil on. Covered even in death, as was the way of the Myriad. And here she laid, humbled by the same gods who'd caused havoc on my friends' lives, on my own damn life. I wondered if they even cared about her anonymous piety, the very reason she had been tossed into a place to be no better than a broodmare.

Making up my mind, I stalked forward a few steps, pulled the cover off her face, and felt relief that her expression was serene. Smooth, pale skin and dark lashes were all I could make out in the minimal moonlight offered by the barred window. Offering a prayer to the old gods, I covered her body even though I knew it would be nothing but ash soon and left the room.

"Mara!" a voice cried out, and, through the increasing haze of smoke, I could see the woman who'd busted the door open running down the hall toward me.

Divine fucking hell.

She spotted me, stopping her running to bend over, hands on her knees as she coughed.

"One more! Mara. I haven't seen—"

She fell into the wall beside her, coughing so roughly I grabbed her elbow before she could collapse.

"With child? Pale skin, dark hair?"

The novice nodded, and I decided I'd tell her once we left. Though she clearly couldn't breathe, she had surprising strength as she pulled away from me, but she kept her hand on my arm for support.

"*Where is she?*"

Jumping as a voice penetrated my mind, I shirked away from her touch. Mind-speaking was about as common as my own vision-weaving abilities, but it still unsettled me. I didn't need someone in the fucking Myriad in my head. I didn't give a damn who she was or what Declan had been doing to them. As far as I was concerned, she brought this shit upon herself.

"Dead," I said, voice monotone. "Come on."

Pushing past her, I started down the hallway, only stopping a moment later when she didn't follow. Peering over my shoulder, I saw her slide down the wall, head in her hands as she coughed, tears running clean tracks down olive skin.

For fuck's sake.

"You'll be dead too, if you don't get the fuck up."

Ignoring me or unable to hear me, I wasn't sure which, she didn't move. Her head tilted forward, and all I could see was the dirty tip of her nose behind that curtain of dark hair.

"I have shit to do. Get up," I said as I approached her. I'd drag her out if I had to, then I'd go help with Rainier. When she refused to move, I bent over her and reached down, tilting her chin up with my fingertip. Eyes I couldn't tell the color of in this light looked back up at me, sadness and hatred whirling behind them.

"It wasn't the fire that killed her. I'm assuming it was Declan's fault. You can't make him pay for it if you die here with her."

Her eyebrows tilted up in the middle, pitiful sadness on her face, before it hardened into something stony. She pushed my hand away and stood, slamming into the wall once more as she started coughing again. My own lungs were aching, but she'd clearly been in the building far longer than me. Though we were farther back where the smoke wasn't nearly as bad, I didn't trust her to make it out.

"Sorry about this," I said as I bent down, picking her up beneath the knees and behind her back.

She didn't fight me, dissolving into a fit of coughing against my chest. Heavier than I'd have thought, I realized the loose novice attire hid her shape. She had been tall for a woman, but what surprised me most was the corded muscle of her legs I felt through the thin, loose pants. She was strong. No wonder she'd been able to kick open the fucking padlocked door. Once outside, I surveyed her as I set her down. I was glad to no longer be touching her, not trusting her to stay out of my gods damned head. Situating her clothing on her body, she winced as she tugged on her shirt, and I saw red injured skin on her exposed arm.

"Shit, you've been burned. Are you alright? The queen is a—"

"Skies, you're lucky you're handsome," she said.

"I'm sorry, what?"

"You'd have to be, because you aren't too bright," she coughed out, and I stared at her. "These are scars, you buffoon."

I studied her arm, realization dawning.

"You winced like it hurt, so I thought it was new..."

"It's fine," she muttered, sounding offended as she tugged her ripped shirt to cover the mottled skin.

I averted my eyes, turning back toward the palace, feeling ashamed. The woman clearly just lost someone she was close to, and I seemed to have insulted her. Pushing the thought out of my mind, I caught sight of riders on horseback, one carrying the novice I'd sent off before going inside the building. At the same time, a Folterran soldier with a crossbow took aim at the rebels, and I knew there would be nothing I could do to stop it.

It was a good thing Lux was there.

White fire drew a line where the soldier had once stood as she veered, scorching a path of earth on her way back toward the palace. I spotted Irses perched on the gods damned fountain, his tail laying in the water below him. He waited for Emmeline—I was sure of it.

Glancing across what I realized was an expansive courtyard with elaborate gardens, I realized most of the enemy had been killed or had fled, making it easier as I urged the surrounding novices toward their ride out of this carnage.

"*Where are they taking them?*" A soft voice whispered in my mind as she put her hand on my shoulder, even as Irses let out a deafening roar. I didn't jump this time, but I turned and scowled.

"Anywhere but here—probably to Evenmoor. Now, hop on." I nodded to the last horse, ready to assist her.

"No, I can't stay—" She shook her head, cutting herself off. "I have to get back to Astana. Take me with you. The king knows me."

I chuckled, guiding her toward the horse as Irses roared once more. I needed to go see if Emma needed my help.

"He told me to help you but didn't tell me to go out of my way. Horse. Now."

That was when I heard the horns.

"Fuck, go on. Now!" I shouted at her.

"No! Take me with you," she pleaded.

"We're getting out of here. Let's go!" The man who'd led the rebel horses yelled out, turning his steed, and his other men followed. The horse this woman was supposed to be on took off, its rider not bothering to wait.

"Fine. Follow me." I took off at a brisk walk, annoyed. "I bet you've never had something this deadly between your legs."

"What did you just say to me?" she shouted as she ran after me, and I couldn't help the grin I shot her over my shoulder.

"Or perhaps you have. I don't know what you're into. I didn't think novices were supposed to—"

I was cut off as my beast slammed to the ground in front of us, ready. Lux was gorgeous, with translucent wings and a rainbow of color on each white scale. Blue eyes that made me want to die blinked down at me, and even I was impressed, although I'd had time to get used to her. I turned toward the novice, expecting shock and awe as she took in the glorious, opalescent creature in front of us. Instead, she looked me up and down, nose crinkled.

"Is that stench coming from *you?*"

CHAPTER 19

Rainier

The smoke grew thick in my cell, and I tried to stay awake as I sat against the cold stone. I considered attempting to crawl into the hallway so the dampening rock wouldn't restrict Em when she found me, but the pressure on my joints as I bent them was too fucking much. So, I sat and waited. For her.

Em was here. *My* Em. Not some gods damned abomination made to deceive me.

I heard a roar from above, and I shuddered, uncertain about what hell Declan was using to defend Darkhold. The knowledge Emma was out there, fighting for me, stirred up something in my gut—pride mixed with nauseating fear. If Declan somehow caught her, all of this would have been for nothing. And the fact she risked herself pissed me off. I had been trying to keep her away from Declan, and here she was, walking straight into the wolf's den.

Because of me.

Dewalt had been right about one thing; she would be angry with him for leaving me. But I had made a promise to the kind novice. The ground shook above me as if something had collapsed, dust and debris falling down. The censer hanging from the ceiling swung in a wide arc, burnt pieces of draíbea falling to the ground.

I took a deep breath and shuddered as I exhaled. Would I be able to look at her the same? She was my wife, my twin flame, the one woman I loved and held above all else.

And I was petrified to see her.

I ran my hand over my face and instantly regretted it, wincing where my eyes were swollen from the last beating I'd received. Why the fuck did Declan bother having my face shaved? For the first time, I wondered how bad I looked. The look on Dewalt's face was—fuck. I must have looked like shit. Glancing down, I noticed my pants hanging off my waist. They weren't my pants, so it was possible they were too large for me. Based on Dewalt's reaction, I didn't think that was the case.

"Rain!"

It was *her* voice. Ragged and terrified, but hers.

Wasn't it? What if it was some sort of trick? What if it was the shifter come to kill me or trick me and execute me early? That would be a blow to Declan's pride, but the end result would be the same. Me, dead at his hands.

"Rainier, where are you?" Her voice was rough, as if she'd been screaming my name for a while.

I palmed the dagger in my pocket, even though I knew I'd be able to tell it was her. I was lucid, thanks to the vomiting Nor inflicted upon me. My throat and abdomen were surprisingly sore from the forceful expulsion of the muck which kept me hazy. But because of it, I'd know her. My Emma would be instantly recognizable. I would know, and it would be fine. I took a deep breath, steadying myself.

"Here," I croaked, and I knew she wouldn't be able to hear me, so I cleared my throat before trying again. "I'm here."

I heard her footsteps before I saw her, the pace quickening after she heard me call out. When she turned the corner and stood in the doorway, the first thing I noticed was the purple bags under her eyes. Eyes I watched widen in shock and something verging on horror. I must have looked worse than I thought. We both froze, and I took her in. Her face was thinner—gaunt. The grief had taken its toll on her. My heart ached at what had happened to us. What she'd been going through without me. The loss of our girl.

But this was Emma. *Her.*

I knew it instantly, even without being able to feel the bond between us, the dampening cell muting our connection. Gods damn, I missed that golden thrumming in my soul. Her beautiful hair framed her face, falling out from her braid. Those eyes were hers, full of life and promise and light. My heart hurt to think the shifter had ever fooled me. Her lower lip started quivering, and my instincts crashed within me. So much of me wanted to go to her, to hold her in my arms, to smell her hair and kiss her neck. But another part of me, the cowardly part, was afraid. Perhaps I feared what I could do to her. If, for just a second, I thought it was the shifter, could I trust myself? Could I stop myself from hurting her? And what if she caught me in a more vulnerable moment? What if I was afraid of not just hurting her, but her hurting me?

"Rain," she whispered. Then she broke, tears streaming down her ash-covered face. I wanted nothing more than to take her in my arms, but I didn't trust myself.

She hadn't taken a step toward me, for which I was grateful. Her eyes traced down my body, lingering where my leg laid propped at an odd angle.

"Broken?"

Her gaze met mine, somber, and I nodded. As she took a step toward me, I forced myself to loosen my grasp on the dagger in my hand, leaving it in my pocket. This was real. This was my Emma. Mine.

When she collapsed to the ground, it took me too long to understand what happened.

"NO!" I shouted.

The woman who stood behind her cackled, sending rage through my veins, and I surged forward, throwing my broken body between Emma and the woman who stole her image. She was alright. She'd be fine. Her divinity would heal her once I pulled her from the cell.

The shifter tossed an ax on the ground, and I stared at Emma's head in horror, terrified she was dead. "I hit her with the blunt end—don't worry. Declan would have my head if I didn't bring her to him in one piece." I tightened my grip on the dagger in my pocket.

"Are you going to drag her there?"

"Oh no, I'm going to shift into Zen and carry her if I have to. He's dead, by the way. Did you know ogres were that flammable? I didn't. Gods, all it took was a spark, and he was done for—a giant flame! It was disgusting and amazing. Anyway, I can't let you die while I carry her out. He has this whole ceremony planned, and he'll be livid if he can't swing your head around. So, you could do me the favor of carrying her, and that way neither of you die in the fire."

"I can't walk, you stupid fuck."

"That wasn't necessary." She sighed, annoyed. "I suppose you'll need to drag yourself then, since I'll be carrying her."

"Why should I even bother? Declan will torture us both."

"Well, I'm sure that will be involved in what happens going forward, but it's better than dying now, isn't it?" She crossed her arms and leaned against the doorway. I stared at her features, pinpointing exactly what was wrong. This Emma didn't have the same spread of freckles across her nose and cheeks. This Emma didn't tug on her bottom lip with her teeth when she was thinking or tuck her hair behind her ear while she fidgeted. Fuck the draíbea for making me think this was her.

"I might be able to walk if you help me up."

"Do you think I'm stupid? I watched you just throw yourself down in front of her. If any moment called for you successfully walking, it would've been that one."

"Oh, fuck off. I was in a hurry to protect her from you. If you help me stand, my legs might hold my weight," I countered.

She sighed, palming her mouth.

"I suppose I'll just carry her and let you die. I'll tell Declan it was too late by the time I got here. I'm doing you a favor, really. You probably don't want to hear him fucking her."

There was a crashing sound above us, and the ceiling shook once more, the censer swaying. The shifter coughed and leaned out of my cell, turning her head in the direction Dewalt had gone.

"Fuck. I'm not dying down here too." Her eyes darted between Emma and me before she skittered past me, just out of reach. When she pulled Emma into her arms, a grunt escaping her lips, I saw regret cross her features. She dragged Emma a step, realizing she wouldn't be able to carry her.

"Should have shifted into the ogre when you had the time," I said, voice calm.

She dropped Emma's limp form, and I cringed as my wife slumped over onto the ground, bashing her forehead. It was then I saw the decision to run on the shifter's face, and I couldn't let her get away. Palming my dagger once more, not sure I'd be able to do much with my aching joints, I cautiously adjusted on the ground where I'd landed.

Emma moaned, eyes closed, turning her head enough so I could see blood trickling from her nose. It was crooked, broken in the last few minutes. My poor love. I lost control of my temper, deciding the shifter would not make her way out of my gods damn cell. She darted to the side as my hand caught her ankle, and she fell, slamming hard to the ground.

I groaned, tugging on her leg as she kicked at me, and my knife skittered across the ground, away from us both.

Fuck.

Scrambling, the shifter kicked at my face, and her heel made contact with my chin, knocking my head back.

"Get the hell off me!" she screamed as I tugged her toward me, and I propelled myself at her, roaring through the pain. My body weight held her legs down as I pulled myself up her prone form. Her shirt moved as I pulled my way past unwelcoming hips and thighs, and a firm, flat stomach without a single gods damn differentiation of that pale skin. Proof they barely fucking tried and had managed to outwit me. Nails clawed at my shoulders as I dug my elbow into that wrong stomach and got my other hand around her throat.

She only had a second to scream as my other hand joined the first, grip tight around her neck. She kicked, trying to buck my body off her. Despite my weakened state, my hold was sure. I looked at my hands, the golden-brown hair spilling over the black stone floor, the rack against the wall—anywhere but at the face looking upward at me, eyes rolling back in her head. I couldn't see that, didn't want to see that. Finally, the kicking slowed and her body fell limp. I didn't move as I held on a bit longer, letting my heaving gasps return to normal.

"She's dead, Rain." I glanced over my shoulder to see Emma sitting up, her hand over her broken nose as she stared at me. Her expression was blank, and I realized what the fuck she was seeing. I released the shifter, pushing away from her body. Unable to look at Emma, I stared at the woman I'd just killed. Nothing changed, the shifter on the ground looking just like the woman who sat a few paces away from me. I'd never thought about what might happen to a shifter who died in another form, but now I knew. I was dissatisfied, wishing to see the true face of the woman who had terrorized me for weeks.

"Go heal yourself," I said, voice cracking.

"I need to heal you so you can walk."

"Heal yourself first."

I didn't look at her as she rose, sighing, and stumbled into the corridor. I stared down at my hands while I waited. Strangling the shifter in front of her would haunt her, and I was so gods damn angry I had to do it. She'd been through enough already.

"Your turn." Cool hands reached down for me as she bent over, trying to help me stand.

"My divinity, I might not be able to—"

"Stop talking and walk," she ordered, pulling me to lean against her.

We stumbled our way out, my weight too much for her, and when I crossed the threshold, I pushed out of her grasp, attempting to get away from her when I realized what was happening. Being in that dampening cell for weeks had made my divinity spool like a gods damn spring, ready to burst. I wasn't sure my body could take it.

The pain was immense.

The ground shook, air blew out the torches, and I heard running water somewhere nearby. Groaning as I curled into myself, focusing every thought and nerve-ending toward control, I barely noticed her hands on me.

Heat enveloped my ankles, my knees, my hips, and I moaned. Gritting my teeth through the pain, it took me a moment to realize the healing warmth was helping balance my involuntary reaction to being free from the suffocating basalt. It still hurt, but I wasn't bringing the palace down around us. Diving deep into the burn, I rocked my body, letting her hands work over me.

"Rain, love, we have to go. Declan's army is just across the plains. We can't face them, not now. It's taking too long to heal you with the lava rock so close. This is the best I can do for now."

I didn't know how long I'd been lying there, but when her voice spoke, it soothed, her fingertips dancing over my face. She leaned against the stone behind her, eyes closed, while she held my head in her lap.

When I pushed to sit, my joints didn't flare with pain. My shoulder and elbow were still stiff in my good arm, and I knew my face wasn't quite right. It felt less tight, but not completely healed. Even so, I was in a much better state after she'd taken care of me.

She stood, using the wall to help her up as she swayed. She clearly hadn't listened to me and finished healing herself. When she held her hand out for me to grasp, I looked up and the angle caught me off guard. How many gods damn times had the shifter stood over me like this, pretending to be the woman I loved? I felt my heart pounding as I stared, and I knew she'd hear it. Her face was a mask of sadness as she watched me.

"She hurt you, didn't she?" she asked, voice quaking.

I didn't have the heart to answer as I took her hand and stood.

I let her lead me through the dungeons, up the stairs, and through a great hallway which crumbled from the surrounding fire. Since the floor to ceiling windows had blown out, we could see smoke billowing forth from the ruin. Gold dripped from the walls, the gilded decor melting and leaving puddles on what had once been rich carpeting. I pulled her back toward me as I spotted a beam about to fall, and I held her close. I tried not to think about it, to think about the shifter I'd just killed. The woman I strangled with my bare hands. That wasn't Emma.

Not Emma. Not Emma.

This is real. This is Em.

And she rescued me. She came for me, this hell where Declan held me, this place that would risk her. She started forward, darting to the side of the hall unaffected by the fallen beam, never dropping my hand. And I followed. My body trusted her, knew this was her. I felt a hint of that golden bond, but I couldn't bear to think about it. It couldn't be intact—I'd feel it more forcefully. And the thought that she didn't have my divinity to protect her had me seething alongside the ache of our broken connection.

Finally, we approached where the fire raged brightest. I'd thought it was her fire, but it wasn't until we got closer that I knew for certain. The white flames had blown out the windows, and I looked for bodies as we walked, but found none. I knew, no matter their alliance, any sort of death would weigh on her. This appeared to be a connecting hall, an enclosed breezeway of sorts to another wing. I didn't remember it from my arrival. It looked ornate, and I had a feeling Declan would be more upset about the destruction of the beautiful parts of his palace than anything else. I caught a glimpse outside and felt my jaw drop.

Everything was on fire.

"How?" I was in awe. She still had divinity left to heal me after she'd done all this. "Are you—you are the Beloved then? We were right?" Her steps faltered for a second before she turned to a window, probably contemplating climbing over and dropping to the ground below rather than forcing our way through the rubble.

"We were right. Hanwen and Ciarden blessed me during—all four gods have blessed me." She wouldn't look at me. I wondered what they'd done, and why she wouldn't meet my gaze. Did it have something to do with Elora? Gods, I'd failed her in so many ways.

"I'm sorry." I didn't know what else to say as I slipped past her, opting to climb through the window first so I could catch her. Sorrow emanated from her as I climbed over the frame, swinging my leg out. Her burdens had been heavy.

"Me too. Go, we need to hurry. Declan rifted to call the army before I found you."

I nodded and swung my other leg over, landing hard on my feet from the small drop. My shoulder ached, and my ribs were sore. The beating I'd received hadn't been exclusive to my face, and her healing hadn't been enough. She climbed onto the frame a second later and turned her body, slipping her legs out to hang down from her fingertips before she dropped. I was there to grab her waist if she stumbled, but she didn't need me.

That hit me harder than it should have.

We were in a small garden area, lush trees and greenery blocking our vision, but I knew what waited was fire and destruction. She pushed ahead of me, and we took off in a run. I heard a rift opening as we approached the edge of the private garden, and as we burst forth into the courtyard, I saw two things which surprised me.

The first was the stream of soldiers running through a single rift. Though we'd fought mostly mercenaries at the Cascade, the soldiers arriving through the rift were Folterrans; black shields with a jade serpent wrapping around bone made it clear. I breathed a sigh of relief when no more rifts opened, grateful Declan didn't seem to have more at the ready.

The second thing which took me by surprise was the dragon charging at us. I threw Emmeline behind me, and she shouted as I turned and drew her sword from her hip. She was yelling as I squared off against the beast, but the sound of carnage drowned out her words. What fresh hell had Declan made for us to face? It wasn't too large, perhaps the size of a small horse, but its maw was open with teeth the size of my hand, and a glint in its eyes told me it sought trouble. Emma latched onto my wrist, prying the sword from me.

"What are you—" I shouted, but the dragon launched itself, jumping from ten meters away and gliding on wings bigger than I imagined, before it slammed down on me. My arm was twisted above me, the sword fallen from my grasp. Claws dug into my shoulders, and I grunted at the weight. I closed my eyes, waiting for the teeth, and nothing could have shocked me more than when a rough, wet tongue slid its way up my chest, neck, and face.

"Divine fucking hell!" I desperately attempted to push the beast off me until Emma rapped it hard on the snout with her knuckles.

She was reprimanding a fucking dragon.

Sounding like a kicked dog, it whined as it eased off me, still hovering as it nudged my chest with its snout.

"He wants pets. But hurry, because we have to go," she said.

I widened my eyes at her, bewildered. Was he her pet? Did this dragon belong to her? I reached out, patting its muzzle, not sure how to pet a creature with teeth like that and rough scales to go along with them.

"Alright, you little shit, let him up."

She shoved at it, and it freed me.

"You have a dragon? How—you have a gods damn dragon?"

"Seven, actually. Come on." She gripped my hand and tugged, pulling us into what had once been an elaborate garden before the mayhem.

Almost stopping in my tracks, I saw what the hell she was talking about. Sure as shit, I counted six other dragons. All but one had a rider or two while the dragons used their mouths or tails to attack the soldiers coming out of the original rift. A second rift opened just as I spotted one of my best soldiers spinning and slicing her way toward us—Shade living true to her name as she moved undetected.

"Come on, you'll ride with me. Can you help push me up?" A giant dragon stepped down from its perch atop an opulent marble fountain, sizing me up in a way which made me worry if it had been fed. Enormous, the grey giant flicked slate wings as he settled, dipping his neck. When he brought his head down to my level, I couldn't help but wonder if he could eat me in one swallow or if he'd have to chew. His large eyes blinked slowly as Emma began her ascent. Green eyes. Eyes that looked like—

"Rain, help me," she said gently.

I put my hands on her hips, hoisting her up that last bit, my movements rigid. Not sure if it was from draíbea or the sheer impossibility of the situation I'd found myself in again, none of it felt real. Dewalt's voice rang out behind me, and I glanced over my shoulder to find him seated in front of a novice. I hoped it was the one who'd helped me. They were atop a dragon the color of a pearl, more slender in build, and he nodded toward me, grim assessment the only expression he wore. A hand slid around his waist and the woman peered out from behind him, a look on her face which told me she was smelling exactly what I smelled earlier in my cell. I felt the hint of a smile as I turned, climbing up behind Emma.

"Call the retreat, Rain."

"What?"

"You're back now, my love. Take your soldiers home."

Shaken, I closed my eyes as I turned my head. Placing two fingers in my mouth, I whistled out the call for a retreat. The answering cry of the soldiers she'd brought sent a surge of emotion through me, and I fought it, suppressing my reaction. I didn't have time to fall apart.

The white dragon launched into the air, and the novice screamed, clinging tightly to my friend.

Shade ran toward the smaller dragon who had tackled me and hopped on with an ever-impressive grace, and they both launched into the air next.

"Hang on tight," Emma said, pulling one of my hands around her waist.

I only hesitated a moment before my other arm joined in, wrapping myself around my wife, feeling those remaining golden tethers hum in delight, weaker than it had ever been. I inhaled deep, trying to breathe her scent, reminding myself she was real, but all she smelled of was smoke. Eyes closed, I buried my face into her hair, loose from the braid now, searching for something, anything, to help me. My nose nuzzled against that spot behind her ear, and she shivered. I caught the faintest hint of lavender and my own soap.

She was mine. She was real. She was here.

"My dear heart," I whispered into her neck, pressing my lips to her skin. Soft, warm, and mine.

She jolted a moment later when a dragon's cry wrenched through the air.

"That hurt, Rain. Why did you do that?" she asked, twisting her body to rub the back of her arm as she turned toward the dragon who had shrieked. A sharp gasp had me looking too, despite my confusion over what she'd just said, and I saw an arrow protruding halfway through the dragon's wing. It recovered, only jostling her riders before righting herself. It continued on, barely affected, and I sat back, running a hand down Emma's arm, recognition swiftly turning to fear and anger.

"You felt that, didn't you?"

"No, I..." She trailed off, uncertain.

"How do you have dragons, Em?"

"I made them."

"What do you mean, you made them?"

"They're—they're made from shadows and memory." The white beast flew a path in front of us, switching sides with the injured dragon, perhaps to better protect her. "That one is Lux, and her memory is one of my sister."

She was graceful beauty and muscle, and the way the rising sun caught on her scales made her almost glow. She was the most beautiful of the seven creatures bearing us southeast toward the Cascade.

"Ciarden's blessing," she whispered.

"You—you felt that though, the arrow?"

"I think so." She slid a hand down to cover mine around her waist.

I held my breath. That kind of power was truly amazing. Unheard of. I didn't dare ask how the god had come to bless her. I knew what caused it. Knew it because I felt it through the bond. I didn't want to make her tell me about Elora, not yet. Part of me didn't want to hear it. I closed my eyes, attempting to dismiss the vision of our daughter covered in blood. The vision of Emma hunched over, crying and telling me it was my fault.

Not Emma.

Drawn from my thoughts at the sound of Dewalt's shout, I glanced over, surprised I heard him. I couldn't understand what he was shouting about, but saw his arms waving wildly, his face angry. It only took a glance at Nor's nauseated expression and her hand clamped over her mouth to realize why. She had vomited straight down his back. I groaned in sympathy but couldn't help it as a chuckle slipped out.

"Oh no, do you think it's the flying? How are you doing? Do you feel sick?" Her concern made my chest tighten, and I closed my eyes, nuzzling closer to her. Mine. Not the shifter, not a dream. Real.

"I'm alright. Because of you." I paused, holding her close. "It was dangerous to come for me, Em."

"I made a mistake in waiting as long as I did. I thought—I didn't want to risk your soldiers after the Cascade, after everything that happened. Shivani wouldn't—I was trying to get her to get you back. But that fucking general...And she doesn't trust me. At all." She shivered, though I wasn't sure it was from the cold.

"Do you want to land? We can try to rift from here to the Cascade. That's where we're going, right?" I asked. The sun had risen, and I realized with a start I should've been dead by now if Declan had his way.

She traced a gentle fingertip over the back of my hand wrapped around her, and I didn't pull away, even though part of me still didn't believe this was real. I was getting used to her again, aching to bridge the gap between us.

"This will be faster. You've felt the bond, right? It's not whole."

"I've been avoiding it, but I can tell it's weaker. When did it..." I couldn't bring myself to finish my sentence.

"Yesterday—the day before? I don't know; it's all a blur. That's how I made the dragons. I couldn't rift to the Cascade, and I—I couldn't stop picturing you. Dead. And I tried to replace it with a good memory. Irses is made from the memory of you throwing me into the lake."

"His eyes...I thought they were like mine." I paused, pulling her close as I reached out to the bond between us to fully inspect it. One thread was torn, and another felt weak. I'd hoped the other two would have been strong enough to keep us connected, but at the same time, I'd spent the last few weeks thinking a gods damn shifter was my wife. No fucking wonder it broke. "It's my fault. All of this was my fault."

"No. Don't do that. You're here. I came for you. I fixed it. We fixed it," she said. Strong and adamant, her voice didn't waver through her clear exhaustion. I felt my own eyelids grow heavy. I couldn't remember the last time I slept, the last time I was comfortable enough to sleep deeply. And, though I wasn't remotely comfortable holding onto a dragon for my life, I grew tired as I pressed my face against her shoulder. Falling asleep was a death wish, but I could finally relax for the first time in weeks. I kept my eyes closed, my arm pinned between her waist and the dragon below us as she leaned flat against its back. I used my body to shield her from the wind, but it felt futile. I hadn't shielded her from enough.

I hadn't shielded her from the worst of it.

"Elora—" Her name hurt as I pushed it out. "I'm sorry you've had to deal with the loss all by yourself. I should never have left you." The mention of our daughter, the sweet girl I'd never know, was an admission of guilt I'd never heal from.

"The loss? No, you shouldn't have left me, Rain. But it will be alright."

"How?" How could we possibly fix the hole left?

"She'll wake up. I'm sure of it."

My heart stopped, and I must have gasped because Emma froze before she turned her head slightly, threading her fingers through my own.

"Rain, Elora isn't dead—well, she was. But I brought her back."

"She's—Elora isn't—?" Every wish and hope taken away from me these six weeks was suddenly delivered back to me, right into my waiting, grasping palms. Was this real or just another trick?

"Elora is alive, Rain."

CHAPTER 20

Elora

My eyes adjusted painfully to the sun shining in through the curtained window. I was confused by the light pouring over my face in an unfamiliar way. I rubbed my eyes, squinting, before realizing where I was. Cyran's room. I sucked in a breath, worried I'd crossed a line again. Each morning that I'd wake and find myself in his room, I would chastise myself for doing it.

Between thinking about what Papa had done to me, Mama lying to me, and remembering the way the mercenaries had taken me, it had been hard to fall asleep. Sometimes, I was angry at Mama for killing Papa, because what if he wanted to apologize to me and he never got the chance? Other times, I felt truly dreadful for not caring. It shocked me that Mama did it more than anything. I cried over the tainted memories I now held of him. A large part of me wondered if he ever was my father. After his accusations against Mama and how he said I was her daughter—not his—how could I not wonder? And Mama clearly had something to do with the Crown Prince's broken engagement. It was all quite strange. Though, when I spoke to her in Cyran's illusion, I wondered if maybe Papa was just upset and delirious. But when Ismene had suggested the Crown Prince might have been my father, I hadn't been able to get it out of my head. Could he be? It was either him or Papa, unless there were more lovers Mama took I didn't know about. I didn't want to think about that though. But in the back of my mind, I wondered about what I thought I knew.

I'd been sobbing for hours when Cyran had opened my door, telling me to quiet down. I'd thrown a book at him before rolling over and trying to muffle my tears with my pillow. When he picked me up, I was surprised, having thought he left the room. He had grasped me with ease, despite his lean frame, and carried me across the hall to his suite. Gently placing me on his bed, he had pulled the blanket around me, reaching out to wipe away a tear. I'd frozen in place until he walked over to the dresser, twisting the key to a music box before settling in on the chaise.

The whimsical tune played quietly, growing slower as the melody continued, and I finally calmed down.

Cyran had been tasked to take me for his brother, to give me to him, and he had kept me as a prisoner. He hadn't been cruel though. He'd been cold at first, but he softened to me much faster than I to him. When he eventually explained how little he cared for Declan and how tied his hands were, I almost felt sorry for him. I didn't think it excused him, but it helped me understand him. His silent and steady presence was a comfort.

The first morning I'd woken in his room, he had told me about his plan with Mama to protect me from Declan. I wasn't sure what I'd done that made him care for me; I'd been nothing but mean to him. Yet, he was taking a risk all the same. Perhaps I was being vain thinking it had anything to do with me, but he'd never stood up to his brother before.

I'd fallen asleep in his bedchamber often after that, the melody of the music box keeping my thoughts at bay. He could have offered me the trinket to take back to my own room, and I could have asked him to borrow it. But neither of us did. He probably didn't think about it, but I certainly did. Did he enjoy my company? I felt stupid for wanting to be around him, but perhaps if he felt the same way, it wasn't so bad.

Last night, we had been keeping each other company, nestled close together on the chaise. He'd been reading me a story from his mother's homeland, translating as he went. It was when he paused in his reading I had thought he was going to kiss me—and I had thought I was going to let him—but at the last second, he dropped his book and then ran out of the room. I had fallen asleep before he returned, kicking myself. I didn't know what I was upset with myself for—being angry I wanted to kiss him or being mad I didn't get to. Waking in the middle of the night, I had been glad to see him asleep in his bed, but I didn't understand why. He was my enemy.

Though, I supposed it didn't mean he couldn't be my friend too.

Cyran was a reluctant companion I'd made out of desperation and self-preservation. Why wouldn't I try to befriend my captor and make him feel bad about what he'd done? Perhaps make him treat me better? Although, to be fair, Cyran had treated me kindly the entire month I'd been with him. Hell, he had even bought me an easel and paints and encouraged me to create. And I did. I'd set it up on the balcony overlooking the pond behind his estate and painted a heron who liked to land in the shallows. I liked to watch as it would dip its long beak down to grasp whatever it could find. I had painted a sunset one day and told him of my plans to paint a sunrise the following morning. And when

I had gone outside after a sleepless night, dawn not having broken yet, he had been waiting with scones and warm tea to share while he kept me company. I'd grown accustomed to him, and that must have been the reason I slipped into that familiarity and convinced myself a kiss was something acceptable. Thank the gods he dropped his book.

It was the memory of his eyes darting to my mouth before his tongue swept over his own lips, my gaze trapped as if in a snare, that I shook out of my mind. He gave me a sleepy grin as the sunlight moved over us. I couldn't help but smile back at him. The thought of his kiss filled me with trepidation and desire, nothing like what happened when Theo kissed me on the road to Mira. I wasn't sure what to think about having had my first kiss with my best friend and less than a month later, I was contemplating my second with someone else. Normally, I'd have talked to Mama about it, but now that I knew of her secrets, I had to wonder if I wanted her input. She didn't seem to have the greatest judgment.

I loved Theo, really I did. He was my first friend, the first hand I held which didn't belong to my parents, the first person who understood me. Every memory of my childhood revolved around him. He was ever-present in my life, and I'd always imagined I'd end up married to him, living in the small home just a short distance from my parents. I imagined a future with Theo, but it was never a very exciting one. I wanted to explore Vesta—drink wine in Olistos, eat the seafood at Nara's Cove, explore the artist's quarter of Astana. But any time I mentioned it, he never seemed too keen. Based on some of our conversations, I supposed he worried I'd meet a conduit or something and leave him behind.

Theo was my best friend; being with him made sense. But when he kissed me, I didn't feel any sort of spark. Not like what I'd been made to expect from my books. When he pulled back, his face illuminated by the fire Papa had built, his deep brown eyes were hopeful and bright, and I smiled at him, trying to hide my disappointment. Everything I should have felt as I watched Theo lean in to kiss me was what I felt when I thought about kissing Cyran. And what did that say about me?

I wanted to kiss my captor. His lips looked so soft, and when he smiled, his dimples distracted me from the fact he was no good for me. Brother to a man who wanted to take me as an unwilling bride, child of a man known for his cruelty. And what his father had supposedly done to my aunt?

Another thing I was mad at Mama for not telling me.

I berated myself over thoughts of Cy's stupid, perfect mouth, even as I smiled at the prince from across the room. His mop of hair was unruly, sticking up at countless different angles, and his hazel eyes looked green in this light. Ismene's room was decorated similarly to Cy's, a deep green paisley pattern on the walls with other earth tones surrounding. But his felt different. Eclectic, the room should have been outrageous, but it worked well—rich, clay browns and mustard seed yellow met in the pillows on the chaise. Deep-red and pine-green clashed in the fabrics of the room. Even the blanket he'd pulled over me didn't match the rest of the colors—a deep blue reminding me of the sea. I was drawn out of my thoughts when I heard loud thumps in the hall, and Cy's eyes shot to his door in a panic as a man burst into the room. I realized instantly who stood in front of us.

"Well, how unusual it is to find you here. Is your bedroom not across the hall?" The sneer on his handsome face made me ill. Declan's eyes moved down my body, and I nearly gagged aloud as I tugged my shirt down where it had ridden up. He looked to be about the same age as Papa—no—Faxon. I glared at him as he continued his frank assessment of me. If anyone else had ever let their eyes have such unabashed freedom as they roamed over me, I would have smacked them. That is, if Mama didn't first. But not Declan, no. I hadn't met him yet, and I'd been hoping to avoid it. His blond hair was littered with wayward strands of silver. With eyes the same color as his brother, I didn't want to fear him, but they held no warmth. They held none of the mischief but plenty of animosity.

"Did you touch my bride, brother? I wish you would have asked first." Declan's eyes never left me, and as I glanced at Cyran, he watched his brother warily. He sat up and spoke, surprising me. For some reason, I hadn't thought he'd say anything. It felt almost like I'd lived this moment before, in a dream or something like it. But not once had Cyran ever spoken up.

"I didn't touch her, and you should leave her be. She just woke up."

"Oh no, I won't be leaving her at all today. She comes with me. Now," he said, voice leaving no room for opposition.

I started from my spot on the chaise, ready to run, but Declan was too fast. He snagged me around the waist, picking me up easily. I flailed, kicking at him, trying to knee him in the groin as I had done to his brother. It was odd—part of me imagined this going a different way. I'd seen it happening differently—seen him pick me up and crush me to his body with my back to his chest. But that wasn't what happened, somehow hoisting me up, so I saw Cy's horrified face over his shoulder.

Cyran scrambled out of bed, his long, strong limbs flexing as he threw himself to the ground at his brother's back.

"Declan, please. Let her stay here. Let them think you have her but leave her with me. Please, brother." Cy looked at me helplessly as he reached out and grasped Declan's belt, trying to haul him backwards.

I shrieked and started clawing and digging at Declan's shoulders when he sent a shadow down Cy's throat, making him collapse to the ground, holding his neck.

"Leave him alone! You're hurting him!" I slapped Declan's back, gouged my nails into his neck, as he stoically carried me out of the room. He was going to kill the best thing to have ever come out of Darkhold. His own brother, the witty and kind shining star who still gleamed despite that horrifying influence.

"YOU'RE HURTING HIM. LET HIM GO," I shouted directly in Declan's ear as he walked over the threshold. As he shut the door, I saw Cyran collapse, chest heaving. Declan had listened, letting him breathe.

"Thank you," I murmured.

Everything went black.

When I woke, my head didn't ache. I thought surely I'd been knocked out, maybe caused by a blow from the wicked prince who had taken me, but the lack of injury told me that wasn't the case. I was confused. It was as if time had jumped, and I'd missed so much. I was sitting with my hands bound by obsidian manacles in my lap, my legs tied together at the ankles. Bouncing along in a carriage, I wondered where we were headed.

"Ah, the princess awakens." I looked up from my lap when the gruff voice spoke, and an old man stared at me. He was old, much older than Old Man McLean, and looked almost just as frail. "It almost hurts to look at you."

"Well, it definitely hurts to look at your ugly face," I retorted. He laughed, and his eyes lit up. Hazel eyes. I froze when I realized who sat across from me.

The king who killed my aunt.

Who sired the evil man who wanted to claim me as his, who wanted to conquer Vesta. The king who sired at least two other children who were the exact opposite of Declan. The witty and scathing Ismene, who would have been my best friend in another life and was desperately loyal to Cy.

Cyran.

I couldn't think about him. He wasn't here, and after what Declan did to him, I worried he was really hurt. I only hoped he'd be alright and tell Mama what happened.

I lifted my chin, meeting the gaze of the man across from me. I wracked my mind, trying to remember facts about Folterra Mama had taught me, and I struggled. She spoke little of Folterran royalty, and now I knew why. I couldn't remember for sure, but I thought King Dryul was born before the Great War. That would have made him over five or six hundred years old. He had the same eyes as his children, and I wondered if all of his children had them. Did he look into them as he killed the ones who dared speak up against him? Cyran had told me that between his father and older brother, they'd killed every other sibling he had, most before he was even born. He and Ismene were the only two left, and he worried they'd both meet the same fate as the others.

"What a cruel twist of fate—that hair. You look so much like your aunt, and it was unfair she looked so much like—" He started coughing, unable to finish what he was rambling about. When he recovered, he asked, "Did you sleep well? You're going to have a busy day."

I ignored him, looking out the window of the carriage. I couldn't see anything but open plain, and I had no idea where we were. We must have been in Folterra still. Perhaps closing in on the Cascade.

"Are you missing a tongue, girl?" The king rapped a cane over my knees, and I cried out in surprise before I glowered at him.

"Eat shit, you moldy, old...turnip." I was annoyed turnips were the first thing that came to mind.

"That's no way for a princess to speak, though I appreciate the creativity. I've lived many years, and never have I been called a vegetable." He gave a wheezy chuckle as his beady eyes tracked over me. "My sister had a mouth on her like that. Didn't do her any good. Your grandfather killed her anyway."

"Lord Kennon?"

He ignored me.

"I think your aunt cursed me, you know, which I might have deserved. But I was avenging my sister and protecting Declan," he muttered to himself. Cyran had said he was losing his mind, but I hadn't expected this.

"Lucia wasn't even born when your sister died, was she?" I argued. Cy had told me little, but King Soren had been married to a Folterran princess at one point. I remembered that, at least.

"No, and that's the rub, isn't it? Born as the Beloved, a threat to Declan, and paid for the king's mistakes in blood. The gods are vicious, are they not?"

I was pondering over what he'd said when I blinked, and suddenly I was seated on a lush pillow inside a tent. What happened? Soft, amethyst fabric rubbed against my legs beneath me, and I was cold in only a thin cotton dress. The dress was white, paired with sensible brown slippers, and I was confused because I hadn't been wearing it before. King Dryul paced around the tent, using his cane to support him.

"Those useless twits. Don't they have any respect? I want to be the one who kills the Beloved," he wheezed. I watched him stumble over a divot in the grass below us. We were clearly in a meadow of sorts, the light smattering of wildflowers a dead giveaway. I moved to stand, but he'd attached my wrists to my ankles. I couldn't walk if I tried. The king's cane got caught, and he stumbled, falling to a knee.

"I don't think you'll be killing anyone, except maybe yourself." The king's eyes snapped to mine, and shadows plumed around him, filling the tent; I couldn't see. He shoved something into my mouth, and dust went down my throat, the makeshift gag unclean. I wasn't sure where it came from, and I tried not to lose the contents of my stomach. I tugged at my wrists, reaching for the fabric.

I heard a strange sound before King Dryul spoke.

"I wondered if my useless sons would send my message."

"I'm here, what do you want?" I gasped when I realized it was Mama, and I shouted through the gag in my mouth.

"It seemed like an interesting bookend. I killed your sister who we thought was the Beloved, so it only makes sense for me to kill you too."

I couldn't see a thing in the dark before the explosion. A bright, white heat knocked me backwards, and I looked up to see blue sky above me, the tent on fire. King Dryul laughed, and I scrambled up. Seeing Mama facing off against the man who now sat in a chair, laughing maniacally, gave me untold hope alongside depthless fear. What if she died trying to save me?

Feeling a soft touch on my shoulder, I nearly jumped out of my body. Before I could even turn my head, a man was face down on the ground next to me, his body twitching. King Dryul looked past me and spoke, drawing my attention to the presence behind me.

"My, you devious thing. This is the only time I haven't doubted you're mine." And he laughed, but Cyran dove forward from behind me and began struggling with the rope holding my legs together.

His eyes met mine, and I wished I had kissed him that night.

Cy felt something for me, or else he wouldn't be here. The way he'd looked at me when his brother took me—I knew it then. And, if we made it through this, if he saved me, kissing him would be the first thing I did.

Mama attacked Dryul again as Cyran finished unbinding my feet. When he took the gag out of my mouth, his thumb traced over my lip, holding my face in his hands for just a moment. It looked as if he was memorizing me, his eyes roaming slowly.

"Cyran, help me; we don't have time for this." My eyes caught with Mama's over his shoulder, and I called out to her when I saw the shadow figure standing behind her.

"Mama, watch out!"

The shadow figure didn't do much damage as Mama's fingertips burst with light when she gripped its arms. The ground started shaking right before Dryul launched his body onto her. Cyran hadn't moved from the spot in which we sat, fingertips tracing my jaw and tucking my hair behind my ear.

"Cyran, come on! We have to help her! I need my divinity!"

"It's going to be alright, Elora. I'm fixing this. I'm going to wake you up. I promise."

I looked back at Mama and the king tussling on the ground and screamed, tears running down my face.

"Shh, Elora. It's alright. Everyone is alright. We are all going to be just fine." He stood up behind me and pulled me to my feet. "I'm sorry." His voice was loud, commanding, and it drew Mama's attention. I was so confused; why was he sorry?

"It's alright, go! Get her out!"

Mama pushed at the king, but he was too strong. Cyran nudged me forward, his palms resting on my upper arms.

When Cyran reached past me, he used his shadows to somehow overpower King Dryul. It made no sense. I'd been practicing my light with him, and he could barely hold me at bay. He wasn't strong enough to do that. No one had ever taught him how to use them at that level of strength, afraid he'd overthrow his brother or father, and he hadn't come to maturity yet. At least, that's what he had told me. Mama sat up, using her light to cocoon around the king as she stood.

Cyran held my head back against his chest as he bent down to speak into my ear.

"We have more time, *min viltasma*."

I turned my head toward him, surprised, and all I could see was his smile. I loved when he called me that. His little, wild thing. I couldn't remember when he'd told me what it meant, but I felt a blush creeping up my cheeks and a buzzing in my chest as he spun me in his arms. Cool fingers grasped my jaw and he tilted my chin up, his eyes landing on my mouth. When I sighed, half in contentment and half in impatience, his hazel gaze moved back up to mine, asking for permission. When I closed my eyes and parted my lips, I felt him move closer, dipping down to meet me. Pushing up on my tiptoes, the touch of his soft mouth met mine, and I whimpered. His hand slid to the back of my neck as he kissed me tenderly, and I melted into his arms. His lips were warm as they moved, and it was everything I'd ever dreamed of in a kiss. Everything I could have wanted.

The characters from my books all spoke of kisses in a way which seemed unattainable to me. Especially after what had happened with Theo. But this kiss, it made me understand. The spark I felt with him was unlike anything I'd ever experienced, and I thought the air in my lungs must have been replaced with a swarm of buzzing bees. When he broke from the kiss and pressed his forehead to mine, I could feel his breath on my lips.

"Wake up, Elora."

CHAPTER 21

Emmeline

My heart hurt in knowing that during our entire time apart, Rain had thought Elora was dead. When I corrected that notion, he'd collapsed against me, freely sobbing into my back. Tears of relief and fear mingled as he held tight to my body. For a while, he'd thought I was dead too. He wouldn't talk about the torture he'd gone through, what Declan had done to him, but I could tell it was brutal. I had seen the table in the corner of his cell; the straps on its surface and the injuries on his body told me its purpose. Seeing him kill the shifter made something so intense stir within me, I wasn't sure I'd be able to concentrate on anything until he told me exactly what happened. But he had barely spoken since I told him about Elora.

Had the shifter assaulted him? Touched him? He'd flinched away from me a few times. Was being pressed against me on top of Irses too much for him? The idea I could cause him any sort of pain, mental or otherwise, broke my heart. I fought every instinct within me to ask him what happened. He'd come to me when he was ready. Rain had waited for me. Steadfast and true, he waited for my mind to catch up with my heart. I would give him the time he had afforded to me, the patience and enduring love he had proven in his actions and words. But it killed me to think I might unknowingly make things worse for him.

The worst part of this was, with our bond incomplete, I couldn't feel his emotions. Was it a blessing to not feel what he felt? To not burden him with my worry? I could feel the bond's presence once he was out of that cell, and as we flew toward the Cascade, the thrumming had become more insistent. I knew from what he'd told me in the past, the bond demanded the connection. Those remaining golden threads hummed in my periphery, desperate. Did the bond care that he might not want to be touched that way? I'd do everything I could to resist it until he was ready. I missed him desperately, every part of him, and I needed us to get back to what we were before. Craved it. But if my suspicions were correct—if the shifter had hurt him...

Gods help me, Declan would pay. He was not long for this world either way, but I would make his death horrific for what he'd done to Rain.

"What's wrong with her?" He cleared his throat as he spoke, disuse making it sound rough.

"She—she's asleep. She won't wake."

"You said you brought her back. What does that mean, Em?"

"I watched her die," I whispered, head turned so he could hear. "Her throat was slit. But something happened, and I brought her back. My divinity."

"Who?"

I hesitated a moment. "It's complicated, Rain."

"How is it complicated?"

"I'm afraid to tell you because of what you might do," I answered.

"What the hell does that mean? What happened to our daughter?" A demand.

"Do you trust me?"

"Of course, I trust you. But—"

"I'm going to ask you to do one thing for me, for her, and that is to promise not to hurt the person who did it. Can you promise me that?"

"Why in the gods' names would you want me to promise that? Whoever hurt her will bleed out slow; I promise you that, Em."

"Even if he were a child in an impossible position, shown a vision of what would happen if he didn't?"

He didn't speak for a moment, but his arm wrapped tighter around me.

"The prince? The boy slit her throat?"

"Elora had to die for Ciarden to bless me," I choked out. "The boy did it because he was shown a vision of what would happen if the Beloved didn't—if I didn't—" I gulped down a breath, struggling to get the words out. And just as I was about to break, when my heart felt like caving in, he laid his head against me and tightened his hold. "Elora died because of me. But—"

"No, don't fucking say that. She's not dead. She will wake." Through my cloak, I felt his lips on my spine. "She has to wake. We have so many things to tell her," he said, and he took a shuddering breath. "*I* have so many things to tell her."

When we finally neared the Cascade, I could see ships on the horizon. Lavenia and Raj had been successful. I felt nothing but immense relief, knowing if Declan took action now, we'd be protected. Rain suspected he would take his time, but still—I was glad to know the Cascade would be fortified if he was wrong.

We landed in the field of wildflowers near the remains of the thorned cavern I'd created. Falling apart with the onslaught of winter, it looked almost skeletal. We hadn't dismounted from Irses, even though the rest of the soldiers had all slid off their beasts. I supposed we could have gotten closer to the fortress, but I didn't want to frighten anyone with the dragons. Glancing over my shoulder at him, I saw him staring at the thorns.

"I saw it," he whispered. "Your shadows and thorns and light. I couldn't get to you in time."

"You've been with me all along." I lifted his hand and pressed it to my heart, letting him feel the steady pound in my chest. His own beat was sure, and he took a deep breath.

"I don't think straight when it comes to you. I lose my fucking mind, and I—I should have stayed with you that day."

Any resentment and frustration I had for him fell away with his words. I hadn't planned to say anything to him immediately, if ever. But now, hearing the regret in his voice, and after knowing what he'd been through, I'd have to take some time to organize my thoughts before we discussed it.

I stayed quiet, and he slid off Irses. I was suddenly exhausted. Steeling myself for the effort it would take to dismount, I froze when I felt his touch on my leg. It wasn't very bright, the winter sun behind a cloud, but his small smile was a balm to my weary soul. He couldn't reach my waist, Irses being as tall as he was, but it was clear Rain wanted to help me down. I twisted, allowing myself to slide from the dragon's muscular body, and Rain guided me to the ground. He let his hands hover over my waist before taking a measured step back. Though incomplete, the bond between us flared to life, golden vibrations and heat taking over. His hands fell to his sides as Dewalt approached, shucking off his shirt.

"What do you want to do with the dragons?" He seemed annoyed. I was about to answer when a breeze struck, causing him to shiver and my nostrils to face the assault of his scent.

"Gods, you need to bathe. You go; I'll deal with them." I turned back to Irses, finding the giant watching me with calm eyes. Rain stood nearby, hands shoved into his pockets and his head down. My chest tightened at the sight. He hadn't returned as a triumphant king, but a broken and bruised man. I tried not to stare at him, not wanting to unsettle him with the sorrow I couldn't hide. He walked over to the woman who had ridden with Dewalt and spoke in a low murmur. Dewalt ignored my command, waiting patiently as I spoke to Irses.

"Listen, I'm not sure you know what I'm saying to you. But this field seems like it might be a good spot for you to sleep?" The dragon shook his wings out before tucking them back in, hunkering down to the smallest size he could. The cold breeze pushed past once more, and goosebumps raced across my skin.

"Do you think it might be too cold for them?" Dewalt asked, voice quiet.

Hyše and Traekka were already curled around one another, but the others seemed restless. I'd have to pull the arrow from Traekka's wing, but I was nervous. What if it hurt me? I was afraid to find just how connected we were.

"You think they might prefer somewhere more sheltered?" My friend continued.

Irses snorted, his breath coming out hot as he looked at Dewalt. I smiled. It seemed as if the beast agreed. I looked around, my eyes catching on the cliff face to the east, overlooking the sea.

"I'm sure there are caves over there." I pointed. "If you can't find one, I can try to make you one? Or I suppose Rain can, since I can't use..." I trailed off, talking more to myself than the dragon before me.

Irses let out a low rumble and bent down, nuzzling against the top of my head. He was gentle, but it felt a bit like being sat upon. Irses let out a small growl, and I turned to find Rain approaching.

"Shush, you," I said, pushing the dragon's head away from me.

"Careful, Your Majesty. The beast's loyalty isn't with you." Dewalt laughed, smiling at Rain. When Rain didn't return the smile, I rushed to explain.

"He's just not used to you yet. He bit Dewalt almost immediately," I offered.

"He's protective. It's a good thing." Rain wrapped his arms around himself, rubbing his biceps, and I realized how cold he had to be.

"Here, take my cloak."

The look I received in return burned a hole through me.

"Absolutely not. I'm sure I can find something here. I probably need to go talk to Ven." Hands in his pockets again, he wouldn't make eye contact with me, and I didn't know why. I couldn't know what was going through his head, but, gods, I just wanted to throw myself upon him. Hold him, weep with him.

"I'll go with you," I blurted.

"No," he replied almost just as fast. His eyes darted to my shoulder before lifting to where I knew Irses hovered, his breath hot. "I'll go change, talk to Ven, and meet you after?"

I swallowed and nodded a moment before Rain opened a rift, stepping through without a word. I turned back to Irses, fighting tears so Dewalt wouldn't see, and rested my hand on the creature's snout.

"Please don't kill any people. Or animals that belong to people. I'll figure out a way to feed you all. Can you keep an eye on them?" Irses let out an exhale of breath as he turned, his wings spread wide, before launching toward the cliffs. All but the injured dragon followed without hesitation. Thyra was fussing over Traekka, and the beast wouldn't let her get close.

"He'll be alright, Emma." Dewalt hadn't left my side, but thankfully he'd kept a decent distance from me, sparing me his stink.

Only Thyra and the novice who'd been sick lingered, and Dewalt followed me as I walked toward Traekka with purpose.

"I know," I said, voice more curt than intended.

"I know you know. I also know it's going to drive you mad until he's back to normal. All I can say is give him space when he needs it."

My touch was soft as the injured dragon let me approach, Thyra and the novice backing away. I let my fingertips graze the muscular wing, and she huffed a pained breath. Ignoring the pinch in my own arm, I pulled gently, stretching the membrane so I could get to the shaft of the arrow.

"You're alright, darling," I cooed.

Thyra had her hand on the dragon's snout, whispering something in her language.

"I don't need you telling me how to handle him," I said, continuing my conversation with Dewalt. "If I hold her like this, can you pull out the arrow?"

My friend nodded, dropping to his knees to get below the wing. When he broke the tip off, my arm flared with pain.

Shit.

"I suppose you have a point. I only had to deal with Rainier for over a decade when he was in a bad mental place. What do I know?" Dewalt said, standing once more to pull the arrow out.

I dropped her wing as pain and relief seared through my arm, and the dragon was in the air a moment later, following the others. I fell on my ass, unable to catch myself. Dewalt's hair was unbound, whipped loose during the flight back, and he stood over me, shirtless, with his hands on his hips.

"Don't you need to go bathe and find some clothes?" I sniped.

Thyra laughed, deep and hearty. "Then how would he show off for pretty woman?" She asked, quiet enough only I heard her.

"What was that, Thyra? Do you need a hug?" Dewalt walked toward her, arms outstretched and his noxious scent filling the air. Thyra backed up, stumbling, disgust clear on her features as Dewalt moved with a purpose. They were tussling a moment later as I pulled myself from the ground.

"Your Majesty?" A quiet voice sounded behind me, and I turned. It was the woman who rode with Dewalt. In the sun's light, I saw the black eye she sported, and I wondered what happened to her. Led by instinct, I took a step forward and lifted my hand. She stumbled back before I realized what I was doing.

"I'm sorry. Can I heal you?"

"You—you want to heal *me*? I'll be fine, it's just a black eye."

"I know you will, but why suffer longer than you have to if I can fix it?" She watched me with a wary gaze, and I saw her eyes dart over to Dewalt. He sighed loudly as he effortlessly held Thyra in a headlock.

"Let her heal you, Nor. She's not going to hurt you." Thyra shoved a thumb into his eye and he yelped, cursing. "Why don't you do something for her stomach while you're at it?"

"It was your stench that made me sick!" Nor yelled at him, and I couldn't help my smile. When she turned back to look at me, her face was flushed. "Is he always so intolerable?"

I snorted as I stepped toward her, lightly tracing my fingertips across her brow. "To be fair, I think anyone would be a bit grumpy with vomit down their back. But he did smell rather putrid; that isn't your fault."

It earned me a smile. She was very pretty, with bright brown eyes, a ring of gold in their center, and there was a sparse smattering of freckles across her light-brown cheeks which told me she'd wear quite a lot of them in the summer. Her dark hair fell in waves over wiry shoulders. She was taller than me, thin, and her clothes hung off her, torn and covered in soot as they were. I wondered why she ended up with us, and I wanted to get to know her since Dewalt thought bringing her to the Cascade with us was a good idea. He could have sent her off with the other novices but had chosen not to.

"Dewalt called you Nor? I'm Emmeline, though you probably know that already." She nodded slightly, trying not to move.

"Yes, I go by Nor."

"Are you from Folterra?" She didn't have the accent.

"No, I'm from Vesta, from the capital." That explained why we brought her with us. I took a quick breath when I realized what it meant.

"Did you live at the temple? Is that where we need to take you?"

"I did, but—no. I won't be going back there. Well, I suppose I do need to go there, but not to stay. My mother..." She trailed off, and I nodded. I studied her face, trying to place her age—I supposed she was in her mid-twenties.

"Will the Myriad not miss you?" Carefully, I listened to her heart; I was uncertain of her loyalties, and I wanted to be sure. Pulling my hand away, my eyes traced over the rest of her for other injuries. Her sleeve was torn, and I saw an old burn on her skin, which she covered with her hand when she noticed my eyes linger there.

"The Myriad will not even know I am missing. They're the ones who sent us there. Master—" She took a deep breath and eyed me warily. "Me and the other novices were all sent to Folterra for Declan to use, degrade, and kill as he saw fit. Between him and the fire, only a third of us survived."

My stomach dropped out. At what Declan had done, but also at what Nor had said.

The fire.

Perhaps she meant a different fire. She couldn't have meant—no. My mouth went dry, and I clenched my fists.

"The fire?" I squeaked out, and Nor looked at me as realization dawned in her features. She swallowed before she squared her shoulders, clearly about to deliver news I wasn't sure I could handle.

"Your Majesty, I know it wasn't your intention, but—"

"It was my fire. My dragons." I couldn't breathe.

She gave the slightest nod.

"Did you do it on purpose?" she asked, and I saw a hint of fear in her eyes.

"Of course not."

I was going to be sick. Turning away from the woman in front of me, I covered my mouth with the back of my hand. Thyra and Dewalt had finally finished tussling, and Thyra was kneeling on the ground, gathering her weapons and bag. Dewalt buttoned a new shirt as he approached, his pack over his shoulder. His stride quickened when he saw me.

"What happened?" Dewalt was gruff in his questioning of the woman, and I would have reprimanded him for it if I trusted myself to speak.

"How many, Nor?" My lungs were tight as I faced her. She looked between Dewalt and me, shame in her features. "Don't. Don't you feel like that. Just tell me."

"Gods damn it. I said I'd tell her myself." Dewalt walked toward me, cutting Nor off, a hand stretched out toward my own.

"It was an accident! I didn't mean to say anything." The anguish in the girl's voice was clear.

"Don't yell at her, D. You knew? Why didn't you tell me the minute you had the chance?"

"I was going to say something! You had creatures and people to heal, and I knew you wouldn't relax until you were done. I thought I had a moment. Fuck, Nor! I asked you not to tell her!"

Anger and guilt flashed across the young woman's face as she spun on a heel, marching toward the fortress.

"I told you not to yell at her. How many?" How many innocent people had died at my hands? The soldiers were one thing, but other victims of Declan's malice? Gods, I was no better than he was.

"Six died from the fire. They were in a building he was keeping them captive in. That's why I left Rainier. He ordered me to go help them."

I started; I hadn't even realized Dewalt had been there and left him. I was so out of my mind when I landed with Lux, I ran inside, not even caring about what had become of Dewalt and Shade. When I'd found Rain alone in his cell, I hadn't even wondered where the two of them were. Hadn't even considered anything other than the other half of my soul. I was angry. Part of me was angry Dewalt had left Rain, but most of my anger was directed at myself.

Mistaking the anger I clearly wore on my face, Dewalt turned his hands up in supplication. "Rainier said he'd deal with you. Please, Emma. You can—Reprimand me if you must, but I was just doing what he asked of me."

I slid to the ground. I hadn't worried about my friend, the man who had helped keep me going these past weeks, and I killed six innocent people. What had I become?

Dewalt sat down facing me. This was wrong. I didn't want his comfort.

"They were on the top floor. I don't think they suffered. You didn't know. How could you have known?"

"What happened to the rest of them? You brought Nor, but how many others were there?"

"About twenty. The ones who left with the rebels were going to Evenmoor."

I nodded, swallowing. "Send word that any who want to come to Astana will be welcome. Were they all novices? All her age?"

"Yes, and some children. I think—I think the children might be Declan's."

"Shit."

"Yeah."

We maintained our silence as Dewalt pulled me from the ground and guided me back toward the fortress. This was my first action in this war, my first real action as a queen, and I killed six innocent people. As Dewalt steered me toward the room Elora and I had stayed in, he murmured something about fetching Rain. I wasn't listening. Thyra left my pack just inside the door, and I kicked my shoes off before sitting down on the bed. I stripped my clothes, the smell of smoke on them a painful reminder.

I began to cry.

The destruction I had wrought was too much. I'd refused to send Cyran to his brother. Refused to trade an innocent young man's death for Rain's life. And yet I'd done exactly that—six-fold. How many of the Folterran soldiers had been innocent? Forced into the life of a warrior by their corrupt monarch? I climbed into the bed, the simple furniture of the fort creaking as I moved. The plain, white linen reminded me of home, of Brambleton. The grey blanket scratched my skin as I pulled it over my naked body. I dwelled in the discomfort. The narrow window let a small streak of mid-day sun into the plain room, illuminating the threadbare tan sofa which set this room apart from the others. I laid there for a moment, blinking up at the ceiling.

I buried my head into the pillow and screamed.

CHAPTER 22

DEWALT

THE MOMENT I DROPPED Emma off in her chambers, I leaned against the wall outside her room. I debated what I needed to do first—all things ranked high on the list. I needed to bathe and get myself out of these clothes. A shiver of delight raced through me at the thought of the bathhouse. It didn't compare to the running water back home, but the steamy mineral baths had always soothed me. I also needed to find Rainier, tell him what happened, and send him to comfort Emma. Though, based on some of the faces I saw him making, I wasn't sure if he'd be of much use. The man was fucking broken, and it pissed me off we didn't kill Declan for it. But Emma was right to have him call the retreat.

When Lux and I first took off, she did a long sweep northward, and I saw the legion. We were barely a match with our entire army—let alone the small group we had, even if we did have dragons. I was surprised by the sheer number Declan had, and I wondered where they all came from. Folterra had never held a candle to our numbers before. I was half-tempted to steer Lux over the soldiers, have her rain down divine hell upon them, but I didn't want to separate from the others. Besides, I didn't know what kind of conduits made up Declan's army, and I didn't want to risk Lux. I didn't know what could take down a dragon, and I didn't want to find out. But now, the Folterrans knew we had the beasts and would prepare accordingly. We needed to be ready too.

The last thing I needed to do, or perhaps wanted to do, was yell at the novice who opened her stupid mouth. I had specifically asked her not to say anything to Emma. She seemed good at opening her mouth when no one asked, and I had the evidence to prove it. When I'd been changing, I picked chunks out of my gods damned hair from what she'd done down my back, and I nearly retched myself. I didn't care if I smelled like Ciarden's ass or she was dizzy from the flying or any other gods damned reason she could've given me; she could have leaned over.

And then she didn't let me delicately break the news to Emma about what happened. I was going to talk to her and Rainier at the same time, so we'd both be there to talk her through it. This shit happened, and as much of a stain on the soul as it was, there was nothing to be done for it but to beg forgiveness and promise to do better. And Rainier and I had been through it enough. We'd have been able to fucking get her through it too. But the novice had blindsided me, and I wondered if she'd done it on purpose.

Everyone within the Myriad could go fuck themselves, as far as I was concerned.

Rainier had to strong-arm me into escorting Emma to her meeting with Filenti, and they'd made her fucking kill someone. And then the very next time I take pity on one of their people? Fucked again.

I was done with it.

I was in a bad mood from being covered in literal shit and vomit and seeing what had happened to my best friend. I hadn't had time to kill enough of them either. Shade killed the guard in the dungeon, and then I went straight to the burning building full of novices, only taking out the one Folterran along the way. I was itching for a fight, and I knew she'd be likely to give it to me.

That was why I chose to bathe first—to douse some of the frustration coursing through my veins. It wouldn't get us anywhere, and it would probably piss Emma off. I'd get accused of intimidating the woman, but something told me Nor wasn't someone easily intimidated. Still, I opted to calm myself instead. Swinging by the room I usually stayed in when we visited the Cascade, I picked up the things I'd need.

The bathhouse was on the eastern wall of the fortress, not very large, and built on a raised platform which allowed hot air from the furnaces to circulate below. It was something Raj and Rainier had added in an attempt to work with the Folterrans in Clearhill, learning about their more complex systems from an older mason originally from Darkhold. There was a large room for men and a smaller one for the women directly beside it, and I strolled into the antechamber and shucked off my pants and boots.

Once inside, I made my way to the pool in the very back, shrouded in shadow and steam, and sank into its warmth. After washing my body and hair several times over, scrubbing my skin until it ached, I finally leaned back, arms spread and head tilted. It hadn't been long when I heard someone come in, quiet footsteps padding across the floor. Keeping my eyes closed, I listened to make sure they didn't come to my pool. There were only a few rules of the bathhouse, and that was an unspoken one. Don't fuck with someone's bath if you can get clean elsewhere. Thankfully, I heard the quiet splash of water across the tall chamber and relaxed.

Until she started singing.

I knew Raj had brought some villagers over from Clearhill, but divine hell, had he really not taught them how to use the gods damned bathhouse? It wasn't as if she had anything to worry about. Not a single man in this fortress would fuck with a woman for fear of death—either by one of their captain's hands or the woman they harassed. Despite that, it annoyed me.

I couldn't make anything out other than her silhouette thanks to the steam and low light in the room. I didn't want to stare, but that *voice*...

I hoped it was the Folterran woman I'd seen hanging sheets in the courtyard. She had been beautiful with a pleasing face, large breasts I'd love to get my mouth on, and sunflower hair. She had smiled at me and blushed prettily, and I'd made a note of it. Maybe she'd help me work out my frustration later. The only thing better than fighting in a battle—which I didn't even get to do—was the ensuing fuck after.

Ven was here, and even though I had yet to talk to her about the bond, I didn't plan on fulfilling any kind of need through her—bond or otherwise. And until I talked to her about it, I wouldn't find release elsewhere either. Our arrangement didn't call for anything other than respect, and I planned to give it to her.

So, instead of approaching the pool, I let my thoughts run rampant. Was it wrong to imagine perfect tits bounce beneath me as golden hair pooled around the pretty face I'd seen? Probably. But it wasn't as if I acted on it. It wasn't as if I *ever* acted on it. The only person I'd had sex with in the last decade was Ven, and most times the bond was the reason for it. Sure, sometimes we'd bring others into it, as we had with the merrow, but that was for Lavenia. Not for me. As much as I tried to convince myself about the Folterran woman, I knew I wouldn't have sought her out even if I'd already spoken to Ven. For the first time, I wondered if my dick would even work without the bond goading it. I couldn't remember the last time I'd been hard without those golden strings being the cause. I'd been able to manage before I bonded with Ven, but I didn't want to go back to that. I didn't like to remember what I was like back then.

I closed my eyes and listened; the voice, high and clear, lulled me into a serene comfort. It was a captivating song about a mother bird coming home to find her nest empty, her baby bird having flown free and never returned. What truly surprised me was that she didn't sing in the common tongue. I recognized it by the melody, a song my older sister had sung to me when I was little. Like my sister Saski, the woman sang in the tongue of the elders, the language predating the gods. Though I didn't speak it, I could pick out a few words I knew. I was surprised to hear the inclusion of the cheeky verse at the end; most people left it out. The mother bird cursing at the father bird for his excitement over a bigger nest was meant for a certain type of crowd. I waited for the curse, the only word meant to be sung in the common tongue, but it never came.

Unable to help myself, I hummed along to the melody, and the fight I'd felt earlier was gone from me; I only felt relaxed. I'd nearly dozed off when the singing stopped. Waiting for her to continue, I kept my eyes closed until I heard the splash of water which told me whoever owned that voice was getting out of the pool.

I should have stayed put, letting her leave in peace, not embarrassing her with the knowledge she went to the wrong part of the bathhouse. Or alerting her to the fact a man was here all along. But I was curious about the woman behind the voice; would she sound as pretty crying out my name?

Fuck, it hadn't been *that* long. The fact I was hard over a voice answered my earlier question.

I thought about Shit River and getting puked on in order to control myself. But I was in a hurry, and it did nothing to help me solve the problem below my waist. Clouds had blocked the windows, and the steam didn't help my vision. Her silhouette wasn't enough, though I could tell she was relatively tall with a lean body, and I wanted to know who the fuck she was. When she reached for her towel, I did the same, but was distracted when she rose from the water. It was when she wrapped her towel around her body, the light shifting in the room and the steam clearing just enough, that I recognized her.

Nor.

Two things happened very quickly. The first thing that occurred was the realization I hadn't even brought my towel over, so I had no choice but to stay put, my cock out of control beneath the water after seeing the shape of her body and hearing her voice. Traitorous, my dick. The second thing was something heavy getting thrown directly at my face with a scream.

"What in the most vile of hells are you doing in here while I'm *bathing*?" The bird's voice was significantly less fucking pleasant when she wasn't singing. This woman who had done nothing but piss me off since the moment I met her had just thrown something at my face. And it didn't feel good.

"What in the most vile of hells were you doing coming into the men's bathhouse while *I'm* bathing?" I shouted back at her while I rubbed my forehead. "I was in here first, you brat."

"This isn't—the tall woman, Teeruh or something, she told me…Men are allowed in here?"

I closed my eyes and breathed through my nose, counting to ten.

"You're telling me you just threw—" I stood, waist deep in the pool, turning to the edge and finding the object in question rolling away from me. Not giving a shit, I gave her a view of my ass as I leaned forward and grasped it. "Why the hell do you have an apple in the baths? You threw an apple at me because you thought men weren't allowed in the *men's* bath?"

She had the decency to blush, and I leaned back, letting my eyes wander now that she wasn't covered in soot and her own vomit. Dark hair not quite as long as mine hung down past small breasts. Dark, thick lashes framed wide eyes, and a hint of pleasant freckles across her face opposed her down-turned mouth. It made her look younger than she was, as if she were a petulant child. In my periphery, I saw the red swirl of skin on her shoulder and noted it extended almost to her elbow. I didn't let my eyes linger.

Letting myself smirk up at her, I brought the apple to my mouth and bit down, licking my lips as I raised a brow.

"Not only were you wrong, you thought I would get something out of this? A contrary novice in a towel? Trust me, if I wanted to see a naked woman in the baths, she would have been willing, and I would have done more than look at her."

She scowled, but her face quickly shifted to a look of horror. "Oh skies, did you hear me singing?"

I laughed, taking another bite of her apple. *My* apple.

"I sure did. You mispronounced a few of the words, bird, but overall, a decent rendition."

Her voice was too good to truly insult, but I was enjoying having the upper hand on her. Her scowl returned in force.

"I did not." She took a step forward, and I noticed her eyes dip down my chest. The water was up to my hips, but it seemed quite bold for a supposed novice to let her gaze linger. Another reason not to fucking trust her. I decided I was done with the conversation as she continued. "I had an apple because I was hungry, and I planned on eating it in my room after my bath, but didn't want to stop and drop it off. I figured it could come with me, but to my delight, it helped me against a would-be assailant instead."

"Do you think an apple to my skull could stop me? Here," I snapped, tossing the core at her feet. She jumped back when it hit her.

She shook her head, anger crinkling up her nose as her brows met in the middle. "What was that for? What did I do to you?"

I raised a brow before turning to hop out of the pool. Even though I'd left my towel in the antechamber, I didn't care what she saw of me. Though she was taller than Ven, I towered over the novice at my full height. She averted her eyes, and I was fucking glad she felt uncomfortable.

"You got sick down my back instead of trying to, I don't know, aim literally anywhere else, and then you told Emmeline something I asked you not to."

"I said I was sor—" I cut her off as I pushed my way past her.

"But maybe I misremembered it. I am the stupidest man you've ever met, after all."

"Give him a minute," Lavenia said, pushing past me to shut the door behind her, preventing my entrance into Raj's study where Rainier waited. "He needed a moment alone. He's not…He's not right. Did he let Emma heal him?"

"She started to. I don't know if she finished. Why?"

"Something he said…" She trailed off. "I don't know what the hell Declan did to him, and he won't tell me."

"He will when he's ready."

"Do you think he might have used a mindbreaker?"

"I don't know, Ven." I rubbed my face, exasperated. I didn't know what she wanted from me. "We won't know until he talks, and he'll probably tell Emma before he tells us."

"I'm just worried." She sighed, leaning against the wall. "Are you coming back to Astana tonight? Nixy offered to rift us. Rainier said he wants to rest before they come back. He doesn't want to deal with our mother just yet."

"I figured I'd stay with them until they were ready to leave. You don't want to stay? What about your army?" I grinned. She laughed, but her smile didn't reach her eyes. She looked beautiful as always, brown skin glowing in the late-afternoon light from the window, but I could tell she was weary.

"I'm tired. Shivani didn't stand in my way, not really. She sort of allowed it to happen." She shrugged. "But you know me. I'm not suited for this. Rainier wants to protect the Cascade for now, in case of retaliation, but he doesn't need me for that. I just want to go crawl into my bed. Mairin's probably there, waiting." She groaned and tilted her head back before looking up at me under heavy lashes. I knew that look.

"What?"

"I know what you like after a battle. I know the bond doesn't need it, but…"

Gods damn it.

I supposed it was time to talk to her. I'd spoke to Mairin on our way to the Cascade and knew my decision was right.

"About that—" I cleared my throat. "Do you have feelings for the merrow?" Her posture shifted, and she pushed away from the wall. "I don't know. Why?"

"Because I'm not doing this again."

"Doing what again? What are you talking about?" She scowled, and I sighed. Rubbing my hand over my face, not eager to have this conversation, I straightened and found my resolve.

"Your relationships suffer because you feel bad for me. I'm not going to watch another woman fall in love with you and get her heart broken. I'm not going to watch you break your own heart to protect me."

"That's not what—"

"It's not up for discussion. I want to break the bond."

"You want to break the bond for *you*, or you want to break the bond for *me*?" she countered.

"It won't take much. Ever since you've met Mairin, it's been weak. Feel it." To illustrate my point, I plucked on one of the golden threads, knowing she would barely feel it. "It got like this with Brenna, but then you fucked that up. Not going to watch it happen again, sorry. If I were compatible with Mairin, then maybe I wouldn't feel like this. We could bring her into the bond with us—if the Myriad would even allow it..." I softened, voice trailing off as I saw hurt cross her features. "Ven, you've been there for me a hell of a lot longer than I deserve. I want you to get what you need and want out of life and not worry about me while you do it."

She crossed her arms, looking up at me with tears in her eyes. "You're not a burden, D. Don't talk that way."

"I'm not here to debate. Do you not see the way she looks at you?" She averted her eyes, cheeks darkening. "She looks at you the way I should," I said. "I'll admit it's not for lack of trying. But it's never been like that between us. Right?" I asked, already knowing the answer. Sure, we appreciated one another's bodies and companionship, but unyielding love? Never.

"Right," she murmured.

"Chin up, kid," I offered, and I couldn't help my grin as her chin jerked out and her eyes went cold.

"Oh, no you fucking don't. You don't get to start—"

"You don't have sex to hold over me anymore. I can call you whatever I want now." I laughed, darting away from her before she landed the punch.

The door opened, and Rainier stood there, eyes tired and posture sagging.

"Where's Em?" he rasped. He sounded as exhausted as he looked.

"In your room." He nodded, about to step past me, and I sobered. "We need to talk."

Walking past them into Raj's study, I gestured for them to join me. Lavenia followed, lowering herself into one of the wingback chairs as I leaned against the desk in front of her. I was pleased with how our conversation had gone. The fact she didn't push back harder told me my decision was the right one. It was strange; I'd been bonded to her for a decade, and it almost felt freeing to end things. Emma had been optimistic about my ability to perform the bond with someone else, but I knew that wasn't in my future. Lavenia could have it though. Lavenia could have what Rainier and Emma found again.

"Two things," I said. Holding up a finger, I continued. "Number one, me and Ven are breaking the bond." Rainier, who leaned against the closed door with folded arms, only blinked at me. "Thought you should know, since our divinity will be affected."

His brows rose before he asked, "Why?"

"Dewalt thinks he's holding me back," Lavenia supplied before I had a chance. She sounded pissed.

"Well, is he?" Rainier questioned, calm.

"It doesn't matter," I said. "I've decided. I assume you'll help us with the dissolution?"

Lavenia bolted up from her seat. "Why would we do that?"

"Why wouldn't you?" Rainier interjected. "You only married because of the bond."

"Exactly."

"What about your title?" she asked. Something twisted in me, seeing her panic-stricken face. I didn't know why she was taking this poorly. There wouldn't be a drastic difference. She rarely weaved visions. It wasn't that often I used her divinity either. I could understand concern over no longer having access to the font, but she could do that with Mairin—if the Myriad could be convinced.

Rainier snorted, answering for me. "Ven, you know he doesn't give a damn about that. What's going on? I thought this had always been the plan. One day, you'd find someone else, break it, and that would be it."

"But neither of us have found someone else. He thinks Mairin is—that she feels—"

"I don't *think*. I know. She has feelings for you as you do for her. Get your shit together."

"Dewalt," Rainier growled in warning.

Turning toward her, it shocked me to see tears in her eyes. This wasn't what I fucking wanted. She ought to be happy. She didn't have to worry about me anymore, and she could have whatever life she wanted with whoever she wanted.

"Ven..."

"I don't want things to change. I—Everything has changed. I'm trying to keep up, that's all." She sniffled, and I didn't know what to do. Glancing at Rainier, I saw he looked equally bewildered.

"It's fine. I'm fine. I'm just going to go. Nixy is supposed to take me back to Astana, so I'm going to go find him."

She was through the door before I could stop her—shiny, black curls bouncing above her shoulders as she left.

Heaving a sigh, I collapsed into the chair she'd been sitting in, my legs over the side and head leaned back.

"Well, that went well," Rainier said, settling into Raj's chair on the other side of the desk.

"Hanwen's fucking ass," I mumbled, and he chuckled. "Not what you thought you'd be dealing with when you came back, I suppose."

"No."

His response had me looking over at him as he studied the grains of the desk. "But you're back. Right?" I asked.

He flipped his hands palm up as he spoke, staring down at them. "More or less."

"I've missed you, brother."

He glanced up at me with a soft smile. "You said there were two things. Surely, the mess with my sister didn't require me as a witness."

"No. You're going to like this even less."

CHAPTER 23

EMMELINE

It was still light out when Rain slipped into the bed, his weight shifting me. I felt the hum of our bond again, and it was vibrating, insistent. He smelled clean, and I wished it didn't hurt that he bathed without me. Rolling onto my side so I wasn't facing him, I began to cry once more, silently, not wanting to bother him with anything. He had to be exhausted. I wasn't even sure what I was crying over. I was overjoyed being able to feel the bond again, no matter that it was incomplete. The missing thread made it so I couldn't feel his emotions or his well of divinity, but I could feel *him*. And he was here beside me.

I could smell smoke, the scent sticking to my hair, burrowing itself in my nostrils, attaching to my soul. Reminding me of what I had done and what I could never forget. I opened my mouth a bit, allowing my breath to escape silently. Rain had enough going on with his own healing. He didn't need to have my own to contend with.

But I was weak.

Every part of me wanted to confide in him, seek comfort in his strength, dig a hole in his chest and hide inside it. The memory of what he'd said when I called him the Bloody Prince came to me, unexpected.

I'm not exactly proud of the blood on my hands.

I'd been mortified, embarrassed I'd said something without thinking and came across as callous in my use of the moniker. But now, I felt a cool understanding I wished I didn't. Had Rain ever killed an innocent? My breath caught, and I readjusted my body. How was I supposed to live with this?

"Would you like to know their names?" Rain's voice was a low rumble behind me which took me by surprise. I swallowed before rolling over to look at him. The sun was setting, and the light in the room had gone dim, but I could still see him clearly. "The novices who died. Do you want to know their names?"

He wore his sympathy clearly on his face. The wrinkles at his eyes were more apparent than they were before he was taken prisoner, probably from malnutrition, and the crease between his eyebrows was accentuated by the frown he wore. He was fully clothed, lying on top of the blankets, and I wondered if that was on purpose. Did he not trust himself since I was naked? My divinity was persistent in the bond's need to grab my attention, and I focused on Rain's mouth. His full lips were down-turned, and I wondered how he knew I was awake and thinking of what I'd done.

"Dewalt told you?" He dipped his chin, and I heaved a breath. "Yes, I want to know their names. Anything you can tell me."

"All I know comes from Nor. I'm sure she'd be willing to tell you more information if you asked her." He watched me, his brows tipping down in concentration. "All the women were around Nor's age or older. Two were from Vesta. One named Sarai came from the temple in the capital and another named Nina from Olistos. They arrived with Nor. She knew Sarai a bit, since they'd lived in the temple together, but they never spoke. She had already taken the vow of silence, but Nor said she spent most of her free time in the library." I closed my eyes, not bothering to fight it as the tears slipped down my cheek. "One woman was from Nythyr, and they called her Henny because she looked after the children like a mother hen. Nor found her huddled over an infant, protecting her from the beam that had fallen on top of them." Rain lifted his hand to my cheek, thumb wiping away one of my tears. "Do you want me to stop? I can tell you the rest later. I—it always helped me to know their names. To humanize my mistakes. It can become easy to willfully forget."

Between my tears and the bond, all I wanted was to be held. But Rain didn't move to pull me into his arms, and I wouldn't ask it of him. Not after what I'd seen with the shifter and the fear I'd seen in his eyes. I'd let him come to me first.

"Tell me. I need to know."

He swallowed, his jaw tense, as if he didn't want to continue. "The other three were from Folterra. Nor didn't know them well. Corinn, Parah, and Louisa. Corinn had just given birth. It was her child Henny died to protect."

I closed my eyes and gave in. Rain pushed my hair behind my ear, traced the skin of my neck and hovered his fingertips over my collarbone as I rode the wave of grief coursing through my body. He said nothing, and I was thankful for it. Nothing he could say would help. We both knew it was an accident. We both knew I'd done it to save him. I wondered if he asked for the names for himself just as much as he did for me.

"Do you want to know the names of the women you saved?"

I inhaled sharply, opening my eyes to stare at him. "Does that matter when I killed the others?"

"Yes. It matters to them, Em." His hand cupped my face. "Every choice, every mistake, every movement has a consequence we can't always foresee. The important part is doing what we can to sway the balance back. Nor lives because of you. Grace and Elsie live because of you. Ysrith and Lisette live because of you." I sobbed as Rain continued. He named each woman and child we'd freed from Darkhold. Every single name, he told me. "You didn't mean to save them. You didn't mean to kill the others. But because of your choices, the balance swung towards goodness, and that's all we can do, dear heart." His hand slid down to my shoulder, and I wiped the tears from my face as I looked at him, his face earnest. "Thank you for saving us."

Squeezing my eyes shut, I blew out a trembling breath. When his lips pressed to my forehead, I swore I almost felt a spark. Heat tore through me, and that gods forsaken bond flared to life. The gesture was intimate, so close to his normal treatment of me, and I wanted to sink into it. But I couldn't trust myself. Even now, I felt an ache between my legs, and I cursed the bond once more. The feeling juxtaposed with my sorrow was more than I could bear.

I was about to tilt my head and meet his lips with mine when his stomach growled, and he looked at me sheepishly, the seriousness of the moment interrupted.

"I had some soup earlier, and now my stomach wants to remind me I haven't truly eaten in weeks. Would you like me to bring back something for you?"

I shook my head. I felt relief at the distance he put between us, while I felt utterly hopeless about the fact we needed it. Letting him bridge the gap between us was going to be a painful game of waiting. I was too heartsick and exhausted to eat, a point I proved the moment he left, crying myself back to sleep as soon as the door shut behind him.

It was dark in the room when I woke, and I couldn't breathe. There was a pressure on my chest and around my throat, and I couldn't understand what was happening.

"Rain!" My voice was a croak, harsh, because I could barely get any air with his hands wrapped around my neck. He was on top of me, naked, with his golden-brown skin on display and his lower half nestled between my thighs. But it wasn't romantic. His touch wasn't tender. He was squeezing tightly, his eyes glazed over.

"Not real. Not real. Not real," he muttered to himself, looking down at my face with an expression of horror. The moonlight from the window shone on him, and I could tell he wasn't truly awake. I slapped at his arms and his back with one hand, using the other to pry his from my neck. Despite my fear, my divinity relaxed before soaring into a frenzied buzzing. Almost sentient, the bond seemed happy it was about to be satiated, then annoyed when it didn't happen.

My husband was choking me, and this stupid, insolent bond was pleased.

"Rain, stop! Me—" I gasped, trying to get a small breath and wheezing as I did. "It's me." He was squeezing so hard I knew I'd have bruises. He thought I was the shifter, and he was going to kill me like he did her. My vision blackened at the edges, and I dragged my fingernails down his back as hard as I could while bucking beneath him. I didn't succeed at much. The blanket slipped off me as I wrapped my legs around his waist, and I tried to pull him off of me at the hips. I hoped the touch of our skin, naked flesh against naked flesh, and the call of our bond would help wake him. His body was warm as it pressed against mine. The weight of him was calming, even with his leaner form, his presence satisfying and everything I wanted. But the pressure around my neck hurt and sent me into a panic.

I closed my eyes and could feel the glow from those threads. He had to feel that. With the way he pressed down upon me, I couldn't tell, but if the bond was doing to him what it was doing to me, I was sure I'd feel the evidence any moment. Perhaps it would be enough.

"Not my Emma. Not real." His voice was louder now, and he squeezed harder.

Despite my vision suffering and the fear of imminent death, my divinity didn't repel his violent and dangerous touch—it reveled in it. The bond clearly didn't care. The bond wanted me to be with him, to renew it, to fix the golden string connecting our bodies. And I wanted it too. But I wanted to continue breathing more. I considered using my divinity on him, burning him to make him let me go, but I knew that wouldn't help us. Knew that to hurt him physically would cause irreparable damage. I couldn't hurt him. I couldn't do what the shifter did to him. Never. As a very last effort from the precipice of death, I might have felt differently. But for now, I was taking small breaths, fighting against him with my arms, allowing myself to get the air I needed.

Feeling the insistent bond gave me an idea though, and not a second too soon. My limbs weren't working as well, my body starved for air, and I was on the edge of passing out. Letting my eyes close, I reached out to those golden threads and plucked.

Rain froze.

He didn't let go of me, but he stopped squeezing so hard. Taking deep, gasping breaths while I could, I stared up at him. His chest heaved for air too, a sheen of sweat covering his naked body.

"Not real. You aren't real. Not my Emma." He stared down at me, still holding my throat, but his hand relaxed. I took another quick breath as I watched his half-asleep mind struggle.

"I'm real, and I'm yours. It's me, Rain." Not knowing what else to do, fear still simmering under my skin, I plucked a thread and pushed my hips up toward him, and I felt him harden against me. His cock slid over my soaked flesh. He wasn't immune to the pull of the bond, and clarity filtered into those pine-green eyes I'd sorely missed. I plucked the threads once more, and his touch on my neck turned gentle. He caressed me, staring at me with confusion as those golden threads vibrated. It was a loud buzzing in my mind, and all I could think about were his hands on my throat and him inside me. An image of him bending me over on the balcony crossed my mind, and I felt him stiffen even further. I wondered if he was imagining the same things.

"It's you? My Em?" Rain tilted his head and spoke low. His anger and confusion turned into raw need. The bond rumbled in anticipation.

"Yours. Always," I agreed. I had wanted to let him come to me, to ask for my touch, to crave it, but I couldn't resist it. Resist him. The call of our bond was one I couldn't ignore any longer. The pain in my stomach—lower—made me ache. I was sick with need. Unrelenting and thorough, it overwhelmed me. I loved it and hated it at the same time. I didn't want this now, and yet I couldn't fight it. I tried. Gods damn, did I try. But the bond wouldn't let me. I needed him to fill me, to lay claim to me once more. He groaned, dropping his head next to mine, his breath in my ear.

"Em, are you sure?" I didn't know what he was asking. Was I sure I was real, that I was his? Was I sure I wanted him? Both answers were yes. He lifted his head to look at me, eyes boring into my very soul—awake.

"Yes," I whispered. He sighed, keeping his hand on my throat even as he lowered his body to mine, the heavy weight of him pressing us together so there was no space between us. I wasn't sure if he thought he was protecting himself or not, with his fingertips on my pulse, but I didn't blame him. "Are *you* sure? Are you awake?"

"I'm here. It's you, Em. Really. I'm so fucking sorry." I shushed him, humming in pleasure as his length pressed harder against my tender, delicate heat. Sliding against my slick skin, I was already wet and ready. I blamed the bond, but it didn't matter. I wanted him more than I knew what to do with myself. "Please?" he asked, and I nodded, pulling him closer and notching him at my entrance. The thick tip of his cock pushed into me, and we both moaned, the pressure and stretch a pleasant pain. He froze just inside me and allowed me to adjust, patient and careful even now. He'd released some of the tension in his hand on my throat but still had me in his grip, and I reached up with my own, covering his, interlacing our fingers over my neck.

He pushed deeper, his hips flexing. They were bonier and almost hurt as he pressed against me, and my heart broke once more. He pulled back before slamming into me, hard, and I cried out his name. He felt huge inside me, filling up every empty part of me. Making up for the lack of him and doing it with a violent precision which should have frightened me. But I'd never been scared of him, even at his worst. He was my safety and my wild. He was my home. He was *mine*.

I was so prepared for him, greedy, and I wrapped my legs around him once more. I had closed my eyes when he first entered me, but I opened them to find his gaze elsewhere. He leaned down, his lips an inch from my collarbone. His hand finally left my throat, and he slid both arms beneath me, coming up my back and hooking his hands over my shoulders, using the position to pound into me harder and faster. Every thrust was punctuated with a whisper.

"Damia."

He kissed my collarbone, licked it, worshiped it, as he crashed against me. The slapping sound nearly undid me, hearing him take me so viciously, making me wetter by the second. I slipped my arms around his body, my fingertips tracing over his skin, and I held my breath, frozen, when I felt new scars scattered over his back. He tensed as I moved my fingertips over them, pushing some of my healing divinity into him as he pushed himself deep into me. He nipped my collarbone before he pulled back a bit to look at my face.

"You saved me." A punctuating thrust. "Gods damn, Em." Another. "You've never stopped saving me."

I reached up with one hand to cup his face while the other still worked over his back. "We saved each other, Rain."

He pulled himself to his knees and picked me up, arms circling behind my back, before he slammed me down onto his thick cock. I felt everything. The short pull out of me before the slam of my body over his, the blood rushing, his heart beating. My heart. I threw an arm around his neck and held on as I tilted my head back and unwrapped my legs from his body, planting my feet on either side of him. I was overwhelmed. He leaned his head down, pulling my nipple into his mouth, nibbling and sucking as he continued to hold me. Tugging with his teeth and healing with his tongue, the slight pain caused everything to throb. Pulling back, Rain licked his bottom lip as he looked over me, reverent.

"The Damia constellation on your collarbone. The shifter didn't have it. But you do." He kissed me there, laving the freckles which set me apart. How we were positioned took the moonlight off him and spread over me instead. He froze, staring at my neck, and I realized I must have bruised already. "Fuck, Em. I didn't—I could have—"

He didn't move, holding me, but I writhed on him, distracting him, looking down to see where he rested inside me. I had taken him completely, and I was comfortable in the fullness. I slid my hand down to my clit, rubbing that sensitive spot there as I moved. He sat still, eyes darting from my face to my neck to where our bodies met.

"You didn't. I could have stopped you before I did if I needed to," I said.

He dropped me, and I slammed onto the bed.

"You should have!" he roared, loud and hoarse. Vicious.

"Rain, if I used my divinity, it would have hurt you. And I refuse to do that."

"So, you let me hurt you instead? What the fuck, Em?"

He was still on his knees, and his cock bobbed between my breasts as I sat up on my elbows. Moving toward him, I pulled him into my mouth, sucking my desire from him. He tilted his head back with a heavy sigh. I slid him deeper into my mouth, letting him push to the back of my throat, before I moved back, sucking tight and at an angle. When I pulled away, a loud popping sound rang out.

"I can protect myself against you, Rain." I turned around and crawled, bending over so I was ready for him. Feeling the vibration of the golden strings, I rubbed my thighs together and reached down, lightly playing with my clit as I looked back at him. And I waited. The insistent buzzing and pulling of those golden threads continued at a milder rate, momentarily satiated, but I knew what it wanted. I knew Rain felt it too, even as he watched me, his erection persistent as he looked me over, throat working as he swallowed.

He moved, sitting on the edge of the bed, facing away from me as he rubbed his fingers through his hair. It had grown a fair amount, and it reminded me of when we were young. I wondered if he'd cut it or keep it. The soft, tight curls begged for my fingers to run through them, but I pushed the thought aside, more concerned about why he'd turned away from me. I sat up, moving to sit beside him. We both sat there, exposed in more than one way, and I leaned against his arm.

"We kissed, but that was it. I saw you—her—naked but never touched her. I didn't want to do what she tempted me with. I only ever wanted to hold you. But now that I can do both of those things with you, and want to, I'm terrified of doing them."

"We don't have—"

"No, that's not what I want. I want to make love to you. I want to renew the bond. I want to hold you. But I don't want to be afraid while doing them. I nearly strangled you to death, Em!"

"But you didn't." I reached out to him, taking his hand in mine and squeezing it. "One day at a time, that's all we can do, Rain."

His face softened as he looked at me, the moonlight highlighting his strong, upturned nose. The light hit his eyes, more grey than green in the dark, and untold emotion lay within them. He pulled me into his lap, situating me on top of him on the edge of the bed. "This way, please," he requested, vulnerable.

"Wait," I said before I reached for my pack, dragging out the dagger I'd stolen from Shivani days ago. I could have sworn it pulsed, the light in the room dimming with it, before I cut my hand. Rain held out his own, palm up, without a word, and I repeated the cut. Taking his hand in mine, letting our blood mingle, I pulled it to my mouth, kissing his knuckles.

"You won't hurt me. I promise I won't let you," I offered, hoping to reassure him.

"I'd rather die than have you hurt. Perhaps I'm a coward, but I've hurt you more than I ever meant to, and I can't let myself do it again. I'm not strong enough."

"You won't hurt me. It's going to be alright," I said as I lifted my body, freeing him from between us, and lowered myself on top of him. His eyes closed, and his mouth parted, a sigh of pleasure escaping as he did. I moved gently, different from how he'd just taken me with rough, precise thrusts. Rocking my body over him as he held me tight, arms wrapped around me, I let the friction and heat between us build. He kissed the top of my shoulder while his hands roamed over me. They cupped my backside, helping pull me back and forth on top of him as I let him fill me so deeply, I didn't think the bond could ever break again. The thrumming heightened as my motions grew more frenzied, my pace increasing as I leaned toward him, about to kiss him. But he dipped his head at the last moment, pressing his mouth to the tops of my breasts.

I did my best to not take offense to the slight, but a tear slipped past my lashes all the same. I vowed to myself to give him all the time he needed to come back to me. I wouldn't let him see my pain when he had so much of his own. His mouth traced kisses across my chest, and I felt the golden light glowing brightly—just on the edge of my vision. It warmed me, warmed us, and I knew we'd make it through this somehow. The tingle in my spine grew, spreading down to where he sat within me, and I felt myself tighten around him. He grunted while he dug his fingers into my hips, leaving marks I'd keep to find in the morning, to make me smile in the memory of our connection.

"The tonic. Oh, gods," I breathed, not stopping, close enough to the crash I wasn't sure I was in control of my movements anymore. His hands stayed on me, guiding me in his lap, choosing not to hear me, or perhaps *needing* not to, and I decided I didn't care.

"Please," he whispered, continuing to move my body, and if this was how he needed to claim me, to come back to me, I'd give it. The risk, the fear, the knowledge we would be able to make it through anything as long as we had each other—it pushed me onward, and I threw caution to the wind. Wanting to take everything he could give me, I flexed my hips, setting a punishing pace. He closed his eyes and tipped his head back, mouth dropping open on a groan. "Yes, Em. Gods, I needed you," he spoke on a shuddered exhale. My own body shook as I pushed us over the edge, heat ripping up my spine.

I felt his heat pulse within me as I dragged it out with each squeeze of my muscles around him. He wrapped his arms around me so tightly, I wasn't sure I'd be able to take a deep breath if I tried. And then I began to cry.

I couldn't stop, the tears crashing down my face as he held me, and I saw a hint of wetness reflected in his own. No words could explain what either of us felt, so we just sat there, holding one another. I traced my hands over his shoulders to the sides of his neck and face. I wanted so badly to kiss him. But I didn't want to face the rejection of him turning away from me again, so I resisted. I reveled in the feeling of our renewed bond, the well of his divinity just on the other side of the threads, and I could feel his emotions again, though less clearly than I remembered. He was content, hopeful, and I was sure my own emotions mirrored it. After long moments wrapped in his arms, I finally let out a long exhale.

"I won't let you hurt me," I whispered. "We're strong enough to get through this. You're strong enough."

And just like that, something happened within him, and my heart stopped. I felt rage flow through him and, a second later, fear. His face shuttered, and his expression grew hard. His relaxed mouth shut tight into a thin line, and he inhaled a quick, panicked breath. He moved me off him before he stood, striding over to the sofa where his clothes laid, swiftly pulling them on without a word.

"Rain?"

He stepped into his pants, the over-sized ones he'd been wearing as we left Darkhold, and pulled them up quickly. I grew anxious and jumped to my feet.

"What's wrong? Where are you going?"

"I can't sleep here." His voice was deep and gruff as he buttoned his shirt, pointedly avoiding my gaze. "I tried, really, I did. When I came back earlier, I saw you sleeping so fucking sweetly, and I know you're hurting. I wanted to be good, to be normal. Climbed into that bed and thought I could, but I—I don't trust myself, Em. I'm sorry."

"I trust you, Rain. I trust me. Stay, please." I grabbed his arm to stop him, and he tugged it free, finishing the buttons on his shirt.

"I'll just be down the hall, alright? Let me know if you need anything?" He stepped over to the door, his hand on the knob as he looked back at me with a silent plea in his eyes I didn't understand. I still felt an undercurrent of fear coming from him, but now there was a sad resignation taking over.

"I need you, Rain. That's all I need. Nothing else." I was begging, and I didn't care.

"I know."

He shut the door behind him as he left.

I sat in an alcove near the dining hall, coaxing my shadows to cover and shelter me. It was nearly dawn by the time I fell asleep, so I was late for breakfast when I finally woke. While grabbing a honey roll from the kitchens, Raj's daughter Marella had tended to me with all her attention, and now I wanted to make myself disappear as I nibbled at the bread, my stomach sick. I felt Rain, knew he was outside, and his anxiety and grief meshed so thoroughly with my own, I didn't know where his feelings ended and mine began.

But I gave him space.

That was how I found myself in the awkward position of watching a conversation between two people who very clearly disliked one another. Only a few steps away, they had no idea I was nearby. Before I could inform them, they'd already started talking, and I didn't want them to think I was eavesdropping, though that's what I began to do all the same.

"Listen, I'm sorry we got off on the wrong foot. I saw your arm." Dewalt's eyes lingered on Nor's shoulder where I'd seen old scars when I'd healed her. "And the whole building was on fire, and I just—"

"It's fine." She looked away, finding something supremely interesting to look at on the stone wall behind him. She heaved a breath. "I didn't mean to tell her."

I stilled, not breathing, when I realized they spoke of me.

"I'm Dewalt, by the way. I don't remember if I gave you my name before you puked on me." He grinned at her, but she didn't return the smile.

"You know what? That was embarrassing for me too. Did you think I wanted to puke on you? Did you think I wanted to get my only clothing dirty?"

"Well, there were pretty endless options of other places to vomit."

She let out a snarl and pushed past him, heading outside. "I'm sorry, it's not often I ride on dragons. And you didn't even have the decency to put me in front. I was trying not to fall off the entire time. You're an ass." She whispered the last word, looking to see if anyone had overheard her. Little did she know I sat just behind her, cloaked in darkness.

"Hey, alright, sorry! I should have—"

She marched outside, and I coaxed the shadows back, letting the darkness swirl over my skin until they dissipated.

"That seemed to have gone well," I offered. Dewalt eyed me in annoyance before it shifted to a softer look which made me feel pitiful.

"Did Rainier not take you to the bathhouse?"

I looked away, attempting to keep my face from showing how his words had wounded me, and caught a whiff of smoke from my hair as it whipped past my face. "He didn't, no. Come on." I stood, heading outside, shivering as the cool breeze hit me. "I need to check on the dragons."

"Did he not come talk to you?"

"No, he did. And then he—he wouldn't stay with me. He thought—" I looked around the courtyard, not wanting anyone to overhear. I needed a friend to confide in, and Dewalt was here. "When I found him in the dungeon, he was killing a shapeshifter who looked like me. Last night, he woke up and tried to strangle me. He wouldn't stay; I think he was afraid of hurting me."

Dewalt closed his eyes, taking a deep breath. He scanned me, and I knew he was looking for any sign of injury. I'd healed them already, even the marks on my hips I'd wanted to savor.

"Divine hell. Just give him time, Emma. He'll be alright. He just needs time."

"I know. But in the meantime, I'm alone again. I don't know if—this is all too much. I can't do this. I killed those women, and I let my daughter die. She might never wake up, D. And now my husband won't talk to me, won't be around me...I'm all alone."

I was crying again and making a gods damn fool of myself. I'd barely cried in the preceding weeks, barely existed, but the moments leading up to our trip to Darkhold and all the ones after seemed to have broken me. I inhaled, trying to pull myself together. Lifting my hands to my face, I wiped my eyes as Dewalt encircled me in his arms, his clean scent enveloping me. He stroked my back, similar to what he'd done when I had accidentally broken the conch shell from Rain.

"You're not alone. You're stuck with me now." He held me at arm's length before patting the top of my head. He was so much taller than me, I probably looked like a child.

"Thank you, but it's not the same," I replied, wiping my nose.

"No. It's not. But I suppose you'll have to settle for less at the moment." He grinned as he put a hand on my shoulder, turning me back toward the fortress. "Go. The bathhouse is on the eastern wall. I'll talk to Rainier. I'll take care of the dragons. Everything is going to be alright."

I had a sick feeling in my stomach as I walked back toward the fortress, and it took a few moments to understand why.

It wasn't me.

Turning around, I scanned the courtyard, looking for him. When I finally found Rain, standing high above the gate on the parapet, his eyes shot daggers at Dewalt. My breath hitched, feeling nausea with a hint of jealousy simmering across our connection. Our friend spotted him too and waved. When Rain didn't return the gesture, I watched Dewalt's steps falter before he strode toward the staircase with a purpose.

Disbelief filled me. He had to know what my friendship with Dewalt was. Rain had to know *he* was what I wanted more than anything. Jealousy had no place between us. I'd promptly dismissed it before with Thyra and even developed a friendship with the woman, for gods' sakes. And even then, I'd had a reason for jealousy. Disbelief gave way to frustration as I stared up at Rain, burning a hole into the side of his face. When he finally looked down at me, I slowly shook my head, jaw clenched.

"No," I mouthed. "Never."

Dewalt came into view from the corner stairwell just as Rain turned away from me, opening a rift and stepping through. I groaned in frustration as I opened my own rift and chose to climb right back into bed.

CHAPTER 24

Cyran

When I woke from the illusion, I rubbed my face in disbelief. Deep blue eyes blinked at me, and she wore a small smile, her lips a perfect, full curve. I swallowed, uncertain of what to say to her. Surely, she wouldn't want to be around me, even though I'd kissed her. Bloody hell, I kissed her in the illusion. But gods, I wanted to do it again. I smiled too, my mouth paying no heed to the fear and trepidation raging within me. She was awake. I had been trying to wake her for weeks, and I finally succeeded.

On my way to Folterra, I'd thought of nothing but her. Hell, even before that, when they took me from the dungeons, she was where my thoughts had gone. I had been fearful. If I wasn't able to visit her in her dreams, would she ever wake? The desperate need I'd felt to fix her and stay with her far outweighed the fear I felt of being delivered to my brother.

I'd visited her in my dreams on the road, and I was selfish in those illusions. I had thought once I arrived in Darkhold I'd be unable to reach her, or worse—dead. So, we'd read together. I'd figured out how to manipulate her dreams more thoroughly than I once had, and could bar Declan from taking her that morning. In that selfish dream, we'd lounged in my quarters for hours, reading and stealing glances at one another.

She had even moved to sit beside me, her soft curls caressing my arm, and I'd wanted to kiss her then. I didn't know why. She'd been the first person to see through me and still wanted to be my friend—despite it. And I'd never denied she was beautiful. Perfect.

And when Emmeline found me, I knew that I'd need to go back. To finish what I had started. I didn't deserve those stolen moments—but I took them all the same. I knew once she woke, Elora would never look at me again, let alone kiss me. But the Elora of my illusions? Of her dreams?

She would kiss me.

I would steal as many kisses from her in our dreams as I could. I would steal whatever moments she would give me, because once she woke and realized what a monster I truly was? She'd hate me forever.

But I'd gotten only the one kiss.

Fate was cruel. I'd have done anything to wake her, even if it meant she'd remember and hate me, but I couldn't have had a few more tender moments with her?

I felt emotion welling up in my throat, and I tamped it down. I didn't want her to see any of it, not when she only just woke. I was sure she had questions for me, and I was afraid of her reaction.

She reached out, fingertips fluttering over my jaw, and I stopped breathing. Was it possible she forgave me? She stared at me with such intensity, I felt naked and raw. Thoughts warred behind her eyes, and I waited.

"I'm *starving*." She coughed after she spoke, her throat dry. "Do you think Cook will bring us something?" I smiled as I thought of the surly man who worked in the kitchens at Evenmoor, and then my stomach dropped out at the thought of him. I hoped Declan took nothing out on the staff. I pushed the thought aside. It wouldn't help me.

"Well, I'm sure I can find you something. But we aren't in Evenmoor."

I held my breath, worried about how this conversation would go. If she didn't know where she was, did she not remember what happened? She sat up on an elbow and looked around the room. I couldn't help but smile as her eyes lit up in delight at the twin bookshelves sitting on either side of the massive fireplace. Though these were her mother's chambers, I knew her room held just as many books, if not more. I'd spent some time exploring the estate once the merrow had brought me from the Cascade.

Elora's eyes moved to the windows, bright winter sun streaming in, and pushed herself up to get a better look at the garden just on the other side. It rivaled in size my favorite garden at Evenmoor. The estate in Folterra where I lived had beautiful grounds, far more exquisite than Darkhold. I thought it was likely the gardeners in Evenmoor had the creative and artistic freedom to hone the grounds into a thing of unrivaled beauty, while my father, and now Declan, ordered the servants by fear.

Elora sat up fully, the massive bed unperturbed by her shifting weight. I supposed I shouldn't have been in the bed with her, but Mairin didn't seem like she would have stopped me. I took a quick breath, eyes widening a fraction, as I realized I ought to go fetch the merrow. But I was stuck, taking Elora in. I couldn't have moved if I tried.

She shook her head as she glanced around, eyes to the ceiling as she noticed the dark beams. The estate was rather modest, as far as royal residences went, but it was beautiful in its simplicity. Declan would have hated it, and the thought gave me some happiness. Her hair was frizzy where she had laid, but it would have been so much worse if Emmeline hadn't kept up with it. I'd watched once, paying attention as she saturated the more tangled area with water and an oil which had a nutty smell to it, using a wide-tooth comb to ease the tension. Her touch had been delicate, reverent, and I had been struck by how much this woman loved her daughter. Had my mother once looked at me like that?

Stopping in the night before, Lavenia had come to check on her, easing Elora as she traded out a freshly laundered silk pillowcase for the one she had been laying on. She explained how the silk would help keep her hair from matting. Though Elora didn't know the woman yet, and Lavenia hadn't been able to truly meet her, it was easy to see the fondness in her expression as she watched Elora sleep. I'd been distinctly jealous and felt rather small about it.

No wonder Elora was the way she was. It made me hurt, wondering how Ismene and I might have turned out had anyone who cared about us still lived. We only had each other. I felt stupid for hoping that maybe one day, Elora could think to shine some of the love she'd absorbed and dwelt in upon me. She looked over her shoulder, the delicate strap of her nightgown slipping down, her golden shoulder in stark contrast to the pale pink nightgown and her white hair.

"Where are we?" she whispered, and I sat up. I crossed my legs as I faced her, taking her hand in mine.

"We are in Astana. This is your mother's suite." I didn't want to tell her yet that not only was Rainier her father, but he was now the king. I figured one thing at a time was best, and starting with her mother's marriage might be easier. Considering that was the smallest of the things to explain to her, I wondered if perhaps I should make us both a drink. I'd seen the sideboard in the living room, properly stocked. It would have given me confidence I was sorely lacking now. Her brows lowered as she looked past me.

"Where is she?" She pulled her lower lip into her mouth, worrying it. Her voice sounded off still, lower. Had I inflicted more lasting damage than just the scar?

"That's a long story." She opened her mouth to argue with me, and I waved her off. "Which I *will* tell you. I just have to get there first. Do try to be patient, darling?" I gave her my most charming smile, knowing it irked her, and was rewarded with her familiar glare.

"Apologies, *Your Highness*." She crossed her arms over her chest, and I averted my eyes, suddenly aware of how improper this was. I felt my skin flush, the back of my neck hot as I stood, walking into the bathing suite, looking for a robe of some sort for her. "Where are you going?" she demanded.

"Hold tight, *min viltasma*." I sucked in a breath, not meaning to call her that so soon. I didn't want to remind her of the illusion and my words to her. Not yet, at least. When I brought out a robe, white silk with blue and purple flowers across it, she seemed nervous. I handed the garment to her and gave her my back as she pulled it on. When I turned, she was looking down and frowning.

"This smells like Mama."

"Well, since this is her suite, I imagine it's her robe." I sighed, ready to delve into the long, convoluted story.

"Did she marry him then? Is this the Crown Prince's estate?" Those beautiful blue eyes met mine, and I sat back down on the edge of the bed beside her. Perhaps this would be easier than I thought. I nodded.

"Yes, they wed. This is their estate in the capital. I've been told which room belongs to you, and I'd be glad to show it to you later. The bookshelves are bigger in there." I gave her a smile, which she met.

"I'd like that." She heaved a sigh, brow furrowing. "So, my mother is a princess, then."

I weighed the options of correcting her, wanting to choose the thing which would upset her the least. I ran my fingers through my hair in frustration, realizing nearly everything would upset her.

"Well, King Soren is dead. So, technically..." I trailed off as her eyes widened.

"Shit. Shit, shit, shit. She's a *queen?*" Her voice rose an octave at the end, and I couldn't help my grin.

"Sort of. I'm a bit fuzzy on the laws of succession in Vesta; it's different in Folterra, though I don't really know them either. No need to really, what with Declan and all. But there has not been a coronation yet."

She smiled, and gods, did I melt in that glow.

"I can't believe she did it. She said she wasn't going to, but I just had a feeling." She tugged that lip back between her teeth. "Is he nice? Have you met him?" Her wringing hands told me she was anxious; perhaps she was more suspicious about him than she let on. When my sister had mentioned it to her, she'd brushed it off as impossible. But some of her dreams made me wonder. Faxon sometimes melded into a man with golden-brown skin and no other discernible features. As if she didn't know enough about the king to fully form him in her mind.

"I haven't met him yet, no. That's where Emmeline is. She went to fetch him."

Elora raised a single brow, commanding more authority than she had any right to have.

"From *where*, Cyran?" she asked. This girl could read me in such an annoying way sometimes.

"My brother took him captive during the attack on the Cascade. He would have been executed yesterday, but we received word early this morning. Your mother prevented it and set half of Darkhold on fire in the process." I smiled, unable to help myself. It was nothing less than Declan deserved, though I hurt for my people. The people stuck under his reign who suffered because of him.

"Fire. Mama has—Cyran, how did I get here?" Her head tilted, confusion morphing into a look I couldn't quite place. Her delicate features screwed up, and I realized with a start she was about to cry. I grasped her hand, pulling it back into mine.

"What's the last thing you remember?"

"I was in the tent with King Dryul when Mama showed up, and then she—she set everything on fire. But it was white, like mine."

I had the urge to run my thumb over her furrowed brow. She was so beautiful it pained me.

"Yes, well, er, your mother is actually the Beloved, not you."

She blinked, her face went blank, and she stared, mouth open.

"It turns out the Beloved is blessed by all four of the gods, which, well, you aren't. But Emmeline is."

"Wait, wait, *what?* All four gods have blessed her?"

"Yes, it's quite surprising. But she is. She was able to defeat my father. He's dead. Declan is king."

"Mama killed King Dryul?" she whispered, amazement on her face, and I felt my lips twitch.

"She did, yes."

Emmeline hadn't even looked at him when he rushed behind her. I wasn't sure she'd even done it consciously; the shadows seemed to have a mind of their own. I had only looked up for a moment, after Elora's eyes went empty. Bloody hell. I didn't want to tell her. I decided to try to skip that part of the story.

"While all of that was happening, King Rainier was overpowered and taken by my brother and has been held in Darkhold ever since."

"How long has it been?" Elora looked down at her hands as she asked.

"Six weeks."

She jumped up, scrambling toward the foot of the bed, and promptly fell to the floor with a cry.

"Elora! Are you alright?" I ran around the bed to her, finding her collapsed on the ground, her hands in her lap and her head hanging low. When she looked up, I saw blood running from her nose. "Shit!"

I scooped her up and took her into the bathing suite where I sat her on the counter as I looked for a cloth to clean her up.

"I hit my nose on the bed frame. It's alright. I'm fine. My legs just...I'm so weak. Cyran, have I been asleep this whole time?"

I grabbed a cloth from within the closet before I came back to stand in front of her. The counter was high, about waist height, so she was taller than me as she sat there on the edge of it. I put both of my hands on her knees, hoping to reassure her.

"Yes, but you're alright. Everyone is alright. Safe."

She narrowed her eyes at me as she took the cloth out of my hands, more forcefully than necessary. "What happened to me? What did you do?" She must have started to remember. I needed to explain the why before I told her the *what*.

"There was a prophecy. I had to awaken the Beloved." She nodded slowly before tilting her head back, the cloth pressed against her nose. "I was shown something I had to do, and in hindsight, every part of me wishes I hadn't done it. I hurt you, and I'm sorry." Those blue eyes watched me over the white cloth as it turned red. "What I did to you caused Ciarden to bless Emmeline and allowed her to kill King Dryul."

She turned on the faucet next to her, spinning a bit on the counter to wet the cloth, not looking at me. "What did you do to me? Why have I been asleep?"

I took a deep breath as I prepared myself for what was to come.

"I killed you." She froze, looking at the cloth in her hand. I squeezed her knees, afraid of losing her. "But your mother brought you back. I'm so sorry, Elora."

She dropped the cloth and turned away from me, spinning on the counter to face the mirror. I held my breath as she pulled her hair behind her shoulders. She traced her fingertip over the long white scar stretching across her throat, and I watched her swallow. Emmeline had tried to heal it, but the scar wouldn't leave her. Just like the scar on my heart to match what I'd done to her. I'd live the rest of my life regretting it, wishing I'd have just let the world burn.

She didn't turn from the mirror as she spoke, her voice almost quiet enough I didn't hear her.

"Get out."

I pulled my hands away and took a step back.

"Your mother brought you back, and I woke you up. I'm sorry, Elora. Please. I thought I had to."

"I said get out." She fisted her hands in her lap as she spun on the counter. Her hands began to shake as her lips flattened into a thin line. I deserved her rage. I deserved so much worse. I was stupid to think she might have remembered what happened and forgiven me.

"Let me help you to the bed at least, your legs—"

She threw a bar of soap from the counter at my face, and it bounced off my forehead painfully.

"I said get out!" Her chin jutted out, and I saw the tears in her eyes. I couldn't just leave her on the counter though. She just woke up, and she was weak; she could fall. I didn't know what to do.

"Come on, *min viltasma*, please let—"

"Do *not* call me that." Her eyes flashed white, and I knew what was about to happen. Still, I couldn't just leave her.

"Stay right here. I'm going to go get someone." I was halfway out the door, hating to leave her, when I heard her collapse to the floor behind me. I stopped, turning as I ran back to her. Stubborn. That's what she was. "I told you to stay put!" I reached for her before I was slammed backwards, white light hitting me square in the chest.

"Bloody hell, Elora! Let me help you, and then I'll go!"

"*Fuck* you, Cyran. Get OUT!" She held her hand up, palm facing me as she screamed.

"Alright, I'll go. I'm leaving. I'm going." I scrambled backwards away from her. I deserved this. Everything terrible that she said to me or did to me was something I deserved ten times over. A hundred times. I'd earned her vitriol. I'd earned her hatred. And that was what I saw in her eyes—hatred and pure anger. Her face was red and blotchy, and her nose had begun to bleed again. I stood up, rubbing my chest where her light had hit me. "I'm sorry, Elora, darling. *Min viltasma*. I'm sorry."

I moved before her light could hit me again, headed toward the door. Not even a second later, I heard a lamp shatter.

CHAPTER 25

RAINIER

I knew how gods damn stupid it was to feel the way I did when I watched Dewalt hug her. I knew it was pathetic, insane, and, most importantly, unfounded. And the look on her face, the words she mouthed to me, told me she felt it and knew exactly how fucked my mind was at the moment. Between my embarrassment of her knowing and Dewalt being completely oblivious to it, I wanted to be alone. That was why the moment I saw my best friend of over twenty years turn toward the steps to bring him up to the battlement, I rifted directly below the gate and made my way out of the fortress. I didn't want to disappear or else I'd have rifted farther away, but I wanted him to know I needed space.

It should have been *me* pulling that fierce, beautiful woman into my arms. It should have been me running my fingers through her hair, down her back, whispering comfort to her. Though, I couldn't help but assume the comfort she sought was because of me. But I couldn't do it. I couldn't risk her. She was too important—to me, to the world. She was the answer, and I was just the man who stood at her side. And if I couldn't be beside her without thinking she was someone else and trying to kill her, then I couldn't be next to her at all. I felt her confusion and at the last moment her frustration, but I didn't know what to do. I had to hope time would make it easier. Time would make me forget the bitch I killed in the dungeons of Darkhold. Time would make me forget what she'd done to me. Em had poured her divinity into my back, deft fingertips fluttering across the skin, moving less smoothly than they once had. I hadn't even noticed the wounds. Would she have helped heal me completely if I had the confidence in my own mind? Heal the wounds of my mind along with those of my body?

It didn't matter; I couldn't risk her.

"Rainier!" Dewalt's shout followed me as I strode toward the cliffs and the massive beasts who circled nearby.

I'd seen them out when the sun rose, and I'd debated between waiting on Emma and going out to see them myself. While I stood on the battlement, I'd felt the bond growing the tiniest bit stronger, her emotions coming through clearer, so I knew she was approaching. I had turned to watch her come out of the fortress. The sun shone down, illuminating her, the act a credit to the gods' generosity. Even just to look at her would have been enough, even if I never could return to her side again. Just to be granted the ability to see her smile, her laugh, her kindness, her strength. All of it. All of her. Even though I noticed she wore the same clothes from yesterday. Had she pulled them back on after I left her last night or had she waited until morning? She looked exhausted, her hair was unbrushed, and I felt my gut twist. But I pushed it aside; I'd feel a hell of a lot more guilty if I had fucking killed her.

When she looked around, I had wondered if she was looking for me. I willed her to look up, to see me, to know I was here. Even from a distance, I was always here for her. I'd be there for her in other ways as soon as I could, but, for now, this would have to do. She'd grasped Dewalt by the wrist, and I felt something stir within me as they spoke in whispers in the middle of the courtyard. I knew it was unreasonable to think she wouldn't confide in him, tell him what happened. I had cringed, hoping she wouldn't tell him too much of the details. He would think I was fucking pathetic for waking up and choking her. For letting myself hurt her. He would think that because it *was* pathetic.

Almost more pitiful was the growl that came out of me when I saw Dewalt pull her into his arms. I couldn't see her face buried in his chest, and my blood heated. I had strained, not allowing my divinity to wrest its control from me and start shaking the ground. Someone cleared their throat behind me, and I ignored it, focusing on my whitening knuckles gripping the half-wall. I didn't give a fuck if he was my best gods damn friend. She was mine. There was no room for jealousy in our relationship—something she'd made clear by how she reacted to Thyra. I knew we were it for one another. Final and complete. But gods damn, did I feel nauseated. I needed her and couldn't have her.

"Rainier, slow the fuck down."

I ignored Dewalt as I kept my pace toward the dragons, almost considering rifting away. But they were too close to the cliff, and I was too on edge to attempt it.

"Shithead!"

I stopped, turning halfway as I waited for him.

"All these years, and I've never wanted to use my authority to chop your head off. But today? I want to more than anything." I gritted my teeth when I imagined his hands rubbing down her back. It was fucking absurd. That was why I kept it to myself. I would have felt this way no matter who it was touching her—because it wasn't me. Out of anyone I could choose to comfort her here, it would be my best fucking friend. What the fuck was my problem?

"Well, it's a good thing I helped save your life then. You owe me, brother." Dewalt clasped his hand on my shoulder as he caught up to me, a slight jig in his step. "I'm not going to let you do it again."

We were rather close to the cliff's edge; I could have thrown a rock over it, let it fall down into the water. The dragon Emma and I had ridden upon, the biggest of the seven, landed gracefully in front of me, back-flapping his wings so he landed softly from a hover. Irses. I liked the name. The different constellations had always fascinated me—ever since I was a child. My mother took little interest in me personally, much preferring to deal with Ven and me together—and rarely at that—but she had a telescope and loved showing me the different wonders the night sky could offer.

"Do what?"

I didn't take my eyes off of the silver-grey behemoth in front of me as I spoke to Dewalt, not sure I wanted to hear what he had to say. Irses lowered his giant head down, blinking at me with my own eyes. She'd made a dragon with a memory of us, and I felt a warmth settle over me knowing what she'd been focused on. I reached for the bond, counting the threads and gently smoothing over them, trying not to touch and disturb her but needing assurance just the same.

"I'm not going to let you shut everyone out and pout for, I don't know, fifteen years," he said.

I grunted at him as I approached the giant before me, jumping back at the last minute as the small, wild dragon came falling from the sky. This one, also a male I believed, was dark-green with eyes the color of the sky. He was rather pretty but obnoxious.

"What's this one's name?" I asked.

Emma had spoken little as we rode Irses, and when she did, it was quiet. I remembered a few dragon's names but not all of them. And certainly not this one. He trotted up, the top of his head nearly eye-level with me.

"She hadn't named him yet. She didn't quite finish with him before we had to leave," he answered.

The dragon nudged me, much more gently than he had the day before, and I reached out to pet his snout.

"You think she'd care if I named him?"

Dewalt snorted as he stood next to us, smoothing a fingertip over the ridge above the dragon's eye. It let out a contented sigh, blinking slowly, and I smiled.

"I don't think she'd mind at all. But you could always, you know, ask her yourself."

I gave a non-committal grunt. She'd clearly told him enough.

"You won't hurt her."

"And you're so sure?"

"You could try, but she's more powerful than you now."

Something tightened within me at the statement. I had never been one to care or think too much about my abilities. Hanwen had blessed me more than most, but compared to my father's gift of that great and terrible fire, I'd never thought my manipulative divinity compared. He could conjure his fire out of nothing. Regardless, I knew how strong I was and didn't hate knowing I could overpower most anyone. But Dewalt was right. She was more powerful than me. At least, to a degree.

"I have access to her blessings."

"Yeah, no shit. You bonded."

"No, the other ones. When I was fighting Declan, my hand—it lit up. I haven't tried, but I assume I have the shadows too."

"Fuck, could you make a dragon too? We could create an army," he breathed.

"How did she do it?"

I reached into my well of divinity and attempted to bring the dark divinity out from within, and, while I didn't know what I was doing, black power curled around my wrist and hovered in my outstretched palm. I made the shadows larger, using my other hand to help cup them. It almost felt like the wind I could pull to me, except icy cold.

"Well, they coated her, the shadows, and I'm pretty certain she just thought really hard about the memory she used to form them."

"What memories did she think of? I know his—" I nodded toward Irses. "But I don't know what I should think about."

"I think she just picked ones that were clear in her mind. Something she could easily draw from."

Before I could think anymore on it, the vision of him holding Emma to his chest and comforting her was in my mind, as clearly as I'd just seen it. I felt the shadows in my hands shift, and I threw myself deeper into the memory, even if I didn't want to. I was committed by then. My friend was doing what I couldn't, and that was all there was to it. Eyes closed, I felt something heavy in my palms and slowly opened my eyes. The dense divinity swirled around its body, and I wanted to see the dragon I'd made with my own two hands. As I pulled my shadows away, it made a strange sound. When it repeated the sound, my jaw dropped.

It meowed.

The black mist cleared, and Dewalt burst into raucous laughter. I couldn't help it as a smile tugged up my lips.

"Well, shit." I said, disappointed. "A fucking cat?"

"At least it's cute. Maybe it will breathe fire or something."

I glared at him then looked at the tiny kitten in my hands. It curled up in my palms, almost too big for me to hold, and licked its front paw. The fur was glossy and black, matching my friend's own hair, but it had bright blue eyes I recognized better than my own. Dewalt tilted his head as he looked at it.

"What were you thinking about? Emma, obviously, but what else?"

"Nothing," I growled. Thankfully, he only raised a brow at me before he turned back to the dragon, who sat down on his haunches, much like an obedient dog. I didn't know if I'd ever seen the creature so still as he watched the small cat in my hands, tilting his head.

"Don't you even think about it." The dragon's eyes cut up to mine. "Leave Yvi alone." I rubbed a thumb over the cat's forehead, tracing the small, white streak on its otherwise solid black body.

"Yvi?"

"It was the cat's name in Elora's book." I set down the feline, and it immediately rubbed and twined itself between my legs before doing the same to the dragon before us, who looked at me and tilted his head again, appearing confused. I chuckled before I reached out and petted his muzzle again. "And I have the perfect name for you."

An hour or two later, I had finally begun to relax. I'd made Dewalt point out every dragon to me, their name, and the memory which had formed them. He wouldn't tell me two of them, claiming he didn't know, but I thought he suspected. The one named Shika, who had black mist which clung to her form and swirled in her eyes, and Ryo, the smallest dragon I'd just named. Given Shika's coloring—deep, blood-red—and the shadows surrounding her, I had a feeling I knew what the memory was, especially because of her name. Ryo, on the other hand, was a mystery. I'd have to ask Emma, but I dreaded the idea. I knew she would want explanations and assurances I wasn't sure I could give.

And she deserved those things, truly. But while Dewalt and I made our rounds with the dragons, I found my mind drifting to the thoughts I'd blocked out. If I poked around the inner recesses of my mind, I found I could penetrate the draíbea fog, and I remembered more clearly things the shifter had said and done to me. Some memories felt so real, I hadn't been able to focus on what Dewalt was saying, forcing him to repeat himself.

The two of us sat on the ground while I used my divinity to throw a giant, compacted ball of dirt for Ryo to chase after and bring back to me. Irses and Hyše, the rust-colored dragon with a temper, looked on with what I could only interpret as agitation, but Traekka and Ifash joined in with fervor. I formed two more balls for them to play with, and all three of the beasts toppled over one another. Using my divinity felt strange after being in the dampening cell for so long, but it was welcome.

"You going to talk about it to someone?" Dewalt pulled me out of my thoughts, and I had to blink a few times to focus on what he'd said.

"No," I answered, shaking my head. What was there to tell? "I'll be fine; I just need to move past it."

Dewalt spoke quietly, a grim look on his face. "And in the meantime?"

"What about it?"

"In the meantime, Emma suffers alone. *You* suffer alone."

"Us suffering is better than me gods damn killing her."

"Like I said before, she's the Beloved, you couldn't kill her—"

"She let me choke her! She wouldn't use her divinity against me. Being the Beloved doesn't mean shit if she won't use it, or if I overpower her. I could snatch her fucking air before she even woke up. We're lucky I didn't do worse!"

He sighed, rubbing his hand over his face. "Fine, don't sleep in the same room as her, but don't shut her out. She needs you to comfort her."

"You seem to have that covered." I couldn't keep the bite out of my voice, and I rubbed my hands over my face in frustration.

"You can't be serious."

Dewalt's mouth was parted as he stared at me. I couldn't wipe the scowl off my face fast enough, unable to play it off as a joke.

"Shit, you are serious. Hanwen's taint. Are you—"

We heard the rift at the same time, closer to the cliff, and I watched the shimmer of it as Emma appeared in front of us, taking a step through. She jolted to a stop, surprise on her face, as her perfect mouth formed a perfect circle.

"Sorry, I—I just came to check on..." She trailed off as she jumped out of the way so the wrestling dragons didn't bowl over her. It appeared one of their dirt balls had sailed off the cliff into the water below, and they hadn't bothered to get it. Instead, they opted to fight over one of the remaining ones. Ryo dropped his and charged over to Emma, and Ifash immediately pounced on the discarded ball.

Emma's face lit up with a smile as Ryo approached her, instantly nuzzling into her outstretched hand.

Gods, she was radiant.

The sun shone on her golden-brown hair, brushed now, and she had some pink to her cheeks she hadn't had before. She wore a loose grey button-down, with black breeches much too long for her—she had cuffed them at the ankle, but the material was too bulky to fit in her boots. Her cloak was the thick, black one she'd worn during our trek through the mountains a few months prior. I couldn't believe it had been that long.

"Hello, little one. Did you miss me?" Her eyes lit up as she gently petted the dragon, and he gave a great sigh before sinking to his haunches. Yvi, who had been lying contentedly between Dewalt and I, enjoying the warmth, ran over to introduce herself. Emma laughed, and I felt delight flutter down the bond, like the wings of a butterfly. I swore the clouds in my mind parted, the hateful memories gone, the fear of what I stood to lose abated. Smiling, her eyes met mine for just a moment, and I realized she probably sensed that small fraction of peace and happiness. I felt her wariness, probably annoyed with me for those mad thoughts of jealousy, but she smiled all the same.

She strode purposefully toward us, and I couldn't help it when my stomach clenched, wishing I could see her collarbone. I wasn't sure what she felt from me, but stopped dead in her tracks, quickly averting her eyes from me to the cat already winding its way through her legs.

"Who is this?" she asked, voice soft.

"That," Dewalt laughed, breaking me free from my internal struggle, "is Rainier's attempt at a dragon."

She snorted before glancing up at me, the laughter stilling on her features when she realized he was serious. "What, really?"

I nodded, grimly. "I suppose it makes sense for you to form the terrifying creatures of myth—it's the least the gods could do."

She smiled sadly as she reached down to scratch the cat behind its ears and run a hand down its back. The feline arched in delight, tail standing straight up. "Well, did you name her?"

The mischievous smile on her face made me feel something entirely too dangerous for me to even consider.

"Yvi. I named that one too," I said, nodding toward the beast watching her in adoration. "His name is Ryo now."

She squinted at me in thought. "Why do I recognize that?"

"*The Discovered Dragon.*" I smiled at her, knowing what it would mean to her. I felt her emotions before she let it show on her face—hopeful joy mixed with sorrow.

"Elora's book."

Dewalt stood and brushed off the back of his pants. "I'm going to head back."

I looked up at him, not bothering to hide my aggravation. Closing my eyes, I inhaled slowly, and heard her heart speed up. I wasn't sure I'd ever get used to the harrowing. Our friend took off toward the fortress at a brisk walk, and I stared at the cat who had made her way back to wrap around my legs.

"I—" Em stopped, looking down from where she stood, the distance between us more than physical. She seemed like she'd been about to say something else, then thought better of it and shook her head. "I wanted to give everyone a day or so to rest, then head back to Astana—to Elora." My heart soared at the thought, and I saw a smile play on her lips as she felt my elation. "Do you know what we should do with them?" She turned toward the dragons in various states of rest, play, and hunting.

"They've been diving for tuna. Do you know what else they eat?" I couldn't risk us bringing them to the capital until we knew what they ate and where they could get it. She shook her head. "Well, they seem to do well here, with the sea. The northern coast is a bit far from Astana. I'm sure we could find them something else. Perhaps, sheep?"

She nodded, pulling that bottom lip into her mouth, and I was jealous for the second time that day. I should be pulling her lip into my mouth, using my tongue to erase any distance. But I still couldn't trust myself, and I almost considered asking her to move her cloak and shirt so I could see that patch of skin, the only thing which seemed to comfort me.

"What if we only take a few to Astana? Leave the rest here. We'd have to talk to Raj first, of course."

She pulled her cloak tight around her as a breeze rippled past. I closed my eyes, frustrated. We were together again; why weren't we warm in bed, wrapped up in one another? The image of my hand on her throat as I moved within her appeared in my mind. It shouldn't have surprised me that she pulled me out of that momentary madness with our physical connection. I was grateful for it, even if it terrified me. We'd renewed the bond; she had my divinity once more, and she was better protected because of it.

"That might be a good idea. Which ones?" I asked.

She turned, eyeing the beasts as they moved. Her gaze immediately turned on Irses as his powerful body dove toward the water, disappearing out of our line of sight over the cliff before reappearing with a tuna the size of a pony in his powerful jaws.

"Irses would come, whether I wanted him to or not. Lux has divine fire—should we bring her?" I contemplated for a moment before nodding. One fire-breathing dragon per location seemed like an intelligent plan. "I thought you might want Shika as your mount," she whispered.

Sorrow. A loved one wrenched from grasp. Vengeance upon the gods. My eyes tracked over the beast, watched her lying curled up with Lux and Traekka, her tail wrapped protectively around the two smaller dragons. The image warmed my heart, thinking of the two I'd do anything to protect. The two I'd die for. I nodded.

"I suppose this little one wouldn't know what to do without Irses—he's kind of taken him...under his wing." She tried not to smile and failed while I couldn't help my grin.

"We can bring him too. Perhaps Elora will ride him."

Once she woke up.

The unspoken part of the sentence weighed heavily on the both of us, clouding the silence between us with heartbreak.

"Is she at the palace?"

"No, the estate. I had a bit of trouble—your mother..." She trailed off, and I stood, brushing off my pants and pulling the hood of my cloak up as the wind whipped around us. Emma's heart beat nearly out of her chest.

"What happened? We haven't had a chance to..." It was my turn to trail off. We hadn't had a chance to speak because I left her—alone. "You said she doesn't trust you?"

"Why do you think she doesn't trust me?" Her eyes searched mine, and I watched them narrow, almost imperceptibly, at the slight swelling I could still feel in my face. "I'll tell you if you let me finish healing you."

She crossed her arms, and I weighed the idea. We were both awake, alert, and I was rather sick of the tenderness. My joints in my arm still ached, and it would be nice not to have so many physical reminders of what had happened. My eyes darted to her shoulder, and I reminded myself the freckles beneath her clothes were there waiting.

"Alright," I answered after a moment. "I would appreciate that. Thank you."

She rubbed the wrinkle between her eyebrows, far more forcefully than necessary. "Don't thank me."

Emma crossed the distance between us and tentatively raised her hand, the touch of her cold fingertips delicate, and I closed my eyes.

Real. Mine. Emma.

When she moved to my shoulder, I winced from the pain, but as the heat of her touch flowed through me, I felt relief. I repeated my mantra until she finished, barely focusing on the story about my mother because her being a pain in the ass was nothing new to me, and I opened my eyes wider than I had in days. My jaw still ached, and I was sure I had a loose tooth, but I didn't bother mentioning it. It would pass.

"We should get back," I said, stepping back the moment she was done. I scooped Yvi up from the ground, figuring I'd make a stable-cat out of her, and turned back to the fortress. I didn't feel like using my divinity, wanting to take my time walking back to the bustle. Wanting to take my time with her.

"Rain." She hadn't moved. I closed my eyes and inhaled. I knew what she wanted, but I couldn't give it to her. "I know you're scared. Talk to me. You won't hurt me."

"I will though. I will if we aren't careful, Em."

"No, I won't let you. Look at me." I couldn't. "Vestana, look at me." Her voice strengthened, and I felt her resolve through the bond.

Fuck, I wanted to be with her. I wanted to be certain I wouldn't have a moment of weakness and accidentally hurt her. I thought I could handle it after she stopped me from choking her. But then she had said something, an echo of what the shifter had said to me, and I was back in the dungeons once more, and the urge to flee came over me.

"I have nothing to give you, Em. Maybe soon. But not yet."

I spared myself from seeing her face break, even though I felt it through the bond. I stopped short when I saw a cloud of dust coming toward us: Thyra on horseback, tearing her way across the field. My heart stopped, and Emma and I stood in silence, watching her. Waiting. I could have made a rift to get to her sooner but didn't, and I'd never felt like more of a coward.

Finally, I saw Thyra's mouth move before either of us could possibly hear her. "She's awake!"

CHAPTER 26

Emmeline

"Go grab what you need—I'll wait."

At his words, I stumbled over myself toward Thyra and her horse before remembering I could rift. Between Rainier's and my own, our emotions were all over the place, crashing and bouncing about, strident. Walking through the rift into my quarters, I grabbed weapons for both Rain and myself, not bothering with my pack, and within moments, I was stumbling back out to the cliff side. The rift was imperfect; I was a hand's breadth above the ground, so I stumbled, and I nearly fell flat on my face before Rain caught my elbow. When he immediately withdrew his touch, frustration and sorrow coming through the bond, I wiped my expression clean. Rain continued giving orders to Thyra, and I shoved his weapon at him before opening a rift to Nara's Cove. The bustle of the port was loud compared to the relative quiet we came from, and the frenzy matched the flurry of emotions overwhelming me.

My stomach roiled. I was terrified. What if she wasn't the same? What if she wasn't herself? I needed her to be alright. The message from Sterling had said she spoke, so that had to have meant she was her normal self. Right? What if she was angry with me? Gods. I had to tell her about Rain—that he was her father. What if she didn't want to meet him? I could tell by the look on his face and the feelings coming down the bond, many of our fears were the same. The odds were good that this first meeting wouldn't go well. But at the same time, I was so thrilled she was awake, I wasn't sure it mattered. She could rage and scream and cry and hate me—I wouldn't care. I had my daughter back. I would do whatever I could to keep her.

I chanced a glance over at Rain, noticing his furrowed brow and his fisted hands. I didn't know what to say to him, what to say which could prepare him for this. I could feel his fear, and there was nothing I could do or say to ease it. Not when the fear clearly extended toward me as well. He created another rift, and we both stepped through without another word, onto a footbridge over a small creek. I immediately went to open another rift, but I struggled to remember the next location in exact detail.

I tried again, frustrated. I wanted to get to her. To get home. She was probably beside herself, wondering where I was. Was she alone? Had Cyran been with her when she woke? Ven or Mairin? When I failed at opening the rift a second time, I started fidgeting. Taking my hair out of its braid and plaiting it once more, tighter, I paced on the bridge, watching Rain below me as he skipped stones on the water, not quite frozen. Though he looked serene and calm, I knew it was a farce. I could feel the tension, sharp down the bond, see it, thick in the hold of his shoulders.

Sighing, I turned away from him and tried once more to open another rift. This time, I was so far, I created a rift back to Nara's Cove.

"Em."

"What?" I snapped, instantly regretting it as I turned toward him. I felt—rather than saw—the small tinge of hurt my sharpness caused.

"Rest." I opened my mouth to argue with him, but he cut me off. "We'll make the next one together."

The quiet way he spoke, the care and compassion in his voice, made me soften. I undid my hair, brushing it out once more, and braided it calmly, giving me something to do.

"What should we say to her? What should I—I should talk to her before you come in. Right? 'You almost died, Elora.' No, she *did* die." My voice broke. "'By the way, the King of Vesta is actually your father.'"

I watched his full lips curve into a smile as he looked up at me, amusement shining through. "I suspect that might cause more questions, considering she might not know I'm king," he drawled. I huffed a laugh despite myself. Warmth from the bond made me look Rain in the eyes, and I wanted nothing more than to throw myself into his arms. But I wouldn't. He wasn't ready. "Just tell her the truth, Em. That's all we can do." He broke eye contact with me, looking down at the stone in his hand as he traced his thumb over it.

"What if she's angry? What if she's upset with me? Hell, what if she doesn't believe me?"

"If she's angry, you will understand because you love her, and you are the most empathetic woman I've ever met. If she's upset with you, you will give her the space and patience she needs to work through it. As for believing you, well, if what Dewalt says is true, maybe I'll be enough proof to convince her." He smiled at me before reaching up and closing his hand over mine where I'd grasped the railing.

"It's not quite as pronounced as Dewalt makes it out to be. It wouldn't have gone unnoticed for so long if it were *that* obvious. He notices it because he knows your face so well. And he knew Lucia's—mine. But perhaps it will help."

He brushed his thumb over the top of my hand as he gazed up at me. But then he pulled away, just as fear and self-doubt ebbed between us. He still wasn't ready. He rested his hand on the hilt of his sword, then pulled it away quickly, almost as if it burned.

"Where did this sword come from?"

He unsheathed it, pulling it out to look at it. Holding it up, he walked into a streak of sunlight and examined it. I hated the thing. I almost felt bad for asking him to carry it for me; since it made me feel sick with dread, it might have similar effects on him. I could feel it from where I stood, a low, repulsive energy. But when Rain looked up at me, awe and confusion on his face, I felt a twinge of pride which made me smile.

"It's Declan's." Shock came rippling out of him, and I couldn't help but laugh. "Well, he was naked when he rifted away from Darkhold, so I suppose that's why he didn't grab it."

"He was naked? Why was—never mind, I don't care." Rain shook his head and went back to examining the sword once more.

"I saw it in his quarters. It glinted in the light, and I—I don't know. I felt like I should take it. But it makes me feel ill."

"It's an elven blade," he said, peering over it. I stared down at it and noticed a golden swirling language inscribed within the steel. It must have only been visible in direct light. His words registered, and I stared at the weapon in disbelief.

"Divine hell, where did Declan get an elven blade? That has to be at least five centuries old—more."

"Your guess is as good as mine. Father has one—er—I suppose we have one. It was something he took from the last elf prince. He challenged him, and the prince lost, or so Father claimed. Truly, this sword could be its twin. The only difference is the stones."

"Your father has Tannyl's sword? Soren was the one who killed him then?" The elf prince had fought bravely during the Great War, but died with the rest of his kin. It had always been a rumor that Soren killed him, but if he had Tannyl's sword, it must have been true.

Already dwindling in number, the war eradicated the pure-blooded elves completely. Unlike their ancestors, any who still had elf-blood in their veins today had little influence over the earth magick, which was their birthright. I'd always found it quite tragic. As the selkies and merrows of the seaborn felt called to the sea, the elves and fae of the forestborn drew their magick from the earth. The more mortal blood flowed in their veins, the less power they could draw. Mairin was a full-blooded merrow, and if she had access to her pendant, her gifts would have been immense.

"He would never speak about his death, but I suspect it was him, yes." Rain traced a fingertip over the delicate script, and I wondered if there was anyone alive who knew how to read it.

"You said it makes you ill?"

My shudder was involuntary.

"I wanted it, desperately. It was almost calling out to me, but when I touched it, I don't know..." A shadow twisted its way up my wrist, and I flicked it away. How could I feel so repulsed and yet drawn to it? "It made me feel sick. Nauseated and angry. I assume you don't feel that?"

He shook his head. His hand had moved away from it when he touched it, but perhaps it meant nothing. He sheathed the blade as he made his way around to the footbridge. I hadn't moved, just staring down at my hands where they wrapped around the railing. I felt his eyes on me, and I forced myself not to look at him. Giving him space, allowing this distance which I hated to my very core, was something he needed from me. I could do that for him. But I detested every second of it.

"You ready?" I nodded and turned away from him, spreading my hands to form the rift. When he put his hands on my waist, I couldn't help but tense. I wanted to melt into his touch, lean backwards into his strength and warmth. My daughter was safe, and Rain was back. Everything I had ever wanted was within reach, yet I couldn't have it. Not the way I wanted, anyway. I stood there, frozen, for just a moment. Allowing myself a second to calm my racing heart and spinning head before I opened the next rift. And right as the sound and shimmer tore through the air, I felt him move, felt his breath against my neck.

And when he inhaled, I stifled a sob.

"You've been using my soap."

I tried to spin in his grip, not sure what I intended, but his hands tightened on my waist, not allowing me movement. All our emotions were so wrapped up and tangled between us, I couldn't distinguish his from my own. But I didn't move, not wanting to endanger this small improvement he'd made. I nodded, unable to speak, stepping away from him into the rift. He followed behind, putting space between us. It was a knife in my chest, but I hid my reaction. He'd given me the space and time I needed while I sorted out my head and my heart. He was patient—until he wasn't—but I'd give him what he needed.

We continued our journey in the same manner, me giving him space and him sometimes closing the distance. Before I knew it, we were back at the apple tree where we'd memorized the prophecy we'd stolen from the Supreme.

"Has he come calling for his book?"

"He offered to heal Elora. I refused, obviously." He exhaled, the relief palpable. "The morning after he offered, all hell broke loose. But she's been at the estate—warded."

Rain moved the earth, snow and dirt churning as his divinity worked. The dirt bubbled up beneath the ground, and a stone box came bouncing out, as if the dirt were a geyser and the box a floating log. I watched him as he pocketed the delicate tome inside, waiting for him to explain what he was planning on doing with it.

"Declan was raping the novices, trying to impregnate them in some sort of bid to impress Rhia." Horror and revulsion raced through my body. Potent. "We know he is Ciarden-blessed, and I suspect Hanwen-blessed as well. I'm not sure about Aonara. But since he isn't Rhia-blessed, he might not be the Accursed. Though he clearly wants to be."

I felt hollow.

"Those women—the women I—" My eyes stung. I hadn't meant to hurt anyone, let alone people who had done no wrong. But innocents who had been raped and held captive by a monster? Even their last moments had been painful because of me. I stilled as Rain took a step forward, eyes on mine. I was sure he felt my sorrow, but he didn't come any closer. "They never knew peace," I whispered.

"They might not have—you're right. I won't pretend what happened wasn't horrible, Em. But I suspect they found some peace in one another."

I took a step forward, still taking Rain in, wanting nothing more than his warm arms wrapped around me, but when I saw him stiffen at my approach, I took a step back. Clearing my throat and my mind, I held my hand out to him.

"Are you ready to go home?"

When he reached back and squeezed, I felt nothing but love, warmth, and concern from him for a few moments before it slowly ebbed into unease. He lifted his hand, and we formed the final rift together.

The elvish woman Dewalt had called upon to form the wards included Rain in her magick boundary. Rain had utilized her services in the past, so it was easy for her to do. I supposed with him back in Astana, it might be safe to lift them.

But I didn't want to deal with that at the moment; the impending collision of two people I loved more than I loved myself was commanding every ounce of my attention. The rift we formed opened into the great room, the high ceilings and wooden beams a comforting sight.

We were home. *Our* home. This place where I'd been dreaming of making memories of the three of us, hoping that despite the odds, we'd get to follow through. And now, standing there in the still quiet, I was overcome by all the emotions I'd been holding at bay. I sunk to the cream sofa and held my head in my hands.

I couldn't see her like this.

I didn't know what kind of state she was in, emotional or otherwise, and I couldn't afford not to be strong for her. Between being strong enough to give Rain the space he needed and hiding all fear and regret and guilt about what happened to my daughter, I wasn't sure I had anything left for myself. I wasn't crying, but it felt like I should have been. I was waiting for the prick of tears at the back of my eyes to take over, but it didn't, and I supposed it was a good thing; I wouldn't have to hide my tears from her.

Gods, I was exhausted.

I heard Rain's footsteps move behind me, coming around to where I sat, and he crouched in front of me.

He had always known when I needed his physical touch, the grounding to reality, and I could tell he wanted to give me that. I could feel the yearning, could see it in his eyes when they met mine. Yet he kept his distance, briefly reaching out to brush my knee before pulling away. And that hurt more than if he hadn't touched me at all.

I inhaled, dropping my hands to rest between my legs. It was quiet, and I wondered where everyone was. It had been half a day since Thyra had brought us the message that Elora was awake. I supposed it was time for Mairin and Ven to be busy at the palace, but I couldn't imagine they'd leave Elora here alone. Cyran must be here somewhere. But considering I didn't hear their voices, and I wasn't sure how she'd reacted to him, I was confused. That was why when Sterling walked out of the dining room, humming a somber tune, I leapt up from the sofa as if I were on fire. Spinning to face him, I took a few deep breaths. He'd scared the hell out of me.

"Your Majesty!" The butler panted, clutching his chest, and I thought he'd have a few more grey hairs because of it.

"Elora?" I rasped.

"She's sleeping in your bed. I got her to eat a bit of soup—oh. Oh." Sterling looked past me, hand still clutching his chest. I glanced over my shoulder at Rain, who stood behind me, and I saw him through Sterling's eyes for just a moment. Saw him the way I did in Declan's dungeon. Thin—far too thin. Cheekbones prominent and pants loose. Eyes not shining quite as brightly.

"Your Majesty," Sterling breathed, a quiver in his voice. The two men looked at one another for a long while as Rain stuffed his hands into his pockets. When Sterling finally crossed the room, it was with purpose. "You're back."

When they embraced, I had to look away.

"I'm going to go talk to her, alright?" I glanced toward the bedroom and back at Rain, who only watched me with an expression I couldn't read. "I'll come for you."

When she's ready. If she wants to meet you.

I didn't want to say it aloud, but his nod and tightening of his mouth told me he knew what I couldn't say.

Straightening, I walked toward that back hallway. She was lying in the bed, asleep with a book next to her. If it weren't for the book and the bowl of soup on her nightstand, I wouldn't have believed she'd woken at all. I sat down on the side of the bed and laid my hand on her hip, gently smoothing the blanket over her. I watched her face, fearful her eyes would stay shut, and I did my best to ignore the thin white scar on her neck. When her eyes fluttered open and they met mine, I sighed, unable to contain my relief.

And when she smiled at me, blue eyes framed by white lashes—bright and *alive*—I came undone.

No amount of telling myself I wouldn't cry, no amount of telling myself to be strong so I wouldn't scare her, could prepare me for the onslaught of emotions which crashed within me. I wasn't sure I said any discernible words as I scooped her up, pulling her body to mine as I sobbed into her hair.

"Mama, stop." I eased up as she pushed an arm between us. "I can't breathe."

"I'm sorry, honey. I just—you're awake."

"Well, I am now," she grumbled, and I laughed out loud at her insolence. Her voice sounded strange from disuse—lower—and I worried about damage I might have missed.

"I'm sorry I interrupted your nap."

She flopped back against the bed, her curls spreading around her. I ran my fingers around a soft spiral, unable to help myself.

"It took me hours to comb it out. My arms hurt."

"Everything is going to be weak for a while. I tried to keep you moving in your sleep and heal you while I did, but surely your muscles have wasted a bit in spite of that. Have you tried to walk yet?"

"Not really," she said, cheeks flushing.

"We'll get you back to normal soon." I reached for her hand, but she pulled it away.

"What happened, Mama? I think I remember, but—I want you to tell me." My eyes caught on the white line on her throat, and I closed my eyes, remembering the gore and blood in vivid detail. Inhaling a shaky breath, I rubbed both hands over my face before looking down at her. Her chin jutted out, and her brows knitted together, a hardness taking over her features I barely recognized. "Tell me," she demanded.

"What do you remember?"

"The tent. I was tied up, and you were fighting the king."

"Cyran untied you." Blue fire flashed at me before she closed her eyes on a sharp intake of breath as I continued. "Elora, I should expl—"

"Don't tell me why. I don't care. It was him, wasn't it? It was Cy?"

My heart broke all over again for her. I knew when she woke, there would be so much for her to understand and cope with. The boy she had trusted, probably had feelings for, had betrayed her. Regardless of his reasons, it was still a betrayal. He'd betrayed all of us, but I had the luxury of distance and age. He had clearly been close to my daughter, and they were so gods damn young. I wondered what I would have done if I were him. Would I have been strong enough to do that to Rain if I knew the world depended on it? Would Rain? The two of us ruined things so thoroughly back then, I had no doubts if we had a bigger decision to have made, we would have struggled with that too.

But Elora had experienced possibly the three biggest betrayals of her life, all in a row. Me and my dishonesty, Faxon doing what he did, and then the boy she'd clearly sought comfort from betrayed her in the worst possible way. And she would have big feelings about all of it, and I couldn't control any of them.

"Cyran slit your throat because of a terrible vision he was privy to."

"I told you I don't care why."

"I know what you told me, and I'm telling you there is more to it."

"You're defending him?" She drew her head back quickly, mouth dropping open, and I hastened to correct her notion.

"No. Never. I'm not defending what he did, and I am sure that what he did will live with all of us for years to come. But," I said, watching her eyes narrow. "He was shown a vision—"

"He said he was shown a vision, and *you believed him?*" Her voice grew shrill.

"Yes. I listened to his heart, and I can tell. He didn't want to."

"Just like you didn't want to keep secrets from me my whole life?" she snapped.

"No. Not like that. What I did..." I sighed. Despite the calm in my words, my heart ached, and frustration coiled within me. I deserved all of this from her and then some. It didn't make it hurt any less. "What I did was a mistake. I was an adult, and I should have known better. For what it's worth, I did it because I didn't want to scare you. Because I thought it would protect you."

"Well, it didn't, Mama. Maybe if I knew, I wouldn't have gone with Papa to Mira." She crossed her arms over her chest with some difficulty, muscles shaky from atrophy, and I raised a brow at her. "Maybe if I knew, I'd have been more careful," she corrected.

"You're telling me you got taken because you weren't being careful? Elora, that's not why it happened."

"No," she huffed. "Fine, you're right. You're always right, aren't you, Mama?"

"No, honey." I frowned. "I wasn't, and I'm not. I would have done so many things in my life differently if I could go back and do them over again."

"Like kill Papa sooner so you could marry the prince?" she whispered and closed her eyes. "The *king*."

Astute, my little sun.

"I would have done things differently with Rain, yes. I would never have married Faxon, let alone kill him."

"Thanks a lot." She glared up at me.

"For what?"

"You wouldn't marry Papa? Maybe that's why you're not mad at Cy—Cyran—because you don't care if I exist."

"Elora," I groaned, rubbing my face. "You are entitled to every opinion and feeling and thought on all of this, but I need you to try to handle these feelings, knowing what I've taught you about me your entire life. Do you truly think I don't care?" Her eyes softened the smallest increment. "Have I left some things out? Yes. But I'm going to rectify that and make a few things clear to you. I have never once regretted you, and frankly, the fact you exist is what has kept me breathing. You are everything to me in this world of shit. You were the only reason I didn't end my life when everything was taken from me. Elora, you are—you are proof of my greatest love. My *only* love."

She blinked up at me, defiance melting away.

"I don't mean Faxon. There is so much love between myself and the man who is your true father. There was then, and there is now. You are the best thing we ever did."

She stared at me for a moment before she squeaked, "The prince? I mean, the king?"

"Yes. And—"

"I knew it," she breathed, and it didn't surprise me she'd figured it out.

"Before you jump to conclusions, I didn't know until recently. Rhia blessed us with you when I needed you most. You look so much like me and with the timing of everything, I truly didn't think it was possible."

"Does he—does he know?"

"Yes, honey." I smiled, hoping to reassure her.

"Was he mad at you?"

Tears filled my eyes, remembering how Rain had reacted to the revelation, nothing but happiness and shock and a touch of sadness for lost time. "No," I whispered. "Not in the slightest."

"Does he want me?" Tentative, shaky breaths came from her slight frame.

"He wanted you before we even realized you were his."

"What about Papa?"

"What about him?" I tensed.

"I mean, Papa…The king is a stranger, and Papa is my—"

"Your father—Faxon—is whatever he was to you. However you feel about him is what he was to you, alright? Rain, as much as he already loves you, will be whatever you want him to be. He knows you already had a man who raised you."

She nodded, averting her eyes, before she replied in a small voice, "What if he doesn't like me or just pretends to make you happy?"

That fear broke my heart, and I wished I could bring Faxon back to make him rue the day he met me. My poor little girl would have a hell of a time trusting anyone ever again, opening her heart up, believing men who said they loved her. The only solace I took was that if there were any man to help prove those words to be true, it was Rain.

"He's not pretending, but I suppose you'll have to give him the chance to prove it. He does like me an awful lot, and, lucky for you, you're just like me." I smiled, and I caught the corner of her lip twitch. "You know, I wasn't much older than you when you were born, and I haven't stopped learning since I've had you." I chuckled before continuing. "Every day, I learn a different way I can be a better mother to you, and I'm sorry you'll only get the best version of me once you're all grown up. But know that I'm trying."

"I know." She wiped her nose, and I stood, situating the blankets over her body. "Mama?"

"Yes, honey?"

"I need to—" She nodded toward the bathing suite, a wide-eyed look on her face.

"Oh, dear, yes. I'm sure you do."

Throwing the blankets off, she spun her body so her legs hung over the edge of the bed.

"I practiced walking a bit with the butler, only because I didn't want to pee in the bed, but he was so awkward about it," she cringed as she stood on unsteady legs. "When I'm done in here, if you think he wants to…Would Rainier—the king—oh, gods. What do I call him?"

I laughed, arm in arm with my girl, and my heart warmed.

"I'm sure we can come up with something."

CHAPTER 27

Rainier

Not long after Emma left to speak with Elora, Sterling slipped away as well, realizing he was late for an errand. After opening a rift into the stable to expedite his journey, I stood in the middle of the great room, looking up at the beams. They came from the trees which stood here before I built the estate, and each one had been cut into shape by Dewalt and I. It had been a particularly bad year for me. Dewalt hadn't questioned me at all when I'd obsessed over painstaking details meant for a woman I thought would never see it. He hadn't even looked at me sideways when I filled a garden for her or when I worked my hands bloody building the house.

Running my hands through my hair, longer than I was used to, I felt extraordinarily out of place. A change into clothes that fit would do me wonders, but I didn't want to interrupt Emma and our girl. My daughter.

Half of me.

Swallowing my nerves, I turned directly to the sideboard near the fireplace and poured myself a drink before stepping out into the garden. It was winter now, just a few days before the solstice, and most of the plants weren't in season. Attempting to put distance between myself and Em, not wanting to have such a clear insight into her emotions because it felt invasive, I walked farther into the garden. Making my way toward the only plant I thought might be in bloom, I turned down a path toward the swing. The winter squill was my mother's idea, wanting me to have a pop of color against the hedges. She had said every garden needed a winter blossom. It was a deep blue, and it surprised me to see the shoots had bloomed through the snow coverage as early as it was in the season. I sat down on the swing and took a long pull of my drink as I stared at the flowers. Hardy, the plants preferred winter, but often waited until closer to spring when the snow had abated to blossom. They were more common in the mountains, and they rarely thrived this far west.

And yet.

Gods, I couldn't wait for her to see the garden in bloom.

I tried to ignore the bond, but it was nearly impossible. Every emotion Emma felt was one I expected—and so full. Robust. I wasn't sure I'd ever felt anything as much as she did. Joy, sorrow, fear, dedication, elation, regret—all were there, and all were strong. I had hoped Elora wouldn't be too hard on her mother, and based on the emotions I was feeling, I couldn't tell. At one point, I felt a sharp dash of amusement, almost causing me to laugh out loud, and I didn't even know what it was about. But the emotion felt so strong, I was almost there with her. I wasn't sure how long they'd be, so I only stayed until I finished my drink before finally heading back toward the estate. I took my time, lingering and attempting to figure out which plant was which beneath the snow coverage. Failing at it, I felt confusion down the bond, followed by overwhelming panic. Stupidly, I ran. I could have rifted right back inside, but I wasn't thinking, anxiety churning in my gut.

I burst into the house as I heard Emma yelling my name from upstairs, looking for me. There was a desperation in her cry which splintered me. Gods, I'd frightened her. Fuck. I felt a thickness in my throat knowing I caused her panic.

"Em, I'm here!" I started toward the front of the house and called out to her. I heard a sound and turned, glancing back toward the open door to the bedroom, only for a flurry of white hair to bounce out of my line of sight. Nervous energy filled me, but the smile brought to my face was more than worth it.

"Divine hell, Rain, you scared me." Emma's voice rounded the corner before she did as she walked back in, and my stomach dropped out.

She was flushed and more beautiful than I'd ever seen her. She'd changed, putting on one of the simple cotton dresses she preferred. But this one was embellished at the waist, tiny flowers of cream and champagne embroidered into the lavender fabric. It was a simple inversion of her wedding gown, and she looked beautiful. I could see her graceful collarbone, that spot where her freckles proclaimed the truth. She was a bit thinner in the face and hips, more noticeable when she wasn't bundled up in layers. I didn't like it at all, knowing the cause of it was stress and malnutrition. As much as a primitive part of me wanted to hate Dewalt for being here and comforting her while I was gone, I was grateful. He'd told me about his and Thyra's efforts to make sure she took care of herself. Both of us needed time and coddling from my cook to get back to normal. Since Sterling lived at the estate and the wards had been no issue for him, he told me he'd been doing the lion's share of cooking. But he was no Deandra, and I was eager to call my cook back.

I stopped thinking about my cook though, the more I looked upon my wife. I couldn't think of anything else when her hair fell in waves around her shoulders. Her eyes were full of warmth and adoration as they met mine, dark blue in this light. I must have still had a smile on my face because her own smile lit up the gods damn room. It was the first moment we'd had since I'd been back that didn't feel tainted. She was happy. She was whole. Her eyes were shining, remnants of the tears she surely shed with Elora, and I felt her overwhelming love—not just through the bond, but even in the air.

"I'm sorry." I set down my glass, not even aware I was still holding it, and I clenched my fist, wanting to close the distance and drag my fingers across her creamy skin. I wanted to count her freckles, kiss each space between them. Gods, she was perfect. Sometimes, on the worst nights in the dungeon, I'd thought all of it was a nightmare. That I'd imagined her coming back to me, only to have her ripped away. But here she was, standing in front of me.

Real. Mine.

"What did you say?" she asked, voice a murmur.

"I said I'm sorry."

"No, no, after that. You whispered something."

I hadn't meant to say it out loud. "I—Sometimes I need to remind myself. That you're real. And you're mine."

Her eyes softened, and I nearly pulled her into my arms until I felt her pity. I didn't need her feeling sorry for me. I had done what I needed to do to protect her, and I paid the price. I didn't want to think about it, so I shook my head.

"How is she?"

Her answering smile could have been the key to the heavens, the answer to a gods damn prayer. "Tired. Her muscles aren't what they were, but she's able to walk for short bursts. We'll have to help her do some exercises."

"Has she been alone since she woke?"

"Cyran woke her, though she wouldn't tell me how. She kicked him out, but I heard him upstairs."

I tensed, uncertain how to feel about the boy. The only thing keeping his head on his shoulders was Em's request. But if Elora wanted me to string him up, I wouldn't fucking hesitate. "And then she's been alone?"

Emma gave a soft smile as she answered. "Mairin checked her over before going on her rounds to the wounded soldiers, and I guess Ven never came back last night. I don't know where she went. We had a system. Dewalt, Thyra, Cyran too. She hasn't been left alone almost the entire time. Mairin left her with Sterling, and he seems to have fussed over her."

"And how did she take it? Does she want to..." I trailed off. Even though my voice was quiet, I was aware of the open door to my bedroom.

"She already knew. Quite perceptive, our girl. Well, she suspected. Apparently, she suspected ever since the last time I spoke to her in one of Cyran's illusions."

"And she wasn't upset?"

"No, Rain. She's nervous, worried perhaps. But not upset." She lowered her voice to a whisper. "I'm afraid you might have your work cut out for you to earn her trust."

I closed my eyes, exhaling with a chuckle. "I wore you down quick enough," I said, grinning at her. I hadn't realized we'd moved so close, and the side of her hand slid against mine. It reminded me just how nervous I was to be around her. I curled my hands, finding my palms sweaty and wiping them on my pants, breaking our connection. Disappointment rippled down the bond, though she did her best to stifle it, and I was sure she felt my shame.

I'm trying, dear heart.

She stepped back quickly before turning toward the hallway leading to our suite. Leading the way as she cleared her throat, Em stopped on the threshold, knocking her knuckles against the door frame. "Elora?" Her voice called out, and I could see over her shoulder to the empty bed. Had she fled from me? Did she not want to meet me?

And then a voice rang, one I'd dreamed of and longed to hear.

"I'm washing up a bit. Give me a minute. Do you know how disgusting I feel? Did you even *try* to wash me? I smell like—"

"Rainier is here with me!" Emma called out desperately, cutting Elora off to save her from embarrassment. I couldn't help it as I laughed. Poor girl. I heard a loud groan, and I chuckled as I strode down the hall.

"Call me when she's ready, Em. No hurry."

But I didn't wait for her to tell me, rushing back into the room the second I heard the bathroom door creak. I stared as my daughter walked into the room, looking annoyed, legs stiff like a newborn fawn. She was shorter than Em, but with that white hair, gods, she looked so much like Lucia. I understood why that was all Emma saw. But as she turned toward me, cheeks rosy and an embarrassed crooked smile lighting up her face, I knew with certainty this girl belonged to me. Similar to the vision I'd seen in Declan's dungeons, her hair was waist-length, with spiraling curls, and her eyes belonged to her mother. But the smile was mine, the upturned nose was mine, the expression she was making, her eyebrows tugged up in the center—mine. She was quiet for a moment, staring up at me, and I wondered if perhaps I was more nervous than she was.

I'd never once been intimidated by a fifteen-year-old, but I supposed my own child was a great place to start.

"Cursing a certain goddess right about now?" she asked, arms crossed. I'd imagined her voice to sound a bit higher, but it was low and a bit raspy.

"All the gods, actually." I gave her a half smile, and I watched as her brows moved down, a glare on her face. "For keeping us apart this long," I finished.

Squinting at me for a second, perhaps to suss out a lie, she finally made her way over to the bed, moving with slow, jerky motions. I considered helping her, but I had the idea she'd be just as annoyed by that as her mother would be. Perched at the head of the bed, hands crossed daintily in her lap, she looked so much like Em and her sister from when we were young.

"Mama, can you fetch me some of that tea you mentioned? I'm getting sore."

Emma's eyes darted between us, uncertain. "Right now, honey?"

"Yes, now."

"Alright, right now. Can—should I bring Rain with me or—"

"Mama." She widened her eyes at her mother, trying to subtly hint something Emma wasn't picking up. "Go get the tea."

I couldn't hide my amusement as I grinned at her. She tapped her fingers on her knees, avoiding my gaze.

"Em, it's fine. Make her the tea. We'll be alright." I gave my wife a smile, and even though she started wringing her hands, she finally left the room. I turned back to face the girl on the bed, looking so small in it. Harsh confidence gone with her mother, my daughter seemed nervous. I worried she might have been scared of me, and I wasn't sure of the best way to approach her. "Can I sit at the end of the bed, Elora?"

Permission granted, I kept my distance as I joined her. I was just about to address her, introduce myself, I supposed, when she took a deep breath and words tumbled out of her mouth.

"I hope you know you hold no obligation to me, and if you don't want to have a relationship with me, I understand it. I don't need it, you don't need it, and I don't want either of us to force something because of Mama. She will just have to deal with it." As an afterthought, she added, "Your Majesty."

I blinked, surprised at the force of her statement. I studied her for just a moment. Gods, she was her mother's daughter. Headstrong, practical, and clearly deluded. If this girl thought, for even a moment, that I wouldn't want her as my child, that I didn't want everything that entailed, I was going to have to set her straight.

"It's nice to finally meet you, Elora. 'Your Majesty' sounds much too stuffy, don't you think? Rainier suits me fine." I smiled at her, warm, still conscious of her wariness. "But on one thing, you are mistaken."

"What?"

"Your mother's wants have nothing to do with it. I *do* need it—a relationship with you. If you're willing."

"It's not like I can stop you, anyway. You're the king. I have to do as you say."

"I'll never ask you to do something you don't want to do."

She jutted out her chin in a painfully familiar way. "So, how is this supposed to work? I tell you my favorite color, you teach me how to fish? You send me to my room if I'm rude to Mama? My last father already taught me how to fish."

"Your favorite color is yellow, and I hate fishing just as much as you do. I also think your mother can hold her own against you."

"How do you know all that?"

"I may have studied up on you," I admitted, a bit sheepishly. I'd asked Em dozens of questions about her before I even knew she was mine. "I'm sure I can teach you other things though, if you want. I'm pretty decent at skipping rocks."

She rewarded me with a small smile. *My* smile.

"I thought old men liked fishing."

Head thrown back, I laughed harder than I'd imagined possible. I felt a surge of elation through the bond a moment before I heard Emma's footsteps down the hallway. The girl next to me was fighting a smile, cheeks darkening and eyes bright.

"How old do you think I am?" I asked, wiping a tear of mirth from my eye as Em stepped into the room, placing the tea service down on the table in front of the fireplace.

"I don't know, forty?"

I snorted. "Close. In four more years, you'd be correct."

"Cy—I was told you both performed the ritual. That's probably a good thing." She lowered her voice to a whisper, exaggeratedly rubbing her fingertip between her eyebrows. "Mama had been complaining about getting wrinkles."

"Little miss," Em's voice chided, and by the gods, I would've had her lay healing hands on my heart if I hadn't known any better. The hammering beat and tightness in my chest was almost too much. Hearing the two of them banter, both pieces of me in the room together, was almost too much to take in. I swelled with pride and emotion.

Emma walked past, carrying a teacup for Elora, and she rested her hand on my shoulder as she passed it over. Lifting my head, my eyes met hers, and I wanted to swim in them. I wanted to pull her into my lap, to cry with her, to laugh with her, to breathe her in. But when my eyes made an involuntary movement, counting those freckles, I knew it was too soon.

But we'd be safe enough for a while. The three of us. I could pretend it was alright. For her, for them, and, honestly, for me. I didn't want to ruin this moment for them, this first chapter in our new lives, as much as I didn't want to ruin it for myself. I put my hand atop Em's, giving her a tentative smile, and emotion flooded through us both, eyes and the bond telling us more than words ever could.

"Sit with us," I murmured, tugging on her hand. Nervous laughter bubbled up her throat as she sat beside me, and I held her hand in my lap. Elora stared at us from her place at the head of the bed, and I wasn't sure what to say. I wanted to learn her, know her, gain her trust. At the same time though, I didn't want to overwhelm her. I didn't know what the hell I was doing.

"Where is Cyran being kept?" Elora asked, more a demand than a question.

I clenched my jaw, ready to kill him, but winced at my tooth, still aching. The tooth had given me issues before, and I considered just ridding myself of it.

"I pulled him out of the dungeons to help wake you. He's stayed here since he came back from Folterra, but we will move him."

"Came back?"

"What do you mean, 'came back'?"

Elora's eyes met mine as we both asked the same question. Em breathed out a laugh, eyes smiling, before she explained.

"His brother offered a deal. Cyran for you, Rain."

My stomach clenched, but I waited for her to continue.

A loud bang cut us off, and I heard my sister's voice, a loud echoing shout.

"Mother! They only just—"

"Rainier, where are you?"

I groaned as the last fucking person I wanted to deal with came stomping down the hallway.

Chapter 28

Emmeline

Without even thinking, I used Rain's divinity to slam the door shut on a gust of wind. Jumping up from the bed, I ran to lock it. "I'm not dealing with that, not yet. You two only just—"

Bang. A demanding knock at the door.

"Rainier, let me in." Shivani's voice grated on my nerves, and I spun, facing my two loves.

"She's not going to leave," Rain offered, rubbing a hand over his face. "May as well get it over with."

Bang. Another request I ignored.

"I'm sure you're right, but—" Clouded with emotion, my voice suffered. "We haven't had enough time. You two have only had a few moments. Besides, Elora just woke up, and…"

I trailed off, opting to protect my daughter. I couldn't tell her Shivani had no interest in her these past weeks, hadn't believed me or wanted to see her. I couldn't do that to her. I hadn't gone into details with Rain, only telling him Shivani didn't believe me, and I tried to convey to him with my expression that I didn't want this meeting to happen without Elora catching on.

When he stared at me blankly, not understanding my meaning, I sighed. Men.

A man who has never been a parent before, I reminded myself. He'd barely been able to protect Lavenia from Shivani's abrasiveness. This would take time.

Bang. Bang. Bang.

"Rainier!"

"Em? Just let her in," he said, giving up.

Elora's eyes whipped back and forth between us, and a red tinge creeped up her neck and cheeks. Nervous.

"Are you comfortable meeting Shivani? She's…still getting used to the idea of having a granddaughter, so you might have to be patient with her." At the sight of Elora's face, slightly green, I shook my head before addressing Rain. "Not now; she's not ready."

"No! I'm fine. It's fine. She's just…Is it true she's the last siphon?"

"Oh gods, don't mention that to her," Rain chuckled. "But yes, she's the last." The banging grew insistent.

"Gods," Elora whispered. "I can't believe I'm about to meet the queen."

"Queen mother now," Rain corrected, gifting me with a smile I felt I should latch onto before it disappeared.

"Are you sure it's alright, honey? I'll make her leave if I need to," I said to Elora.

"Mama, it's fine. She's going to knock the door down if you don't."

I turned toward the door and unlocked it, stepping back as Shivani came slamming through and pushing past me.

"You're home," she said as she leaned over Rain, drawing him into a hug that surprised the hell out of me. His confusion through the bond told me he felt the same. A second later, she pulled back, cupping his jaw so tightly in her hand he winced.

I sent out a shadow, not even thinking, wrapping it around her wrist and pulling it away from him.

"What the hell do you—"

She cut me off with her tone, fearful anger making her words shake as she yelled at her son. "Don't you ever do something like that again. And to tell me your true heir right before you performed some sacrificial—How was I supposed to interpret that?"

Rain rubbed his jaw, appearing rather sheepish as he looked up at Shivani.

"I'm sorry. For what it's worth, I didn't intend to be captured, Mother. Speaking of my heir, you haven't met yet." Rain nodded toward Elora whose mouth had fallen open.

"No. I'm not your—no," she stuttered, eyes whipping over to me.

"We'll talk about it later, honey," I replied, stopping myself from shooting daggers at Rain. I reminded myself Elora was not a fragile doll, but a real girl growing into womanhood. Coddling her would do her no good—but still. She'd been through enough lately, and I wanted to help guide her through it as gently as possible. She was still wrapping her head around the fact he was her father; we didn't need to add anything else to it. But Rain didn't know what he was doing either, and the sudden intrusion didn't help anyone.

Shivani straightened, turning toward Elora so I couldn't see her face. But when she crossed her arms over her body, I tensed.

"Hello, Elora. I'm glad to see you've finally awakened. I know your mother was worried sick."

My stomach clenched. Her tone was cold, and it was clear in her posture she was merely being polite. I held my tongue, glancing at Rain, who still rubbed his face.

"Are you alright? In pain? Did I miss something?" I asked him.

"It's just a toothache. It's probably loose. I ought to just pull it—it's given me trouble before."

"The milk tooth?" Shivani asked.

My heart stuttered, and Rain turned to look at me, no doubt sensing my reaction through the bond.

"It's nothing, Em. Just a tooth that never fell out. I think I need to pull it, though. It sits below my other teeth and aches sometimes."

Elora's eyes widened.

"Do you have it too?" I asked Shivani.

"How did you—Mine fell out when I was a child, but I never grew in another. Same spot, though." Shivani's brows furrowed as she turned to look at me, arms still crossed.

"Third from the back, right side," I whispered.

Rain's smile lit up the gods damn room as he turned toward Elora, understanding dawning.

"What?" Shivani glanced between her son and me, and I felt a tear trickle from my eye. I knew it in my heart, knew it in every part of me. Rhia had even confirmed it in my dream. But gods did having this tangible evidence feel gratifying.

"Me too." Elora's voice was quiet as she spoke. Hesitating for a second, she opened her mouth wide, pulling her lip down, and I laughed. A joyful thing—light.

Shivani turned back toward Elora, and her arms fell down to her sides.

"You have it too?"

It was nice to see Shivani unraveled.

"I've been keeping an eye on it, since it wants to sink into her gums." My voice dropped low as I added, "Like her father's, I suppose."

"You weren't lying," Shivani whispered.

Rain's smile left, and a low rumble came up his throat, his anger simmering along the bond.

"You will not accuse my wife, your queen, of being a liar again. I don't care if you're my mother," he gritted out.

Shivani didn't turn, eyes pinned to Elora, and my daughter averted her own, looking down at the bed next to her.

"I suppose I was wrong."

"You suppose? You're not very good at apologizing," I said, voice cold. "Between this and your insistence on listening to General Ashmont, I think it best if you leave until you can come up with something better."

"I—I'm sorry," Shivani offered, pleading eyes turned toward her son.

"Not my apology to accept." Rain shrugged.

Before Shivani finished her slow turn toward me, I made a decision. It would have been easier if I just accepted the apology as it was given, letting us all move on with this new confirmation. However, not only had Shivani insulted me by calling me a liar, she'd all but accused me of conniving to put Elora on the throne, and her inaction nearly cost me Rain. Considering Rain never left the dungeon, Declan clearly had no intention of actually trading the boy.

It had gone too far. Once, when I was young, I might have accepted that treatment. Hell, I'd accepted quite a bit from Faxon. And that hadn't gotten me anywhere. I'd been isolated, made to live with the past by myself. I'd been made to handle my emotions by myself, raise a daughter alone, and live through the ache of separation from the man who was literally the other half of my whole gods damn soul. I'd spent the past months learning from my mistakes, learning about myself, and it was safe to say I'd discovered my spine.

"Nothing you can come up with on the spot will be enough. I might not have been doing what was best for the kingdom before," I said, voice clipped and precise, "but now, I am doing what is best for me and my family. You need to leave."

To my surprise, Shivani dipped her head, quietly slipping out of the room with one last glance toward her son and granddaughter. I waited with bated breath, bracing for Rain's response. His relationship with his mother was complicated, and I didn't want to make things difficult for him. The bond was unusually silent, though I thought I felt a flicker of something, and I finally lifted my eyes to his.

And I saw fire.

Banked, just a glimmer, but it was there. He hadn't looked at me like that, not since he'd been back, and it caught me off guard. Even the night before, when I'd brought him back from the brink of something dangerous with our physical connection, he hadn't looked at me with anything more than reluctance and heartbreaking love. His gaze had held no heat. Through the bond, I felt just a hint of that warmth, and it ebbed and flowed, as if he were trying to hold it back.

"She seems...special," Elora said, breaking the trance between Rain and me.

He closed his eyes, a smile tipping up the corners of his mouth as he said, "She's something, I'll give you that."

I caught myself staring at the two of them, a meter apart, and I suddenly felt bone-tired. It was unwelcome. With the two of them only just coming back to me, it felt as if I should have been jumping for joy, holding them and laughing and crying, but I struggled to keep a yawn at bay.

"Uh, so what happens now?" Elora asked, and it startled me to realize she wasn't directing her question toward me. I'd expected her to look to me to navigate this, but she was looking at Rain.

I could tell it surprised him too.

"Well, long-term or short-term?" He replied, a laugh hiding behind his words.

"Both. Either. Do you even know?"

I snorted, the sound startling me. I was so tired, I wasn't sure how I still stood.

"Come here, Em."

Words I didn't know I needed to hear dragged me toward the two of them, sitting me beside him. An arm supported my back as he pulled me against him. Gods, I'd missed his warmth.

"Long-term? I think we'll need to figure that out. Folterra and Declan—Did Declan, did anyone hurt you or touch you? Other than what..." His voice trailed off.

Other than what Cyran did.

Elora crossed her arms, looking at the ground, and I reached over, putting my hand on her knee.

"No. Other than the mercenaries forever ago, everyone was decent enough. Even King Dryul wasn't that bad. He just seemed old and crazy. Declan looked at me a certain way, but no one touched me."

"That is lucky for them."

I felt like an outsider to their conversation in the best way. I allowed myself to relax against his shoulder, content for the first time in weeks. We were together, and they seemed to get along well enough. Part of me thought I ought to stay alert to help them through this awkward beginning, and I tried. I tried to listen to everything they were saying to one another, but my body had finally had it. I didn't quite understand it. Though I hadn't slept well the night before, I had slept better than I had in weeks, knowing he was back. I should have been more awake than I had been since that awful day. I wondered if it was because I'd been forced to stay awake under those conditions, running myself ragged with a cause to work for. Now that I'd achieved and attained everything I could ever want, aside from vengeance, my body would tolerate no more.

"Mama, are you falling asleep?"

"No." I jolted upright.

"It's the middle of the day," she sassed.

"I haven't been sleeping well."

She looked sheepish as Rain dragged a hand up my back, resting his palm on the back of my neck. I closed my eyes once more, hoping it meant he wasn't afraid of hurting me. Or at the very least, trusted me to stop him.

"Do I have a room here? Cy—Cyran said something about my bedroom."

I straightened, stretching out my arms and legs as I yawned. "Yes, of course you do. I've been sleeping in here with you for now. We can keep doing that if you want to, or I can sleep in your room with you, or whatever you want."

"Is Cyran still here?"

"He is, but we will find somewhere else for him to stay. He's been staying in the room across from yours. I didn't know what—Elora, I want you to know I almost had him executed. But, because of Mairin, I decided to leave it up to you. I suggest you speak with her about the boy—she can read his aura," I added, realizing she might not yet know what Mairin was. She only stared, and I didn't have it in me to explain. "You'd still be asleep if it weren't for what he's been doing. Do you remember any of the illusions?"

"Some of them," she responded, voice sullen.

"Well, whatever you choose to do with him, I—*we*—will support your decision."

Rain's hand stilled on the back of my neck before he finally said, somewhat reluctantly, "I'll have Sterling set him up elsewhere."

"Will you show me to the room? I'm already tired. You'd think I'd be fine since I slept for over a month, but I'd like a nap."

"It's because your body isn't used to this much activity. We'll work on strengthening your muscles," I explained. "Do you think Dewalt would help with that?" I addressed the man beside me.

Rain nodded.

"Who's Dewalt?"

I chuckled, peeling myself from the bed and opening a rift into the bedroom Rain had suggested for her all those weeks ago. When he'd been waiting for me to say yes to him. I didn't even hesitate an entire day, but even that felt like such wasted time now. Perhaps if I'd said yes before the palace, things with Soren would have gone differently, and we could have made it to the Cascade sooner. I shook my head, dismissing the thoughts.

"Well, I suppose he's your uncle," I said, grasping her hand, but she froze, not allowing me to pull her up. "Do you need Rain to carry you, or do you think you can make it to the bed?"

"No!" She was quick to deny the help, and her face turned red. "I can make it. You—I know you did the bond, but I wasn't expecting *that*." She gestured toward the rift.

"Ah, yes. There's more I'll have to tell you later."

"I remember the light—that fire—The fire isn't his, is it?" She nodded toward Rain as I pulled her up, and he chuckled. "Where did it come from?"

She clung to me as we made our way through the rift and across the room to her bed, where I pulled back the duvet for her to climb beneath. I hadn't done practically anything to the room to make it her own. I'd have to send for her things from Brambleton, although part of me wanted to retrieve them myself. She'd grown up in that house, and though Faxon tainted many of them, we had made some wonderful memories there. I wanted to say goodbye.

"It's quite a long story, but right now, you should rest. I don't know how much longer I can stay awake either. Someone will wake you for dinner."

After getting her settled, I stacked a few books on the nightstand for her and sat down with her hands in mine. I'd let the rift close, not sure if she'd want Rain to hear our conversation, and I leaned forward, pressing my forehead against hers. I was so gods damn relieved and grateful to be here with her, to be able to talk to her again. What she had been through was more than I could pretend to understand, but I'd do my best to protect her. I knew Rain would do the same.

"I'm sorry for everything, Elora. I love you."

"I love you too. I'm sorry you saw me die," she whispered.

"Don't, baby. No." I gasped and barely held my tears back. "I deserve to have that memory for the rest of my days. It was all my fault. Cyran—"

"I *liked* him. I thought—I thought he liked me too, and I'm embarrassed. He was only kind to me so I would trust him." Anger and heartbreak warred in her voice.

"I know you liked him. I know. He fooled me too, honey. But, for what it's worth, I think he does like you. I think he just—He felt he had a duty to make sure his vision didn't come true."

Another boy who chose duty. Not unlike the man who waited downstairs. The stakes with Rain were much lower, yet, the idea was the same. Elora swallowed, sitting back against the headboard.

"I think I'd like to be alone. Can you lock the door? At least, until Cyran isn't here anymore?"

"Of course."

Moments later, after kissing Elora on the forehead, breathing in that summer scent of her, I passed Cyran's room and heard the beat of his heart. It was slow, telling me he was probably asleep. Everyone needed rest, it seemed, and though I'd do as Elora asked, I'd have Sterling organize it as soon as he returned rather than uproot the boy while he slept.

When I turned the corner to the top of the stairs, it surprised me to see Rain starting up them.

"She's going to rest for a while. I'll have Sterling deal with the prince when he gets back, so don't bother with it."

When he continued climbing the stairs, I stopped, confusion flooding me.

"I'm going to get some rest too," he explained, offering no clarity.

"I'm barely standing myself." I took a step down so I stood a head above him.

"You can sleep in the suite. I'll stay in the room next to the prince."

"Her door is locked, and she doesn't want to see him. I don't think he'd try anything, and I definitely don't think she'd let him if he did."

"What? Gods, that wasn't even something—" He shook his head, blinking, as he rubbed a hand over his jaw. "I didn't even think about that. I'm going to have to think about things like that. Divine fucking hell."

I laughed softly, but when I realized if that wasn't his reason for going upstairs, it meant he had another.

"Rain..." I trailed off.

"It's not safe yet."

"Well, unless you intend on kicking Mairin out or using your sister and Dewalt's room, you're going to have to build another wing."

"Ven and Dewalt have a suite in the palace. I'll sleep in their room."

"Or you can try. With me."

"I—Em," he murmured. "I don't trust myself."

Give him time.

"Alright," I said.

He was with me, back in my presence, and it should have been enough. And yet, it almost felt like he hadn't returned at all. There was no grand return, no reunion. Though we'd renewed the bond of the body, I had been too scared to truly inspect the other golden strings, fearful they'd grown weaker. He was here with me physically, but was it enough? Was the bond of our minds still just as strong? Would it ever be the same again?

I swallowed, moving aside so he could continue up the stairs. And when he did, I tried to swallow the emotions, did my best to protect him from the guilt I knew he'd feel if it came down the bond. I bit my lip as hard as I could as I took my final step and glanced up at him over my shoulder. He stood there, watching me, and I could see the turmoil on his face, feel it in our connection. Inhaling deeply, I calmed myself and turned away from him. He needed my patience, needed my soft. If I pushed him before he was ready, I was no better than those who tormented him. Slowly, I made my way past the front entry, down the small hallway into the great room, only to find him standing in the hall leading to our suite. I hadn't even heard the rift.

His hands were in his pockets as he leaned one shoulder against the wall. Just the weight of his hands made his spare pants from the Cascade hang low on his hips. He had rolled his sleeves up, the corded muscle in his arm flexing, and I knew he'd clenched his fist within his pockets. His emerald-green gaze met mine, and a flicker of nervousness was replaced with something else. Determination perhaps. I pushed my hair behind my shoulder as I approached, allowing him to see the freckles he said looked like the Damia constellation.

"You stood up to my mother quite well today."

I laughed, stopping far enough back to give him space. "I called her a coward and told her to get the fuck out not even a week ago. I'd say I was rather tame today."

Tracking his movements, my eyes dropped to his feet as he took a step forward, easing the distance between us.

"You're anything but tame, Em."

My heart hammered beneath my skin, and I hoped he wasn't listening for it. I wasn't sure I'd ever get used to him being able to harrow.

"It was quite nice to see her taken by surprise," I murmured.

"She made it harder for you, didn't she?" Another step. I nodded, afraid of moving and threatening our progress. "I want to know everything. The hard things. I—When I thought Elora was dead, I thought you'd never forgive me."

"I'll tell you—but not yet. I don't want to burden you. Your burdens are heavy enough."

Another step, and the toe of his boot touched the toe of the slippers I wore.

"We made a promise, Vestana."

I blew out a breath, smiling at his use of my new surname. "What's that?" I asked.

"*I will shoulder your burdens and swallow your secrets.*"

"I think we should take into consideration whose burdens are heavier when we begin sharing them. Whoever has the heavier load shouldn't take on more if the other person can reliably carry it on their own," I rambled.

He was so close to me, banked fire dancing in his eyes and a small smile playing on his lips. I grew nervous. I wanted to obey, to share what I'd gone through, but I wanted him to share too. And I doubted he was ready for that.

"I think that line is open to interpretation. How about you give me a burden, and I'll give you a secret?" he asked.

"Fine."

"Fine?" That crooked smile lulled me into compliance.

"I'll start with a very easy one. Barely a needle of hay to add to your stack."

"Please do," he said, grinning.

"Even in her state, Elora tossed and turned so much. I woke up with bruised shins quite often, but I didn't want her to wake alone."

"Are they better now?"

"What?"

"Your shins. Are they better? I'll heal them for you. I can do that now, you know."

Though his eyes glimmered with mischief, I felt something through the bond which didn't quite match, making his comment feel forced.

"I'm alright, thank you. Rain, you don't have to do this. I know you're trying for me, but please. Don't force yourself to stand here and talk to me if it hurts you."

"I haven't told you my secret."

"Rain."

"When I thought you were both dead, I wanted to follow. Tried to follow by harassing Declan. I don't know how long it was before he told me you survived. I stopped egging him on after that. "

"Gods, Rain. I'm so sorry. We're all fine—safe."

"I'm not done." He put a hand up, brushing my hair away that had fallen forward, darting his eyes to my collarbone, before gently pushing me back against the wall. "When I thought you were both dead, I wanted to die too. To join you. Not a single part of me wants to live without you. And it's fucking killing me that I'm afraid to touch you, to kiss you, when there's nothing I want more."

"I won't let you hurt me," I whispered. "I promise."

"And what if you don't have a choice? What if you don't wake up to stop me next time?"

"That's not going to—" I gasped when he traced my jaw and his hand brushed my hair behind my ear. "Happen," I breathed.

His fingertips dragged down my neck, crossing over my shoulder. "How can you be so sure?"

"The bond won't let you; *I* won't let you."

"You'll use your divinity against me? You'll burn my flesh to stop me?"

"I—I don't know if I can promise that."

"Then I don't see how I can try. Not yet, anyway." He withdrew his touch.

"No, I—if I hurt you, it could send us back to the start. I know she hurt you."

He leaned down, lips hovering over my skin, before pressing them to my shoulder. I was frozen, pressed against the wall, dying for his kiss to move, to trace my jaw, to find my own lips parted and waiting.

"I'd rather that than be afraid of you not using it when you need to."

His mouth moved against my skin, following the path up my neck like I wanted.

"Can I touch you?" I asked.

A brush of his lips against my jaw, as he whispered, "Yes." I slid my hands on either side of his waist, pulling him closer to me as his hand rested on my shoulder and his thumb grazed my skin. "Promise me, Em."

"I can't. I won't hurt you."

"If you don't promise me, I can't kiss you. And I swear on all the gods if you don't let me kiss you right now, my divinity will bring the walls down around us."

"Kiss me anyway," I said, as his hand moved up to cup my face. Insistent green eyes simmering with that tempered heat stared down at me, and the crease between his eyebrows added to his intensity.

"Promise me," he whispered as his mouth lowered to mine, echoes of his last kiss hovering between us. When he'd told me goodbye at the Cascade. When we stood to lose or gain everything.

"I promise," I breathed, unable to deny myself this. Unable to continue existing without him.

And when his lips made contact with my own, it was with the lightest touch. A whisper of motion I wouldn't have noticed if he wasn't here in front of me. But then I met his movement, pulling him toward me by the waist. I hadn't realized how much I had yearned for his lips on mine until they were there. When he'd turned away from me the night before, it had hurt, but I didn't realize just how badly I needed it until now. It was like the kiss we shared against the table in my little house in Brambleton. An end to our separation and the promise of more.

His thumb caressed my cheek as he deepened the kiss. Still feather-light and gentle, but undeniably him. I whimpered as emotion flooded our bond. Contentment and relief mixed with unyielding affection and desire. After my initial pressing, I wanted him to lead what passed between us. So I let him pull away, even though I never wanted him to stop.

"You taste like home," he said.

Tears I hadn't realized were waiting crashed down over my cheeks, and he leaned forward, kissing each one before dragging his lips back to mine, their salty caress making me feel so gods damn alive.

He moved with purpose now, his tongue parting my lips and sneaking in, twining with mine. Allowing me to hold him tight, our bodies aligned, and I pulled him flush against me. As much as I might have tasted like home to him, it was his embrace, his touch, his grounding presence which was my home. I could tell he was still afraid to touch me, only allowing his one hand to cup my jaw while the other braced the wall. But he didn't hold back with this kiss, the desperation and need running through the bond between us so potently I didn't know what to do with it. He slid his leg between my own, his thigh pressing against me and providing pressure I needed. A slight moan slipped out which he took, stealing the sound with his mouth, and he dropped his hand from the wall, placing it on my shoulder.

"Real. Mine."

"Always."

I tugged his lower lip into my mouth, nipping softly, and his hand slid from my shoulder up to my neck. Knowing the roughness of his touch was likely a result of my playful bite and the tension between us, I hated myself for not being able to push the thoughts of the night before out of my mind. When he'd stolen my breath from me, left bruises on me, because he thought I was someone I wasn't. I'd convinced him I wasn't afraid, that the risk was worth it, but the harsh grip, no matter how harmless, set me on edge. It was only when I noticed them crawling up his wrist in my periphery, I realized I could use my shadows to stop him without hurting him. It calmed me in an instant, and I was eager to show him.

Letting the shadow circle tighter, I coaxed them to pull his hand away from my neck.

"See? I can stop you," I said, just as I felt fear through the bond.

He jolted away suddenly, pulling his wrist from my grip.

"Let go," he demanded, stern, and I was confused. I had dismissed my shadows the second I felt the fear, and yet they continued to twine up his arm.

"Let go!" He shouted, stepping away from me, stumbling backwards.

"I did! Rain, I—I don't know why—" I stuttered, trying to coax the shadows away, but they wouldn't listen. They twisted up his own neck, and I summoned my light into my hand, hoping to banish them that way.

It reminded me of—

"Gods, Rain, they're *your* shadows. I forgot you have them too. They do this when—"

He was breathing fast, mouth open and panic in his eyes as he slid down the wall. I was afraid to use my light on him and hurt him. I'd never burned myself, but I'd seen what divine fire could do. Perhaps he could use his own to stop them.

Dropping my fire, I knelt in front of him, on my knees between his outspread legs, as I put a hand on either side of his face. I held his head, making his frenzied eyes meet mine. His eyes were wet, and he heaved a sob, the terror down the bond so profound I knew it would haunt me for the rest of my life.

"Listen to me, you can do it. Send them away."

"I can't," he gasped, and the shadows slipped around his torso.

"Yes, you can, love. Call upon your light," I urged, voice steady and sure despite my own heartbreak. A flicker came from his fingertip, and the shadows only repelled a small amount. Keeping one hand on his face, I held the other between us, cupping a small flame. "Like this, Rain. Watch me."

And he did. His breathing slowed as he watched my flame, and he made one in his hand to match it.

"Focus on the light. Good. They're already going away. Breathe."

His frantic heart had slowed, and I allowed my hand on his face to caress downward, tracing my fingertips over his shoulder.

"Almost there. Look at me, Rain."

His eyes met mine, filled with sorrow, and I noticed all the shadows were gone. When I leaned in, trying to soften his terror with a kiss, his emotions through the bond and the obsessive attention to my shoulder gave me pause. Brushing my hair away, uncovering the small spot over my collarbone, I sat back on my heels.

"It's alright. It happens to me sometimes too, when my thoughts go dark. Irses was a mistake made by one of my outbursts."

"I can't touch you anymore. Not yet."

"You didn't hurt me."

"No, I didn't. This time, it wasn't even about hurting you." I held my hands in my lap, letting him speak. "When you used the shadow on my wrist, it reminded me of the straps—" He cut himself off, angrily rubbing his chin.

"From the rack," I whispered. "Rain, I'm sorry. I was just trying to show you I could—"

"I know. I could feel your excitement when you realized it. But it's not going to work. I can't be around you until I work through this shit, Em."

"Stay in your sister's room. I understand." Gods, did it pain me, but I understood.

"Being around you and not being able to—it's fucking torture." He shook his head before standing and opening a rift without even looking at me. He'd barely returned, and I'd already lost him.

If I even got him back to begin with.

CHAPTER 29

LAVENIA

Three Weeks Later

When I finally began to feel like myself again, I'd been staying at the palace for nearly a month after Rainier kicked me out of the estate. I hadn't wanted to go all the way to my own estate. Surprisingly, it had been a blessing. I felt for Emma, knew whatever reason he had to sleep in my room rather than with her was going to torture her. But it gave me some distance from everyone, Mairin included, and I could come to terms with the way things had changed in my life. The merrow had been avoiding me anyway, but this way, it made me feel as if it were my decision. Since no one did a single thing for winter solstice, it was easy to avoid everyone. I didn't think anyone was in the mood for celebration.

So many things had changed, and it was nice to have time to get used to it. Emmeline was back with a niece I still hadn't met, Rainier was king, the mental bond between Dewalt and me had already severed, and I could no longer use his divinity. The other threads were fading, and I avoided inspecting them more thoroughly because I didn't want to think about it. Those threads had been an ever-present part of me for ten damn years. Not having them made me feel naked.

Dewalt had taken me by surprise. I knew it might happen one day, but I thought it would be me who decided it. That I'd be madly in love with someone, and we'd part ways for the better. But this felt like he was leaving me high and dry with little warning. And the way he'd looked at me when he announced it to Rainier made me feel awful. Pitied. It still annoyed me that he couldn't give me an hour to get used to it before he had to go say something to my brother. The only thing we'd agreed upon was respect, and, though I was glad he had the decency to talk to me about things, it didn't feel like a mutual agreement.

"Ven, I need you to act as emissary."

Drawing me out of my thoughts, Rainier clapped a hand to my shoulder. We'd been in a council meeting, deciding what to do about Folterra, but I hadn't moved since it ended. It was just the two of us left.

"Where? Nythyr? When?"

"After the coronation. And no, not Nythyr. The seaborn. Mairin mentioned finding allies among her people."

"The merrows haven't been involved in conduit squabbles in centuries. What makes her think they'd want to be involved now?"

I ignored the nervous pinch in my stomach over Mairin not bringing it up with me.

"You two didn't discuss this?" he asked.

"We did," I lied. "I just didn't think her reasons were good enough. But you must have?"

"I think Declan doesn't have many people to rift his army, or else he'd have attacked at the Cascade after Em—after I was saved. And if the seaborn can help us with the Mahowin Strait, I'd not only be arrogant, but stupid not to ask for it."

He pulled out the chair to sit beside me, long legs crossing at the ankles beneath the table. Rainier had put some weight back on, but he was still quite a bit leaner than before his time in Folterra. He still looked tired though, as if he wasn't getting enough rest.

"What am I supposed to offer them?"

"I trust you to use your judgment. See what they want, and if it's within reason, promise it to them."

I stared at him for a moment before tossing my head back to laugh. "Father would have set your leg hair on fire for that, at the very least."

"It wouldn't be the first time," he laughed, but the smile didn't reach his eyes. Our father used his fire to punish in cruel ways, albeit rare. His father, though, our grandfather, had been a monster from what we'd heard. So, we'd been lucky.

"He wouldn't have trusted anyone to do what you're asking of me."

"Get to your point, Ven. He's dead, and I am not." He sighed, propping an elbow up on the arm of his chair, rubbing his forehead.

"I don't have a point. Thank you for trusting me," I said.

"Don't go thanking me yet."

"Why not?"

"I only have one captain to spare at the moment."

"No," I snapped.

"Ven, she—"

"Please, don't say—"

"Dewalt is occupied, and Raj is busy taking over Ashmont's duties." He shook his head, mind already made up. "I don't trust anyone else to escort you."

"Rhia's tears, Rainier. Please, I'm begging."

"It's been—what? A year, now?"

"Yes, but—"

"I'm sure she's over it. You've moved on too. You'll have Mairin. Brenna won't bother you while you're with the merrow."

"I'm not *with the merrow*. It's complicated."

"Oh?"

Gods, I hated that tone. I didn't want to talk about how she'd been avoiding me and how badly my feelings were hurt by it. "I'm not *with* the merrow, just like you *are* with Emmeline," I gritted out. "Complicated."

"Fair point." His tone was crisp, but I didn't miss the sad dip of his shoulders.

"Are you still sleeping in my room?"

"I *said*, fair point."

"I don't see why you're staying away from her."

"I don't see why you're continuing this line of conversation when I clearly don't want to talk about it," he retorted.

"Maybe that's the problem, brother. Maybe you need to talk about it."

"Not to you, I don't."

"Then who?" Are you talking to Dewalt about—"

"Are *you* talking to Dewalt?"

"Divine hell, you are a pain in my ass," I snapped, exasperated.

"As you are in mine, little sister."

"Listen, when you're being stupid, it has to be someone's responsibility to inform you. I thought Emma was going to take over that role—"

"Oh, she still does. She barely spoke to me at all last week." A heavy sigh escaped from his lips as he tilted his head back.

"I don't think that was all about you," I offered. She finally had her first courses after drinking from the font. Notoriously brutal, she wasn't prepared. No one had told her what to expect, and I was disappointed in myself for failing her in that regard. Mairin had mentioned it in passing during one of the brief moments we'd ran into each other in the barracks. She'd had to go no sooner than she'd told me, and I'd almost chased after her.

"No, I know it wasn't. I could—you know, they ought to warn us."

"What do you mean?"

"Feeling her pain through the bond was awful."

"I promise you, it was worse for her."

"Gods, you ass. I know that." He scowled. "But I couldn't do anything. Not being able to fix it for her? Was yours that bad?"

"Do you not remember?"

"No, why would I remember that?"

"Because it was on one of our fucking trips to Nythyr. When we took a few days in Pelmuzu? I was laid up in the inn. I didn't get to go to any of the wineries the entire time. I was furious."

"Oh, I remember now. Gods, Dewalt and I drank so much that…" He trailed off when he saw the look on my face.

"I know. Ass. I'm surprised Emma's came so soon, though. Mine took almost two years."

"Of course, it started when I couldn't be there for her."

"Wait, you still refused to be around her? Even with the pain?"

"Well, no. I—Elora has been sleeping in there off and on. I couldn't just barge in."

"You could have asked her."

"And given her some sort of hope?" He tsked. "No. That wouldn't be fair."

"So, there is no hope for you to get better then? She is to live in your suite with your daughter while you stay a safe distance away? Rainier, you barely seem to have tried. You won't talk to anyone about it, least of all her."

"Table it, Ven. I don't know what you want from me."

"Treating her like she is something you can break is what has caused all this heartache between the two of you. The fact she hasn't kicked your ass tells me she is taking it better than I would have thought, but you're being unreasonable."

"She's the fucking Beloved, Ven."

"So?"

"*So*, if something happens to her, it's not just *my* world that is destroyed."

"And meanwhile, you're destroying *her* world yourself."

Shooting daggers at one another, we finally relaxed after a few moments of heavy silence. I loved my brother, and the thought of what he had gone through during those weeks and the thought of losing him had nearly torn me apart. But I hated watching him throw away what they'd worked so hard for. I hated how he let what Declan did divide them.

Emma was being much more patient with him than I would have been.

"When Dewalt came to me at the Cascade, I thought the two of you had discussed it." The tone he used as he changed the subject told me our conversation about Emma was finished, but he seemed to hold genuine concern.

"He sprang it on me just a few minutes before that."

"Shit. Why would he do that?"

"Things were—I'll spare you the details, but things had been off since Mairin came around."

"Was Dewalt right?"

"That she has feelings for me? I don't know. I doubt it."

Considering I thought she was avoiding me, it seemed Dewalt was wrong.

"Perhaps it's something to discuss with her on this trip," he said.

I sighed, standing from my seat. "Where are we going? I don't even know—"

"Northeast of Olistos."

"Divine hell, that far?"

"Brenna is coming with the *Netari* to Northport. She'll wait there until after the coronation."

"Why the *Netari*? Do you expect trouble?"

"We're sending a dragon with you, and the *Netari* is the fastest ship with room for it."

"And you think this is worth it? Asking the merrows for help?"

"If they say yes, they'd be invaluable."

"I suppose I don't understand. How are they supposed to stop the ships from crossing?"

"The Sea Queen."

I snorted. "The Sea Queen?"

"According to Mairin, she truly exists."

"Exist*ed*. Dead. Gone. Ancient."

"I suppose you'll have to ask her about it, considering what she told me."

"What do you mean?"

"Mairin is the last daughter of the Seaborn Queen."

Sterling met me at the door, letting me in with haste, the frigid wind carrying snow into the estate and whipping my cloak around me. I hadn't been here since I'd returned from Folterra, and I was kicking myself for it now. I'd wanted to give Rainier and Emma plenty of time to adjust as a family, though my brother was clearly wasting that time.

Emma had invited me over to meet Elora last week, but both Dewalt and Mairin were invited—I didn't want to deal with them both at the same time. It was cowardly, and I'd made an excuse. I glimpsed myself in the gilded mirror in the entryway as I marched toward the stairs. Snowflakes melting in my curls, they glistened, and I was grateful I didn't look more windswept.

I hoped to sneak in and speak to the merrow and leave before anyone knew I was there. Quietly running up the stairs, I heard humming from the room I knew Emma had reserved for Elora, and I stopped, undecided about what I should do. It would be quite rude to not introduce myself, but I wasn't sure if Emma or Rainier would want to be here for it. They'd been quite protective of her, understandably, and I didn't want to cross any lines. It was stupid of me to even come. It was possible Mairin wasn't even here. Slowly, I eased backward toward the steps, when a sweet voice rang out.

"Mama? You're back early. Good. I need my charcoals from downstairs, and since you won't let me go downstairs...Mama?"

Well, now's as good of time as any.

"Hello, Elora. It's Lavenia. Your fa—Rainier's sister. Can I come in?" Taking a step toward her door, I waited for her reply.

"Uh, sure."

Rounding the corner, I found a much more vibrant version of the girl I'd watched sleep for weeks. Cheeks bright and eyes shining, she sat at the desk which had clearly been brought in from another room, shoved tight against the bookcase on the wall. Sheets of paper covered every bit of the table—sketches of people, flowers, trees, and animals in various stages of completion. She had a small glass of water and a paintbrush, with a few different pigments sitting in front of her.

A cord pulled her hair back, and I took some joy in seeing the shining curls. Emma had fine waves and clearly knew little about curly hair like her daughter's. It had amazed her when the oil I brought made working through the tangles easy. She used it regularly while Elora slept, doing as I'd shown her. If she had gone much longer without waking, I would have suggested doing something else with it to protect it, but with Emma's constant attention and silk pillowcases, I was glad to see how healthy it looked considering the poor thing had slept on it with little movement for six weeks.

She turned in her chair, looking up at me, and all I could see was Lucia. I knew she was my niece, half of my brother in there somewhere, but that girl on the chair was my best friend, especially with her hair pulled back. I'd been the baby, annoyance to my brother and Dewalt, and Lucia had been kind to me from the very beginning. My heart ached. It wasn't often I thought of her anymore, but when I did, the pain still felt fresh.

I knew she was always on Dewalt's mind, and, while I didn't blame him for it at all, I'd healed after all these years where he had not. For so long, it felt like I couldn't properly grieve her. With Rainier being heartbroken over his friend's death and Emma's leaving and Dewalt being a shred of a person, I felt selfish for my feelings.

I was still young, only sixteen, but I was the only one who held it together during that time. Someone had to. Though Rainier protected me and talked to me like I was a nuisance, I knew I was the only reason those two made it through those first few years. It was by divine intervention that they didn't die from the alcohol and draíbea they poured into their bodies.

Lost in my thoughts about those years of pain and hardship, I leaned against the door frame, not sure what to say.

"I know I look like her," she said. I smiled, and she returned it; it took my breath away. Gone was Lucia, and in her place was my brother. The curve of her lips and the crinkle at the corners of her eyes weren't present in sleep. But looking at her now, it was interesting to see all the people who made her.

"You do, but you look like him—Rainier—too. Your expressions."

"That's what Dewalt said."

"Ah, you've met Dewalt then?"

"He helps with my exercises every day." There was a tightness in my chest. I would have known that and could have come with him if I wasn't busy wallowing in self pity. "I can walk for quite a distance now, but Mama still won't let me do the stairs. She won't even do them with me. She opens a rift and makes me go that way."

I chuckled, then said, "I'm sure she's just worried. You'll be going down stairs in no time."

"Will you take me? I want to get my charcoals, and I was using them in the dining room yesterday."

She looked down at the ground, not making eye contact with me, but little did she know, I was just as mischievous as her when I was young. "You've met your mother, right? I wasn't born yesterday. She'll have both our asses."

"If she catches me," Elora offered, entirely too nonchalant before tugging her bottom lip between her teeth.

"And if you fall and get hurt?"

"I'll say I went by myself. You were never here," she added, and I laughed out loud.

"Then why wait until I'm here? Why not just do it yourself from the start?"

"Alright, maybe I'm a little scared to do it all on my own. But now that you're here..."

She stood, barely coming up past my chin. She was a little spitfire.

"Emma made it seem like you were well-behaved. Obedient, even."

"Yeah, well, things change," she replied, a hint of darkness in her voice. Eyeing her, I wondered how she was handling all of it. The world had thrown a lot at her all at once.

"Things do change, that's true. And just so you know, change doesn't get any easier, even when you're old, like me and your mother."

"You're not that old."

"I performed the bond a decade ago. I'm closer to your mother's age, even though I look closer to yours."

"Who are you bonded to?"

"Uh, no one, anymore. I was bonded to Dewalt until recently."

"Oh. Uh..."

I forced a laugh, wrapping an arm around her and turning her toward the door.

"It was a mutual decision, little one," I lied. "Are you sure you don't want me to just get the charcoals and bring them back up?"

"Actually, I plan to stay down there. The lighting is better in the dining room."

She swiped most of the papers from the desk into a leather folio, and I noticed one looked like a certain prince we both knew. I said nothing though and instead pulled it from her and placed it under my arm. "You'll need both hands," I explained.

A moment later, with one hand on the banister and the other arm looped with mine, she tentatively took one step down.

"Let me know if you need to stop."

She nodded but didn't speak as we continued our way down each step, and before long, we were both at the bottom. When she turned toward me and gave me a hug, I froze. I hadn't expected that at all.

"Thank you, Lavenia," she said, pulling away from me. "Mama and—they talk about you a lot. You gave her the oils for my hair." She grinned wide. "Thank you."

"Don't mention it," I replied, feeling pleased to have helped her.

She cleared her throat and fiddled with her dress. "She told me about how—how you were the first person she told about me getting taken."

"She was very frightened—understandably."

"And I imagine you were angry?" she asked as we made our way down the hall toward the living and dining area.

"Why would I be angry?"

"Well, because she showed up out of nowhere to ask for help. I don't know. I'd be pretty mad if my friend hid from me and all of a sudden just showed up. It's nice of you to forgive her."

Pulling out a chair for her at the dining table, I placed the folio next to the array of charcoals and blank paper left behind from her previous session. "There was nothing to forgive. It was hard on all of us when your aunt died, your mother especially."

"She said he didn't know about me. Is that true?" She sat down in the chair, squeaking across the wooden floor as she pulled up close to the table.

"If he would have known about you, there's nothing anyone could have done to stop him from finding you. I could have found your mother for him—he asked me to do it. But I refused to compel your grandfather. I wanted to respect Emma's wishes. But if I knew you were his? I would have done what he asked of me."

"You really think Mama didn't know? I mean…I've read enough books." She flushed. "How could she not know?"

I laughed, more out of surprise than anything else. "Your mother lets you read those kinds of books?"

"Well, no. But I've snuck some of hers. I'll be sixteen in a few months. It's not like—"

"You don't have to explain." I waved away her embarrassment. "I haven't asked about the specifics of the situation because I don't want to know. But I'm confident your mother wouldn't have kept you from Rainier if she knew. She's a good person, Elora."

"I know," she said, a bit too quickly. "Thank you for bringing me downstairs. And for finally coming to meet me."

"I'm sorry—"

"I'm kidding. Not everyone has time to rearrange their schedules for a secret love child."

I snorted. "Have you called yourself that in front of them?"

"What do you think?" She smirked, and I chuckled, easing into the chair beside her.

"You think you can show me how to draw like that?" I asked, nodding toward one of the charcoal drawings.

"No," she replied. I barked a laugh. The girl was a delight, so much like both of her parents. A sly smile tugged at her lips as her cheeks pinked. She slid a blank sheet over to me as she said, "I can certainly try, but I'm not even that good with them. I'm better with paint."

The two of us sat together for the better part of an hour, and I doodled with no real finesse as I learned about the girl beside me. Though I'd seen Rainier and her white hair made me think of Lucia, her personality was pure Emma. Granted, she looked like her too, but her mannerisms were her mother's. Her kindness and sense of humor belonged to her too. She was a sweet and funny girl, and time got away from us.

By the end of the hour, black dust covered her hands and face, her animated style of speaking causing her to move her hands everywhere and make a mess. She strategically avoided mentioning the father who raised her in her stories, but I could tell it saddened her. I couldn't imagine how she felt. Moments of fatherly love and kindness between Soren and me were near non-existent, but it seemed Faxon had truly cared about her until he found out the truth. I couldn't imagine it. Elora didn't deserve that.

She poked fun at my stick figure drawings as she sketched out the figure of a tall, lean man. Leaving his face blank, she focused on the posture, hands in pockets and a foot kicked up as he leaned against a wall.

"Who's that?"

"Just a figure study," she answered before wadding the paper up into a ball and throwing it into a small pile she'd made.

"Your mother mentioned you've had a few visits from your old friend, Theo? Is it him?"

"No, it's not him. But—" She grinned, her face lighting up. "Theo does come and play card games with me. I'm glad he's here. It...helps."

"I imagine so. You've known him a long time, right?"

"As long as I can remember. He's my best friend."

"Those are good to have," I replied, heart twisting. "Do you have feelings for him?"

Wide eyes met mine, face flushed in embarrassment. "I don't think so. I don't know. He kissed me once, but..." She trailed off.

"But?"

"But it didn't—I didn't...feel...I don't know."

"It didn't feel like you'd die if he didn't kiss you again?" I asked, smiling even though my stomach was starting to hurt.

"Exactly!" she exclaimed. "I love him—*as my friend.*"

"It's important to have best friends. It's hard when lines blur. Have you told your mother about your kiss?"

"Gods, no! You're not going to tell her, are you?"

"Should I?"

She groaned. "Please don't. She might not let Theo come visit me anymore without a chaperone."

"Is there a need for a chaperone?" Given what she'd said about not feeling much from their kiss, I still asked just in case.

"No! I think I'm going to tell him we should just be friends."

"That's probably a good idea. Friends are important, and if he's a good one, he'll understand."

"He's the best," she whispered. Part of me wondered if she wished she felt something, and I understood more than I could say.

"Emma is going to singe both your asses," a familiar voice trilled behind us, and I turned to see the woman I'd come to visit leaning against the archway into the dining room. My heart rate sped up, nearly bursting out of my chest.

"Not if she doesn't find out," Elora said, mischief in her tone.

"Oh, it's too late for that." Another familiar voice rang out, and Elora's eyes widened before darting to the grandfather clock in the corner.

"You're home early," the girl squeaked.

"Not too many people to see today, darling," Emma said as she stepped into the room, unwinding a scarf from around her shoulders. Cheeks pink and eyes bright, she looked better than the last time I'd seen her, but she wore her sadness heavy on her face.

Gods, my brother was stupid.

"I did just fine, didn't I, Lavenia?" Elora asked, attitude in her voice, and I cleared my throat.

"We were very careful," I offered, as Emma turned squinting eyes toward me. "She wouldn't have gone if it—"

"Oh, don't take the fall for her," Emma laughed as her face softened. "I know how coercive she can be."

She stepped forward, running her fingers through Elora's hair and leaning down to kiss the crown of her daughter's head. "Did you finish the garden piece?" Emma murmured to the girl, her chin resting on top of her head as she put her arms around her. It was sweet, and I smiled as I watched the two of them. From our conversation, it seemed as if Elora was still trying to wrap her head around everything and figure out parts of her mother she didn't quite know. I wondered how Rainier was fitting into all of it.

"Ven? A word?" Mairin asked behind me.

I closed my eyes, exhaling softly. I'd come here to speak to her, so I didn't know why I suddenly regretted it. Pushing my chair out, I stood and wadded up my drawing and tossed it into the center of the table with the rest of the scraps.

"Thanks for trying to teach me your ways, Elora."

"Thanks for helping me irritate Mama," she said. Emma pinched her, and the girl squeaked as her mother pushed me out of the way with her hip, stealing my seat at the table.

Chuckling, I turned and made my way over to the merrow. Looking infuriatingly beautiful with fire and autumn curls and plump curves that didn't stop, she watched me as I walked over before leading us out into the great room. Somehow, she set me on edge, making me feel vulnerable. I didn't want to admit to myself that she'd hurt my feelings by keeping her distance these past few weeks since I'd moved into the palace.

"We need to speak about a few things," she said, voice low.

"Yes."

Her gaze tracked over me, moving from my booted feet up to my face, not stopping on the features she'd once paid attention to before. Waving her hand for me to follow, she didn't even bother looking at me.

"You've been avoiding me," I accused.

"Spare me. I'm not—" She sighed, grumpy. "Lavenia, I've been giving you space. But with our upcoming trip, I thought we should talk."

"I had some things I wanted to talk to you about too."

She led us toward the front of the estate, bringing us to the study, where she closed the door behind us.

"The Sea Queen, huh?" I asked, voice tighter than I intended. I watched her freckles blend into the rosy blush painting her cheeks.

"How does one bring that up? Being a merrow is more than enough to elicit fear, but to mention my mother? Besides, she has hundreds of children."

"But you're the last daughter. Mairin…"

"So?"

"That has to mean something. Are you in line for—for a throne?" I asked.

She threw her head back and laughed. I tried not to look at the long line of her throat and the freckles across the ample swells of her breasts.

"My mother would have to die for that, and, well, she can't."

"What do you mean, she can't?"

"I mean, I spent a few hundred years trying."

My jaw dropped, and my blood ran cold.

"Wha—what?"

"The seaborn aren't like you. My mother encouraged it." She shrugged. As if that was why I was dumbstruck. Although, to be fair, I should have found attempted matricide more shocking.

"How old are you?" My voice cracked.

"Oh. Four hundred and something. I forget now. Closer to four hundred than five hundred."

"And you didn't bother mentioning that?"

"Why would I mention it? I've only been land-side for about a decade."

"Why wouldn't you?" I started pacing as she removed her cloak, tossing it onto the back of a maroon wing-backed chair which clashed horribly with her hair.

"Didn't seem relevant." She dropped to the sofa. She wore a dark green blouse with a leather corset over it, and I averted my eyes before I got lost in her body. She was larger than other women I'd been with. Shorter than me with a wide frame, I found her mesmerizing. Her sturdiness was alluring as I thought about her thick thighs squeezing at my head when I'd been between her legs. The swell of her stomach where I kissed it. The dips and valleys of plump soft skin were a place I could call home. I hadn't been with her since before Dewalt ended the bond, and I was angry I hadn't realized the last time was the last time.

"Alright, Mairin. Whatever you say." I shook my head, irritated, as I turned toward the door.

"I wanted to give us a chance to discuss things before we were stuck on a ship together."

It hit me like a slap.

Stuck.

She didn't want to be on the ship with me. I felt foolish for how often I'd thought about her.

"Well, go ahead then." I crossed my arms. "Say what you need to say so you can go back to giving me space."

Patting the spot next to her on the sofa, her voice grew soft. "Sit next to me."

"I'd rather stand."

"Fine. If you're going to be difficult…Ven, look at me."

As stupid as I thought my brother was, I exceeded it when I obeyed her.

"*Sit next to me,*" she said again, secondary lids lowering down over her eyes as the compulsion in her voice forced me to move.

"That's not fair. I wouldn't do that to you. I hate using it."

"That's just one of the many differences between us. I will not feel guilty over using my gift." She'd proven her point by forcing me to sit beside her, though I sat as far from her on the sofa as I could manage.

"I don't like you very much right now."

"Liar." Her smile looked extra toothy at that moment, and it made me realize how little I knew her. Not only was she a merrow, but she'd lived for centuries before I was even a thought.

"You're not my favorite person right now, that's for sure."

"Because I've been giving you space?"

"Space I didn't ask for," I replied.

"That's what I wanted to explain."

"Considering you didn't tell me you were over four hundred years old, I'm thinking it was a good idea you gave me space."

"I don't make it a habit of telling people things about myself when I haven't decided whether or not to invest in them. It's kept me safe."

"Then why are you telling me now?"

"It is relevant to what we will be doing. I want to make sure you know the important things."

"Alright. Anything else?" I didn't know what I had wanted her to say. That she had decided she wanted to invest in me?

"Rainier arranged a meeting with me and Brenna a few weeks ago."

Divine hell.

"And?"

"And she asked about our relationship."

"Of course she did." I rolled my eyes. "And you felt the need to answer her, I presume."

"She wanted to warn me."

"To warn you?" I barked a laugh. "*She* called things off with *me!*"

"Not about that. She wanted to warn me about your visit the night Dewalt told you he wanted to end the bond."

My stomach dropped.

"I didn't—we didn't—I just wanted to talk to her," I stuttered.

"I know," Mairin offered, calmer than I would've expected. "She didn't accuse you of anything untoward."

I exhaled a breath of relief. "Dewalt just took me by surprise, and Nixy got me drunk at a tavern after he brought me back to the capital, and I found myself at Brenna's, and I—"

And I went to someone who I knew once loved me, who had once wanted to be with me. I went to seek validation from someone whose love I'd never doubted when I had it.

"I had suspected you might react that way. Told Dewalt as much. Brenna told me you don't know how to be alone, and I think she's right," Mairin said.

I stared down at my hands in my lap.

"Gods damn it, Brenna," I muttered. "Wait, he talked to you?"

"He did."

"Care to share?"

"He had a suspicion he wanted to verify before he made his decision." She shrugged.

"And whatever it was made you want to stay away from me."

"No. I wanted to give you space to learn to be alone. But this is me telling you I give that space reluctantly. That I would much rather fall asleep beside you and listen to you talk in your dreams. That I would much rather bury my head between your legs and hear your sweet moans as you clench around my fingers. This is me telling you to figure out who you are and what you want."

Explosive heat tore through me, and my lips parted. I sure as hell hadn't been expecting that.

"Tell me when you know," she said, leaning forward and pressing a soft kiss to my lips. "And don't lie to me just because you miss my tongue."

"Know what?" I asked on an exhale.

"Who you are."

CHAPTER 30

Rainier

I UNDERSTOOD NOW. It might not have been in the same way she felt it, but the imposing black structure housing the Myriad Seat made me fucking nauseated to look at now. Knowing Em was nearby was enough to make me worried, given we knew the Myriad had hidden the true prophecy. I didn't even want her in Lamera, let alone a few blocks from the Seat, but here we were.

We had agreed to confront the Supreme after we retrieved Elora and settled into some sort of routine. Because of what had happened though, it had taken quite a long time to get to that point. Knowing how close this man was with Queen Nereza, I had to play my cards right, ensuring every accusation had basis. I wasn't wholly convinced of the Supreme's innocence, but I'd known the man since I was a child. I couldn't understand what he stood to gain if he banded together with Declan; he already had the Seat. He already held power in every city of Vesta. And we had a history of a working friendship together. It made little sense for him to be involved, and from what Nor had told me about operations in the capital, I didn't think he knew what was happening.

But he did know about the true prophecy. That much was clear.

Steeling myself, I moved up the final few steps, wary about the impending suffocation of my divinity. I eyed the drakes on either side of the giant doors, dragons made stone. The likeness was uncanny. I'd have to research how long the basalt monstrosity had stood in Lamera. The gods hadn't walked the earth for millennia, but had some of the drakes survived for longer? I was about to push my way inside, when I hesitated a moment, feeling my way across the bond with the lightest touch, not wanting her to know I was checking in. When we were farther apart, it was hard to feel her emotions unless I actively attempted it—something I'd learned well in recent weeks.

She was nervous, but nothing more than what I'd have expected. Withdrawing back down the bond, I took the final step and was about to push through the door when a rift opened behind me, and Emma stepped through, running up the steps.

"I felt you. Are you alright?" she asked, breathless.

"I'm fine," I snapped, annoyed. "Go back. I don't want them to—"

The door creaked open, and the Supreme himself peeked his head out, a wide smile appearing on his face.

Too late.

"Your Majesties, please. You must be freezing. Come inside," the man said as he took a step back, allowing us room to pass.

"Actually, Emmeline was just—"

"Saying that, myself. It's the wind that gets you. The cold isn't so bad," she interjected, giving me a look as irritation fluttered down the bond.

She stepped past me, not even hesitating to cross over the threshold. Where was the woman I'd had to practically drag up these steps? Had she really gotten that brave, or was it a show for me? I couldn't tell what she was feeling, the bond silent once we stepped inside. I tempered my breathing, trying to calm myself. My hand rested on the hilt of my sword as my fingers twitched. Em flicked her hood back, freeing her hair from her cloak. Back straight, head held high, I wondered how she ever doubted her ability to be my queen.

"I was sorry to hear what happened at the Cascade, but I was ecstatic when I heard your daughter woke," the Supreme said as he led the way toward his quarters. I only grunted in response, but Emma flicked icy cool eyes over her shoulder at me before clearing her throat.

"It has been arduous, but all is well now. How did you know about our plan at the Cascade without us telling you?"

The Supreme's steps didn't falter as mine did. Blunt and direct, I hadn't expected her to ask him in that manner, though I supposed it served her purpose when he answered, unfazed.

"Why, Shivani mentioned it when we corresponded over your ritual. It feels as if there is more to your question, my dear." Opening the door to the room we'd met in all those weeks ago, his footsteps silenced as he trekked across the plush carpet. "Have a seat, and we'll talk about it."

As we sat on one side of the desk, my chest went tight. Distracted by her questioning and confidence, I hadn't even noticed the trapped feeling of my divinity. My heart raced, and I slid my hands down over my legs, wiping my palms off.

"Tea? Water?" the Supreme asked, standing at a sideboard behind his desk. I shook my head, but Emma's hand slid over, wrapping around my knee.

"Water for us both, please," she said as she squeezed. I sat perfectly still, and it was only then did I notice how hard she shook. She was putting on a show. For me? For her? It didn't matter. I slid my hand over the top of hers and interlaced our fingers, closing my eyes as I inhaled deeply.

"So, it appears you mistrust me."

The clink of the glass on the wooden desk had me opening my eyes and finding my voice. "No, we just wanted some clarity on a few things, and to inform you of something you may not know."

"Oh?"

"My mother told you about our plans at the Cascade?"

"Yes, when she arranged borrowing Hanwen's dagger for your ceremony. Which she has yet to return, I might add. Not the first artifact Astana holds, of that I am sure." A slight brow raise was his only tell.

"So, you've realized by now what we know."

"Please, enlighten me," he said, tone dry but not unkind.

"The prophecy the Myriad spouts is a lie," Em snapped, her cool facade slipping. I squeezed her hand atop my knee.

To my surprise, the Supreme bowed his head. "A lie by omission, but yes, I suppose it is a lie all the same."

"Why?"

"Fear."

Silence. Just for a moment, as we both looked at the Supreme, not a sound was made. He ran his hands through his dark-brown, disheveled hair. He'd let it grow long enough I couldn't see the scar I knew ran from ear to ear over the crown of his head. His tired eyes met mine as he heaved a sigh.

"My predecessor didn't want people to know about the Accursed. A conduit blessed by all four of the gods is something near impossible to imagine, let alone understand. And for one to be at odds with the Beloved, the face of all which is good? It was a decision made before I took this role, one with which I agreed."

"Are you the only one who knew the true prophecy?" Emma asked.

"No."

"Who else?"

"Every master and mistress knows. And Nereza."

"You thought to tell one monarch but not the others?" My voice belied my annoyance, and Emma's thumb rubbed over my little finger where it rested. Her confidence and calm soothed, and it prepared me to have it out with the Supreme.

"Nereza and I have known each other for a very long time."

"I've known you my entire life."

"Yes, and you're just a babe as far as being a king is concerned."

"So, my father knew?"

"Your father," he sighed, before rubbing his face. "Your father didn't want to know anything. There is more I've forgotten about your father than you've ever even known."

That surprised me. It was always my mother who dealt with the Supreme and the Myriad. And yet, he claimed to know my father that well? "And my mother?"

"No. She knows nothing. The way the—I couldn't tell her without Soren."

"And Folterra?"

"Yes. Declan believes he is the Accursed because of it. Or yearns to be—I don't know."

"Our spies tell me he plans to make moves on Lamera first. That he's building an army and plans to bring it across the Mahowin Strait. Do you expect Nereza to come to your defense when he does?" He only stared at me, eyes darting over to Em. "You've hidden this information from Vesta, whom you share a continent with, who hosts more of your temples than any other kingdom. And yet you expect us to come to your defense when a product of that information comes calling?"

"I swore a verit oath to only tell the sitting monarchs. I could not tell you until your father died, and since then you've been occupied. It was not for lack of trying—unless you mean to tell me you have received none of my correspondence since your return from Folterra?"

I wasn't sure if I'd received anything from him. It wasn't impossible.

"I realize how this looks." He held out his hands in supplication. "I assure you, I only knew about the Cascade because of Shivani. A smarter man would have never shown the texts with the true prophecy in them until I was prepared to explain it. Perhaps it was subconscious. The weight has been heavy on me all these years because of Soren's reluctance to hear anything. After Larke's death he—" He shook his head. "Despite my attempts, I could not convince Soren to meet with me about the true prophecy. That is why I convinced Shivani, and Medina before her, to allow me to build more temples in Vesta. To watch for any signs of the Accursed. To be ready."

It had been a long time since I'd heard Medina's name. She'd died in childbirth along with the son who might have been king instead of me. I'd always wondered if it was their death which turned my father's heart to stone, but perhaps it had been after Larke's demise when it hardened.

"I apologize, truly. If I had come to Astana, perhaps you'd be more willing to forgive my errors," he said, voice somber.

I wished we were speaking with him in Astana too, for a few reasons. Not the least of which was being able to hear his heart and have a better estimate of the truth of his statements. I wanted to believe him. He'd always been kind to me, warm even, when my father never had been.

"You will need to come to Astana either way," my wife spoke up, and I glanced sideways at her. The Supreme only lifted his eyes to hers, a slight tilt to his head. "You need to clean out your temple. Do you claim no knowledge of what Filenti has been doing? I suppose you know about the task he asked me to complete?" Her brow arched, and her voice held strong.

The Supreme looked confused as he said, "The same task I asked of Rainier. To prove your abilities to protect one another. I'll admit, if you came here for your task, I would have spent a considerable time questioning you. Your divinity was no match for his, as far as I understood, and I worried the bond might not have held. But I see now, I was wrong. Did he question you?"

A cold laugh crossed her lips, sending shivers up my spine. I rubbed my thumb over the back of her hand, wishing I could take away that memory for her. "He forced me to kill a woman with my harrowing. A mistress. Miriam? Does she mean anything to you?"

"No." He shook his head. "I do not believe it. Miriam was seized with apoplexy."

"I watched her die. I assure you, it was at my hand." Her voice shook.

"Why did you not mention it when you were here for the font?"

"Because we didn't know if you ordered the task, and we needed to complete the ritual. I wasn't risking you preventing our access," I snapped. "She needed my divinity."

The Supreme's mouth was parted, looking between the two of us before holding his head in his hands, elbows on his desk, looking as human as I'd ever seen him.

"I—I am finding this difficult to understand. I—Filenti wouldn't do—He has been in charge of the temple in Astana for decades. He prefers to worship Hanwen. He is just and fair. This makes little sense to me."

"He is trafficking your novices," Emma said quietly, and I wondered how she was feeling. So much had happened since she came back into my life, and I knew certain aspects had to weigh heavy on her soul. I hadn't even given the dead mistress a second thought, and I understood now why she so badly wanted to come with me. She needed to make sure Filenti would pay. I had been surprised to find out she hadn't gone to deal with the master herself while I was in Folterra but glad she showed restraint. It was one thing to steal a book from the Supreme, but to kill one of his masters would have consequences which I hoped to avoid.

My wife explained what Nor had told her when they'd sat together in recent days. I'd originally planned on talking to the woman myself, but I changed my mind at the last moment. Considering how she'd helped me, I shouldn't have, but her face was a reminder of those days spent in the dampening cell. I listened with rapt attention, starved for details Emma had refused to divulge. It was a brilliant and effective strategy of hers—denying more than the bare minimum to me while I did the same to her.

I fucking hated it.

"Your masters in the capital are all complicit. We've been watching and have intercepted thirteen women over the past three weeks."

I knew about the guards she'd placed near the temple, hiding in plain sight. I knew they'd intercepted the women. But I didn't know how she'd done it without alerting the masters of what we knew.

"Now, I find it hard to believe that all of *my* masters—"

"Would you like to know how many children? Girls. All younger than my—*our* daughter." Her voice held steady—a viper waiting to strike. Deadly, dangerous, *mine*. "Six. Six girls. Two of which haven't had their first blood."

Divine fucking hell. She hadn't told me that.

"Now, that's enough. There is no way this is true. I'll summon Filenti right—"

"Do it. Summon him," I said.

The Supreme blanched as he glanced between the two of us.

"You truly—" He shook his head. "This is madness. No, it's simply not happening."

"It is, and this is me telling you to deal with it. You will come back with us to Astana, and you will put him down. You have always treated me with kindness and respect. It is because of this, I do not accuse you of having anything to do with it. But the more you hesitate, the more I wonder if perhaps I am wrong about that."

Em's hand squeezed my knee, and in my periphery, I caught her staring at the Supreme, flint in her eyes.

"Rainier, I assure you, if I knew about it, I wouldn't have—"

Emma cut him off, her voice stone. "Just because you didn't know doesn't mean you aren't responsible for what was done. It was your responsibility to know. You will be lucky if Rhia doesn't smite you herself for what they have done in her name under your nose. The novices we rescued from Folterra? Most of them chose to come to Vesta. Do you know how many were pregnant by rape?" When the Supreme didn't answer, Emma scooted forward in her seat, body shaking with rage instead of fear. "Over half of them," she said. "And some of them on their second pregnancy. *You* let that happen."

"I'll gather the High Masters now." He exhaled a breath, shaking his head. It seemed as if he truly couldn't believe it.

"Good," I said as he rose.

"If you wait here—"

"No," Emma snapped, eyes darting to me. "We'll wait outside."

He simply nodded, holding the door open before saying, "Give me a few minutes."

She rose, and when her hand left my leg, I felt a twist in my stomach.

It was a few moments later when we sat beside one another on the bottom stair outside, she tentatively reached out with that same hand. She offered me the touch I needed desperately and had been avoiding entirely.

I allowed myself to take it.

"Are you al—"

"How are you—"

A breathless smile lit up her features, and the warmth she radiated filled my chest. "Me first. Are you alright? I thought because of the..." She hesitated.

"The cell. It wasn't pleasant, but I'm fine. You?" I squeezed her hand.

"It actually wasn't as bad as last time, and I don't know why. Maybe because I was more worried about you."

I looked away, her scrutiny feeling too thorough. She'd always seen down to the soul of me, and I couldn't let her see my want. Not yet. I was getting so much better. I'd told myself if I went more than a week without having a nightmare, I'd go back to her. I hadn't mentioned it to her, not wanting to get her hopes up. The longest I'd gone was five days, and the thought of her asking with expectations only for me to dash them was not something I wanted to deal with. Tonight would make six days, but I worried coming here would set me back. The more stress I was in during the day, the more likely I saw my dead daughter or my hands wrapped around Em's throat. Or the worst nights when I saw Vondi. I'd truly failed the boy, and no amount of remorse would resurrect him.

The clock tower chimed noon, and Emma jumped up with a start, dropping my hand along with my heart. "I thought we'd be halfway back by now," she exclaimed.

"In a hurry, Your Majesty?" I stood, taking her hand back into mine, and she looked at me out of the corner of her eye, wary. I hated it.

"I have things to attend to, yes."

"What things?"

"Things I'll tell you once you share my bed again," she said, and if it weren't for the lip quiver she hid by biting it, I would have believed her rancor.

"You know Sterling reports to me, right? I know what time you leave every day." Without telling me a single thing about it. She left with different people each time too. Dickey, Thyra, Dewalt, Mairin, even my gods damn sister went with her. And not a single one would tell me where she went. Dewalt had assured me she was safe, but the fact he wouldn't tell me more than that pissed me off more than it should have. Dewalt was my best fucking friend, and the two of them conspiring together to keep a secret irked me.

"I know," she answered simply.

"I suppose I'm going to have to follow you if I want to find out?"

"No. You'll have to come back to me, Rain." She withdrew her hand from mine.

"I'm trying."

"You don't need to try. Just come back. Gods, if I have to tie you to the bed so you can't hurt me, I will. Just...How do you expect to be around me again without *being around me?*" Biting, her words were laced with frustration, and I wanted to take that away, but I wasn't ready to put her at risk. Why couldn't she understand that? I was staying at the estate with her. I was interacting with her at dinner with Elora every night. I thought I was being reasonable.

It didn't matter that we hadn't had a real conversation. Or that I couldn't concentrate unless I could see those gods forsaken freckles.

"I've tried being patient, I've tried giving you space, and I don't know what else to do. I thought you were going to talk to Dewalt, or maybe Ven. Anyone. You've shut us all out. You've shut *me* out," she whispered. "You feel how weak the threads are." Blue ice met my gaze when I looked over at her. "Time's almost up, Rain."

Echoing my own words from the fall, her chin jutted out. I fought myself to put a hand on either side of her face and pull her mouth to mine. She was right. It wasn't just the Body either which was weak. We needed to talk, to connect.

"Tonight. I will try tonight." Her lips parted, and I only let my eyes dart to her collarbone for a second before they returned to tracing her perfect features, more beautiful each day, I was sure. Her cheeks and the tip of her nose were pink from the cold. The furrow between her brows relaxed, and the wind kicked up along with her heartbeat. Not sure if the wind was from either of us, or from the winter weather, I took a step toward her, closing the distance. "At some point though, whether or not we need it, I wouldn't mind either of us being tied to the bed."

Her face flushed, not from the cold this time, and she pulled the hood of her cloak up. "You can't say things like that." Though there was irritation in her tone, her lips twisted up at one side.

"And why not?"

"Because you'll make me want them."

"And what's wrong with wanting that?"

"Everything, when I don't know if you'll be able to give it." She crossed her arms, turning away.

"Tonight is only the first night. We have plenty of nights for us, for *me*, to figure it out. Imagining you that way is quite the incentive, you know."

"Who said I want to be the one tied up?" She laughed, her nose crinkling. Gods, I missed her. It wasn't that I didn't want to be around her. I wanted it more than anything. But until I stopped having nightmares and panic attacks, I didn't want to risk it. Only one night had been as bad as the night in the hallway. I'd woken up covered in sweat and shadows, and I'd done what Em taught me, using my light to brighten the room and banish the dark. "After all, you're the one you're worried about," she said.

"And you're not worried?"

"No." Definitive, confident, and final, her voice didn't waver as she gripped my hand.

I had to break my promise sooner than I thought.

When we had returned to Astana, Emma went off to do whatever it was she refused to tell me about, and I accompanied the Supreme and his High Masters to the temple. Having brought a few members of my guard along with us, I positioned them out in the street, waiting to apprehend Filenti or the other masters who might have run.

But none of them were in the temple. There were a few novices in the building, going about their tasks, but they all deferred graciously to the Supreme. One novice hadn't spoken their vow of silence, and they explained no one had seen the missing masters for the last day.

The ground rumbled beneath my feet as I struggled to get my temper under control. I had wanted this so badly for Em. I was kicking myself for not taking matters into my own hands, respect for the man I'd known my whole life and fear of his alliance with Nereza be damned. I should have dealt with Filenti the moment he made her fucking kill that woman.

Fuck.

Though the Supreme intended to stay in Astana for a while, aiding in a High Master's takeover of Filenti's role, he gave his full permission for me to rid the capital of the missing masters if my men found them first. By whatever means I chose.

Not knowing where they were unnerved me, and I decided to tell Em as much when she returned to the estate that night. She wore common clothing—her old boots, a stained pair of breeches, and a plain black button-down shirt beneath the winter cloak belonging to her sister. She didn't fit the image one might expect from a queen. I studied her frame, looking for any hint of where she might have been. Her hair was slipping free from her braid, and her face wore a grimace. Massaging one palm with her other hand, she winced, and I grasped it in mine, gently rubbing away the soreness. Whatever she'd been up to was painful for her.

Though I doubted she would tell me, especially since I was about to break my promise, I thought perhaps a bit of my own transparency would help her understand.

"Filenti was gone. The other masters too," I said, watching for a reaction which didn't come. "And because I fear where they are and what they might do—*to you*—on top of a bad day in Lamera, I am certain to have a nightmare. I can count on it at this point. Tonight isn't a good night to start, but—"

She tugged her hand free from mine and spun on a heel toward my suite—*our* suite. She'd come back late, Elora already asleep in her room, so I walked after her, keeping my voice low as I called out to her.

"Em, I'm sorry," I said, reaching for the hand she wouldn't let me grab as she stalked toward the bedroom.

"I'm tired, Rain. I don't think you—Do you think I don't have nightmares? Over losing you? Over what I did to those women? Over what I saw happen to our daughter? Do you think I'm unfamiliar?" She bit out the words but lost her steam halfway through, as if it exhausted her just to talk about. Yanking her cloak off and sitting on an armchair to unlace her boots, she sighed before continuing. "Kingdoms, years, and utter devastation, Rain."

She looked up at me as she pulled the braid out of her hair, her ocean depths drowning me.

"It means—"

"It means I'll wait." She nodded as she cut me off, standing to wiggle out of her breeches. Gods, the way she swayed made me twitch, and I wanted to toss her on the bed and use my fingers and tongue to make those hips grind up into me.

Too bad I'm a fucking coward.

"Just—You can't tease me like this, alright? I have left you alone, done what you asked of me. And I'll keep doing it. But don't make me think I'm getting you back when I'm not," she said, trailing off into a whisper. I closed my eyes, clenching my fist. Gods, I didn't deserve her.

"I'm going to kiss you—if you'll let me," I added.

"That's not fair. You know I'd never turn away your kiss."

Cheeks still pink from the cold, standing in nothing but her shirt and thick socks pulled halfway up her shins, wavy hair tumbling past shoulders rounded with rejection—the sight of her made me think I was strong enough to stay. It was dangerous. Crossing the distance between us, I allowed my hand to snake up her neck into her hair, and she bowed into my touch.

Leaning down, I whispered, "You're too important." I pressed my mouth to her jaw, just under her ear. "You're the answer to everything." Another kiss, moving toward her lips. "I want to be selfish with you. I want to take risks to be near you." She tilted her head, giving me a better angle to pepper her skin with soft kisses. "But you're the Beloved, and that makes you the answer to all of it."

Moving to her mouth, our breath mingled as my lips hovered over hers. Wide blue eyes, unencumbered by frustration or fear or hesitation blinked up at me, hiding nothing.

"Too many people depend on you, depend on *me* to protect you. We have to fix all of this. If not for our future, for Elora's. I can't risk you."

A tear slipped forth from her lashes, and I closed my eyes, finally pressing my lips to hers. The kiss had little passion but instead held every emotion we couldn't explain. When she finally pulled away, pressing her forehead against mine, I would have changed my mind if she hadn't slid her hands up my chest, holding me there as she took a step away.

"I understand," she whispered. "I'll wait as long as you need me to."

Less than an hour later, head in my hands as I sat on the edge of the bed upstairs, I reached out, using Emma's divinity to listen to the heartbeats in the vicinity. It was no surprise Elora's heart was steady, just on the other side of the hall. I'd peeked my head in to say goodnight, in case she was still up. We'd had a cordial sort of friendship so far, but my favorite part was when we said goodnight to one another. She'd been thinking of different names to call me, each one more ridiculous than the last. She had called me Snoots the night before after she witnessed a sneezing fit, and I'd laughed so hard it brought a tear to my eye. She eventually just settled on calling me by my name. It didn't hurt, not truly, but I yearned for a day when she might think of me as something more.

The girl had a wonderful sense of humor, but I wondered how much of it was for show. Occasionally, I'd find her staring off in the middle-distance, eyes glazing over. And her drawings of the prince were hard to miss. I wanted to respect her wishes, wanted us to pretend he never existed. Considering I wanted to ensure he no longer existed at all, it wasn't an easy task, but I did my best. Tonight was the most fatherly I'd felt toward her when I had picked her book up from where it lay, pages bent under her elbow, and blew out the lamp on her nightstand.

A smile on my face thinking of my daughter, I reached farther, finding Mairin's faster beat next to Elora's room. Her heart always beat faster than everyone else's, and I assumed it had to do with her being a merrow. Next was Sterling, his beat slow and steady as he slept in his quarters off the kitchen. Less pinpointed, I cast the net of my divinity farther, counting the five soldiers I had on watch outside of the estate. I'd brought them with me after my visit to the temple, and it made me feel more assured of Em's safety. Even though we still had the wards up, I couldn't be too careful. Those checks out of the way, I reached out once more. To *her*.

She wasn't sleeping, I knew that. I'd heard the bathwater running after I left her suite. But her heart raced, and I felt something through the bond.

Lust.

Fuck.

One of the golden strings vibrated, and I felt it in my gods damn balls. I was hard within seconds. A clear mental image of her naked body in the bathtub assaulted my senses. I kicked myself for taking the time to check every heartbeat on the grounds before I got to hers. Desire and longing flooded the bond, and I wondered if she'd been keeping it at bay until she felt me.

Divine hell. She had to be close, her heart pounding fast.

Spearing my thoughts at the bond, I let her feel my desire as I fisted myself, stroking my length to the beat of her heart. She caressed the threads between us, letting me know she was there, and gods, if I didn't consider racing down the stairs to her. But the thunderous beat reached a tipping point, and I was about to finish. Relief and love and longing passed down the bond to me, flowing through my body, and the thread between us glowed brighter in the recesses of my subconscious, pushing me over the edge with her.

"Come on," she whispered, tugging my hand as we raced down one hall of Crown Cottage.

I didn't know how she'd come all the way to my rooms without alerting anyone, though it shouldn't have been any wonder considering Dewalt's nickname for her. She always brightened when he called her mouse. It surprised me she didn't wake him or bring Lucia with her. Something about her wanting only me had my heart speeding up.

I shouldn't have been thinking about her like that.

It was a good thing I hadn't fallen asleep yet when she rapped on my door, quick and quiet, and started whispering nonsense I couldn't understand. I'd pulled on my breeches in a hurry and thrown my robe on. When I had opened the door, she bounced on her toes, a gleam in her eye which brought a smile to my face.

"I found it," she'd exclaimed, beaming.

"Found what?" I'd asked, distracted by the wide smile on her face. Always so serious, it was rare I got to see it on her.

"Oh, come on." She had scowled and grabbed my hand before running down the hall.

That had been all she'd said, repeating it every few minutes when she deemed I wasn't fast enough. Heading toward the northwestern corner of the estate, I wasn't surprised when we found the tower and climbed the steps. As we made our spiral ascent, I took a peek through the window, questioning why exactly it was called Crown Cottage. Though it was the most humble estate the Crown owned, it wasn't a fucking cottage.

Finally reaching the top of the tower, she pushed against a dusty door to a storage room, cringing as it creaked.

"You came up here tonight?" I asked, confused.

"I told you I'd find it for you."

"Find what for me?"

She glanced over her shoulder and glared, tossing her head so I'd follow her. "Would you just come here, you oaf, and help me?"

I took a few steps into the room. The ceiling was tall and pointed since it was at the top of the tower, complete with a loft full of junk.

"It's up there," she breathed. "I'm almost certain."

"Em, what are you even talking about?"

"I told you not to call me that."

"Emma," I said, enunciating the second half of her name. "I was half-asleep. You're going to need to be more specific."

Setting her oil lantern down on a crate, she pulled a sheet down off the wall, the dusty window she unveiled allowing the light from the full moon to illuminate the room—and the dust.

And her.

Divine hell, when had she gotten so pretty? Her hair was tied back in a braid down her back, but some of it fell down into her eyes, loose from our traipse to the tower. She blew it out of her face as I stared at her before her eyes shot to mine.

"What?"

"Nothing." *I cleared my throat.* "What's up there? Is there a ladder?"

"If there was a ladder, do you think I'd need your help?" *she snarked.*

"Alright, smart ass. Need me to hoist you up there?"

She started moving crates out of the way, stacking them how she wanted, before beginning to climb. "Just make sure I don't fall," *she said.*

She scurried over the edge of the loft a moment later, and I squinted up, unable to see what she was doing. A moment later, she peeked her head over, smiling down at me. "It's here. I was right!"

"Hanwen's ass, what is it, Highclere?"

"Here, take it," *she said, lowering down a long, black box. Heavy, she dropped it into my arms before she climbed down herself. She didn't need a ladder or me, as it turned out. She took the box out of my arms, grunting as she did, before leading us back down the steps to a lower level of the tower, through another storage room which had access to a balcony.*

"Let me carry that," *I said, to which she harrumphed at me and slammed a shoulder into the door, attempting to get outside.* "Well, can I get the door at least?"

"Hurry; I'm excited," *she mumbled, a sheepish grin on her face.*

Having to provide a bit more force than expected, I got the door open, and we stepped out onto the balcony. It was well into spring, my birthday a week away, but the wind was still crisp; she shivered as she set down the box.

Her robe had come untied, and I glimpsed the thin nightgown beneath it.

And the tight buds of her nipples pressing against the fabric.

She gave a strangled cough, and my eyes moved up just in time to see a pink blush creeping up her cheeks, visible even in the moonlight. I averted my eyes to the box as she tied her robe shut.

"Open it," *she croaked, clearly embarrassed.*

If anyone should have felt that way, it was me, not her. I had just been ogling her, shame the last thing on my mind. Dipping my head, I knelt and began fumbling with the silver latch. It was stuck.

"Turn it, idiot," she laughed, and I let the sound push my mortification away. Doing as she'd said before lifting the silver fastener, I held my breath as I lifted the lid.

A telescope.

Resting my hands on my thighs, I stared down at it. I'd made an offhand comment about the activity I'd once enjoyed doing with my mother, and she'd remembered. That had been last summer. And she had said she'd find it back then, but I'd forgotten, or possibly hadn't taken her seriously. This was the same one I'd remembered from when I was small. The brass instrument was stored at its full extension, spanning nearly the length of my arm. The velvet lined case was a bit moth-eaten, but it seemed in decent shape.

"Are you—is it alright that I—you're not mad, are you?"

She stood next to me, looking down nervously. Surging to my feet, I put my hands on her arms, staring down at her.

"I'm not mad. I'm the opposite of mad. This was—wow, I can't..." I trailed off, eyes moving to her mouth as her tongue darted out, wetting her lower lip. Everything in me wanted to kiss her, but I forced myself to take a step back. "This is the kindest thing anyone has ever done for me. I'm surprised you even remembered."

That pink flush creeped up her cheeks again.

"You seemed so happy when you talked about it. I couldn't find it last summer and didn't have time to look when we were here for Solstice, but I had a feeling it was up here. It was the first place I thought to look when we got here last week." She was talking fast—frantic. Nervous? "And I wanted to give it to you for your birthday, but I knew it was a full moon now, and I thought you might want to use it, and—"

I pressed a finger to her lips, "Shhh." She swallowed as I stepped closer to her. "We might be able to see Damia or Urepa, but it's too bright to see the others tonight." Voice low, I moved my fingertip to her chin and tilted it up. "Thank you, Em."

I had decided I was going to kiss her, was bending down to bring my lips to hers, when her eyes flared. Panic flooding her features, she leapt forward, encircling her arms around my body so tightly it knocked the wind out of me. I laughed, rubbing my hand down her spine, and then wrapped my arms around her, returning the embrace.

"You're welcome," she mumbled against my chest, muffled by the fabric of my robe.

But when I let go, she fell backwards.

No, I pushed her.

I rushed forward to catch her, but my hands moved of their own accord, shoving her from the tower.

*Shouting, I raced forward, gripping the railing.
But when I looked down, she was gone.*

CHAPTER 31

Emmeline

Kicking myself for drinking a glass of water before sleep, I climbed out of bed and tiptoed across the cold floor to the bathing suite. Still dark, I was grateful when I realized I'd have a few more hours to sleep once I climbed back into the warm bed. Finished and padding my way back across the room, a gentle rumble in the earth below me stalled my footsteps. Soft, I would have slept through it if my bladder hadn't roused me. A sick, fearful feeling made my stomach drop and my heart race. It only took me a moment to realize it wasn't me, but Rain through the bond.

Not hesitating, I opened a rift into the hall outside Lavenia's room. I hated that he slept here, away from me, but at least he was nearby. At least I could rift straight to him if I needed to. Hand on the doorknob, I waited. I wanted to give him space. I didn't want to push him when he wasn't ready for me. But he didn't seem to be improving. Would I have to push him further than I wanted, just to get a reaction?

I felt another low rumble in my chest, an echo of what he was doing to the earth below us, and I pushed my way into his room.

"Rain?" I whispered, unable to see in the pitch dark. When he didn't answer, I pulled a flame into my hand and could barely make out his body on the bed, twitching in his sleep. A fine layer of shadows coated him, nothing compared to that day in the hallway, and I could see a faint sheen on his skin. He was having a nightmare.

I froze, uncertain of what to do. If I woke him, I was sure he'd yell at me for coming to him during the time he felt most likely to hurt me. But I wasn't going to leave him, to let him suffer. Nodding to myself, I decided. Crossing over the threshold of the room in easy, confident strides, I tossed my robe onto the foot of the bed before climbing into it behind him.

"You're alright," I whispered, as I encircled his waist with my arm and pressed my chest to his back. Using my other hand to dig my fingertips into his hair, I stroked his scalp, soothing him the best I could. I hoped my gentle movements wouldn't wake him but would be enough comfort to pull him from wherever his mind had sent him. "I'm here. You're safe—we're *all* safe."

Pressing my body tight against him, I tucked my knees behind his. He was so much larger than me, and I was so gods damn grateful to feel the weight he'd put back on in recent weeks. He wasn't back to his normal self, but getting closer, though he still looked haunted more often than not. Molding my body to his, I felt his breathing slow and calm.

He slept shirtless, and I pressed my cheek against the warm skin of his back. Though he was sweating in his sleep, I didn't mind, the touch something I craved. I'd taken a few moments adjusting to the lack of light, the moon barely peeking through a narrow opening in the curtains, and I watched as his shadows slowly receded and the sick feeling in my stomach faded away. Instead, I felt contentment and a hint of melancholy, but the ground no longer rumbled.

Tightening my arm and nuzzling against him, I breathed in his scent. The intoxicating smell of him, those moments after a spring storm, mixed with the sweat drying on his skin. I hadn't been this close to him in weeks, and I reveled in it. I only planned on staying for a few moments before returning to our room—alone. But when it became harder and harder to keep my eyes open, finally drifting off to sleep with ease for once, I decided to stay.

When I woke, he was gone. His side of the bed was made, not even an indent on the pillow to prove he had been there. I stretched before rolling onto my stomach, burying my nose into the bed, breathing him in. Shameless, I didn't care how pathetic it was. I missed him. My husband, my twin flame. Laying flat on my stomach, I turned my head to look out the window. Facing the front of the estate, I couldn't see the garden, but I could see treetops. Stripped of color from winter, they swayed in the breeze. Snow fell from the sky, fluffy as it drifted down. Sighing, I sat up and rubbed sleep from my eyes. I didn't know what I expected. Did I think Rain would wake up and be thrilled? Did I think he'd stay and yell at me? I thought anything would have been better than what happened. Which was nothing.

But when I looked at the nightstand on my side of the bed, my breath caught in my throat. He'd left me a shell. I wondered where he got it. Did he have a collection somewhere? It wasn't as if either of us had been to the beach since Mira. Unless you counted the Cascade, which I didn't. It was tiny, no bigger than my pinky fingernail, but it was a perfect, tiny cowrie shell. Bleached white from the sun, I wasn't sure how he'd even noticed it to pick it out at all. I was afraid of losing it, but I didn't want to leave it there either. I wanted him to know I saw it and knew he'd left it for me.

Carefully plucking it off the table, I opened a rift into my suite and found Elora sitting on my bed. It took me by surprise. I normally woke before her, but not this morning, evidently. I glanced at the clock behind me on the mantle and had to take a second look. It was past mid-morning.

"Finally," she sighed, crossing her arms over her chest before looking me up and down. "Where did you sleep? He told me not to wake…oh. Oh gods. Ick."

I nearly laughed at her repulsion.

"I *slept* upstairs. But, eventually, he'll be alright again, and we'll both sleep down here—permanently."

She gave an exaggerated shudder before standing. "I know. It's just strange. All of this is strange."

She wore a long dress, dusty rose in color, cinching at her middle. Elora's frame was narrow, slimmer than I'd ever been, and this dress highlighted the fact she indeed had a waist—tighter than she usually preferred. She'd pulled her curls back halfway, and I could actually see her eyelashes, which told me she'd darkened them with kohl. I was instantly suspicious.

"You look lovely. Is there any sort of occasion for it?"

"I'm sick of looking like a boy." I laughed, not sure what she meant. "The only time I'm allowed out of the estate is to train with Dewalt and Theo, and I can't wear dresses or look nice for that. I want to look pretty, and I want to *go* somewhere."

Inhaling became difficult. "Elora," I started.

"No, please, Mama. I'm losing my mind. I'm never going to get back to normal if I'm stuck here all the time. Please," she said, hurrying across the room to me.

We still hadn't talked about our time apart.

"Elora, I—"

"Thyra already said she'd escort me." I raised a brow. "I knew you'd say no outright if I didn't come up with a plan. I don't even want to do much. I just—it's just me here half the time. He—Rainier—is doing king things, and you're busy healing people. And since you won't let me go with you…" She trailed off.

Peering down at her, I tried to read her expression. I'd failed her once again. While my daughter had been at home alone, I'd been out healing people. I'd been by her side every hour for a week, drawing with her, reading with her, just being with her, but eventually she grew annoyed with me and asked for space. And I'd been having dreams of women dying in a fire, so I'd thought to channel some of that guilt into helping people with my healing. But it appeared I'd given her too much space.

"I'm sorry, Elora. I'll be home more. I thought you wanted—"

"I did want space. I *do* want space. I don't know—I'm just feeling suffocated. I thought it was you, and that's why I told you to back off. But I still feel like this. I think..." She tugged on her earlobe. "Cyran used to go into town with me. He took me into Evenmoor while I was staying there. I think I've changed too much. I'm not just a child anymore. I want to go do things. Be a person." I nodded slowly, thinking it over. "Rainier said it was alright with him if it was alright with you. Especially after I told him Thyra already agreed to it."

"You asked Rainier?"

"Well, yeah. I mean, he's—I need his permission too, don't I?"

My chest somehow tightened and expanded at the same time.

"Well, where do you want to go?"

Her face lit up. "I need books here, and Rainier mentioned a line of credit?"

I laughed, folding her into my arms. "Let me get dressed, and I'll go with you? *Not*," I blurted, "to escort you. That's Thyra's job. But I'd like to spend the day with you before I check on my patients. If you'll have me?"

"I'd love that, Mama."

Curled up on a comfortable sofa in a back room of the giant bookstore, my daughter and I read the books we'd picked out for one another, her head in my lap as she stretched out. A fire roared in the grate beside us, warm after our short trek through the snow. It hadn't slowed down since the morning, and I wondered if we'd be snowed in tonight. She was nearly halfway done with the book I'd chosen for her, a story about a girl trapped in a tower by an evil king. I knew she'd like it; the girl ended up escaping and falling in love with a shifter on her way to her home kingdom. A romantic, my daughter.

The tome she'd picked for me was a collection of elven stories. They reminded me of a darker version of the story collection of elvish princesses and humans turned into frogs which sat on a shelf back at home in Brambleton. I was reading a short story about the elf king who had grown so old the blood which had once run golden in his veins had turned black. Though they'd all been dead for centuries, it was known elf-blood was made of something precious, part of why they'd been hunted and killed to extinction. Though powerful from the earth magick they possessed, the elves eventually lost their battle. I wondered if black blood was only a myth or if it was true. In the story, King Wuehlnar had to be put down by his seven sons, much too evil to submit on his own. But that wasn't the case for most elves. Most let themselves fade without fighting their eventual deaths.

I glanced down after finishing the story before moving onto the next, and I noticed Elora carefully wipe her face free of a tear.

"Honey?" I asked, gently running my hand down her arm.

"I miss him," she whispered. "I know I shouldn't but...I do."

Not quite certain of who she was speaking about, I dragged my fingers up to her hair and started lightly massaging her scalp. "That's alright, Elora. You can miss whoever you want."

She sat up abruptly, turning so she was next to me.

"Did he hate me?" Still not sure if she spoke of Faxon or Cyran, I just tilted my head to look at her, not wanting to ask and upset her. "Papa," she clarified. "He—I know I'm not his, but I *was* his. Does that make sense?"

"You *were* his, baby. I'm so sorry for what he did. I knew he wasn't a good man, but he wasn't as bad as his brothers or the other men who my father could have forced me to marry, but if I had known he could do something like that, I never would have—"

"Stop, Mama. That's getting annoying." Cautiously, I sat up straighter. I hadn't meant to upset her. Her frustration felt almost like a slap. We'd had such a lovely day together, and I didn't want to ruin it. Her features softened as she looked over at me. "This is about Papa and how horrible he is. Was. Not about the mistakes you made. You keep doing that. You keep making it about how you messed up. It's not all about you."

My mouth snapped shut, and I nodded. She was right. This wasn't about me. This was about her sadness over the man who raised her. It wasn't fair or right of me to turn her grief into my guilt.

"Was he so angry at you for what you did that it made him hate me, too?"

"I don't know." I'd already explained to her that I'd done nothing wrong to Faxon. I hadn't known, hadn't thought it was possible for Rain to be her father. "He might have thought I did it intentionally. That I'd known you weren't his and fooled him into raising you."

I stopped myself from laughing at the idea. If I had known she was Rain's, I would have left Faxon the moment I realized. If I had thought it was possible what we did had created a child, I would have refused to marry Faxon when I did. I'd have told Rain everything. I never would have let him go.

"But that's not my fault," she whispered. "Papa almost got me killed. Did get me killed? I don't know anymore." She sighed, tilting her head back against the sofa. "The shifter's father took the girl fishing in this book. It reminded me of him."

"That's normal, Elora. You miss what you thought he was. I—He had moments of kindness with me. I won't say I miss him, but I mourn the good parts of him. And it's alright to feel that way. It doesn't make what he did any less terrible."

She leaned her head on my shoulder, turning the book over in her lap to hold the page.

"Would you have married Rainier if you knew I was his? Would they have made you? Oh gods, would we have been *murdered*? They murder bastard children all the time in books. Am I still a bastard since you're married now?"

"You know, I don't know. I'll have to ask." I chuckled, cutting off her rapid-fire questions. She would go for an hour if I let her. "But no, we wouldn't have been murdered. He would have protected us with everything he had. I don't know what I would have done. I suppose I would have started by letting him know he had a perfect little girl. I wouldn't have told him about your eyes, though." I smiled. "I'd have let him figure your light out for himself the first time you cried for him. Just like I had to."

I heard her smile when she said, "It doesn't happen that often anymore. I've gotten better at controlling it."

"That's wonderful, honey. I'm—I haven't told you how proud of you I am." I rested my head on hers. "You're stronger than anyone I know. Stronger than me, that's for sure." I turned, pressing a kiss to the crown of her head. She smelled of citrus and sunshine, and I breathed deep.

"I didn't really do anything."

"I wouldn't call biting someone's ear off nothing. Learning how to walk again? Forgiving your short-sighted mother? Getting to know Rain?" She snorted as I slid an arm around her shoulders. "How is that going? I've tried not to bother you both about it, but I can't help but wonder."

"He's very kind. He seems to enjoy my company. I don't know. How's it supposed to go?"

"Well, I suppose just getting to know one another is the first step."

"Uh, well, I guess that's going fine. He doesn't like fishing, so at least I'll never get dragged along for that. And—" She grinned, his crooked smile spreading wide on her face. "He thinks I'm quite clever. *He* likes my jokes."

I chuckled, rolling my eyes. "I like your jokes too, Elora."

"Not as much as he does. He really laughs, not like your laughs, where you pretend to think it's funny so you don't hurt my feelings."

About to argue with her, I stopped when Thyra stormed into the back room where we sat, looking between Elora and me. She'd been chatting with the shopkeeper, the small man I'd met before—Reminy—and by the look on her face, it seemed someone we knew had come into the shop. She widened her eyes at me and then glanced over at Elora. I picked up her meaning, but so did Elora.

"Why hasn't he gone back to Folterra?" She snapped at me, whipping her head off my shoulder to look at me.

"We aren't forcing him to go back to Folterra. If Cyran wants to coordinate with the rebels while safe in Astana, we aren't going to stop him."

"Mama, he ki—"

"I know what he did. And I know why he did it. Your blood is on all our hands. His, mine, Faxon's. You miss Faxon, you've forgiven me, and something tells me you miss Cyran too. I know how sorry he is, and I know you are soft-hearted behind all of that sass and *justified* anger."

Thyra nodded at me, backing out of the room and leaning against the door frame, blocking anyone's entrance. I felt the heat of Elora's glare on the side of my face, but I turned to look at her with a brow raised.

"If it was different, if you had to do what Cyran did to save the world, to save me, for example, would you have?" Her jaw clenched, her temple flexing. Gods, did she look like Rain when she was mad. "I'm not forcing you to talk to him, to even look at him if you don't want to. We can slip out the back entrance here, if you'd like. Besides, if you avoid him long enough, he'll probably leave and go back to Folterra all on his own. To be honest, I hope he doesn't. At least here, he is better protected." Glancing over at the clock on the wall, I felt bad. We'd only been out for a couple hours, and I didn't want to cut it short for her, but I couldn't stay. "I have to go. Do you want me to take you back to the estate, or do you want to stay with Thyra?"

"Stay. I'll stay," she nearly shouted.

I chuckled, pulling her closer to me. "Your legs aren't too sore?"

"I'm fine, Mama. The only thing that might ruin my day is a person out there." She nodded toward the door Thyra had passed through. "And Thyra will keep him away if I ask her to, right, Thyra?" she called out.

"Right, Your Highness," my Second replied. The face Elora made at the title caused a laugh to force its way past my lips.

"Get used to it, Princess," I chided, standing up and pulling on my cloak.

"I'm not a princess yet. You said the council members—"

"Your—Rainier has no qualms with forcing council members to bend to his will on things that are important to him."

And you are important to him, I said with my eyes.

"Ugh, fine." She laid down on the sofa, stretching her legs out and tossing her book over her face. "How long can I stay?" she asked, voice muffled by the book.

"Dinner? Is that good? Thyra? Have her home by dinner?"

"Yes, Your Majesty."

"Thyra," I warned.

"I call you what you want when we are at estate, but here? No. It would be disrespectful," she answered, never turning away from where she scanned the room with her eyes.

Rolling my own, I bent over and pressed a kiss to Elora's forehead.

"You don't have to kiss me every time you leave, you know."

"Oh, but I disagree."

Sneaking out the back door after exchanging goodbyes, I looked down either side of the alley and opened a rift. Doing a quick sweep of the street, ensuring no one heard the rift or saw me walk through it, I determined I was safe to proceed. Leaning against the corner building, I pulled my cloak tight and my hood low. I fumbled for gloves to keep my hands warm. Normally, I rifted elsewhere and rode alongside Dickey or Mairin. Dewalt and Thyra had each come with me once. Dewalt didn't approve of it, knowing it would probably make Rain angry.

Come on, Dickey.

It was late-afternoon and the snow had started to pile up, but I'd wanted to check on a specific woman before her husband returned for the day. Dewalt had threatened to tell Rain what I was doing unless I promised to bring a chaperone with me, no matter how silly I thought it was. He'd determined Dickey was adequate company, so he was the one who came with me more often than not. But he was late. I'd told him I was spending the day with Elora and what time he was supposed to meet me, but after ten minutes of waiting, I took matters into my own hands.

Turning west onto the street, I walked past quite a few rundown row-houses in various stages of disrepair before I found the one I recognized. Blue paint chipped and peeled from a shutter which barely clung to the side of the building, and a crack ran through the bottom corner of the window. There were three steps up to the front door, but the bottom step was crumbling; I carefully skipped it, waiting patiently once I rapped on the door. Rubbing my arms beneath my cloak, I shivered as snow began to settle on my shoulders.

A child no older than six opened it and stared up at me in silence. They hadn't been there the day before, and I wondered why.

"Hello, sweetheart. Is your mama home?"

The child nodded, opening the door wider. Desperately in need of a bath, their hair was matted, and I could see dirt on their face. All they wore was a long shirt to their knees. I stepped over the threshold, assuming Francine was in the single bedroom. The home was small, and she had told me another family stayed above them, using a stairwell in the back garden.

"Francine?" I called out, making my way through the house. Though the child looked filthy, the home was tidy, if in need of a wipe-down. Considering she only had use of the one arm, it surprised me she kept it as tidy as she did. I knew she was likely tired, considering I'd had to re-break her arm the day before. Francine knew I'd have to come back and finish healing her; the twist in her shoulder made mobility difficult. And I had planned on convincing her to leave the man who had done it to her.

I'd wanted to take it into my own hands and rid the world of the scum, but it would have meant exposing myself, which would mean I wouldn't have been able to help anyone. The council had already deemed this activity too unsafe for a queen, and I'd done it anyway. I had to maintain my secrecy and anonymity. The way I worked necessitated trust, and it was clear Francine didn't want to leave the man. She even denied he'd been the one to do it to her. I had to prove to her that I could be trusted, or this wouldn't work.

Peeking my head into the back room, I saw her curled up in the bed, worn out from the day before I guessed. Burgundy hair spilled over her pillow, and the blanket was pulled up past her neck.

"Francine," I whispered. "It's time for our next session."

Walking around the foot of the bed, I nudged her through the blanket and was immediately discomfited by the stiffness.

"Francine?"

Though I heard the heartbeats of the child and others, likely her upstairs neighbors, Francine's own chest was silent. Hurrying my steps, I pulled her hair away from her face and nearly vomited at what I saw. Wide and unseeing eyes looked back at me. Her nose was broken, and purple fingerprints covered her neck. I screeched as I jumped away, turning to leave, to run, to find help. She was irreparably dead, and I needed to get the child out before the man who did this returned.

Stumbling over myself out of the back room, I couldn't find the child anywhere. Running to check the garden, hoping they'd only wandered so far, I didn't expect to get hit over the head so hard I blacked out instantly.

CHAPTER 32

Rainier

Waking up with her arm around my waist had been a gods damn dream after a slumber full of endless nightmares. It had taken a moment for me to understand it was real. I had breathed deep, inhaling the scent of her. She'd gone back to using her soap—I'd brought mine to the bathing suite attached to my room, not giving her much of a choice. I had taken a moment, just a moment, to close my eyes again and relax.

And yet my heart started to race.

Pounding frantic beats against my chest, a small flicker of fear had untucked itself from between my ribs and fluttered up my throat. All because I couldn't see her. Logically, I knew I was in my home in Astana, but this sick panic knew no logic. I'd gotten better, yet somehow worse, in recent weeks. When I wasn't around her, I tricked myself into believing I was fine, and I'd start out warm with her whenever I did see her, pushing myself to hope and try—and then something small would ruin it. Her divinity had calmed me, reminding me it was part of me when I heard her heart. Slow and steady, it beat in time with her soft breaths. I was nearly calm when I heard a soft snore, and I smiled, letting it ground me.

I had cursed myself for scheduling this early meeting with my mother. Slipping out from beneath her arm, I had moved about the room quietly to get ready. She had slept deeply, needing it, and I had tried not to look at the dark circles beneath her eyes, for which I was surely responsible. And when I turned to go, leaving behind the surprise of a shell for her, I had stopped myself.

One kiss. I could hold it together enough to press my lips to her forehead, smooth in her sleep, not wrinkled by stress and frustration. I had tugged the blanket up to better cover her, and done just that, my mouth whispering across her skin, not firm enough to pull her from slumber.

It was the thought of that kiss which motivated me to deal with Shivani and get it over with quickly. Small progress was better than no progress. I hadn't told her, not wanting to get her hopes up, but I'd been practicing banishing my shadows with Dewalt. Em had suggested we learn from Cyran, but I'd immediately dismissed the idea. I had no interest in dealing with the boy—unless it involved dealing with the way his head still rested on his shoulders.

Walking toward my mother's private quarters within the palace, I pondered what I'd been dreaming of the night before.

Her, of course.

An old memory, a fond one. We grew close that summer, but neither of us ever crossed the line of friendship, despite both of our separate desires. It was the next spring, before the summer it all went to hell, when I finally decided I couldn't live, couldn't *breathe*, without pressing my lips to hers. Her finding the telescope for me marked a change between us though. I had felt stupid for being so touched by it, but she'd remembered and wanted to do something nice for me. Me and her sister always had people fawning over us and doing things for us, wanting our attention and praise, but it was that action from her which meant more than all the rest.

It hadn't hurt that over the past year, she'd grown into the most beautiful girl I'd ever seen. Inside and out, she had been perfect. Still was. Gods, I was fucking lucky. But of course, the memory had turned into a nightmare. I'd hurt her, been the one to make her fall. It wasn't hard to figure out why my mind had gone down such a path.

Rapping lightly on the door to her suite, I entered Shivani's room, steeling myself for the onslaught of planning and questions she would bring down upon me. The coronation was in one week's time. I had hoped I'd be back to my old self again by then, but I'd had to readjust my expectations.

I stopped dead in my tracks when I saw my mother on the sofa, knees curled up against her chest as she wiped tears from her eyes. A plate with a half-eaten honey roll sat on the end table beside her, and the curtains hadn't even been drawn. She was crying in the dark.

"Mother?"

She sat upright, placing her feet on the ground and clasping her hands in her lap.

"Good morning, Rainier. I didn't expect you so soon."

"I'm late."

"Oh? I hadn't even realized."

Cautiously walking past her to the window behind the sofa, I drew the curtains and allowed light into the room. She still wore her robe and scarf from sleep. Always perfectly dressed and manicured, she hadn't let me see this side of her since I was a child.

"Are you alright?"

Deep brown eyes blinked up at me, and she shook her head as she stood. "I'll be right back," she said as she took a step toward her bathing suite.

I grasped her wrist as she walked past, not sure where the urge to comfort her came from. Though I didn't blame her for listening to Ashmont, nor did I resent her for choosing the route I would have chosen myself when it came to Declan, I was angry with her for how she made Em feel in my absence. The point of sending the message to her from the Cascade was to ensure she would take care of my girls if I couldn't. And from what I'd been told, she had thought Em a liar. It was up to my wife to decide to forgive her, but I'd forever hold some anger over it. No matter if Em accepted her apology or not. Even so, I felt myself trying to bridge the distance.

"What's wrong?"

She tried to jerk her arm away, but my grip held firm.

"Nothing. I lost track of time. Let me freshen up, and I'll be ready to discuss our plans."

"You were crying. Why?"

"Unhand me, and let me get dressed."

"Get dressed, then we'll talk about why I found you crying," I said, loosening my hold. She glared up at me but turned toward her bathing suite, gliding away gracefully.

Moments later, she swanned out, wearing a long, flowing emerald-green dress. Loose and unembellished, it was a dress more casual than most she wore. She'd swapped out her plain, silken scarf for a golden one with black vines twisting in a pattern. The skin under her eyes was puffy, the only evidence of her tears.

Ignoring me, she moved past me to sit at the table where notes and charts took over every bit of space.

"Nereza is sending two of her daughters to the coronation," she said, not looking at me. "I presume they'll have questions. Enough people saw Keeva packing her things and that squall rather conveniently sank the passenger ship. I assume we shall blame it on that?"

Her words were a smack, and I sat down heavily into the chair beside her. "Gods. I don't know where to start. Divine hell, Mother. Conveniently sank? What the hell is wrong with you?"

She shrugged, eyes lowered to the list of topics to discuss. "I am nothing if not pragmatic. I feel for those souls who perished, but it provides us a rather convenient explanation for Keeva's disappearance. Unless you intend to tell them the truth?"

"Gods, no." That would sign Em's death warrant. I'd take the blame for it before I'd tell them the truth.

"Exactly. Would you have me not extend the invitation? Though they opened the pass for his mercenaries, it seems Nereza has not yet allied with Declan. She is close with the Supreme, and I suspect she will do nothing without his input. It is good you brought him in. Filenti outstayed his welcome."

I nodded, analyzing her. Her words and motions were detached, delivered in a way to unsettle me. She'd been manipulating how I reacted to things my entire life, and I knew what it was when I saw it. "What were you crying over?" I demanded.

"I wasn't crying."

I sighed, rubbing my hand hard against the stubble on my jaw. I had forgotten to shave. "Why bother to lie? I could bring Dewalt—er, no, I suppose I can't do that anymore. I could bring Lavenia in to make you tell the truth."

"You wouldn't."

All I did was raise a single brow as I leaned back in my chair, crossing my arms.

"Then I would know I was right—that I have truly failed you."

"What?"

She sighed, shuffling papers in front of her. "Nothing."

"Divine hell, Mother."

"I know you both say you didn't know, but you didn't keep her a secret from me did you?" she asked.

I stared at her a moment before asking, "Who?"

"The gi—Elora. Your daughter. Did you decide to hide her from me? From the Myriad?"

I blew out a breath, long and low. "No."

"I cannot help but think you didn't trust me back then. You never told me the two of you..." She trailed off, but her meaning was clear.

"Most young men don't take it upon themselves to tell their mother after the first time they've been inside a woman," I said, stone-faced. She cringed in response.

"No, I suppose you're right. The year after the other Highclere girl died, I thought—"

"Her name was Lucia."

"The year after Lucia Highclere died," she amended, "we grew close. Close enough for you to tell me about the ring you had made. I just—" She scrubbed her hands over her face. "Did you miss out on years of your daughter's life because of me? Or your father? Because you were afraid I wouldn't stand with you and whatever you chose to do?"

The vulnerability in her question surprised me.

"No, Mother. No."

"You're not just saying that to protect me from guilt?"

"Do you think so little of me and so highly of yourself? Do you truly think anything you said or could have done would have kept me from my own flesh and blood? Do you know me at all?"

She groaned, burying her head in her hands. I'd never seen her so disheveled. "I have a control problem," she mumbled, and I barked a laugh.

"You don't say."

"There is much you don't know about my life before I married your father. And when you were finally born, my first instinct was to push you away to protect you."

"To protect me?"

"I know it makes no sense. Anything and everything good in my life became corrupted. I thought the best way to protect you and Lavenia was to distance myself, controlling your lives from afar. Soren allowed me to make many choices regarding how you were raised only because of my detachment. But I think I did you a disservice. Did *us* a disservice."

I took a moment to mull over her words. "He didn't want you close to us?"

"He wanted to raise you both a certain way. He—his life wasn't easy either. I think it was his own way of protecting you. The rotating tutors and maids, never having a constant in your life. He wanted to prepare *you*, especially. He viewed attachments and affection as weakness."

I snorted. My love for my girls, my reliance on my friendships? Those were the strongest parts of me.

"I'm sorry, Rainier. I have always wanted what was best for you. I thought surely she would have told you before now, and it seemed like treachery to me. You send that message and then disappear?"

"Emma would never do anything to harm me." A vivid image of her sinking her blade into my stomach came back to me, a phantom twinge of pain just next to my navel. "Nothing she couldn't heal, anyway. And she wouldn't do that to Elora."

"I know that now. I do. She—she is a better mother than I am."

"Yes."

I hadn't intended to say it out loud, but the word struck a blow with her, physically knocking her back into her seat. After a quiet moment, she started laughing to herself, and I wondered if she was having a mental break.

"She threw a dagger at Soren," she chuckled, eyes closed. "And I was too afraid to start a war."

"Well, to be fair, those are two vastly different things."

"I'm still shocked your father didn't kill her. You're the only reason he didn't."

Remembering the words he'd said to me that day had rage bubbling beneath my skin.

Is her cunt that sweet?

And then worse, what he'd unknowingly said to Em about his own kin.

Pray to the gods the dark prince thinks the same about your daughter.

"You mean he only spared her because he didn't want to have to kill me too."

"No." She shook her head. "He said little those last days, but he said he was scared for you."

"Scared?"

"'Love will be his greatest punishment,' he said. 'I'm scared he won't survive it.'"

Frozen, I watched her as her eyes lifted to mine, curious whether I'd see her shed tears over the man who sired me. I certainly hadn't.

"Was it that much torment for him to love you?" I chided, but I wanted to change the topic. I wasn't ready to think about how fucked my relationship with my father was. At my comment though, my mother threw her head back and laughed.

Boisterous, she went on for several moments before finally catching her breath. Wiping away tears from her eyes, she struggled to get out her words. "Soren has only loved one woman his entire life, and she is long dead."

"Larke."

"Yes. Larke. And supposedly he killed her, so when he said that love is punishment, take it with a grain of salt. He was the one doling it out." All I could do was nod. Gods, I envied Em sometimes. Her father was just shy of his seventieth year. She didn't have to sift through centuries of history to learn about him.

"My point was, Rainier, that Emmeline threw a dagger at Soren over an untoward comment. I can only imagine what she would have done if he hadn't called off his order. And yet, I sat here and weighed the merits of sending an army after you. She set Darkhold on fire for you. She would've set the *world* on fire for Elora."

"You're not wrong." Em was a gods damn force to be reckoned with. I was fully convinced that if she didn't have Elora to think about, she would have been in Darkhold with or without an army days after I was taken.

"I hope I haven't ruined things irreparably with her and Elora," she said.

"It is time for new beginnings in Vesta. You can be part of that. It won't hurt to try, anyway."

"Speaking of new beginnings." She inhaled. "Coronation."

And with that, for the rest of the morning and far into the afternoon, we discussed the logistics of the coronation and the ball. I felt a bit anxious throughout the day, eager to get back to the estate. Though I wasn't ready to share her bed, I was eager to share this conversation with Emma. Just to talk to her. At the very least, I wanted to laugh with her about Shivani's tantrum over my refusal to hold a festival. I almost thanked the gods for Declan putting us into a state of war because it allowed me to cancel it completely with no qualms. If I could get away with it, I would have canceled the coronation as well. But between the council members and my mother, I wasn't going to weasel my way out of it. The good news was they agreed to bypass any vote about Elora's legitimacy.

"Elora Vestana. At least it sounds nice together," Mother said, and I choked on a breath.

"I hadn't even—what if she doesn't want it?" I stuttered. I had yet to prove myself to this girl. She had a man who raised her, even if he ended up a monster. "I suppose she could change it to Highclere if she doesn't want to keep Faxon's or take mine."

"Why, in the gods' names, do you think she wouldn't want your name? You're the king." Incredulous, my mother clearly had no experience with what my daughter was going through.

"I don't know. Change? Accepting me? It's a lot for a child to think about."

"She could not do any better than you as a father," she said, resting a hand atop mine. "You are everything your father was not. I don't know where you learned it, because it certainly wasn't from him, and it's not as if I fulfilled that role for you. But I have no doubts she will accept you. Fickle is the heart of a young girl, but I have utmost faith she will see you for who you are."

I nodded, trying to convince myself to believe her. I found myself grateful for our time together, and I wondered if I had been right about new beginnings.

A fist hammered on the door of Shivani's suite, and before I could even stand, it was bursting open and shadows I hadn't summoned had crawled up my arms as I retrieved my sword. Dewalt was already talking when Dickey ran up behind him, panting and running his fingers through his hair.

"—dead body—"
A dull roar.
"—the queen wasn't there—"
A rushing of blood through my ears.
"—no sign of struggle—"
The room went pitch black, and the earth shook.

CHAPTER 33

Dewalt

"Rainier!" I shouted his name as I rushed toward him blindly. "Your light. Remember what she showed you. What we practiced." I was halfway across the room when the shadows thinned, and Shivani fell to her knees. His hand was in hers, and I realized she'd siphoned away his shadows.

"Divine hell, they—gods," she breathed. "I've never felt something like that." She coughed. "They're demanding, aren't they?"

Rainier had doubled over, hands on his knees, panting.

"Fuck!" he shouted, and the ground shook beneath us. "Elora? Is she with her? Is she safe?"

"She's never taken Elora with her before."

"Elora is with Thyra. Emmeline sent a message, told me what time to meet her. I was only a few minutes late. I ran into someone." Dickey turned a violent shade of red as he rushed out the words. I glared at the boy, annoyed.

"See? Elora is safe. It's possible Emma changed her plans. She might have gone to the city guards about the body," I said, remaining calm. In the back of my head, I knew I was wrong. Thyra had gone with Emma to the woman's house the day before, and I regretted not being the one to go with her since it was a repeat visit.

"You said Em was safe too. You promised me, D." He ground out the words.

"I did. She *was*." Gods damn the stubborn fucking woman for going off alone.

"You swore I didn't have to worry about what she was doing, that you'd protect her. Where is she?"

I stared at him for a moment, blinking. I had promised, but so had she. Fucking hell.

"I don't—"

"*Where is she?*"

"Let's go check the estate, just to be sure. Open a rift." I knew it was a waste of time, but I had some hope she hadn't strayed from our plans to keep her safe.

I'd already impulsed her a few times, and knew she would have found me if she could have.

He rubbed at his chest, closing his eyes and breathing hard. Was he checking their bond, feeling over those golden strands? An ache started in my own chest, thinking about the ones I'd once shared with Ven. A phantom pain I still felt occasionally, but I didn't regret my choice.

"She's there, but I can't—it's like she's asleep," he whispered, rubbing harder at his chest. His throat bobbed before he addressed me, vicious and targeted. "Where, Dewalt? I swear to the gods if she is hurt..." He trailed off before pinning me with hate in his eyes. "She is my *gods damned soul*."

"She's been healing people." I braced myself. "In the Wend."

The ground shook hard enough, I heard more than one person scream within the palace as Shivani lowered herself into a seat.

"My gods," she murmured, rubbing her forehead. "You stupid—"

"The Wend? You have got to be fucking kidding me. You let her go to *the Wend by herself?*"

Before I could defend my decision, he was opening a rift and stepping through, nearly getting hit by a carriage. Dickey skittered through behind him, and I followed. And to my utter surprise, Shivani came through behind me.

"What are you doing?"

"I—I do not know," she said. "Helping?"

"Where?" Rainier demanded, shoving past a few people who gawked at us, completely oblivious to the dropped jaws he left in his wake.

"The row-houses on Tembris," I said as I pushed past Dickey to stand on Rainier's left, covering his weaker side on instinct.

"When this is done, I'm going to fucking kill you," he muttered, teeth gritting as he walked with purpose down the street.

"Hanwen's ass, she wasn't supposed to go alone. We'd discussed this. Dickey was supposed to be with her."

"Cover your ears, Dickey," he said, not bothering to see if the boy obeyed. "And what the fuck is Dickey going to do? He's a boy who barely knows how to use a sword. Divine fucking hell, Dewalt. I was trying to trust her decisions, and I thought, like an idiot clearly, that I could trust yours too."

One hand on his sword and the other holding a fist of divine fire, he didn't bother looking at me. I could taste his disappointment and anger. I heard a sniffle from Dickey, telling me he'd heard every word. His head was dipped low, and I knew he felt dejected for having disappointed us. But I couldn't bring myself to care. We were in a load of shit between the two of them.

"She was determined, and it's not as if she's weak. She's never gone alone before. Not until today anyway," I said, shooting a look at Dickey to see if he had anything else to say about it.

"I was only a few minutes late," he groaned.

"Northern end or southern end?" Rainier asked, turning down a road running adjacent to Tembris.

"Barely on the northern end. Close to the fountain," Dickey offered. "House with blue shutters."

"I know the council forbade her from doing this—for *good fucking reason*. I didn't stop to think she'd do it anyway or that you'd help her. Gods, of course she would have done it anyway. Fuck!" He shook his head. "Has anyone recognized her?"

"She usually only heals children or the elderly. Everyone has been too grateful to question her," I answered. She'd been careful until today for whatever gods damned reason.

"How many people has she helped? Fucking hell," he muttered, walking fast enough that Shivani and Dickey struggled to keep up.

"She's been going every day for the last couple of weeks. Not that many. Two dozen?"

Cutting across an alleyway which would spit us out near the fountain, he slowed his pace as he scanned the houses. If I hadn't known they were full of people, I'd have thought they were abandoned, they were in that poor of shape. Doors hung off hinges, and many didn't have panes in their windows anymore. It was the worst part of Astana, and of course, the place she wanted to help the most.

Because of course she didn't want to make my life easy.

"One of us always escorts her. In and out, no questions, no money. Nothing." I should have known better.

"So, three people who are highly visible as the queen's companions? Hanwen fucking help me. And today's patient?" he asked, walking out on Tembris with his head down, considerably calmer than just a moment before. A predator on the prowl, his grip on his sword didn't change.

"Uh, a woman. I know that. Dickey?" I asked the boy who huffed as he kept our pace, Shivani a few steps behind him.

"The one whose husband..." He trailed off.

"*Fuck*." We were in such deep, unyielding shit.

"Explain. *Now*," Rainier demanded, and the ground shifted the slightest bit below us as we approached the fountain. Dry over the winter, it seemed to house at least two vagabonds judging by the piles of belongings inside it.

"She normally doesn't go back to the same house twice, but I remember her saying something about the woman's shoulder. I—uh, fuck. Emma thought the husband might have hurt her. The body must have been the wife, not—"

"*Not* Em," Rainier said, clearing his throat. "I feel her but..." He hesitated, stopping on the sidewalk beside the fountain, staring up at the house with blue shutters before looking north down Tembris. "She's that way, but I can't just follow it blindly. She's too far."

Nodding, clearly deciding what to do, he pivoted toward the house Emma was supposed to visit before speaking curtly. "Mother, go back to the palace. All you're doing is garnering a crowd."

He was right. Everyone on the street had either run into their homes or boldly stared.

"As if you're not?" she retorted, and I heard him sigh.

"On your head," he replied. "Dickey, I thought you said there was no one else here."

"I did. Just the b-body."

"Then why do I hear a heartbeat?" He raised a brow, unsheathing his sword as he kicked in the door in one smooth movement. I rested my hand on my own and filed in after him. There was no sense in everyone brandishing a sword in such tight quarters. I had to keep reminding myself I couldn't compel anymore, and having my hand free would make it easier to weave a vision if needed.

Rainier held a hand up to stop us as he crept through to a back bedroom. The house was tidy, even if plaster was flaking from the walls and cobwebs coated the corners of the room. The home didn't look lived in. Nothing boiling in the hearth, no wood in the stove. I peeked my head out a back door leading into an enclosed garden, and I saw nothing strange. A moment later, Rainier came out of the back bedroom, carrying a small child.

"Here, Mother," he said, gently handing the bundle of filth off to Shivani. It surprised me to see her take it in stride, holding her arms open wide. "Do either of you know the name of the man who lived here?" Rainier looked at both Dickey and me with an expression of such distaste, I felt my stomach plummet. I wondered if perhaps he wasn't lying when he said he'd kill me.

"No," we said in unison.

"For fuck's sake. Did she know? Did she even think to look into that?" He swore under his breath. "Gods damn it, Em."

The ground below us shook, and Shivani took the child outside into the garden.

"I'll go ask the neighbors," Dickey offered, and Rainier responded with a quick tip of his chin. I started rambling the moment the boy left.

"I'm sorry. She usually has someone with her, and—"

"Stop talking before I take the breath right out of your gods damn lungs."

"Rainier—"

"I said *stop fucking talking*. We never found Filenti. He has nothing to lose."

"What would they—"

"Hanwen take my divinity, I swear on every star in the night sky if you do not shut the fuck up, I *will* kill you. I trusted you, and you let her work in the Wend. *Without any protection.*"

Rather than continue arguing with him, I stopped talking, pulling my braid loose. Thyra had plaited it the night before, far too tightly, and it was killing me. Rubbing at my scalp, I blew out a breath. He was right. I'd tried to convince her not to do it. At the very least, I'd made her agree to a chaperone—and I was angry with her for ignoring our deal. But at the same time, she was a grown woman.

"What did you expect me to do? You know her. She was going to do whatever she wanted. With or without me."

Before I had a chance to react, Rainier had an arm barred across my chest, shoving me against the wall near the back door.

"I expected you to *tell me*."

"And she asked me specifically not to tell you. You want me to disobey my queen?"

"I want you to respect your fucking king and your gods damned *brother*. You know the shit I've been fighting with this." He gestured to the shadows creeping up his arms, moving quickly toward his shoulders. "I swear to the gods, if something happens to her—"

"Thomason," Dickey shouted, running back into the house and gaping at the two of us, mouth open. Rainier hadn't hurt me, but he dropped his arm all the same, though he didn't back away. "And he works at the mill."

"Which one?"

Dickey looked panicked before backing out of the door a step. "I'll go ask."

"No, don't bother. She's to the north. It has to be the Nordingtree mill."

He stepped back from me, attempting to open a rift.

"Fuck!" he shouted, punching a hole in the wall when he couldn't do it. Shadows whipped around his body before he banished them within a second. It was the fastest I'd ever seen him control them. If he wouldn't have beat my head in, I would have commended him for it. But he was too stressed to open the rift, knowing she might be in danger. I needed to walk him through it.

"Feel for the bond. She's there. Focus on it, and stay calm. Breathe in."

"It's not that. I don't remember the mill. It's been years. I've stayed away from the capital for too long. Fucking hell. I don't remember it." He trailed off, voice going quiet.

"Then we'll ride. I'll grab us some horses. You'll have to give me a few minutes; I doubt I'll find any on Tembris."

"It's at least an hour's ride. Dickey, how long has it been since you were supposed to meet her here?"

The boy dipped outside to get an eye on the clock tower. "Just under two hours," he said, coming back a moment later. It had taken Dickey some time to run to the palace and get through the various guards to speak to me. And, of course, I'd been all the way at the barracks, on the other side of the grounds from Shivani's quarters.

"What do you want me to do?" I asked.

"Go back in time and tell me my wife wanted to heal people in the gods damned Wend."

I understood his anger, but now was not the time. "This could have happened anywhere. Fuck, the Bell Street Butcher from a few years ago lived in the fucking Brigand, Rainier. That's the nicest neighborhood in Astana. Poor men aren't the only men who abuse women."

"Is that supposed to make me feel any better, you fuck?"

"I should have told you, but I thought she'd be smarter than just going off on her own." He lifted his eyes to mine and stared blankly. "Alright, fair," I said, and Dickey snorted behind me.

"Just give me a minute to remember," Rainier said, as he slammed his body down onto a wooden chair.

Shivani came in a moment later, and the child followed behind her, tentatively sneaking out behind her billowing dress.

"Robbie says his Mama has been asleep since Papa came home and told him to get out of their room. They were yelling a lot. Do you want to tell them what happened after?" She knelt beside the boy, and I felt a pang. I'd never seen her be soft like that to Ven, let alone Rainier.

"Papa left for a while but came back with a wagon. He said Mama was sick and a lady would come help her. Is she gonna be alright? She wouldn't wake up. Is she dead?"

"Oh, darling. We will talk about that in a few minutes, but can you finish telling them what you told me?" Shivani closed her eyes, pained, as if she didn't want to force the child to keep talking. Wanting to comfort him instead. It was out of character for her. He gulped, nodding as he brushed his long, ratty hair out of his face—dark brown with hints of red.

"He hurt the lady who came to help Mama. Papa made me wait in the garden, and then he hit her when she came out. He put her in the wagon with the other man and left."

"The other man?" Rainier inquired, quick and precise. The boy jumped, moving behind Shivani.

"Did you know the other man? Does he work with your papa?" Shivani asked, rubbing a hand down the boy's arm.

"No. It's the man who usually wears white."

Fuck.

"From the temple?" Shivani prodded, and the boy dipped his head.

The ground trembled once more.

CHAPTER 34

Emmeline

I WOKE WITH A knife to my throat as someone shoved a gag into my mouth. My hands were bound, nearly numb, and I could barely move. Freezing, I glanced down, relieved to find myself fully clothed, though my cloak was halfway torn. Covered in a fine layer of snow, I was drenched. My braid soaked through my shirt, heavy against my chest, and my breath puffed out in a cloud in front of me.

Ignoring the man who knelt beside me, I blinked, my vision doubling. My back was pressed against a stone wall, and water trickled nearby. Light filtered in through cracks in the wooden walls across from me, and a few snowflakes drifted down from the ceiling. Looking around, I saw sacks of what appeared to be flour leaning against the wall. It couldn't have been long since I was taken; my head didn't hurt bad enough for me to have been knocked out for an extended time. The knife pressed harder against my throat, right across the artery. One wrong move, and I'd be dead.

But I could still use my divinity. Wary of the knife held to my throat, I chose to do something discreet with it while I found my bearings. Closing my eyes, I willed it to heal the back of my head where I could tell my scalp had split, dripping blood into my hair. I shivered, and the man in front of me laughed, the scent of alcohol on his breath.

"She's freezing. You sure I can't warm her up?"

A cold *tsk* had me looking up at another man who hovered over me, and a cool trickle of fear iced down my spine. The master with the letter opener. The man who had handed me a letter opener to slice my palm to prove my divinity and sneered at the handkerchief I used to clean it. A neat black beard and bright amber eyes stood out against alabaster skin, and his clothing, though plain, was equally tidy.

"If you put your own beast of a child in her, he'll have to wait. So, no. If you can't control your vile urges, hand me the knife," the man said. I couldn't remember his name, wasn't sure if I ever even knew it. But he was one of the two men who had stood alongside Filenti, forcing me to kill Miriam. "I know she can heal herself, but I don't know if she could survive us cutting your spawn out of her to ready her for the king."

A shiver wracked through me, the cold and fear creating a maelstrom of nervous movement through my body. The master smiled as he knelt beside me. Using his index finger to tilt my chin up, he chuckled before speaking.

"Filenti and Andron will be here soon, and we'll be on our way. Andron will rift us."

I glared at him as I tried to spit out the gag. The other man laughed and pressed the knife close enough I felt my skin break.

"Easy, Edrick. If she's dead, she can't carry a babe. Stop," the master said.

"You said you'd pay me."

"That was before you killed your wife. You made this harder on us."

"She talked back to me."

"You weren't supposed to kill her. Just do enough harm to get *her* to return."

I closed my eyes, leaning my head against the stone wall. Edrick pressed the dagger closer. I'd been set up; they'd been watching me. I sighed, and I felt a single tear roll down my cheek. It burned against my face, salty rage. I'd made a mistake. Perhaps Rain had been right in every choice he made when it came to me. Maybe I *couldn't* be trusted to take care of myself.

Thyra and Dewalt were too recognizable. Hell, I'd made Elora dip her hair in brun root, and it had done nothing. I was stupid to think I could have blended in. My desire to do something blinded me—my desire to be useful. Elora needed space, Rain wouldn't let me help him, and I was drowning in my guilt over the women I'd burned alive. Sway the balance toward good. That's what I'd been attempting to do. What place needed more good done for it than the Wend? It had called out to me, and I felt the pull in my bones to do what I could there.

Though, I should have known better. No good deed, and all that. But I was reckless, and this was my fault. I hadn't even thought to listen, to use my harrowing at the door, before I went into my patient's home. My chest ached. Francine had died to trap me. Sorrow wrapped its way around my heart, and my insides clenched tight.

"The bitch deserved it. We got her, didn't we?"

"And there are too many ways this can go wrong because of you now. Just one more time. That was all we needed."

Anger lancing through me, my eyes whipped to Francine's husband. The man who'd beaten his wife so severely, it was going to take me two visits to ensure she kept shoulder mobility. He was supposed to continue beating Francine, luring me back to heal her. A whisper of a shadow skimmed over my skin, down near my ankle, and I waited for the men to notice. I didn't breathe, didn't move, just let the shadow hover over my skin. I just needed a moment. A single moment, and I could use my divinity to kill them both.

Glancing between them, focusing on one another in the argument, I made my move. No longer listening to the men, I closed my eyes nearly all the way, letting them think I wasn't paying attention. Instead, I willed my shadows to travel up Edrick's leg, twining around his calf without touching him. I needed to make sure I'd have enough time to get away.

A few things happened in quick succession. Just as I was about to tighten my rein on the shadows, a door banged open in my periphery, light and snow pouring into the room. The storm had worsened significantly, the wind pushing the door wide. As my eyes rounded at the intrusion, the newcomer shouted, and the master in front of me had his own dagger to my throat.

"Drop them, now."

I did the opposite, allowing the shadows to climb up Edrick's body. He fell over, tugging at the bindings I'd created out of nothing—the act futile. I tested my limits, allowing the shadows to keep moving and sliding up around his neck. They needed my body, after all, to carry a baby. They wouldn't hurt me.

The master in front of me pressed the dagger in farther, leaning in to whisper with hot, rancid breath on my ear. "I don't care if you kill him. You turn the shadows on me though, and I'll slice your neck open and fuck the hole it leaves. I'm not dying over you."

He leaned back, staring at me with golden eyes. I let my own convey my message as I allowed my shadows to squeeze. Not breaking eye contact, I continued choking the man who laid at my feet. The master chuckled, allowing the blade to once more break my skin.

"She is not as confident as she seems. I can hear her heart racing," the familiar voice said, moving farther into my line of sight.

Before I could act, I heard a rift open behind me, knocking me forward, and I grunted when a sharp pain rasped across my neck. My shadows dropped, and I would have gasped if I didn't have the gag in my mouth. I watched, eyes wide, as blood sprayed out onto the dusty wooden floor below me. Instinct overtaking me, I rolled to my shoulder, just enough to draw my pinned arms up and press my hand to my neck, stopping the bleeding as I used every bit of my divinity to heal myself. Blood bubbled past my fingertips, my racing heart working against me. The fact I could still breathe told me the wound wasn't deep, but gods, did the floor turn red all the same.

"Divine hell, Andron. You couldn't have been more careful? Get the collar on her."

Just as I finally caught my breath, the blood slowing as I panted, cool metal closed around my neck with a clang, and the touch of it on my skin burned. My breathing turned into a hiss, and I choked on it, coughing. Divinity stamped out, I knew obsidian was inlaid within the collar.

"Truly, could the lot of you have made this any more difficult? I think not."

The cool, pinched voice of the master who forced me to stop a woman's heart seared my mind.

I had high hopes you'd be successful.

Haunting grey eyes appeared in my mind, dark brown hair pulled back into a severe bun. A sacrifice. I'd thought of her words frequently since that day, especially after what happened at the Cascade.

They suspect you are not what you appear.

Had she known I would be the Beloved? Had the seer known? Told Miriam she had to die—for me? To fulfill the prophecy and bring peace? Watching Elora sleep, not yet waking, I'd thought of my success in bringing her back. I'd started her heart, just as I was supposed to do for the mistress. I might have been able to save her, and the knowledge of it cut deeper than having to do it in the first place.

"Deal with the drunk. We're not taking him."

"Why bother? He's worthless. Just leave him here," Andron, the man who clamped the collar around my throat, said as he sat up, straddling my hips. I bucked, trying to throw him off. My arms were trapped beneath me, still tied at the wrists and tucked under my chin from healing myself, but I tried to push up on my elbows. I couldn't do much before Andron threw me back down to the ground. His knee pressed into the center of my back, and my face slammed to the ground, blood and dust mixing into small clumps beneath my cheek. His full weight on my back was painful, and my breaths grew labored.

"He knows the route we are taking, and I don't want them compelling him for the answer." Filenti looked down at me, a sneer on his face. "Can't have her getting free."

"I told you we should have taken her that day."

The master I woke up to, the trimmed beard and amber eyes, had scrambled backward after I fell onto his dagger. From where I was pinned, all I could see was his leg and my blood saturating his pants. I felt dizzy from blood loss or the knee to my back; I wasn't sure.

"You know we had to be certain, Tor. I wasn't going to deal with—"

"I know, I know. How do you know she isn't already with child?"

"She had her courses last week, and he hasn't slept in her bed since. It will be fine."

Though I was growing drowsy, barely able to follow their words, the confidence in his voice surprised me, and my eyes snapped to his.

"She wonders how I know that," Filenti said, tilting his head as he knelt, a fingertip reaching out to brush my hair off my face. I reared back as much as I could with Andron on top of me, not wanting the stain of his touch. "Servants like to gossip, *dear heart*."

I thrashed, trying once more to push the gag out of my mouth with my tongue.

"Careful. You'll break open that pretty neck again," Filenti said, thick dark brows arching in mock concern. "I quite like my own, so we need to go. Andron, deal with him." Filenti nodded toward the drunken man as he pulled himself to his feet.

Andron finally climbed off me, and I could take a deep breath, though the burn around my neck stifled it. My chest hurt as I breathed, and I wondered if a rib was broken. Rolling onto my side, out of my smeared blood, I stared at the ceiling as I found my bearings. Being deprived of oxygen, blood, and divinity left me weak. The wind outside roared, though it could have been the ache in my head, and horses spooked outside. The first master, Tor, approached me, and pulled me up to my feet, a rough hand positioned in the crook of my arm, and led us to where Filenti stood.

"What do you want me to do with him?" Andron asked as he knelt over Francine's husband.

"You have a dagger. What do you think?" Filenti said, as he grasped my other arm, pulling me tight against him. He brought his mouth low, close to my ear. "Why didn't you bring Miriam back? Restart her heart?" Though I was already shivering, my cloak discarded and clothes soggy thanks to the snow, goosebumps of disgust traveled down my spine. My hands were even more numb than before, and I clasped them together, threading my fingers for warmth. Filenti rubbed a hand down my arm, and my stomach roiled. Movements still sluggish, I jerked away from him.

"We know you can, so why didn't you? Because she was part of the Myriad? One of us?" He yanked on my arm, hard, and I stumbled into him, unable to catch myself properly with my wrists tied. The master steadied me before grasping me by the chin, bruising me as he turned my head, and I cried out in pain around the fabric in my mouth. "You wouldn't have been able to take the vow of silence. Pitiful creature. Your sister was far more obedient."

I blinked, taken by surprise for just a second. And when Filenti laughed, I took the opportunity I had, the one and only moment I might get, and kicked him as hard as I could in the side of his knee. And he fell. I swung out again, aiming for his chest, but he grabbed my foot, pulling me to the ground with him. I was kicking furiously, grunting and screaming through the gag. Tor stumbled over, reaching for my hands, and I reared back before swinging my head forward and bashing him in the skull. It hurt, and when I fell back, the reverberations rippled through me.

On instinct, I attempted to reach out and listen for the heart of anyone who might be outside. The only salvation I could think of. And of course, I heard nothing because of the collar. Given we were in a mill house, the millstone and flour giving it away, I knew we were on the outskirts of the capital, and I'd be lucky if anyone was nearby. I tried to pull myself up, but I was still shaking—from cold, blood loss, bashing my head against both Tor and the ground. It took me a beat to understand. Rain. He shouldn't have expected me until dinnertime, and it was still far too light outside, even with the snowstorm. But still, I felt the rumbling in the earth. It grew stronger by the second, and I knew he was on his way to me. My relief found its way out of me in the form of hot tears burning a trail down my frozen cheeks.

The ground shook hard, rattling the wooden shelves on the wall. I wasn't sure if Rain just didn't bother to control it, hoping to intimidate, or if he truly couldn't while knowing I was in danger. It didn't matter. The result would be the same.

"Andron, come on. Make the rift." Having finished off the man I'd half-killed myself, Andron stood and obeyed. I wasn't going to let them take me anywhere. Tor was doubled over, nursing the broken nose I'd probably given him, when the door burst open and knocked him over. Bright and blinding, light poured in, the wind whipping through, making it harder to see as it carried the snow with it.

Momentarily distracted, Filenti's hands closed around my ankles once more, and I started kicking. I didn't fight for myself, but for my family instead. Rain was still dealing with the nightly torments from his time in Folterra, and I couldn't let this happen to him too. He wouldn't come back from it. I was worried enough as it was that he wouldn't come back from his time in the dungeons. But if I was taken from him? It would only get worse. Elora was still finding her footing in this new world, and she'd need me. It was with determination to see him through his pain and see her through this transition that I fought, the rumble in the ground growing louder and more forceful.

The door stayed open, wind and snow whipping around the room. I was so gods damn cold, but fear and fury heated my body. Filenti lost his grip on one leg but held onto the other while I kicked out, my boot making contact with his eye.

"You bitch," he spat as he let go of me. Scrambling backward, I did my damnedest to slide my wrist out of the rope. I'd be able to do more if I had both hands. Andron dropped the rift he'd made, clearly unable to hold it open without his full concentration. I scrambled to my feet as both he and Tor, blood running down his face, approached me, and I backed away until I stumbled into the millstone.

I could barely stand, the ground shaking so forcefully, and I struggled to balance without being able to grab onto anything. I only had to make it a few more moments. Rain would rift the second he could. He'd get here and stop them. Just a little while longer, and I would have his help.

Tor realized it too, rushing me as he said, "Rift, now."

In the scuffle, my gag had come loose to an extent, falling down my chin.

"Your plan won't fucking work," I choked out as I thrashed beneath Tor, my legs pinned by his upper body. "I can't have more children," I said, not sure if it was a lie.

With the millstone behind me, I had nowhere to go, and he dodged me as I swung my tied fists toward his face, figuring he'd expect my kick. He crowded me, wrapping both arms around me and picking me up at the waist, dragging me backward to where Andron struggled to open a rift. I could barely stand upright, and I worried about the mill house falling apart, the structure holding the giant stone fracturing and sending it crashing to the ground. Rain had to be close. Filenti was next to the other master, screaming into his ear. Tor buried my face in his chest as I struggled, trying to pull away, stomp on his instep, anything, when I heard a voice I recognized.

"Masters, please. Let us discuss what you're doing."

Tor froze, barely holding onto me, and I stumbled back.

"Y-Your Holiness," he stuttered out, and I looked over his shoulder. Sure enough, the Supreme stood in the doorway, white robes billowing out with the wind. He wore a thick, white cloak embroidered in gold filigree, and his hands bore white gloves. Lit from behind by the dull white of the storm, he looked sent by Aonara herself. But what did he expect to do? He was a healer, and he didn't appear armed.

"The rift," Filenti hissed, paying no heed to the Supreme.

"You won't be able to rift. The mill house is warded."

"Who?" Filenti demanded, turning to face the Supreme.

"A former novice. She was quite eager to help me in my task of finding you. You'll recognize her?"

Nor stepped into sight behind the Supreme, and I blinked in surprise. I hadn't seen her since building the dormitory for the novices we'd recovered from Darkhold, and the past few weeks had been kind to her. I knew she'd been training, something Elora had mentioned, but I had heard little more. Still narrow, her face looked healthier, the dark circles she had worn gone. Her clothes were dark, not the white of a novice, and light brown eyes stared at Filenti with powerful hatred.

"Of course, she's fucking elvish," Andron murmured to himself.

I hadn't realized it when I met her, but looking now, I could see a slight point to the tips of her ears, barely noticeable. She had at least a drop of elf-blood. I slowly backed away, trying to put as much distance between the three men who still carried at least one dagger amongst them. Snow pinked by my blood was slick beneath my feet, and I slipped, falling to a knee. In an instant, Filenti was behind me, tugging on a fistful of my hair.

"Break the ward so we can go. We'll leave her."

"Why would I do that? The king will be here any moment. Can't you feel that?"

"How did you find us?" Tor asked, hands loose at his sides as if he'd given up.

"I didn't. She did." He nodded at Nor. "She remembered the men who helped ferry her across to Folterra. She's been waiting for you to make a misstep and alerted the city guard and me as soon as you did. I assume they're not far behind the king."

Nor and the Supreme set after us on their own? I glanced at the woman, her face set in a grim line. On the ground were markings, the side of a circle. Had she been drawing the boundaries and uttering incantations this entire time? Andron tried once more to open a rift and failed, and I hoped her ward would continue to hold.

The shaking ground caused me to pitch forward, and I would have fallen on my face if Filenti didn't have a grip on my hair. He stumbled too though, and the twist of my body told me my rib was definitely broken. Groaning, I tried to steady myself the best I could.

"I told you. I'm barren. I'm of no use to Declan," I gritted out, and Filenti jerked my head back.

"We'll leave it up to him to decide."

I heard Rain's rift before I saw him. Filenti pulled me up, putting his blade to my throat and holding my body in front of him as a shield. I closed my eyes, remembering Elora being held in the same manner. I lifted my hands, grabbing onto his wrist and tugging it away from me, but he was stronger. Both Tor and Andron fell to the ground twitching, holding onto their throats as my husband pushed his way past Nor and the Supreme, Dewalt following behind a moment later.

"Let her go," Rain demanded. An avenging god, his dark cloak billowed behind him, and his anger turned his expression to stone. He held one hand in front of him in a fist, giving himself a physical control on his divinity. Nonplussed by the twitching men on the ground, his eyes were on Filenti. An idea came to me. The Supreme was right there, and he could heal me as long as we were fast enough. I silently pleaded for Rain to look at me, to see the plan I'd worked out. With my hands on Filenti's wrist and Rain taking his breath, it wasn't likely he could do enough damage that the Supreme couldn't fix it.

"Do you have the mark?" Filenti's breath was hot in my ear. "Is it in as delicate of a place as it was on your sister?"

My stomach folded over on itself, and I wanted to retch. I knew what he spoke of, aware of my sister's birthmark just below her hip—a spot of white shaped almost like a star.

"You're disgusting. Let go of me," I said, twisting in his hold, moving so the blade wasn't over my artery.

"She said the same thing," he rasped, and I threw up my elbow, trying to hit him in the chest. The blade bit into my neck, and I heard Rain yelling. He must have realized his only option was to take Filenti's air, because the master stopped talking, and his veins bulged out of his neck as he pressed his blade against my skin. I held onto his arm, doing my best to keep the blade from digging in too deep. When Filenti fell to his knees, bringing me down with him, Rain was there, grabbing at his wrist with me, lending me his strength, as Dewalt pulled back the master's head.

When blood sprayed over my face, I feared it was my own, but the hand against my neck went limp.

"Holy gods," the Supreme whispered. Rolling flat onto my back, out of the master's grip, I saw Dewalt standing over me, holding the severed head of the man who'd just tried to kill me. He tossed both his sword and bloody trophy down as my husband pulled me into his arms.

"Show me, let me see," Rain said, voice frantic as he tugged at my braid.

"It's not bad, I don't think," I replied, closing my eyes as I reached up to where the blade had pressed against me. Finding only a small trickle of blood, I sighed, thankful it hadn't been worse.

"There's so much blood," he whispered. "Please," Rain said, calling the Supreme over.

"Old blood. Healed myself the first time," I croaked. "I'm alright."

I adjusted, about to sit up, but he held on so tightly, I couldn't move. I opened my eyes and looked up at Rain, finding him blinking rapidly as he cupped my face. The Supreme knelt and placed a cold hand on my neck.

"It looks worse than it is," the Supreme reassured Rain, a tight smile on his face.

"Thank you," I whispered, looking up at the man as he healed me. I shuddered to think what would have happened if Nor and the Supreme hadn't intervened with the ward. He looked down at me with sad, brown eyes, and started to say something before hesitating and closing his mouth.

"Go on, out with it." Rain adjusted me in his hold, pressing me tight against his body as the Supreme pulled away. Rain stood, picking me up easily, my legs tucked over his arm. The Supreme flinched at the harsh tone before righting himself and standing, careful to not touch his white clothing with bloody hands.

"I was going to say I was sorry for not believing you at first. Filenti has been a faithful servant for a very long time. I am…distraught I didn't see it sooner."

"Where has he been assigned? Which temples?" Dewalt's voice was a whip cracking behind me, and I tensed. Rain held me tighter, and I relaxed into it, the touch more than I'd had in weeks.

The Supreme winced and took two large—and wise—steps backwards. "Ardian. That's where he was before I assigned him to the capital."

Dewalt closed the distance the Supreme had created, and I reached for his arm, knowing why rage flowed from him. I had the same questions. But it wasn't as if the Supreme could answer them—not now anyway. I'd request a list of names from him, and we'd do our own research.

"D," Rain's voice was a growl, and I studied his face, the rage radiating from him still potent even without being able to feel the bond.

"Dewalt, can you find the key to the collar?" I asked, diverting the male attention and posturing. I watched as Nor dragged her foot through a marking on the ground outside as she cut her palm over it, red drips steaming in the snow.

Moments later, Rain opened a rift which brought us all into the temple, and then he turned and created another which opened up in front of the comfortable cream sofa at the estate. He set me down gently. Exhaustion and relief hit me so hard, I stumbled through it in a daze toward the sofa, only remembering at the last moment I was covered in blood.

"Fuck off," he barked behind me, and I turned to see Dewalt's face on the other side of the rift as it closed.

"Why didn't you—"

Rain strode toward me with purposeful steps, riding a wave of fury in his eyes. Gripping my face, a hand on either side, his lips crashed into mine. Desperate, searching, panting, Rain kissed me so hard, I reached up and grabbed his wrists. I lost my balance, twisting enough to bring a cry to my lips. He jolted back and stared at me, chest heaving.

"My rib. I think it's broken."

His hand dipped beneath my shirt, reaching up to palm my side where I held it. His hand was warm against my skin, still wet from the snow. A fire roared in the grate behind me, and I closed my eyes. The heat of his healing divinity, the comfort of his presence, and the crackling fire brought me peace.

"Elora?" I asked.

"At the palace with Thyra. I suppose she got to see her new quarters."

I deflated a bit, knowing he'd been trying to make it perfect for her. He should have been there when she saw it for the first time.

"I'm sorry."

"Are you?" he snapped, and my cheeks flushed with shame as he pulled away from me.

"I am. For all of it."

"You didn't tell me because you knew I wouldn't approve."

"Partially, yes."

"And the rest?"

"Bartering," I said, hanging my head. "I thought maybe you'd be desperate enough to know..."

"Desperate enough to know where my wife was going, endangering herself, working *in the Wend* with no guards? Desperate enough that I'd what? That I'd—"

"Not everyone who lives in the Wend is a criminal," I argued.

"You think I don't fucking know that, Emmeline?" he growled. "What you did was reckless all the same." Frustration flared down the bond between us, red and hot.

"I won't argue with that."

"I trusted Dewalt—Thyra and Dickey too. And I trusted *you* to not be so thick-headed." He stepped back, nostrils flaring.

"Well, maybe if you trusted me more, I wouldn't have found myself desperate to do something, to feel useful. Elora needs space, and you don't trust me enough to protect myself against you. What would you have me do? Sit here alone? I've been alone for half my fucking life, and it's nothing I want to repeat," I snapped.

"How can I trust you to protect yourself from me, the other half of your soul, when you can't even protect yourself from men who beat their wives? From thieves and murderers? What did you think Dickey was going to do to help you? Do you see how stupid that is?" he yelled as he paced in front of the fireplace, one hand on his sword, the other on his forehead.

"I made a mistake!" I yelled back at him, cursing my inane heart for making tears well up. I hadn't thought things through—he was right. But I hadn't intended to hurt anyone or endanger myself. My only intention had been to maintain my sanity, to do something about the guilt which tore at my insides. The guilt I couldn't even talk to him about because he was dealing with his own demons. "You never would have let me help them if I told you!" I shouted, willing my tears away.

"Wrong!" he roared, and the ground shook beneath us. I wasn't sure whose divinity was out of control between the two of us, but I felt the whisper of a shadow on my skin. "If you would have told me you wanted to do something so gods damned dangerous, I would have tried to convince you otherwise, but..." He shook his head, wiping his brow. "Em, if you would have insisted, I would've seen to it that you could do what you wanted—*safely*. Because, truthfully, I don't know if I could ever tell you no. Maybe it's you who doesn't trust me."

His words hit me like a punch to the stomach. Perhaps I didn't trust him to react reasonably because nothing about the situation between us was reasonable.

"I am not strong enough for this, for this distance between us. I am not strong enough," I said, voice breaking.

He whirled on me, and the frustration he'd been holding onto tightly turned into rage—rippling black down the bond. For the first time since he'd choked me in the bedroom, I was afraid. When his eyes darted to my shoulder, clothed and bloody, I ripped my shirt away, tugging it down off my shoulder.

"It's me. You feel me down the bond." I plucked gently at those golden threads, hoping it would be enough. He froze. I watched him blink a few times, and I wondered if he felt my fear. Rubbing his hands over his face, he groaned before turning away from me and opening a rift.

"I miss you," I whispered. Our quarters in the palace were in sight past his silhouette. It took everything in me not to beg him, not to plead with him to stay. It felt selfish to desire his presence so desperately, when I seemed to be the last thing he needed. But I was broken too. I didn't know if he heard me as he stepped through, letting it close behind him. Tears I'd held at bay slid down my cheeks.

I'd never felt more alone.

CHAPTER 35

Elora

I stretched in the morning winter sun shining in from my balcony. One thing I wasn't sure I'd ever get used to was the comfortable bedding. Yvi was curled up at the foot of the bed, and she tilted her head back to look at me before flopping backwards and stretching her paws out. Tiny claws dug into the bedspread and got stuck. She panicked and started to flop about and tear it up, so I sat up quickly, tugging her claw free. She flew off the bed and slammed to the floor.

"Stupid little monster," I said, laughing. She spun before launching herself beneath the bed. I didn't think she'd like it as much as the bed at the estate. Boxes of art supplies sat crammed beneath that one, providing her ample hiding spots. There was nothing for her to hide behind here. Not yet, anyway.

I couldn't believe all the things he'd done for me. Rainier. My father. It was very strange to think about. So, I thought it best to mostly just not think about it. But it was harder to do so in the midst of his generosity. The suite he'd chosen for me was on an exterior wall with a small balcony. Double doors opened up to a view of the bustling capital below me. I saw linens strung up between houses, greenhouses and aviaries on rooftops, and hundreds of people carrying about their day. And beside the double doors, he'd placed an easel. He hadn't been here when I arrived, and I hadn't yet thanked him.

He'd been off getting Mama out of trouble.

Even stranger to think about than Rainier as my father was to think about Mama and all the trouble she seemed to get into. Thyra had told me all about how she killed and put to sleep a tírrúil on the road and how she threw a dagger at King Soren. That one made me scratch my head a bit. Thyra wouldn't tell me what the king had said to warrant her reaction, but something told me Mama was a bit reckless in her actions. The fact she was sneaking about healing people though, that didn't surprise me in the slightest. That's what she did. That's what she'd always done.

When Rainier returned the night before, he'd knocked to tell me and Thyra that Mama was safe and sound, but I was on the verge of sleep and never got more clarity about what happened. I decided to ask him about it. I wanted to be told all the details, wanted to be part of it. I knew Mama claimed I wasn't the Beloved, but she'd claimed so my whole life; I wasn't sure if I should believe her or not.

Crawling out of the bed, I tugged the golden bedspread up. It wasn't nearly as pretty as it had been before I got into it, but since I'd never get it the way it was, I didn't even bother. After changing into a simple peach-colored dress, I was sitting in a chair beside the fireplace and reading one of the many books on my shelves when a light rap on the door drew my attention.

"You may come in," I said, and Rainier peeked in a second later.

"Good morning, Elora. Are you busy?"

"Not exactly," I said, gesturing to the book. "Nothing I can't put on hold."

He shuffled into the room, hands in pockets and looking nervous. It was so strange. He was the king. I should have been the nervous one. Casting his eyes about the room, lingering on the light green sofa beside me with golden-yellow pillows, he took a few steps farther into the room.

"Do you like it? I know it's not like what you had in Brambleton, but I tried to make it nice for you."

"I do. Did Mama help you?"

"A little. She gave me enough information to do the rest on my own."

"Oh, then I suppose she's the one who told you I liked yellow?"

Beaming, he nodded. "Yes. Spring colors."

"Ah, that's why. If only she remembered that I actually hate yellow."

His eyes widened as he took in the goldenrod bedspread, the pillows on the sofa, the wallpaper. "Oh gods, I'll have them—"

"I'm teasing! I love it. Yellow is perfect," I said, feeling bad for upsetting him. He was so nervous. I smiled and set down my book before standing.

Should I hug him?

A grin spread across his face, and it made me feel infinitely better. He was always joking and bantering with Dewalt when he'd sat in on our training, and he'd seemed funny and kind even the very first day I met him. I'd wanted to make him feel more comfortable with me, but his panic made me regret it.

"Oh, you got me, didn't you?" He laughed.

"Sorry," I said. "I couldn't help myself."

"You get that from her."

"Get what from her?"

"The inclination to vex me," he replied, grinning. I giggled and gestured to the sofa beside my armchair for him to sit. Though he appeared startled, he recovered and we both sat.

"And what do you think I get from you?" I asked it before I could stop myself.

"I've heard you're quite stubborn, but I suppose you could get that from either of us."

"True."

"I think I'm far more charming than your mother. And you're quite charming yourself."

"You think I'm charming? I would not have said that."

He shrugged. "You're funny without being unkind. Easy to like. I think that's charming, although definitions may vary. You get your charm from me." He winked.

"Isn't thinking yourself charming, in fact, not charming?"

"Another thing you get from your mother—contrarian." He chuckled, and I realized I wasn't so nervous anymore. He sighed and adjusted, resting his ankle on his opposite knee. Seated on the sofa like that, he didn't look quite so royal. He wore a plain button-down shirt tucked into brown breeches, and the black boots he wore weren't new, but worn in.

"I'm sorry the paints and canvases haven't arrived. I realize it looks like I know very little when all I supplied was an easel. But I promise more is coming. I didn't know what kind to get you, so I ordered a little bit of everything from a shop in the artist quarter. The shopkeeper suggested oils might be too much at first for you to master, but I got them anyway."

His smile was sheepish, and I didn't know what to think. "Mama and I just mixed our own. I read somewhere about using egg whites as a base. The shopkeeper might be right." Thinking of all the things Papa used to buy me—books and jewelry to gain my affection—I turned to Rainier. "You don't have to buy me things, you know."

"I know."

"Mama did good, even though we didn't have a lot of money. I was happy. She always got me whatever I wanted."

"I know she did. That doesn't surprise me at all. I just—" He leaned forward, clasping his hands together between his legs as he stared at the floor. "I know this is a strange transition for you, and I wanted to help. I knew you liked to paint, so I wanted to give you the space and supplies to do it."

"Uh, well, thank you. I really appreciate it. Do—Do you like to paint? Do you have any hobbies?"

Lifting his head, a smile brightened his features. "Well, when I find the time, I like to stargaze. It's something my mother did with me when I was very young and something your mother renewed in me when she was your age."

"Were you the one who taught her all the constellations?"

"I won't take credit for all of her education, but I definitely used it as an excuse to spend time with her."

"Oh, of course," I said, fighting a smile. "Did you, uh, did you really love her that whole time?"

"Absolutely. It was quite inconvenient, but yes. I fell in love with her while showing her the stars, and I'll love her until the last one falls from the sky."

It was strange to think about Mama being with me and Papa, all while the Crown Prince of Vesta pined after her. All along, he loved her. It was the kind of love from my stories; I never thought it could be real. A memory of Mama crying popped into my head, sudden and surprising. I'd forgotten how often she used to cry. But she hadn't in a long time, had she? Or maybe she just got better at hiding it.

"Sometimes, I think—do you think if I didn't have my light, you and Mama would have ended up together again sooner? If we got to stay at Ravemont?"

"Elora, I'm not sure that's worth thinking about. I know we're certainly not thinking about it, so neither should you."

"But—"

"No. There's no way to know what might have happened differently, and letting our minds wander down that path won't take us anywhere worthwhile. All we can do is take what we have now and live in these moments." His voice was firm, but he wouldn't meet my eyes. Did he blame my light? Or was it something else? "We shouldn't waste the time we've been given."

"Alright," I agreed, not feeling quite satisfied. "Uh, well, in that case. Can you rift me back to the estate?" I asked. "I'm supposed to be training. You could join us?"

"I'd love to. Do we need to leave now?"

"I only have fancy princess dresses here, so yes, we should probably go now."

A crisp nod and an easy smile had him up from his seat in a moment. While I waited for him to get his cloak, I wondered why I was ever frightened of him.

"This is so awkward," Theo whispered beside me, and I snorted. "I thought they were friends. The captain is his Second, isn't he?"

"He is. I don't know. I think it's something to do with Mama secretly healing people."

Rainier and Dewalt were supposed to be showing different sword grips, but really it had turned into the two of them arguing over which ones were better or worse and why. Theo and I hadn't been listening for the past several minutes, but I didn't think they noticed.

"I heard something in the barracks, but I don't know if it's true."

"Tell me," I replied.

"Well, the queen was supposedly helping people in the Wend."

"The Wend?"

"Er, it's not the best area in the city. Lots of criminals and just not a good place to go for anybody, let alone the queen. And something bad happened last night. I think she got hurt."

"She's fine. I saw her inside when I was changing. Her and Dewalt were talking about something, but she seemed fine."

"She can heal herself, silly. Of course she's fine. Doesn't mean she didn't get hurt."

"Alright, fine. But still," I whispered.

"Let me see the stance Dewalt has taught you both." Rainier commanded, clearly irritated with his friend. Both Theo and I moved, bending our front foot at the knee and keeping our back leg straight.

"Chin down, Elora," Dewalt reminded me, and I obeyed.

"Now your swords," Rainier added, and we held our wooden practice swords in the stance we preferred to start with. Dewalt had shown us a few and let us pick which one felt most natural to us.

"Elora should be in a guarding stance," Rainier said. "Theo is fine doing overhand."

"She wanted to start on the offensive, and I agree," Dewalt argued.

I looked at my friend out of the corner of my eye and had to try hard not to laugh.

"Relax," Dewalt sniped.

"I like it better when Thyra trains us," Theo whispered as we stepped away from the arguing men.

"Me too. She said we can go to the bookstore today if I wanted. Do you want to come with us?"

"Always," he said, and I noticed the tips of his ears go pink. "I like spending time with you."

"And I, you." I ignored the meaning behind his words. He hadn't tried to kiss me again, thank the gods, but I had a feeling I'd have to talk to him about it.

Kissing you felt like kissing a brother. Let's just stay friends?

"If you'd allow me, I'd love to go somewhere for dinner with you. J-just the two of us. There's a cafe in the artist quarter that has apple cider still. If you wanted. I mean, if you wanted to go with me. Not if you want apple cider. Unless you don't like apple cider? Oh gods, I don't know if you even like apple—"

"Hey, breathe." More than just his ears were turning red. I hadn't wanted to talk to him about this so soon. "I don't think I'd be allowed to go anywhere, just the two of us."

"Oh, that's true. Maybe Thyra would go with us? And just watch us eat?"

I scrunched up my nose. "That's weird, Theo."

"Yeah, I guess it is. Well, I don't know. Maybe we could have a picnic here?"

"Where? There's snow everywhere. I-I don't think we should—"

"Am I a bad kisser?"

My eyes rounded. "Theo!"

"Shh," he replied, nodding at Rainier and Dewalt, who still weren't paying attention. "Well, am I?"

"Theo, I don't think that—"

"This shouldn't come as a surprise to you, b-but you were my first kiss, and I bet it would be better if you let me try again."

I closed my eyes, mortified and wishing I was anywhere but here. "I don't plan on kissing *anyone* for a very long time," I hissed.

"Was it because of him?" I heard his scowl. "He didn't *do* anything to you, did he?"

"Divine hell. No. Cy didn't—Cyran didn't hurt me."

Other than the obvious.

"I guess I just thought there had to be a reason you haven't kissed me again. We've been training together every day for weeks, and I feel like we're back to normal. I thought maybe I did something wrong."

I sighed. "We *are* back to normal, and that's the whole point. You're my best friend, and we were best friends for a long time before any kissing happened. I just want to go back to that, Theo."

When his warm brown eyes met mine and I saw a shimmer of a tear, I wanted to cry too. But I had felt nothing when he kissed me, no matter how much I wanted to. I wouldn't think about the other kiss I'd had. *Refused* to think about it. It wasn't even a real kiss. Theo was the only person I'd ever truly kissed, and it didn't feel like I thought it was supposed to.

Cy's kiss, though. Cy's kiss felt right.

It hadn't been real.

"I'm sorry. The last thing I want to do is pressure you. You're my best friend too. I'm probably just lonely. With Ma and Benny in Mira, I thought coming here would be better than staying in Brambleton."

"Can't you go to Mira with your family?" I asked, regretting it instantly when his face crumpled.

"There's no room for me at my aunt's house. But maybe there's even less room for me here," he said, turning toward his pile of things he'd brought with him. "You're a princess now. What was I thinking?"

"No, Theo, I didn't mean it like that."

"Mm."

"No, seriously. I just meant—if you're lonely—"

"I know what you meant."

"Theo."

"It's really fine. I—" He closed his eyes as he turned to face me. A curl of auburn hair fell down and rested on the center of his forehead. "It was my fault for expecting something else when I should just be grateful that you're even here, alive, after what he did to you. I love our friendship, and you're right. Alright? You're right, Elora. I'm sorry for saying all those things. But, while my pride is still salvageable, I think I'm going to go. I'll see you tomorrow?"

Dewalt stomped over, looking as if he'd eaten something sour, and clapped Theo on the shoulder. "I know we got little done today, you two, but your stances looked good," he said before turning and projecting his voice. "No matter which one was correct, it looked good."

Rainier didn't reply, opting instead to stare with disdain.

"Tomorrow you'll be with Thyra," Dewalt continued, grinning despite the murderous look on his friend's face.

"Sounds good. See you tomorrow, Elora," Theo said, starting down the drive before I could reply.

I called goodbye after him, feeling all the world like the worst friend to ever exist. Rainier and Dewalt came to stand on either side of me, both of them crossing their arms and watching as Theo moved out of sight.

"Everything alright between you two?" Rainier asked, quiet and curious. I pulled my cloak around me, uncertain if I wanted to answer.

"I suppose."

Dewalt snorted. "She supposes."

"Shut up, D. Go find somewhere else to be."

"Can do, Your Majesty," Dewalt taunted, before ruffling my hair and striding toward the estate, leaving Rainier and me alone.

"He's a good boy, Theo."

"He's my very best friend."

"Friend is the important word, isn't it?"

"The most important."

"That's good. I'm not going to pretend your mother isn't the better one to talk to about this, but," he began, clearing his throat. "I think, if you give him some time, he'll realize your friendship is the most important thing to him too."

"I hope so."

"He will. Just give him some time to lick his wounds. You're worth it."

Rainier put his hand on my shoulder. I could tell he was tempted to pull me closer to his side, and I spared us both the awkwardness of him asking by leaning into his side and putting an arm around his waist.

"Thank you," I said as he turned us, his smile wide as we walked toward the estate. His grip on my shoulder held strong, almost as if he was afraid I'd push him off me.

"Let's go in before there's another blizzard."

I didn't bother searching for Mama once inside, heading straight to my room to change into something comfortable and dry. Opening my door and kicking off my shoes, I froze as I saw the package on my bed. A small box wrapped in brown paper sat there with a folded piece of parchment beneath it. Crossing the room in a single bound, I snatched the folded piece of paper and broke the wax seal immediately.

I had a feeling I knew who it was from.

Narrow, loopy handwriting filled the page, and my heart stuttered when I read the greeting.

Min viltasma,

Part of me knew I should have thrown the letter straight in the fire, but the other part of me, the one who missed the bastard, was stronger. I kept reading.

I will be the first to admit that I delivered this package to you by a rather nefarious method. I paid a child to bring it to your butler. A gift for the newest princess from a far-off lord in Olistos. I know, I know, I shouldn't have involved a child—a young boy of only seven, at that! And yet, I was desperate. Sterling is quite the dour man, I must say.

I digress. I know you do not want to see me, and this is not to say I blame you at all for it. Yet, I must ask you to reconsider.

Wait!

I laughed and hated myself for it once I read the next line. He knew me too well.

Wait! Do not throw the letter away just yet!

Now, having spent my birthday alone this year (it was quite sad), I was hoping you'd consider making your absence up to me by allowing me to create the most wonderful of illusions for you for your own birthday before I return to Folterra. I know it's early, and your birthday is months away, and I know I have no right to ask this of you. What I did was unforgivable. But ever since you told me about your last birthday, I've been thinking about a way to make this one special for you.

It had horrified him that I didn't have a cake for my birthday. I had to explain it wasn't the cake that upset me, but that Papa had forgotten to pick it up. I never thought he actually understood, though, considering his father probably never once cared about his birthday. Mama had been working for Mairin that week after an accident at the forge, and she'd asked him to do one simple task for my birthday. After she apologized to me, I had heard her harsh whispers for an hour while I hid away upstairs.

Once I leave for Folterra, I won't bother you again. If you never want to speak to me or think of me ever again, no one would blame you. I wanted to give you plenty of time to decide.

The gift in the box is something that made me think of you, but I must divulge there is an ulterior motive to it. I had it enchanted by an elvish woman. I have a matching one, and it will warm when you wear yours. If I find mine heating, I'll assume you'll welcome me into an illusion. I can't exactly check any other way, considering the king has banished me from his estate.

I will understand if you choose to melt it down and turn it into a talisman of hatred for me, or if you have your parents open a rift over the ocean and drop it. But for my sake, I'll be hoping and pretending you'll consider my offer and allow me to truly apologize.

Fretfully and frightfully yours,

Cy

Inside the package was a delicate bracelet made of white gold with four tiny sapphires shaped to resemble leaves in the center. I stared at it for a long moment, *too* long, before closing the lid and shoving it into my nightstand. That it wasn't its beauty causing my fingertips to hover was more frightening than I cared to admit.

CHAPTER 36

Emmeline

The night Rain walked through that rift into the palace, I realized I was going to have to be more aggressive in my approach. I'd given him time and space, but it felt like every step forward came with two steps back. Every time I felt him pulling away, he searched me for a sign that it was actually me, not the shifter. Any kind of strong emotion had him worrying. And I decided exactly what I needed to do to help remove his fear.

I'd been patient and understanding, but it wasn't getting any better, and I didn't know what to do. I couldn't continue living in this loneliness. I needed my partner, my equal, and I needed him to understand that. The day after he left the estate, I ran my idea past Dewalt, and he agreed it could only help. He wasn't as optimistic as I was, but he did what I asked of him and made the arrangements. The elven woman met with me the next day, and I was thrilled, if scared, to continue on my plan. That had been yesterday, and today I'd gone through with it. It was one more step toward making Rain see me and know it was me without hesitation. It wouldn't fix things, but it would make a difference. I didn't think I'd ever be able to convince him I would use my divinity against him, but if I could make him more confident to be around me, it was a start.

"I told you it hurts like hell," Dewalt said, raising his voice from beside me.

"You didn't say it would be this bad," I whined.

He laughed, and I gritted my teeth the final few moments of the ride back home. Turning up the long drive, the tall trees lining either side, I finally caught sight of the estate. I'd never tire of seeing it. It stood out starkly against the sparkling snow, and I was eager to witness it in all the seasons. The grey-stone sparkled, frost settling in the crevices, and the rich oak accents and covered porch were nothing if not inviting.

The estate had been painfully quiet the past few days, Mairin my only company. Rain had called Deandra and Melisse back once he'd returned from Darkhold, but Melisse had handed in her resignation after what happened with Filenti.

Considering a gossiping servant had provided them with personal information, I was happy to accept. I doubted she'd had evil intent, but it still hurt. With Rain staying in our quarters in the palace, and Elora exploring the suite he'd had readied specifically for her, I was lonely. But it gave me time to sort out my own emotions about the distance with Rain, and what I planned to do about it.

Thyra and Dickey made their way across the lawn from the stables, trudging through the snow. Dickey had thrown himself prostrate at my feet the morning after the ordeal with Filenti, tears and snot running down his face as he begged forgiveness. No matter how many times I told him to stop, he wouldn't have it and had been doing more than I asked from him, going out of his way to do things for me. He had been giving special care to Bree, and it seemed he intended to continue with that endeavor as he approached my mare. Gentle with him, she suffered through his attentions.

I caught sight of Sterling standing on the porch and was surprised by the worry across his features until I saw Rain step out from behind him, hands in pockets and a cloak billowing in the wind, his face a calm mask. No crooked smile graced his features, and his nod was crisp. It startled me, not expecting him, and when I traced the bond, curious about his emotional state, I realized he had it locked down. I couldn't tell what he was feeling. Whatever he felt wasn't overwhelming him, though, or else he wouldn't have been able to stop me from feeling it.

I stared for a long moment, equal parts confused and angry. Shutting me out like that wasn't something I would have expected from him, even in his weakest moments. It hurt far more than I ever would have thought. I only had a moment to sit with the notion when I felt a hand slap to my thigh.

"Come on," Dewalt said, reaching for my hips. Normally, I would have had a funny remark to toss at him, not allowing him to help me. But my shoulder ached, so I was grateful for the assistance, not wanting to move more than I had to. Twisting my other leg over the saddle, I allowed my friend to grab me by the waist and pull me down.

"Do you trust me?" he asked, keeping his hands on me.

I shook my head, confused, before blinking up at him. "Yes? Are we asking stupid questions today?"

He chuckled, leaning past me to grab my pack from Bree, but pressed surprisingly close against me. "I'm going to encourage the man," he whispered, close enough to my ear to make me shiver.

"Dewalt, no," I said, but he ignored me as he placed my pack on my good shoulder, delicate in his touch. "I don't know why you think that's going to do something."

"It might, it might not." His hair fell down into his eyes, black silk he'd left unbound. A mischievous grin crossed his face as he leaned closer, using cool fingertips to tuck a strand of my hair over my ear as he brushed a kiss to my cheek.

"Enough," I said, but the word was lost in the wind as a rift opened behind Dewalt, and Rain stomped through, anger and jealousy slipping down the bond even as he fought to keep it tamped down. "Rain, he's just—"

Rain grabbed Dewalt by the collar and turned him around, punching him in the face with a loud smacking sound.

"Rain, don't!" I shouted, frustrated with both men. Dewalt was on the ground as Rain stood over him, chest heaving. "You can't be serious."

"Oh, he's serious," Dewalt said, scrambling to his feet. "You should move."

I crossed my arms, having every intention to ignore him. But then he dove at Rain, shoulder slamming into his midsection, and both men were on the ground within a moment. Rain pounded on Dewalt's back, his skull, fighting against the man who pinned him. Dewalt reared back and punched Rain in the head, hard, and the sound made me feel ill. The horses both spooked, cantering away toward the stable, and Dickey went chasing after them.

"You stupid—" Punch. "Stubborn—" Punch. Dewalt didn't hold back as he slammed his fists into Rain's sides, and he only stopped talking when Rain grabbed him around the neck and rolled him off.

Thyra came to stand beside me, arms crossed. "Do you want me to separate them?"

"No," I said. Watching Rain stumble to his feet and spit blood on the snow-covered ground had me seeing red. "Let him get it out of his system." I shook my head. Jealousy and anger still rolled down the bond toward me, and all I could do was make sure he felt my disgust and disappointment in return.

"Em," he muttered, and I ignored him.

"Thyra, walk with me?" I asked, leading her to sit on the porch beside me. Turning our chairs to face the two men still tussling on the ground, she let out a low whistle. Both of them were soaking wet, and the snow below them had already turned brown from the mud they were kicking up beneath it. Rain sported a busted lip, and Dewalt had a black eye. Yet, they continued. They'd wrestled when they were younger, always fighting and showing off, but never had I seen them actually draw blood.

"Do they do this often?"

"Not so bad, no. Usually it isn't so important—why they fight."

A mirthless laugh crossed my lips, and I crossed one of my legs over the other. I had worn thick black breeches, warm, and my old boots. It was too cold for the blue cloak I wore, and I missed my black one from Lucia. I had high hopes the seamstress who supplied my wardrobe might fix it after my struggle with the rogue masters. Pulling my extra cloak closer to my body and the hood up over my head, I turned to Thyra.

"It's not a true fight, though. Dewalt was antagonizing him on purpose."

"Does it look like it matters?" she asked, nodding at the two men as Rain pulled Dewalt to the ground by his hair.

"It should," I mumbled.

"Men are not bright, Your Majesty."

Snorting, I rolled my eyes before letting out a heavy breath. "In my heart, I know I didn't make a mistake by choosing to accept Rain and accept this love. But a part of me wonders if he doesn't get past this, is my life going to be the same as it has been? I've loved him most of my life, and now that I can finally have him, he won't have me. It's painful, even if his intentions are good."

"Misguided," she countered, and I nodded in agreement. Rain straddled Dewalt's hips and landed a heavy fist to his friend's jaw which made me flinch.

"I can't watch this," I began, but was swiftly distracted by the hawk shooting down from the sky, transforming into Shivani's servant Warric. Naked, he rolled to his feet before pivoting to face me, an envelope in his hand. Had he carried it in his beak?

"Hey!" Rain called out behind him, and both men—*children*—who'd just been rolling on the ground followed the shifter.

"Your Majesty," Warric said, bowing low. I ignored his nudity and greeted him with a tight smile. "You received an urgent message at the palace, and the queen mother bid me to bring it to you with haste." Handing over the letter, he immediately shifted back into his hawk form and shot back into the sky, circling lazily above us. It wasn't sealed, and I felt more than a bit perturbed that Shivani clearly opened it. I read it twice and handed it over to Thyra before turning to go inside.

My father was dying, and he had things he needed to tell me.

Elora didn't want to go to Ravemont, and I didn't blame her. She'd been drawing in her room while I was gone with Dewalt, and she showed me each sketch before I had a chance to tell her about Lord Kennon. She had been so excited to show me how her figures had improved after she'd picked up a drawing guide at the bookstore. When I finally got around to telling her, she didn't have much reaction other than to make sure I was alright. She was getting used to her life here, and she'd never had a chance to be close to her grandfather. Part of me was hesitant to leave her for a few reasons. By not forcing her to go, I felt almost as if I had failed as a mother. That I hadn't instilled in her some sort of love and respect for the man who had sired me. My own relationship with him was complicated though, so I couldn't expect it to be different for her. Part of me didn't want to go myself.

Another reason I didn't want to leave her was obvious. The past two days she'd been at the palace were torturous. I knew she was there, safe, and Thyra checked in on her for me. And yet, I'd been far more nervous than necessary. Would I be able to stomach the separation? Even if only for a few days?

But she'd stopped me, anticipating my fear, promising to do anything and everything Thyra told her to do. My Second had instantly offered her services, and I was grateful for her. The woman had become a close friend, to both myself and my daughter. They immediately discussed Elora's schedule, Thyra commenting on her sketches.

I had relented, agreeing to the arrangement, before Rain and Dewalt even came inside. Coming down the stairs from Elora's room, I felt their gazes on me from the threshold, and I ignored them. I would inevitably have to speak to Rain and explain to him that I wouldn't be going to the coronation. I didn't have to be there by rights, and the purpose was to solidify him as king. I'd be queen in name only, and perhaps only ever in name, if Rain never crossed this chasm between us.

But the distance between my father and me only had one opportunity to be fixed, if his nurse's letter was to be believed. His mind had been wasting away. I'd witnessed a hint of it when I saw him months ago at Ravemont, and I'd pushed it aside. Elora was my priority, and I ignored my gut, which told me he wasn't quite right. Now, he only had a few moments of clarity each day, and I'd need to make use of those hours to make any sort of amends with him.

So, I packed a bag. Difficult to do while minimizing movement of one arm, I did my best. I hoped I'd be able to rift myself back to Brambleton, everything blanketed by snow, but what was the alternative? Any other travel wouldn't get me there in reasonable time. Methodically, I rolled up shirts and pants, shoving them into the bag neatly. I began to feel guilt over the fact I'd found out my father was dying, and I felt nothing. I didn't feel sad or worried. I didn't feel much at all. Regret, perhaps, but nothing so potent I couldn't function.

I was grabbing a few things from the bathing suite when Rain came to stand in the doorway, taking up too much room in my physical and mental space. I wasn't ready to deal with him.

"Thyra told me your father is dying," he said, voice quiet. I pointedly avoided looking at him as I walked back into the closet, ignoring his red and bleeding knuckles. All I did was nod as I pulled another sweater off a hanger. "We'll be leaving tonight?"

"*I'll* be leaving tonight," I corrected.

"I'm going too."

"No. I don't know if I'll be back in time for the coronation."

"They can't have a coronation without me. They'll wait."

"People are traveling, already on their way. I intend to stay at Ravemont until…after. There will be things to take care of." A thought occurred to me. "Will Ravemont belong to the Crown after he dies?"

"It will belong to you."

"And I belong to you, the Crown."

"Your heart belongs to me, not your property," he said.

I stopped what I was doing, lifting my eyes to his. "It doesn't feel like much of me belongs to you anymore. I certainly own nothing of you. Your ire, perhaps. I do own that."

"Em," he started, but I picked up my pack, carrying it past him to our bed. *My* bed for the last few months. I picked up the sweater I'd laid on it, tugging it on over my button-down and scarf. Hissing through the pain in my shoulder and neck, I stayed quiet enough I didn't think he heard me. I wouldn't let him know about it. I didn't want to give him that yet, still too frustrated about his behavior with Dewalt.

"Do you mind?" I asked, as I tugged at my breeches. I had a thick pair of soft leggings I planned to wear beneath them, an appropriate dress for the weather and the mountains.

"Do I mind what?" He asked, though it was clear he knew what I meant.

"I'm trying to change my clothes."

"I'm not stopping you."

His eyes raked down the curve of my thighs as I dropped my breeches. I ignored him as I finished ripping off the pants and quickly started yanking my leggings on. He took a step forward, his fingers twitching at his sides. When I pulled the breeches on over the leggings, I struggled. I was about to lie down on the bed and try to pull them up that way, when he reached out and gripped the waistband and tugged hard. Heat flared in his eyes, and I gulped audibly.

He cleared his throat and stepped back.

"You used to be close to Kennon. Well, closer than I was with my father. How are you feeling? I didn't realize his illness was this bad when we were at Ravemont."

"What do you mean?"

"That Gemma woman. His nurse? I thought…"

"Divine hell. Of course. I—With everything going on, I forgot to…" Incredulous with my own stupidity, I began to laugh. "I thought she was…I thought he'd taken a lover or—or wanted to wed again. Why did no one tell me?"

"I assumed you knew, I suppose. And we had more pressing issues. I guess that means you weren't close."

"No. We weren't. Definitely not since…" I trailed off. Since our lives changed forever. "I'm indifferent." I didn't tell him I felt guilty about it, but I was sure it ebbed its way across the bond. "Can I borrow one of your winter cloaks? Mine is with the seamstress."

"You don't need to ask. What is mine is yours."

Swallowing the knot in my throat, I trudged back to our closet and grabbed one of his cloaks, dark brown and soft. It was too long, but I'd make it work. He followed me, clearly on the verge of saying something. Opening one of the built-in drawers, I grabbed a few pairs of thick woolen socks. I heard him doing something behind me, but I focused on my task. There was one pair in particular I wanted. Knitted with thick fleece, I could pull them up to my knees. Finally finding them, I didn't bother to speak to the man behind me as I left.

"I'm not sure when I'll be back, but I'll send a letter if it will be longer than a week," I called over my shoulder as I went to find Sterling to give him a last update. I considered bringing Bree with me through the rift, nervous about my skills and memory, remembering the difficulty in getting to the Cascade. What if I found myself stranded halfway back to Brambleton? I'd have to return to Astana and bury my pride enough to ask Rain for help.

"Wait, Em," Rain called, footsteps echoing on the wooden floor behind me as I passed the cream sofa and headed toward the kitchen. I didn't slow down because I couldn't. I was heartsick and frustrated and numb.

Not finding Sterling in the kitchen, I sighed, turning around as I leaned against the archway into the dining room, eyes on the ceiling. I didn't want to look at Rain, knowing he'd see to the heart of me. Knowing he'd see just how little I wanted to do this alone.

"Do you know where Sterling is?" I asked.

He came to a halt in front of me, not speaking, as I continued to not look at him. When I finally caved, crossing my arms as I took him in, I groaned in frustration. He'd done as I had and layered warm clothing over what he wore. A bigger pack than mine lay at his feet, stuffed full. He wore one of his winter cloaks, dark pine green, hood already up. Though his wounds from fighting with Dewalt had been healed, I saw the blood left behind on his face and hands. Anger flared through me at the thought. Not only was it stupid he didn't trust his best friend, but his reaction meant he didn't trust me. That he thought I could entertain something so deranged, so impossibly wrong? I was mad all over again.

"Did you fix Dewalt too?" I asked.

"Yes."

"Did you apologize?"

"Not yet."

"Do you intend to?"

"Yes," he gritted out.

"Good. I'm sure the two of you will have plenty to talk about while I'm gone." I grunted as I adjusted my bundle on my shoulder. His hand darted out, and he took it from me, tossing both of the packs onto his back.

"*We* will have plenty to talk about while *we're* gone."

I sighed, rubbing my face with both of my hands. "I have nothing to discuss that we haven't discussed already. If I am to be your wife in name only, it is quite unfair for you to give me any sort of hope for something more."

"Please," he breathed, letting me feel his vulnerability, letting me see it in his emerald eyes. The hints of gold were barely visible in the low light, and I realized I missed him more in these last few weeks than I did all of our years apart. But if he planned to tell me I could only expect more of the same, I didn't know what I'd say to him. I wouldn't leave him; I would be here with him for the rest of my life. But I didn't know what to do.

I needed him to let me in. Not just for him, but for me too. I needed him. Every time I saw Nor or any of the former novices in their dormitory, my stomach twisted, and I wanted to vomit. Logically, I knew it was an accident. Even though I'd sat with Nor for long hours, exhausting every bit of knowledge she could give me about the women who'd died. Even though I'd said multiple prayers to the gods, done everything I could to help those who survived, the ache still ran deep in my soul. And then I came home to an empty bed, and no one to share that burden with.

Least of all the other half of my soul. Was that why we struggled? One soul, too bruised to heal separately? Perhaps this distance between us made it worse in more ways than one.

"Alright," I acquiesced, and light shone in his eyes once more. "But we speak on my terms. And I am angry enough with you right now that I don't want to talk for a good, long while." He nodded, clearly serious in his intent to obey my wishes, and I fought the twitch of my lip. "Does Sterling already know of our plans?" I asked. He nodded once more, and I rolled my eyes. "You may speak when spoken to."

A low growl made its way up his throat before he said, soft as velvet, "A dangerous way to speak to a man, dear heart."

And despite myself, my traitorous body tensed and heated under his gaze. I closed my eyes, banishing images of us tangled in our sheets, his hands on my waist as he guided me on top of him that night when I accepted everything we were and would be. The image was a cruel one to conjure.

"This is only because I don't think I can rift to the plains alone."

"I can't do that either, but lucky for us, Ven's estate sits farther east. It will make our rift to the mountains easier so we don't have to stop in the plains. It's too hard to pinpoint a place to rift to out there."

I nodded as he turned away, spreading his hands in front of him. Looking back over his shoulder, he smiled. "A little help?"

Hands on his hips, I leaned my forehead into his back, caressing the bond between us as I sent my divinity to combine with his.

"I have to pee, and then we can keep going."

"I buried Faxon that way," he replied, pointing to a patch of trees off the entrance to the cave we'd slept in months prior. Before the Faxon comment, I'd been thinking about what we'd done that night, and I knew he was thinking about it too. When I'd made a choice to take something for myself for once, to accept him as my twin flame, it had been a turning point for us both. The heady attraction weighed heavily on my tongue as the bond glowed golden.

But his comment threw me, and I looked at him, eyes wide, not sure how to react.

"Sorry. Was that—I meant nothing—well…I meant that. I wholeheartedly think you should piss on his grave if you want to, but I understand if you…don't…" He trailed off, unable to continue as I held my stomach, a single tear rolling down my face from trying not to laugh. It was absurd. My feelings about Faxon and his betrayal were complex. I hated him for what he did, for what

I'd been made to endure with him, but it almost felt like it wasn't anger for me to own. That belonged to Elora. I knew I had every right to hate him, every right to do what I did to him, but I'd barely spared a thought for him since the day Rain put him in the ground. I wasn't sure I wanted to start now.

His suggestion took me by surprise, forced me to think about Faxon, specifically watering his grave in my own special way, and it took all I had not to laugh out loud. Rain's smile only grew, crooked and perfect, and the biggest I'd seen it since our wedding.

"Do you need my help to stay upright while you do it? So you don't fall in the snow?" he asked, a brow kicking up to match his smile.

I choked on my laugh and shook my head. "I think it might be more insulting to not give him a second thought," I answered.

I wandered away, plodding through the snow. I didn't go too far, not as worried about my modesty as I was about getting soaked from the snow and creatures wandering at night. With the new moon only a few days past, it was still quite dark despite the blanket of white. Either way, the snow came nearly up to my knees in the deepest parts, and I didn't feel like dealing with that. Finding a hollow beside a pine tree, I took care of my business before heading back.

"Rain?" I called out, and he was trudging through the snow a second later. He'd brushed against a branch on his way, and tiny snowflakes had landed on top of the hood he wore, and a few dusted his cheeks and lashes. Gods, he was beautiful. His breath puffed out in a cloud in front of him, and I wanted to be closer. Wanted to watch our breath mingle. I wondered if he could feel my affection. I wasn't hiding it, but I wasn't shouting it either. Still dreadfully hurt over his choices to shut me out, and decidedly angry over his scuffle with his friend, I focused on why I'd called him over.

"Where is he buried? You said it was under a bush?"

He nodded, gripping my elbow as he moved us closer to the cave. "I placed a stone, but it's probably buried," he said. "Oh. Well, shit."

He gestured to the bush in front of us, and I couldn't help but laugh. The bush of winterfrost roses was in full bloom. The faintly silvered edges of each petal and the fact they were blooming in the middle of winter was the only sign they weren't ordinary roses.

"I wouldn't have picked this bush if I'd have known. He doesn't deserve it," Rain murmured, and he placed his hand on the small of my back. Gods, no matter how frustrated I was with him, no matter how much I willed my spine to remain steel, it turned into a ribbon at the attention. Folding in soft, shining waves, I bent to his touch.

"It's not a bad thing. Winterfrost roses are—well, look at them. It's the dead of winter, and they're beautiful. There is beauty in Faxon's death, in his betrayal. If he hadn't done what he did, if we never would have known?" I stepped forward, taking one of my gloves off, and plucked two roses from the bush. "You get to be a father because of what he did."

The look on his face was contemplative as I gestured for him to turn. Digging deep into my bag hanging from his back, I tugged out a handkerchief to fold the flowers in before carefully placing them in my pack. I'd press them the first chance I could. I told myself I kept them for Elora, but truly, I didn't know why I felt called to keep them.

"Shame on you for saying something like that. Now I can't piss here," he laughed, and I gave him a look over my shoulder as I marched past him. "You're right, Em. What he did changed my life. I suppose it's a gift."

"Of course I'm right. Besides, I never said you couldn't empty your bladder there. The bush might need watering."

His laugh echoed, but the fact he didn't follow immediately behind me told me he was taking me up on the idea. Trudging through the snow, I made it back out to the cave entrance. It looked so much bigger without Rain's guard and the tents inside it. I shivered, my wet pants sticking to my skin, and I coerced my divinity into my palm and crouched, holding a divine flame in my palms to warm my legs.

"Can I show you a trick?" he asked, voice quiet so as not to startle me, even though I'd heard him approach. When I looked up at him, I noticed his eyes dip to my collarbone for just a second before landing back on my face. I'd been paying attention, waiting for him to have some sort of reaction, and he'd made it a few hours. Satisfaction and sadness mingled, and, while I was sad he was still dealing with those thoughts, I was pleased with the choice I'd made.

"You might not have issues with it, but the colder the water is, the more I struggle. But it should be warm enough against your body." His eyes skated down my legs before a twitch of his fingers coaxed the water out of my pants. He'd done it at the lake too, and I was kicking myself for not thinking about it.

"This entire time, I could've been using your divinity to dry myself," I groaned. "I've had wet breeches for weeks!"

A soft smile met me. "You try?"

"Well, I'm dry now," I said, and immediately regretted the words. I ran to the safety of the cave as malevolent glee crossed his face, and he bent down to pack a snowball.

"It's a fair fight, Highclere. Come out," he taunted.

"I'm on the Vestana side now. It's not sporting to attack your own!"

"Oh, but three versus two was sporting?"

The twins and Dewalt up against royalty. We had won every single time.

"I think so. Lucia barely counted." She couldn't have hit a target if it was a meter away. I was rethinking my hiding place. Though there were a few stalagmites farther back into the cave, they weren't wide enough to take cover behind. Feeling devious, I opened a rift and stepped out behind Rain and packed my own snowball as he whipped around to face me. It would hurt my shoulder to throw, but it was a sacrifice I'd have to make.

"Rifting is cheating!" He yelled as I formed another rift which opened behind him, and I threw the snowball, hitting him square in the back of his head.

"Oh, you are going to pay for that," he said as he took off in a run toward me, snow flying behind his feet as he struggled through it, and I opened another rift. Just as I stepped through, Rain turned, anticipating that I'd open it behind him, and he lunged at me.

Twisting out of his grip, I laughed and took two steps before he was on me again, tackling me into the snow. He rolled me over beneath him, and I hid my grimace as I adjusted my scarf.

"Are you alright? I hurt you," he said, low and quiet. His face was in shadow, the stars lighting up the sky behind him, and I could barely make out the concerned look in his eyes.

"I'm fine," I whispered. Blinking, I stared dully at his silhouette and realized shadows coiled around his arms. "You didn't hurt me, Rain. It's me, and you didn't hurt me."

He inhaled quickly and pushed himself to his feet before offering his hand to pull me up and, shadows already gone, using his divinity to whisk the water from my wet clothes.

"I want to get out of the mountains before we stop for the night," he said, voice gruff as he turned away from me and opened the next rift.

CHAPTER 37

Dewalt

Annoyed, I marched into the estate and straight up to my old bedroom. Lavenia's room. I figured I still had clothes in the closet, and I was caked in filth. Rainier had healed me, and after they left for Ravemont, I'd helped Thyra and Dickey with the horses. It was nightfall by the time we were done, and I needed to bathe. I'd been guilted into mucking out the stalls, so I never bothered changing out of my bloody clothes. Rounding the top of the stairs, I slammed right into someone and nearly tumbled backwards.

"Shit!"

Ven's hand shot out and grabbed me by the forearm, pulling me vertical before I fell down the steps. "Sorry! Are you alright?"

"I'm a lot better than I would have been if I actually fell. Thanks for grabbing me." I clapped a hand to the side of her arm and moved past her. She hadn't spoken to me in weeks, and I didn't know if I blamed her. I hesitated for a beat, not sure if I should speak to her or apologize or what, but ultimately opted to give her space. I started down the hall, intending to bathe and change, when Ven cleared her throat.

"You know, you never thanked me. Not once."

My hand stilled on the doorknob.

"You know I'm grateful. I thought I made it clear. You didn't have to perform the ritual with me."

"Not for that."

"Then what, Ven?" I leaned against the door frame, crossing my arms as I turned to face her.

"The balcony."

My stomach twisted. "That was what, fifteen fucking years ago? Even though I'm sure I thanked you back then, I'll do it again. Since you're clearly still pissed off about it. Thank you for stopping me from falling off the fucking balcony."

"Try it again, but with the truth."

"What do you mean? I almost fell. You grabbed me so I didn't. End of story."

"You were about to *jump* off the balcony," she said.

"No, I wasn't. I was acting a fool. Fucking around."

"You know, I spent probably five years of my life keeping the two of you from killing yourselves. But I don't think Rainier ever actually considered doing it on purpose. You can say you were fucking around all you want. But we both know the truth. And you never once honestly and openly thanked me for it. Not with all the weight that gratitude deserves. That I deserve. You want to know how I stopped worrying about you so gods damn much? The bond. Because I could feel you at the other end. Because I knew you weren't fucking dead."

The air in the hallway stilled, and I didn't move. She took a step toward me and stopped, her face carved out of stone. She'd never looked more like Shivani. The low lamplight at the end of the hall did little to illuminate the shadows on her face, and I didn't know what to say. "It's not your decision that upsets me. It's the fact you had so little fucking consideration of me and my feelings when I've considered yours for *years*, D. That was a conversation we should have had."

"I knew you wouldn't listen."

"You found time to talk to Mairin, so you could have found time to talk to me. Even if you thought I wouldn't have listened, you owed me the decency to fucking try. You owed me that."

"I'm sorry," I said—helpless. I barely had any fight to begin with when it came to her, but whatever remained left me upon hearing the disappointment in her voice.

"I'm starting to think that I was so worried about you and Rainier, I didn't have a chance to learn who I am and what I want out of life. Hell, part of me wonders if you both let yourselves sink as low as you did because you knew I'd be there to make sure you didn't go too far. The woman you loved died, and he lost the woman he loved. I know that. But neither of you," she whispered, angry tears threatening at her lashes, "Neither of you cared to ask me how I was. They were my friends too. It was my tragedy to grieve too."

"You're right." I didn't know what else to say. She *was* right. Rainier and I were both selfish in our misery. I had never once put voice to my actions that night on the balcony, and she was forcing me to do it. It had been a moment of weakness. I wouldn't have thought about the enticing edge, an end to the constant ache if it hadn't been Lucia's birthday. In those early days, it wasn't safe for me to be alone on anniversaries. I'd been alright the week before, the anniversary of the day she'd died. But it was too much to get through both so close together.

"You know, part of me worried you'd both leave me too. And then where would I be?" Her arms were crossed tightly over her body, making herself small, but she held her neck straight and head high. Elegant.

"You're right about all of it. I was selfish, and Rainier was selfish. We shouldn't have burdened you with our grief like that. Not when you had your own."

"No, you shouldn't have. We were all too young, but I was only sixteen. I should have been sneaking around like you two did. I should have had friends. But I was too afraid to make any because then you might think I didn't need you. That you didn't have any reason to—to stay."

"Ven, I—" I took a step forward, reaching out to her, but she shook her head. I probably knew her boundaries better than anyone, and she wasn't finished talking. I didn't interrupt her.

"I'm glad you feel confident enough in me and in yourself to make this decision. But if you would have let me be a part of the conversation, I would have sat down with you and explained my fears. I've had a lot of time to think about this, and I just have to get this off my chest before I leave tomorrow."

"Leave?"

"We are headed to Northport in the morning. I came by to grab a few things I left here."

"I thought you were going after the coronation."

"I don't quite feel like celebrating. Not to mention, who knows when the coronation will be now. We can't afford to wait, not with Lamera under threat."

"Shit. Alright, well, I hope you'll be careful."

"I will." She looked down at the floor, poking at something with the toe of her boot.

"You wanted to get something off your chest?"

"Yes." She sighed. "If you would have come to me, I would have tried to make sure you'll be alright. I'm about to be gone for gods know how long, and I won't know that you'll be fine. You've been...decent for a long while, but I'm afraid."

"I'm fine."

"That's what you said back then too. And then I found you weeping on the balcony."

"Low blow. I already feel bad enough. I don't want to think about that too hard right now."

"Fine. Can you do me a favor?"

"What?"

"You don't have to talk about it with me or with anyone, really. But I want you to think about that night, those first few years, and look at them for what they really were. Stop lying to yourself." I nodded, clearing my throat and looking down at the doorknob near my hip. Anything to not look at her. "And, while I'm gone, be careful?"

"I'll do my best."

"Better. Do better than your best." She inhaled deep. "Thank you. As mad as I am, I can't help but worry."

"I'll be fine."

"Are you just saying that to shut me up?"

"No. I actually talked to Emma a bit about all this." I pretended to not see the hurt in her eyes. I'd gone to someone other than her, and that had to sting. I continued, "I don't know if I ever could have what the two of them have, but I think you could. I'm not ruling it out for me either, but I'm not optimistic."

"We both could have it."

"Maybe. Anyway, I'm doing alright. I promise I'll steer clear from any and all balconies while you're gone."

"That's not very funny."

"I think it's at least a little funny."

She huffed a laugh. "You're such an ass."

"It's part of my charm." I pushed off the wall, shoving my hands into my pockets.

"Well, I suppose I should go. Early morning," she mumbled.

"Ven?"

"Yes?"

"I'm sorry."

"It's alright."

"And thank you. Thank you for giving me a reason to stay."

I was in a strange mental state when I finally went downstairs. I'd mulled over what Ven had said to me while I bathed, and I sat there until the water grew cold. There was a lot I tried not to think about from those early years after Lucia died. I hadn't been a good person or a good friend. I'd justified it in my mind, but that wasn't fair. I was living my hell. Sad and fucking angry, every morning I woke up I wished I didn't. It wasn't like I was actively seeking an end to my misery, but I did a lot of dumb shit that could have very easily done it for me. I still didn't know if I really planned to jump that night or if I wanted to fall, which was nearly the same thing.

But not quite.

I didn't want to die. I just didn't want to live.

That difference meant something, and I wasn't sure why.

I had always thought Ven asking for the bond was for our mutual benefit. To find out she counted on it to make sure I was alright made me feel like a piece of shit. She deserved better. I should have gotten my shit together back then, so she didn't feel she needed to tie her fucking life to mine. And then I went and chose to end the bond without giving her the respect she deserved. Fuck. I was going to have to make it up to her once she got back.

I was brushing out my hair as I ran down the stairs, fresh from the bath and hoping to get a late dinner, when a chorus of feminine laughter echoed from the front sitting room. Altering my destination, I explored the noise. I'd expected Thyra and Elora, but Nor was a surprise. I found Elora sitting on the ground in front of the sofa while Thyra pulled her hair into a loose braid. Nor sat at the table beside them, a book open in her hands. She was pink-cheeked and grinning, and I looked at the title.

Ruminations on Marital Bliss.

None of them noticed me as I leaned against the door frame.

"A woman's sensitivities are too volatile, and thusly, it is a man's duty to protect her from such excitation. The femininity of a decisive woman is a bane and should be avoided." Nor projected the words, wrinkling her nose as she spoke.

Thyra snorted as she tied a string in Elora's hair, ending the braid. "Where did you get such stupid book?"

"It's an old Myriad text. I found it in my mother's belongings," Nor replied, slamming it shut and tossing it on the table.

"Well, is your father a blissful man? Unburdened by a decisive, excitable woman?"

All three heads snapped toward mine when I spoke, and Elora jumped to her feet.

"Were you eavesdropping?" she asked, hands fisted at her sides.

"Just for a moment. Don't worry, I didn't hear anything else about a man's duty. I'm not sure how appropriate that book is for a child once you get to the more instructive parts."

"I skipped those," Nor said, arms folded. She wore a dark brown dress, simple, which contrasted and complimented her freckled fawn skin. Long dark hair lay in loose waves down her chest, and she looked significantly healthier than the last time I'd seen her.

When she'd seen my dick.

Gods, had that been truly necessary? Judging by the pinched look on her face as she glared at me, I didn't think it had affected her too much.

"I'm almost sixteen. It's not like I don't know," Elora blurted out.

Nor's eyes widened, and I stifled my laugh.

"And that is something that none of us here will be talking about to you, Princess. That is conversation for your mother," Thyra said, chuckling as she stood. "Come, bedtime. Miss Nor will need to get back to dormitory soon."

"You're a lot less fun when Mama is gone, you know that?"

They both headed to the stairs as Nor gathered her cloak and shoved the book into her bag. I watched her for a moment, still suspicious of her presence.

"So, why are you here? What could you possibly have in common with a child and a soldier?"

"Skies above. The queen has questioned me thoroughly, and I've answered all of them satisfactorily. I don't answer to you."

"I suppose that may be true, but I don't trust you."

"Good thing I don't care."

She started toward the door, and I blocked the archway, not allowing her to pass.

"They've been through enough, *we've* all been through enough, at the hands of zealots. If you're here for some sort of scheme—"

"I'm the only woman in the dormitory who wasn't raped by Declan. And they all make sure I know they hate me for it. That's why I'm here. Thyra and Elora don't look at me like I'm less than dirt. Her Majesty knows and trusts me enough. Does that make you feel better? Can I go now? It's late, and I need to get back." Shocked into silence, I didn't move. "Oh, and I haven't seen my father since I was a child after he poured boiling oil all over me. So, no, he is not a blissful man. Satisfied?"

She buttoned her cloak under her chin and tossed her hood up before shoving past me.

"You don't have family to stay with?" I blurted, not sure what the fuck I was even saying. I remembered she was from Astana, and that was why she'd been eager to come back.

"I did. But my mother died while I was in Folterra."

"I'm sorry for your loss."

"I'd have thought you would know better than to toss meaningless platitudes at me." I blinked at her. "Yes, I know all about your dead first love. Everyone likes to make excuses for you. Did you know that?"

"Excuse me?"

"Some of us don't let the bad things consume us. You might consider it."

"You don't know what the hell you're talking about."

"Maybe not. But maybe I do. Goodnight, Captain."

She shoved past me and marched out the front door into the snowy night. I stood there for a few moments, not sure what to do with myself. On one hand, I thought Emma allowing Nor to be around her child meant she'd made absolutely certain the woman could be trusted. But on the other, Emma had trusted Cyran, and we saw where that got us. But wouldn't it give her all the more reason to ensure Nor was safe? To be completely positive? The women we'd rescued from Folterra were novices, part of the gods damned Myriad, but they all seemed to be victims. Except for Nor. I wondered why.

Wondering why someone wasn't raped by an evil man was a strange train of thought, so I dismissed it. I supposed it was time for me to go back to the palace and get some rest, but that would take me on the same path as the woman who had just lambasted me. The woman who left on foot to trudge through the snow late at night. A woman who Elora and Thyra liked and Emma seemed to trust.

Hanwen's taint.

Not long later, me and my horse caught up to her, and I watched her struggle through the snow for a moment before I cleared my throat.

"Go away!" she shouted back at me.

"I'm headed back to the palace anyway. It's near midnight, and it's going to take you hours to get to the dormitory at this rate. Consider it a truce." She stopped, turning to look up at me. "For now," I added. Couldn't have her thinking I trusted her. She rolled her eyes and turned forward, trudging through snow which had to be freezing against unclothed skin.

"What possessed you to wear a dress and not pants?" I asked.

"Great divine, you do not stop, do you?" she snapped.

"Stop what?"

"Provoking, goading, irritating, vexing."

"I've been told it's charming."

"They lied."

"Nor, just get on the horse."

"I'm fine." She stumbled.

"Fine, freeze. Far be it from me to stop a woman from freezing to death when she is clearly so determined."

I wasn't going to argue with her. Passing her, I continued on my way, annoyed. Even though the moon was just a fucking sliver, the road was dead going into the city. Safe enough. I convinced myself she'd be fine. And if she wasn't, it wasn't my problem.

But when I glanced over my shoulder a few minutes later and didn't see her behind me, I somehow made it my fucking problem and backtracked to see where she went.

"Nor?" I called out. Either side of the road was forest, and, though not known for vagabonds or criminals, I realized it wouldn't be the worst hiding spot for someone wanting to do harm to a young woman walking alone near midnight. Fuck.

"Nor!" I shouted once more, looking for her footprints in the snow. Once I found them, I saw a long trail going off the side of the road down a steep slope. Had she fallen? It was just a hill, but with the height of the snow and where the hollows from the pine trees sat, it was possible she fell and was struggling to climb back up.

Jumping down from my horse, I went to find her. It only took me a few moments to spot her, a dark spot against the white. She'd dropped her bag, and the contents had spilled out as it tumbled down the hill.

"You alright, Nor?" I called out from above.

Her voice was clouded with tears as she replied, "I'm fine."

"Need help?"

"No. This is the last of it," she said, wiping a hand over her eyes before turning to face me. She kept her eyes averted as she clambered up the hill through the snow. "I dropped my bag, and it spilled everywhere. Half the things are probably ruined now."

I held out my hand to her as she approached the final lip she'd have to climb over to get back onto the road—the steepest part of her ascent. She hesitated for a second before she gripped my hand, and I pulled her up.

"Let me take you home. It doesn't sit right with me to have you walking alone out here. It's cold, and it's late and I don't want to fi—"

"Alright." My mouth snapped shut, surprised she'd given in so quickly. By the look on her face, it had surprised her too. "Only because I'm tired."

"Uh huh," I replied before directing her and helping her onto the horse. "You can sit in the front this time. I'll try not to get sick down your back. If I feel the need to expel the contents of my stomach, I'll direct it to either side. Don't worry."

"Skies above, you're the worst. I couldn't help it. I said I was sorry."

Settling in behind her, I caught a whiff of her soap. Something citrus—bergamot, perhaps. It didn't make me nauseated, so we were already off to a better start than our last trip together.

"I'm actually just teasing, Nor. What kind of name is that, anyway?"

"It's short for something."

"Are you going to tell me?"

"Why would I tell you? You'll probably try to hold it against me."

"Is there a way to hold someone's name against them?"

"I don't know. I'm sure you'll find a way. You seem bound and determined to hate me."

I sighed, rubbing my face. Maybe it was time to turn over a new leaf in all aspects. "Listen, I'll be straightforward with you. That dead first love? Lucia Highclere."

"I know that. Martyr Lucia," she whispered.

"So you know why she died."

"Because she was the Beloved."

"She wasn't, though, was she? And I don't know if they thought she might be one day, or what, but the Myriad said she was, so she was a target. And she died. Whether they meant it or not, the Myriad is responsible for her death."

"I can understand why you'd think that."

"You can probably also understand then why anyone in the Myriad makes my fucking skin crawl."

"Did Lucia willingly tie herself to the Myriad?"

"No. They forced her into it when she was small. Eight or so, I believe."

"And her parents chose that life for her?"

"Yes."

"Will it humanize me for you to know she and I have that in common?"

"I shouldn't need to hear that to humanize you," I mumbled, feeling guilty.

"No," she agreed. "Most novices get to choose. But I didn't. We ran from my father, and this was where we ended up. My mother was devout, and they helped us."

"I suppose it was probably the lesser of two evils."

She nodded and was silent for a while. Finally, the dormitory came into sight on the edge of the city. It was strange to be out this far, away from the bustle, but it was the only place Emma had found to build it. The council had wanted to give her an old barracks, but she'd gotten her way and had built a new home for the displaced women.

"Honor," she said.

"What?"

"Nor is short for Honor."

"Your name is Honor," I repeated, a brow raised.

"I told you my mother was devout. She preferred to worship Hanwen, even though our divinity comes from Ciarden."

"The mind-speaking. My divinity is from Ciarden too. Hanwen, though. That surprises me."

"Why?"

"Most women prefer Aonara or Rhia. Not the God of Wrath. War."

"Justice and honor. Fairness. She—she made a lot of mistakes, but she wanted to be like Hanwen. Even after she started doing the things they forced on her, she hated it. I think it's what got her killed and me sent to Folterra."

"She was part of the trafficking?"

We had reached the dormitory, but neither of us moved.

"Yes. Filenti forced her. She had smuggled out some of the younger girls he had selected. She'd always done what they said to do since she was a mistress, but those girls were young—thirteen or fourteen—so she refused. I was sent to Folterra the next week. I don't think her death was natural like they said."

"They?"

"The novices left behind after Filenti got caught. A fit of apoplexy, they said."

My stomach dropped. A mistress who died suspiciously?

"What was her name?"

"Miriam."

CHAPTER 38

Emmeline

I LOOKED DOWN AT our pile of bags and wood in the snow and then looked back up at Rain. He was bringing one last armful of kindling over, having told me to sit on a rock and wait. Though relatively smooth, the stone was cold, and my ass was freezing. Normally, I would have helped, but I was exhausted. Sore too. He'd been quiet, almost reticent, after he thought he'd hurt me when he tackled me in the snow. I didn't bother trying to address it. There was no point. Patient and undeterred, I would wait for him, even if it killed me in small amounts every day.

"Now, if this isn't alright, just say so, but I don't think we have another choice. Without a tent, it makes the most sense—out of the wind, no snow—"

"I already said it's fine," I sighed. Truly, I was too tired to care.

"Are you sure?" When he saw my facial expression, he gave me a crooked smile and turned to open the rift without another word.

If I thought the cavern on the eastern side of the Alsors was beautiful during the day, it was transcendent at night. A narrow streak of moonlight shone down into the shallow pool, and the glow of the moonfish shimmered off the stone walls. Breathtaking, the luminescent sparkle the creatures gave off was unlike anything I'd ever seen before. No wonder they were thought to be god-touched. My divinity hummed, calling out to the cavern, and I rose from my seat on the stone and grabbed our packs.

"Do you feel that?" I whispered, and he cocked his head.

"I—maybe? It feels…different," he said. "It's faint."

My divinity rose to a fever pitch, and I was sure my chest was vibrating. "It's not faint for me. It's frenetic. Wild."

I took a step forward, about to walk through, when I felt his hand on my wrist.

"It doesn't feel unsafe, does it? Not like the Seat, right?"

"No, no, nothing like that. My divinity wants to be in there. As if maybe it could…rest."

He let go as I pushed ahead, one foot in front of the other, unbothered. The pull of my divinity and the fact I'd been there before and had been able to leave made it easier for me. I knew how to rift now, and the cavern did feel safe. When I stepped through, my divinity settled and calmed, almost like it dispersed to fill the area. Rain followed behind, lugging armfuls of wood and letting the rift close behind him. I sighed, rubbing at my chest. It was as if a pressure had been lifted. I'd been forcing myself to use more divinity than I normally would, just to keep it at bay. But here, I felt peaceful.

I moved closer to the small pool in the center, crouching to see the moonfish as they bumped blindly around, their glowing scales casting opalescent light around them. I heard Rain setting up the logs nearby, using the hole in the cavern above us to vent the smoke as he lit it with his light.

"You know," he said, "I wish I didn't have the fire. I expected to have your healing and harrowing. Nothing more. It's not fair to complain. You didn't ask for this either. But the fire...It's not something I enjoy using."

I didn't turn to look at him, skittish. One wrong move and he'd shut me out and stop talking. "Because of Soren?" I asked, dipping a fingertip into the water as he built up the fire behind me. I could feel its heat, hotter than a standard fire because of the divine flames, and the light cast our silhouettes upon the wall in front of me. Rain was crouched, facing the fire itself, and I watched the curve of his strong back carved out in stark relief on the stone.

"Mmm, partially. Because of him, but also because of you."

"What do you mean?"

"You're the Beloved. The gods blessed you, not me. I shouldn't have this. I don't want the shadows either. All this belongs to you."

The moonfish started swimming down the stream, out toward the lake. I wasn't sure if they didn't like the light or the heat, but I stood and watched the pond clear over several moments as I thought over what Rain said.

"All but one of my blessings came after we performed the ritual. The shadows and light belong to you just as much as they belong to me. And you were part of my first blessing—with Rhia and Elora." I hesitated, not sure if I should share the rest with him. "She came to me in a dream while you were gone."

I watched his shadow as he stood, removing his cloak and putting his hands in his pockets as he spoke.

"The goddess? Was the dream that realistic or do you truly think it was her?"

"It was her; I could tell." His shadow nodded. "I was right when I guessed she was the reason Elora came to be. She didn't come right out and say it, but, since you stopped before—" I blushed despite the fact that this man had been inside me a few times since that first time. "If Rhia hadn't intervened, it was unlikely we would have had a child from it."

"Do you feel any sort of way about that?" he asked, carefully weighing the words as he spoke them, taking a step closer to me. I didn't know why I faced the pond, looking down into it. The moonfish were all gone. I took my other glove off, the warmth of the cavern making them unnecessary, and lifted my hand to the steady stream of water coming down from above. Frigid, I pulled my hand back quickly.

"I'm glad she intervened, if that's what you mean. I'm glad I have a daughter, and I'm glad she's yours."

"I'm glad she's mine too."

"She offered to do it again."

He stilled. "Do what again?"

"Intervene. She wouldn't promise that I'd get you back, but she said she could give me a babe since I hadn't had my courses yet."

"And you said no?"

"How could I say yes? Not without you." I shook my head, and he took a few more steps until he stood just behind me. "She was quite cruel about it." I inhaled quickly, trying to avoid tears, but my voice still shook. "Said it would have been a boy. I'm sorry if I missed our only chance to have another. With the way my body barely held onto Elora...A goddess blessing might have been the only way." I suddenly felt nervous and tried to change the subject. "Gods, it's warm in here now."

A deep breath and a sigh came from behind me. "I don't need another babe from you," he whispered, and I closed my eyes. "I can't say it won't be fun to try though. If you're warm, I'll take your cloak."

I chuckled and turned just as he reached to unfasten the snap at my throat. The action between us was fumbled, his hand grazing roughly over my shoulder, and I wasn't able to contain my hiss of pain as I jerked away from the movement.

"Divine hell, Em! What was that?"

"Sorry. I'm fine," I said, stiffly shucking off my cloak and tossing it toward our packs.

"No, you're clearly in pain. You've been favoring your arm all day. Why haven't you healed yourself? " His eyes narrowed. "Is that why D helped you off the horse?"

I was about to tell him what it was, but his comment set my blood on fire all over again. "Dewalt helped me off my horse because he's madly in love with me, obviously. I thought you noticed?" I marched over to my pack, pulling out the attached bed roll and wicking away the water with Rain's divinity as he'd shown me.

"Oh, don't do that."

"Do what, Rain? That's why you punched him in the head, isn't it? Male peacocking?"

"It was idiotic. We can agree that I acted a fool. Wait—peacocking? Like the bird? Nereza's birds?"

"Yes. They show off for their mates with their big, stupid feathers and their insufferable egos."

"I've seen her peacocks, you know. They're quite beautiful."

"Irrelevant. One can be both visually appealing and unbearable."

His grin was a lazy one, slow-forming and intentional as he crossed his arms. I stuck out my chin, and he dropped his posture a second later.

"I healed Dewalt and plan to speak to him about it when we get back. He knew it would rile me, and I was already angry with him because of the Wend. For allowing you to—"

"Allowing me to?" I barked a laugh. "I am his queen. He didn't *allow* me to do anything."

"It's the Wend, Em! Divine hell. You'd never even been to the capital until a couple months ago."

"I'd never been the Beloved until a couple months ago, either. I made a mistake with the Wend, but only because I didn't think about the familiar faces who went with me. Not because I shouldn't have been doing it."

"Then why was I forbidden to know what you were doing?"

"Because I knew you wouldn't approve."

"And you didn't think you could convince me otherwise."

I sighed, throwing my hands down at my sides. "With how things have been, with you not even risking being around me, what was I supposed to think? I don't know what you would have me do, Rain. I had to do *something*."

"Are you already bored with this life?"

"I'm not bored," I said, voice clipped. The insinuation I'd risk my safety out of boredom made me want to slap him. He'd deserve it, and I doubted I'd regret it. "I had to do something because I've been stuck in my head. You won't let me in, and I can't get out. If I couldn't fix you, and I couldn't fix me, at least I could fix them. It's what I do! What I've always done, Rain."

He looked as if I'd actually slapped him rather than just thought about it. "I'm sorry," he said.

"It's fine." I busied myself with my pack again.

"No, it's not."

"Alright, it's not. You're right."

"You're struggling over the novices, aren't you?" I dipped my head, not trusting my voice. "Oh, Em," he whispered, and he took a few steps toward me. I stood, rebuking the motion with my own. "I suppose I thought you would talk to Dewalt about it," he said.

"I didn't want to talk to Dewalt about it! I wanted to talk to you!" I shouted, my words echoing. "And if you thought I'd talk to Dewalt about it, why wouldn't you ask him about me? About how I was doing? Then you'd have known I was keeping it all to myself."

"I'm sorry. I've been wrapped up in my own issues. I—you and Dewalt—"

"Aren't married. Aren't bonded. Aren't two parts of one *soul*, Rain. You might not need me to get through what you've been through, but I need *you*. It's as if you forget who we belong to."

Standing to face him, I ripped my sweater off and unraveled my scarf from my neck, careful with my tender skin. My hair fell in a soft wave, and Rain didn't notice as he lifted his chin and crossed the distance between us.

"You mistake me. I need you more than I've ever needed anyone. Staying away from you has been—" He shook his head. "A fish without water. The tides without the moon. A flower without the gods damn sun. You are my heart and soul. You are the reason I draw breath. That's why I've been so fucking scared to hurt you. I refuse to live in this world if you're not a part of it, and if I somehow was the reason for it? I want to escape those thoughts, but the worst part is that I shouldn't. When I wake up in a cold sweat and have to remind myself where I am, I'm grateful it's not by your side."

It hurt, but I understood. It wasn't as if I didn't think he was struggling too. I knew he was, but he seemed so content to wade through it without me. "I know sometimes you have a hard time telling it's me. But I want to help you. I want us to be able to help each other."

"Yes. I know it's you, I do, but it's a lot easier when I can see your skin." His eyes moved to my collarbone as I knew they would. Though I wore a shirt, without the scarf he could see my neck. He blinked, and I tossed my hair over my shoulder.

"What—"

"That's where I went with Dewalt," I murmured.

He stepped forward, and I watched as his hand lifted and dropped a few times. I started unbuttoning my shirt, allowing the top of it to fall open. There was no sensuality behind it, no attempt to draw his attention to my breasts, as I slid the shirt off my shoulder.

I closed my eyes as his fingertips reached out and he traced the swirling ink winding between my freckles. The flowers mirrored the shape of the Damia constellation, and their petals and vines twisted and turned over my skin. Lilacs, violets, lavender—all flowers from the garden he'd created for me—formed a scattered trail across my shoulder and up my neck. It had taken a few hours for the elvish woman to paint the designs on my skin, and she had to do it twice. The first time, I'd stupidly let my divinity heal it after she uttered the incantation, and the ink was immediately gone. She was quite pressed about having to paint it a second time, strongly implying she wouldn't do it a third. I didn't blame her. After the second time, I'd held my divinity back and let the ink and incantation sink deep.

"Damia," he whispered, pressing his lips to the freckles I'd left alone. I didn't want to take the markings from him, but I'd wanted to give him more. Something he could see without me having to pull away my clothing, the hint of it peeking up my neck. I shivered as his lips and fingertips traced my skin. When he finally pulled away from me, tucking my hair behind my ear, I opened my eyes. The gold in his own shimmered in the firelight.

"You did this for me?"

"I did it for us."

When he dipped his head toward mine, I turned mine away.

"Em," he murmured.

"I told you I'd wait, and I will. For as long as it takes. But I have to protect myself too."

"From me."

"Isn't that what you've wanted all along? For me to protect myself from you?"

"Not like this, no."

"You can't have it all, Rain. You can't have me when you need me, only to forget me when I need you."

"If you think I've forgotten you for a single minute, you're wrong. You're all I fucking think about."

"You could have fooled me."

"The years apart from you were easier than these few weeks. You have consumed me. You think I don't want to be near you? With you? Inside you? Gods, to finally have you back and be forced to stay away? I went to a fucking mindbreaker, Em."

"You did what?" I exclaimed, whipping my head back to face him.

"To remove the memories of the shifter, but I guess they used one on me in Folterra. I can't get rid of them. They're too tangled. I'll go mad trying."

"Rain—"

"So, it's funny you say I forget you. When I quite literally cannot forget even a fake, corrupted version of you. But I hear you, and I'm not going anywhere."

"Don't feel like you have—if it's too much, I—"

"There hasn't been a gods damn moment since I've met you when you haven't been too much. You eclipse the fucking sun, Em. I ought to be used to it by now. You've been so brave. You saved our daughter, you saved me—gods, what can't you do?"

I didn't move as he finished unbuttoning my shirt and slipped it off my shoulders.

"I'm sorry I haven't matched your fortitude. A flaw I'm going to begin to rectify tonight. I'm—I have to trust us, trust *you*."

"It's not your—"

"Do you remember our last time here? You faced your fear. I helped you face it, and you stood beside me in this beautiful, god-touched cavern. It seems as good a place as any for you to help me face my own fears. Help me, dear heart."

His fingers found the buttons of my breeches, and he unfastened them, tugging them down and struggling with the leggings I wore beneath. I didn't move, afraid for more than one reason. He knelt, tugging at every barrier to my skin until his thumbs grazed my legs. I stood bare before him—in both heart and body.

He stayed where he was, sliding calloused hands up the outsides of my thighs, past my hips, before settling them on my waist. Leaning forward, he pressed his lips just under my navel. My limbs were frozen, stuck like stone. I was waiting for his shadows to make an appearance, for him to stop what he was doing and break me apart again.

His lips and hands forged a path downward.

"Let me," he whispered against delicate skin, pressing a soft kiss to the juncture of my thigh.

I relaxed the tiniest bit, and he could tell, dragging his hands to my backside and gripping me. He dipped, kissing and licking his way over to that sensitive spot, and I closed my eyes. A sigh fought its way past my lips, and, tentatively, I rested my hand on his shoulder.

"You're divine. The greatest thing the gods have ever done was design for me to taste you for eternity. Now, spread your legs wider."

I hesitated, still waiting for the pain.

"Don't keep me from what belongs to me. Spread your legs, and show me that pretty cunt."

His words reached low in my stomach and squeezed, twisting. He pressed a kiss to my clit and breathed deep—inhaling me. Ripping his shirt off, he tossed it behind him before gripping one of my thighs, pulling it up to rest on his shoulder. Nearly losing my balance, I latched onto his head, trying to dig my fingers into his hair.

"That's right, put my tongue where you need me." My skin muffled his voice.

"Rain, I don't—are you sure?"

I tugged on his hair, pulling his head back so I could see him, and he licked his lips as his eyes met mine. He didn't say a word in reply, but slid his hand up the inside of my planted leg, and his fingertips found me slick and wanting. Circling my entrance once, he pushed in two fingers, and I moaned, my hips twitching forward.

His other hand slid behind me, palming my ass, drawing me close. And he feasted. Ravenous, his lips and tongue roamed across my skin as he stroked relentless fingers inside of me. Thorough, unyielding, and punctuating, he coaxed me to the edge. Sucking my clit hard, he pulled me closer against him with a firm hand, and I wondered how he could breathe. He didn't stop, didn't slow down, just kept an unremitting pace. Part of me wondered if he was being so rough to punish me, but I dismissed it. Even if he was, he knew part of me needed a bit of pain. The sting made the pleasure all the sweeter. Moving up to a tiptoe, I held onto his hair and neck for balance, body jerking as he added a third finger and thrusted. I groaned, eyes rolling back.

Still moving inside me, Rain's lips left my skin as he tilted his head up.

"I need you closer when you come on my tongue," he panted.

"I'm a-about to," I sighed as his fingers curled the slightest bit, making my knee buckle.

"Not close enough." His fingers abruptly left me, and he adjusted, one hand wrapping around my thigh on his shoulder while tugging on the back of my other leg. When he moved, pulling me toward him as he started leaning back, I realized his intention.

"Rain, I don't know—"

"I do. Closer, Em. I want to drown in you."

Hand clasped to my thigh on his shoulder, he leaned back on his discarded shirt, unfolding his long legs as his muscular abdomen bent me to his will, bringing me along in his slow descent. I barely kept my balance as he guided my body. I landed hard, a knee on either side of his face, and I leaned back, keeping my weight off him.

A ghost of a touch on my knees, he healed the ache in an instant.

"Love, I—" I squealed as his hands cupped my ass and dragged me onto his face. Without a moment's hesitation, his tongue moved in a forceful path up the center of me, and I shuddered. If he couldn't breathe before, he certainly wouldn't be able to now. His touch roamed up my hips and sides, and even as I tried to lift, his hands settled on my waist and pulled me down.

"I'm going to smother you," I gasped as he turned his head, pressing a kiss to my inner thigh.

"You're not. Now use me."

His tongue parted my needy flesh, sliding wet and warm over touch-deprived skin. Rough hands moved to my hips, dragging me back and forth atop him. The friction from the scruff on his face was a delicious hurt, and I tilted my head back on a moan. Using one hand to guide my body, he slid the other up, tracing gentle fingertips past my ribs, cupping my heavy breast in his hand. Rubbing his thumb over my nipple as he focused his attention on my clit, he drew sounds and pleasure from my body, dragging me toward a climax I was sure would leave me shattered.

His desire for me to ride his face drove me wild with need. Of all the ways to bring me pleasure with his mouth, he chose the one which made him the most vulnerable. I was probably reading into it more than I ought to, but, especially after everything he had been through, the weakness he experienced when he couldn't see my collarbone, this felt like *more*. I'd relaxed, widening my stance and lowering onto him, and I lifted on my knees, suddenly uncertain. Within a second, he dropped my breast, and both hands grasped me tight, roughly yanking me back down. A punishing nip to my clit with the faint hint of teeth sent sparks of want up my spine. I felt shadows coil on my skin as pinpricks of sensation threatened to overwhelm me.

Looking down, I realized the shadows weren't mine, and I froze. This was too much, and he wasn't ready for it. Relief found me when green eyes met mine, a roguish sparkle in them. Coaxing his shadows to twine on my thighs, holding me exactly where he wanted me, he continued his attentions. With both hands free, he allowed one to slip back up to my breast, tweaking a nipple, while the other reached behind me and cupped my backside. He nibbled my clit, sucking and laving with his tongue.

"*Oh, gods.*"

A prayer and praise in one, I dragged out the words. And then I moved. One hand threaded through his short curls, and the other held my own hair off my neck as I rocked on him. He groaned into me as I ground my hips, accepting what he wanted from me. I let myself sink lower, as I had been before, and my hips worked over him. Erotic sounds filled the cavern; my moans, his soft grunts, and the wet mess he'd made of me warred for dominance. A wandering hand slid across my ass, fingers pressing, roaming. I didn't stop him as I continued moving my body, undulating a beat onto his face. When a fingertip paused in its wandering, exploring one spot more thoroughly, the sound I made deafened the rest, a rough groan breaking past my lips. The wicked man chuckled into my skin as he pressed a kiss to my burning flesh and sucked roughly on my clit. Gods, I had missed him. He was the only one with such power to weaken me in this way, to make me feel as if I was on the edge of life and death, teetering between absolution and damnation.

My pulse scorched a path between my legs, the fire building, as he speared his tongue into me. I felt my orgasm build. A long exhale of breath against my clit made my internal muscles clench as he continued to devour me. My divinity stretched and roamed, almost like a cloud of shimmering birds in the air, twisting and turning as it expanded. As if it searched for a place—a home. I held onto him as I moved, using my other hand to grab my breast, increasing the pleasure. A long, decadent pull on the most sensitive part of me sent me over the edge, legs twitching and thighs trying to snap together as I came. My hips bucked as I pulled on my nipple, crying out as he licked and sucked me through my release.

Dropping his shadows, his hands clamped over my legs, and he slid me back toward his chest as he panted. Looking down at him, I grew embarrassed over the sheen of my desire I'd left behind, and when he gave an imperceptible shake of his head, I knew he felt it through the bond.

"Do not be ashamed of what your body does for me; I told you I wanted to drown." A wicked grin.

I lifted one leg, about to climb off him, and he tugged me back, pressing a final kiss to my oversensitive clit. I lost my balance and toppled over in a shriek.

I started laughing, spent, and he rolled onto his side, joining in with a smile and running a hand up my thigh. He quieted as I continued chuckling and just watched me. I had collapsed on my back, my hair spread out beneath me, and I knew the angle he saw me from wasn't all that flattering, and I began to fidget.

"Quit that," he said.

"Quit what?"

"Giving me that look."

"What look?"

"Like I should be anything less than awed by you."

I snorted, sitting up and tugging my knees to my chest. "This is what I missed the most—while you've been gone. Laughing with you. I thought maybe we'd used up all the good moments. That this hell has been some type of penance for our joy."

"If it is, that's bullshit. We've both earned any joy we can take—tenfold. And I plan to keep it."

"Speaking of planning, you didn't tell me about the last council meeting. Have they gotten over the dragons?"

Rain rolled onto his back, laughing. "You're going to talk to me about council meetings and dragons when I'm hard as a diamond?"

His tented pants proved his point.

"I'm sorry, I've just missed talking—"

"I'm teasing," he said as he rose. After shimmying out of his clothing, he stood fully nude before me. It was the first time I'd seen him that way in weeks. Of course, my eyes were drawn to the thick erection he sported, but the lean lines of muscle leading there from his abdomen distracted me. He'd gained back some of his weight and muscle, but he was still more lean than he had been before Darkhold. It shook me to see that even a month of comfortable eating hadn't wholly fixed him. "Come here." He held a hand out to me and helped me stand. Leading us to the pool where the moonfish had been, he dipped a toe in.

"I figured the fire was heating it too much if the moonfish fled. It feels comfortable if you want to join me."

"That's not warm." I nodded toward the trickle from the ceiling of the cave.

"I think we can manage avoiding it," he replied. The side we stood on was a gradual decline, and he walked in slowly. "Alright, I'll admit it's still a bit cold. Come, keep me warm. Don't make me drag you in here like I did the last time we visited this place."

Shooting a devastating grin over his shoulder, I took a moment to admire him. Halfway turned to face me, the indentation of muscle over his hip was stark, countered by the rounded curve of his backside. My eyes were drawn downward, where I found the only remaining visual evidence of his turmoil in Folterra. A scar the length of my hand ran down the back of his thigh, puckered at the top.

"What's that from?" I pointed.

"I actually don't know. I woke up with it in the dungeon."

"Have you tried to heal it since you've been back?"

"No."

"Why?"

"I don't know. A reminder, I suppose?"

"You need to be reminded?" I moved forward, stepping into the cool water and wincing as I let my fingertips brush over the top of the scar.

"A scar I can see helps me remember the memories are lies."

Raising my hand to his lower back, I walked my fingers across skin peppered with old wounds, and I remembered his words to me. "Your scars are proof."

He cocked a brow and smiled sadly before continuing into the water. "That they are."

Turning to face me and walking backwards, he grabbed both my hands and led me into the water. It was shallow, waist high where we stood, and he dragged my body against his.

"You'll be in all future council meetings."

"Really?"

"You should have been in them already, but I was afraid talking about Declan and Folterra..." He trailed off.

"Would trigger the thoughts about the shifter."

He nodded as he brushed my hair off my shoulder. "We believe he's going to make moves on Lamera first and use it to push east."

"Is Nereza going to help defend the Supreme?"

"That's what we're working on. I've already sent soldiers. I left word for Ven to leave now. We need the seaborn. With them, we might be able to avoid any confrontation in Lamera—especially if Nereza cooperates."

"Your sister is going to be furious with you for making her miss the coronation."

"You know, I think she might be relieved. She's got a lot on her mind. I told her to take Hyše with her. I hope that's fine. And no, the council still isn't over the dragons."

"Hyše was the best choice. She's ruthless. But the others? They're harmless!" He smiled down at me, and gods had I missed it.

"While I don't agree with you, that's not the issue. They don't like knowing you can make them."

"Then tell them I can't make more; that it's dangerous."

"Ah yes, I should make it public knowledge that you're tied to the dragons and when they hurt, you hurt. Good thinking."

I slapped his chest as I leaned back on a laugh. "Irses is probably just as mad as Ven. I wish I'd gone to see them before we left."

The dragons we'd brought from the Cascade had been living near the hot springs I'd visited with Shivani and Lavenia. The same family who tended to the cabin agreed to take them on with the added benefit of extra pay. Ryo had grown quite a bit in the last few weeks, and I'd planned on taking Elora the next time I visited. Now that Rain seemed to be ready to move forward with caution, perhaps we could plan the trip together. Though I couldn't help but feel like maybe he was just on the edge of slipping away from me again. My stomach was already twisting with anxiety over it.

"You're nervous." He wrapped his arms around me, pulling me flush against him. The cool water and the serious conversation had calmed him down some, but not enough I didn't feel every bit of him bob against me beneath the water.

"I just don't want you to go back to—to before—to when—"

"I won't." Confident in his words, he pressed a kiss to the crown of my head. "The tattoo was brilliant. Really. I've only had to look once, and it instantly helped. How did you think of it?"

"I always caught you looking at my collarbone like you wished I was naked, but not in a fun way."

He laughed. "You naked is always fun."

"Dewalt told me about his tattoos, and I didn't think it was a bad idea."

"How bad did it hurt? I've always been too chicken to get one."

I blinked at him. "You? Chicken? I just assumed you didn't want one."

"No. I was scared to get one. Dewalt always whines so much, but you haven't been nearly as dramatic."

"The worst part was right after she finished the incantation, and I had to do that part twice." I pouted and explained what I meant.

"It has to be strange to repress your healing like that." He swiped his thumb over my lower lip as I nodded. "Has anyone else seen it yet?"

"No. Only you."

"Good. I think I need a better look," he said as he grabbed me around the waist, lifting me as he sank into the water. I wrapped my legs around him with a yelp, and he supported me with both hands cupping beneath me. Holding me close, he peered down at the ink on my shoulder.

"Lilacs, lavender, violets—what's that one?"

"Delphinium."

"Delphinium," he repeated. "Is that in our garden?"

"I think so. It wouldn't have bloomed yet, but I suspected. They were on that first dress you bought me though. The ruined one."

"Keeva," he growled before shaking his head. "You left the freckles."

"I did, just in case. I wanted you to be able to see them."

He pressed a soft kiss to my skin, a satisfied sound rumbling in his chest.

"Oh, look," he said as he turned me to the side so I could see out to the lake, a tiny sliver of water and stars. I could just make out the glowing trail of moonfish swimming outward.

"I hope we don't get them eaten. They don't blend in, do they?"

He chuckled, pressing a kiss to my cheek as I stared out. "Gods, I love how your mind works. I think: beautiful, once-in-a-lifetime sight. You though, you think they're going to be eaten, and it's going to be our fault."

"Well, it feels sacrilegious. We shooed them out of their god-touched pool."

"I think shooing the fish out is the least sacrilegious thing happening here. I just made you cry out to the gods while you rode my face."

I buried my head in his chest as his rumbling laughter rolled over my body, making my heart take notice and relax by a fraction. I wasn't sure how long it would take me to be confident that he wasn't going anywhere—that he wasn't going to shut me out at any moment.

"If anything, I'm probably more god-touched than this cavern."

"Ah, then the pool belongs to you." I could hear his smile.

"Yes, I was just kind enough to share it. The fish knew we needed privacy."

"Oh, I'm sure," he said as he squeezed my bottom. "Well, we wouldn't want to waste their consideration, would we?"

"It would be rude to waste it." Lifting my head from his chest, I pressed my lips to his jaw, slow and open-mouthed, before asking, "Have you started taking the tonic again? We were fine last time, but with everything going on, I—not that I'm ruling it out, but—"

"I started taking it again when we came back to Astana. With the bond, I figured we'd—"

"Have to."

"Don't say it like that. Not while I'm holding you and my cock is aching to be inside you."

"Your cock is aching, or you are?"

"You want to argue semantics about this?" He reached down, grabbing his length and rubbing it against my still sensitive clit.

"You know I always want to argue semantics, even if you're inside me. Even if I'm squeezing you tight, stretching to take you deep—"

"Gods, Em. You're going to make me finish just from talking that way. Everything is aching. My cock, my gods damn soul. I want to be so close to you, so deep I can't move, can't breathe without feeling you. I'm convinced you're the only reason I exist."

Notching him at my entrance, I pumped his length twice, and his head tilted back on a groan. But no matter how much I wanted to sheathe him inside me, I wasn't going to let him get away with this distance, saying nothing.

"Promise me you won't shut me out again. That you won't stay away to protect me."

"I promise I'll try not to."

"Not good enough," I said as I slid my hand down his length, rough. "If you want to sink this thick, perfect cock into my tight, warm *cunt*," I said, enunciating each word with a stroke as I used his own filthy language against him, "Then I need more than trying."

"*Fuck*, dear heart, you're going to kill me," he hissed, closing his eyes. "I promise."

A quick pump of my hand.

"I *swear*."

"Then take what's yours," I whispered.

And he did.

In one precise, vicious stroke, he slammed me down onto his cock as his hips bucked upward, lifting me out of the water. Invading and consuming, his body claimed mine, and my fervent heart began to mend. My back arched as I grabbed onto his shoulders, my hair dipping into the water behind me. His thrusts demanded, and my body acquiesced. Opening for him and accepting him, my muscles loosened, and the tension ebbed away. He leaned down, dipping to caress my breasts with his lips, slowing his movements even as I writhed on his hardness. My divinity expanded and glowed on the edges of my vision. I'd never felt so in tune with it. Closing my eyes, I moved my body on his, whimpering as he slowed me, dragging me up and down his length.

"Greedy thing," he murmured, carrying me to the opposite end of the pool where a rock ledge waited. "You need me just as much as I need you."

"More. I've always needed you more."

Setting me down on the edge, caging his body around me, he pressed into me so hard I gasped. He was so deep, my eyes rolled, and my head fell back on a moan. My divinity soared and stretched, and I let it crawl to life on my skin. I let it be, didn't contain it, didn't ask it to do my bidding. It caressed my skin, raising goosebumps on my flesh.

"You never needed me. You *wanted* me," he argued.

A deep thrust meant to pierce my heart. He grabbed my legs, spreading me, holding me tightly as he used his cock to give pleasure and proof to his words.

"They're the same. I wanted you; I chose you."

I braced myself with one hand on the ground beside me as I wrapped the other around his neck. When he pulled nearly all the way out of me, I looked down, watching as he slammed back in. Seeing my arousal glisten on his length as he disappeared within me turned me molten. It was me soaking into his skin, my body which gave him pleasure, my soul with which his was entwined.

Gripping my thighs, he tugged me close, crowding me. Hands moved to my hips as he pounded into me. Forehead to forehead, our breaths mingled as his body slammed against mine. He slid his hand between us, using his thumb to press down on my clit as his hips moved slower against me.

"But you thrive without me, Em. Always have and always will. Me? I'm half a person without you. That's true need."

I bit my lip as I looked up at him, the deliberate thrusts while he put pressure on my clit nearly too much. But I still noticed something like hurt dancing in his eyes. And when I saw the vulnerability, he rubbed me with more pressure, wanting to distract me, wanting me to let it pass, but I wouldn't allow it.

"Every moment we've ever been apart, I spent waiting. Wanting to claw my—" I gasped as his thumb circled faster. "Claw my way to you. To fight you and let me love you."

"Even after I left you that first time?"

"Yes," I hissed as he slammed into me once more, my breasts bouncing from the force. "But I didn't think you wanted me."

"Then why did you fight me so hard when you found out I did? That I've never stopped wanting you?"

"Wanting to love you—" Thrust. "And fight with you—" Thrust. "Doesn't negate that you left me."

He slid deep and froze, leaning forward and gathering me close in his arms. I wrapped my legs tight around him. There was no room between us, no space for unspoken words. The bond between us trembled and sparked, matching the electric energy of our divinity.

"And when you gave in, I left again, didn't I?" he whispered into my neck, voice thick. "I didn't mean to this time, Em."

He moved slowly, pumping in and out of me. He brushed my hair out of the way and was careful as he kissed the ink on my skin. Unlike the marks on my feet, burned upon me when I'd tried to run from Faxon, this was a brand I'd chosen. His and his alone. There would be no one else, regardless of his propensity to leave me, physically or otherwise.

"Never again." He vowed with gentle thrusts. He'd sworn first with words and now wrote promises on my flesh, and our trust—a fraught, tenuous thing—budded and flowered. I hoped one day, that trust would be second-nature, that we wouldn't have to try for it, but I'd work every day to have it with him.

He grabbed my thighs, spreading my legs farther. "Need to get deeper," he grunted as he attempted to do just that. Lifting one leg so my foot rested on the ledge, I opened up for him even more. The ache was deep and thorough as he pushed into places I didn't realize were possible.

"Rain," I panted, and he lifted his gaze so his eyes met mine.

"Mine," he uttered, choked with emotion, and I watched as a tear broke from his lashes and its descent cracked my heart in two. Swiping my thumb over it, I cupped his jaw, pulling his mouth to mine.

"Always," I whispered on his lips. And then they were on mine, and words didn't matter anymore. Promises didn't matter. Past hurts and haunts meant nothing when we came together this way. His tongue sought entrance, and I opened for him. He stole my moan with his mouth as he slid his hand between us once more, circling my clit with force.

"Give it to me," he muttered against my lips.

My body tightened, a taut thread about to snap. The building pleasure rolled through me, causing goosebumps.

"Too much, too much," I whispered, closing my eyes. My legs shook as he continued his movements, and, arms around his neck, I pulled him close, attempting to still his hand with the press of our bodies. It only seemed to stir him further.

"Need to feel you fall apart." He nipped my jaw and nuzzled into my neck, lips moving against fevered skin. "It's me you come for, my cock filling you, my name written on your gods damn soul."

"Only you. Only ever you," I groaned as warmth traversed my spine. I'd never had such intense pleasure build up for so long, and I didn't know what to do with myself. Our divinity sang, and I could feel the harmonic melding of our souls. The cavern amplified all of it, and lightning danced along my pebbled skin. When I opened my eyes, I saw their glowing reflection in Rain's own. Faint whorls of light came to life on my skin, emitting a gentle glow. The light was soft, so unlike the divine fire I could call to my hand.

"A shooting star. Did you fall from Damia just for me?" He pressed his lips to my luminescent skin, unaffected by the sight as he wrote his urgency on my clit with skilled fingertips.

Chest full, my breathing quickened, and my mouth dropped open on a silent scream. The pressure between my legs relieved in a final crash, long and complete, and my body moved of its own accord, folding backward. It was too much. A cool breeze blew through the cavern from the lake, and even the touch of air was too much for my overstimulated skin. I was sobbing, though no tears fell, overwhelmed with the touch.

"Perfect," Rain grunted as he moved inside me with a fury while my body pulsed around him. "Squeezing me so gods damn tight—*fuck*."

Tears formed in my vision as he barreled into me. Deep, forceful thrusts as he panted on my lips had me crying out. My fading release climbed once more, sooner and more forcefully than I'd have thought possible. I groaned, shock moving through me as scars of light on my body pulsed along to my heartbeat.

"Another. Give me another, dear heart," he demanded.

"I can't," I gasped.

"You can, and you will."

He gently lowered me, laying me flat on the ground while pulling me closer to the edge of the pool where he stood. One hand on my thigh and the other moving against that sensitive spot, giving me the friction I needed to give him what he wanted. I reached up, using both hands to grab my breasts, pinching my nipples and giving myself the small pain to go along with the overwhelming pleasure. And when that pressure burst, and I came screaming his name, Rain finished too, a loud, stuttering moan on his lips as he spilled into me. He panted as he looked down at me, brows gathered in the middle with his mouth open. Eyes soft, his gaze slid over me, blissful. He gave a soft sigh of contentment before collapsing forward into my embrace, his head resting between my breasts.

I slid my fingers into his hair, massaging his scalp, relishing the closeness I'd been craving, I'd been dying for. I closed my eyes as my divinity settled, slowing with my breaths. Rain's breathing slowed as well, and we laid like that for long moments until I finally realized he'd fallen asleep half-standing and still inside me.

When I roused him, his eyes met mine, and he said, "Mine."

CHAPTER 39

LAVENIA

I hadn't intended on confronting Dewalt. Reflecting on those early years when it was just the three of us helped me understand why I felt the way I did. I hadn't resented him back then, would never have made him feel like he was a burden. But now that he seemed stable, and had been that way for a while, it seemed safe to tell him what I'd been feeling all those years.

There was something to be said about feeling like a caretaker of someone else's happiness; it could make you forget about your own. I hated seeing him and my brother hurt. I didn't resent them, not truly. But it was seeing Dewalt nearly kill himself by accident a few times which set me on edge, and when I suspected he was going to do it on purpose? I stopped sleeping soundly.

I'd been close with Lucia, so when she grew close with Dewalt, so did I. He became my best friend too. The three of us had been attached to one another. Even though they grew feelings for each other, I'd never felt as if I was intruding or an afterthought. But once she died, a part of him did too. It became my responsibility to make sure the rest of him didn't. It was something I was far too young for. Who could I go to? My brother was nearly as bad. No, it was up to me to keep them whole. And I hadn't wanted thanks or needed it. I'd craved no sort of recognition for anything. But the unceremonious way in which he dumped the bond had hurt my feelings. It reminded me of how little they thought of me during those years.

It was a gods damn relief to tell him. I hadn't realized how heavy it had been weighing on me. I wouldn't take any of it back, wouldn't have changed any of my actions, but my realization had me demanding what I deserved.

It was a huge change for me, and I surprised myself when I'd said it.

It was with that newfound confidence I wore on my frame, we arrived in Northport. Nixy had rifted us, and we'd somehow corralled Hyśe through it. The dragon was on the smaller side but fierce despite her size. Mairin had been the one to convince her to take those tentative steps through the opening, using a dead pheasant as a lure. Body lowered to the ground, the dragon prowled through like a cat before shaking herself, great wings spreading out from her body.

She'd been made from the memory of Emma killing Keeva, and it gave her an intimidating look. Inky black scales and wings were contrasted by orange eyes, probably drawn from the light of a torch. Mairin threw her head back and laughed when people started shrieking on the streets of Northport. Her smile was contagious, wide and bright. I stifled my affection.

"Oh, we should have thought about that," said Nixy.

"There's the *Netari*." I pointed to the ship anchored in the bay. "You two rift over, and I'll fly?"

I scrambled atop Hyše within a moment. I hadn't been able to ride a dragon yet. Emma had commissioned special saddles for them, and I was excited, if a little scared.

"You have any idea what you're doing?" the merrow called out to me.

"Not at all."

I heard her laugh alongside Nixy's rift, and I tried to squeeze my legs together and lean forward like I would with a horse. The dragon didn't move, probably didn't even notice me squeezing its sides. I remembered Emma's instruction to just speak to them, and though dubious, I attempted it.

"Up?"

With my tentative command, Hyše launched into the sky on a powerful thrust of her legs and a flap of her wings. I shrieked, unable to contain my surprise. Gripping onto the pommel, farther forward than on a horse's saddle, I let loose a yell as a smile lit up my face. I knew Brenna was aboard that ship, and the coming days would not be pleasant for me. This felt like one last moment of freedom.

Swooping in a circle over the ship, the dragon found a place to delicately land, claws made to tear and rip touching down softly.

"If you want to fly over us, you can," I told the dragon after sliding down from the saddle. She took off a moment later, and a group of soldiers and sailors, all shocked into silence, met me with curious stares.

"Your Highness," a gruff voice said from behind me, and I turned to face Beau, the captain of the *Netari*. It had been quite some time since I'd seen him. What little hair was left on his head was still blond, but his long beard had gone white.

"Beau!" I shouted, crossing the few steps to meet him and pulling him into a hug. We clapped each other on the back before separating. His grin was missing a few more teeth than the last time I'd seen it.

"How's Melina?"

"Still mean as a snake and pretty as a peach. And Dewalt?"

I swallowed, not sure why the question set me back. Dewalt was still my friend, after all, and it was only expected for him to ask. Still, I cleared my throat.

"He's—"

"Ah fuck. I'm sorry. I forgot. Brenna told me about the bond."

Oh, hell.

"We're still friends, Beau. It's not some sort of heartbreak," I said, even though it felt similar. Not a romantic hurt, but a deep one all the same. "He's got his hands full training Rainier's daughter."

"I couldn't wait to ask you about that." He put his arm around my shoulders and led me to the captain's quarters. "There still hasn't been any formal proclamation, but it's true, then? The king has a daughter? Nearly grown?"

"It's true." I nodded. "She's almost sixteen."

He shook his head and swiped a hand over his brow as he fell into his chair and kicked his boots onto his desk. I sat across from him. "He kept it a secret all these years?"

"No, not quite."

"No." He gasped. "*She* did?"

"She didn't know."

He steepled his fingers on his stomach as he lifted a brow. "But she knows now? That makes little sense."

"The 'she' you speak of is your queen, my sister, and my friend. You'd do best if you mind that, Beau."

"Lavenia, you know I mean nothing by it. I'm not the only one confused. That's all it is—confusion."

"It's not their duty or mine to explain it, but she's his. Doesn't matter that it took some time for him to know it. She might not have been raised near him, but gods, she is familiar." I smiled. "Besides, you should be happy. It means I'll never sit on the throne."

He guffawed and slapped his knee. "You'd be a good queen. Don't kid yourself."

"I won't waste my breath on arguing with you. So, have you ever met with the seaborn before?"

"Met with them? Nah. Encountered? Yeah. Rare, though. They've kept to themselves as long as I've been at sea."

"And the Seaborn Queen? Any stories about her?"

"Just that it's probably a mistake to seek her out. But your brother assured me you had something she'd want."

"Some*one*. Her only daughter."

"No shit?"

"No shit. The spitfire with the red hair. Mairin."

"Why is she with you?"

"She's land-bound. She's been living in Vesta for the last decade. Mairin is a longtime friend of the queen, and she's a good person."

"But she's seaborn. What is she? A merrow? A selkie?"

"Merrow."

He shivered. "Ever seen her in her true form?"

"No." Gods, I'd never even thought about it.

"Vicious creatures, I tell you. Unsettling."

"Well, I don't think she can shift into it without the pendant. Someone destroyed it."

"You think she plans to request another from her mother?"

"What do you mean?"

"I don't know. I've heard the Seaborn Queen has the magick to do it but rarely does. You get caught, you reap the consequences, you know?"

I nodded, but the information whirled around my mind. I couldn't blame Mairin for wanting to replace her pendant, but it took me by surprise. Especially considering what she'd said to me the other night.

"All I know is I'm supposed to be gaining us an alliance, and the merrow is going to help me. What she does after is her decision."

"Aye. Well, I know Brenna was waiting to speak to you, so I won't keep you."

I blew out a breath and rubbed both my hands over my face before standing.

"You didn't, did you?" He raised a brow and gave me a disappointed look. "I told you to stay away from her."

"I don't want to talk about it, Beau."

"I told you that wouldn't end well. I suppose I wasn't wrong?"

"No, you weren't."

"You oughta listen to me, girly."

"Yeah, yeah. Wish me luck."

"Godspeed."

When I found Brenna and Mairin playing cards below deck, my stomach caved in on itself. Was it just the discomfort of seeing the woman I used to love sitting and talking to the woman I—well, who knows what I felt for her? Or was it something akin to jealousy? I didn't want Brenna near Mairin, but what could I say?

"Finally. Done fucking around with Beau?" Brenna gritted out. Her pin-straight black hair was cut short in the back, falling at an angle to be longer in the front. Dark eyes I swore didn't contain a fucking soul looked up at me, nearly black in the low light.

"Good to see you too, Brenna," I deadpanned. I swore I saw Mairin smirk out of the corner of my eye, and I tried not to think about how every bone in my body was on high alert around her.

The air below deck was stale. It was almost too warm, even though the flight with Hyše had nearly frozen me solid. Emma and my brother both had fire to keep them warm, but I did not. But dozens of bodies below the deck made for cramped quarters and stagnant air. Or perhaps it was the heat of a certain merrow's gaze on the side of my face. I hadn't talked to her about our prior conversation, and I didn't intend to anytime soon. I was sad about how things happened with Dewalt, but after getting my feelings out there and voicing them to him, it was almost freeing. And it made me consider what Brenna had said to Mairin, and what Mairin had agreed with.

I did need to find out who I was.

"Good isn't the word I'd use."

"Oh, cut the shit," Mairin interrupted, to my surprise. "I didn't sign up to be miserable for weeks while the two of you do whatever the fuck this is. Get it out of your systems now, or I'll hold one of you under compulsion until we're done."

"I can compel too," I pointed out.

"Yes, princess, but you don't like to use your gifts."

I rolled my eyes and crossed my arms.

"You have five minutes." We both just looked at the merrow. "I'm serious. I'm not putting up with this shit for weeks. Do your worst, then move on. I'll cover my ears."

I blinked as Mairin did just that, and I didn't know what to do with myself.

"Believe me, I tried to get out of this. I don't want to be around you just as much as you don't want to be around me," the dark-haired woman beside me murmured. She was short in stature, like Mairin, but that was where their similarities ended. Where Mairin was supple curves and soft, rounded stomach, Brenna was narrow and muscular. Both of their bodies were beautiful, but I'd have been lying if I said I wasn't partial to the merrow. But that had nothing to do with, well, anything.

"I don't care in one way or another about being around you. We both have a job to do, and I know you and Beau will do it well. I have just as much respect for you as I always did, though now I lack affection."

She scoffed. "You didn't respect me when we were together."

"I did. Why would you say that?"

"If you respected me, you wouldn't have led me to believe we had a future when you did not intend to be with only me. And then to come to me when Dewalt ended the bond? A smack in the fucking face." Her laugh was cold. "And my stupid ass actually thought—"

"I shouldn't have come to you. That was wrong of me, and I'm sorry."

"An apology. I should write this date down."

"Come on, Bren. I don't know what you want from—"

"You ladies done? I don't want to hear any more bickering or I swear I'll close your mouths for you. Your auras are hell to look at," Mairin interrupted.

"What's the strategy for the Sea Queen?" Brenna asked, switching directions with ease. She would probably do exactly as Mairin asked. But I was still itching from the conversation. She'd ended things with *me*. Should I have been quicker to end things with Dewalt or set her expectations differently? Absolutely. But when the subject had been broached, I felt like ending things with Dewalt meant things with her would be permanent from that point forward. I couldn't end the thing he relied on without the best reason, and I didn't know if she was that reason.

"She'll come," Mairin shrugged. "The ocean speaks to her. Once we get near her palace, I'll dip a toe in, and she'll come. Sentimental, my mother." A cocky grin formed on her face as she looked at me, but I could tell she was nervous. "And as for strategy? There is nothing to do with her other than hope she doesn't ask for too much."

"What do you think she'll want?" I asked.

"Probably me. Or perhaps you. I'm hoping neither, though."

"Me?"

"She'll have interest in any…friend of mine. But that cost is much too high. Your brother said to use reason, and we won't be giving you to my mother. Don't worry."

"And you?"

"Well, we'll just have to see, won't we?" Her smile seemed forced.

Hours later, the two of us stood at the ship's stern watching the sunset, and I slid my hand closer, where we both gripped the railing. I couldn't help it as I rubbed my pinky up against hers. I was trying to keep a distance between us until I figured out what she asked of me. Did I want something with her? Did I even know what I wanted? But I'd sat with the thought of her giving herself to her mother for Vesta, and I'd only grown more agitated.

"You're her last daughter. She'll probably kill you."

"She was more fond of me than she ever was of my sisters. It's possible she won't."

"But you threaten her crown by existing, do you not?"

"Ven, tell me, how is a merrow without a pendant going to become the Seaborn Queen? The ability to live in the ocean isn't a suggestion; it's a requirement. I am no threat to her."

"Still though. Why endanger yourself?"

"The seaborn have their own prophecy, you know—about the Beloved and all that nonsense?"

"I didn't know that. What does it say?"

"It isn't just about uniting the Three Kingdoms. It means the forestborn and seaborn too."

"All the pureblood elves are dead."

"But their children live. Those with elf-blood in their veins. And don't forget the fae, even if they've hidden for centuries. That has to count for something. And if I have the chance to help, I will."

Spotting a speck of a ship on the horizon, I shook my head before focusing on the black dot. "I don't want you to help if it means sacrificing yourself," I mumbled.

"I don't know if you have any say in the matter."

"I want say in the matter."

"It's too early for that."

"What do you mean?"

"You're not ready for that with me."

"What?"

"You only get a say if we belong to one another. You're not ready for that. Not yet."

"Says who?" I knew I wasn't ready, but I wanted to hear why she thought it.

"Says me. And your aura. It's...brightened in recent days. But I want confident, glowing, and indisputable. Then you can have a say."

"I'm trying."

"These things take forever. It's a good thing we have time."

"Unless you sacrifice yourself!" I nearly shouted.

"You let me worry about that, sweet." She put her hand atop mine, and I tried very hard not to think about what I'd do if push came to shove. The Seaborn Queen would certainly kill the only threat to her throne, but would she kill me? Even if the odds were barely better for me than they were for Mairin, I wouldn't let her sacrifice herself.

CHAPTER 40

Elora

I put on and took off the bracelet no less than a dozen times after Thyra shut my door behind her. Finally, after the last time, I tossed it across the room and watched as it hit the door and slid down. I rolled over, pulling the blankets over me. That damn bracelet had put me in a state ever since I opened his letter.

The villain. The enemy. My murderer, friend, and savior—all in one.

What was I to do with that? Mama had begun to explain over several conversations what Cyran had done and why—but I never listened. I didn't want to know. She hadn't been forceful about it, opting not to harass me when I clearly wanted nothing to do with it. But she made it clear he'd had no choice.

I considered talking to Rainier about it after his commentary about Theo, but something told me he was far less hospitable toward Cy than Mama was. I was afraid his opinion was too close to my own. I wished there was someone I could talk to who didn't know either of us and could tell me what to do. An outsider. There was no one to talk to about Cy, no one who would listen, anyway. I didn't have anyone to talk to about anything, really. I'd been able to talk to Theo, but then I'd hurt his feelings. Every time I talked to him, I only made it worse. It didn't feel fair to confide in him.

I was lonely, even though I was surrounded by people every day. That was the only reason I slipped the bracelet on. And off and on. And off. The prince wanted my company, was desperate for it. And he was a good listener. He always respected my boundaries, and I never had to ask twice with him.

I supposed I'd have to be more clear with him in the future so as not to walk away with a slit throat.

If I ever spoke to him again.

Yvi batted the bracelet around on the ground, and I threw a pillow at her, groaning as I flipped onto my back. The fire had grown dim, and I was restless. I'd had nothing to be indecisive about in my life. The worst of my worries was not being able to mix the right paint color. That was it. And keeping my divinity secret—that too. But that wasn't much of a problem. I was allowed to show Theo, and he was the only person I was ever around anyway.

The idea of reading a book until I fell asleep crossed my mind, and I was immediately out of the bed, running over on tiptoe before a devious little cat could swipe at my feet. She was Ciarden's mischief all in one tiny body; I was certain of it.

The Discovered Dragon caught my eye, not quite pushed all the way onto the shelf. Mama had told me she'd found Cyran asleep while reading it to me one day, so I shied away from it at first. But Yvi, the demon-cat, latched onto the bottom of my nightgown, and I grabbed it quickly before batting her off me. Pain shot through my foot as I made my way back toward the bed, stepping on the gods forsaken bracelet the dumb animal had moved right to where she knew I'd step on it. It had to be intentional. I picked it up before crawling back into bed. Yvi was already there, having balled up into a circle on my spare pillow after I smacked her off my nightgown. She rolled her head backwards, exposing her chin to me, and I gave her precisely three scratches because any more than that, and she'd grab my hand with her front paws and attack with the rear ones. Mama had already had to heal me twice.

Sitting up against the headboard, I cradled the book in my lap. Lighting the lamp on my nightstand, I couldn't help my smile. It was beautiful. I'd never seen anything like it. Mama and I always had simple lanterns with a brass bottom and a plain, glass shade. This one was special, a hanging lamp. The base led to a swan-neck which dangled the oil from a mosaic glass tiled globe. It was beautiful—something Rainier had picked up on a visit to Nythyr, he'd told me. One of the times he'd been looking for Mama. I still couldn't believe that part of their story. He must have loved her so much, even after all that time.

When I finally got around to opening my book, it startled me when a slip of paper fell out of it. I recognized the tidy scrawl in an instant, matching the letter he'd sent me days before. Tilting it toward the light, I puzzled over the meaning. Disjointed words and phrases littered the paper. I flipped it over, confused. I sat up, swinging my legs over the side of the bed, and held it closer to the lamp, leaning down. The mosaic titles were beautiful, but they didn't give good light to see by.

"'Fix the memory,'" I whispered, reading the words aloud. "'Give a happy ending.'"

They were notes. An entire page of notes, front and back, on how to wake me from my slumber. The bottom right corner of the page detailed the dream I had about Declan taking me from his room.

"'Fight for her,'" I breathed.

At the bottom of the paper, he'd notated a page number and beside it had scrawled in hurried strokes, *If this is what it feels like, then I am ruined.*

Knowing the story like the back of my hand, my stomach tightened. The page Cyran had noted was towards the end, when the cursed dragon broke the spell. With shaking hands, I flipped to the back of the book in my lap, noticing doodles and notes in the margins. I only spared a half of a second of frustration for him writing all over it, too nervous for what I would find. Trembling, I found the page I was looking for, and exhaled a shaky breath as I read the passage he'd marked. A single question mark in the margins and a blot of ink underneath, as if he'd let the pen hover, and it dripped onto the page.

If I am the moon, then you are the sun, fireshine. You shine your light upon me and brighten all which is cold and dark within me. You have taught me to forgive is divine and even I, a loathsome creature, am deserving of it. I spend every moment wishing for more with you. More quiet, more talking, more kissing. Just more. If you never wish to look upon me again, Alina, I understand. But know, I am ruined for having loved you.

I slid the bracelet onto my wrist.

I opened my eyes and looked down at my feet. Bare, my feet sank into the earth. Wiggling my toes, I lifted my head and took in my surroundings. I stood in a glen beside a stream, surrounded by mossy rocks and steep earth climbing high above me. Out of one fissure in the rocks came the source of the stream—a tiny waterfall. The streambed was made of grey pebbles, smoothed by the white frothy water. A tree covered with more of the soft moss stuck out awkwardly from the path I stood on, arching over the stream. Its branches were nearly entwined with another tree jutting out from the cliff face, close but not quite touching. Near sunset, the dusky sky and fine mist made the glen hum with something akin to magick. It reminded me of the stories of the fae—forestborn like the elves, less human in design who lived as one with nature, their presence more myth than anything else. I spotted a dark red mushroom and smiled, imagining a pixie built her home beneath it.

When the first firefly appeared in front of me, I gasped. "Oh!" I lifted my hand to my mouth in surprise. I turned, wanting to witness the whole glen filled with fireflies as the sun went down. Cyran stood a few paces behind me, hands shoved deep into his pockets. He was also barefoot, well-tailored brown breeches on his form. His white shirt with laces at the collar resembled what Theo and Papa wore when they worked outside. His dark-brown hair was tousled, as if he'd spent countless minutes running his fingers through it. He wasn't wearing any of his jewelry, looking as plain as he did the last time I'd seen him. That had been nearly a month ago now, and it surprised me he hadn't gone back to dressing the way he had when I met him. At the very least, I had expected him to have pierced his ear again.

"Hello, Elora," he said. Hazel eyes met mine, and I tried to steady my nerves. He didn't know I'd found his page of notes. Or had he expected me to find them? I supposed when I woke and kicked him out, he wouldn't have had the time to gather anything. But he had to have known I'd read my book and see his drawings in the margins. I shook my head, not bothering to think about it. What would I say anyway? *Do you love me, Cy?* No. You don't hurt the people you love, let alone kill them.

"Cy," I replied, wincing when I realized I'd meant to call him Cyran and forgot.

The glow of fireflies surrounded him, blinking to life as they rose from the ground. I watched one as it meandered on its lazy flight over the stream. Turning to follow it, I smiled as I watched hundreds of them flicker throughout the glen.

"I, uh, brought us a picnic. Are you hungry?" he asked, and I glanced over in time to see him running his fingers through his hair.

"I'm—I don't know. It's a dream, right? Am I hungry?"

"Gods, I didn't—" A shaky laugh. "I hadn't even thought of that. Well, I eat in my dreams all the time, even though I'm not hungry. But it's light. If you don't want it, we don't have to—"

"I want to," I said, not sure why I wanted to protect his feelings. He smiled, and his dimple appeared. "Unless it's poisoned."

The reaction was barely noticeable. I wouldn't have seen it if I hadn't been looking for it. He squeezed his eyes shut tight for a moment before taking a step toward me.

"I have not poisoned it. And even if it were, there is nothing I can do to you in an illusion that will have a lasting effect. Physically, at least," he added, giving me a strange look.

I looked up at him, waiting for him to explain. He was taller than I remembered. Nearly as tall as Rainier. As he approached, I peeked down at what I was wearing. Thankful I had worn the thickest of my nightgowns, I almost wished I'd worn something prettier to bed.

"I hope the things I say to you have an effect outside the illusion. But that's it. I don't plan to do you any harm," he uttered, intense eyes on mine. His accent was going to kill me if he didn't. I breathed deep and regretted it instantly, his orange and ginger scent no less captivating in an illusion.

"You've found oranges in Vesta?" I asked, trying to give my mind something to latch onto that wasn't *him*. But the citrus fruit he loved so much was part of what made him, wasn't it?

"I, uh, was practicing before I came to you. I've been craving an orange, so I made one when I finished. You smell it on me?" He smiled. "I know I'll still crave it when I wake, but—" He shrugged.

"What did you have to practice?" I asked.

"The fireflies. It was hard to make it so they blinked independently."

"Ah." I nodded, looking around at all that he'd created with a new appreciation. "Is the stream not difficult?"

"Surprisingly, no. Water is easy."

"Are oranges part of the picnic?"

"They can be. Would you like an orange?"

"Yes. And I'd like to see what else you came up with."

He swallowed, walking up the path toward an area above the spring, just over the waterfall. It was flat with tidy grass, and a blanket waited on the ground. Deep mustard yellow, it reminded me of the pillows in Cy's bedroom, and I knew it would be soft. A small wicker basket sat on one corner of the blanket, full of what I assumed was our picnic. Rubbing his hand up the back of his neck and into his hair, he waited for me to say something.

"You're being...awkward," I said.

A sly smile crossed his features as he dropped his hand. I barely reacted in time as his other hand tossed me an orange. Catching it, I glared at him.

"Would you like me to peel it for you, *min vil*—"

His words cut off at the jerk of my chin. I didn't want him thinking he could just go back to calling me that.

"I've got it," I said, stubborn as I peeled at it with my thumbnails. I wasn't used to the skin of the fruit, and it was difficult. Apples were better because their skin stayed on. Groaning internally, I realized I'd be smelling it on my fingers. Smelling *him*. His expression gave away nothing as he watched me struggle. Folding his long legs under him, he sat on a corner of the blanket, waiting for me as I fought with the damn orange.

"Are you sure?"

I chucked it at him, hitting him square in the chest before it bounced over the cliff behind him. He controlled his smile as he looked up at me.

"Do you want another?"

"No!" I grunted, sitting down across from him on the blanket. "What else is in there?" I nodded toward the basket. I was in a sour mood now. It was stupid of me to wear the bracelet. I clearly wasn't ready to be around him, and I didn't know if I ever would be. I'd only come because of one thing he'd written, and it might not have even meant what I thought it did.

"Where do you want me to start? Your most favorite or your least favorite—but still something you like, of course."

"Most favorite."

"I hoped you'd say that," he said, giving me a soft smile. Gods, when he spoke quietly like this, his accent and tilt of his lips made me almost forget what he'd done to me. Reaching into the basket, he pulled out a small package wrapped in brown paper. When he opened it, unveiling the raspberry cream puffs within, I instantly started salivating.

"Here," he said, passing the entire parcel over to me. Grabbing one and taking a bite from it, equal parts raspberry filling, cream, and pastry, I closed my eyes and sighed. Gods, they were delicious.

"It tastes just like Cook's," I offered, talking with a mouthful of dessert.

"He made them often enough that month for you; my memory is fresh."

I sobered a bit at the mention of my time in Evenmoor with him. But I came here to see him, to let him try to apologize. Letting negative thoughts distract me was counterproductive.

"I brought the bubbly wine you liked." He conjured a small glass out of the air before pouring a measure for me. Mama hadn't let me have alcohol on more than a rare occasion, but Cyran and Ismene drank it nightly. I didn't like it much, but Ismene had finally found one I liked after a few weeks. Only one glass had me giggling and light-headed.

"Thank you," I said, taking a sip from the proffered glass. "Uh, so what have you been doing since I saw you last?" Gods, this was painful.

"Mmm," he murmured, biding his time by taking a long swig of his own wine. As if I wouldn't notice that was exactly why he did it. "I've been corresponding with the rebels in Folterra. They, uh, they want me to come back. I had told them I'd come back once my business in Astana was finished."

It took me a moment to realize *I* was the business.

"But you're still here. Why?"

Pain crossed his features, and I forced away my urge to care.

"I've been helping Mistress Imogene with her errands for the dormitory."

"Mistress Imogene?"

"I heard Emmeline call her Nana once."

"The little old lady?" I asked. I knew she had much to do with Mama's upbringing, but I'd only met her once since I'd woken up.

"Yes. She's—I think she invents more errands for me just to keep me around." His dimple appeared with his grin. "I've been staying there. At the dormitory," he clarified when I tilted my head in question. I hadn't wondered where he'd been. Not even once.

I didn't say anything else, just looked at my hands as I brushed them off on my nightgown. He cleared his throat and took a deep breath.

"Declan beat me." I lifted my eyes to his, but now he was the one looking down at his hands. "I want to start off by saying this isn't an excuse. What I did was unforgivable. I don't deserve your forgiveness, but I don't know. I just...I don't want you to think I did what I did because of you."

I stared at him, waiting for him to look at me, but he didn't.

"My father hit me only once before my mother took me away to one of the farther keeps in Folterra. When she died, I was sent to Declan. Ismene's mother died within the year, and she was sent there too. My brother took his rage out on me and Ismene. Once he started hitting Ismene, I started taking her punishments for her. My brother is evil. He wanted to start the slave trade again. I know I told you that already, but I need to tell you again. He has always been more in tune with the shadows than I have, and half the time I think he's almost influenced by them. He wants to unite the Three Kingdoms under Folterran rule. He claims it is his birthright. It would be hell."

"Alright. So, you killed me to what? Help Declan? Did he force you or something?"

He grimaced when I said he killed me. Hazel eyes darted to my neck and then moved away just as quickly. "Did Emmeline not tell you any of it?"

"I want to hear *you* explain it." I knew what Mama had told me, but something wouldn't let me believe her.

He sighed. "My brother didn't force me to hurt you. I wouldn't have done it. I'd have slit my own throat before doing it to you if it was just a matter of Declan telling me to do it."

"Then why didn't you?" He stared at me, and I continued. "Kill yourself instead of me?"

My stomach twisted over the hurt in his eyes, but I forced myself to ignore it. He deserved this. I had done nothing to him but trust him, and he had repaid me in the worst way.

He inhaled deep, then said in a rush, "I was shown a vision by a seer of the whole bloody world ending in flames. Everyone would die or be enslaved. It was hell, Elora." His jaw hardened and brows furrowed as he looked at me. "It was you or the rest of the gods damn world. Your mother needed her last blessing to prevent what happened in my vision, and your death made Ciarden bless her."

I didn't know what to say. What could I say to that? Did I even believe him? I crossed my arms over my chest, protecting my heart both mentally and physically.

"I'm going to hold the illusion so I can give you the second half of your gift, but I'm going to go because I don't think you'll enjoy it as much with me here." The glen fell away, and we stood on the grounds of Evenmoor. The sun cast a bruised glow over the sky, and I saw the reflection in the pond I'd once looked at from my balcony. A heron stood in the water, unmoving. And on the bank stood an easel with all the paint I could possibly need.

"Cy, you don't have to go," I said.

"I think I do. I just hope you know I realize now it was a mistake. I should have let it all burn. Either way is hell for me, but in one outcome, I made it hell for you too. I wish I could take it back."

And then he was gone.

CHAPTER 41

Rainier

I WOKE TO DARKNESS and smoke. For a brief moment, I was confused. The hard ground we laid on and the scent wafting into my nostrils brought me back to that dank dungeon cell. But when she moved against me, and her hair got stuck to my beard, I breathed a sigh of relief. It had only been a few days since I'd shaved, but it was long enough I had to pick her hair out of it. Her smooth arm was across my chest, and she'd nestled into the crook of my shoulder. As my vision adjusted, I peered down at her tattoo. Took in the constellation of flowers on her skin she'd had imprinted on her body—for me. She said it was for us, but if it weren't for my problems, she wouldn't have needed to do it.

My twin flame.

Whoever had painted the tattoo had been talented. The flowers weren't filled with color, but black outlines made up the detailed petals. I counted the blooms, appreciating their formation to mirror the freckles. She was real, and she was mine. She'd put painful marks on her body to help me escape the torments of my mind. It was just one of the few painful things she'd done for me in her lifetime. Between this, what she had to do to get me back, and giving birth to our child—nearly dying from it—I owed her everything.

I traced her skin with a soft touch, delicately brushing her hair from her shoulder so I could better see the ink on her skin. Comforted and pacified, I looked up, trying to understand why the cavern was so smoky. No light shone down from above, even though it was definitely daytime. The only light I could see by was what filtered through the crack out to the lake. Was the hole into the cavern covered somehow?

I gently adjusted her as I moved my body out from beneath her. She was sound asleep and so gods damn beautiful. The blanket was pulled up to her waist, and as I jostled her, she murmured quietly before tucking her hand under her cheek. I wanted to ignore everything else and lay back down beside her. Lying on her side, her breasts pushed together, her skin was tantalizing. I wanted to kiss every bit of exposed flesh. And then I wanted to expose more and kiss that too.

That single act she'd done for me had changed so much. It was a final push I'd needed to be less fearful around her. I'd been on the verge of working something out with her, but then she'd risked herself with the fucking Wend, which had me so angry, all the progress I'd made had been lost. I still didn't intend to leave that topic alone though, not satisfied with how we'd left it. But I'd felt so helpless, like there was nothing I could do but wait. Speaking to the mindbreaker hadn't helped, and I had resigned myself to struggle through it. But she'd taken a decisive action, one which brought her pain, and did something about it. She was a gods damn force.

And when we'd come together in the cavern, making love within the pool, it had mirrored our moment in the lake months ago. Had both moments been equally restorative? The cavern itself felt different than the last time. Em had mentioned it—her divinity wanted to rest here. I could sense the feeling, not nearly as much, in my own. Perhaps it was only the blessings from Aonara or Ciarden which wanted to rest here, and she had significantly *more* of that than I did. Either way, the cavern had helped in some way to heal us both. And because of it, I'd continue to allow us to heal—together.

I quietly pulled my breeches and boots on, grabbing my cloak and wrapping it around myself. When I rifted out, I wasn't sure I'd even be able to see where the top of the cavern was, but I'd try. The rift I'd opened was beside the tree I'd pushed her up against in the fall. Where I'd shamelessly ground against her, showing her the evidence of what she fucking did to me. My cock jerked at the memory. The memory of when I'd told her that not only was I not her friend, but there was no moving on for me. Emma had written her name in blood on my soul.

Turning toward the mountainside, I blinked at what I saw before letting a laugh take over.

Irses popped his head out from under his wing, blinking at me with what I could only describe as a glare. He stood, stretching his wings, and smoke drifted into the sky behind him. He'd sat on top of the hole into the cavern, blocking it. Ryo launched into the air behind him, and I groaned. The two of them were so attached to her. Protective hounds—though how could I blame them? Ryo had grown quite a bit and was already larger than Hyše, and before he could crash into me to lick me—as he was wont to do—I opened a rift back into the cavern. Emma stirred at the sound. The winter sun streamed down from above, warming her soft pearlescent skin, and she rolled onto her back. Nipples pink in the sunlight hardened as I watched. She stretched both arms above her head, eyes closed. Gods, she was perfect. It hit me then how fucking lucky I was. To finally be reunited with her after all those years, to survive captivity with Declan, and then to be back beside her? Staying away to protect her felt like a waste, but I couldn't regret it.

I'd just have to make the best of it. Beginning her morning with an orgasm felt like a good place to start. Bright blue eyes opened slowly and peered up at me as I approached.

"Why is it so smoky in here?"

"Long story," I said, kneeling beside her and pulling the blanket down past her navel. "Well, short story, but I'll tell it in a minute."

I bent over and kissed her stomach.

"Where were you?" she asked, tucking her arms under her head and smiling.

"Investigating." Kissing up her torso, I tugged her nipple into my mouth, and she hissed, arching.

"And what did you—"

An earth-trembling roar from an angry dragon interrupted her, and she sat straight up.

"Was that a dragon? Did they follow us?"

I groaned, flopping onto my back. "Irses and Ryo found us, yes."

She jumped to her feet as a slightly quieter roar sounded. She was naked still, and I let my eyes caress her in all the ways my hands wanted to. That round and perfect swell of her backside jiggled as she took a few steps to her pack, and I was on my knees before I knew it. I grabbed her by the hips and nipped at her as she bent over.

"Do you really need clothes right now?"

"If I'm going to shut those two up, I ought to put some on, don't you think?"

"Let them roar."

She laughed as she ignored me, pulling on fresh underthings. "We'll have them upsetting people if I don't deal with them." She tugged on her breeches and pulled thick woolen socks on, and I snagged her boots, holding them open for her to step into before lacing them. "Well, that was nice of you," she said.

"I have my moments. You plan to take them with us to Ravemont?"

"I don't know if I have much of a choice. I don't even know how they found us."

"They must have sensed you somehow. I'm surprised the ones we left at the Cascade haven't made it over to Vesta." Groaning, I pulled myself to my feet and dressed as well. "You know, you never told me which memory you used to create Ryo."

Sheepishly, she glanced at me over her shoulder as she buttoned her shirt. "Remember when you tackled me and tore my cloak?" The echo of my own words to her from the fall, when she'd found the cloak I'd had made for her all those years ago, brought a smile to my face.

"Wait," I started, my lip twitching as I fought back a smile. "Is that why he likes to knock me down and lick me?"

"I have no idea," she said, but her own grin spread wide. She tidied her pack and then opened a rift, tossing the charred remnants of our fire through it. I couldn't help my grin when I saw the rift she'd made led to the same tree mine had. She remembered it just as well as I did. Respectful of the gods-touched cavern, she removed every trace of us before peering into the pool in the center of the cave.

"They're back."

"How many do you think got eaten?" Her horrified look over her shoulder brought a smile to my face. "I'm teasing. I'm sure they're all fine."

"Oh, but what if they're not? It's not like we'll ever know. Now I feel bad," she whined.

"Come here," I chuckled as I tossed my pack onto my shoulder. Taking hers as she neared, I brushed her hair out of my way and leaned in. Grasping her chin, I turned her head slightly, looking at the flowers climbing up her neck. "You're beautiful. Your heart, your mind, all of it." She smiled, soft and shy, and averted her eyes. "Look at me, Em. You are the only good in me."

"That's not true. You're a good man, Rain."

"There's a reason they call me the Bloody Prince. You don't know what I did in Varmeer. And that was a world that still had you. That's why I've stayed away from you—because a world without you in it is one I would lay waste to and have no remorse."

"Don't say that." She brought her lips to mine, softly pressing a kiss to the corner of my lips, just above my chin, the other corner, my nose. "You're good on your own. You just want to be better because of me. And I feel the same way about you."

Pressing her lips to mine, she wrapped her arms around my neck as she stood on tiptoe. A loud crashing echoed above us, and she pulled away on a gasp.

"Gods damn dragons," I grumbled.

The dragons absolutely would not go through the rifts with us, and Em didn't want to leave them behind. So we rode them to her home. She'd offered Irses to me, considering Ryo was still on the smaller side, but the larger dragon had expressed his discontent by huffing at us both and refusing to allow me to climb onto his back. Stubborn, jealous monster. I was rather annoyed about our change in plans because it took all fucking day. Traveling with my guard took us three days from her home to the mountains, and it took us nearly twelve hours to travel the same path by dragon. Rifting would have been far quicker. We'd only stopped once to warm up and eat before we were on our way again. Even though it was dark by the time we approached, we skirted south of Brambleton proper, not wanting to frighten anyone or alert anyone of our presence. News of the dragons had likely spread throughout the kingdom by now—or would soon enough. But, still.

Em had opted to stop at her home rather than go straight to Ravemont, and I didn't question it. This trip was for her and her father. Dismounting the dragons in the clearing where my soldiers had once camped, she patted her loyal pets and asked them to stay put. I didn't understand how they knew what she was saying, but Irses curled up as I built a dirt enclosure from the ground to help protect them from the cold.

"We are going to have to practice this with you."

"I told you, I can barely do it at all. It was...difficult at the Cascade when I had to—to bury the soldiers."

Of course it was Em who had to help Dewalt and the others handle that. Fuck. It should have been me.

"It will just take some time and practice," I replied.

She crouched, slipping a glove off her hand, and pressed her fingertip into the dirt. Concentrating, her eyebrows scrunched up, and I felt the faintest rumble in the ground.

"Well, that's a start."

"I'm trying to be precise about it. It's all or nothing for some reason."

I knelt beside her and put my hand on the small of her back. I smoothed over the bond, and she shivered as I poured some of my divinity into her, trying to help her coax it to do her bidding.

"You're moving it, not getting rid of or adding to," I whispered, realizing why she was struggling. "Use your divinity as a shovel." She huffed a laugh as the tiniest bit of earth parted, leaving a hole. "There you go, Em."

"A shovel?"

"That's how my father taught me. Hanwen spent some time as a farmer. Did you know that? He hated it so much, he focused his divinity into making it easier. That's where it comes from."

"So, what you're telling me is your divinity comes from the laziest god."

"*Our* divinity." I grinned. "I don't know if I believe it though. Imagine Hanwen as a farmer. Why would he do that? For fun? Because he was bored?"

"Why do those fucks do anything they do?" She asked, looking cross, and I failed at keeping a straight face.

"Why, indeed."

She stood, concentrating on the ground below her, trying to build more of a barrier for the dragons before she harrumphed in frustration. "Would you just do it? This is going to take me forever."

I smiled and did as she asked, then followed her through the rift she made for us.

"Oh," she whispered as we stepped into her kitchen. I slid closer, placing my hands on her hips.

"What is it?"

"It's so…small. And it's falling apart." She spun to face me and looked up with panic in her eyes. "Why did I ever let you come here? Oh gods, this is a mess." She put her hands on my chest and backed me up toward the rift she'd already let close.

"Em, it's fine. What are you doing?" I laughed. "This is your home, Elora's home. It's perfect because it was yours. But if you've become too accustomed to a lavish lifestyle in these past few months, we can always continue on to Ravemont."

She glared up at me, and I held her face in my hands before pressing a kiss to her forehead.

"I don't want to go to Ravemont tonight. The letter, uh, the letter his nurse sent said he acts up at night," she murmured.

"How so?"

"I guess he barely talks at all anymore, but when he does he gets confused. He asks for me or Lucia, gets riled when his schedule changes. She said it's at its worst when the sun goes down."

"Did she say how long he might—"

"Weeks maybe? He's incontinent, and it's hard to get him to eat."

"Gods, Em. That's horrible." I pulled her into my arms. Her voice hadn't wavered, but I could feel the sorrow and regret through the bond.

"It's fine. I mean, he was always going to die one day. I just wish I had more time with him now that…now that I can."

"Did you not see him all those years?"

"Once a month for about five minutes. I think it hurt him to see me, and it only got worse after my mother died."

She'd been truly alone. I could count on one hand how many people she had to talk to and even less she could trust. My heart ached for her.

"We'll go first thing in the morning and spend as much time there as you want."

She nodded against my chest. "I'm hungry," she said as she pulled away from me. "I ought to have some potatoes in the root cellar. Maybe some green beans?"

"I'll get them."

A few minutes later, I came back into the house with what she'd wanted, dropping them off at the kitchen table. I heard a curse and found her soaking wet and struggling with the window in the study.

"What are you doing?"

"Being stupid."

I laughed, reaching past her to pull the window down. "Is that so?"

"I tried your little water from the well trick," she said, glowering up at me as water dripped from her brow and the tip of her nose. Whisking it away from her face, I conjured it into a ball, letting it hover over my outstretched palm.

"Try to separate it into droplets," I instructed.

She screwed up her face, concentrating, before releasing a sharp breath. "Ever since the Cascade, your gifts have been harder to master."

"One more time?"

"I have enough water for dinner."

"You're going to quit on me, Highclere?"

She set down the pot of water she'd managed to fill and rolled up her sleeves.

"You can't call me that anymore," she said as she crossed her arms and focused on the water hovering over my palm.

"Unless you can separate this water, I'll call you—"

The water burst, spraying me in the face.

"You deserved that."

"I suppose I did," I laughed, bringing the pot she'd filled to the hearth.

Later, after all the potatoes had been peeled and tossed in the pot to boil with the green beans, she wiped her hands off on a rag and leaned against the table.

"What should I do with this place?" she asked.

"Whatever you want to do with it."

She blew out a breath. "Help me think of something. I know I can do whatever I want, but I don't know *what* I want."

"Well, I'm sure you probably want to help someone. Is there a family in town who could use it? One of your patients?"

"Oh gods." She straightened, bringing her wide blue eyes to mine. "I just realized. What have they been doing without me and Mairin?"

"There is no other healer?"

"Not any good ones," she murmured as she worried her bottom lip.

"Well, there's a good idea. We can find a healer and offer this home as part of their wages."

"They can't afford to pay a healer here."

"We'll pay them then."

"What?"

I nearly laughed at her surprise. "We'll give them the house to live in and an allowance to live off of as long as they're serving the town."

"You'd do that?"

"Yes, but, more importantly, you would. And you're the queen."

"The council will allow that appropriation of funds?"

"They allot certain funds for special projects. This can be one. If I have to divert some funds from the sewer system, I can. I'll do some of the work myself if I have to."

"They approved of that? Nobody told me," she said.

"Fuck. Yes. That was why I was at the estate when you came back with Dewalt."

"Ah, that's why you forgot. Distracted by punching your best friend in the face."

I averted my eyes before mumbling, "Let's not bring that up."

"He and Thyra kept me sane while you were gone. I don't know what I would have done without the two of them." Quiet, she stepped toward me as she spoke, and I couldn't bring myself to look at her. I'd acted foolishly.

"I'm happy you had them. Ven said Thyra slept in your quarters," I said.

"To keep me from going to Folterra alone."

A shuddering breath left my body. I could only imagine. I finally met her gaze, and I wasn't surprised to find her looking furious. "Thank the gods she stopped you. Divine hell, Em. You would've gotten yourself killed. I'm shocked no one got hurt when you did come."

"Dewalt made me eat even when I didn't want to. Made me talk. Let me tell him how angry I was with you."

"Angry with me?"

"For trying to sacrifice yourself for me, for getting yourself taken, for leaving me again." Her voice shook.

"I'm sorry, Em. I don't know how many more times I can say it or try to make it up to you," I said, resigned. "I won't apologize for trying to protect you. I just won't. I do apologize for how I chose to go about it though."

"I'm not asking for that. I'm just telling you that Dewalt is one of the best friends either of us could deserve, and you hitting him was insulting to both of us. He would never do something like that. He only did what he did to piss you off. You had to know it wasn't real."

"I know. It's just—seeing how close the two of you got while I was gone had me thinking some stupid things."

"Like?"

"It's so idiotic, I don't even want to tell you." I ran my hand over my jaw as I looked toward the hearth, the hypnotic bubbling of the water an easy distraction.

"Well, now you have to," she said, grabbing my hands and tugging me closer. Always drawing my attention back to her.

"My mind just went to really dark places the last few weeks. They were all irrational and self-destructive. They're embarrassing."

She just stared up at me, blue eyes patient.

I sighed. "I didn't let myself think about it too long, but you're the closest thing to Lucia he has."

"And you worried that since he couldn't have *her*..." She trailed off.

"No, I didn't truly worry. But I avoided him, avoided seeing the two of you together. And it's stupid. You needed someone to comfort you, and I sure as fuck wasn't doing it."

"But you trusted me."

"Of course I trusted you, Em."

"Until you saw him help me off the horse." Disappointment dripped from her words.

"No! I just hit my breaking point. And he knew it too. He was staring right at me, trying to rile me."

She sighed, a chuckle betraying her serious demeanor. "Men. He did ask for the fight, I'll admit. I told him to knock it off."

"Thank you for that," I laughed. "I think part of him was itching for a fight. We argued—*we're not done* arguing over the Wend." I gestured between us. "*You and I* are not done arguing about that."

"We are nowhere near Astana tonight, so let's hold off?" she asked, threading her fingers through my belt loops and pulling my body to press against hers.

"We are definitely not done talking about this, but, while you might not have told me what you were doing, I had secrets of my own."

"What do you mean?"

"The Wend is a shithole, but it's that way because?"

"I—there's a lot of crime there."

"Why is there crime there?" I prompted.

"I mean, I don't know. I saw the city guard making rounds, but—"

"There aren't a lot, and they're green, too. The ones assigned to the Wend are put there because—"

"Because the people who've been part of the guard longer don't want to be there," she said.

"Precisely. Not to mention, I don't know how many people have the guard in their pockets. I've actually been looking into it. Ever since you requested to start helping people there." Shame coursed from her, and I ignored it, pressing on. "It makes little sense for the richest district with the lowest crime to have such a high percentage of the guard."

"No, it doesn't. But more members of the guard doesn't feel like a solution."

"You're right. It's not going to stop them from being poor, and that's part of the problem. I've inherited quite a bit of shit from my father's reign. I didn't know where to start, but between the Wend and the sewers, I've been enacting plans to better Astana. I'm surprised we never ran into each other."

"What do you mean?"

"Did you never go toward the southern end of Tembris?"

"No," she said, "Dewalt wouldn't let me go that far. It was his hard limit."

"I've been overseeing the restoration of the rowhouses on that end. Really, I already did this once before with the Cascade and Clearhill, but that was on a vastly smaller scale. I figured the first step was to make everything look nice, give people better housing, tidy everything up. We had to knock down one of the buildings, and I started plans for a garden. I, uh, hoped you'd help me with it."

She played with a button on my shirt, a thoughtful look on her face. "Of course."

"And, I'm working with Durand to form some sort of arrangement with experienced merchants who can help open some shops. There are people who could thrive here with a little help getting started. Maybe open some sort of market too? What do you think?"

"Food. Yes. Brilliant, Rain." She stood on tiptoes to place a kiss on my jaw, and the adoration I felt through the bond set my heart aflame. "I think that's the solution."

"You think?"

"People only thieve because they need to, and they're doing it within the Wend. They're starving. Why else would they take from their neighbors? And of course that leads to violence."

"So, we bring in food."

"It's a start, I think." She tugged on my collar, pride radiating from her frame. "Oh!"

She shoved past me, and I turned to see her reaching for some rags, about to grab the pot boiling over.

"Wait, Em, let me. Go open the door."

She only hesitated for a second before doing as I bid, and a cold rush of air burst into the tiny home. Using my divinity to coax about a third of the water out of the pot, I formed it into a ball as I walked it to the front door, extra cautious because of the boiling water steaming in the air.

"I overfilled it," she said, sheepishly.

"I'm not sure if it's cold enough; I think it is, but watch," I replied as I used my divinity to shoot the water past her out into the night. A gust of wind blew at the most opportune moment, sending tiny ice crystals which formed from the boiling water flying into the air. She whooped with glee, just as I'd hoped she would.

"It froze! Gods, that was so fast!"

"It has to be extremely cold to do it that quick. Thank Aonara we had her fire on the trip here. We'd have frozen to death in the sky without it."

"That reminded me of something I used to do with Elora in the wintertime."

"What's that?"

"Snow taffy."

"Snow taffy," I repeated, and she laughed.

"It's maple syrup. You pack the snow and boil the syrup. When you pour it onto the snow, it cools it. The minute—and I mean down to the second—Elora saw the first snowflake, she'd start shouting about snow taffy."

"That sounds adorable."

"It was." She smiled, though I felt her sadness over the bond. I tried not to think about it. I'd lost the opportunity to make those memories with them, but I would not spend my time mourning. I'd make whatever memories I could with my daughter.

"Come, I have some things to show you," she said.

She led the way upstairs and brought me into her bedroom, lighting the lamp with her divine fire. The last time we'd been here, she'd forced me to help her make her bed. I'd thought then that it had been a taunt. That it was a way for her to send the message she'd been with someone who wasn't me. I wasn't sure what was worse anymore. I wasn't glad she was unhappy and unfulfilled, not by any means. But would she have been able to find fulfillment with someone else anyway? I knew I hadn't. If I could have gone back and not slept with the women I did, I would have in a heartbeat. There wasn't a single gods damn one I didn't regret after.

But my frustration over what I thought was a taunt was why I'd let her believe the number of women I'd been with was so high. A dozen women over the course of sixteen years wasn't much, but the court gossips thought I slept with every woman I spoke to. And I let them make those assumptions, wanting them to think I was some sort of rake, so I'd be left alone. By the time I'd been set right about Emma's experiences, it wasn't as if I could tell her it was only a dozen women. A dozen was still far more than I wanted to lay claim to. I didn't think it would help anything, so I kept it to myself.

I was on the verge of telling her though, those thoughts brought to mind by her old marriage bed and my desire to tell her every passing notion which weighed on me, when she dragged a trunk over from the corner of the room and directed me to sit on the edge of the bed. Settling down onto her knees beside the chest, she pulled out a folio and reached inside.

"I commissioned a sketch artist in town every few years. Mother and Father had us sit for portraits every other year, if you remember. The whole ordeal with hours of sitting frozen, the big, puffy dresses—it was miserable. I didn't have the money for that, and truly I don't know if I'd have put her through it anyway, but I could afford a sketch. The woman was quite good." A sad smile crossed her face as she looked down at the stack of drawings. My stomach knotted in anticipation. "Mistress McNish passed last year. She'd spend the whole day with us, just chatting and sketching. She wouldn't let me pay her the very first year. Elora had been such a joy, she said our company was payment enough."

I stopped breathing as she passed the first one over to me. A toddler with short, curly hair sticking straight out from her head smiled at me. She wore a nappy and nothing else. Hands on her hips, a round swell of a belly stuck out.

"Perfect. Of course she was. Is. Gods, Em."

"Not included was the ribbon I'd tied in her hair a dozen times that day. She took it out no sooner than I put it in."

I laughed, holding the portrait closer to examine my daughter. "Is that a dimple?"

"Yes, she lost it when she lost her baby fat."

"Her hair," I murmured, awed by the unruly curls she got from me.

"I didn't know what to do with it at that age, so mostly I didn't do anything," she admitted. "She's six in this next one."

Trading out the portraits, the little girl looked much the same, and yet so different in the next one. Her curls had grown vulnerable to gravity and rested on her shoulders. The dimple was much more slight, and yet the artist had still captured it.

"She's not smiling as much," I mumbled.

"She was missing both her front teeth, and she didn't like her smile."

"Did she have a lisp? Ven had one when she lost her two front teeth."

"A small one, yes." Em's whole face lit up as she smiled.

The two of us spent a while going through the remaining three portraits, and I was able to watch my girl grow in a way. Once finished, Em pulled a soft yellow blanket from the chest. It was in wonderful condition, and I found it hard to believe it was Elora's from infancy.

"Mother made this for her. My father brought it with the news of her death."

"Lady Highclere didn't seem like the type to make anything."

Em laughed, unfolding and refolding the blanket, yellow like butter. "No, she didn't. But Father insisted it was her. I meant to ask Nana about that. Perhaps she made it instead."

"How is Nana doing? I haven't asked about her." Hadn't asked about a lot of things.

"She loves it. The girls in the dormitory love her, and it keeps her busy." The woman was a great fit to help transition the novices back to life as free women. Emma had been wise to ask her to do it.

"I have a few more things in there to show you in the morning when it's light out. Drawings and stories she wrote. Oh, wait," she said as she placed everything else back in the trunk. "Look. I made this for her to wear on her first birthday."

She stood, walking over a dress made for a doll. Yellow with white flowers and frilled edges, it couldn't have fit a real child.

"It's tiny."

She laughed. "Elora was tiny, Rain. She was always small for her age."

Not sure why it affected me more than any of the rest, I wrapped my arms around Em's waist and pulled her close. Pressing my face into her chest, I inhaled. That faint lilac scent permeated through her clothes. The thought that the two of them were here for so long, vulnerable and unprotected, pained me. I was so gods damn lucky they were alright, and they were mine. Lucky I'd been given this chance.

"You did so good, Em." I turned my head so she could hear me, but didn't pull away. She gently pulled the dress out from between us and set it on the foot of the bed before wrapping her arms around my head. She straddled me, lowering herself to sit on my lap. My head slid up her chest, and I listened to her heart. A steady and calming beat met me, and I squeezed her tighter.

"I could have done much better with you," she whispered.

"Not better, just different. She's perfect, Em. You're perfect." I pressed a kiss between her breasts.

Suddenly, she gasped, and her heart raced. At first, I thought it was from my touch, anticipatory, but then I felt her anxiety.

"What is it?"

"What? Nothing."

I pulled away and gave her a look. She sighed, hanging her head.

"I know you probably don't want to sleep in here. We can sleep in Elora's bed."

I made a face, instantly repulsed. "I'm not going to make love to you in our daughter's bed."

She snorted. "You planned on making love to me tonight?"

"Every night I can, dear heart. I suppose I could make you come on the floor or against the wall if you don't want to use the bed."

"This bed, it…I don't want to make you uncomf—"

"How many times have you finished in this bed? How many times did you ride your hand and think of me?"

A red flush creeped up her cheeks, and I tugged her close and kissed her neck.

"A few dozen at least," she replied.

"That's it?"

"I didn't keep track."

"Well, I didn't keep track of how many times I fisted my cock to thoughts of you, but it was certainly more than a few dozen. Gods."

"Do you want me to say hundreds? Would that make you feel better?"

"Only if it were true."

She sighed before tipping her head up toward the ceiling and scrunching her nose.

"What's that face about?" I asked.

"You're making me do the calculations."

I barked a laugh. "I'm just being facetious, Em. Don't worry about me. I know I made this sweet cunt wet just from a memory of me. You're probably wet right now."

Her breath stuttered, but she ignored me. "Close to four hundred times, I'd guess. That accounts for twice a month."

I dipped my head and kissed her shoulder, tugging the fabric of her shirt out of my way. I was gentle on the ink, even though I wanted to trace every path carved across her ivory skin.

"Now do the calculation for twice a day."

"I did not!"

"I'm not talking about you." I grinned, and she jumped to her feet.

"You did not."

I couldn't help my joy around this woman, now she'd forced me to look it in the eye and take it. "Not that often, but close. Take your clothes off. This bed should know what I'm truly capable of." She shook her head, smiling and rolling her eyes. "I can help you if you've forgotten how to work buttons," I offered.

"I suppose I can change into something more comfortable," she said, a coy smile playing on her lips.

"I've heard nudity is quite comfortable. As is being bent over on the bed with your thighs spread."

"You're incorrigible."

"Intractable, truly," I agreed.

A sly smile crossed her features as she unbuttoned her blouse. "Fine, I'll undress, but you're only allowed to make love to me in whatever I put on."

"It doesn't matter what you wear, I'll take it off anyway."

"No, that's part of the deal. You can't take it off."

"Then how am I—" I argued, but she cut me off.

"I'll make sure you have access."

"Fine."

"Close your eyes."

I obeyed, laughing at her for what she was doing to me. As incorrigible as I might have been, she was my match in every way. No one could counter me like her. No one could put me in my place like her. I heard quick footsteps and the squeak of wood against wood as she opened a drawer. There was a flutter of fabric as she changed, and I was tempted to peek at her. Finally, she grabbed my hands in hers and told me to open my eyes.

I blinked a few times as I took her in.

"What do you think?" she asked, fighting a smile as if her life depended on it.

A sack. That's what she wore. A hideous brown sack hanging nearly to the floor. No shape, nothing. There were no sleeves to it, so her bare arms stuck out from either side.

"You're a rectangle."

She burst out laughing, and I took the moment to pick her up and toss her on the bed. The fabric of her dress was rough, and I couldn't imagine it felt good on her soft skin. I ripped my own clothes off as she laughed. Her eyes heated as she took in my nudity.

"Where did this monstrosity come from?" I asked, tugging at the nightgown.

"Theo's mother gave it to me. I pretended I liked it, and she gave me three more."

She sat up on her elbows, and I tugged the dress up, rolling her over onto her stomach.

"On your knees, Your Majesty."

"You don't want to see this beautiful nightgown?" She rose onto her knees and shrieked as I pulled the gown up and exposed her bare ass. Plump, round, and inviting, I nearly groaned at the sight.

"The view I have now is better. Put your elbows on the bed."

I pressed down on her upper back until she lowered, and the gown slid halfway up. Rubbing my hands over her ass and up her body, I gripped and massaged her, loosening any tension in her muscles. I had her moaning without even touching her waiting heat. And when I touched her there, parted her sweet flesh and dipped my finger inside her, I grumbled my approval when I found her soaked. When she pushed her hips back toward me, trying to take my finger deeper, I laughed.

"So needy. You ache for my cock, don't you, Em?"

"Always," she replied.

I dipped down, replacing my finger with my tongue. Licking her from clit to entrance, I groaned against her. I wasn't sure if I'd ever get enough of her. She hummed in pleasure as she moved her hips, granting me a better angle. As much as I loved to taste her though, I needed to be inside her more. Moving upright, I slid my hands from her hips up to her waist, my thumbs bracketing her spine. When I sheathed myself inside her in a slow stroke, her low, throaty moan tugged on something deep within me. Completely seated, I stilled, allowing both of us to get used to the feeling. The angle made her so tight I had to grit my teeth.

Hands on her ass, I guided our movements. She gripped me tight as I slid out slowly before pushing back in. Her knees were close together though, and I knew I could get deeper. Nudging her legs open, she repositioned and moaned when I thrust again, going farther than before. I continued moving, dragging out of her and forcing my way back in—languid movements requiring every bit of self-control I could muster. It was excruciating torment to go so slowly, but I wanted her to savor it. To feel every bit of me I had to give her.

She twisted and looked over her shoulder at me, stretching her arm back to grip mine while she rested on her other elbow. Clasping my hand around her wrist, I held onto her as she looked up at me. Eyes I wanted to dive into met mine as I moved faster. Even though I was the one fucking her, barreling us both toward release, the grip on my arm told me how much she wanted it. How much she wanted to work with me to give us both what we needed. An active participant in our meeting of flesh and melding of desire. Holding that arm back, I used my other hand to guide her ass as I picked up my pace. She bit her lip as she bounced from the motion. Panting, her mouth opened on a silent scream as I pumped into her.

She gasped, dropping her face into the bed as I let go of her hand. Grabbing her with harsh fingertips, I pounded hard into her. Watching her ass bounce, seeing the jiggle of sweet flesh I wanted to bite, nearly undid me.

Putting my knee on the bed, I bent over her body, sliding her gown up and brushing my lips across her shoulder blades. She was so gods damn perfect. Her bravery and courage over the past few months were nothing short of extraordinary, and I couldn't be more proud of her. There was nothing she couldn't do. And in turn, there was nothing I wouldn't do for her. She'd shown me the lengths she'd go to for me, in so many ways, and I needed to get out of my head and make her know I'd do the same.

Climbing over her, both knees on the bed, I yanked the horrifying gown over her head, and she flattened, laughing as she pulled it down off her arms.

"I said you had to leave it on," she whined.

"You also said I'm incorrigible. What did you expect?"

I'd slipped out of her when I pulled the gown from her body, and as she moved back onto her knees, I splayed a hand on her backside, forcing her flat. One knee on either side of her legs, I slid back into that wet heat. She groaned and arched her spine as she reached back, running her fingers over where we connected.

"*Gods*," she murmured.

"I know, Em. You feel how good you take me? Gods damn made for me."

Her whimper told me she agreed, and I decided I needed to be closer. Needed to feel more of her skin. Sliding my hands over her body, I leaned down over her, kissing a path up her spine before bracketing my arms on either side of her. I buried my face in her neck, breathing her in as I pushed deep inside her. Gripping her throat, I turned her head to the side and kissed her the best I could from that angle.

When she laid her head down and grabbed my hands on either side of her, pulling me forward, I had no choice but to collapse on top of her. My elbows bracketed her own, and every part of our bodies aligned. I settled my legs between hers, my chest pressed to her back, and I relished the closeness.

"I'm too heavy," I panted into her ear even as my cock moved within her.

Pulling my hand, she brought it to her mouth and kissed.

"Harder," she demanded in a whisper.

Using my elbows as leverage, I lifted my hips and slammed into her as hard as I could, and she moaned on my hand, biting my knuckle. She pulled my other hand close, and I crowded her. And yet it still wasn't close enough.

I wanted to wring pleasure from her every single night, wanted to write my name in her flesh. Her body was mine and mine alone. There were nights during our time apart—forced and self-inflicted—when I thought about how close we'd come to losing one another forever. To never having this chance. If Faxon hadn't found out about Elora's paternity, would we have ever found each other again? Would she have continued to live unhappily with him, even after Elora had grown and left? The idea maddened me. Short, punctuated thrusts to ease my frustration over those thoughts had her crying out. I could feel her clenching around me and knew she was close.

I bent down and nipped her ear. "Do you need my hand to come? Or will my cock be enough?"

"Don't you dare move," she ordered. "Keep going."

I obeyed, maintaining a steady pace and feeling her tighten around me as her moans turned high-pitched. Biting the inside of my cheek, I stopped myself from finishing so she could ride out the full wave of her release, squeezing my length. She bit down hard on my knuckle, and I lost my resolve. The pleasure was too much. Those delicate internal muscles fluttered around me, and I grunted as I spilled deep inside her. I laid there for a moment on top of her as we both caught our breath before realizing I was crushing her.

Using my hands to walk my body up and take some weight off her, I was on my knees between her legs, hands on her ass as I pulled out of her. She made a noise, wincing at the absence, and I watched as I dripped out of her. The glint of her wetness on my cock, the mess we'd made of one another, was enough to satiate some primal instinct of mine. The sight was enough to draw a grumble out of my chest as I used my thumb to circle her entrance, pushing my release back inside and drawing a whimper from her lips. Though I was on the tonic, part of me wished I wasn't. I knew the timing was wrong, knew it could risk her, but it was just one more way our rash decisions had robbed us. And I wanted it. I wanted to experience everything with her.

She sat up on her elbows, arching her back as she turned her head to the side to look at me.

"There are towels in the hall closet," she said, voice raspy from her cries.

"I'm content to watch you like this."

"Rogue."

"*Your* rogue," I corrected.

"Well, you're going to have to help me clean myself up if you want to be fed."

"And why's that?"

She gave an exaggerated sniff in the air while making a face. "Burnt green beans."

Gods, how she healed my soul.

CHAPTER 42

Emmeline

We'd never bothered to ward Ravemont, the cost outweighing the risk, so I could have rifted straight inside if I'd wanted. But for some reason I didn't know, I opened the rift outside near the fountain instead. Emptied for the winter, a thin layer of snow covered the bottom of the water feature. I wrung my hands as I stared up at the statue of the little girl. The dandelion she had once held had broken off since my last visit. I didn't know why I was nervous. Rain put his hand on the small of my back as he moved to stand beside me, sensing I needed his touch.

"How is it so similar and different all at once?" I murmured.

"Time makes us look at things differently."

"This is only the second time I've been here since Lucia died. Winter makes it worse, I think. It's...dead."

"It's not your home anymore. Places we used to call ours never feel quite the same once we've left."

"Does Crown Cottage feel that way to you?"

He sighed. "Crown Cottage changed once *you* left. I still visit regularly, but it hasn't been the same, no."

"I'm surprised you still went. What with Dewalt, I mean. That had to be hard for him."

"Dewalt is actually why we went. He wanted to visit more often than I did."

"He probably feels closer to her when he's there. Most of my memories with her are here—once you lot went to Astana for the winter. And of course, from before we were cursed with knowing you," I added with a grin.

His hand slid to my waist as he tugged my body against his. "The feeling is mutual, Em."

The sun came out from behind a cloud, blinding us with its glint on the snow. I took a deep breath. I didn't know what I was waiting for. It was my father. We'd once been close—though it felt like a lifetime ago. Steeling myself, I broke from

Rain's grip on my waist and moved toward the front door. Mister Carson had it open by the time I reached the bottom step.

"Your Majesties," he said with a deep bow.

"Oh gods, not you. Please don't."

"Get used to it, my queen," Rain murmured under his breath, a smile in his voice.

"I'm serious, Mister Carson. Please don't address me like that. You've seen me get my nappy changed. Emmeline is fine," I said.

A red flush creeped up the butler's neck, and I stepped past him into the foyer to save him the embarrassment of replying.

Ravemont was quiet. It seemed the butler had dismissed some of the servants, and those who remained did their best not to be seen or heard. Even when I'd been here during the fall, it hadn't been like this. On our flight to Brambleton, I had thought a lot about my father's behavior during that visit. He'd seemed confused about Elora. And now that I knew Gemma, the woman he'd shared my secret with, was his nurse? I wondered how long he'd been ailing. There were many questions I had, and I wasn't sure I'd find all the answers.

"I'll go fetch Miss Gemma. If you want to wait in the front sitting room?"

I nodded, though there was a sting to the words. Ravemont had a multitude of rooms which served various purposes. The front sitting room was where we met with formal guests. It reminded me just how much this wasn't my home anymore. It would make sense if Mister Carson chose that room because of the Crown, but my sensitive heart took it the worst way possible. I was a guest—a stranger.

But I was, wasn't I?

The older servants knew me, but they knew a different version of me. They knew an Emmeline who loved and fought with and kept secrets from her sister. They knew an Emmeline who didn't understand grief and guilt and regret. When I'd been grieving my sister and going through pregnancy alone, I'd been locked away, only visited by Nana or my mother. I certainly hadn't been around anyone enough for them to know me. They didn't know who I became when I was forced to move forward on a new path on my own. They didn't know who I was as a mother. They didn't know how reconciling myself with the past gave me a new future. I was someone new, made by my own decisions.

Rain and I only had to wait a few moments before Gemma came bustling into the room.

"Your Majesties, I must say he is doing rather well today!" she exclaimed, much too loudly. Her crimson dress made of velvet seemed much too fine for a nursemaid, but I supposed she was paid generously. Her blonde hair was pulled back into a chignon, and she clasped her hands together in front of her. "I'm sorry about these circumstances. I wanted Lord Kennon to tell you back in the fall when you were here, but he refused because of what you were going through. Didn't want to be a burden, he said."

"How long has he been sick?" I asked.

"Mister Carson and Nana pressured him to hire me just over a year ago," she replied, crossing over to the high-back chair across from me. The leather gave an annoying squeak as she sat, putting me more on edge than before. Rage tore through me when I realized Nana had known for a year and hadn't told me in the past few months. Rain slid his arm down from the back of the sofa, resting it around my waist. He could sense it.

"How did it start?" Rain sat forward in his seat as he spoke, maintaining contact with me. Grounding me as he always did.

"The servants noticed he was getting confused more often, having volatile changes in mood, forgetting things. Nothing too horrible, but still concerning."

"That started a year ago? Why did no one tell me?" I asked.

"It started quite some time before that, but they didn't do anything until then. He didn't want anyone to tell you." She gave a sad smile. "I was going to let you know once it got to this point, regardless of his wishes."

"He didn't seem this bad when I saw him last. He rode to meet me by himself three months ago! And now he's only got a few weeks left?"

Rain's thumb moved soothing circles on my side as he tightened his hand around me. None of this made any sense. The fact he was sick, that he didn't tell me, and he'd gotten so bad so quickly—how? I was angry with him for not telling me. I could have visited more frequently or tried to repair what had broken between us. Gods, in the years since Lucia died and then Mother soon after, I had desperately wanted some sort of relationship with the man who had bounced me on his knee and taught me how to tell time and helped me with arithmetic. And now there wasn't time for that. Even a year would have been more time.

"I rode with him to your home. He only crossed the meadow by himself. It was a great argument we had, but the man insisted. It was going to be the last time I planned to pacify his pride. He couldn't even remember half the servants' names by then. His mind has been failing him for a long time, and now his body has caught up." I swallowed hard, controlling my reaction. "I'm sorry, truly. I wish I had better news for you," she said.

"You said he was doing alright today?" I asked, voice thick.

"Yes. He just had his breakfast, and he won't need to nap for a few hours. He was very pleased when I told him you were here. You arrived much faster than I thought you would have, although you are able to rift, aren't you?"

"Yes ma'am," Rain replied, dipping his head.

"That'll do it." She stood, brushing down her dress. "He's in his suite. He remembers who you are today, but sometimes he forgets the details. Do not be too hurt if he calls you by your mother's name. It's purely accidental. He could always surprise us and recall all the things I reminded him of yesterday. It's hard to tell what it will be each day. I do think it would be best if only the queen goes in," she said, leading me toward the door before addressing Rain. "Your visit made him quite excitable, sire. I hope you will forgive me for my reluctance to see him agitated again."

Rain dipped his head and began to sit back down, but he was quickly on his feet a moment later. My hand had reached for him of its own accord. Her casual referral to me as queen had unsteadied me, but then she'd said Rain couldn't go in with me. My heart started racing, and it felt like something was squeezing my chest. When I started feeling dizzy, I realized I couldn't take a deep breath.

"Em." Warm hands held onto mine, thumbs rubbing the backs of them. "Em, look at me." Pine-green eyes filled with concern met mine. "Breathe with me. In." He inhaled, and I mimicked the motion. "Out." We both expelled a breath.

"If you need to go in with—"

He shot a look at Gemma, silencing her.

"It shouldn't be something I have to do alone," I said, stifling a sob.

"No, it shouldn't," he agreed.

"They should be here. It's not fair."

"They should, and it isn't fair."

"It should be the three of us, not just me."

The realization hit me: once my father died, I'd have no family left, aside from the one I'd made. It was something I couldn't bear to think about.

"You said he doesn't remember half the servants?" Gemma nodded her head in answer to his question as Rain gently guided me back to the sofa we'd been sitting on. "Any of them my size?"

"Rain, you don't have to—"

"Brilliant, Your Majesty. I'll be right back."

Rain kept his own breeches on, but a few minutes later, he was following behind me into my father's suite wearing Mister Carson's jacket. It was far too small, and I was sure we'd have to replace it after Rain was done with it. Seeing him struggle into it helped calm my nerves. He couldn't lift his arms, and it was comical to look at. I'd told him he didn't have to do that, I would be fine, but he persisted. I had just needed a moment to calm myself. It was a panic attack. I'd had them before, but it had been long enough I'd forgotten what they felt like.

When my father rolled his head on the pillow to look up at me, I realized the ruse might not have been worth our time. The way his eyes couldn't focus on me made me wonder if he would have even noticed Rain.

"Hello, Pa," I said quietly, using a name I hadn't used for him since I was a child. I didn't plan to call him that, but seeing him lying in the bed looking small and weak had my gut twisted and mind addled. His hair, normally perfectly combed, was a mess. He wore a linen shirt, loose on his thin frame, and my eyes were drawn to the stains on the front. Porridge, it looked like. His skin sagged from his face, evidence of weight lost too quickly.

"Why, hello sunshine. Come here," he said, lifting a shaking arm from the bed. My chest tightened at the endearment. He had once called me sunshine and Lucia stormcloud, just to be contrary, aggravating the both of us. I hadn't heard him say it once since my sister's death. Rain took a seat at the chess table along the far wall as I moved around to my father's side of the bed. I perched on the edge, just next to his hip. The faint scent of urine reached me as I adjusted.

"How are you feeling?" I asked.

"I've felt worse," he replied, coughing on a laugh. I reached for his frail hand, and he patted my own before clasping them together. "It's awful, getting old. You were smart to put it off."

Not understanding his meaning at first, it took me a moment to realize he knew about the bond. Gemma said she had reminded him of things, but I was pleasantly surprised. "I'm sorry you weren't there. It was all very sudden."

"Nothing to apologize for, my sunshine girl. I'm glad you're finally getting some happiness. What's that?" he asked, pointing at my neck.

"It's a tattoo." I hadn't once thought about having to explain it to anyone.

"It's pretty."

"Thank you," I replied, surprised that was all he had to say.

"How's Lucia?"

A quick cut I wasn't expecting.

"Do you mean Elora, Pa?" I corrected gently.

"Yes, who else?" He sounded frustrated, and I remembered Gemma's words warning me to approach situations such as this carefully. I wasn't supposed to draw attention to his mistake.

"She's well. She's still got some healing to do, but I'm very proud of her."

"There's a rumor going around." He raised a brow as he looked up at me, eyes the color of my own curious. I chuckled, squeezing his hand.

"You have time to pay attention to rumors now?"

"Elora belongs to the Crown Prince? That's what the servants are saying."

I stilled, uncertain of what to say. I didn't know if he'd be upset, and Gemma had insisted it was paramount not to distress him. But I wouldn't lie. Not bothering to correct him about Rain's royal status, I answered about our daughter.

"She does."

"I'm sorry, sunshine."

My brows furrowed before I said, "I'm not. I'm ecstatic she belongs to him."

"Not that. For pushing you on Faxon when you were with child."

"Oh."

"Your mother and I, well, it doesn't matter now. I think we made a mistake. Faxon wasn't—"

"Faxon is dead, and I'd prefer him to remain so. Even in conversation."

He nodded, chin wobbling. "You'll have to ask your mother about our reasons."

I bit my lip and nodded, fighting the urge to correct him. Why make him live through her death again in his feeble state?

"I've missed you, sunshine. I wish you came to see me more often."

He started coughing, turning his head to the side, and it saved me from having to bite my tongue. Visiting Ravemont had been forbidden. It was hard to reconcile this sweet, dying man with the man who'd forced me upon Faxon and allowed me to be isolated for over a decade. It was a war of heart and mind within me, and I glanced over at Rain for a burst of confidence. But Rain's eyes were wide as he looked at my father—coughing fit passed.

"Pa?" I shouted in a panic, fearful of what I might see.

"Your Highness?" He croaked out, using his sheet to dry his spittle-covered lips. "Why are you—" The coughing began again.

"Oh, gods," I murmured. "Pa, Rain is here with me for support."

He flopped onto his back, panting, with eyes closed. "That makes sense."

Rain had stood, shrugging off Mister Carson's jacket to reveal the plain black shirt beneath. He looked between my father and me, clearly uncertain of what to do.

"Can you send in Ginny?" My father decided for us, and I assumed he meant his nurse. "I need her," he added, with an uncomfortable clearing of his throat.

"I'll get her, Pa. I'll be staying a while, alright?"

"Yes, dear."

Rain followed behind as I moved toward the door, a comforting hand on the small of my back. I glanced over my shoulder at my father, looking so small in the great bed which had belonged to my mother's ancestors for centuries. His eyes were closed, and he'd thrown an arm over his face, my stomach twisting at the sight. I was struck then by how unfair it was for him that I would be the one at that bedside as he left his mortal body. It was the first time I wasn't upset over the fact he loved Lucia and my mother more, instead wishing he had anyone left who cared for him as they had.

"I don't know. It doesn't feel like a good idea."

"We don't have to if you don't want to," he replied, though he seemed a bit forlorn. "It's an apple orchard now."

"What is?"

"Where it happened. Dewalt's idea. We expanded the olive grove too."

I sighed. "I'm surprised he was the main reason you visited. I would've thought he wouldn't want to..."

"He didn't want to leave that fall. We almost didn't, in fact. When I tried to see you and you wouldn't see me, I threw a tantrum like a petulant child, and he relented. I'm tempted to give him Crown Cottage, to be quite honest."

"Can you do that now that you signed their paperwork?"

"I let him keep his title." I raised a brow, surprised he could do that. "Perks of being king, I suppose. Although, I made sure to mention it to the council right after recounting my time in Darkhold. I think they felt sorry for me."

"As they should," I said, somber over what he'd gone through.

"Anyway, he's still a duke, and I can assign any land to him I might want. I don't know, though. If I give him Crown Cottage, then he'll never give up her ghost."

"She'd be so angry he's doing this to himself. I can hear her now, pacing the hall and yelling at me about it."

Rain chuckled. "She'd have thrown something while yelling about it, I'm sure. Highclere women, always throwing things."

"Excuse me, Lucia was the one who—"

"Dagger at my father." I glared at him, but kept my mouth shut as his lips kicked up in a crooked smile. "Elora does it too. She threw her practice sword at Dewalt last week. She claimed it was an accident, but I could tell it wasn't."

"I wish I could say that didn't sound like her."

"I can't believe how much Highclere she has in her. But when she makes the same faces I make? Gods, it stops me in my tracks every time. It's more often than I'd like to admit that I wish she looked like me. Just so we'd have known sooner, but also because half the time I don't believe she's mine."

"Why don't you believe she's yours?" My stomach tightened.

"Relax, Em," he said, brushing his knuckles against mine. "I have not a single doubt in my mind that she's mine. I just can't believe I'm this lucky. It's all so new, I have to remind myself every day. Don't you worry that pretty head of yours."

"I'm sorry. Your mother—"

"Speaking of my mother," he interrupted. "I know thinking about it is going to send you into a tailspin of stress and anxiety. Can I redirect you to something else regarding her? It's about Crown Cottage."

"Oh?" He was right. I didn't want to talk about how horrid she'd been during his absence.

"When I went back to Ravemont and found out you were gone..." I winced as he continued, nonplussed. "She was staying at Crown Cottage. We only slept there one night after I found out about you. She stayed up that entire night and did something for me to make me feel better."

"You told her about us?"

"She knew I brought your ring with me that day."

"This ring?" He nodded. "You've had it this whole time? What were you planning on—Rain, *what?*"

"I told you I came to my senses, dear heart. After you wouldn't see me that fall, I went and tried to get my head straight for a while. But when I realized what I should have known all along, that I'd been a fool, well, I wasted no more time. I suppose it would have been the summer after Elora was born. I was going to make you my bride—whether you liked it or not. But you were already gone."

"You held onto it?" I whispered.

"Obviously."

"For over a decade?"

"Well, what else was I going to do with it?"

"I don't know. Give it to someone else? Sell it?"

He laughed, brows pitched up incredulously. "'Here, Ven. A ring for the woman who has ruined me for all others. But you can wear it if you want.'"

"Alright, fine. But you still could have sold it or given it to the treasury, or, I don't know—"

"I wore it around my neck for a time. Does that count?"

"Gods, Rain."

I stopped myself. In that moment, I felt horrible for how much he'd been affected and the lengths he'd gone to while I was throwing myself into raising Elora to avoid thoughts of him. He was performing grand gestures, and I was evading. I had my fair share of lonely nights, the profound ache of my broken heart, but I tried to hold myself together and raise an ornery little girl. Shame and guilt took root, and my gaze settled on my lap. How could I deserve him when I'd tried so hard not to think of him?

"What's this about?" he asked, tilting my chin up with a fingertip. Gods, that cursed bond.

"Nothing."

"Em," he growled in warning.

"Nothing. I just—" He used his fingertip to turn my head toward him, and I sighed. "I just feel ashamed. You were getting rings made, going to Ravemont to make these dramatic declarations, and I was just in Brambleton changing nappies and teaching her letters and trying not to think of you. I feel bad about it, that's all."

"I hurt you, Em. I said things I can't take back. I'd all but sent you away. Of course, you tried not to think of me. What's important," he grinned, face lighting up as he continued, "is that you failed at it. I know you thought of me despite your best efforts."

"That's true," I relented. "Still."

"Our past has framed us and made us better. It was hell, but now we're here." He pulled me into him, and I rested my head on his shoulder. "You got us off topic, my wife."

"I'm—"

"Gods," he exclaimed. "My wife. Truly, I never thought I'd say that phrase about anyone, let alone you."

"Now who is off topic?"

He slid an arm around me. After we took leave of my father, we had meandered our way around the estate, finding ourselves in the drawing room. We'd sat beside one another on a chaise and hadn't moved since. It was soft, and though we'd slept comfortably enough the night before, the hard ground hadn't done us any favors.

"Ah yes, where were we? My mother." I made a sound in my throat, and he shook with laughter. "She cleared out a room for me. I added to it over time—whenever we visited. I think you'd like it."

"She cleaned out a room? I don't understand. You had rooms there."

"You should let me take you. We can rift right in. I've been there recently enough."

"I don't know. I don't want to see where she died."

"We won't," he assured me. "I promise."

"Fine, we can go after dinner. But I have a place I'd like to stop first."

"Oh, gods," I groaned, hands on my knees as I sent healing divinity into my aching joints. "That was stupid."

Rain chuckled from somewhere above me, moonlight streaming down behind him, casting his face in shadow. "It wasn't the smartest thing I've seen you do. Your knees aren't made for that jump anymore."

"Clearly," I snapped, and his laugh brought a smile to my face. Wanting to see if I could coax the light under my skin as I had the night before, I closed my eyes and inhaled. I tried for a few moments and only managed to conjure the divine fire in my palm. Ever since we'd been in the cavern, my divinity had settled almost, nearly back to how it felt before the Cascade. I could tell there was something lingering deep though, Hanwen's vast power waiting for me to awaken it. Giving up, I started for the back of the wine cellar.

"White or red?" I called out.

"No preference. Whatever you want."

I didn't think he'd ever liked wine that much, not like his sister. Pulling a sweet, fruity wine off the shelf, I released a plume of dust into the air. When I sneezed, my fire went out, and I nearly jumped out of my skin.

"Regretting sneaking now, Em?"

"Is it even sneaking?"

"Not with all the noise you're making, no," he said. Fighting a grin, I opened a rift and shoved the bottle of wine at him, and he chuckled. "Didn't want to climb the ladder like old times?"

"I wasn't sure my knees could take it," I replied, and he took my hand, dragging me toward the hall. "Where are we going?" I asked.

"You'll see."

He headed toward the northwest corner of the estate, away from the grounds I wanted to avoid.

"How many staff are here?" I whispered.

"Just two. They're new."

"Mister Handry is gone?"

"Died a few years ago. His nephew is the caretaker, actually. We don't keep a full staff when we're gone, of course. The new Mister Handry and his wife and two boys live in the guest rooms. Your rooms." He squeezed my hand as he slowed his gait to walk beside me.

"That's good. I only had happy memories in the guest suite. It should stay that way."

We continued along in silence, and I smiled when I realized my muscles remembered this place. Without a hint of moonlight getting into the interior hall, I knew we were just past the library, and I had a suspicion about where he was taking me. We needn't bother to keep quiet, the guest rooms on the other side of the estate, but we still moved with silent grace.

When we reached the steps of the tower, Rain nudged me forward to lead the rest of the way up. I assumed his mother must have done something with the storage room we traipsed through regularly to get to the balcony where we once watched the stars. Surprised he'd told his mother about it, I was even more shocked when I opened the door. Tapestries lined the walls, and they had brought in furniture and rugs. Rain lit a lamp behind me, and low light filled the room. The furniture was covered with sheets to protect them from dust, and Rain moved past me, uncovering a sofa in the center of the room.

"Our chaise!" I exclaimed, rushing over. It had once rested in his bedroom, and I'd snoozed on it with my feet in his lap more times than was proper. Plopping down on it, the cushions were as soft as I remembered, and I traced my fingertip over the dark gold filigree design.

Rain moved toward the far side of the room and pulled a sheet off what turned out to be a sideboard. When he opened the cabinet though, he jumped back and swore.

"What is it?"

"Nothing—" he began, before sighing and cutting himself off. "I went to get some glasses out, but there's old draíbea in here."

"Oh, we don't need to smoke any of that; just the wine is fine," I said, confused.

He laughed without humor. "I'm never smoking this shit again."

I turned from where I sat, watching him in the dim light of the lamp. His hand rested on the cabinet door, and I studied the lines of his face. Tight and tired, he looked down at the drawer inside the cabinet. It took a moment for me to realize.

"Darkhold. You smelled like it."

"A censer suspended from the ceiling where I couldn't reach, and they gave it to me in my meals."

"Oh, Rain. Here, let me," I said, but he yanked the drawer open and grabbed it before I could even get up. Only when he stalked past me toward the outside door, small satchel in hand, did I begin to smell it. When he flung the doors open and threw it over the balcony, the wind whipped into the room, carrying the thick, cloying sweetness to me. I'd never liked draíbea, something Lavenia and I usually abstained from while the others partook. The one and only time I'd tried smoking it, I kept seeing things out of the corner of my eye. It wasn't a relaxing experience for me, but Lucia had enjoyed it well enough, calling it an escape from the truth.

If they'd been making him breathe it the entire time? Between that and the mindbreaker, no wonder he'd been so worried about accidentally hurting me. The lines between true and false would have been hard for him to see. My heart ached for him, and I felt the ebbing panic through the bond.

Unmoving, I held my breath and waited for the shadows to overtake him. I wanted nothing more than to approach him, though I didn't move, afraid to make it worse. But he surprised me. Rain stood there for only a moment, and took a deep breath, rubbing at his sternum.

"Em, come here."

Thankful I still had my cloak on, I moved to stand beside him in the doorway. But as I approached, I felt a slight tug from my chest, almost as if one of those golden strings between us was being tugged toward the balcony outside. Glancing up at Rain, his confusion told me he felt it, too.

"It feels…important."

"It does," I agreed.

Following the sensation to where it tugged us, we found ourselves on the western facing side of the tower. When the feeling on that golden string abated, we stood square in the middle of the balcony, almost exactly where he'd once had his telescope set up. Many hours on many nights, I'd snuck up here with him, and we had watched the stars. Though our first kiss was in the meadow, this was where I first fell in love with Rain. If asked, I couldn't have pinpointed any one night in particular, but it had flowered over quiet nights spent together, heads huddled close as he taught me the constellations. I remembered one night in particular when I finally had realized what it was I'd been feeling. I'd left in a hurry, not bothering to say goodnight.

He'd kissed me the first time the very next day.

"It's a perfect night for it. No moon," he said.

"It is. What do you think that was? That feeling?"

"I don't know, but it's passed now."

"Mmm," I hummed. "I wish I understood all the implications. The bond, the Beloved, my divinity—all of it. I don't like not knowing."

"I don't like it either. Maybe next time a god shows up in your dreams, you should ask them." He chuckled when I glared at him. It wasn't as if Rhia had been forthcoming. He faced me, pulling my hands into his, and lifted his eyes to the stars. "Damia," he said on a sigh as his lips lifted into a beautiful smile. "My deliverance."

I lost track of time as I watched him, the smile on his face softening as he stared into the sky. "Do you still have the telescope?"

"It's inside. Would you like me to get it out?"

"I thought you might want to test me," I said, my smile meeting his.

"Oh, you test me every day, Emmeline," he teased, though he went inside to fetch the telescope anyway.

"And that one?"

"Irses, the death-bringer," I recited.

"Wrong, that's Damia. Try again," he said.

"Shit. Irses, the hope-bearer."

"There you go. Servant to which of the gods?"

"You and your trick questions. Irses was no servant."

"Yes, he was," Rain argued, and I pulled my face away from the telescope and straightened as his hand rested on my hip. He'd leaned down beside me—too close.

"No," I insisted. "Rhia released him from servitude."

"But he was a servant before that, so my question still stands, Highclere." His grin was both handsome and annoying. Though we both stood at our full heights, no longer huddled around the telescope, his hand hadn't moved. I did my best not to draw his attention to it, in fear of him moving away.

"Hanwen."

He cleared his throat to say something, smiling with a raised brow as I cut him off.

"And before that, Ciarden, and before that Aonara, but originally he was a servant to Rhia."

He pursed his lips, clearly disappointed I hadn't fallen for his trickery.

"I guess you do pay attention sometimes," *he grumbled.*

"I'm always paying attention."

"Well, that's just not true."

He withdrew his hand, slow, looking at me in a way I longed for and dreaded at the same time. The torch in the bracket had nearly burnt out, but I could see the heat in his green eyes. When the royals had returned the week prior, I'd been eager to get back to Rain teaching me constellations, but in the back of my mind I was more eager to learn him. He'd let his hair grow longer on the top, though still short on the sides, and some of the shining spirals spilled across his forehead. Not knowing what possessed me to do it, I reached up and pulled a curl down, watching it bounce when I let go.

He frowned, not quite annoyed.

"Em," *he said, voice full of something I suspected would break my heart.* "In the fall, when Lucia and me—"

"What about it?"

"I won't be here as often, and I—It's all going to change," *he said, the sound of his heart nearly drowning out his words.*

"You're my best friend, Rain. That will not change."

His throat bobbed, and he looked away.

"You're my best friend too. I just—I wish things were different. I don't want to lose you."

"You won't. I promise you won't."

Even if it killed me to know he'd bonded with my sister. Even if I only saw him once a year, even if I married and raised a family, even if I grew old and wrinkled and he didn't age a day, he'd always be the person I would long to speak to and confide in. He'd become so much more than a friend over the past year, and I couldn't bear to think it would end.

The beat of his heart thundered against the silence. Thick in the air between us, I could feel that change. I could see it just on the edge of my vision, golden and warm.

I was in love with him.

And wasn't that just the worst trick of all?

CHAPTER 43

Rainier

My father had been ill off and on for years before this past autumn, and I was used to seeing him frail. I harbored little affection for the man, so it didn't bother me to see him that way. But it was different with Em and her father. Despite their estrangement, sorrow and regret filled our connection, and I wished I could take some of it from her like I did the pain. Holding her each night, I shared the load to ease her headache caused by the use of her divinity. Though she needed me to accompany her the day we arrived, the shock of seeing the man who raised her on his deathbed wore off, and she no longer required my presence. I still went with her, sometimes only lingering in the hall, but always nearby to step in once she wore her divinity out.

The day we arrived was Lord Kennon's last lucid day. He hadn't had many as of late, and it seemed we were lucky to see it. After having the nurse show her exactly what needed to be done for the man, Emma only required help in the mornings. She spent every day with her father, trying to heal him and get him to eat. The first couple of days, when his conversations lessened and grew more addled, he'd tormented her with questions about Lucia and Lady Highclere. I knew it hurt Em to talk about them as if they were just in another room, unable to tell him anything in fear of upsetting him. He'd grown quite bothered when she wouldn't bring his wife to visit.

Each night, Em crawled into bed beside me, mentally and physically exhausted, her divinity suffering. Though Hanwen had blessed her with more divinity than either of us could have imagined, she used every bit on Kennon each day. For whatever reason, she hadn't been able to dip into it as far as she had that day at the Cascade, and since our night in the cavern, she said her divinity almost felt normal again. She succeeded in making her father more comfortable, but each day, it was as if she hadn't even touched him, his state just as bad, if not worse, than before.

It felt like prolonging the inevitable. Eventually, she thought to heal his mind rather than his body, but she'd compared it to what the mindbreaker had done to Faxon.

"There's nothing to heal," she had said in a horrified whisper.

After that, she stopped trying, and I knew it killed a part of her to give up on him. There were no words to soothe I didn't try, but I knew her grief was something she'd have to work through on her own. I wondered if she ever debated stopping his heart to end the pain. If she did, she never said it, and I never mentioned it. She'd already been forced to use her harrowing that way when she didn't want to. I wouldn't recommend putting her through it again.

We hadn't yet been at Ravemont for a week when I fetched my telescope from Crown Cottage, setting it up in the back garden. It wasn't the same, nor was it as convenient as the balcony, but she hadn't wanted to risk rifting away in case her father worsened. Kennon was falling asleep earlier and earlier each day, and as selfish as it was, I was happier for it. It was hard on Em to see him fade away and her unable to do anything for him. The sooner he slept, the more rest she got. I was eager to show her the telescope, so the moment I felt her cool relief, her father finally finding sleep, I rifted to her.

When I met her in the hall outside his bedroom, she jumped in surprise. "Rain!" she squeaked, clutching her chest.

"I'm sorry. I didn't mean to frighten you."

"It's alright," she breathed as she leaned against the wall and wiped her brow. "I had to help move Pa. Mister Carson hurt his back the last time Gemma needed help changing him."

"Why didn't you call for me? I'd have helped."

"He already pitched a fit because I was there. Imagine if the King of Vesta saw him that way."

"He wouldn't even recognize me."

"He might. He called me sunshine again today." A small smile raised the corners of her lips. Her eyes were half shut as she lifted her hair off her neck. She was worn out. "It's so unfair, isn't it?"

"It is."

"Not about him dying." She tilted her head back, resting it against the wall and completely closing her eyes. "He—he's had this in him the whole time; he just chose not to. He hasn't called me sunshine in over sixteen years, Rain. It's almost like he died a long time ago. I don't—" Exhaling, she opened her eyes and slid them to mine, resolve taking over her features. "The father I knew died with Lucia, and I never got a chance to know this new one. It's strange to mourn now when I've been mourning him all along. And now I get to see glimpses of the old him. It's bullshit."

"Parts of all of us changed irreparably that day."

"Don't defend him." Her right brow lifted as she looked at me.

"I'm not. I don't have to imagine what it's like to lose a child because for weeks I thought I had. And what I have with Elora isn't near what you had with—"

"Better. It's better. Or will be, at the very least." She dropped her hair and pushed off the wall to face me. The cross of her arms and the stubborn tilt of her chin had me taking a step toward her.

She'd finally put some of her weight back on, her hips and thighs softening and filling her clothes out once more. I'd been worried about her, knowing it was stress and unwillingness to prioritize herself which had made her soft curves harden. I loved her body in all its forms, but there was something to be said about being able to grab a handful of my favorite parts. But I uttered nothing to her about it; I learned early on that a woman's body was none of my gods damned concern.

Well, unless I was drawing gasps of pleasure from this woman's body in particular. *That* I would make my concern.

"Sometimes I wonder if they wished it was me instead of her," she admitted.

"Don't fucking say that. Don't even think it."

"It's hard not to think that. If I had died, Lucia would be queen beside you." I barely stifled my reaction, revulsion-caused goosebumps spreading over my skin. "There would be no second household for my father to scrape the funds together for. I doubt my mother would have taken my death as hard as she did Lucia's. I've had a lot of time to think about this, Rain. I don't hold any bitterness over it—well, not too much anyway. It is what it is. But I don't think Lucia would have let him treat her the way I've let him carry on all these years."

"Either way, he had you, and he wasted it. What Lucia would have done doesn't matter because she's not here."

"Maybe I should have tried harder."

"You were barely more than a child when you left, Em. And you had your own to raise."

"It's clear he cared about me, the way he's been talking to me these past few days. Maybe if I would have pushed for more, I might have noticed he was ailing—before it was too late. He was short with me this past year, worse than normal. He didn't even ask about Elora half the time. I thought he didn't care, Rain," she whispered, and I folded her into my arms.

"Don't be too harsh on yourself. Did he ever make more of an effort? All the years before then?"

"Well, no."

"So, the conclusion you came to was reasonable."

"I suppose," she mumbled as she wrapped her arms around my waist, and I rested my chin atop her head. The calm rhythm of our hearts beating together made me grateful for this melancholy sort of respite.

Perhaps it made me a bad person or an irresponsible failure of a king. My father never would have dropped everything, certainly not amid the impending war, to comfort his wife. Perhaps with his first one, but not with my mother, his third. No, he was raging at me from the afterlife, questioning himself for raising such a fool.

I knew everything was in hand though. Between Lavenia's choice to make way to the seaborn, my directions for Raj and the council, and my Second's knowledge and determination to protect our kingdom while Thyra protected Elora—I was surprisingly confident. I'd put everything in Dewalt's hands when I left, knew he'd follow through with what was expected—even if he had to work with my mother to get it. Funny how I trusted him with Vesta's armies, but I'd still beaten him to the ground with my fists. It hadn't been because of that kind of trust though. By not telling me something he knew would have angered me, something he knew was dangerous for Em, he violated our brotherhood. Still, though, that didn't give me the right to behave as I did.

"Being here again is strange. Not in a bad way or a good way, just...strange," she said, pulling away from me.

"How so?"

"So much is different, but so much is the same. It feels so easy to slip back into a routine here. Do you ever—?" She stopped speaking, brushing her hair from her face. She looked so beautiful and yet so heartbroken. "It's silly because, of course, you've never felt like this." She averted her eyes, and I held her hand in mine.

"Ask me anyway."

"Do you ever feel stuck in the past? I don't think—" She tugged her bottom lip between her teeth, rolling it for a second before she continued. "This is hard to explain. But I feel like I've just been stuck in place and everyone has grown up around me. I've just been trying to catch up with the rest of you, and I'm having a difficult time adjusting to it. Being here is making it worse."

"It's expected that you feel left behind. You *were* left behind."

"At my own fault," she muttered, hugging herself.

"Doesn't matter, Em. We had each other; you only had Elora."

"But I could have had you. All of you. You three had lives, lovers, battles—the list goes on. You negotiated agreements with other kingdoms. I could have tried to contact you all those years, but I didn't think you'd care."

"Em—" She cut me off with a jerk of her chin, and I slid my gaze to hers. In her eyes I saw storms, and I wanted to weather them with her. Of course I'd have cared.

"And now that I know I could've come back, I'm having a lot of regrets. I have to wonder if—"

"What good does wondering do? You're trying now. You're catching up, we're making up for all of it. Wondering does nothing but bring you sorrow."

She sighed, and her shoulders rolled inward. "You're right. I think being here isn't good for me. It reminds me of all the things I've ruined. All my hang-ups and misgivings."

"You couldn't have ruined us by yourself. And you did something pretty wonderful on your own. You didn't ruin Elora at all."

A hint of a smile played at the corners of her lips. "If anything, she ruined me."

Grabbing her at the waist, I yanked her against me, forcefully reminding her I needed her close. "If anything, dear heart, *you* have ruined *me*."

Though the curves of her body had changed with time, they fit better against me than I ever could have imagined. How rare was it to find someone to complete me so wholly? She relaxed, letting me support her in my hold.

"As hard as it is for you, I think some part of me needed to come to Ravemont," I said.

"Why is that?" she asked, held tilted to look at me.

"I have good memories here. It—it gets me out of my head. Astana has been...difficult."

She lifted her hand to caress my cheek before saying, "I know. This time away has brought you back to me. I wonder if we'd still be stuck if we never left the capital."

"It doesn't matter. We'll get through it," I said. "I'm sorry your memories here are hurtful ones."

A small smile lifted her lips. "Not all of them. Not the ones with you or the others. The bad ones are the ones from after."

"After Lucia died and before Elora was born," I said. It killed me to think of her so gods damn alone.

"But we're here now," she said, voice watery. "Together."

I nodded, pulling her close and resting my chin on her head. It was hard on both of us to think of our missed time together, and I held her for a few moments. "Hard day with your father?" I finally asked.

"He barely spoke. Only remembered my name to yell at me to get out."

"I don't think it's going to get any better, do you?"

"No," she said, leaning back to look up at me. "So, why were you lurking in the hallway?"

"I want to show you something."

We spent the night in calm serenity. Enraptured by the night sky, we stayed warm by lighting a fire beside us. By the time we finished stargazing, enough snow had melted nearby that a small stream of water flowed down the slope behind us. When we returned to her old bedroom, I turned my attention to the constellations on her body, worshiping each freckle, curve, and indentation. Gentle and sweet, we reconnected in the quiet. I hated to be grateful for Kennon's ailing health, but it had afforded us something we needed desperately.

Time.

"It's strange to be in here with you," she said, rolling over to face me. Dwindling light from the fireplace graced her features as she propped herself up on an elbow.

"And why's that?"

"It feels like we're breaking a rule or something. Like someone's going to come in and scold us at any moment."

I chuckled as she leaned in and gave me a soft kiss. It was moments like this, laughter and love intermixed with heartache, which made us whole again. The perfect mold of her body against my own as I tucked her into my side was something I would never take for granted.

And later, when I woke with a start, Vondi's forever young face the only thing I could see, she jolted awake too. She sat up, grabbing my hand and holding it to her chest. She pulled her hair from her bare shoulder, making sure I could see her tattoo in the dim light.

"Real. Yours," she whispered.

"Always."

A moment's pause hung heavy in the air between us.

"Are you alright?" she asked.

"It was Vondi again."

"Do you want to talk about it?"

During one of our somber nights the past week, I'd told her about the little boy the shifter had tormented me with. Sparing us both the risk of her condemnation, I hadn't told her the details. The way she'd called me the Bloody Prince in the lake told me she either didn't believe the story or hadn't heard it. Part of me wanted to deprive her of the knowledge. She'd no doubt see me differently if she knew the stories were true. But the past few days had emboldened me, and I knew I needed to open up to her. So when she asked, I decided to tell her.

"What do you know of Varmeer before I...handled it?"

"Not much. It was a settlement first, right?"

"Yes. Vestian and Folterran at first. By the time I arrived, the settlement had merged into one, and Dryul had decided to claim the island. He sent forces and built a fortress on the northern side, put it under the control of one of his generals, Brunel. I wanted to just let him have it, but my father viewed it as a threat. Which, as it turns out, he wasn't wrong. They were poised to use it as a launching point for an assault."

"So, Soren made you handle it?"

"Yes. That's why I was there." I inhaled deeply. "Vondi was born on the island, and he never left. He is dead because of me."

She said nothing, waiting, her expression concerned and nothing more. I sat up to face her, tracing the ink on her skin as she pulled the blanket up to keep her warm. It surprised me she didn't immediately jump to tell me I was wrong, but she'd learned recently that sometimes we make lasting mistakes. The weight of our decisions could sink us if we let them, so I opened my heart to her so she'd do the same with me if she needed. I was hers just as she was mine, and we'd promised to shoulder one another's burdens. I'd been unwilling before, afraid of weighing her down further, but perhaps we could help each other float. Letting her know the extent of my greatest regret, save for what I did to her, was terrifying but something we needed.

"His father was a foot soldier forced into the Folterran army, and his mother hailed from Olistos. They'd tried to find peace on the island to be together, and they had it until Dryul decided he wanted to claim Varmeer. Vondi's father had died in a skirmish with soldiers my father sent ahead of me. The boy and his mother lived alone on the southern shore, where my contingency waited. Folterrans to the north, and my army to the south. His mother—uh, she didn't do well after her husband died. Vondi had to take care of himself. Became a good little pickpocket. I used him for it and sent him into a den of wolves."

"He spied for you? Why didn't you use Aedwyn?" She didn't ask with judgment, just curiosity.

There was a pang in my chest when I thought about the shifter twins. With Aerfen dead and no sight of Aedwyn from any of our spies, I had a feeling he was dead too, and I mourned their loss. "I didn't have the shifters yet. They were minor, the things I asked of him. Most of the people who lived on the island just put up with Brunel. Honestly, it was peaceful enough before my father decided to take it back. So, the town was still active. I asked him to eavesdrop at a pub or monitor some of the general's men. Things like that."

"But something happened," she said. Pulling my hand into her lap, she rubbed a thumb over my palm, pressing hard. I couldn't help the soft grunt which escaped my lips.

"Yes. A relative of his, a distant cousin, I think, was part of Brunel's inner circle. Vondi thought he could use that to his advantage and get me something more useful. He started giving me more detailed plots, and we stayed one step ahead as the Folterrans tried to run us off the island. I didn't know where he got the information, and I was too naive and excited to use it to ask. I thought he was getting lucky." Shaking my head, I wiped a hand down my face. I was so gods damned stupid. "A supply shipment from Folterra was set to come to the western shore, and I hoped to intercept it and sink it before it reached the docks. But it was an ambush. It's how I got the scar on my back."

"It was a trap, wasn't it? To hurt you and prove—"

"To confirm he was the one giving me information, yes. If only I were as wise as you to see it sooner." I gave her a tight smile, but all she did was cock her head to the side as I continued. "The healer could barely close me up once Thyra and Dewalt got me out. By the time I realized the truth, finally conscious, Brunel's men had already killed him."

"How old was he?" she whispered, still rubbing circles on my palm. Her eyes stayed fixed on me in the low light, that familiar wrinkle between her brows showing her concern.

"Eleven."

"Oh, Rain." Her words were barely more than breath, and her thumb stilled for a moment before she brought my hand to her mouth, softly pressing her lips to my knuckles. "You were wounded. You couldn't—"

"They flayed him, Em. Put his little body on display." I'd grieved for the boy so often over the years, I barely had a reaction anymore when I thought of him, numb to it. But seeing the tears spill down her rosy cheeks made the horror and pain feel fresh. "They tore his skin from his body because of my ignorance. I should have known."

Her head tilted, and the tracks on her face glimmered in the low light. "But you didn't do that to him. It doesn't make you the Bloody Prince. They're the ones who tortured a child!" Her voice went high-pitched, and I worried she'd wake someone.

"You truly don't know?"

"Don't know what?" She frowned.

"What I did after? What I did when I saw his body…That's how I earned the name."

"No, I don't—what did you do?"

"I went to the fortress with no plan. It was reckless. I didn't wait for Dewalt or any of my guard, I just went. It was the middle of the day, so there was no stealth to my approach; I just moved. I don't know if it was Hanwen's blessing or what it was, but something came over me. I don't remember any of it past riding there. Not until…"

The images haunted me. The rage burning beneath my skin, waiting for an outlet, had taken the path of least resistance through my divinity.

"Not until what?" she prompted after a moment. I stared at the hand she held, blinking as I cleared my thoughts.

"I supposedly killed the archers first. Took all their breath at once." Disbelief fluttered down the bond, but I continued. "The gate was open—it was midday after all—so I strolled inside. But I wasn't done. When Brunel ran into the courtyard, flanked by the men who hurt Vondi I killed them all with barely more than a thought."

"How?" she breathed.

"I realized what I was doing as I was doing it, but blood is mostly water, isn't it?" She nodded slowly, squeezing my hand tight. "I coaxed it to fill their lungs, to choke them on their own blood. The ground turned red because of me. That's why they call me the Bloody Prince. The rest of the soldiers within the fortress stopped rushing me as they fell victim to the same thing. It only took a few dozen men falling before everyone else stopped, just watching as I choked their comrades to death."

"But Rain, I—when I healed Elora…I don't remember it. I couldn't have controlled my actions, just like you—"

"I realized what I was doing when there was time to stop. I chose not to."

A tendril of her hair fell from behind her ear, loose and wavy, as her eyes met mine. I couldn't tell what she was thinking, and there were so many feelings moving between us down the bond, I couldn't differentiate our emotions. Using my free hand to rub my chest, I stayed quiet, waiting for her anger. I should have told her about the worst things I'd done before she swore her life to me. The most important thing I learned with her was honesty, and, though I didn't lie, it wasn't as if I had been forthright with her.

"If given that choice again, right here, right now, would you still choose it?"

"Yes." The word slipped from my mouth before I even understood her question. "But I'll never use my divinity that way again. It felt so fucking wrong, Em."

"Good. I don't think you should regret it. Those who would do that to a child or stand back and allow it to happen are owed no mercy."

"I don't regret it, but I do hate that my actions with Vondi were what led me to the breaking point."

"It was a mistake, Rain. Did they leave Varmeer after that?"

"I let those who wanted to surrender go back to Folterra, yes."

"Sparing them and protecting Vesta from their plans had to have counted for something. Swayed the balance back to good. I know it doesn't bring Vondi back, but…I'm sure there were other children who would have died if not for the way things played out."

"Probably." I swallowed. "Anyway, I try not to think about it, about him, but Declan's mindbreaker gave one of my memories to the shifter. She struggled to make herself sound like him, so mostly she just leaned against the wall and stared at me. But the memory they'd taken, it was…from after he died."

She swore and threw herself across the bed into my lap. One of her arms wrapped tight around my neck while her other hand snaked up, and she drew it across my brow before cupping my jaw. Dropping her forehead to press against mine, I couldn't stand the look on her face, so I closed my eyes. I deserved to see what my actions had wrought; what I didn't deserve was her pity.

But what I felt over the bond wasn't pity—it was pain and grief.

"I'm sorry you've had to live with that memory. I'd take it from you if I could." I felt her breath on my lips as she adjusted in my lap, situating herself as she pressed her body against me. She shuddered as her skin touched mine, and she began to rub her hands over my chest and shoulders. "You're cold," she offered, and I opened my eyes.

"And you keep me warm."

We held each other as we fell back asleep.

Nearly a week later, we woke to news of Lord Kennon's passing overnight. He'd gone in his sleep—peaceful. Emma hadn't been able to get any words out of him for several days before he died, but she'd stayed by his side the entire time. Mister Carson had been the one to knock, just after dawn, and I was careful not to rouse her as I rose to answer the door.

Crawling back into the bed, I had pulled her into my arms and gently woke her. When I told her the news, the first thing I felt was her relief, followed on swift wings by guilt. I'd done my best to reassure her how normal those feelings were for someone grieving a recent loss of a loved one, let alone someone with whom she shared a complicated history. I didn't think it helped her much, but I also knew she'd have to muddle her way through it, as I had with my own father these recent weeks. Although, I surely hadn't felt nearly as much guilt as she did.

When she asked me to handle the burial with Mister Carson, I didn't hesitate to help her. She'd been by Kennon's side for nearly two weeks, and I wanted her to rest—mentally and physically. If I could give that to her, I would.

Which was how I found myself with Mister Carson, standing in the lantern's light in the Highclere family crypt. I hadn't been down in it when they laid Lucia to rest, but I'd been outside it. Northeast of Ravemont, it was closer to Tuaman Cliffs than I remembered, just far west enough to be dug into the rolling hills which graced Eastern Vesta. The Highclere ancestors must have desired a nearness to the sea. I swore I could hear the waves crashing against the shore even from our distance away. There were a half-dozen different iron doors inset into the hills, and I remembered the vivid green grass which sat beneath the inches of snow. The last time I'd been here, it was early summer, a year after Lucia died. Dewalt had asked me to come along with him, and I couldn't tell him no. Once he and Ven bonded though, it was her who went with him when he visited. At first, I wasn't sure how Mister Carson kept them all straight, but as he explained which ancestor each crypt housed, it was clear the Highclere family just expanded in order each time. Pointing out the door farthest to the north, I'd only hesitated a second before following the man.

"It needs a bit of a dust-up, don't you think?"

I grunted in assent as I leaned Kennon's sword against the wall. Though the interior walls were the same limestone rock Ravemont was built from, the work was patchier, allowing dirt from the earth above to fall between cracks and flake to the ground.

"Cover your face," I ordered, doing the same for myself with my cloak, and I coaxed a breeze down which carried much of the dust and debris along with it.

A few stubborn cobwebs clung to the walls, but the exterior chamber appeared clean enough.

"There's only three vaults in this crypt; theirs is the one on the right," the butler explained as he used his lantern to light a torch he'd brought, placing it in a sconce.

Following the man's instructions, I left the entryway, and I coaxed a tiny flame into my hand to light my path. A moment later, Mister Carson's footsteps echoed behind me as I turned through the archway into the vault. I stopped short as I saw the four tombs resting on platforms within the room. Two rested in the center of the chamber, flanked by an aisle on either side, and then two more sat flush against each wall. There was room for more, but this vault had clearly been outfitted for Em's immediate family. It made my fucking skin crawl. Crossing the threshold, I urged the flame in my hand to grow. It resisted, and I huffed in irritation. I wasn't very good at it yet. The divine statuary at the back of the vault was in bad shape. Aonara had fallen into Rhia, and her arm had broken off. Ciarden was covered in cobwebs, and Hanwen's face had crumbled to dust.

After repeating the earlier process of using my divinity to clear out the vault, I traced my fingertip over the name on the tomb beside me. Natara Highclere had no fanfare even in death, her name carved with no indication of who she was when she lived.

"I suppose this one is his?" I asked Mister Carson, nodding toward the tomb beside Natara's.

"Yes. They'll etch his name when they seal it," he explained, joining me beside the long, narrow box. "The stand beneath it is for resting this piece, if you'll help me place it there?"

He set down his lantern on the ground beside us as I let the fire in my hand extinguish.

The stone top was heavier than I'd anticipated, and once we finished moving it, I peered inside the empty box, not sure what I expected to see.

The sheer emptiness jarred me. The thought that everything Kennon Highclere had ever been would rest inside a wooden casket, then inside this stone tomb, inside the vault, inside the crypt had my breathing growing shallow. I glanced up, looking at the tomb which belonged to Lucia—or perhaps it was the empty one which would have one day belonged to Em—and I leaned heavily against where Natara rested.

Was there a service when my father was placed in the royal crypt? I hadn't even asked, and no one had mentioned it. When it came to me, I had wanted death, been pleading for Declan to give it to me, and was prepared to face it and welcome that eternal slumber. But staring at the quiet finality of it made me squirm. I needed to be outside.

"All done?" I asked. Before Mister Carson even answered, I was pushing off from where I stood to open a rift, but the sound of stone scraping behind me had me turning around. "What—" I cut off my own words when I saw the stone top had slid from my touch, revealing a glimpse into Natara's tomb. I conjured a flame in my hand once more, far too big, and leaned over to look down into it. It wasn't right. "Where is the casket? Why isn't this tomb sealed?"

"Your Majesty?"

"It's not sealed, Mister Carson, and I don't see a gods damn casket."

I started sliding the stone top, my heart racing in my chest. The butler moved to the other end, frazzled the best way to describe him, and helped me move the top to the stand beneath it as we'd already done for Kennon's tomb.

There was nothing inside it.

I took a step back, wiping my hand down my jaw. "Explain."

"I don't know. I wasn't here when she died; I was visiting my sister. Imogene handled all of it. She told me they put some of her belongings in here, at least."

"What do you mean?"

"Well, since there was no body, Imogene said they—"

"No body?"

"They never found her, just the note." He looked at me in confusion, as if I should have known what he was talking about.

"I'm going to need you to explain."

"Surely, you know—Lady Highclere jumped from Tuaman Cliffs."

I was taken aback. Em had never mentioned it, and I vaguely remembered Natara's cause of death being described as a sudden illness all those years ago. "So, there was no body," I drawled, my words slow as I struggled to piece it all together.

"No, but Imogene still had a casket full of her belongings placed in here, as far as I know. I believe some jewelry and books, something for Kennon to..." He trailed off as he peered down into the empty box.

"The door wasn't bolted, was it?"

"No, it wasn't."

"So anyone could have come in here..." I trailed off as I glanced toward the tomb on this side of Natara's. Lucia's name had been carved into it, and my stomach dropped. If things from her mother's tomb were missing, it was possible her resting place had also been tampered with.

"Oh, no," Mister Carson whispered, holding his lantern up higher as he tracked my gaze, and we saw a slip of fabric stuck between the tomb and the stone top.

CHAPTER 44

Dewalt

Rainier had only been gone for one fucking day when things started going to shit. That was why, nearly two weeks later, I woke before dawn, waiting for Raj to arrive. His letter arrived the day after Rainier left, and it had come with two dozen women and children. Shivani had been surprisingly helpful, coordinating with Nana and the novices to find places for them to stay.

Raj had heard through the rebels in Folterra that Declan planned to take over the Cascade using the full might of his army. Bly had ridden Ifash north toward Darkhold, and nearly got shot off the dragon by a volley of arrows before they got away. Thankfully rider and steed had made it back unharmed, but it had confirmed the worst. Each day since, the people living in the Cascade and those whose homes we had rebuilt in Clearhill were slowly but surely evacuated to Vesta. Some of them went to Nara's Cove and some to Mira, but all the soldiers came to the capital. Rainier had sent ten thousand men westward to Lamera, so I felt confident in keeping the rest in Astana. I had a strange feeling about it all, and I knew better than to ignore my gut.

I yawned, tugging on my cloak. Bly and Raj, along with Raj's children and their nanny, as he put it, were going to be riding in on the dragons sometime close to sunrise. I'd been staying at the estate, and it worked out for all of them to arrive there first. The family who had been taking care of the dragons near the mountains were distant relatives of Raj's and would come later in the day to take both his children and the arriving dragons back to the Alsors. The other beasts had been thriving there, although Irses and Ryo had disappeared since Rainier had left. That very first dragon she'd made was so gods damned attuned with Emma, I was sure he had gone after her.

My hair was bunched up under my cloak, and I was busy tugging at it when I went out the front door, so I didn't notice her sitting there at first. Nor cleared her throat, and I nearly jumped out of my skin.

"Fuck!"

"Sorry," she said, though her small smile told me she wasn't sorry at all. "I didn't mean to startle you."

"What are you doing out here? It's early as hell and colder than an elvish kiss." I stilled, remembering how she'd created the wards around that gods damned mill to help rescue Emma. Glancing over at her, hoping I hadn't offended her, I couldn't help it when my eyes were drawn to her lips. I flinched as I caught her eyebrow raising. "I didn't mean to—"

"I'm barely elvish. I wasn't taught enough to put this elf-blood to use, so you can stop thinking about my kiss." Her lips turned up at the corners, and if I didn't know better, I'd have thought she was teasing me. But then her mouth formed a frown, and she peered up at me over the blanket she had wrapped around her. "What is it with that saying anyway? Where does it come from?"

"I...actually don't know where it came from."

"It sounds offensive. Perhaps you shouldn't say it unless you know the meaning behind it."

I paused, tilting my head in consideration. "You're right. I'll have to look into it. I'm sorry." Her eyes widened in such surprise, I rolled my eyes. "Your mother wasn't elvish, then?"

"No, she was a conduit. I remember little about my father, but he hated the elf-blood enough to—I was never permitted to learn, and my mother kept me away from it once we moved here."

"Enough to what?"

"Nothing."

Sighing, I took a few steps off the covered porch to look toward the southwestern sky, eager to spot the dragons and go back inside. I knew Miriam was a conduit, but I didn't want to tell her daughter how I knew. It had shocked the shit out of me when I realized who her mother was, but how was I supposed to tell her that? How was I supposed to tell her Emmeline had killed her because the woman had asked for it? Besides, I didn't owe her anything more than what I'd already given her. I'd inform Emma as soon as they arrived and let her handle it. Though, the thought of burdening my friend more for this woman also pissed me off. I didn't bother to look over my shoulder as I asked, "Why are you here, Nor?"

"Do you mean why am I still here?"

That caught my attention.

"You slept here?"

"Thyra invited me over, and I drank too much wine. I thought you might have accosted me and yelled at me if you saw me stumbling home."

"I was here all night; I wouldn't have seen you. I *didn't* see you." My eyes narrowed as I turned to face her. Hurt flashed across her features, and I decided I only imagined it when she tilted her head back and closed her eyes.

"I assure you, I was drinking my sorrows away with Thyra, nothing more. It was very kind of her to entertain me, even after she found out I'd never had alcohol before."

Watching the skies once more for a sign of the dragons, I couldn't help it when my voice softened. "Sorrows?"

"I'm going to collect the rest of my mother's things in a few hours." Casual as I turned to look at her, I finally noticed the dark circles under her eyes in the early dawn light, and how her dark, mussed hair fell thick around her face. She'd dragged a blanket outside with her, and she looked far less self-assured than she normally did with it wrapped around her. Different from the first day I met her, it annoyed me how aware I was of myself when I was around her now. Careful with every interaction, I always did my best to maintain some sort of distance, artfully curating all of my responses to her. Because I didn't trust her, because we'd gotten off on the wrong foot, because she'd clearly had a shit life—I didn't know. But it annoyed me that every muscle in my body tightened around her in some sort of instinctual reaction. I struggled to know if it wanted to fight with her or get away from her. But I did neither.

When her gaze lifted to meet mine, I realized I'd looked at her a beat too long.

"At the temple?" I asked, taking one step down off the porch.

"Yes," she whispered. "We had a suite there. Before..."

Before they had shipped her off to Declan for breeding. I cleared my throat. "Are you going alone?"

"Thyra was supposed to come with me, but Elora asked her to go with her when—"

"She has that lunch with Shivani today, doesn't she?"

"Yes. The queen mother is terrifying though, so I'm glad Thyra is going with her."

I chuckled, but something twisted inside me. Going to the temple was the last fucking thing I wanted to do, but it would be shit of me to let her go alone.

"Any of the other novices available to go with you?"

Nor laughed, harsh and cold. "Skies, what do you think?"

"Oh."

"You're not doing a very good job convincing me you aren't stupid, you know. I will not ask that of them. They hate me enough as it is."

"It's not your fault he hadn't gotten to you yet," I blurted, annoyed at her insult and frustrated with the situation, and her breath hitched. Why was it such a struggle to maintain control around her? "Sorry, I didn't mean—"

"It's fine. I knew what you meant. Anyway, I'll be alright. I've known the Supreme for a long time. He let me know Filenti's replacement planned on getting rid of her things in the next few days, so I said I'd do it today. It'll be fine. I don't need an—"

"When?"

"Two hours from now," she said, almost suspicious.

"If Raj ever shows, we'll leave straight after." I jogged down the steps and looked to the west, spotting a few black specks toward the horizon, and hoped it was the man in question. I waited for a response, but when she didn't answer, I turned to face her. The wind kicked up, and I regretted not braiding my hair back, the cool air whipping it in my face.

"This feels like a trap," she said from her bundle on the porch.

"Suit yourself. I figured Rainier or Emma would have volunteered to go with you, so I was offering the same courtesy. If you don't want—"

"I want. Yes, please." Breathless, she stood, pulling the blanket tight around her. Large eyes ringed by dark lashes blinked rapidly as she looked down at me, and I lifted mine to the sky once more, grateful when I saw Raj was indeed nearby. Seeing her relief over something so simple was painful, making me feel bad for the suspicion I still harbored for her.

Until I remembered exactly what I'd agreed to.

What the fuck was I thinking?

I'd gone with Emma to the temple three months prior because I'd be damned if the closest link I had to Lucia was going to put herself anywhere near those lying shits. And I'd failed her then. I'd let her out of my sight, and they made her kill the mother of the woman who stood beside me now. But this was Nor's old home, so when I followed behind her down the hall and up a staircase, it unnerved me how the path was second nature to her. She knew this place, had lived here and learned here for the greater part of her life.

It felt like a betrayal. Nor was part of the very system which I held responsible for the death of the only woman I'd ever loved. She would have said the prayers, held the vigil, uttered devotions to *Martyr Lucia*, as they called her. Fuck, I hated that. Lu wasn't killed for her beliefs; she was killed for theirs. It wasn't right. She died for her gods damned identity and what it meant to the Myriad, and it wasn't even accurate.

She'd died for nothing.

Being here and not burning it down felt like the worst sort of disrespect I could imagine. With Emma, I had known Lucia would have wanted me to protect her sister—even though my protection had meant nothing. But with Nor, her identity was an affront to everything I'd hated the past sixteen years.

Slowing, I realized her footsteps had faltered. I stopped at the last second before running into her. The woman stood stock still at a plain wooden door. We were three stories above the ground level, the rich tapestries and carpets giving way to plain stone floors and undecorated walls. She must have counted how many steps it took to get here from the top of the stairs, because otherwise, the door didn't stand out at all.

"Do you need a key?" I asked.

"I have it," she said, rubbing her thumb along the glint of silver in her hand I hadn't yet noticed. Her eyes didn't leave the door. "The Supreme gave it to me weeks ago, back after the Filenti thing. I'd been putting it off. I probably wouldn't have come at all if I hadn't known her things would get tossed out like rubbish if I didn't."

I swallowed. Rushing her didn't feel like the right thing to do, but I wanted to get the fuck out of the temple. It had been a mistake to offer my presence. I was a traitor being here. "Do you want me to pack it up for you?" I asked. The sooner we gathered her things, the sooner we could go.

"I don't know if I even want to take anything," she whispered before shaking her head. Resolve taking over her, I watched as her spine straightened. She'd tucked her thick waves up into a bun on the back of her head, all loose wisps carefully slicked back. An elegant neck tapered down to a high collar—modest. When she picked and tugged at the clothing as we rode into the capital, I wondered why. But seeing her here, I realized it had to be because it wasn't the clothing of a novice.

"You lived here too; surely you have belongings of your own you want?"

"I wasn't allowed to have anything material. I was about to take the silent oath when…everything happened."

"And you had to get rid of your things?"

"Yes. After three years of silence, we're allowed to have our own possessions once more, and then two years after that, we can speak again if we desire it."

Nor unlocked the door and stepped through, a vacant musty scent drifting toward us.

"How old are you?" I asked.

"Why?" She shot a scowl over her shoulder at me, dark brows furrowed.

"I thought novices took the vow at eighteen, but you seem older."

Her shoulders relaxed as she replied, "Oh. I didn't want to, and since my mother was a mistress, it afforded me certain liberties. But you're right. Most take it at eighteen. I'm twenty-five, and my time had run out."

She stalked across the room to the heavy draperies and flung them open. I stood in the doorway as I took in the space. Small, there was a round table with two chairs in the middle of the room and a narrow bed shoved against the wall. A bathroom door stood ajar, and Nor moved toward the closed one beside it.

"You both lived here?"

"Yes."

When she opened the closed door, I understood, and it appalled me. A small pallet rested inside, just big enough for a grown adult to curl into. A dress like the mistresses wore hung above it, and a novice's cloak hung beside it. "Fucking hell, Nor. You slept on the floor?"

"I slept on my pallet," she retorted, no small amount of annoyance in her tone. "Mother had a bad back," she added as she knelt to dig through the blankets on the ground.

Wiping my hand over my jaw, I took a few steps into the room and looked at the wall across from Nor. A tapestry of the richest blues and golds hung behind a dresser, easily the most expensive thing in the room. A depiction of the old gods creating the new ones, all life as we knew it pouring out of the font. Every animal imaginable was visible on the tapestry, the intricate threads weaving a pattern of gold between them and their source.

"She had enough for this tapestry, but not for another bed?"

"I loved that tapestry when I was small," she said as she stood and closed the closet door. I wondered what she'd been searching for but decided not to ask.

"And now? Do you realize how gods damned expensive it was while you were sleeping on the floor?"

"Where would a bed have gone, *Walt*?"

There my muscles went again, spasming in irritation. "Beside hers, turn them out."

"The table and chairs are in the way."

"The table and chairs could have gone into the closet."

She paused for only a second before rushing out, "It doesn't matter, anyway."

"Well, do you want it? Perhaps you can sell it and buy yourself a bed."

"I live in a dormitory. It has a bed."

"You know what I meant."

"I know you are being awfully judgmental of something you know nothing about."

"Oh, I probably know more than you, Nor." I turned to face her, not realizing how close she'd been standing beside me as we both looked at the tapestry.

"I don't think I know anything," she whispered as she stepped forward, tracing her fingertip over a loose golden thread.

I watched her, itching to put my hand on her shoulder in comfort. My tone had been too harsh for her, I realized. Her mother had lived here and raised her here, and she never got to say goodbye. It was something I had to keep reminding myself. This couldn't have been easy for her. I nearly kicked myself for softening to this woman. She didn't move as I glanced over at her, eyes drawn to a single strand of shorter hair she hadn't gathered into her bun. Angular cheekbones swept up to delicate, slightly pointed ears, and I noticed a rough red mark on the tip of the one facing me, and I wondered if it was a burn to match her arm.

"Turns out none of us do; don't scold yourself over it," I said, voice more soothing than I intended to be.

When I heard a sniffle from her, I turned away, allowing myself to be distracted by a glint of gold resting atop the dresser. Taking a step forward, I froze when I saw the portrait inside the tiny gilded frame.

"Lu," I breathed, unable to stop myself as I reached my fingertip out. It was a miniature, but unmistakably her. Long hair hung down straight on either side of her face, a light smirk playing about her mouth. It matched the one given to me all those years ago, and I wondered how many copies were made. The artist had mastered Lucia's expression with very few lines, but the effect of seeing her was immediate. "Why did she have this?" I demanded.

"Ah, she—skies, I'm sorry, I shouldn't have—"

"Why did she have this?" I repeated.

"I don't know. It was a recent addition. I think she found it in storage somewhere. I remember her saying she felt a kinship with her, which, frankly, I didn't understand. But I didn't argue with her." She hesitated, looking at me with something like panic. "I don't know. I'm sorry. My mother was strange, I don't know why she—"

"Do you want it?" I asked.

"The portrait?"

"Yes. Do you want it?"

"I—no, I suppose not."

"May I?" I asked, picking up the miniature and holding it between my fingertips before she could respond.

"Sure, yes. Good, take it."

I said nothing, just looked down at *her*. My old copy had fallen apart years ago, and I hadn't looked upon an image of her since. There were likenesses of Lucia displayed at the temples, but considering I didn't make it a habit of going to them, I hadn't been able to look upon her in years. Unless one counted Emma, which I tried not to, it had been over a decade since I'd seen her face. I only allowed myself a moment before shoving her portrait in my pocket. It helped ease some of the guilt of being here.

"I'm finished. I got what I came for, and I want nothing else."

"Not even the tapestry?"

"Where would I put it?"

"Your room at the dormitory?" I realized the suggestion was foolish as soon as I said it. She did me the favor of not calling me brainless, merely giving me a look with a raised brow instead.

"A tapestry like this deserves a home, and I don't have one of those. Never really have. A place to rest my head doesn't count."

"You're right." It shocked me we had something in common. Ever since I joined Rainier's guard, I'd gone from the barracks to the home belonging to Lavenia to the room I slept in at Rainier's estate. None of it was mine. None of it was permanent.

We left the room then, and I watched her pat her cloak over her chest, ensuring whatever she'd grabbed from her pallet was safe, and I nearly took the stairs two at a time to get out faster.

"Turn right," she said out of the corner of her mouth, and I followed her command without question. I knew it was something I'd ponder later as I tried to sleep—the why of it—but I listened all the same. She took a few steps past me down a dark hall, peering over her shoulder a few times as she picked up her speed.

"Where are we going?"

Instead of answering, she reached back and grabbed my hand, and I only had a moment to prepare before she spoke in my mind. "*Filenti's study. He obviously had connections—with Declan, other temples, the men who helped move us. I want to see if I can find anything useful. I want them to pay.*"

Not even bothering to reply, I let her tug me down the corridor. The idea was a good one, and clearly she needed me to be quiet. Lit by a solitary torch at the end of the hall, I could barely make out anything other than her lean silhouette in front of me. She was tall for a woman—nearing Thyra in height, but not quite.

Peeking over her shoulder one last time, she knelt in front of the last door on the left, fumbling with the lock.

"Here, let—"

The quiet creak of the door swinging open cut me off, and she stood, holding her finger to her lips before pulling me in and shutting the door behind us. The room was small and plain. Cold and stark, it matched the man who I'd beheaded only weeks prior. Nothing adorned the walls, and a threadbare carpet stretched out beneath my feet, the only comfort in the room the empty fireplace. The oak desk was cleared off, and everything on the bookshelf behind it was tidy and organized.

"Where should I—"

With rounded eyes, she shook her head and moved behind the desk. Clearly, she expected me to shut my mouth and let her work. She dropped to the ground and started picking at the lock on the bottom-most drawer. Rolling my shoulders, I strolled over and leaned across the desk, chin propped on my fist.

"Where'd you learn to pick locks, Nor?"

She glared up at me before looking back down, shoving a pin into the mechanism and biting her lip in concentration.

"My mother taught me when I was little."

"Your mother. Why?"

"Just in case."

"In case of what?"

"My father," she replied, offering no further explanation. She made a face as she pulled on the bottom lip of the drawer. Her nose crinkled, and the tip of her tongue darted out between her teeth. Her skin was lit by the small sliver of light the parted curtains allowed, the color reminding me of the wheat fields my family had grown, and the stubborn set of her jaw eased into relaxation as she pulled the drawer open on a sigh.

"No," she breathed as we both stared down into an empty drawer. "He stored letters here. I know it. I know he did."

"He must have taken them out before everything happened."

"Then why lock it after?"

"Is there a false bottom?"

She leaned to the side to compare the depth of the outside of the drawer with what we could see. She tapped the bottom, but the sound it made yielded nothing. I moved to where she knelt and tugged at the drawer, intending to pull it out.

When the bottom fell to the ground with a clatter but the drawer looked intact, it was clear I was right. The only thing that fell out was a small, wooden ball, nearly perfect in shape, and it rolled across the floor to rest against Nor's knee. She stared at it for a moment before picking it up and palming it, her lips tilted down in a frown.

Worried someone might have heard, I hurried to put the drawer back together while Nor sat immobile on the ground. The clock tower chimed midday, and she shook her head with a start.

"Oh, skies, we have to go," she murmured, rubbing her thumb over the wooden ball and staring as if in a daze.

"What is it?"

I slid the drawer back in, carefully maneuvering around the shocked woman on the ground.

"Nor," I said, voice firm. "Get up."

She complied, still staring at the ball.

"What the fuck? Give it to me," I said, holding out my hand. She obeyed with reluctance, and I shoved it in my pocket. Hooking my arm in hers, I tugged her out of the room, doing a final scan to ensure we'd left it as we found it, and locked the door behind us. She leaned against the wall, breathing heavily. I dragged her halfway down the corridor before peering back at her, and I found tears running down her cheeks.

"Nor, what is this?" I stopped, producing the ball in my hand. Resting a hand atop her head and worrying her bottom lip, she inhaled deeply.

"That was my father's."

I looked down, examining the toy. It was completely smoothed down from a combination of expert carving and time.

"The man your mother ran from?"

"Yes," she whispered.

"He must have known who your father was. Used it against your mother."

"You think he threatened her? The Supreme was the only one who knew, I thought. I don't even know. I was only six when he did this." She gestured toward her shoulder, and I grimaced. I'd tried to forget her father was the one who did that to her, but, gods, at the age of six? Blood pounded in my ears, and my mouth went dry

"Do you think she would have done the things she did without being threatened?"

She tilted her head in thought right as I heard footsteps coming toward us from the end of the hallway. Though the corridor was dimly lit, I could see the whites of her eyes as they widened in panic. Grabbing my hand, she spoke in my mind, loud enough I winced.

"*Kiss me.*"

"What?" I whisper-shouted back at her.

"*We're not supposed to be here. Kiss me, so we have a reason.*" Ready to argue with her some more, I didn't have a choice when she yanked me closer to her, an iron grip on the back of my neck. Her lips were soft as they met mine, and she spoke in my mind once more. "*Act like you don't hate this, please? It might be the Supreme.*"

Her tongue prodded at the seam of my lips, and I hesitantly opened them, allowing her to kiss me more thoroughly as she stood on her tiptoes. The person at the end of the hall stuttered a step or two, and I realized she was right. And suddenly, I felt senseless as all hell. The ruse required me to look like a lustful fool, mind taken over by my dick. The only solace I received was in knowing she appeared wanton as well, unable to control herself.

Well, if she wanted a performance, I'd give one.

With a chuckle, I put one hand on the wall beside her head and pressed against her lithe body. She hummed in surprise, and my other hand found her waist. She smelled clean and warm, and a part of me wanted to nuzzle into her neck. A small sound slipped up her throat as I dipped my tongue into her mouth, rubbing it against hers, and I nearly moaned in satisfaction. Finding joy in her reaction, even if she was the last person I cared to affect, my hand found the edge of her shirt. Instinct had my thumb dipping under it to rub her velvet skin. Thoughts blank, I let my body move, and she had nothing to say as I pinned her against the wall. My body responded, cock jumping to attention, and it shocked me when she pulled me closer, one hand at my neck and the other on my belt loop. My hair swung down, covering us from view, and she tentatively reached for it, gently running her hand through it. Biting back a groan, I resisted as she tugged me flush against her. She didn't need to feel how fucking hard I was from a gods damned kiss. Fuck, with her, of all people.

As the footsteps grew closer, and I heard a chuckle, I reared back from her in a start, realizing only at that moment what I hadn't thought of in the past several minutes when her soft mouth moved against mine. My hand drifted upwards, thumb rubbing my lower lip as I stared at her. The Supreme said something, and Nor laughed, breathless, murmuring her apologies as she tugged me along behind her.

"*Thank the gods I just kissed you myself. If I would've waited for you to figure it out, he would have known something was off. Skies above, he might still think it.*"

I said nothing, swallowing in a panic as I watched the first woman I'd kissed since Lucia died burst from the dreary temple into the midday winter sun.

CHAPTER 45

Emmeline

I'd been in a daze ever since we buried my father. We had to get back for the coronation, and, though they hated it, I was able to corral the dragons through our rifts. They'd enjoyed themselves on the coast after following us from Brambleton to Ravemont, and it was likely the only reason I could get them to listen to me: they were well-fed and thus, well-behaved.

While thoughts of my sister's grave being robbed—her gods damn skull missing along with her jewelry—haunted me, the true source of my uneasiness came from the fact my father had never told me what truly happened to my mother. She'd been so distraught with grief, she jumped from Tuaman Cliffs. Why hadn't he told me? Why hadn't he shared that burden with me?

And he was dead, so it wasn't as if I could ask him. I spent an entire day digging through his belongings with Rain. I was too angry with Mister Carson to ask for his help. I knew it wasn't his fault, not really. It was my father who hid it, but I was sore over being the last to know. His study and bedroom turned upside down and inside out didn't reveal my mother's note. I didn't know what I wanted from it, what I wanted it to say, but I was devastated when we couldn't find it.

We had just left Brambleton and were halfway to the Alsors when I realized Nana hadn't told me either. The only reasonable answer to my questions was that he must have convinced everyone I knew the truth, and since those who saw me these last few months hadn't any reason to speak of her, my knowledge of the truth wasn't verified. It made sense, honestly, that my mother would have done that. The light went out in her eyes the moment my sister died. I swore if she could have lain alongside her for burial, she would have. I had been angry with her all these years for her pushing me away, for not making an effort for her remaining daughter, but I largely forgave her upon her death. But this reopened the wound, and I didn't know how to feel.

She couldn't help it, and the grief she felt had clearly overwhelmed her. It was wrong of me to be angry with her for jumping. It was wrong of me to be upset. I knew it, and yet, I couldn't help my feelings either. Wasn't I worth staying for?

Stuck in my head for the better part of a day, unwilling to voice my thoughts to Rain for fear of him thinking less of me for my selfish attitude, I was in a sore mood by the time we reached the cavern we'd stayed in a couple weeks prior.

"Well, let's have it." His voice startled me as I laid down on my bedroll, my back to his side. He'd been staying close to me but giving me space, saying all the right things, giving me all the gentle caresses I needed without pressing, but I could tell he was done waiting and was ready to push me to speak.

"There's nothing to say."

"There's an awful lot you're thinking." He tugged on one of the golden threads between us, the vibration of our connection resounding in my mind. "And feeling."

"It's just something I need to work through myself. You don't need to worry about it."

"And yet."

"And yet you're going to?" He rolled over, throwing an arm around my waist in answer. I closed my eyes, inhaling. "Promise not to think less of me?"

"I could never think less of you, Em."

I sighed, threading his fingers with mine and pulling his arm tighter around me.

"Why wasn't I enough for her? Hell, for either of them? Why wasn't I enough for them to care, for her to...stay?"

He said nothing, just nuzzled closer and waited.

"I know she couldn't help it. Her mind made her think...I know no one would choose to do what she did if they thought there was another option. But in my mind, I'm having a hard time reconciling that not only did they ship me away, I wasn't enough for either of them to find some sort of joy or happiness or will to live. I understand their actions to an extent. For those few seconds after Cyran...Elora..." A shudder rolled through me, and he tugged me ever closer. A bittersweet sadness and grief made its way across the bond to me followed by a muted rage. He'd been holding onto his anger over the boy's actions, letting Elora and me lead the way, but I wondered, if given the chance or our approval, would the princeling survive Rain's wrath? "I'm not sure if I would have been able to stay here without her. But, if I had another child—I don't know. Even the thought of abandoning any child for any reason is just too much. I could never do what they did."

"No, no, you couldn't."

"Am I selfish for being upset with them? Is there any point in being upset? They're both dead."

"You're allowed to feel however you feel, dear heart."

"Lucia wouldn't have let them—"

"Lucia would have done a lot of things differently than you. You did what they asked of you, out of guilt or regret, or just the need to do what they seemed to need after Lucia died. Right?"

"Yes. I didn't want to upset them, so I—"

"Lucia wouldn't have cared about their feelings," he scoffed. "But she always did what she was told. She wouldn't have reacted any differently than you did. And who knows? Perhaps your mother would have reacted the same way had it been you who died."

"No, Lucia was the golden one. They barely would have missed me."

"And fuck them for making you feel that way. You're just as important as her. More important than anyone—to me."

"Except Elora."

"Without you, I wouldn't have her. Different kind of important."

I rolled over, rubbing my hand over his chest, thinking as I snuggled farther into his hold. "I'm mad that I'm mad. Does that make any gods damn sense?"

"Absolutely. It's alright to wish it did not affect you." He paused, brushing my hair out of his stubble where it liked to roam, and I smiled at the motion. "I still can't believe Kennon didn't tell you."

"I wish I were more surprised, truly. He kept telling me to find her. I thought he meant—" I swallowed. "I guess he meant something else."

Rain settled his body against mine, breathing slowly, and I knew he was fighting sleep. He'd been waking with me, and since I'd barely been sleeping, I knew it was taking a toll on him.

"I'm sorry, Em. You deserved better. I wish they'd been better for you."

"Me too."

Dewalt's arms were crossed as he leaned against the wall. We'd only just arrived home, and I'd sunk into one of the high-backed chairs in the dining room, missing Elora. She was at the bookstore with Thyra and Theo, Dewalt explained, and I didn't bother hiding my disappointment. I wanted to hug her, hold her, and make sure she knew I would never do to her what my parents did to me. I had to wonder if any parent had any idea what they were doing. Were we all just trying to do better than our own?

Thankfully, Faxon had left most of the true parenting to me, only taking time to do fun things with her. Never once did he have to take on the true toll of fatherhood. I was responsible for every bit of who she turned out to be. He might as well have been a neighbor, someone there only to bring her joy and leave the rest to me. I was eager to see Rain interact with her, someone so much better and more suited to be her father. I'd given them ample space, not wanting to upset Rain or intrude on them getting to know one another, but I'd watched the two of them together and had burst into tears when I saw her lean into him and his arm wrap around her. It was everything I could have ever dreamed and everything I never thought I'd have. I was eager to see it up close.

But first, it seemed I would have to bear witness to Rain's distress about his best friend.

"D," he murmured, clearly surprised his Second was in the room. He dipped his chin, awkwardly moving past Dewalt to slip into a seat across from me.

"Gods, and here I was, thinking you were going to make this as uncomfortable as possible," Dewalt replied, a lazy grin on his face.

Rain's head snapped up, and I took a small amount of joy in seeing his irritation. It wasn't anything they couldn't get past, but I looked down at the table as soon as his eyes darted to mine. I refused to help him out of it.

"I'm sorry I hit you, Dewalt."

"What was that?" I had to cover a laugh with a cough as Dewalt called Rain out for speaking in barely audible tones.

"May Hanwen shit on you," Rain murmured under his breath, and I leaped out of my seat and nearly ran for the kitchen. It wouldn't do for them to see my eyes watering, trying to hold back my laughter. Since Sterling wasn't present, likely gone into the city for some errands while Elora and Thyra were gone, I found my distraction in putting on a pot of water to boil for tea. I glanced around desperately for something else to do in the kitchen, but of course Sterling had prevented that by keeping the estate in pristine condition. I was beginning to worry one or both of the men had left, the silence so long and thorough, when Rain finally spoke.

"I shouldn't have hit you, Dewalt. But you—"

"Ah, ah. Anything after a 'but' undoes the apology, Your Majesty."

I didn't bother hiding my smile in the safety of the kitchen.

"You were goading me."

"No shit."

"You wanted me to hit you."

"That I did."

"Divine fucking hell, then why am I apologizing?"

"Because she wants you to," Dewalt whispered, entirely too loudly, and, though I couldn't see it, I knew Rain was glaring up at his Second.

"Be that as it may, I *am* sorry," Rain offered, and I felt his reluctance through the bond.

"Don't be. I expect you to lay me out if I'm the one being dense. Just as we've always done."

I hid my snort when I reached for the porcelain container decorated with a golden vine, which held the green tea. Dewalt cleared his throat, and I swore I heard his foot tapping.

"I swear to the gods, I'll do it again—Gods damn it, Dewalt. What do you want from me?"

"You know what I want."

"No."

"Go on, say it."

I felt my brow pinch, wondering what he wanted, right as the water came to a boil. Not bothering to heat the kettle first, I dumped the tea into the bottom and poured the hot water over it. I leaned against the counter, settling in for it to steep while the two men finished their conversation. Rain must have said something, because Dewalt was laughing. Leaning over the slightest bit to peek into the dining room, I watched as my friend doubled over, his loose hair catching the light.

"You're welcome. And I know I was right, but, gods, do I love hearing you say it."

"Em, you can come back out now. I'm sure you've had enough of the entertainment," Rain grumbled.

Pulling the corner of my lip into my mouth to fight a smile, I carried the kettle and a few cups out on a tray, gently placing it on the table beside Rain. The moment I set it down, he was wrapping his arm around my legs, pulling me down into his lap.

"The Cascade has been evacuated," Dewalt said.

"What?" Rain's grip on my body tensed.

"Declan's army positioned themselves to take the Cascade. Triple how many came in the fall—his soldiers, not mercenaries. You said if—"

"I know what I said." Rain cut him off, propping his elbow on the arm of the chair. "I just didn't expect Declan to do it so soon. You got everyone out?"

Dewalt nodded. "And everyone from Clearhill who was willing as well."

"And Lamera is still his target? You positioned soldiers in Nara's Cove too, like I asked?"

"Of course. Did you doubt me?" Though his tone was jesting, I saw something in Dewalt's eyes which told me it might have been a valid insecurity.

"Gods, no. Besides Ven, you two are the only ones I trust to rule in my stead."

"You trust us quite a bit then, you'd say?" Dewalt asked, and I knew where he was going with it before the slight hint of a smile curved his lips.

"Don't—" I started, but Rain interrupted by snagging a teacup from the tray and pretending to throw it at his friend. Dewalt flinched, ready to catch an object hurtling at his face, before chuckling and relaxing against the wall as he had been before. I changed the topic, eager to move on from past unpleasantness.

"Anything else? Is Shivani eager to move on with the coronation? Or perhaps the opposite?" I asked, unsure if she was truly willing to hand over full control to Rain. Though I hadn't been to the council meetings, I knew Rain had been running them since he'd been back, so I was hopeful she was ready to give up control.

"Ah, she, uh. Fuck. Elora has been visiting Shivani while you've been gone," he offered, rubbing his hand along the back of his neck, clearly nervous about our reaction.

"Why?" and "What?" came out of our mouths at the same time, both Rain and I clearly confused.

"Listen, she sent a letter addressed to Elora. I read it before I gave it to her," he added, giving us a searing glare as we protested. "I'm not stupid. She apologized for not reaching out to her sooner and invited Elora and a chaperone to dine with her. Thyra went, and she claims it seemed as if Shivani truly wanted to get to know the girl. She said she was kind." Rain and I exchanged a glance. "I know. They've repeated the meal a few times."

"Gods," I sighed, not prepared for Shivani's change of tune. "Should we be worried?"

"We should always be nervous about my mother and whatever ulterior motives she might have. But, I don't know, she seems different. Without my father around, she's...warmer. To me, at least. I think we should take it a day at a time with her."

"She'll know you're back by now. I expect the coronation will take place in a few days' time. Meanwhile, two of the Nine have been eager to meet with you and your new bride," Dewalt said with a raised brow, and my stomach dropped.

"Which ones?" Rain's voice dropped low as his thumb dipped beneath my shirt, rubbing soothing circles on my hip. It didn't stop my racing heart, but it was still a comfort.

"Who do you think she sent?" Dewalt countered.

"Fuck."

"No, no. What does that mean? Who?" I jolted forward, hands pressed flat atop the table.

"The Scythe and the Scar."

"Oh. That sounds ominous."

"It is." Both men spoke in tandem.

"Don't they have real names?" I asked. Neither of them answered, and that unsettled me all the more.

"They're the only two? Any word from our spies about the Silence? Did she stay home?" Rain asked.

"No one spotted—"

"Who is the Silence?"

"Well, that's the point. We don't know. She's the sister who hides her face and her voice. Green eyes, tall build—that's all we know," Rain explained. I wondered if he found it annoying I'd kept my head in the sand, hiding from all knowledge of anything outside Brambleton. I knew the Nine existed, but nothing more.

"She was spotted in Nythyr the same day her sisters arrived, so if she plans to come, she'll be late."

"Good."

"Did..." I hesitated, not sure if I wanted to bring her up. "Did Keeva have a name like that?"

"No. Those three are Nereza's prized possessions. She wants their reputation known. Keeva fashioned herself as the deadliest, but the Silence is far more deadly. Her death toll is unknown." Rain's breath was warm on my shoulder.

We heard the front door slam open on a gust of wind, and Elora's laughter echoed. I put my hands on the arms of Rain's chair, about to stand. Uncertainty flooded over our golden bond, and I threaded my fingers through his as he wrapped his arm around me.

"Let her come to us. If we're going to—I want her to see us as we are, as we're meant to be. Not as it has been. Unless you think we should ease her into it?" he added in a panic.

Before I could move, the girl in question cleared her throat from the archway. "What in the name of all the gods is on your shoulder, Mama?"

Stunned, I didn't move for a moment before bursting into laughter. Weariness, grief, my reconciliation with Rain, and the desire to see and hold her was too much.

"Come here, honey. Hug me, and take a closer look."

Her eyes darted to Rain for a moment before she dumped a stack of books on the table and made her way around it.

"*The Discovered Dragon* has a sequel," she breathed, excitement lifting her lips into a dazzling smile. "It's about Alina's sister and her love interest." She traced her fingertip over the swirling ink on my skin and looked over my shoulder at Rain, posing her question to him. "Can I get one?"

"Elora Mae. No. You're too young," I replied.

"I didn't ask you; I asked him. He gave one to Uncle Dewalt."

"That's different," Rain said, shifting beneath me.

"You did what?" I whipped my head around to face him, catching Dewalt attempting to slink away out of the corner of my eye. "No, no. You two did what?"

"It was just one, and it's almost completely faded," Dewalt supplied, the tops of his cheeks turning red. "How do you even—" Thyra sauntered into the room, arms crossed with a devilish smirk on her face. "Oh, I'm going to kill you," he growled at my Second.

"Hold on, someone explain."

"Dewalt has tattoo on his ass." Thyra barely managed the words before Dewalt lunged at her, and she dodged out of the way.

"You gave Dewalt a tattoo on his ass?" I asked my husband, twisting to look down at him.

"He lost a bet when we were young," Rain answered sheepishly. "It was not well done."

"Wait, what? I didn't see it back at the lake."

"I assume you weren't examining his ass that closely for an old, faded tattoo, dear heart." He scowled at me, and I couldn't stop the laughter from bubbling over.

"Gods, how long ago? Did he have a tattoo when—"

"Yes. I gave it to him before we came back that last summer. It's a letter F."

"F? F for what?"

"Fool. I lost the bet too. He just lost it first."

"And what kind of bet did you both lose?" I asked, voice soft as I ignored Dewalt and Thyra's rough-housing, which had moved out into the great room.

"I think you know."

I smiled sadly as I cupped his cheek.

"Gods, the point is, Mama, Rainier gave him a tattoo, one of the awful ones where he poked him a bunch." I turned my attention toward my daughter, though I squeezed Rain's hand tight in mine. "I'd get a nice one. A dragon maybe, oh, or a silhouette of Yvi. I wouldn't get a letter on my backside," she scoffed. "Besides, I wasn't asking *you*. What *he* says is actual law."

I smiled, a brow lifting at her resourcefulness.

"You had to know I'd choose whatever your mother said, right?" Rain's smile was loud in his voice, and an ache pulsed deep in my chest.

This was how it should have always been. How could I simultaneously be so heartsick over all we'd missed, and so appreciative for what we had now? I'd been grateful and so happy they had a chance. The distance I'd felt with my daughter after I'd failed her and the distance I'd felt with Rain had kept me from feeling the full weight of all of my emotions about the three of us. I pulled Elora against me, one hand in her curls, and, after a moment, I felt Rain shift. Leaning forward, he pressed his chest against my back and wrapped both of us in his arms. Elora was stiff for only a second before she melted into me.

"I love you so much," I whispered into her hair. "You're so resilient, more than I ever was. You make me so gods damn proud, you know that?"

"Stop, Mama," she said back, though I wasn't convinced it was what she wanted.

Rain didn't say a word, just squeezed tighter. I couldn't wait for the day the two of them had a relationship where he could say the things I knew were on his heart. But he wouldn't risk telling her before she was ready.

"Does this mean I can get a tattoo?"

Rain shook with laughter as I said, "Absolutely not."

I was exhausted. We had stayed at the estate until Elora went to bed, taking our time to visit with her, before we rifted to the palace. Our meeting with the sisters was an early one, and we wanted to be well-rested for it. Once we arrived, Rain was quiet once more, and despite the logical side of me trying to soothe my anxiety about it, I let it get the better of me. I was afraid our return to the capital would bring those horrible memories and thoughts back to him, and he'd push me away once more. My heart had raced, and it was the only reason Rain knew anything was wrong. But instead of coming to me and holding me, he'd demanded an answer about it from across the room. Distance separating us—protecting us.

But when I had disrobed in reply, pulling my hair to my unmarked shoulder, his posture had softened and he had held his head in his hands. I wouldn't accept his apologies, only asking he let me approach him. And he had. It would be a long road before he was himself again, but when his lips grazed my inked skin and he didn't hesitate to put his arms around me, I knew we'd be alright.

After he'd finally drifted to sleep, his arms wrapped around me while I lightly scratched his scalp, I'd had my own inner turmoil to deal with. The fear I felt surrounding the meeting with Keeva's sisters had me nearly chewing a hole through my lower lip. They would know I killed her the moment they looked me in the eyes. And while I wasn't frightened for myself, I didn't like thinking about the potential impact my actions could have on the kingdom.

That was why, when we finally made our way to the meeting, my eyes were bloodshot, and I held tightly onto my coffee which Rain had ordered brought to us. I was twitching with nervous energy when they finally walked into the council room. The Scythe was nearly the same height as Thyra, but her biceps beat my Second's by a long shot. Her arm was nearly the width of her head. She paced the room, looking at the clock on the wall every few moments before casting a haughty glare at the door we'd be walking through. It was Rain's idea to watch them through the slit in the wall, a thin tapestry hanging over the opening to disguise it. I hadn't a clue it existed, though it made sense given his father's paranoia.

I'd only ever seen likenesses of Queen Nereza, but the Scythe appeared as if she could be her true daughter rather than an adopted assassin. Nereza was renowned for her beauty with long, dark hair she always wore unbound, thick full brows, and golden skin. The Scythe wore her hair short and didn't have the voluptuous curves her mother was known for, but she resembled her at the very least. Unlike her sister.

The Scar was likely my height, hard to tell while seated, and I never would have guessed she was an assassin. She wore an old wound across her face, starting at one temple and crossing over her nose, puckering near where she probably once had a dimple to match the other. I wondered what could have possibly done that to her, and why it hadn't been healed by a conduit. Certainly, Nereza had more than a few in her employ. I'd always thought assassins were meant to blend in, no discernible features to give them away, but these two stood out. The Scar sat patiently at the table, hands neatly crossed in her lap. Though she was narrower in the bust and wider in the hips, we looked similar. Her features were lighter than mine, almost as if she were the mid-point between Lucia and me. Her thick blonde hair was pulled back into a tight bun, and she appeared as if she allowed no room for distraction.

Their hearts beat in opposition, and I was fearful about why.

"Help me, dear heart." Rain whispered, lips touching my ear. "One beat is racing while the other is not?"

"Yes."

"I thought so. It's harder to pinpoint than I realized. And the other is almost sluggish in comparison?" When I nodded, he put his hands on my hips. "It's odd, don't you think?"

"You're significantly calmer than me. Listen," I murmured, pulling his hand to my chest.

"You have nothing to fear. The ship she boarded sank. That's all there is to it, Em."

"What are their real names?"

"The Scar is named Jesmine, and the Scythe is named Penelope."

"Penelope." I retorted, dubious.

"I didn't name her." He shrugged. "Are you ready?"

"As I suppose I'll ever be."

When we walked through the room, both women stood, their vast height difference far more noticeable. The Scar—Jesmine—wasn't as tall as I thought, perhaps a hand shorter than me.

"Your Majesties," they said in unison on a bow, only offering the faintest hint of an accent.

Rain nodded, and I dipped my head, still becoming accustomed to the genuflections.

"Your Highnesses," his voice rumbled, and I echoed, feeling uncomfortable before shaking it off. They knew who I was. They knew I didn't know what I was doing. Faking it to make things better wouldn't earn me any favors with them. I attempted normalcy and projected warmth. I had held no ill will toward Keeva until she broke my bones and tried to kill me. Perhaps the two of us could salvage whatever alliances Nythyr and Vesta had once hoped for—with kindness alone.

"Jesmine, Penelope, thank you for coming to celebrate the coronation," I offered, nodding toward each of them and Rain's grip on my hip squeezed. Confused at the look on the Scar's face, I continued. "Has your stay been comfortable? I'm sorry the festivities were postponed; that was my fault."

"He didn't prepare you properly," she said, a rueful smile curving the side of her mouth left untouched by injury. "I am not the Scar. She is." The shorter woman who wore the injury nodded toward the taller one, and my stomach tightened.

"She is the reason for this though," she added, tracing a fingertip across the old wound.

"I'm sorry. I didn't mean to off—"

"My sister, *Penelope*, is a bitch," the taller woman, the real Scar, I supposed, said, a smile on her face showing extraordinarily white teeth. Almost too white. Unsettling. "Don't mind her."

"I apologize," Rain said, pulling me against him and looking down at me. "That was my fault. I forget sometimes how little you've been privy to these last years. Surely, the two of you understand? She's been away for a time."

"We've heard enough," the shorter woman, Penelope, said. "You are the one who outshone Keeva."

"Our condolences," Rain swept in, putting on airs of royal grandeur, smoothing over the situation at hand. I'd heard stories, but seeing him work his charm was amazing. No playfulness or mischief or crooked smile graced his features. Only a polished royal stood beside me. "I do fear it was my fault she met her end." My body tightened in response to his words, and he squeezed my hand before he continued. "She was eager to leave because of me. The weather wasn't good for it, not with the autumn squalls Seyma's Gulf gets. I'd have insisted she stay if I'd have known what would happen."

"Our sister was always a hard one to deter when her mind was made up," Jesmine said before nodding to the table between us. "Let us sit?"

As Rain and I sat down across from the two of them, I'd noticed their hearts had traded beats. Jesmine, who had paced and seemed nervous, had a slower beat while Penelope, who had been slow and calm, was now jittery, her leg bouncing beneath the table.

"Did you kill her?" Penelope blurted, just as we pulled our chairs in. My jaw dropped, and Rain swore.

"What in the gods—" he began before Jesmine cut him off, nostrils flaring.

"Divine hell, Pen. Are you trying to get us all killed? They kill us, Mother kills them all. Shit!"

"It just doesn't make any sense. Keeva wasn't in line anymore, not with marrying him. None of the others—" The small blonde woman shrieked when her sister slammed a hand down on the table between them.

"Shut the fuck up, Penny."

"Alright, what's going on?" Rain demanded. There was something more to all of this, and I didn't know if it would work out in our—*my*—favor or not.

Jesmine dropped her head in both hands, elbows on the table in front of her. The two eldest daughters of Nereza, Queen of Nythyr, Mother of the Nine, were supposed to be formidable, but they were doing little to convince us of such.

"Who killed our sister?" Jesmine said, staring down at the table. Penelope crossed her arms and hardened her features.

"Your sister drowned at sea when her—" Rain began, quiet tone doing little to hide his aggravation.

"We know she never boarded that ship." Jesmine lifted her gaze to mine, and I swore I saw fear in her eyes. "We just need to know if it was one of you or one of our sisters."

CHAPTER 46

LAVENIA

WITH FAIR WEATHER AND open seas, the trip to the horn of Olistos should have taken two weeks. But Seyma's Gulf was treacherous without massive squalls nearly upending the ship, let alone with the type of weather the gods had decided to curse us with. We were approaching the end of our third week on the water and still had days before reaching the horn. After rounding it, we'd still have to head east for a while, to reach the Seaborn Queen. Sometimes I wondered if travel by land would have been faster.

I'd been at sea enough in my life to have discovered my sea-legs, and yet I was finding myself trying not to vomit more often than not, the tilt of the deck precarious at best, downright deadly at worst. Mairin spent most of her time with her eyes on the horizon, and part of me wondered if it was as a lookout for her mother. Oddly enough, it was Nixy who spent most of his time with me. He had sworn up and down he knew a cure for my sickness, and after an hour of my head being in a bucket, I finally caved, demanding for him to show me.

Starting on the inside of my wrists, Nixy used a surprisingly gentle touch to firmly press deep into my skin. But when the first few spots did little to ease my nausea, I grew irritated with him, trying to push him away from where he pressed into my back.

"This is pointless."

"Hold still, Venia," he hissed, a soft grunt of a breath puffing over my bare shoulder. I'd stripped down to my thin undershirt, the fabric an easier barrier for him to dig into. I was shocked the man had made no crude comments. It had been a few years since I'd been around him, and it seemed he'd matured. Or so I hoped. He was a few years younger than me, and ever since he joined the guard almost a decade prior, he'd been trying to bed me. Though I'd made it abundantly clear to him it would never happen, and I only saw him as a friend, if that, he had always burned for my attention. This was the closest he'd ever been to seeing me naked; I had braced myself for his commentary, and he surprised me by not saying anything stupid.

"It hurts," I whined.

"No shit. I can't get to the right spot if you keep wiggling away from me. Do you want to stop getting sick all over the ship or not?"

"Alright, Nixy." I sighed, straightening and bracing myself. "Do your worst."

"If it works, you have to do something for me," he said, digging into a spot on either side of my spine. I worried he'd not only fail, but I'd start pissing blood.

"I'm not going to sleep with you."

"That's not what I want. Gods. I'd like you to call me by my name."

I snorted, but he didn't say anything, just continued kneading my skin. The ship rolled, knocking me backward into him, and my stomach rioted. Fumbling for my bucket, I nearly missed as Nixy held it under my mouth, a steady hand on my back.

"Divine hell, Ven. Desperate measures, as they say. Lie down."

"Very funny," I said, wiping the spittle from my mouth.

"I'm serious. On your back." He patted his bed, the bunk below Brenna's, an expectant look on his face which turned faintly irritated after a moment. "Aonara's tits. I'm not going to do anything you won't thank me for later." He grinned, deep brown eyes twinkling, though I could tell he meant me no harm. Glaring daggers at him, I did as I was told, lying down and crossing my arms over my chest.

"Fucking hell, Venia. Would you put your arms down and relax? I'm not going to look at your tits any more than I already do." He rolled his eyes and pushed up his sleeves, revealing umber forearms more muscular than I remembered. He wasn't unattractive, not by any means. But he was young, and between that and his unyielding eagerness, I found him annoying. Dewalt had been the only man I'd found attractive in the last decade or so, and that was only because I hadn't ruled out the idea the gods themselves had chiseled him from stone.

Mairin was Dewalt's opposite. I knew it would do me no good to think of those full, rounded curves or her plump behind and the way her breeches clung tightly to it. Gods, when she bent over after dinner only hours before, ass within reach, it had taken everything in me to keep my hands to myself. If Dewalt had been hewn from stone, Mairin was molded from clay, Rhia's soft fingertips gifting her with elegant abundance.

Thinking about her body that way was quite the stupid thing to do when Nixy leaned over my prone form, pressing on my upper abdomen. Tempted to cross my arms over myself again, nipples hardened from arousal thanks to the merrow, I closed my eyes and thought about just how little she'd spoken to me in the past few weeks. Though I'd been staring into the bottom of a sick bucket more often than not, she had kept away. She'd even refused to sleep in the bunks Beau had gifted to us below the captain's quarters. Instead, I shared with only Nixy and Brenna, an uncomfortable affair all around, while Mairin slept in the berth with the other sailors. She truly wanted me to find out who I was now that I was free to do it, and she'd barely entertained me in recent weeks. In fact, part of me wondered if she spent time with Brenna on purpose, just to keep me away. She knew I wanted nothing to do with the woman, so she provided a good barrier.

Part of me wondered if she'd realized wanting to be with me was a mistake and was letting me down gracefully.

"What the fuck are you doing? *Don't move.*" Compulsion heavy in my voice, Nixy froze, straddled atop me, thumbs pressing into my stomach. My eyes had snapped open the second he threw a heavy leg over my body, and he was about to topple over now that I'd prevented him from moving. "*Explain.*"

"I have to press on both spots beneath your breastbone. I couldn't reach properly, so I straddled you." Voice stilted, Nixy answered under the compulsion, unable to lie.

"*No other motivation?*"

"No. But—" He sputtered a bit, fighting my divinity. "I knew the view would be good, and I wasn't wrong."

I was about to reprimand him when the ship hit a wave, and he fell over, still stuck in the same position. Laughing, I released him from the compulsion and sat up. He brushed himself off and rubbed a hand over his head, hair shaved short, before glaring up at me from the ground.

"Not coughing your guts up, I see."

"Shit. I'm not."

"I'm going to have a lump," he said, rubbing his head once more. "Between that and the favor I just did you, I want mine. Call me Hawley."

"Hawley Nixy? Did your parents hate you?"

"You know my surname is Nix, not Nixy." He scowled, dark eyebrows knitting.

A loud thud resounded from above us, and I knew Hyše had returned. Since it was too early for her nap, it meant the weather was about to somehow get worse.

"Alright, *Hawley*. Keep working your magic," I said as I laid back down. "Don't read into it though," I added, after noticing the hint of a smile at his lips.

A roar from a dragon woke me hours later, Nixy's hands the reason for the best slumber I'd had the entire time I'd been on the ship. I'd barely opened my eyes when, just a meter above my head, a grappling hook burst through the hull, sending ocean water and splinters of wood flying at my face. I screeched, covering my eyes, and two sets of hands were pulling me backwards off my bed.

"Fucking hell!" Brenna's voice called out as Nixy turned me around to look at my face. Hyše screeched, and I heard the tremendous flap of her wings as she must have taken flight. Shouts and screams followed by clashes of metal followed swiftly after.

"I can't see shit," Brenna murmured, backing away from the porthole window. "It has to be pirates, right?" she whispered, voice trembling. I'd only ever seen her this afraid once, back on Varmeer. The sway of the lantern above us cast a ghastly glow over her features, and she looked ill.

"You think it's the ship that's been following us?" I asked. It had kept a distance, just on the horizon, but the gulf had always been a massive thoroughfare so it wasn't too strange. Beau hadn't worried, so I tried not to either. But now? I regretted not being more vocal about my discontent. Loud thuds resounded on the other side of the door to our quarters, thumps of boots hitting the ground after leaping down the ladder.

"Mairin," I breathed, realizing only then she was already part of the fray.

And then I heard her sing.

"Gods, no," I uttered on a breath. Pulling my breeches and boots on faster than I ever had in my life, I reached for my sword and was at the door within a moment.

"What are you going to do, La—Your Highness? You can't go out there." Brenna grabbed my arm, pulling me away from the door, and I shook my wrist free from her grasp.

"Awful convenient time to treat me like royalty, don't you think, Bren? Fuck off."

I moved forward, grateful to see Nixy already armed and ready to follow.

"*Slit your throat,*" I ordered the first pirate I saw, blocking my way to the merrow whose call I could not resist. A shaft of moonlight from a grate above her shone down across her hair, glowing a dark burnt-orange in the low light. She hadn't made it far, still singing from the row of hammocks she'd been sleeping in, head tilted back and voice clear. I was careful to avoid looking at her face, not wanting to be swept up into the song.

Nixy shoved past me, slipping a dagger into the back of one of the attacker's necks as the merrow's call distracted him. I didn't know what to do—go find Beau or make my way over to Mairin. My instinct told me to go to her, but she was holding her own and Beau might need me. Glancing over at her only the once, I followed Brenna, climbing the ladder to find our ship's captain.

It was a mistake.

A sturdy woman slammed Brenna backwards, holding her in place with a thick, muscular frame. About to compel her to let go, I felt a knife press against the side of my throat, and I froze.

"Well, hello there, Ven. Nice to see you again."

Fiona.

Gods. Damned. Fiona.

Or that's what I thought her name was.

It had been nearly a decade since I'd seen her—fucked her. D and I had been visiting Olistos one year when my brother had been in Nythyr. Olistos first and Lucia's tomb after. That had been the plan. But we'd been waylaid by this ruthless little bitch.

She didn't look much different at all. Shorter than me with alabaster skin and stormy eyes, her dark brown hair was still a mass of curls she did little to tame. But now, with her tricorn hat atop it, she actually looked like what she was.

A fucking thief. A pirate. A gods damn miscreant.

She'd played me well. Dewalt too, but I had been her mark. The absolute fool I was. I hadn't thought about it in a long time, but I sat here, reliving every moment which led to the biggest confrontation my mother and I had ever had—when we lost an entire shipment of Nythyrian wine, meant to last for gods only knew how long. And Fiona had been the reason for it.

Shaped like an hourglass, her body had earned not only my attention but Nixy's too. He'd been so angry she went to bed with me—until he found out what happened after. Then he'd laughed until Dewalt, still naked from chasing after her that morning, smacked him over the back of the head.

Tied against the mast between Brenna and Nixy, a chain of basalt wrapped over us, there was nothing any of us could do except wait for the fray to finish. When Mairin's song stopped abruptly, I leaned forward the best I could, retching.

"That's not, fuck—is that the wench from—"

"Shut your gods damned mouth, Nix," Brenna murmured.

"It's her," I croaked, stifling my cry of rage when I saw two people dragging Mairin up the ladder, the bag over her head unable to hold all of her long, fiery hair. After hauling her up, the merrow was dropped rather gently on the ground between me and Fiona. I tugged against my bindings, desperate to get to her. Because of how carefully the pirate put her down, I didn't have fear about her being alive, but I stilled, watching for an intake of breath. Only when I saw her chest rise and fall did I allow myself to look up at who carried her. One was the muscular woman who'd slammed into Brenna, and the other was one of the most beautiful people I'd ever seen.

"Tetty wears a rune, drawn on them by a seaborn with elf-blood. They can't be compelled," Fiona said, a smirk on her face as she offered an explanation I didn't care to hear, nodding toward the attractive pirate. I knew the compulsion aspect was supposed to be the shocking part, but the fact a seaborn had mated with an elf was more surprising to me. The seaborn had always been purists, not wanting their blood to dilute at all—by order of their queen. My eyes slid over to Tetty, expecting to see evidence of the rune plastered on their forehead, but it was clearly hidden. Tall and narrow, they walked over to the bitch I once knew, leaning down for a kiss as they tugged Fiona close. They had cropped blond hair, half of it pulled back on top of their head, and Fiona reached over to them, running a soft hand down their cheek. The intimacy between them was clear.

"And you know I can't be compelled," Fiona said, a grin kicking up her lips. "You remember that well, don't you?"

Fiona sauntered over, the full moon shining down on her form. She wore boots laced up to her knees, in good shape if a bit damaged by saltwater, over form-fitting breeches and a loose tunic. Her coat hung low, and she wore multiple layers beneath it, jackets and belts which hid her frame. But I could tell her hips and breasts were still to die for, and I wanted to make her jump off the side of the gods damned ship.

"Don't you, princess?" She used the tip of her saber to tilt my chin up.

"Still don't have your pendant, I see. Couldn't sell enough of the stolen wine?" I made a face, mocking her. "Sad, little thing misses the sea. Too bad."

"Take the merrow's eyes," Fiona barked, not looking away from me.

"What? No!" I shouted, rearing back. "Don't. Don't take her eyes!" Tetty stood over Mairin but didn't move, waiting. "Fiona, please."

"Mmm, hearing you beg sounds just as good now as it did back then."

"Fi," Tetty murmured, taking a few steps toward the veritable demon who stood over me. Tetty rubbed their neck, worrying their bottom lip. "Fiona, remember what we discussed?"

"You're no fun, my star."

"Think of the fun we'll have once you get what you want."

"But I want that now." Tetty pressed a hand to Fiona's back, gentle. I didn't know what the hell I was witnessing, but Tetty tempered the woman who still balanced my chin on the end of her blade. She blew out a breath, rolling her eyes before tipping her head back to me. "Fine. How much do you think the Crown will ransom for your ass?"

"What?" I nearly laughed.

"Ransom. The concept isn't a hard one, Princess."

"I don't know. I'm not taken captive often," I retorted, and I swore Mairin shook with laughter. Relief spread through me as I watched her stir. I couldn't keep my eyes off the merrow, needing to see her face just to know she was alright.

"Look at her once more while I'm talking to you, and I'll take her tongue, too."

"I don't know, Fiona! Fuck! Probably enough to get your audience with the Seaborn Queen."

"How do you know—" Tetty began.

"Why else?" I interrupted. "It's been a decade since Olistos. You should've had the coin by now. Did the wine not sell quickly enough?"

The tip of the saber sliced into my skin, and I felt my blood drip. "You know what? Queen Estri likes shiny things. What's shinier than a princess?"

Mairin's body thrashed, her feet knocking Tetty to the ground. Fiona swore, kicking the merrow—*my merrow*—in the stomach, and I was shouting, my screams breaking through the silence. Tetty stopped the woman from killing Mairin, and all of us were on the ground panting within a few moments.

"I'm going to make you crawl for her," Fiona growled. "Start begging."

And I did.

CHAPTER 47

Rainier

I was sweating beneath the heavy regalia, the sheer number of people in the throne room adding to my discomfort. The sun had made a rare appearance, almost like a message, but it shone down through the skylight above us—and gods was it warm. Sitting on the throne my father had once dominated didn't feel nearly as awful as I thought it would. In fact, the dread I'd felt for this ceremony and the relief I'd experienced at its postponement had been unnecessary. The first half of it had gone well. The two of us had traveled separately from my estate in the gilded carriages my mother had insisted upon; Elora accompanied her mother while my own mother accompanied me, the cries and shouts from the crowd overwhelmingly positive. I'd missed Em, sore over the fact we didn't travel together, but neither of us had much time to dwell on it when we arrived at the palace, both of us ushered off to dress in the proper finery.

The Supreme presided over the entire thing. A grating irritation on my soul, considering everything which had happened with the novices, but I tried to ignore my vexation. He'd been kind to me my entire life, and he had tried to help Em when Filenti and the other masters had taken her. My hands were tied. My mother wanted the ceremony to go like my father's had, and I didn't care enough to fight with her. Though the Supreme wasn't nearly as old as my father, he had attended the coronation in his youth, and few of those who attended still lived. It was the Supreme or Lord Kress from my council who would be an authority on the subject, and I couldn't stand the latter.

My scrutiny moved to my council members, all of them seated on either side of the dais, wearing burgundy robes and looking just as warm as me. Lord Durand had even brought a fan, and I was impressed by his foresight. I could have ordered any of my subjects to do the same for me, but that wasn't something I was interested in doing. Just because I was a crowned king now didn't mean I intended on abusing it. Instead, I discreetly used my divinity to send a breeze throughout the room. I heard more than one person sigh in relief, and I smiled.

Gripping the arms of the throne, I adjusted my body, looking up at the door Emmeline would walk through at any moment. *Should* have walked through ten minutes ago. I would have been nervous if I hadn't sensed her through the bond. She seemed rushed, perhaps a bit agitated, but an undercurrent of excitement pulsated through, and I knew she was coming. When the doors finally opened, a loud echo resonated through the room. And as she stepped in, flanked by my mother on one side and my daughter on the other, my breath caught. My mother's sour expression was expected. She'd been present for my own crowning but had scurried off to ensure Em would be ready for hers, and it wasn't long after when I felt my wife's irritation. I hoped she gave Shivani as much grief as she deserved.

As the three of them made their way down the steps, I stiffened, remembering Em's last experience in this room, and I worried she'd think about it too. The black carpet covering the stone steps had been brought out for the ceremony, along with the dark blue banners which hung down flaunting the Vestana family crest. I'd requested the sheer black silk behind me to hang lower, blocking the headless likenesses of those the Vestana family had proudly slain, knowing Em wouldn't like to see that reminder of what she was now part of. The council members had insisted upon bringing out the gilded ceremonial chairs for their seats, but other than those few changes, the throne room remained largely the same. I wondered if it was a mistake, afraid I should have changed it more. But Em didn't falter. My queen was sure and steady as she descended the stone stairs.

Elora tripped down a step, but she caught herself quickly, grabbing onto Em's arm for support. Her cheeks flushed instantly, horror fluttering over her features, and it made my heart sing when her eyes sought out mine for reassurance. She was clinging to Em, but that girl was mine—and she knew it. I smiled, my chest aching, and nodded. Her posture straightened, and she recovered, striding forward with confident steps. Just a small thing, her reliance on me in that moment, but, gods, I would think about it for the rest of my days. I hoped she'd always look to me when she needed it. It struck me that one day she would make this journey on her own. Once I died, this throne would be hers. Did the thought cross her mind? Though my mother would have fought it, if I'd have died in Darkhold, Elora could have been in my place right now.

It startled me, discovering how much I needed to teach her. My father knew with his age his days were numbered and pushed me into learning about my role early on. But just because I *could* have centuries to teach Elora didn't mean we *would* have all of that time. I'd need to speak with Em about it, and we'd have to discuss her education. The robe she wore was far too large for her, and I realized with a start it was the one I had worn when I came to maturity, officially capable of leading Vesta if my father died. Lavenia had gone through the same ceremony though, so why my mother hadn't given Elora a better fitting garment, I didn't know.

As for my sister, her absence was noteworthy. Not once had I done anything like this without her. By my side for every event neither of us wanted to attend, and she missed this one. It was for a good cause, but still—I loathed it. I had heard nothing from her since she left for the Seaborn Queen's territory, but I knew the waters were precarious this time of year in the gulf. I'd instructed her to stop in Olistos on her way back and send a message, but I still waited, nervous about how things were faring. I was so gods damn grateful for her willingness to step up as an emissary. I'd underestimated my sister, and I planned to make up for it as soon as she returned. We'd been experiencing tremendous storms on our western shore, and though I was grateful they stood as a barrier against Declan and Folterra, I worried for Ven. Seyma's Gulf was bracketed on the north and south by land, and I hoped it would be enough to shield them from ill weather while the *Netari* navigated treacherous waters.

Both my mother and my daughter joined the standing crowd on the steps, on even footing with me. Elora stood between Dewalt and my mother, appearing nervous once more. I couldn't help my smile as my best friend elbowed her, and a grin spread over both their faces. When my daughter clapped her hand to her mouth, stifling a laugh as Dewalt whispered something, my mother shot him a glare over Elora's head. He'd thrown himself into training my girl, preparing her for anything which might come her way. I'd worried at first it might be too hard for him, considering how much she looked like Lucia, but I soon understood their differences were enough; he didn't seem to struggle. Lucia might have been opinionated, but she mostly obeyed. She had her limits, certainly, but Elora took after her mother quite a bit. And, perhaps foolishly, I hoped part of her rebelliousness came from me. Either way, Dewalt had been better than I'd ever seen him despite breaking the bond and his work with Elora.

The Supreme cleared his throat, and while everyone else's gaze snapped to him, I watched Em. My wife. Hair swept up and back, fashioned into something regal, she held her head high, showing her tattoo with pride as she finished walking down the last few stairs, a few steps below me on the central platform. I suspected she'd pulled her robe farther off her neck to give me a better view. We'd only been back for a few days, but word had spread about the marking the new queen wore. Other than Dewalt, no one else knew the reason for it, even if they might have suspected. It was important to her that it was my secret to keep and reveal as I saw fit.

Perhaps one day I'd speak about it. But not now, not with a change of power, not when I'd been held captive for weeks. The sad fact was that my subjects would look to me for strength with the threat of war looming, and even the slightest question about my ability to lead could be detrimental. But something irked me about that. I didn't care about looking weak for them—with Em as my strength, I could do anything. Maybe they needed to see that too.

Until then, the ink climbing up her neck was mine to look at, mine to know the reason for. A reminder of her love—just one of the many sacrifices she'd made for me. She caught my attention as she approached. With a slight tickle of nerves moving down the bond, her cheeks flushed, and she gave me a small smile before kneeling on the dais below me. I hated that this was part of the ceremony. Though she didn't kneel for me, but the reverence of the Crown itself, it made me uncomfortable. Clearly sensing my annoyance for the custom, she raised a brow before lazily tracking her gaze over my body.

Mischievous, my queen.

I returned the favor. While I was dressed in the same black attire from our wedding beneath the matching robes we wore, Em had on a simple white gown I'd never seen before. I didn't know how she convinced my mother to allow her to forgo the ermine cape atop the long, sapphire velvet train of the robe, but she looked no less royal. The dress itself was simple—straight and modest across the top, with delicate gold lace adorning the bottom. Beautiful, strong, and capable, she situated her gown around her before lifting her head to the Supreme.

He repeated the ceremony with her as he had done with me. Two novices strode forward, fully covered, and handed her both a set of scales and a sword to represent Rhia and Hanwen's blessing.

"With wisdom from Rhia, swear to go forward with intent in your mind and heart to bring Vesta's people peace, but with Hanwen's wrath, do not forget to execute justice to the wicked."

Emmeline bowed her head as I had done before passing the items back to the novices. Two more took their place, one holding the same candlestick as they'd held for me, while the other held a small bowl full of water from the font.

"As Aonara brings light to Ciarden's dark, so shall you swear to bring balance to this blessed kingdom."

Taking the vessel in one hand, Em used the candlestick to light the votive floating within. Using both hands to cradle the bowl, candle discarded, she waited for the Supreme's nod.

Em declared, voice loud and resolute, "I do so swear."

I used my divinity to shake the earth, amplifying the stomping of feet surrounding us as she rose, gracefully making her way to the throne beside me. Only a quick display of nerves struck her after she sat, her hand making its way up to smooth the line between her brows. The volume in the room grew to deafening even after I'd stopped my divinity. I'd grown distracted, watching my mother wrap an arm around Elora, when I felt Em's touch, reaching between us to take my hand in hers.

"My queen," I murmured, letting the rest of the din fall away. If I had to choose only one color to see the rest of my life, the specific blue of those love-filled eyes which looked back at me would be it.

"Unreal," she whispered. "All of this. It's unreal."

"It is. Unreal, but it's ours."

Em made a face when she reached up, fork still hovering in front of her mouth, as she adjusted my crown. We'd been permitted to take the velvet capes off, leaving the coronation regalia with the servants in the throne room. Neither of us wanted to wear the heavy ornamental crowns either and instead opted for lighter counterparts. My own circlet I preferred had been confiscated, and my mother had given me something she insisted was more 'king-like', though I couldn't understand why. It was nearly the same as my old one, but with a sprinkling of black sapphires inlaid. Em wore the same diadem from our wedding ceremony, and she looked even more beautiful now than she did the first time I saw her wear it. She dropped her hand when Warric strode across the room, clothes barely pulled on.

"Your Majesties, I am sorry to interrupt your meal, but I come to you in haste. Some sort of explosion occurred in Evenmoor—the ground shook all the way in Mindengar. It seems most of his soldiers are marching north past Darkhold. Perhaps because of the storms in the south? We've received no word from the rebels yet."

"Thank you, Warric," I said as I pushed my chair back, using a napkin to wipe my mouth.

"Do you think it was a rebel attack? Or do you think—"

"They'd have told us if they planned to make moves on Declan." I cut her off as I stood, offering Em my hand.

Swiftly making our way across the hall, I spotted Raj seated between his two children, in the capital for the coronation. Both more well-behaved than I'd ever seen them, I wondered if their elven-tutor might have used her magick on them to get them to behave as such.

"Raj, a word?" I hated to interrupt, but I didn't want to deliver such news to him in front of his children. Though I didn't ask her to, wanting her to be as involved in this as she wanted to be, Em took Raj's seat and engaged with the children, distracting them while I spoke to their father. I could tell she was listening though, her head cocked at a perfect angle which elongated the elegant curve of her neck, while she asked Raj's son about his favorite part of the ceremony.

"When?" Raj asked, clearly expecting some type of order.

"Tomorrow. I want you in Lamera. I'm going to send Ashmont to Nara's Cove just in case. They're not leaving from the Cascade, but from the north instead."

"The storms," Raj murmured.

"I don't anticipate them getting very far from the north either, at least not quickly, but I want to be ready. I suspect he'll try to take Lamera with little bloodshed."

"They'll find it a difficult task," a low, seductive voice piped up from behind me, and I cursed myself for not checking my surroundings. The Scythe barely came up to my chest, but I didn't like her sneaking up on me like that.

"And why is that?" Raj snapped, and the woman's face turned to stone, not a single muscle out of place.

"My mother owes the Supreme a favor." She shrugged before spinning on a heel and melting back into the crowd who mingled after their dinner. Drawing a hand over my face, I gave Raj a look and knew he'd investigate whatever the fuck the assassin had been speaking about. While we hadn't revealed that Em had caused Keeva's death, we insisted their sister died at sea, and they had left our meeting without saying much else. They had, however, asked for our discretion, and Em had given her word. I felt her guilt down the bond, and she'd silenced me with a wicked mouth and dexterous hands when I tried to discuss it with her afterward. The burden of a taken life, no matter the reason, was a heavy one, and, though I yearned to lighten it for her, I knew she wouldn't want that. Instead, I strove to give her the silent assurance she needed that I'd be here for her through it.

The crowd wasn't too loud, thankfully, considering half of the guests had already left because of the postponement. It didn't feel right to celebrate anyway. I glimpsed Elora chatting with Theo, tugging on one of her curls and twisting it as she spoke—a nervous habit I'd noticed she had—and I wondered if she required intervention. A moment later, a clattering of broken glass drew everyone's attention, and a clearly drunken Prince Cyran threw himself to the ground to help clean up whatever mess he'd made. When I'd seen him on the guest list my mother gave me, I'd insisted upon his removal, but she'd thrown a fit and told me Elora demanded it. *His brother knows he betrayed him, and he has no one*, she'd supposedly said. I wasn't as surprised by her compassion as I ought to have been.

"Which captains await me in Lamera? With Brenna gone, I assume you want Dewalt here?"

"Of course he does," my friend said, sauntering up and butting into the conversation. I was getting rather aggravated by all the interruptions, though I supposed I was the one who decided not to call a formal meeting.

"Can I have Thyra at least?" Raj asked, complaint in his tone.

"That's a question for my wife," I said, inclining my head toward the woman in question, who sat with her head close to Raj's daughter, Marella. I suspected Em was orchestrating a friendship between his girl and our own. "Are you going to send them back to the Alsors?"

"I suspect you'll be summoning the dragons to Astana, so no. My family won't be there to care for them. They can stay here. Aida will keep an eye on them."

"Where is she tonight?" Dewalt asked.

"I told you to bring her," I added, and Raj cleared his throat, a sheepish look on his face as he brushed his thumb to his nose, clearly embarrassed.

"Wasn't feeling well, she said."

"You're allowed to move on. Marella seems to like her." Surprisingly gentle, Dewalt spoke quietly. He'd left his hair down, and he tucked it behind his ear as the two of us swiveled our attention to him.

"Oh, you're the master at moving on now, are you?" Raj retorted. For the first time in my long relationship with the two of them, I felt like an outsider to the conversation. Before, while my love hadn't died, I'd still been able to commiserate with them, missing Em and full of regret as I was. But now, I couldn't help but feel they might begrudge my newfound happiness, whether they wanted to or not. Although, Raj seemed to be trying to move on.

"I think what Dewalt is trying to say," I interrupted, "is that if you're feeling embarrassed with us about it, there is no need. We're happy for you."

Raj dipped his head before clearing his throat. "Alright, gods, what is this? A sewing circle?"

"I resent that remark, General," Em interjected, joining us by pinching Raj in the side.

"Your Majesty, forgive me, I—"

"Marella just finished telling me all about how Aida has been teaching you how to patch your own clothes, so she no longer has to do it. It would seem your sewing circle is serving you well."

Dewalt guffawed, and Emma shot him a dark look. "Don't act as if I didn't hear you telling him to move on. It's quite interesting what the young ones notice, you know? Elora was just telling me earlier today about how much attention you've paid to a certain nov—"

"You've made your point," Dewalt drawled. "Nor is dangerous. I've been paying attention to protecting your daughter."

"For which I am grateful. I'm curious to hear about how escorting the woman to the temple protected Elora?" A picture of innocence with her hands clasped behind her back, Em awaited his answer, and I felt her dry amusement for just a moment before she let the man off the hook, addressing Raj instead. "You want to take Thyra with you?"

"Gods, Em, what *didn't* you hear?"

She turned her grin upon me, a smile shining like a beacon directly to my soul. "I hear *everything*. You'd be surprised how motherhood makes one adapt."

I shook my head, smiling, finding myself wanting to pull her into my hold. Each moment wouldn't be enough with her.

"You may take her, Raj. As long as your first embroidery project is delivered to me?" Her voice was so sweet as she asked, and Raj ran his hand through his beard, the silver more apparent among the otherwise black hair which graced his russet skin. He clearly hadn't realized she was only using him for her amusement.

"Of course, Your Majesty," he replied, failing to hide his gritted teeth. She snorted and rolled her eyes, deserting us to speak to Marella once more.

"Enjoy the rest of your meal, Raj," I said as I dismissed him.

"I suppose you'll have to inform the Supreme?" Dewalt asked.

"I suppose so," I sighed, scanning the room to find the Supreme and my mother in conversation, heads tilted toward one another as Shivani laughed, smiling brightly.

"She's different now, isn't she?"

"It would seem," I agreed.

"I hate to celebrate a man's death, but—"

"It was far past his time to go."

Taking a sip of my drink, I observed Em introduce Elora and Theo to Marella and her brother, Jesper. My daughter's smile was shy, one I'd seen grace her mother's features a few times before. Theo said something to both girls, and they took a moment to look at one another before bursting into a fit of laughter. Em immediately sought me out, eager for me to witness the sweet interaction, and my throat tightened.

With Declan finally making moves, this moment could be one of our first and last happy ones, and I felt sick to think about what might come to pass. Declan believing he was the Accursed, and Emma undeniably being the Beloved meant her role in all of this was something we needed to discuss.

It wasn't the first time I'd wished I'd laid a full-out assault on Folterra the moment I'd recovered. But we didn't have enough soldiers to reliably rift the entire Vestian army to Folterra, and the ships we had wouldn't be enough either. Between that and the winter storms I knew would wreck the strait, it made little sense to risk my people. From our spies' reports, Declan had a far larger army than we'd ever considered between his own people and mercenaries he'd either purchased from Skos in the east or Qirus in the west. No, defensive positioning was the best path forward. I had to trust the plans I'd made with my advisors. Dewalt spent so much time with his head in books of military strategy, he would have made sure I knew of any better opportunity.

Emma straightened, turning to give me a strained smile, clearly feeling something through the bond. Checking on Elora before she made her way over to me, her gaze flitted around the room as she approached.

Assessing any threats.

"Hey," she whispered, pulling both of my hands into hers, beautiful full lips pulled down into a frown. "I know," she said. "I'm afraid too."

With the touch of her skin on my hands calming me, I leaned forward, pressing a kiss to lips made to both tempt and soothe me. The thought of not being able to protect her, of her being the one meant to end all of this, was going to send me to madness. With a sigh, I cupped her jaw and gave in, promising in my heart to relinquish any sense of control I ever thought I had. But it didn't mean we'd go into it ignorant of just how fucked we were by this prophecy.

A loud screech and a clattering of dishes gave me an idea I wasn't sure would yield fruitful results, but an overwhelming sense of rightness overcame me.

"Have you forgiven the little prince?" I asked.

CHAPTER 48

CYRAN

It had been a month since I first appeared to her in the illusion of a glen near Evenmoor. A full month of Elora continuing to wear the bracelet. I hadn't made myself known to her the entire time, but I continued to appear in her dreams. She still had nightmares, and they were far worse than the ones I'd helped her with in Evenmoor. Remarkably, the one in which I killed her wasn't the most frequent anymore, but, instead, the one haunting her was an altercation with Faxon. The one which had caused me to use a mindbreaker upon him.

She'd never told me about the whole conversation they'd had that day. In fact, she had tried convincing me nothing dreadful had happened, and the red mark on her face had merely been a product of the cold. Had she thought I couldn't see the imprint of his hand? When the shadows had whipped their way up my arms as I left her room, intent on doing everything in my ability to ensure he wouldn't hurt her again, she'd started screaming my name as Ismene held her back.

I still didn't understand why she wouldn't want me to punish him for what he'd done. I'd never killed a man before, but the rage I felt deep in my bones told me I could have done just that if I had allowed myself. But at that point, the seer had already told me what would happen. What I'd have to do. And I didn't want to cause her any more pain in the time we had left. It was already unfair I was going to have to hurt her, and I resisted every urge within me to grow close to her. But gods, had it been futile. The verit oath I'd sworn about keeping her from harm forced me to act. So, I didn't kill him, knowing she'd hate me for it, but I made it so he couldn't hurt her.

It took a few days for her to speak to me again afterwards.

More often than not, when I would find my way into her sleep, it was Faxon who haunted her. Who slapped her, whispered in her ear, and sometimes it was he who slit her throat. And it was me—a dream version of me—who held her as she died. I made myself endure it with her the first few times until I could no longer bear it. It was torturous. I found myself going to bed earlier and earlier to guarantee I'd make it there in time to intervene. I did my best to form illusions to intercept and interrupt the worst parts, but the fact remained: I played a part in those agonizing moments.

A new pain I hadn't predicted was having to watch her dream about her bloody friend.

It made sense she had dreams about Theo, and, of course, all of them were pleasant. Theo laughed with her, practiced sparring with her, ran barefoot through a meadow with her. In most of the dreams of him, they were both younger by a few years, with fresh faces and easy smiles. I knew I had no right to be jealous or upset, but I hated it. Her dreams of Theo never devolved into a torment for her. Her dreams of Theo were everything she deserved.

The one and only time I ever noticed any kind of discomfort in regards to Theo was during a dream I could tell came from a memory. And it didn't last very long. She sat on a log beside him in front of a fire, travel gear on the ground beside them. Faxon snored on his bedroll on the other side, just out of sight. She was tense, her shoulders nearly touching her ears, and her posture was stiff. And Theo, the lanky, awkward idiot that he was, leaned in with pouty lips and closed eyes. Her cheeks had pinked, and I made shadows swirl around the whole scene when her gaze moved to his lips. The dream had ended then, and when I woke up in my uncomfortable bed in the dormitory, I'd felt sick to my stomach. And lost.

So very lost.

She had *kissed* him. Laughed with him, smiled with him, had *fun* with him.

I could never be that for her, and I was sure she would never want me to be. Why would she? I was the son of a brute, raised by my brother, who was even worse. Gods, I wasn't any better, was I? I was a murderer. Killer to the best thing I'd ever known. There was no way she could ever look upon me with the same fondness she reserved for him. And I was a witless fool for ever thinking otherwise.

She'd seen me at the feast. She was with him, and she saw me. Watched me make a mess of myself, drinking myself into oblivion. I still didn't know why I even went to the ceremony. Hell, why was I even still in Astana? Perhaps I should have been in Evenmoor all along. Maybe Declan would have hesitated before destroying the mines.

Clearly premeditated, word had spread about his burning of the basalt mines just on the outskirts of Evenmoor. Elora's father had been kind enough to send a messenger when details of the attack came with the dawn. I had a tenacious ache in my head, my nausea even more imperious, and I couldn't control myself, retching on the poor man's shoes.

The man—Warren, I thought his name was—had barely reacted as he explained something about the porosity of lava rock and what happened when water trapped inside heated too quickly. The gist of it was, my brother caused a massive explosion, which, if it didn't kill on impact, the inhalation of obsidian dust had kept anyone from fighting back as a portion of his army slaughtered those who dared stand against him. With most of the rebels gathering in Evenmoor, how many of the Folterran resistance had died at his hands?

Had Cook survived? Magdalena? My sister? I doubted he would have let Ismene return to Evenmoor after moving her to Darkhold to be near him. I'd barely been able to see her more than a few times while I'd been in Vesta, and it terrified me. Every visit was a risk, a chance her defiance would be found out. She'd passed on helpful information to me the last time I saw her, and I hoped my warning to Nigel and the other rebels went heeded. She'd known he was planning something which involved fire, but it probably hadn't been enough.

I regretted not seeking out the help of King Rainier. I should have asked him to assist and protect the rebels. How could I ever expect to be better than my brother if I didn't have any idea how to lead? How to safeguard my people? The death of those who dared stand against him, of those who—rather stupidly—thought I was somehow a decent choice all weighed heavily upon me. What kind of king could I ever be?

The second wave of queasiness had moved up my throat, and the messenger had dismissed himself before he fell victim once more to the contents of my stomach. I'd gone back to sleep fitfully, attempting to forget it all.

"Are you going to be in there all day getting sick, or are you going to come help me with the stable? Mistress Imogene wants it done before nightfall." The last damn voice I wanted to hear rang out, drawing me from my self-indulgent wallowing.

Making a face and mocking Theo's words, I pulled myself up and waited for the contents of my skull to catch up to their new, vertical position. "I'll help with the stable, but I doubt I can rule out the potentiality of more vomit."

"Serves you right."

That motivated me, and I stood up quickly, immediately regretting it. After a deep breath, I pulled on my lowliest set of breeches and boots and my cloak before thinking better of it. I only had the one cloak, and mucking the stables in it seemed a poor idea. Instead, I layered on another shirt and a thick jacket, hopeful it would keep out the chill well enough. Theo had already gone outside when I made my way down the hall. I didn't bother hastening my steps, knowing nothing but annoyance and shit waited for me.

"Hasn't he realized he has no place here?" I heard Theo's voice on the other side of the door, and my heart stopped beating in my chest as I waited to hear who he might have been speaking to. There was one person who could reply and ruin me, and I held my breath.

"Listen here, boy." My stomach twisted into a knot, but I loosed a sigh, listening to the gods damn King of Vesta's tone turn reprimanding. "Anyone who flees from the Umbroth reign will find a home in Vesta."

"But, *he's* an Um—"

"Ah." Though I couldn't see it, Rainier stopped Theo from speaking. "Though you are my da—Elora's friend, I am still your king. In my stead, the queen pardoned the prince, and I upheld that decision. Elora gave her approval as well. If that girl, your *friend*, has the space in her heart to let him live here freely, I expect the rest of my kingdom to make an effort."

I swallowed, shock at his words filling me with far too much exhilaration. I hadn't known Elora said I could stay. I heard footsteps approach, and I pushed my way through the door quickly, squinting thanks to the winter sun. I didn't want either of them to know I'd overheard what they said.

"Your Majesty," I said, sweeping into a bow. "Has Mistress Imogene gotten to you, too?"

The king blinked at me for a moment, taken by surprise. I'd barely interacted with him at all, cowed by the idea of him doing to me exactly what I deserved after harming Elora. Though he stood barely taller than me, his physique was true to any warrior, shoulders broad and muscled, clear to any observer, even beneath his thick cloak. Any time I'd been near him, I searched his face for similarities to her. The one thing which stood out to me every time was her smile, and it was gifted to me, albeit on his face, when he threw his head back and laughed.

"Nana put you boys to work?"

I couldn't stop myself as my brows shot up to my hairline. "Nana?" I sputtered.

"Oh, yes. She must see something in the two of you. She'd never let me call her anything else," he chuckled. "Unfortunately, I do not have time to help with whatever tasks she's assigned you. Theo, you'll have to make do on your own today. Tell Nana it was my fault."

From behind Rainier, Theo shot daggers at me before groaning and heading toward the stable by himself.

"Finally rifting me back to Folterra?" Even after what I'd overheard, in the back of my mind, I'd always wonder when my time had run out. Uprooted from place to place, I'd never known stability. How could I possibly expect it in enemy territory after I'd proven myself a wretch?

"Do you want to go back to Folterra?" He pressed his lips together, as if he wanted to speak, but stopped himself.

"One day, I suppose I'll be expected to, won't I? After the Three Kingdoms are rid of Declan? Unless this is all an elaborate ploy to—"

"It is no ploy, princeling. You're the one who—" He shook his head, glancing at the sky above us. "After Declan has been deposed, you will be king, and you will be expected to rule. Am I right in assuming you know very little about ruling?"

I plucked at the sleeve of my jacket before replying. "There was no need or desire—from both parties, to be fair. I never allowed myself to have any interest in it. Though, I recognize now that was a mistake."

Rubbing a hand over his brow, the king approached. He only looked a little younger than Declan, but I knew my brother outmatched him by at least a couple of centuries. Truth be told, I didn't know how old Declan was. The two men couldn't be more different. My brother was obsessed with his appearance—a single fleck of lint would ruin his entire week—while Rainier seemed to care very little. He wore comfortable clothing, not bothering with finery. And the shadow of a beard on his face would have made Declan ill.

"I make no judgments about what you know and what you do not. I knew very little at your age," the king said.

"Well, now Folterra is going to suffer more than it already has."

"A desire to avoid their suffering is half the battle. You can only be responsible for what you do. The wars of our ancestors can stop with us. I do not resent you as an Umbroth, just as I hope you do not resent me as a Vestana."

"No, no resentment. You've been far kinder to me than I had any right to experience."

"That we have." He raised an eyebrow, daring me to have a smart-mouthed retort. When I remained silent, he continued. "You only have two women to thank for your continued existence. If it were up to me, even now I don't know if I particularly like seeing your head attached to your neck. I need you to repay their kindness."

"Anything, of c-course," I stuttered, nervous.

"Well, firstly, I need to know. Do you regret it?" Jaw tight, he stared down at me, his temple throbbing.

"I haven't stopped regretting it. If I could go back and change it, I—" I shook my head. "Only the gods know how many times I prayed to take it all back. To let me start over. I would never have hurt her. I will never hurt her again, I swear to you."

"You speak as if you might be given the chance to harm her," he said, scowling. I hung my head as he exhaled slowly. When I chanced a glance at him, he only stared at me, arms crossed as he chewed on the inside of his cheek. Finally, he took a deep breath before continuing. "Emmeline and I have Ciarden's shadows, and you've had them your entire life, have you not?"

"Shortly after I was born, I'm told. One of my brothers startled me during a nap, and Magdalena could barely find me within the nursery."

"Do you remember them?" he asked, voice rough. It wasn't a secret that Declan killed nearly every person who could come for his crown.

"I remember Emmett. Sophia too. But none of the rest."

He grimaced. "You would have been quite small when they died."

I nodded before clearing my throat. "You and the queen need help mastering the shadows?"

"Yes. There's something else though." He pulled a parcel out of his jacket, handing it over. Small, the brown packaging around it crinkled in the quiet.

"What is this?" I asked, as he handed it over.

"I have one scholar who is working on this, but I don't want it widely known, not yet anyway. I know you were tutored in the Old Language, and—"

"How do you know that?"

"Spies, Cyran." He sighed heavily, and I felt rather brainless. "Besides, it is to be expected, as you are royalty. It's been twenty gods damn years since I was taught. I can only assume you remember far more than I do."

"Do you need it to be translated?" Curious, I unfolded a corner of the paper wrapping, and he stopped me with a shake of his head.

"Not here. And no, I don't need it translated in its entirety. There are a few pages at the beginning in the Old Language, handwritten. I'll do anything to have some sort of leg-up on your brother. I want you to just focus on the note. I have someone looking into more details about what the prophecy entails. He has far more resources than anyone I know. He's willing to work with you as well."

"Alright. I-I wasn't very good at the Old Language, but it was only a year or so ago. I'll certainly try." I dipped my head, not willing to make eye contact as I asked, "You trust me with this?"

"No." The blunt retort nearly pulled a laugh from my lungs. "But I don't trust anyone, and it just felt right to ask it of you. It might be a mistake, but if we are to rule together, there must be some sort of trust between us. For what you did to my child, I shouldn't trust you."

Shame. Complete and utter shame.

"And yet?"

He assessed me, arms crossed and brow furrowed. "I'm learning to trust my instincts. And for some gods forsaken reason, I feel compelled to put faith in the child who killed my daughter. It makes little sense, but here I am."

Not knowing what to say, I bowed my head and pocketed the book. "I'll have it to you as quick as I can. You can trust me. I'll swear a verit oath if you—"

"No time. Are you ready to begin?"

"Now?" I sputtered.

He nodded and opened a rift into the bookstore I'd frequented far too many times in hopes of seeing *her*.

"She wouldn't even look at me, Iz," I whined. After discovering my intuition was correct and Ismene was in Darkhold, she could tell something was wrong and refused to talk about anything else until I told her what it was.

"Well, you can't exactly blame her, can you? I'm honestly surprised she didn't stab you the minute she woke."

"I'm not so sure she wouldn't have if given the opportunity." I shook my head and blew out a breath. "Though I'm quite certain you enjoy calling me thickheaded, we have other things to discuss."

"Yes, and they're quite a bit less amusing, so humor me a while longer." Hazel eyes darker than mine stared just past my shoulder, and she absentmindedly braided her long black hair. She looked well, significantly better than she had the first time I'd visited her in an illusion. Even so, since she was in Darkhold, it couldn't be pleasant for her. I wanted to see her smile, so I gave in.

"The man at the bookstore, Reminy is his name, is quite timid, and he was forced to intervene with a rather nasty patron giving one of his clerks a tongue-lashing. We had been working on the, well—"

"The incredibly secret thing you cannot tell me about, yes, go on."

"And, well, the poor man. Iz, you know I had to say something!"

"Always getting yourself into trouble, big brother."

I rolled my eyes. "You know I hate when you call me that."

"I don't care," my sister said, grinning ear to ear. Her birthday had been a few weeks after mine, and it was the first one we hadn't spent together since before her mother died when we were ten.

"Well, anyway, this crotchety toad of a woman was mad because she'd bought a book and the second half of it was bound with missing pages or something, and the clerk went to replace it but there weren't any more—oh, none of this matters." I fluttered my hand in dismissal. "She was quite evil to them both, so I came out and told her to choke on a tit, and it was a whole ordeal. Then Elora came in with her guard, and she had the woman escorted out."

She stifled her laughter to ask, "And she didn't speak to you?"

"No!" I wiped my hand down my face, pacing. I hadn't bothered making a full illusion, only a sofa in front of a fire, so I couldn't quite see, but I didn't feel like using my divinity. "Reminy asked where Thyra was—that's her normal guard," I added, forgetful about which details I'd told my sister before. "And then she made herself scarce, hiding away in the back room."

"Well, did you go speak to her?"

"Why would I? She didn't even look at me."

"Was she wearing the bracelet?"

"I don't know; she was wearing a cloak."

"Sure, but didn't you feel if yours was warm or not? You had it enchanted, right?"

"I wasn't wearing mine."

"What?" she exclaimed.

"It's been too warm to wear. It got irritating."

"Cy! She's been wearing it? Have you appeared to her since that first one?"

"No," I mumbled, bracing myself for my sister's indignation. She stood, black nightgown rippling around her.

"That was a month ago! And she's been wearing it ever since? No wonder she wouldn't even look at you, you imbecile!"

"I just—I wanted to make sure she really forgives me," I confessed. "Not just because I told her a sad story about a sad prince who lived a sad, lonely life. I figured she'd come to me when she really forgave me, not just...out of pity."

"Cy," she breathed, shoulders dropping, fight leaving her frame. "When did you take your bracelet off?"

"A few days ago."

"Cyran Speelglen Umbroth—"

"Goddess, save me, do not call me—"

"She wore that gods forsaken bracelet for nearly a month, maybe more! Who knows? Not you, since you took it off!" Ismene shouted, crossing the distance and grabbing me by both arms. "She would have taken it off by now if it was just out of pity. She probably thinks, well, I don't know. But I'd have done the same thing if I'd been inviting someone into my dreams every night for a *month*, and he never showed up."

"I did show up."

"You just said you—"

"I've been helping with her nightmares, but I haven't exactly let her see me."

My sister's jaw dropped, and the light of the fire behind her flared as she stepped back.

"You love her."

"Well, maybe." I started. "I don't—"

"Oh, dear brother. She is going to *ruin* you." She gave me a soft smile as she tilted her head.

"She already has."

CHAPTER 49

Emmeline

"Truth," Lucia said, tossing a grape into her mouth and biting down as she leered toward Dewalt, her teeth vicious and snapping. He shoved her away at the shoulder, and she laughed, tossing her head back. White, silky hair, iridescent in the setting sun, fell back from her shoulders. Dewalt poked her in the rib, and she swatted his hand away. His gaze rested on her for a moment longer, and I could tell she had grown uncomfortable in his perusal. "I'm fine, stop," she whispered, and I wondered what she meant.

"What's the first thing you'll do as queen?" I asked, leaning back onto my palms. The five of us had been in the meadow for hours, lazing about and drinking Nythyrian wine, and we'd only just decided to take a break from the hot sun, meandering over to the creek and the shade the willow gave us. I was getting drowsy. I was glad she picked truth, or I would've had to think of something for her to do. The question rolled off my tongue easily, the answer something I'd wanted to know for a while.

"When I'm queen? Skipping the princess part, are we?"

"My father is as old as dirt; it won't be long," Lavenia laughed, tugging her knees to rest beneath her chin as she wrapped her arms around her legs. "Besides, you can't really do anything as a princess," she lamented.

"Fine. Let me think," Lucia grumbled. She sat across from me, legs tucked in such a way she looked regal, even if she was sun-drenched and worn out like the rest of us.

"You already told me some of what you want to do," Rain interjected, leaning forward, elbows resting on his knees. It bothered me she'd told him and not me. She'd been increasingly distant over the past few months, not talking to me much at all. And it bothered me even more they were having conversations without me. I had no right to be upset though. But still. I thought it was going to be different, now that he'd kissed me beneath the same willow tree under which we now sat. But in front of the others, he was unchanged. To me, everything had changed. And it wasn't as if we'd only kissed the once. No, we had been sneaking back here for weeks now, progressively more careless about it than the time before. Fumbling hands had laid waste to each line we drew for ourselves, and the only thing keeping me from doing more with him was because I knew it would kill me to have to stop. And one day, we'd be forced to. I never wanted to experience that pain with him.

Dewalt cleared his throat, and I glanced over, drawn out of my jealous confusion. He stared at me with unwavering eye contact, head lifted high. It made me wonder if he knew.

"What's that?" I asked. "What—what did you say you'd do?" I demanded of my sister, reminded of how annoyed I was with her for not telling me things.

She made a face, crossing her eyes at Rain. "Outlaw the Myriad robes. All that white? It's unsettling. But that's not a real answer."

"No, it's not," I agreed.

"Well, what would you do?" she snarked.

"I-I've never thought about it," I stammered, doing my best not to look at Rain. Gods, if he thought I'd ever considered... I knew what I was to him. A friend he liked to kiss, to pass the time. He'd be with my sister, and that would be it. I didn't want him suspecting I thought more about us than I should. My feelings and how they'd grown didn't matter.

"Liar," Rain said, turning toward me from where he sat beside me. Heat rose up my chest, blanketing my skin in humiliation before he continued. "Everyone has thought about how we would rule. Even Dewalt," he added.

"Yes, I've thought quite a lot about what I'd do if I became queen. I think the dresses will look much better on me than they would on any of you," Dewalt said, grinning at each of us while Rain laughed beside me. Lavenia groaned, throwing grass at both of them.

"Go on, Em. I know you've thought about it."

The warmth I exuded based on that one syllable, his nickname for me on his full, kissable lips, was almost too much to bear. It would be obvious to anyone who looked at me exactly what I was thinking.

"I, uh, well, I'm just one of a lot—" I cleared my throat and wrung my hands in my lap. "I know there aren't so many conduits left anymore, but there are a fair amount of healers," I started, feeling silly around the four of them. They were more powerful or rare than I was by a long shot.

"And?" Lucia pressed, encouraging me to continue. If there was one thing I knew about my sister, it was that she believed in me. She'd never doubted me in all my life. We'd argued and had our spats—sometimes I wondered if she didn't enjoy having me as a sister—but she never made me feel as if my ideas or dreams were lesser for not being as divinely blessed as the rest of them.

"Well, I think it's rather cruel for healers to charge for their services." Feeling Rain's gaze on my face made me nervous. We'd talked a bit about these types of things before—he was my best friend, after all—but we'd never talked about me. The ways the Crown could enact change was a frequent topic, but this was something I could do, with or without his help. "It tires me, certainly, but our ancestors were blessed with the ability to heal, and I received those gifts. It seems a waste not to use it, don't you think?" When no one spoke for a moment, I panicked, feeling the need to fill the silence, and my eyes caught my sister's. "I know I'm not truly blessed like you and Rain—Rainier—"

"An ordinary conduit like the rest of us," Ven interjected, laughing, and she broke the tension, all while Lucia studied me. When my sister cocked her head to the side, her eyes glazed over for just a moment before a small smile curled up one side of her mouth.

"I think if anyone could do something like that, it would be you." Sincere and soft, my sister's voice soothed my nerves.

"She's right, Em. And you three aren't just ordinary conduits," Rain murmured, a mild frown crossing his features.

"Besides," Lucia said, "I've never been able to heal anything more than a papercut. Your divinity is far more useful than mine. You all have more useful divinity than me and Rainier." She cast a glance over at Dewalt, something in her voice sounding like a plea, and I wasn't sure what it meant. When he wouldn't look at her, her attention fell back on the two royals. "You know, it's quite unfair neither of you inherited the siphoning."

"Thank the gods," Lavenia said. "We'd have to deal with Mother more if we did."

"Rainier is powerful enough without being able to siphon. Between the earthquakes and the divine fire, no one will stand a chance against the two of you," Dewalt said as he stood, abruptly starting for his horse grazing in the meadow.

"Come back here, scoundrel," Lucia called out, bounding after him. He started running, a laugh echoing on the breeze as his hair fanned out behind him.

It wasn't long before Lavenia followed, shouting at them to wait for her. With just Rain and me left beneath the willow tree, the mood shifted, the air growing thick with something.

"I didn't know you wanted to donate your divinity like that," he murmured, laying back and clasping his hands over his stomach.

"Not just mine. I'd love if others would too. And it doesn't have to stop at healing. I don't know. Dewalt could weave visions for people who are bedridden or—or Lavenia could make murderers confess..." I trailed off, feeling a bit ashamed of my excitement. It was unlikely for such a change to be enacted, let alone by someone like me.

"Well, we have some conduits who compel criminals already, but you're right. More conduits could put their divinity to work for the good of the kingdom."

I laid back on the grass beside him before he grunted and pulled me over, nestling me in the crook of his arm. It wasn't the first or even the second time we'd laid under the willow tree like this, but every time it made my heart beat wildly out of my chest, certain he could hear it. His never sped up quite like mine did, and I wondered if it was because he didn't care as much about me as I did him. If this didn't mean the same thing to him as it did to me.

"What's the first thing you'll do as king?" I asked, shifting to press more of my body against his. It was summer and hot and we both smelled faintly of sweat, but I had quickly become addicted to him. I couldn't get enough. He'd been my best friend for a while, but something had changed between us during all those long nights at his telescope, during shared glances and quiet moments. And once he finally kissed me? It was all over for me. I didn't—couldn't—think about how it would have to end eventually, wouldn't dare dream it might last. Until then, I'd soak up every moment with him I could. I knew in the back of my mind I wasn't being very kind to my heart, but I didn't care.

He sighed, bringing his hand up to massage my scalp. It took all I had to keep from making a noise of content. "The first thing I'll do will be bury my father, I suppose."

"You know what I meant," I said, lightly smacking his chest. His other hand drifted up, and he weaved his fingers through my own, holding both of our hands over his heart.

"I know. I've just been so hung up on what not to do, how not to be like him, that I haven't thought too much about what I'd actually do. I don't want to be like him, Em."

"You won't be."

"But what if I am?"

"You won't be." I shook my head, adamant. "You couldn't be like him. I'm sure it will be a lot to think about at first, but you'll figure it all out. I believe in you."

"I won't even know where to start, really. I imagine it will be quite lonely," he said.

"Well, I suppose you'll have Lucia—"

"You'd be better at it than she would."

I stilled, unsure of what to say. Not allowing myself to look into it too much, I pulled my hand off his chest and sat up, adjusting my dress. He followed suit, running his fingers through my hair and tracing his fingertips down my back as he spoke.

"Don't get me wrong; she'll be great at most of it. The people will love her, she's a beacon of peace and prosperity and all that. But I think she expects it all just to fall into her lap from the gods. You wouldn't be afraid to put in effort and thought. You already have more ideas about how to improve things than I do. I wish you were the—"

"If wishes and dreams meant anything, I'd let you finish that sentence," I interrupted, a tightness in my chest making my teeth clench. His hand met my cheek, turning me to look at him with a gentle touch.

"I wish you could be my queen, want it to be you. I could see you wearing a crown."

He pressed his lips to mine, soft, and pulled away when I didn't kiss him back, confusion in his eyes.

"The difference is one day, you will wear a crown. You on the throne? That's inevitable," I explained. "You can't say things like that to me, Rain. You'll give me hope."

"Hope for what?" he asked, a grin spreading on his face, and I didn't know why it would make him smile.

"Hope that this could happen." I gestured. "Us. It's not fair. It's already bad enough I have to think about you and Lucia—"

"You'd want an 'us' to happen?" I wouldn't look at him as I nodded, staring down at the ground. Mortified to have to admit I wanted more from him, I bit my lip. He cupped my jaw, reaching his thumb across my lip and freeing it from my teeth. "Don't think about any of that. Think about this," he said, leaning in and kissing me again. Thoroughly. His hand slid to my neck, pulling me closer. His other hand rested on my waist, and he tugged me toward him, eventually settling me in his lap. I let myself give in to his touch, the sweet caress of his mouth on mine. It wouldn't last forever, this easiness between us, this madness which had me straddling his lap and aching for more.

"Maybe, Em, maybe we—" he whispered against my lips before stopping himself. "I've never felt this way about someone before."

"You've never felt like kissing someone before?" I hedged.

"I've never felt as if I could spend every moment with someone, and it wouldn't be enough. As if the sky could crash down around us, and I wouldn't care."

I lifted my hand, brushing one of his curls off his forehead. I was unusually aware of my body; my skin felt flushed, and my heart hammered in my chest. To allow myself to be told such beautiful things when I knew the truth of the matter was *torturous, and yet I couldn't wait to hear the next thing he'd allow to pass over his perfect, damning lips.*

"Em, I think I'm in—" *I cut him off, pressing my lips to his, not allowing him to say the one thing which would cut me the deepest once this was all over. I cupped his face with both my hands, allowing myself to do as I wished. I'd grown quite adept at kissing him, but we'd always stopped, panting and unfulfilled, before anything more. And I decided something, then and there. If he loved me and I couldn't let him say it, I wanted to show him with my body that I felt the same. But he broke off our kiss as I rolled my hips on him, his breath a gasp and his words frantic.* "Not here. The cavern. Tonight," *he whispered, eyes searching mine. I took a quick breath, uncertain of everything else. Everything except this one thing.*

"Tonight."

I had forgotten so many of our conversations, our tender moments wrapped up in each other that spring and summer. Rain had been so focused on not becoming his father, and yet it was one of the first things I accused him of when I came back into his life. He'd been so worried about it, he hadn't had any time to think about what his life would be like and what he could do with only the council to stop him. And yet, he'd grown into a leader as the Crown Prince, doing things his way before he even had the full power of the Crown. He'd won the approval and love of the people of Vesta long before the coronation; the ceremony the day before had merely been a formality. It was probably a relief for him he'd behaved as a king all along, and now he had no limits to enact everything he wanted.

The memory wasn't a sad one, not in the way it could have been, and I had allowed it to guide me along the halls of the palace, following the golden tether on my soul, knowing he was at the other end. It was late, the lantern in my hand the only barrier between me and a pitch-black corridor. I realized halfway down the hall I could have held light in my palm, but, by then, it was too late. When I stepped into the throne room, I looked down the steps and found him sitting similar to the way I'd imagined so many times before.

In my imagination, Rainier had forever been twenty years old, sitting with one foot pulled up, arm resting on a knee, and a crown falling off his head. The real vision wasn't too far off. He wasn't wearing the crown, and one leg was crossed over the other, still just as relaxed as he'd always been in my mind. His gaze didn't move up from the floor, but I saw his lips tip up in a smile and felt a faint hint of amusement down the bond as I made my way down the stairs.

"You found me," he said.

"Were you hiding?" I asked, tracing my gaze over the tilt of his head, the arch of his neck, the long line of his leg.

"No, dear heart. Not hiding. Ruminating."

"Oh?" I sat on the edge of the dais, gathering my nightgown and robe to sit delicately.

"You have a seat beside me, you know," he grumbled, staring pointedly until I moved to the throne beside him. "Better. I like you sitting there."

"Did Cyran say yes?"

"I don't think he felt he had much choice, but yes. He got straight to work with Reminy. I found my old text from back when I was taught, and I'm hoping it helps him."

"On the Old Language?" My jaw dropped as he nodded. "You just...lent that to a Folterran prince? You do realize how rare that book probably is, right?"

"I can do what I want now, remember?" He chuckled, though it felt hollow.

"What were you ruminating on, love?"

"The path we took to get here. The gods couldn't have made it any harder on us, could they?"

I tucked my legs up beneath me, turning on the throne beside him. It had been surreal, seated there beside him, the same diadem I'd worn for our wedding resting far heavier on my head than it was in reality. Even in my wildest dreams of Rain and a future we could have created together, I had never once imagined being his queen. I'd imagined him as king countless times. I'd imagined him seated on a throne, though the one in real life was far less impressive than the one in my mind. It had been massive, gilded and ostentatious, like the ones in Elora's storybooks. Though it was still impressive, almost large enough for us to sit side by side, it still wasn't as grand as I'd always dreamed. I'd also never pictured a queen's throne beside it. Even when Lucia had been alive, I'd never once seen her seated beside him. Rain had been alone in every version I'd imagined; I wondered if it was because I'd wanted him to be alone if it couldn't be me, or if it was an act of self-preservation. Putting my elbow up on the arm of the throne—*my* throne—I rested my chin in my hand and gazed upon my husband. Rainier Vestana, a king of the Three Kingdoms, and owner of my mind, body, and soul. I could have wept.

"They say it is pressure and hardship which makes the most precious of gems," I said.

He grunted in assent, turning toward me, and the thin glint of moonlight coming in from above illuminated a sheen in his eyes.

"I've changed my mind. I want you sitting here." He rubbed his palm down his thigh, and I was reminded of the thick layer of corded muscle beneath his breeches. I stood, leaving my robe on my own throne, nearly giggling to myself at the sheer absurdity of it.

"Do you remember that day beneath the willow? The last day?" I asked, perching myself on his knee, sitting daintily in his lap. The throne we sat upon was older than King Soren; I was afraid of breaking it. But Rain wasn't having any of it, using his strong grip to move my legs to either side of his own, a symmetry to the memory I'd mentioned. The soft velvet of the fabric seat felt nice where it touched the skin of my bare leg, my nightgown sliding up as we adjusted.

"Do I remember the last day we had together before it all went to shit? Yes," he said, amusement clear even with his dry tone.

"Do you remember what we talked about?"

"You'd told us about wanting to help people with your divinity, and I told you I wanted you as my queen." I leaned forward and pressed my lips to his forehead, and he grinned up at me. "It appears the gods have listened to at least a few things I've asked for."

"We also talked about how much you didn't want to be like him, like your father."

"We did, yes."

"I'm sorry I ever compared you to him."

"You already apologized for this," he said, leaning forward to trace his lips over my jaw as he spoke. "And I've forgiven you for everything—from the moment I met you until the moment I draw my last breath. You don't need to apologize."

"I know. Still. I'm sorry I ever—" At the look on his face, I cut myself off, shaking my head. "What you did at the Cascade and with Clearhill...it has to hurt knowing Folterra holds it now. And after what happened in the fall."

"The people are safe. That's what matters. Raj and Dewalt did everything right."

"They did what you'd taught them to do, trusted them to do, expected them to do. You've been a king far longer than Soren has been dead." He dipped his head, pulling my sleeve down and tracing my tattoo with reverie, his lips and tongue moving in tandem to worship my skin. "My king," I whispered.

"I was going to tell you I was in love with you that day. But—"

"But I wouldn't let you."

"I regretted never saying it," he murmured, hands sliding up and down my sides, caressing the curve of my hips up to my waist.

"I regretted not letting you. You know, in all my imaginings of you on your throne one day, there was never anyone at your side."

"Because you knew it could only ever be you."

"Did you ever picture anyone else?"

"You should know by now, Em. If I ever thought of anyone, it was always you. But I did imagine this," he said. Dipping his head once more, he pressed soft lips to my collarbone.

"Kissing me?" I teased, my hands tracing his shoulders.

"Taking you. Right here. In this very spot." His hands gripped my hips tight, and he nipped at my exposed skin.

"Tell me more," I said, letting my head tip back as his mouth moved upward toward my neck.

"My mind is rather creative, but it always starts out with me kissing you as if I'll never be able to again."

"A good start," I affirmed, tilting his head up with my hands and doing just that. My thumbs caressed his cheeks as I deepened our kiss. Sliding my tongue against his, he opened for me and matched my movements. Our kiss grew more persistent, desperation for one another clear. His hands drifted, lazily brushing over my back, pushing my hair behind my shoulders, caressing my ribs, always moving. My own slid down his neck to his shoulders, the movements in complete opposition to the frenzied kisses we shared. Heat built between my legs, and I could feel his hardened length between us. Gasping for breath, I pulled away before resting my forehead against his.

"And what comes next?" I panted.

"Usually one of two things," he said, mischief in his crooked smile. "I either use my tongue on that sweet cunt until you scream my name or you take me in your mouth and make me forget mine."

"I think we have time for both," I said as I slid down off of his lap onto my knees, unfastening his breeches and tugging at his pants before he could get a word in. He lifted his hips with a soft grunt, and he unbuttoned his shirt as I tugged his breeches down. Moments later, the image of his strong, naked body on the throne of one of the most powerful kingdoms our world had ever known made my thoughts go erratic. My divinity heaved in my chest, a cool breeze whipping away shadows from my fingertips.

From my knees, I shouldn't have felt as powerful as I did, but every great king required an equal partner. And he'd announced me as such by choosing me, I'd proved it by saving him, and the people had accepted it based on their cheers of approval in the streets the day before. If I had earned the unyielding love and the look he wore on his face, I was just as powerful on my knees as I was on the throne beside him.

I grasped him in hand, swiping the bead of moisture with my thumb as I swirled it over the thick head of his cock. He closed his eyes on a sigh, a smile curling up the edges of his lips. Both of his hands moved to grip the arms of the throne, and he leaned back, positioning his hips closer to me. I moved nearer, spreading his legs so I could sit between them. There was a balance here—in the vulnerability which came from submitting to one another in this way, we found power.

Sliding my hand down, I dipped forward, licking up the side of his length, sucking and tonguing a path up the evidence of his arousal. And when I took just the tip between my lips, he shuddered, exhaling roughly.

"Gods, your mouth will be my fucking ruin," he growled, knuckles white as he held onto the throne.

Our eyes met, and I held his gaze as I took him deeper, my hand sliding down the length of him to work in tandem. He watched me, enraptured, eyes aflame with lust and life. Using one hand to tenderly tuck my hair behind an ear, his hips twitched upward, and everything between us boiled down to this—trust, understanding, and this gentleness existing alongside our desire and passion.

His soft sigh as he closed his eyes was enough to turn me single-minded toward bringing rapture to his body. We'd had such peace since our visit to Ravemont, and our few days back in Astana had already taken their toll on him. He was weary, and the responsibility of our roles weighed far heavier on him than they did on me. While I learned my place, attempting to understand how I could assist him with the kingdom, I would help release the tension in other ways.

I bobbed my head up and down, using my hand to help with the length of him. His breathing grew ragged, and his thigh shook. I massaged it with my free hand, and I felt the most exquisite roll of affection down the bond. It glowed bright between us, strong and shining. It had never been so firm, even before everything happened at the Cascade. Gentle fingertips traced my brow before he gathered up my hair with both hands, allowing a glimpse of the precious ink which announced my devotion.

"How are you mine? You're so beautiful, I don't even know what to do with you," he whispered. I took him deeper until I felt the press of him against the back of my throat. He moaned, ending the sound with a curse, and he gave the most gentle press of his hips, clearly holding himself back. Still, I took him, swallowing, until I felt a tear run down the side of my face. Breaking free for just a moment to gasp a breath of air, I wiped spit off my chin before continuing my efforts, more forcefully than before, pressing him farther back with each downward motion. I picked up my pace, squeezing a bit tighter with my hand until he was cursing again. One hand still held my hair while his other grasped the throne once more.

"Divine hell, you're so good. So *fucking* good, Em," he panted. "I need to taste you."

But when he reached for me, I pressed my palm against his abdomen, pushing him back and holding him in place. He'd never finished in my mouth before, and I didn't know why I wanted it so badly in that moment, but I did. I didn't want there to be anything unknown between us.

"Em, I'm going to—"

"I know," I said, popping him out of my mouth for a second before replacing it, continuing my effort in earnest. I wanted to taste him. And a moment later, his hands gripped the armrests, and he grunted, moaning my name as he spilled down my throat. I swallowed him greedily, gently running my nails up his thighs, shivers and chill following in the wake of my fingertips.

"It would seem I'm the one who did the taking," I said, beaming up at him as he collapsed back into himself.

"Only a goddess should have this type of power, dear heart," he replied, and I laughed, standing and wiping my mouth. His heart was still beating quickly as he tilted his head back and closed his eyes. "Come here—I want to look at you."

I stepped between his legs as he leaned forward, lifting my nightgown at the hem and tugging it over my head. He surprised me when he wrapped both his arms around me, pressing a kiss between my breasts and holding himself there.

"Could die happy here. So soft," he murmured, pressing kisses to my skin as he withdrew from me, sliding his hands down my sides, rough palms grazing my body. I felt his length twitch against the front of my leg.

"Already?" I asked, and he laughed.

"Almost. It doesn't take me long with you," he said, and his gaze turned searing as his hands slid down, thumbs tracing over my sides and stomach, the pressure of his fingertips changing as he found the smoother skin, scars of my body's growth and change. His touch was lighter—reverent, almost.

"Did they hurt when you got them?" he asked, and the only thing keeping me from laughing aloud was his expression and the grave seriousness I felt down the bond. And as silly as it was for him to ask, I didn't want him to be ashamed of such an innocent question.

"They did not hurt. They itched a bit sometimes, but no. It happens slowly enough it doesn't hurt."

"I wish I was there to rub lotion on you," he said. Fingers hitching into my underwear, he slid them down until they fell at my feet, and I stepped out.

"I wish you were there too, and I'm sorry you weren't."

"Don't say sorry. Can I hold you for a minute?" he asked.

Wordlessly, I moved, and he situated me across his lap, my upper body turned to curl into his. Though the throne room wasn't cold, it wasn't warm by any means, and I needed him closer. I felt his cock twitch against my leg again, growing more insistent, but he ignored it, nuzzling into my neck.

"I'll never waste another moment with you. I'll never take any of it for granted," he said, voice low.

"Neither will I," I promised.

One of his hands slid down, squeezing my backside before he adjusted me, bringing my back to his chest. His other hand moved, tracing gently over my hip, down to where I knew I was wet, my body eager. His cock stood erect between where my legs rested, ready for me. When one fingertip circled my clit, the touch a weightless tease, I tilted my head back, resting it against his shoulder. I loved being with him like this. Tender moments when time stopped and it was just the two of us. Just him, pressing a kiss above my ear, inhaling as he did.

Moving his touches down farther, he teased my entrance before dragging my wetness back to my clit, rubbing more thoroughly. And, though I knew he wanted to taste me, and I'd said we had plenty of time, my patience had worn thin. Reaching down, I grasped his length, moving him up as I slid forward. Using one hand to grip the throne for balance, I notched him at my entrance. When I'd moved, his hand had fallen away from my clit, and he grabbed me by the waist, helping me find my balance as I slowly lowered myself down atop him. Legs spread on either side of his, I braced myself as I moved while he guided me.

"Gods, I love when you take what you want," he groaned, gripping me tight as I leisurely slid down his length. I was in no rush, wanting to draw out the pleasure for as long as I could. Glancing over my shoulder, the light of the moon shone down on him, illuminating the adoration and need etched in his face. Jaw tight, he grunted as I lowered myself completely, circling my hips before stilling. I rested there, fully filled with him, and he leaned forward, pressing a kiss to my spine.

"What I want is you. Always has been," I said. And it was true. I'd have spent the rest of my days wishing things had been different and feeling guilty for every errant thought about him. I never escaped them for long either. It would have been miserable.

He slid down a bit further in the throne, giving himself more leverage to push up into me. I continued, lifting and lowering upon him—slow. He gripped my hips, supporting me. His grasp on my skin was bruising, punishing almost, as if he was holding back with every bit of his control. He let me continue my slow pace, movements languid. I knew eventually he'd lose control, unable to stop himself. But I continued to slowly bounce atop him, and his little breaths of pleasure spurred me on until I picked up my speed.

I paused, my foot slipping on the ground, and he took the opportunity to wrap both arms around me and tug me backward onto his chest. One hand slid down to touch where he sat within me, his fingertips rubbing circles on my sensitive clit as he held me tight. A gentle nibble on my ear sent goosebumps across my flesh, and my body warmed against his, sinking back into his embrace.

"You're everything I could ever want," he said. "And you're mine." He punctuated his words with gentle upward thrusts, and I writhed atop him. With his fingertips circling me, bringing me closer and closer to that precipice, his thick cock filling me so deep, I closed my eyes as his other hand came up to massage my breast. He held me that way, pressing up into me slowly and surely, as I relaxed against him. A rightness came over me—an absolute certainty which I'd only started to realize was content. I'd never felt so loved and satisfied in my life.

He moved my hair out of the way, enabling him to press his lips to my neck. I felt my body tighten around him, tension rising and breath shaking, and he could sense it too. He changed nothing about what he was doing, maintaining the perfect pressure and pace. I couldn't help it as I started moaning, the sound echoing in the large chamber, my cries of pleasure bouncing off the stone walls. I brought both my feet up to the edge of the throne, opening my legs up wider for his access, and I ground down on his cock as his hand moved in a frenzy. A tingling started from where our bodies met, spreading upward and outward. Everything tensed within me, and Rain pushed deep, holding me at the ideal angle as he rubbed that spot. My body pulsed, and my legs began to twitch, the pleasure too much. My hips bucked, my natural instinct to pull myself away from the demanding rapture. Panting his name, I allowed my head to loll against him.

"Calling my name so sweetly while you're squeezing my cock so tight?" He growled against my neck, sending shivers down my spine. "My wicked little thing."

I shuddered as he withdrew and drove into me again during the muscle spasms and the gasping, my breath catching in my throat as he drew out the sensation. When I tried to snap my legs shut, he used one hand to hold my thigh while the other continued its assault on my clit.

"Take it, Em, take the pleasure like you take me. Come for me," he commanded.

The ground shook as I obeyed, the overwhelming crash causing my legs to shake and my body to jerk forward as my moans turned into a scream. Pinpricks of gold appeared in my vision as I closed my eyes, our bond shining bright. There was a loud crash behind us, something shattering as it fell. I jumped, about to climb to my feet as Rain pulled me back and started laughing.

"That must have been quite good for you," he said, chuckling even as he continued pushing up into me. The sensation was too much—I was still so sensitive, and my leg twitched. "That was all you, dear heart. You probably just destroyed one of the statues."

"I did?" I gasped. "Oh, no."

He laughed. "I don't care about them. You'll get used to making the ground shake. I plan to keep pleasuring you to that point as often as possible."

I swatted at his arm, and he pushed up into me again, causing a moan to rip free from my chest. Leaning forward, I pulled myself off of him, turning before settling into his lap once more.

"I like seeing the look on your face when you come," I said, leaning forward to lick his lower lip. He grabbed himself, lining up his cock with my body, before he slammed me down onto him. My head dropped back, and his hands gripped me once more, tight as he held me in place. His hold guided my body, moving me up and down his length, until he groaned with frustration.

"What is it?" I asked, just as he stood, a small grunt crossing his lips as he picked me up and walked to the edge of the dais. "Am I too heavy?"

"Don't insult me," he quipped.

Wrapping my arms and legs around him, I held on tight as he turned, laughter on my lips. He dropped to a knee, gently laying me down on the steps leading up to the thrones. I leaned back on my elbows, my hair splaying on the dais behind me.

"Couldn't fuck you like I need to and still see your face," he grumbled, dropping his body to mine, covering me, before sliding into me once more. I moaned, and then he was moving. Rough pounding thrusts, deeper and more aggressive than the gentle way I'd ridden him, had me grabbing onto his shoulders. My nails scraped down his skin as he slammed into me, my mouth open on a silent scream.

"Oh, gods," I panted, biting my lip. The flare of gold on the edges of my vision, those beautiful gilded threads, drew my attention, and I closed my eyes. Though my skin hadn't begun to glow, my eyes did when I opened them, but it was all the better so I could see the face of the man who took heaving breaths above me, staring down at me reverently.

"Beautiful, Em," he breathed, placing a soft kiss to my forehead as his hips moved in opposition, nothing tender about it. I mirrored his movements, doing my best to meet each thrust. A step dug into my back, and I didn't care, grabbing him to better pull him toward me. He dipped his head, lips grazing over the lilacs on my skin, harsh breaths panting. His hand dipped to my thigh, pulling it up around his waist, caressing the length of my leg as he moved it. His rhythm grew stuttered and soft grunts spilled from his lips, his brows drawing together. I pulled his face to mine, kissing him with abandon, until I felt him pulse inside me. Gasping for breath, his mouth open and eyes closed, he pumped his body into mine, filling me. When his jerking hips stilled, he dipped his head lower, all but collapsing atop me.

"My queen," he murmured into my shoulder. I closed my eyes, letting myself dwell in the moment, before staring up at the stars through the skylight above. I couldn't tell which constellation I looked at, but that didn't matter. I'd love him beneath it all the same.

CHAPTER 50

Rainier

"What's this?" she asked, toeing the rubble from the statue she'd broken. Back in her robe, hair a tangled mess down her back, I watched her as I tugged my breeches back on. Between her breaking a statue and my ass somehow detaching the cushion on the throne, the entire room was in a state. I couldn't help my grin over it. I hadn't been allowed in this room until I came into my divinity, and I would have had my ass singed if there was any damage done. We'd done more to it in an hour than had probably been done in the past thousand years.

Pants on and barefoot, I approached, glad she'd slipped her shoes back on before coming to inspect.

"I believe it was Larke."

"No, I know," she said, melancholy emanating from her. "What's *that*?"

Pulling divine light into her hand, she gestured toward the base of the statue. Larke's disembodied stone hand still clutched a likeness of a rolled-up piece of parchment, evidence of the treaty broken by her demise. Most of her arms were in tiny pieces on the ground, but the rest of the statue remained intact.

Bending over to grab the piece, ready to tell Em what it was, I stiffened when I saw the stone treaty was open, a hole no bigger than my fingertip at the end of it. Bringing it closer to Em, using her divine light to see, I heard her intake of breath when she saw what I did. There was a tightly rolled scroll shoved within the hollow interior. I took a closer look at the opening, realizing it wasn't broken, but there was a spot for a lid. I didn't know how many times I'd seen that damn statue, not even realizing there was a hidden compartment.

"Can you try to get it out?" I asked her, knowing her smaller fingers would be better suited for the task. After letting her divine light fall away and leading me to the center of the dais to use the moonlight, I held up the piece of statue as she got to work.

"We're going to be lucky if I can get this out in one piece, Rain."

"I know. What do you think it is?"

"Maybe a copy of the treaty?"

"That would be pointless."

"What else could it be?" she whispered, tugging cautiously. It was a tight fit, and the scroll had opened a bit inside the thin opening, so she had to be gentle with it.

"Maybe something about what happened with Larke?"

"I've always wondered…" Suddenly excited at the prospect of an answer to the five hundred-year-old mystery, she perked up, a small smile curving her sensuous mouth. I let myself stare at her as I held the heavy stone, and she made incremental progress.

Being with her in the quiet dark, doing something which felt an awful lot like something I wasn't supposed to be doing, reminded me of those long nights at Crown Cottage. Sneaking around, stealing wine and moments with her. Gods, I had loved her for so long, and it took me far too long to realize it. Everything would have been different if I only spoke up sooner. I dismissed the thought just as quickly as it had come. We were going to have to stop thinking about the past. All it did was haunt.

Finally finished, Em pulled the scroll free, dropping to her knees in front of me for the second time that night, and I took a moment to adjust my already hardening cock as I placed the broken piece of statue back with the rest of the debris. She was going to be the death of me.

By the time I returned, she was gently unrolling the scroll in the patch of moonlight from above.

"It's hard to read. If you want to hold it open, I'll use my light. Unless you want to try?"

I shook my head. Though we'd practiced since Ravemont, I didn't have nearly the level of control she did. It was humbling and amazing to see how much better she was than me; and she made it look so simple. The healing came more naturally to me than the light, though I still wasn't as good as her. Kneeling, I held the parchment open, careful not to be too rough with it. It was small, barely wide enough to warrant it being wrapped so tightly. Her eyes must have been better than mine though, because I could barely even see the writing on the page.

Once she held the fire in her hand beside me, we both leaned over it, trying to make out the words.

My sweet star,

I know now you … received my letter. If only I could have … … after it happened, perhaps you wouldn't have done this. Perhaps you … have chosen to take the only light in my life away from me. And ... I do not know what to do with myself. How can I be ex ... ... to ... ... on? I would have loved ... and the ... even if it belonged to him. I would have done anything .... I know you know this now. If only you knew sooner. ... I think you knew, and you did this anyway. Those are my weakest, angry moments. Please ... give me for them. I will forever mourn the ... of your light.

S.

Though parts of it were illegible, the gist of the note was clear.

"Is S..." Em trailed off, sitting back on her heels, dropping her fire and looking to me for an answer.

"It has to be. My father had to have written this."

"Alright, alright. Imagine a candle," Elora said. "It's steady, right? It's not flashing or smoldering or, I don't know, doing whatever it was you just did."

I snorted, rubbing my palms down my thighs. Elora and I sat facing each other, cross-legged, on the floor of the living area in my estate. She'd chosen to be near the fireplace, *'just in case,'* she said, as if the proximity to a place meant for fire would keep me from burning down my home. It would've been better to sit in the bathing suite with the water running. At least I was skilled with that. The light had come second nature to Em, but she struggled to put words to her guidance. Elora had overheard, gleefully ready to help. The relief down the bond Em felt was quickly controlled, and she cast a sheepish smile in my direction. I wasn't pressed about it, more than willing to spend time with our daughter. Em picked up on it too, offering to check in with the prince and Reminy who worked tirelessly in the bookstore.

"A candle, yes. Steady."

"Now, I can't make my flame quite as big as Mama, and I know Aunt Lucia's divinity was different too. Who knows if yours is the same as ours? It could make it harder to master. I don't know. But, the important part is the control. When you use your divinity, you have to be calm about it. It's..." She trailed off, rubbing her forehead in frustration, and the gesture was so much like her mother, my heart warmed. "I'm not explaining this very well."

"I understand what you mean. I don't have to think about my divinity when I use it, but I do struggle to rift when I'm anxious or frightened. Let me try again."

I closed my eyes, centering myself, putting both hands on my knees. Palms up, I breathed deeply as I summoned the divinity within me to bring forth the light. It was attached to the bond between me and Em, firmly entrenched in our connection. Every bit of her divinity I could use was dependent on it. When our bond was thready and unstable after I returned from Darkhold, her divinity had been difficult to use. But now, it had never been stronger, so I shouldn't have had any trouble with it. Although, perhaps that was exactly why I struggled; I'd never experienced it at full capacity.

"That's it, you're doing it!" Elora's sweet voice sang, and I grinned with my eyes closed, trying to stay centered and keep it going for as long as I could. I felt the warmth of the fire on my skin. "Bigger," she said, and I attempted to grow the flame as I was told. "No, not bigger, no, no, *taller*," she corrected, and the heat in front of my face told me I had redirected as she wanted. "Alright, tiny flame now, no bigger than a thimble."

The last order was more difficult than the rest; coaxing all that divinity back down into a small flame took significantly more effort than creating the flames to begin with.

"Now put it out!" She sounded so thrilled with my progress, I opened my eyes early, watching as the flames extinguished in my hand. And when I did it successfully, she squealed, lunging forward and hugging me. I froze for just a moment, completely unsure of what to do, before I wrapped my arms around her—lightly—and hugged her back. She smelled like summer and youth, and gods damn, it took everything in me to control my overwhelming emotions before she ended the embrace.

"You did it!" She beamed as she sat back on her heels. "I think we've probably done enough for one day. That's how burns happen, and I don't know how good you are at healing yet." She laughed, and I stood, pulling her to her feet with me.

"Thank you for helping me." I looked down at her and resisted the urge to pull her in for another hug. I'd done well at letting her lead things, and it seemed to serve us well. I didn't want to ruin it now.

"We can work on it again tomorrow?" she asked, hopeful. She *wanted* to help me.

"After your training with Dewalt and Theo?" She made a face and rolled her eyes, a noncommittal shrug completing the reaction. "Is that so?" I asked, chuckling.

"I'm not very good with a sword. It's heavy, and I would much rather use my divinity. And Theo is a bit overbearing," she added, glancing up at me nervously.

"He just worries about me, but I'm fine. He can't wrap his head around the fact that I'm fine."

"I'll admit, it's hard to understand how you could be," I said, hooking her arm in mine and leading her towards the garden. The sun had been kind the past day and melted all the snow. It was likely we'd get one or two more storms before the season was over, but it made for a nice change of view. Stepping outside, I used my divinity to remove some of the water from our path, creating one made of dirt rather than mud.

"Do I have a choice? There's nothing I can do about any of it," she replied.

"So you forgive the prince? Since there's nothing you can do about it?"

"To an extent. I still don't want to be around him though."

"I know we've told you this already, but your mother and I think it's rather admirable of you to allow him to stay."

"It's only because his brother would kill him otherwise," she said. "I don't want him here, but I don't want him to be killed either."

"It would be alright if you did."

She stopped dead in her tracks and turned to face me. "No. It wouldn't."

I said nothing as she tucked her arm back in mine, and we continued on our stroll. I didn't know what to say, so we walked in silence for a while. Sometimes I wished she didn't have so much of her mother's empathy, but perhaps it was a good thing. He'd have been dead by now if she didn't. And maybe it wasn't the solution.

"When I was younger, a few years ago, maybe, Mama saved a man who had been pushed into a well. Someone got him out, but he was really hurt, and she saved him," she said.

"I didn't know that."

"And afterwards, when Pa—Faxon yelled at her for it, she yelled back at him about how it wasn't her decision if the man was worth it or not. And I agreed with her at the time. But when he told me later that the man was a bad man, and he hurt a little girl like me, I was mad too." I stayed silent, allowing her to continue, uncertain of where her story was going. "I was mad at Mama for doing it, and when she realized I was avoiding her, she sat me down and told me why. She said it wasn't her choice about what happened to the man, but if she didn't save him, she was taking away the choice of the little girl he hurt. And she said that if someone ever hurt me like that, I should be allowed to decide for myself what happened to the person. She didn't want the death of the man to be on the little girl's conscience." She took a deep breath before continuing. "And as much as I hate Cyran for what he did, I don't think he did it out of malice. I don't want his death on my conscience. He—he told me Declan beat him."

I had no doubts the boy had told her the truth. He had made himself small around me, and though he had a healthy dose of bravado when he spoke to me, I could tell it was forced. Knowing what kind of man Declan was made it even more likely.

"Well, we won't send him back to Folterra as long as you don't want us to. I should have checked with you to see if you were alright with me asking him to translate the note. I'm sorry I didn't."

She laughed. "I don't mind. He's probably bored senseless. Mama mentioned it to me. If it helps you both figure out more about the prophecy, I know it will be worth it." She nodded, almost as if she were convincing herself, but I let it go.

"Did she tell you he's going to teach us how to use our shadows? Is that alright with you?"

She said nothing for a moment, and I worried every bit of effort and connection we'd made was about to be undone.

"Cy is a good teacher. He helped me a bit when I was having trouble. I was...very upset about things with—" She cleared her throat. "Faxon and Mama. I was having problems with my light. And he helped me."

"Divinity is tricky when our emotions are overwhelming. Like how Em—your Mama—" I corrected. "—made the dragons. She had more control over it by the time she made Ryo."

"Ryo?" Elora jolted to a stop.

"Yes. I, uh, wanted to take you to see the dragons soon. I thought Ryo might be the one you'd choose to be yours." Gods, how was I such a nervous fool over a child? She was mine, and, while I had every right to worry about what she thought, I still felt silly.

"I get a dragon?" Eyes wide, her smile spread over her face, and I relaxed in one to match it before nodding. "I'm—that's amazing! I'm surprised Mama remembered that name." I cleared my throat, not certain if I should correct her, but she read my body language despite my hesitation, shock etching her features. "*You* named him? Did you read the book too?"

I nodded.

"Alright, so what do you think about Ryo? Do you think he took too long to come around to Alina? When I made Mama read it, she said if he would have just told her his feelings sooner, she would have understood him, but I think—"

I threw my head back and laughed, eager to continue speaking to her about her passions. We spent the rest of our time together discussing her book, and I had four more added to my mental list she had ordered me to get through. And, though I'd never been much of a reader, I knew I'd absorb every word in haste just to hear her speak to me about them. By the time we returned to the estate from our turn around the garden, I needed to leave to meet with Cyran, and, by the look on her face, it surprised me that Elora didn't request to come with me.

After receiving news from Dickey—who'd turned into my errand boy more than anything else—I met Em at the palace where we were to work with Cyran. We were early, and I had been pacing for a few moments before Em snagged my wrist, pulling me to sit beside her. We were in the council room, and I'd just explained how my mother had gone off to the hot springs once more, making her unavailable for the dozens of questions we had.

"Love, she couldn't have known I was going to break the statue of Larke and unveil a five century old secret love letter."

"No, but I'm sure she knows something," I said.

"She might, but is it that important?"

"It might be. If the treaty wasn't actually broken, then—"

"Then Declan has already broken it by now. Do you think his mind would be changed by the fact your father might not have been the one to kill her? I don't think he cares."

I sighed, leaning forward and holding my head in my hands. "You're right. I just—"

I struggled to put into words what I was feeling. There was very little I knew about my father, and all of it was carefully curated. Based on his reactions and what the kingdom believed, he'd killed Larke. But my mother said he had loved the woman, though she'd committed atrocities he wouldn't speak of, and the Supreme had admitted Soren had been hard to deal with after her death. Em's hand dragged up my back, rubbing soft circles up my spine, and her voice matched it.

"I want to know just as much as you do, but it is not so pressing as the rest of it. You leave for Lamera soon, and we have the prophecy to worry about, and Declan will not stop because we find out the mystery of two dead monarchs." She spoke sense. Even so, there was a nagging feeling in the back of my mind which told me I needed to know now.

"I didn't know she was with child," I said, closing my eyes as Em rubbed my shoulder blades with more force. "It makes it worse."

"Only if he actually killed her. Either way, it's sad but...you don't think someone killed her because of what he wrote? About the babe not being his?"

"Honestly, I cannot fathom the idea of my father being willing to parent, let alone love a child who didn't truly belong to him."

She made a thoughtful sound just as the door to the council room slammed open, and Cyran swaggered through. I did my best to hold my tongue, though I felt amusement from Em, which made it difficult. For all he was, for all the fear he held for us, he hid it well. Standing tall, he took us in and removed his cloak, shaking his mussed hair out of his eyes. Gods, that age. He was far better than I ever was at faking it, I'd give him that.

"Before we begin, Ismene told me last night that Lamera is a distraction. With most of your forces amassed to the west, he expects it will be easier to march northward from Nara's Cove."

"He told her this?"

"She overheard it, but I trust her."

I nodded, grateful Dewalt and I had made a contingency plan in case something like this happened.

"Any news on the rebels? Were you able to appear to any of them?"

"Nigel was the only one I could appear to, and he wasn't quite right. I think he was injured in the blast; his dreams were hard to work in. But nearly everyone we had contact with is dead."

And with that sobering information, the three of us worked in near silence, coaxing the shadows to do what we wished, and considering how much more I felt in control at the end, it seemed Elora had been right. The prince was a good teacher.

CHAPTER 51

Elora

I WAS ALMOST CERTAIN Cyran came into my dreams—and often. Unless I was dreaming of him that much, unable to escape thoughts of him even in unconsciousness. I'd been wearing the bracelet ever since I first put it on, and he'd never once come back to speak to me. I didn't understand how I was the person who'd suffered at his hands, and yet I felt irreparably guilty over how I treated him after.

He had *killed* me, so why was I feeling like the villain? It perturbed me. But I wasn't convinced he wasn't watching over me in sleep, even if he refused to come talk to me. I hadn't had a true nightmare the past month. Each time something upsetting would start happening in my dreams, it would end, and I'd remember nothing bad past the first moment. I swore, though, shadows permeated my vision a few times.

I'd almost considered going with Mama and Rainier to the palace, sitting in on their little lesson with Cy. Could I ever fully forgive him? I'd had to learn to walk again, legs too weak from being bedridden, and I didn't even want to think about the effort it had taken me to train my bladder again. Was it all too much to forgive? Wandering into the bathing room attached to my bedroom, eager to wash my face and sit down to draw, I pushed away thoughts of interrupting their lesson. What could I say to him?

Glancing up at the mirror when I was finished, my eyes were drawn to the thin white line across my throat. I'd finally made Mama stop trying to heal it a few weeks past. Every time she looked at me, she couldn't help herself as she stared at it, and her eyes would grow wet before she'd fuss over me. It annoyed me to no end. I'd taken to covering it with my hair, ashamed that it seemed a beacon of my stupidity and overeagerness to trust someone I shouldn't have.

Maybe once I owned my naivety and stopped being ashamed of it, I could move past things with Cyran. I could stop thinking about him, stop letting him own so much of my time. We both had an abundance of regrets. If I had died, he'd still be tortured with thoughts of me, but I hadn't. Thanks to Mama. So, there was no sense in either of us torturing ourselves any longer. We couldn't be friends, but I could give him the forgiveness we both needed so we could go our separate ways and never speak or think of one another again.

Sweeping my hair back, I revealed my scar, ensuring not a single curl fell down and obstructed the view. I'd been wearing high-necked clothing, far more modest than I'd ever worn before, and I decided I was done with that. There was a beautiful yellow frock, made of the finest velvet, the neck quite low for me, which I tugged out of my closet. Struggling to put it on in the growing darkness, I sighed, tossing it on the bed before lighting the lamp. Glimpsing myself in the mirror once more, determination filled me. This would end it, and it was something I needed to do.

"And where are you going at this hour?" Mama's voice lilted out of the great room, and I cringed. I'd been hoping to slip out to the stable with no one knowing.

"It's not that late," I said, peeking my head into the room, finding her sitting sideways on the sofa and looking at me over the back of it. The fire was the only light in the room, and I wondered if Sterling had been dismissed right after dinner. It wasn't like him not to light any lamps. "We only just ate dinner."

"And normally, you're in for the night by then. So, my question still stands," she murmured, and as I approached, I realized it was because Rainier was asleep on the sofa curled up around her legs, arms wrapped around her thighs and using them as a pillow. He snored softly, and she tilted her head back on the sofa to look up at me. I'd never seen her so happy. She seemed tired, certainly, but content. Her fingertips drew light circles on his scalp, and when she glanced down at him, a soft smile formed on her lips. She had quite a pretty smile, I realized.

"I, erm, well, I was going to talk to Cy. Cyran. The prince," I stammered. I hadn't intended on anyone seeing me, so I didn't know what to say.

"Oh?" she asked softly.

"I haven't told him I forgive him, and I think we both need that."

"Mmm."

"He thought he was doing the right thing, and maybe he was. Without me dying, then you wouldn't have been blessed by Ciarden. Perhaps Dryul would have killed you, I don't know." I straightened myself, attempting to stand as tall as

I could. "He thought he was doing the right thing. I would have done the same," I lied.

I never could have done that to him, but I would have liked to think I could.

"You think?" she asked, and I immediately knew what she was doing.

"What? You don't think so?" I snapped, immediately regretting it when Rainier stirred. Mama watched me patiently until he settled once more in her lap.

"I don't think so, no," she finally said.

"And why's that?"

"You couldn't do that to someone you loved, no matter what you thought about it being the right thing."

"Who says I love him—*loved* him?"

"Your eyes told me, baby girl. Right before he did what he did."

"Well, clearly I don't know what love is."

"And I'm sorry for that, Elora." She sighed, staring down at my sire, the man she'd loved all of my life, even with the time and distance between them. "Do you want me to rift you there? I don't want you going out this late alone, and it's cold." Even though I tried to control it, my brows shot up, and she chuckled. "You're almost sixteen years old, and I know more than I care to about what you're feeling. You're either going to sneak out later, or I can take you there now. One involves significantly less work for both of us."

"Alright," I said, drawing out the word. "Is there a catch?"

"How long do you think you'll be? I'm afraid I'll only be able to give you twenty minutes or so because I am barely awake right now."

"I can say what I need to say in twenty minutes."

She nodded, and gently removed herself from Rainier's embrace, settling a throw pillow under his body to ease the transition. He turned his head toward me as he adjusted, and I realized how much younger he looked in his sleep. I had grown quite fond of him, though I was still wary of the idea of him being my father. My lunches with Shivani had helped me have more of an appreciation for him as well. Mama had been dubious about the meetings when she found out, but I'd managed to convince her. She preferred me only to go when Thyra could accompany me, but when she sent Thyra off to Lamera, I whined for a while about my new routine. She'd given in quickly afterwards. It wasn't that I wanted to see Shivani as much as it was about wanting to hear her stories. Her opinion, which didn't seem high of anybody—Aunt Lavenia included—knew no bounds when it came to him. And it didn't seem as if anything she told me was untrue or some manipulation to get me to like him. She genuinely thought the world of him. The day before last, she'd mentioned he was going to stand with the soldiers who were preparing for Declan's army's arrival, and her worry permeated her slim frame. It had clearly rubbed off on me, anxiety curling in my stomach as I looked at his sleeping face.

Was I about to lose another father?

I dismissed the thought, grateful for Mama electing to stay with me, promising to protect Astana, of more use here than on the front with Rainier. I knew she hated it though, especially after what happened at the Cascade when he'd been captured.

"The prince is probably back at the dormitory now," Mama said, turning and opening a rift to the moonlit street outside it. I'd never get used to her being able to do that. "Nana's room is the first room on the right when you go inside. She should be able to show you to his. I'll be back in twenty minutes?" I nodded. "Don't make me come searching for you, Elora," she warned, and I knew then this was a test. The better I did, the more freedom she'd allow. With all the intrigue and shops and activities Astana had to offer, I wanted to pass it.

The rift closed behind me, and I exhaled before planting my foot on the bottom-most stair.

"Elora?" A voice cracked behind me, and I turned, surprised to see Theo walking up the lane, and I kicked myself, forgetting he lived there too.

"Hello, Theo." I groaned internally, frustrated with the predicament I now faced.

"You've never come to see me before. Can I show you around? The dormitory is—"

Deciding to get it over with, I let my words rip between us. "I'm not here to see you."

"Oh. I—Mistress Imogene usually goes to bed by now, but I'm sure—"

"She's here to see me." His words curled around my spine and tugged it straight, the accent clear and crisp as the winter air around us. I hadn't even heard the door creak open behind me. Seeing the shadow of Cyran's tall form spill onto the ground, stretched and bigger than life, Theo's feet coming to rest just inside the outline of his head, I grew nervous. And when his hand rested on my shoulder, I closed my eyes.

"Yes, Theo, I've come to speak with Cyran. I won't be long," I said, ignoring my friend's expression as I turned to face the prince. Surprised to see him wearing a dangling earring and two long intertwining chains once more, the top buttons of his shirt unbuttoned, I almost tripped forward into his arms. He looked like himself again. The hint of a smile formed at the corner of his mouth as he grabbed my elbows, steading me.

Clearing my throat as I regained my balance, I stumbled up the step and walked past him into the dormitory. "Take me somewhere we can talk," I demanded.

He breezed past me, leading the way down the hall, and I followed. I heard Theo walk in behind us, blowing out the oil lamp on the table by the entryway, plunging us into darkness. By habit, I conjured a flame in my hand. Cyran stuttered a step, almost causing me to set his back aflame as I nearly ran into him. He led me down one hallway and up a stairwell, and I barely paid attention to anything until he stopped in front of a door, pulling out a key from a chain around his neck.

It was only then I realized how bare everything was. Wooden floors and plain plaster walls, with no color or decoration or warmth, made up the dormitory. And when his door creaked open, it sent a twinge of pain through me to see it matched the rest of it. The moonlight came in through a slim window, illuminating a rumpled bed made of white linens, and a small desk and chair tucked away in a corner. He lit the lamp which sat on the desk before sitting down on his bed.

"So, what do I have to thank for this visit?" A single brow raised as he tilted his chin to meet my eyes. He folded his hands in his lap and crossed his legs at the ankle, waiting. He looked both impatient and nervous at the same time, and I let him suffer a bit. Crossing to the single chair, I removed my cloak, folding it lengthwise before laying it over the back. And when I finally sat down, it was with some satisfaction I watched his eyes dip to my scar, unobscured by my hair or clothing. His throat bobbed, and I leaned back in my seat, watching him as he grew increasingly agitated, the evidence of his betrayal staring right at him. I made myself take a deep breath. I wasn't here to make him squirm.

"I've come to return this," I said, taking the bracelet off my wrist from where I'd worn it the past month, noticing he didn't wear one of his own. "And I've come to ask you to stop coming into my dreams." His face flushed scarlet, and I knew I had been right all along. It gave me the confidence to continue. "I forgive you. The decision you had to make was a horrible one, and I do not envy it. You barely knew me, you thought you—"

"I knew you, Elora," he whispered, eyes downcast. "I knew you, and it should have been enough to stop me."

My chest tightened painfully. "It doesn't matter. If you hadn't done it, who knows what might have happened? Dryul might have killed me and Mama anyway. There's no sense in—" I stood, hoping it would give me more confidence to handle this as I wanted without letting emotions get the better of me. It was a mistake, considering he looked up at me with doe eyes from across the room. I closed mine, balling my fists at my side.

"I forgive you. I thought I felt something more for you, and I thought you felt the same. But if you felt for me even a fraction of what I felt for you, I don't know how you could have done what you did. I could never have done that to you." I threw my hands up, calm demeanor ruined. "Hell, to anyone!"

"You never could have done that, I know. You're right." His hair fell down into his eyes as he stared at the ground.

"But you might have saved so many other lives," I whispered. "So, how could I possibly fault you?"

"Elora, I didn't know then—"

"No, please, Cy. Please don't make this harder than it needs to be." He reached up, swiping a hand over his mouth and jaw and remaining silent. "Seeing you is too difficult, but I don't want you to get hurt by going back to Folterra. I just...I know you feel guilty, and that's why you're in my dreams. But I don't want you there anymore. I don't want to think about you." I sniffed, not realizing I'd started to cry. "I will stay away from the bookstore until your project for Rainier is done, but after that, we should work out a schedule so we don't run into one another."

"Elora..." Whatever pain I saw on his face was tenfold for me. "*Min viltasma*, please."

"I don't think I'm asking for too much, Cy." He stood, unfolding his lean body and standing tall. Gods, it was unfair how he looked, given what I'd come to do. He shouldn't look as handsome as he did all those nights in Evenmoor. "If there's any decency within you, you'll accept what I say and let our friendship end. Gods, I don't even know if friendship is the right word. What do you call it when you betray someone who cares about you—but for good reason?"

"I cared about you too, Elora. I still care about you. That's why I don't like to see you suffer in your sleep. Knowing I might be the cause of those horrible dreams? It's painful."

"Well, I don't want your help anymore."

He dipped his head before crossing over to open the door for me, surprising me.

"I respect your wishes, Elora. I will be sorry for the rest of my life, but I won't give you any more trouble."

I swore I saw tears in his eyes, but I wouldn't let myself give into them as I grabbed my cloak and moved past him.

"Be well, Cy." I hesitated, hand on the doorknob as I started to pull it shut behind me. "I have no ill will towards you. And thank you for what you did to help fix things." He didn't meet my eyes, just turned away as I shut the door.

It was a few moments later when I sat on the steps outside, waiting for Mama to show up, when I began to wonder if I was just one more person on a long list who had turned their back on him when he needed them most.

CHAPTER 52

DEWALT

With the information gifted to us by the prince, Rainier and I had spent hours upon hours in the council room, which had eventually turned into a war room. Raj was already in Lamera and Ashmont on his way to Nara's Cove, and we had to coordinate the movement of soldiers, sending messenger crows and Warric to spread the word. We didn't plan on leaving Lamera undefended, but we'd received word this morning that Nereza had her own soldiers positioned on the Aesiron Bridge, ready to defend the Supreme if necessary. It made sense to pull our own soldiers back. Though we planned to leave for Nara's Cove in a few days' time, there was plenty of preparation still to be done. Rainier left with Emma at the end of the meeting, fetching the dragons from the hot springs to bring south. He planned to bring the fire breathers with us but leave the rest to protect Astana.

I had an hour before training with the children, and I decided I'd earned myself a nap, making my way toward Ven's chambers within the palace. I'd moved my things back there since the coronation, but once she returned from her journey, I was going to have to find new accommodations. Perhaps I'd buy a house.

Turning the corner, not paying attention and fumbling with the cuff of my sleeve, I ran straight into someone and knocked them to the ground. Apologizing, I offered my hand to help the person up before I realized just who it was.

"It's always you, isn't it?" I said, pulling my hand away as I glared down at the woman on the ground.

"I could say the same," Nor sniped, before scrambling to her feet and running a hand through her long dark-brown hair.

"What are you doing here?"

"I tutor Lord Durand's children now," she said, but she looked down at her hands, which she quickly slipped into the pockets of her loose, flowing pants. She still wore styles resembling that of the novices, just not in white. It irked me it was something I'd paid attention to. *Everything* about the woman irked me. Her fucking mouth—the way it was soft and sweet and warm, and the sounds she'd made as I kissed her.

As *she* kissed *me*, I reminded myself.

I hadn't been the one to permanently implant herself into my mind as the only person I'd kissed since Lucia. Sure, I'd had lovers, but not once had I ever kissed them. Not even Ven. No, I'd saved that because I didn't want to erase Lu's memory from my lips. And she took it from me. She'd had no right to do that. And I'd been thinking about it ever fucking since.

"The Durands' chambers lie on the western side of the palace. What are you doing here?"

"Nothing," she said, far too quickly.

"What was it you shoved in your pockets, Nor?"

"Nothing."

As she tried to make her way past me, I snatched her wrist, dragging her into Ven's chambers despite her fighting against me. She tugged her arm hard, and the sound she made told me she hurt herself. I eased my grip.

"What are you doing on this side of the palace?" I demanded, gritting my teeth as I shut the door behind me, tucking my hair behind my ears. I'd enunciated my words as if I were compelling her, and my annoyance was reborn when I remembered I could no longer do that.

"I was in the library doing some research, alright!" she shouted, arms crossed as she glared at me. One hand drifted up to massage her shoulder, and I remembered her burns there. Emma had mentioned something about a salve to help ease the aches, and I wondered if she'd ever delivered it. And with a start, I realized I'd never told either Rainier or Emmeline about Miriam and her daughter. I'd have to make it a priority.

"What kind of research?"

"It's none of your business, gods damn it!" And then she covered her mouth with her hand, the tips of her ears and her cheeks turning bright red. I couldn't help my amusement.

"Is that the first time you've cursed, little novice?"

"Shut up," she snapped.

"I should have known when you skipped the curse in the sweet song you sang in the bath," I said, stepping toward her. "So, what were you researching, songbird? Would you like some help?"

She stepped backward, finding herself pressed against the desk behind her.

"I found what I needed," she gritted out, frustration I wasn't sure was directed at me laced her words.

"And what was that?"

"Skies above, would you just leave me alone?" she groaned.

"No. I don't fucking trust you. You are—you're dangerous, and I want to know what you are up to."

"How am I dangerous? I have no desire to harm anyone; I don't think I could if I tried. I am a victim of circumstance and men who sought to hurt me." With a sniffle, I watched her hands ball into fists at her sides. "And it seems I still am."

"I am not here to hurt you. Gods, if anything, *you've* hurt *me*," I blurted in exasperation.

"How have I hurt you?" she whispered. She smelled as good as she had the last time, and that pissed me off all the more.

"By cursing me to think of your lips when it's the last gods damned thing I should think about. You're part of the Myriad, and—"

"And you blame them for her death," she finished.

"Yes."

"I am not part of the Myriad. We parted ways when they shipped me off to—to Declan."

"It doesn't matter."

"Doesn't it? You don't trust me because of something I had no control over being a part of." Her eyes were always changing, reacting to the surrounding environment. Today, they looked more green than brown, and her pupils were dilated.

"I don't trust you because of that, because you hid your identity as one of the elven—"

"I didn't hide—"

"What else are you hiding?" My limbs moved of their own accord as I stepped even closer, tucking a wayward strand of hair behind her ear. Feeling the skin there, rough and scarred, I trailed a finger over it. Ear barely pointed, it occurred to me someone might have tried to hide her elf-blood. Her reaction was immediate and involuntary as she shuddered.

"The elf-blood," she breathed. "My ears were pointed before he cut them..."

Hot rage ripped through me, and I clenched my fists. "Your father did this too? I thought he was elvish."

"He is. He—his ears are not pointed, though. He can hide it, I suppose."

"That makes no sense."

"Or maybe he cut at his own. I do not know." I hadn't even realized how close we stood until I felt her fingertips flutter on my side. "Why do you hate me?"

"I don't hate you. I just don't trust you."

"Because I make you forget about her."

"What? No." I reared back. "Because you are full of secrets and—and temptation," I stuttered.

"Now who sounds like a zealot? I am full of temptation? I put you off guard because you want to rut me, is that it?"

"*Rut* you? Gods, you were truly raised by the Myriad, weren't you?" I couldn't say she was wrong though, could I? Ever since that gods forsaken kiss, I'd thought of it more than once. Would she take the lead like she had in the hallway? She flushed, cheeks reddening as her eyes darted away from me.

"You hate yourself for it." Her voice dropped lower. "I'm sorry I went into the wrong baths. I—I shouldn't have been there. You shouldn't have—we shouldn't have seen one another." Though her voice shook, she found her confidence a moment later. "Still, though. Ever since then, I've seen the looks you give me. My mother taught me what to look for when a man..." She trailed off as she pulled her hand away from me abruptly, clearly realizing what she'd been doing.

A pang of guilt took root in my stomach. For knowing how she must feel about men after what her mother endured, and gods only knew what else she'd seen. For knowing she was right. How was the first woman to affect me this way part of the very organization which had killed Lu? And a tiny part of me was angry it wasn't Ven who'd been able to affect me so. It would have been easier. But my frustration renewed at the thought of her finding me lecherous, looking at her in some perverted fashion.

"You're the one who kissed me, Nor," I retorted.

"Only as a ruse!" she exclaimed.

"If it were only for a ruse, you wouldn't have parted my lips with that wandering tongue. You wouldn't have given me those little moans of pleasure. You wouldn't have pulled me closer. Don't pretend your thighs don't slicken every time you think about that kiss."

Pinned between me and the desk, her lips parted, and I heard the hint of a stuttering breath. Perhaps we both had something we needed to get out of our system. The idea of kissing her again didn't bring me disgust when standing this close to her.

"I won't pretend you're not a good kisser," she whispered, eyes on my lips.

"I'm good at other things too," I said, tugging at the loose pants around her hips, not thinking. When she gripped my wrist with one hand, tight, I froze. But she didn't pull me away from her. After a moment, her grip loosened, and I continued my path. She never let go, but she let my hand wander as her breaths grew stuttered. Her other hand returned to my side, her fingertips trembling as she moved them up my skin. Tracing down past rough curls, I found her heat as she let out a gasp.

She was wet as hell.

"You can claim it's 'only a ruse' all you want, but this mess tells me otherwise," I said, leaning forward and pressing my lips to the side of her neck. I wouldn't kiss her on the mouth again, no. This would be just what I needed to get her out of my gods damned head. Circling her entrance for a second, I pulled my finger toward that tender, sensitive spot, using her wetness to glide across her skin. Her hips jerked, giving me better access. "Now who wants to *rut?*"

"If you're going to be cruel to me, stalk me all over Astana, there should be benefits to the arrangement, I'd think." Her voice stuttered with her breath.

"Some bravado for someone who has probably never been touched here before," I whispered, lips close to her ear. "Unless you've done it yourself." She jerked away from me, tightening her grip on my wrist, but I swore she tugged my hand closer to her body. "You hate this just as much as I do. Is it some sort of elven trickery? Some cursed elvish nonsense?"

"Are you asking me if I've—if I've seduced you with magick?" I wasn't sure what made her stutter—her fury or the way I rubbed her clit.

"Well, I can't think of any other reason I'd—"

"You truly think you are the only one to suffer a loss of someone you loved. You are not the first, and you won't be the last. You don't have to prove your suffering by withholding joy or—or pleas—"

I slipped a finger into that tight heat and drew it out slowly. Gods, she was tight. Slick with need, she still clamped around me. She took a deep breath, chest expanding as her mouth dropped open. Her thick brows furrowed in frustration as she glared up at me.

"If I withhold pleasure, it is for someone else's benefit, not my own," I said.

"I'm trying to speak to you about—"

"About how your pussy is eager for my touch?" I slipped another finger in beside the first, and she exhaled forcefully, shaking as she lurched forward. She dropped my wrist, planting her hand on the desk beside her. I didn't care to hear what she had to say—about accepting joy or otherwise. Not for a few reasons. One being the obvious—I was two knuckles deep in her sweet warmth—but the other was because I'd heard it all before. I didn't think I was proving anything. I'd wondered myself why I wasn't like the other people I knew who could move on. Hell, Raj's wife had only been dead for five years, and he was bedding a beautiful woman who seemed to care about his children and fuss over him. And he was happy. I'd never been married to Lu, though I'd thought about it. I'd been nothing more than a friend until that last year with her. And yet, I was living my sixteenth year without her, still hanging onto her memory. It wasn't that I didn't long to be free of the past. Even more so now that Rainier was living his. Without the option? These past months since Emmeline had been back made me fucking crave freedom from Lucia's memory. I worried I'd never get it.

Maybe the novice was right though. Maybe that was why I hated her. Because I couldn't help but look at her the same gods damned way I had looked at Lucia.

"Such a filthy mouth," she said on a sigh. "It serves you well in being distracting."

"Is my hand not filthy too? You grind on it so well."

"May the gods forgive me for it too," she murmured, closing her eyes as I continued dragging my two fingers in and out, gaze tearing down her body as she writhed for me. "Maybe you will too."

I froze, fingers stilling. "What do you mean?"

"Because I shouldn't add to your regrets. You're trying to prove something to yourself, aren't you?"

She moaned as I pushed my fingers in deeper, tilting her head back so her long waves flowed down to the desk. Free hand planted on the desk beside her, I crowded her body as I pushed my fingers in and out, palm pressing hard against her clit.

"And what could I be trying to prove? That my dick can still get hard despite you being a novice?"

"Our time in the temple already proved that," she said, staring hate at me along with a coy smirk.

"Gods damn it all, Nor," I said, right before I surged forward and claimed her mouth. The mouth which had haunted me every fucking day since I first tasted it. This time it was me who pried her lips to part, me who swept my tongue into her mouth and traced and battled her own with it. Me who moaned into her as her fingernails traced a path up my side. Me who plunged my fingers into her wet pussy as she leaned back on the desk for support, legs drifting farther apart to make room for me.

"I don't know what it is you're trying to prove, but something tells me you're failing at it."

Her voice in my mind was less jarring this time, a soft purr to match what I hoped I was making her feel. I deepened our kiss and angled my hand, using my thumb to rub that sensitive little nub.

"*Oh, skies,*" she said, sounding breathless even in my mind. I didn't think she meant to say it to me, and I smiled against her lips. I didn't understand it, this desire to make her scream my name and rid myself of her for good. Using my free hand to boost her up, I let it slip down to her pants after, about to rid her of them completely, when I knocked something off the side of the desk. It landed with a clunk, and I wouldn't have thought anything of it if the glare of the sunlight reflecting off it hadn't shined right in my eyes. Pulling away for just a moment, I glanced down.

The gilded miniature portrait of Lucia sat right in the middle of a ray of sunlight warming the ground.

I extricated myself from Nor and stumbled a few steps backward, stomach lurching.

"Get out," I barked. "What the fuck am I—you need to leave."

"Dewalt," she said, adjusting her pants as her gaze followed mine. "It's alright. It's not broken. Here, let me—"

"Don't touch it," I demanded, quiet and full of anger I didn't know where to direct. She looked up at me from where she knelt, pity and confusion warring in her eyes. I fucking hated it. "Just go, Nor. This was a mistake. I wasn't thinking. You should leave." Wiping my clammy hands on my pants, I nodded toward the door to encourage her.

"I—uh, you're right. That was a mess. A huge mistake." She nodded, brushing her hair behind her ear, and I felt guilty when I saw her injured skin. And when she adjusted, her blouse moving on her shoulder, the evidence of her abuse fully revealed to me, I regretted the coarse words I'd said to her. She was used to men being rough with her, and she probably deserved some gentleness. It wasn't me who could give her that though. She walked past me to the door, eyes darting away. It made sense for her to feel that way; we both knew I wasn't stable at the moment. How could I go from distrusting her, from questioning her every motive, to having my fingers in her and kissing her like I'd been kissing women haphazardly for the past sixteen years? And then to dismiss her because of a picture of the long-dead woman who'd held my heart hostage? Fucking hell.

Truly irrational behavior.

One of her hands rested on the doorknob while the other moved to her mouth. To wipe away the trace of me.

"I-I need to tell someone something, but I'm afraid. I thought maybe after this—whatever this was—I could have told you." She wouldn't look at me and started scratching at her wrist.

"What is it, Nor?"

"No, I—never mind, it's not important." She turned the knob.

I softened my voice as I adjusted my clothing. "You can tell me. Why are you afraid?"

"The things you helped me gather? I'd stolen my mother's locket the day before Filenti dragged me off. Hid it in my pallet."

"And?" I prompted as she toed the ground.

"Filenti knew who my father was as well, had something of his, according to my mother. But in the locket were two tiny portraits of my parents. Somehow, I think she still loved him, despite everything. And it's so tiny, I—"

"Do you know who your father is?" I pushed her toward the point. I needed to rid myself of her before I did something stupid.

"That ball," she whispered. "I recognized it."

"The one in Filenti's drawer?"

"Yes."

"Gods, Nor. Get to the point."

She strode across the room, tugging the necklace out of her pocket and opening it as she grabbed my hand and placed it in my palm.

"I don't remember my father, not really. I remember he was blond, and that's it. Does that—is that Declan? I never saw him while I was in Folterra."

I peered down at the tiny image. It was nearly impossible to tell.

"I was born in Folterra, and that ball? Declan had a collection of them, all whittled to perfection in that same way. He gave them to the women he—the novices that he..."

"Divine fucking hell, Nor."

"He didn't rape me because I—because I think I am his daughter."

CHAPTER 53

Rainier

Elora's shriek was blood curdling in my ear, and I couldn't help but laugh as I wrapped an arm around her.

"I've got you. I won't let you fall," I said, loud enough for her to hear me in the wind. Though I couldn't quite make out what she muttered in response, I saw her knuckles whiten where she held on to Ryo's neck and felt her nails dig into the arm I put around her waist. Glancing to my right, I saw Em watching us from where she sat atop Irses, her hair blowing in the wind. It wasn't as cold as it could have been, but we'd made the dragons stay low to keep us warmer, not wanting to deal with the hassle of divine fire.

We'd only been able to corral the dragons through one rift, and they wanted nothing to do with another. My heart had soared when we worked together to get them through it. The beasts had been sleeping in a cave near the hot spring, and I created a sunken path which rose high to either side, coming straight out of the mountain. They had no choice but to enter it when they came out. I kept the rift open and rumbled the earth beneath them to encourage them to move. Em had covered the top of the path with shadows, hoping they'd stay beneath it, and, thankfully, they had made their way toward the end of our makeshift tunnel. Elora had run along after them, shouting at them and urging them toward the rift. She'd been afraid at first but quickly came around, especially after Ryo licked her, covering her torso and face in dragon spit. She was no longer scared at that point and only wanted vengeance. Sadly, our plan didn't work a second time because the dragons had all launched into the air the moment they went through the rift.

It had taken Emma shouting at Irses at the top of her lungs for several minutes for him and Ryo to land. The others didn't risk it. Elora and Em both decided it would be best for Elora to ride with me, and gods, I had been giddy about it.

Her screeching though; I worried for my ears.

As we came upon the outskirts of the capital, people gawked. They'd gotten a glimpse of the dragons when we'd taken them to the hot springs, but with how low we were flying now, the people ran out of their houses to see the visions of fiction in the flesh. Ryo vibrated with energy, and I could tell he wanted to perform some sort of trick because of all the attention, and I clamped my legs tight on either side of him.

"Not now, boy," I said, leaning forward to pat his neck near where Elora clung tightly.

I visited a few times during those weeks I was avoiding Emma, working on training him for Elora. I'd kept up my visits since we returned from Ravemont, but I hadn't tended to them as often as I would have liked. He'd made extreme progress. He did even better with Shika's presence to our left; the blood-red dragon with curling shadows around her body frightened him. Though she looked terrifying, she was quite gentle, and had quickly grown to be my favorite dragon. Irses still hadn't quite warmed to me, but we had an understanding by now—a begrudging respect. We both were fiercely loyal to the woman who rode atop him, and that was all that mattered.

When we finally landed at the estate, it was midday, and I was beyond tired. We'd been up at dawn for meetings with my council, then Em and I went to retrieve Elora before fetching the dragons. Holding the rift open for as long as I did while rumbling the earth had taken its toll on my divinity, and I wanted to nap.

But I knew I would find no rest, already late for my meeting with Reminy. I slid down off the dragon and helped Elora after.

"Wasn't that bad, was it?"

"It was amazing!" she shouted, cheeks pink and hair windblown.

"You were screaming your head off," I countered, grinning at the girl who stood bouncing on the balls of her feet.

"Alright, yes, but it was just, oh, it was exhilarating," she breathed. "I can't wait to do it again."

"I, uh, when I'm back...after Nara's Cove..." I trailed off when her expression grew somber. "What is it?"

"I wish you weren't going there. I know you have to, but it...you'll be alright, won't you?"

The ache in my heart pulsed when I realized she was afraid, and then I had to stop myself from smiling over the fact she was worried for me. She was my daughter, and I would love her until the day I died. But in the back of my mind, I'd wondered when she'd feel the same about me being her father, if she ever would. It seemed she might get there one day.

"I'll be alright. I won't be involved unless Declan is there. He's too strong for my soldiers to take down alone, but I'm not repeating the mistakes of last time. I was worn out and weak the last time I faced him. I won't do that again."

"Alright," she said, albeit warily. "When you're back from Nara's Cove?" she prompted.

"I can teach you how to ride Ryo on your own? I don't want you—I'd rather you not try to ride the dragons while I'm gone. I don't want you to get hurt."

A slow smile spread on her face, and I saw Em out of the corner of my eye, feeling all too many emotions spreading between us down the bond.

"That sounds like a great idea."

"Good." I cleared my throat. "Em, we have that meeting with Reminy, and I have a few last-minute things to do before I leave. You ready?"

"Can you rift me into the city with you? I, uh—" Elora fiddled with her clothing as a flush rose up her cheeks. "Cyran asked me to meet him one last time—to say goodbye. I think he's, uh, finally accepted that we can't be friends."

"That should work," Em said slowly, eyes lingering on Elora as she turned to me. "I have to stop at the novice dormitory instead of meeting with Reminy, anyway. I'll take Elora, and—"

"We're actually meeting at a cafe by the bookstore. Rainier can take me?"

"We'll figure it out. You probably want to go change considering you smell like dragon spit," I said, and Elora gifted me with her laugh before flouncing inside.

"The actual contents of the book are—I'm not sure if you'll be able to do much with it. It seems to just be conjecture. The author of the text drones on and on about what 'bloom, blood, and bone' could mean. There is, uh, evidence, I suppose, of a ritual which took place a few years before your father was born which could summon the gods? But I'm not sure if it worked, or if it would help you."

"What do they think it means?" I asked, leaning forward with both hands spread wide on the table. Reminy had collected all of his notes and texts he'd used to cross-reference what he'd found in the original prophecy book in tidy piles.

"So, the author of this text disagrees, but another person believed it went with the next line. Bloom would go with betrayer, blood with the body, and bone with bane. That if you could source those items, you could summon the gods? While the author disagrees, it seems that he'd read other stories about being able to force the gods to perform some sort of favor. It also seems that body and Beloved were once synonymous. That the body is sacred and beloved, I suppose. It could be either; I'm not sure."

"Bloom with betrayer, blood with either body or Beloved, and bone with bane?"

"Yes, it would seem. I found this text here," he said, sliding an older book in front of me. "This is written by the person our author seems to disagree with. He believed it was meant to be the bloom of the betrayer, blood of the Beloved, and bone of the bane. And if collected, well, they could invoke a favor from the gods."

"Hmm," I murmured, standing up and crossing my arms. "A favor from the gods would be quite fortuitous, especially for the Accursed."

"Indeed, Your Majesty." The small man pushed his glasses up his nose before replacing the book in his neat stack. "I'm sorry I do not have more information for you. It was quite…taxing to read a few dead men argue back and forth. I got through an entire pamphlet before I realized it was just name-calling."

I laughed, but it felt forced. "Thank you, Reminy, for taking on this endeavor for me. And the boy's translation? He didn't bother you, did he?"

Reminy pulled a folded sheet of paper from the stack and handed it over. "He didn't bother me. It was nice to not have to switch directions in thought. What he translated was more informal than what I did. It seems a few centuries stood between what was printed and the note inside. It appears it was some sort of gift."

"I'll let you get back to work, friend. Thank you for your help."

He nodded and ran a hand through sleek, black hair. "Do you, erm, do you know when that big woman will be back?"

I blinked at him for a second before realizing who he meant. "Thyra? Elora's guard?"

"Yes," he replied, gulping loudly.

"She's riding to Nara's Cove now, but, if all goes well, she'll return with me."

"She is very intimidating to the patrons who like to yell. Her presence has made my life far easier."

He dipped his head, running off to the back office as I sat down at the table with a smile, unfolding Cyran's translation.

My dear friend Zaph,
This is the only book I could find about what you wanted. I don't know why you're so obsessed with the prophecy. Didn't the original seer say it wouldn't come to pass for another five hundred years? Maybe more? Even with the font, we might be dead

before then. At the very least, we'll be old enough we won't be able to do much about it.

As for your letter, do not be worried. He is surprisingly kind. I wish you wouldn't be so difficult about it. And, honestly, what I do with Tannyl is none of your business, is it? You don't see me asking about the things you do with the novices. I can't help but wonder if it is jealousy which you harbor toward Tan. You promised nothing would come between us.

Anyway, I wish you luck with this prophecy nonsense. I don't know what kind of favor you could possibly want, anyway. But please don't ask me for any more help. The king is nice to me, treats me fairly, and I do not want to ruin things here.

All my love,

L

I read it a few times and compared it to the original on the desk. With the words translated for me, I could catch a few of them. The prince had done a good job. I sat there for a moment, one ankle crossed over my leg as I leaned back. Pondering over what I'd just read, it seemed clear to me this note was from Larke. Did I only think that because she was on my mind after what we'd found the other night? She spoke of the king in this letter, and I assumed she meant my father. She'd clearly stolen the prophecy book from our libraries, if that were the case. But between her letter and my father's, something had gone sorely wrong. I'd done nothing but think about what could have passed between the two of them since we'd discovered his. He shoved her out of a tower, or so the stories went. In this letter she said he was kind, but clearly spoke of some sort of relationship with Tannyl. Had my father found out and done something to her?

I closed my eyes and rubbed my temples before dragging myself to my feet. I knew Em said it wasn't important right now, but something was driving me to figure it out. The last time I'd ignored my gut instincts, I'd set into motion sixteen years of torment. Grabbing the book and Cyran's translation, I opened up a rift into my mother's chambers.

The fire was lit, and the late afternoon sun shone through the windows at the end of the hall.

"Mother?" I called, hearing her doing something in the back of her chamber.

"Rainier? I wasn't expecting you," she said, coming out of her bedroom with a comb in one hand and a bottle of oil in the other. Eyeing me and what I carried, she walked back into her room. "Bring a bottle of wine," she called out.

I chuckled, grabbing a bottle and two glasses from the sideboard within the living area of her suite before following after her. Her room was the same as

I remembered it, jewel-toned greens and blues with white, flowing curtains. I remembered being young and watching them blow in the breeze from an open window as Ven and I took a nap on her bed. It was a short memory, not too important, but I'd remembered my little sister curled up between me and my mother, and I had wondered why Shivani never spent more time with us that way. I knew now, I supposed, but it was a bitter sting of a memory.

"Open the curtain for me a bit more, would you, dear?" she asked. The window in her bedchamber faced the west, so it would only get brighter for a while before sunset. After doing as she bid, I sat on the edge of the bed while she returned to her vanity. I watched as she parted her hair, taking a section and twisting it back away from her face.

"So, my serious boy, what is it?"

I frowned at the endearment as I brought the book and Cyran's translation out, gently placing them beside me on her bed. I'd left the scroll of my father's in my bedchamber, not willing to damage it. With it being rolled as it was, I knew it wouldn't stand up well to disturbance.

"I found an old letter from Soren to Larke."

"You did." Not a question, but a statement. "When you broke her statue, no doubt?"

"You knew there was a compartment in it?"

"I did. The dead are best left as such, Rainier," she said, an eyebrow raising as she looked at me through her mirror.

"Did he kill Larke?"

"No."

"Why does everyone think he did?"

"Because," she sighed, leaning back as she tied off the twist she worked on. "The assumption was made, and his council didn't work to prevent the word from spreading. And he didn't care."

"How do you know this?" I demanded, suddenly irritated. She sectioned out another piece of hair. Why was I the only one who thought this truth important?

"Your father got very drunk on our wedding night, and he told me I had no reason to fear him throwing me off a balcony. After some prodding, I only found out a bit more, but enough to know he hadn't done it to her. She jumped."

"What? Don't spare me the details."

She finished the twist and started brushing the rest of her hair back into a bun, decidedly continuing her motions in a weighted manner. Slow and methodical, she seemed in no hurry to tell me anything. "Larke was...torn between two men. Your father and the elf prince."

"Tannyl."

"Yes, the very one." She leaned forward, clipping a bead to either twist before pulling them back to join her bun. I was growing impatient, and observing her do something I'd watched in moments of adoration during my childhood made me more annoyed as each minute passed. "Larke had both men and found herself pregnant. When Tannyl died, it seems she blamed your father and threw herself off the balcony."

"Gods, Mother. How can you be so detached?" The way she'd said it in a bored, monotone voice unsettled me.

"It happened a few centuries before I was born, and I don't think your father was ever capable of love again. If I think about it too hard, I make excuses for him. But I cannot and should not make excuses for how he treated me and how it forced me to treat you and your sister." She turned on her seat and smoothed her dress down before elegantly lifting her chin to speak to me. "I do not see how or why it is important, considering everyone in the story is dead."

"Did he kill Tannyl?"

"Now that, I do not know. Anything else?" she asked, straightening her collar as she glanced out the window.

"I suppose not. I found a note I think is from Larke in a book I believe she stole. Do you know who a Zaph is, who she might have been—" Shivani had stood, walking over to the window in a daze, clearly not listening to me. "Mother?"

"Fire."

I rushed behind her, first noticing the massive plume of smoke coming from the northern end of the capital—where Elora was. When the massive winged creature I didn't recognize as a dragon flew over the palace, it drew me from my stupor.

"Elora's at the cafe on Armista," I said, right before opening one rift to get my sword followed by another which opened up into chaos.

CHAPTER 54

Cyran

"You're going *where?*" Elora's voice was shrill as she slapped both of her hands palm down on the table between us. The cook shot a glare at me through the kitchen window, and I ignored him, preferring to look upon the girl across from me for the last time. Besides, the place was empty, so it wasn't as if we were bothering any customers.

"Pelmuzu isn't quite so cold as it is here, and I've heard it's lovely in the spring."

"Cy, you can't be serious. You're just going to give up your kingdom to your brother like that?" Her brow furrowed, reminding me of the girl I'd met this past autumn. The girl who'd promptly brought me to my knees and then somehow stole whatever was left of my heart.

"Well, no. I planned to hide there for a time, gain friends and riches, then purchase mercenaries to eradicate my brother. Unless your father does it for me first, of course. Then I'll pay him back, I suppose."

"You can't go to Nythyr. That doesn't make any sense."

"And I can't go back to Folterra, not now. The rebels are all dead. Dec saw to that."

"What about your sister? You're just going to abandon her too?"

"Ismene won't leave."

"When did you decide?" she whispered. Her blue eyes welled up, and she tugged one of her curls over her shoulder, twisting it around a finger. She wore her hair pinned back, forcing me to stare at her scar—the evidence of my betrayal.

"After our discussion," I said, after only a moment's hesitation.

"Cy," she breathed.

"Please don't call me that anymore."

"Stay here," she pleaded. "I didn't ask you to leave Vesta. I just needed to draw a line between us."

"And I respect that, Elora. I didn't ask you here to make you feel guilty. I only asked you here to say goodbye. And to tell you sorry once more. I have nowhere to go in Folterra, and I can't stay here. Nythyr is—"

"You *can* stay. I—" She tugged her lower lip into her mouth and fidgeted in her seat. "I *want* you to stay."

"*Min viltasma*," I murmured. "I cannot stay because I will never be able to—to—it is difficult to be in your proximity. This capital is not big enough to put enough space between us for me to not think about you. The way you bite your thumb when you concentrate. The freckle on your right ear. The face you make when I annoy you. All the ways I have hurt you and betrayed you." She clasped her hands together and leaned forward as if she was about to argue with me, but I cut her off. "Your forgiveness was a gift I will never deserve. But I cannot go home, and I cannot live like this."

"Like what, Cy?" she whispered.

I sighed, pulling on my hair with my elbows on the table. She was going to make me rip out the contents of my soul and lay them on the table in front of her, wasn't she?

"In Evenmoor, you made me feel as if I could do anything. As if I wasn't an Umbroth. Other than Ismene, no one has ever seen me without that dark stain. Until you. Others have tried since, I suppose. Your mother and father try, but they'll always see me as the boy who tried to take something precious from them. But you, even when you screamed at me and kicked me out, I didn't think it was because you thought I was evil. It was because I-I betrayed you. Because you trusted me, and I ruined it. But you forgave me anyway, Elora. Killing you will be the greatest regret of my life, even if you're sitting across from me—living, breathing, *smiling*." I laughed, bitter. "It would seem as if saving the rest of the world came at the cost of my own happiness. And that has to be alright. Because *you* are alright."

She reached for me but jumped when a loud booming sound shook the building. Dust fell from the rafters, and the cook's head popped up to the window. "What in the gods' names was that?" he shouted.

I stood, shoving Elora behind me as I approached the door. When I cracked it open, she wrenched at my arm, trying to pull me back.

"Cy, no. This is—no," she implored.

Shaking her free, I leaned out, finding nothing awry. I saw a few other faces doing the same as I did, looking up and down the street. It was well past lunchtime but before the dinner crowd, so the street was rather empty. I saw a horse galloping off to my left with its rider chasing after it, but other than that, nothing seemed amiss.

Until the woman across the street looked above me and let out a harsh scream before falling back into the building behind her. Eyes wide, I backed up, hand searching for Elora.

"Get back, Elora, I—" My own words dried in my throat as a long—*far too bloody long*—arm swung down in front of the door. I couldn't even see it in its entirety, but the pale, creamy skin at the top led to blackened, hand-like claws at the bottom, swaying at the height of my chest. I'd seen nothing like it ever before. Elora screamed, grabbing my jacket and pulling me back to her just as shadows erupted from me, shoving the door closed and holding it tight. My divinity had yet to manifest so strongly, and, by the gods, I was grateful it had chosen this moment. I heard a clattering behind me and glanced back just in time to see the cook run out a back door.

"Elora, go, follow him. Get out. I'll hold it back," I ordered, just as the creature began beating at the door, a loud slamming sound punctuated with high-pitched screeching. My heart raced, and I did my best to solidify the shadows standing against the beast. It soon began beating at the wall beside the door, and I spread my shadows wider, protecting the front of the building.

"I'm not leaving you," she said. Moving to stand beside me, she lifted her hands up to her chest and drew divine light into her palm. Growing it into a large ball between her hands, she turned to face me with a set jaw. "We'll back towards the door together, and if it gets through your shadows, I'll be waiting."

"*Min viltasma,* please, go on," I pleaded.

"How sssweet," a voice hissed from outside the door, and I swore I recognized it.

The banging continued, the entire front of the building shaking. I grimaced as I felt it penetrate my shadows. I couldn't see the creature beyond them, but my divinity loathed it, whatever it was. It was pure evil and ready to kill me the second I broke. "Elora, go!" I fought back tears. "I will die loving you—now go!"

She blinked at me, moving to stand between me and the shadows holding the creature at bay. "Would you stop fighting with me and just do what I say? I'm not leaving you, and if you don't shut up, you're going to get me killed. Again. If you truly love me, you'll listen to me!"

She punctuated her words with a swift kick to my shin, and I swallowed, nodding. "Alright, Elora. Alright." My voice cracked as she moved to stand beside me, growing the divine fire between her hands. She transferred it to one hand, making the large glowing sphere spin above her outstretched palm as she used the other to grab my elbow.

"I'll lead the way," she said, and she navigated me past a table and around the corner of the bar, which led to the kitchen. It was harder to control my shadows the farther away we moved.

"Elora, get ready to run. I don't know if I can hold the shadows that far. I can shield us, but—it stopped," I said, realizing whatever it was no longer pecked at my shadows. In the span of a heartbeat, the roof of the building was torn off. I moved all my shadows toward Elora, about to cover her as she released the ball of fire toward the ceiling, igniting the roof and the creature. It had long legs, triple-jointed, and unsettlingly human feet. It screeched, scrambling backward for a moment before tossing something down through the massive, flaming hole.

My blood ran cold when I realized it was a body wrapped in a Folterran burial shroud.

"Cy, come on," Elora tugged at my arm, dragging me towards the door just as I recognized the raven hair sticking out of the top.

"Iz," I breathed, every muscle in my body frozen in place. "Iz!" I shouted, doing my best to protect Elora with my shadows as I ran toward my sister. Elora's shout was my only warning as one of those long arms shot down in front of me, and one of my shadows tried wrapping around it. The creature broke free, raking its claw through the air, and it tried to grab me before I jumped back.

"Little prince," the voice spoke, drawing out the word in a hiss, and the body of the beast came into view above me. If a human's limbs were stretched and blackened, eyes depthless and jaws opened in a gaping wound, it would look like the creature above me. The wings spreading from its shoulders were black and leathery, enormous to carry the weight of its massive limbs. "Your brother isss looking for you," it said a second before a blast of Elora's fire hit it. Launching it away from the wreckage we'd made of the roof, loud wings snapped as it took off.

"Was that—that was Cook, wasn't it? From Evenmoor?" Elora said, voice shaking with horror.

I dropped to my knees, coughing as a beam toward the front of the building fell, ash and smoke filling the room.

"Cy, we have to get out!"

"It's Ismene," I said, rolling my sister over. I peeled the shroud back. Hazel eyes a mirror of my own stared back at me—lifeless. Her lips were parted, her face pale, and her skin cold. Bruises covered her neck, tiny scratches in her skin from where she must have tried to pry her attacker away. I leaned over her, looking for something—anything. I heard Elora's sharp intake of breath as she moved to stand behind me. "We have to find your mother. Go find her!" I shouted. "Go!"

"Cy, the building, it's—"

"She brought you back, gods damn it. Hurry!" Elora said nothing for a moment, and I lifted my hand to brush the dark hair off my sister's face. "GO!" I bellowed, whipping my head to look back at Elora.

"She's dead, Cy. Come on, please." Elora hooked her arms beneath my armpits and tried to drag me backward, but I wouldn't let go of Iz. *Couldn't* let go of Iz.

"She's my little sister, I can't—I can't."

When surprisingly cool hands pressed on either side of my face, and the only eyes to look at me with kindness in these recent years moved into my line of sight, I dragged my gaze from Ismene's body to look up at Elora. "Please, Elora. Please," I pleaded.

"Cyran. There's nothing we can do. You have to—"

Another creature flew over, and I watched as a giant boulder hit it, knocking it out of its flight. When it came tumbling down upon us, I used the last bit of my divinity to cover the three of us and pulled Elora into my arms.

CHAPTER 55

Emmeline

I was just sitting down to tea with Nana in her room in the dormitory when I heard a thundering of hooves outside. With the dormitory being on the outskirts of the capital, it was unlikely it was someone just passing through.

"I'll be right back, Nana."

I'd been eager to see her since we returned from Ravemont, to ask her questions about my mother, and demand she explain to me why I was never told about how she died. I was angry with the woman, but I knew there had to be some sort of explanation.

"It's probably just Cyran. Theo is out back with the horses and said one of them was missing."

"He's—yes, it might be him," I said, not bothering to explain. Her room was right off the entryway, easy for her to keep track of all the comings and goings, so I was outside within a moment.

Dewalt swung off his horse, hair a flyaway mess as he strode toward me, sounding as if he was apologizing. "I should have mentioned it sooner, but forgot to tell you when you came back, and she's about to—*oh fuck*, here she is," he said, just as Nor came flying down the road behind him. "Her mother is Miriam. The mistress. I told her what happened. I'm sorry. The one from—"

I stared at him blankly, and I barely had a second to react before Nor was behind him, flinging herself at his back, nails dragging at his face and skin.

"Nor!" I shouted, but her own cries drowned me out.

"You knew! You knew she killed my mother and didn't tell me!" Tears streamed down the woman's face, mixing with the sorrow in her eyes as she wrapped one arm around his neck, trying to pull him to the ground.

"Nor, stop. It was—she—" I started, trying to say too many things all at once.

"You!" she screamed, pointing a finger at me over Dewalt's shoulder.

"Me," I said firmly. "*Not* him. Let him go."

When she didn't do as I commanded, I let my shadows gently ripple toward her, and she detached herself from Dewalt before I had to use them.

"Don't. Don't use the shadows on me," she mumbled, wiping tears from her eyes.

"And Declan is her father," Dewalt said, wiping blood from his neck. He was calm as he said it, unnervingly so.

I stared between the two of them, jaw dropped, unable to process what they were telling me.

"What is going on over here?" Theo's voice cried out from the side of the building just as Nana opened the door, probably about to ask the same thing.

"Nothing!" Nor, Dewalt, and I all spoke at the same time. Theo and Nana watched warily, but the boy turned, shaking his head as he went back to work.

"A lot of the novices are inside doing nap time. Just because these old ears can barely hear you doesn't mean the babes won't," Nana scolded before heading back into the dormitory.

"He said she made you do it?" Nor whispered, tears dried and arms crossed over her chest.

"Yes. She—she spoke into my mind and told me...I suppose I now know what she meant when she said the Myriad suspected I wasn't what I appeared to be. I—Filenti had told me to stop her heart and start it again."

"Then why didn't you?" she demanded, cutting me off.

"Do you want to go sit—"

"No, I want answers." Her jaw was set, and eyes, which I now recognized as the Umbroth hazel, glared down at me. I needed to know more about that, but gods, I had to explain myself. Dewalt turned his body, so he stood between us, watching us both with caution. I made a note to reprimand him for not giving me more warning.

"Your mother told me not to start her heart again. She said if I did, we would die anyway and thousands more too, because they would know what I was. A seer told her. I know now she meant I was the Beloved."

Nor's posture eased a bit, face softening when she saw my own sorrow. "I knew she had begun meeting with a seer. They don't like seers that much. The Myriad, I mean. So she did it in private. I wonder if they caught her." She shook her head, chewing on the inside of her cheek. "Filenti orchestrated this?" she asked, and I nodded. "You said she spoke to you? Did she say anything else?"

I closed my eyes, imagining the woman who might have looked like her daughter a long time ago, the only similarity their dark-brown hair and tanned skin. "I suppose the message she had was for you. She asked me to tell you she was sorry she wasn't better."

The girl nodded, and I watched Dewalt's hand twitch as if he wanted to reach for her. She brushed away a tear with her thumb, nodding. "That sounds like her. I'm—I'm sorry for assuming the worst."

"Don't be. Please, don't be sorry," I said, pausing to breathe for a moment. "I'm glad I could give you her message. And I'm sorry I didn't know how to fix it. I hoped it was a trick, but it made no sense. She was asking me to kill her. What could I do? Why would she lie about that?" I crossed my own arms over my chest, hugging myself in light of the memory. Her death had haunted me just as much as the novices. Knowing it wasn't me who deserved peace at the moment, I did my best to comfort the woman in front of me. "She prayed for me, and I gave her the sacred words. For whatever that's worth."

Nor started nodding, a tear slipping down her cheek. "It's worth so much. Thank you." She let her arms fall to her sides, staring down at the ground for a moment. "As for Declan being my father, I just figured it out, and I'm still not sure I'm right."

"What makes you think that?" I asked, mind racing.

Nor explained what she'd discovered, pulling out a locket to show me. It was too tiny to confirm whether or not the portrait was of Declan, but the rest of the story made sense.

"I took you to get your things a week ago. Why didn't you tell anyone before then?" Dewalt demanded.

"I was looking for portraits of him in the library when you ran into me," Nor's soft voice spoke as her cheeks reddened.

"Wait. Your mother was a conduit, right?" I asked, and before she could finish her answer, I continued. "So that means Declan has elf-blood. Dryul took an elvish woman to bed?" I asked, looking more to Dewalt for an answer, his knowledge about historical matters surpassing mine.

"It does surprise me. He was obsessed with breeding strong conduits, which the elvish blood would be counterproductive in that case. Unless she was pure elf. Is Declan even that old? Perhaps it was a tryst of the heart," he said. I knew I didn't imagine his cheeks flushing as he turned his body to face away from Nor. There would be time for that subject later, and I filed it away. Pushing my thoughts back toward Declan and his probable daughter, I pondered what this could mean.

Disgust filled me. "The Myriad sent you to Folterra. With the other novices."

"I thought he hadn't gotten to me yet," she spat. "It seems he has some limit to his depravity."

I heard a screech, almost like a dragon, and lifted my gaze to the skies, expecting Irses or Ryo, come to harass me. They were on the opposite end of the capital, making use of the ample estate grounds. Behaving, I hoped.

"This tea is going to get cold, Emmeline," Nana's voice said behind me, peeking her head out the door to frown at me.

"Be right there," I called, just as Nor's face blanched.

"Nana, close the door right now! Close the door!" she shouted, and I whipped around.

Horror gripped me. Moving in complete silence as it climbed down from the roof onto the overhanging porch was a vile creature with long legs and arms, the body of a woman, and giant wings of a bat. Lanky blonde hair hung down in front of her face, and as she tilted her head, I realized her jaw was hung open at an awkward angle, maw twisting.

"Get inside, Nana!" I screamed, pulling my divine fire into my hands. But it was too late.

The creature pounced, reaching down and grabbing the tiny woman who'd been more mother to me than my own. She twisted her body, breaking Nana's back as I watched my flames descend upon the beast just a second too late.

CHAPTER 56

Rainier

My mother leapt through the rift behind me, grabbing onto my back to steady her. The row houses where the cafe sat were on fire, the white flames spreading from the central building. I had opened the rift in an alley across the street, not wanting to step right into the middle of an attack. One of the winged creatures spiraled to the ground behind the buildings, wings aflame. Despite my fear for her, pride surged through me. It didn't last long before the beast I'd seen sail past the palace swooped down, about to take the place of the wounded one.

"That's her fire, isn't it?" Shivani asked, and I ignored her stupid question.

"Take some of my divinity. *My* divinity, not the fire. I don't have enough to spare."

My mother's hand was cool on my wrist as she siphoned some of my power, the feeling not dissimilar to getting blooded by leeches. I used my own divinity to dislodge earth from the road and tossed it at the creature about to land on the roof. It dropped; I couldn't tell if it went behind the building or in it, but fear flooded through me. I might not have hurt it enough to make a difference if it fell right on top of her. Stepping out of the alley, I counted six more creatures flying in our direction.

"Put the fire out. There's a well nearby. I can feel it."

"Where are you going?" my mother demanded.

"Where the fuck do you think I'm going?" I yelled, dragging her behind me as I shouldered my way through the few people screaming and running in a panic. "Get inside, go into your cellars if you can," I bellowed just before I kicked in the flaming door of the cafe.

The rafters were aflame, and white heat licked down the walls. A beam hung down from above, and I stepped around it. Smoke was funneling out of the hole in the roof, but it was getting to be too much—and I worried the entire fucking thing was going to collapse. Cyran had created a shield, his shadows solid against the injured beast clawing at the dome around them. It hunched over it, barely able to move with all its limbs and wings. Praise the gods he'd been with Elora and that he took his promise to never hurt her again a step further, protecting her too.

It cocked its head to look at me, and a flash of recognition hit me just as it stretched a clawed limb toward me. Conjuring Emma's fire, I hit the creature with her light, unsheathing my sword the moment my hands were free. Between the boulder I'd thrown at it and the fire, its wings were destroyed, only leaving long legs taller than I was and arms nearly just as long.

"You ssseem well, Your Majesssty," it hissed, and I recognized the mottled face as one of the guards who Declan had used to torment me.

"So, you didn't burn with your ogre friend," I replied, looking around for something to use as a shield. I hadn't had time to grab one, and those claws looked wicked.

"I died by a ssslave woman'sss ax," it slurred as it staggered toward me, body hovering above me on spindly arms and legs. I got a good look at his claw as the beast lunged. Human in form, three curled talons jutted out of the second knuckle. "Declan made usss ssstronger."

I lured him into lunging again and promptly cut off his hand. The beast scrambled backwards hissing, trying to reach the stump but failing because of how gods damn long his revolting limbs were. In my periphery, I noticed the shadow shield dissipating, and I moved to put myself between the beast and my child. A horrifying idea occurred to me, and I nearly lost my balance when the beast lunged.

"Elora, are you in there?" I shouted. I'd do what I could to protect Cyran, but if my daughter wasn't even there, then—

"I'm here!"

Warm relief slid through my veins. "Good. Stay there!"

"I don't know if—"

I didn't hear what else she said as the beast staggered toward me, screeching and wailing. I cut off another chunk of its long arm, but instead of skittering away, he came at me with force, the other claw slicing deep into my shoulder. Staggering back, Cyran's shadows whipped around my ankles, allowing me in. The creature realized it the moment I did, running forward on its three remaining limbs, but was stopped by the blast of fire Elora sent right at its chest, dismissing the shadows and knocking the creature away with enough force, it fell on its back. I rushed forward, dodging scrambling legs as it tried to right itself and failed. It twisted, attempting to bite my leg before I plunged my blade through its heart and twisted. Its limbs curled in upon it, not unlike a gods damn spider. It startled me, thinking it wasn't dead as the heavy limb moved past me. When I pulled out my sword, a muddy substance poured forth, and a few wisps of shadow plumed out, floating up into the smoke.

Turning around, I looked Elora over to see she was unharmed. Fists clenched and jaw set, she was her mother's daughter. The prince was on the ground at her feet, leaning over a body.

"It's his sister," Elora said, barely loud enough for me to hear over the fire. "Cy, we have to get out of here."

"Heal her," the boy demanded, voice a harsh croak as he finally looked up at me with watery eyes. The girl on the ground was long dead. There was no way my divinity could bring her back from that. And I had an entire city to defend with at least six more beasts nearby. A beam fell down behind us, blocking our path back to the street, and Elora tugged on Cyran, attempting to make him stand.

I turned to open a rift, ready to throw the two of them through it, but I couldn't do it. "Fuck," I sighed, closing my eyes and centering myself.

"I said heal her!" Cyran screamed up at me, tears streaming down his face. "Please!"

"I'm sorry, Cyran. She's dead. I can't—I don't even know how Em did it with—she's too far gone. Now, come on. Let me get you two somewhere safe."

"Will you try?" Elora said, and I eyed her for a moment, knowing the outcome but weighing my daughter's heart. She needed me to try. So I crouched in front of the prince and put my hand on the girl's neck.

"There's nothing there for my divinity to latch onto. I'm sorry."

"Try harder," he sobbed. When his hand wrapped around my wrist, I knew he'd remember this moment for the rest of his life. Though the remnants of the roof above us creaked, and I didn't know how much longer I had before those creatures came crashing down upon us, I offered him what I'd have wanted.

"Cyran," I began, waiting until his eyes met mine. "Your sister is dead, and my divinity will not work on her. But while I still have any left, I have to do what is right by my kingdom. Those screams outside? People I can help. And this girl you swore you would never hurt again? You have her to protect with me."

The boy stared at me, tears trickling down from eyes full of guilt. I recognized it, having seen it in Em's eyes. *'Why not me?'* If Em's lingering sorrow was any indication, he'd ask the question for years. But he nodded quickly, standing as Elora grabbed his hand. Water fell from above, my mother having finally figured out how to use my divinity, and the ensuing steam caused me to cough.

I dragged them both out the back door of the cafe into a small courtyard where we could breathe before I attempted to rift once more. Frowning, I rolled my shoulders and spread my hands wide. The spot where the villainous creature had gouged my arm ached, even though I'd used Em's divinity to heal it already.

"It's not going to work, Rainy."

I whipped around, pushing both children behind me as I searched for the voice above us. A voice which had haunted my nightmares. Cyran cursed behind me, and I heard Elora's sharp intake of breath. It only took me a moment before I pinpointed him, picking his way across the wood shingles, held afloat over the holes in the roof by his shadows attempting to bridge the gaps. Declan looked the same as he had during my time in Darkhold.

"Nice of you to visit," I called as I desperately attempted to open a rift once more. Whatever he had done had worked. "Stay behind me," I murmured as Elora peeked her head around me.

"Warded. Finished the circle while you lot were dealing with my itzki." He used his shadows to move down from the roof into the courtyard. I backed up with Elora, spreading an arm out to force Cyran to step back too. The earth began to rumble a split second before I used my divinity to draw forth the rocks nearby to throw at him. His shadows squelched my efforts, spreading to the ground to work as a barricade.

"Aren't they magnificent? It's too bad you killed Vincent. Victor?" Declan shook his head, hands held behind his back as he took a few steps. His blond hair was tied back, and his teeth glinted in the sunlight. "The itzkim haven't been seen since the gods walked. No drakes, but I couldn't be outdone by your whore. So, I brought them back."

Since the last thing I wanted was to hear him speak, I drew Em's fire into my hands, worried about taking too much from her but not having much of a choice, and I sent a wall of flames toward him, cutting the courtyard in half. I wasn't confident enough with her fire to get close to him.

"Itzkim were conduits who stood against the gods, punished for it. You are no god," I barked, shoving Elora and Cyran back toward the building. I heard the loud beat of wings and knew we were fucked. "Get out to the street. Find Shivani," I urged.

"I'm not leaving you," Elora argued, twisting her body away from where I pushed her shoulder. "Gods, are all of you so stupid? I'm not going anywhere!"

"Do I not stand in defiance of the gods now?" Declan yelled out, his shadows attempting to muffle the fire as he spoke. "A symmetry I enjoyed. No, I suppose you are right. They may not be true itzkim, however, I think I did quite well. You should see the one hunting your wife right now. They keep their memories, you know. I'd be more worried about her other hunter though. He has a bone to pick."

"Cyran? Use your shadows to get her out. Drag her if you have to," I ordered, tossing the command over my shoulder.

"No, no," Declan said, sending a snap of shadow over the flames. I dismissed it with my wind, but I paled when I realized his shadows had changed. Something harder for me to fight against.

"Cyran, take her and go!" I bellowed. Declan's dark divinity had turned into something different. Almost flame-like.

"My little brother has some sort of gift, doesn't he? Gets her to trust him, kills her, somehow convinces all of you to forgive him. Then he lures her here to the capital? Which, of course, would bring you to me. It's only a matter of time before the Beloved joins us."

"I didn't—" Cyran stuttered behind me. "I didn't lure you, I swear. This is—he's lying. Elora, look at me. I didn't."

"Silly little fool. Did you think I would not notice our sister sleeping without the necklace?"

When Declan burst through the flame in the center of the courtyard, I was waiting, allowing the fireball I'd held in my hands to launch toward his chest. A shadow whipped in front of him, flicking the fire away, thrusting it past me into the smoldering cafe, and the back wall burst into flames. When I pulled the earth up below him, he used the shadows to stabilize him. And when I broke the earth apart to fling it at him, only a few small rocks met their mark, most of it knocked away with ease.

"You both have to run. I'll make you a path," I said, all the while manipulating the earth to assault Declan. When a rock hit his temple and he cursed, I couldn't help my grin. "Over the hedge, go on."

"I'm not leaving you!" Elora screamed, stepping out from behind me to throw a dozen smaller fireballs at Declan. One of which hit the end of his tunic, but he promptly snuffed it, the dark power rolling over him. I glanced over my shoulder to check on her, and thank the gods I did. I tackled her away at the very last second, the itzki leaping down from the top of the building snatching Cyran instead.

"No," she cried out, reaching past me toward where the beast hovered in the air, the boy wrapped in its arms.

"Up," Declan snarled, and the beast moved farther into the sky.

Scrambling to our feet, I kept Elora behind me as I conjured fire in my hands. And this time, I could feel Em. She was using it. She needed it. I took the small bit

I had, using my wind to push it at Declan with force, satisfied when he staggered back, grunting.

"Your mother needs her fire. Elora, I—"

"Together. Use your air," she said, moving to stand beside me, a burst of her flame going straight toward him. Her flame wasn't strong enough to hurt him too badly, so our best bet was to try to build her flames to something devastating. Amplified by my wind, I whipped it around him, his body stuck within an inferno, slowly closing in on him and cutting off his air.

"Bloody fucking hell!" he screeched, black flames coming up to shield his body, which he spread outward, absorbing the divine fire. "All of this for just a bit of blood."

His eyes narrowed on Elora beside me, and before he moved toward her, I darted forward, sword at the ready, as I pulled every drop of water from the well the next courtyard over and dumped it over him. And when Declan fell to the ground, my sword poised to strike, he grinned.

Elora's scream ripped through the air, and I watched as the prince plummeted to the ground.

CHAPTER 57

LAVENIA

Wrists sore and knees bloody, I woke from a restless sleep, back aching from how I'd leaned forward in unconsciousness. Tied to the mast as I was, alone, I was shocked I'd been able to rest at all. Someone had taken pity on me and brought me a spare piece of sail, though the thin fabric did little in the way of warmth. The shouts of pirates throughout the night as they plundered the *Netari* had kept me from sleep, but now it was the silence which had woken me. By the time I opened my eyes, it was to face the full assault of the winter sun shining directly into them. I had yet to feel the effects of its warmth but knew I'd be grateful for it soon. I closed my eyes once more, thinking of the reason for the silence, and I smiled. The racket of a dragon rising to hunt and bring its catch back, tearing it apart on the deck to eat, was missing. And I felt relief because of what the quiet lack of raucous sounds meant.

Hyše was gone.

The dragon had escaped. That flap of wings I'd heard when I was below deck meant she had gotten away. The pirate's ship was armed with massive mechanical crossbows, and I was shocked she'd been able to flee unscathed. I didn't know how it might help us in the future, but I had hope she could be used to sway the odds in our favor.

Tetty and another pirate had taken Mairin over to their ship first, and though they struggled to carry her, limp as she was after being beaten into unconsciousness, they were gentle with her. I had to be grateful for that. No matter how thoroughly I had begged her, Fiona took every excuse to hurt Mairin. If I didn't speak quickly enough, if I didn't address her properly—almost everything I did earned my merrow a beating.

Tetty had intervened more than once, and even though they were there with Fiona, helping the bitch hold us captive, part of me wondered if they were just as much of a victim as we were. They didn't seem keen on the merrow's behavior. The two of them had a few whispered conversations which seemed to grow heated as they continued. When Tetty escorted Brenna and Nix over next, I had wondered if the two of them only lived because of Tetty's intervention. Brenna had glanced over her shoulder to look at me, tied once more to the mast with bloodied knees, and I saw fear in her eyes. But I wasn't worried.

I was meant to be bait for Queen Estri; Fiona wouldn't kill me.

"What happened to those gold beads you used to wear? They were so pretty," Fiona cooed, crouching down to look me in the eye.

I said nothing as I glared up at her.

"There wasn't much of value on this ship, other than what I've already claimed. Shame. I'll have to find you something lavish to wear for when we meet with Estri."

"You sound quite familiar with her," I forced out between gritted teeth.

"She's quite familiar with my family. I've owed her a visit for quite some time." Her eyes darkened before she reached a fingertip beneath my chin and tilted it up. "I regretted leaving that morning, you know."

I couldn't help it as a laugh burst forth between my lips. "When? When you shimmied down the trellis or when you commandeered the shipment? Or was it later when you had that first sip of stolen wine?"

She sat down on the ground, legs spread and arms resting on her knees. "When I didn't get off for months without thinking about it." She shrugged.

"Divine hell." My laugh was bitter. "It wasn't because of what you did? Not an ounce of remorse?"

"About doing it? No. About doing it *to you?* Maybe. You were quite nice for a royal. And you knew what you were doing with your tongue. And, well, the duke..." She tilted her head, a knowing smile on her lips.

"I get it, Fiona. The sex was good. Any other stupid shit you want to say?"

She guffawed, taking her hat off and running her fingers through her hair. I saw a few grey hairs, and I wondered just how old she was. She was a merrow, after all. If Mairin was over four centuries old and barely looked older than me, how old was Fiona? She clearly didn't know Mairin was Estri's daughter—her *only* daughter. Mairin was much more enticing than I was.

"Tetty is quite soft-hearted. I met them not long after you."

"Ah, but you didn't thieve from them."

"I would have if they had anything worth stealing. They stole my heart instead."

"Oh, for fuck's sake," I said, exasperated.

"This is important, Lavenia. Listen. They're ill. The pendant isn't for me. The pendant will grant Tetty access to the font."

"Is Tetty not a conduit? Can't they just perform the ritual? Gods, what the hell, Fiona?"

"I started out wanting the pendant for me, but when I found out Tetty was going to—Tetty took care of their mother when she died from this, and because of how fucking bad it was, they plan to—before it gets too bad…" Fiona shook her head and cleared her throat. "Tetty is a conduit, but the Myriad won't let me drink from it. And Tetty won't perform it with anyone else. They won't ever be granted access unless I intervene. So, I made a deal with someone," she said, moving to sit cross-legged. "I get a pendant, they'll give me access to the font. Estri doesn't take too kindly to the exiled unless they come with something worthwhile. You're my something worthwhile."

"You think the Myriad will actually allow Tetty access without doing the ritual? Why don't you just steal some of their casks? It would be easier."

"The water from the casks hasn't worked. You think I haven't tried that?"

"Oh," I whispered. "You're taking them to the Seat." Fiona nodded. "So, you plan to use me to convince Estri to give you your pendant, then you're going to use it to leverage your way into the gods damn Seat in Lamera?" Hysterical, I laughed once more. "You're insane. Truly."

"Come on." Fiona was rough as she tugged me to my feet, dragging me toward the gangway. "I already made the deal, Princess." She sneered. "I won't have to leverage shit after Estri. I'll just have to get Tetty there. They're my *everything*. I'll do whatever it fucking takes."

I never saw Beau again, and Fiona, still a merrow even if landlocked as Mairin was, compelled the rest of our crew to stay on the sinking *Netari*.

Over two weeks passed, and we were much farther east than the horn of Olistos. We would stumble upon the Seaborn Queen any day now. Nix, Brenna, and I had all been thrown into a cabin beside Tetty and Fiona, and they kept Mairin locked away from us, forcing us into submission. By the time they untied us, we were too far away from anywhere useful Nixy could have rifted to, but that didn't stop Fiona from keeping him chained in obsidian at the wrists. I felt bad for him, knowing it chafed his skin.

More than half of Fiona's crew had a compulsion rune, so she didn't bother with me. I supposed it made sense if they were seafaring, more likely to stumble upon a merrow, but it surprised me considering Fiona was one. Hadn't she needed to force them to act on her behalf, or were they that loyal to her? She didn't seem like someone stable enough to garner loyalty, but clearly I was wrong.

I'd been able to talk to Mairin through a grate a few days prior to ensure she was even alive. Unable to speak freely, it was difficult to comfort one another. Either way, we were heading to the Seaborn Queen, but I'd expected to go freely and without the threat of Fiona over our heads. I'd expected to come offering something from Vesta which Estri might want, but, now, I was the gift being offered.

Mairin was worried about it. Though I couldn't see her, I knew she had probably bitten her nails down to the quick. Though rare, she did it when she was anxious, and I'd only seen it two times—once when she treated Elora and again with another patient with mortal wounds. During that week, when one soldier lingered between life and death, she'd bitten her nails to the point of bleeding. I hated it. And I knew the thought of me being given to Estri would have set the bad habit off.

The merrow had done her best to calm me, assuring me everything would be alright, and I wouldn't have said it gave me hope—but it certainly didn't dash it. Fiona clearly knew nothing about Mairin, and that was the ace up our sleeve. Perhaps Estri would take offense to what Fiona had done and rid us of the problem.

But I was a soft-hearted fool, and I felt bad for Tetty. Their illness was noticeable once I paid attention. At first, I thought it was vision-related only, causing them to stumble, but now and then, I noticed their arms and legs spasming. Fiona would make a big fuss about getting Tetty into their cabin so she could rub their fatigued muscles. And when their speech slurred one night when they delivered our meal, I realized it was affecting many aspects of their life.

I didn't blame Fiona for wanting to get them to the font.

Brenna stirred, stretching her legs, and it drew me out of my thoughts. Nixy snored softly, and his foot tapped against something metallic, telling me he was precariously close to the waste bucket we'd been given. Thank the gods a sailor had emptied it earlier, so there was only piss in it now. There was nothing less humanizing than having to shit in a bucket in front of two people who I'd either had sex with or who wanted to have sex with me. But the pirates wouldn't let us out, even with the runed sailors as escorts.

Brenna groaned a bit, and it sounded as if she massaged her leg. It was dark where we were, no windows, and they hadn't even given us a lantern.

"Why am I awake if you refuse to sleep?" she asked, not bothering to quiet herself. Nixy slept on despite it.

"I'm sorry. I don't even know what time it is anymore, but I'm not tired."

Though I couldn't see her, I felt her eyes searching for me in the dark. "You'd do the same thing," she muttered.

"What?"

"As Fiona. You'd do this for someone you loved."

I snorted. "Hurt people to save someone? No."

"Not even for Dewalt? If you had to go to the end of the sea and barter with the Seaborn Queen?" I couldn't place the tone of her voice.

"I don't know. I—" I hesitated, not wanting to upset her, but decided I didn't care. "I don't think I've ever felt that strongly for *anyone*. If it was as simple as bartering, sure, but not this."

"You feel that strongly for *everyone*. Do you mean you haven't held someone above all the rest? Now *that*, I could believe. If it was anyone you cared for, you'd have done this in a heartbeat. But that's the thing. With loving everyone so fiercely, you don't have any left over."

"This feels like an argument for the sake of arguing."

"And what if it is? Humor me."

I chuckled, pulling myself up into a seated position. "Fine. I feel strongly for the people I care about, yes."

"You have all the love and conviction for people you care about, but you don't save any extra for the one person you should hold above the others. You never could do it with Dewalt, and you never bothered to with me. Do you think it will be different this time? With her?"

"With Mairin?"

"No, with Queen Emmeline," she huffed in annoyance. "Yes, with Mairin."

"She's a friend who I care about."

"You begged on your knees until they bled."

"I'd have done that for anyone I care about. I'd have done it for you, even though you hate me."

She was silent for a moment, and I listened to her calm breathing. "I don't hate you." I couldn't help but laugh at her words, and she joined in a moment later. It was a soft sound I hadn't realized I'd missed. "Alright, I don't hate you as much as I used to. We weren't compatible," she admitted.

"No?"

"I hated everyone but me and you. Still hate everyone. You loved everyone so much, you didn't have enough left to love us—not fully."

"You don't hate everyone. You're kind, Brenna, I—"

The screech of a dragon interrupted us, and we jumped to our feet as Nixy jolted awake, knocking over the bucket, and the reek of piss filled the small cabin. Boots pounded away from us, and Nixy was shoving past me to throw his body against the door before I could move. A loud thud reverberated from above, and we all flinched.

"Come on. We have to get to the dragon. Are you ready?"

"Mairin is below, Nix. I can't leave without her."

"I'll get her," Brenna said. "I swear. But you have to go. Get to Hyše."

Nixy kicked near the doorknob, and it slammed open. He led the way, finding the ladder which led to a trapdoor, and without hesitation, flung it open. Brenna slid past me, moving toward the other end of the ship. I groaned, my eyes adjusting painfully to the sun. Nixy charged through, grabbing a saber from the limp form of a body lying still on the deck. Though his wrists were still cuffed, preventing him from rifting, Fiona had given him some slack, and he tossed the saber to me before snagging an abandoned weapon laying at his feet.

Chaos reigned.

Hyše circled from above, diving past flaming arrows to tear pirates from the deck before tossing them. Most of her marks went flying into the water, but I understood the source of the loud thud from moments ago as one man fell back to the deck, an earsplitting crack telling me he didn't survive the fall. It also explained the abandoned weapon.

An arrow hit the dragon, going through her wing, and she screeched—flying farther out to sea before turning back, a dot against the sun. Nixy crept over to a barrel and knelt behind it. I joined him, unnoticed.

Fiona clambered out of the same trapdoor we'd come from. "Find them!" she screamed. She wasn't wearing shoes, her hat missing completely, and Tetty slipped on a rung as they climbed up behind their partner. They both appeared disheveled from sleep, and though it was midday, I wondered if it was because Tetty's illness necessitated rest. They wobbled on their feet, and Fiona gripped their elbow to steady them.

It was then I heard the song.

I couldn't understand why Mairin would even bother, not in this chaos, when more than half the people on the ship were unassailable by her song. But gods, it was beautiful. I searched for her, doing my best to find her without revealing where Nixy and I hid. When I finally spotted her across the ship, Brenna was beside her, doing her best to hold off any of the attackers who didn't fall victim to Mai's song. I watched as they crossed the deck together, surprised by the way they moved as one. Where Brenna's sword missed, Mairin carried a small dagger.

They'd spent a lot of time together while Mairin gave me space, and I wondered if that was the reason for their harmony. Far closer than was comfortable, I heard Fiona join her in song and panicked.

"Don't look either of them in the eyes, Nix. I don't know what Mairin is saying, and I don't—"

A loud roar came from overhead, and I ducked on instinct, not even realizing Hyše had returned. And she dove, landing just long enough for Mairin to climb on her back, Brenna scrambling up behind her. Then they were in the air again. When I stopped hearing Mairin's song, I realized it was the dragon she'd been calling to. She'd summoned her own means of escape after Brenna got her loose.

Relief flooded me as Nixy grabbed my arm, dragging me toward the prow.

"We have to get where they'll see us. Come on."

We made our way slowly, avoiding the pirates who'd run to the railing, shooting flaming arrows at the dragon as she flew farther away. Fiona had stopped her own song and was screaming at the top of her lungs while Tetty watched on in silence, arms crossed tightly over their body. We got as close to the prow as possible, hiding behind barrels and spare rigging when my eyes deceived me.

Or so I thought.

Climbing a rope up the side of the ship, I saw a man whose legs and torso were swiftly changing from a speckled grey to an iridescent shimmer before fading away to a golden-bronze.

"Selkie," I breathed. And not just one, I realized. The entire ship was being overcome by the seaborn shifters, each of them climbing nude up the side before clambering over.

Why had the shifters come?

And why did none of the pirates move? Why did no one fight back? They were outnumbered two to one by the selkies, but that shouldn't have stopped them. Another roar sounded as Hyše circled back, and Brenna pointed us out on the prow, causing the dragon to change direction.

It took me far too long to understand what I looked at as a large tentacle flew out of the water, thicker than a tree trunk and far longer than the tallest one I'd ever seen. It was a dark red color, though the suckers on the interior were nearly white. I couldn't stop the scream of terror which bubbled up from my lungs as it slammed into Brenna. She fell for far too long before smacking the hard surface of the water.

And then the tentacle wrapped around Hyše's leg. Another lifted out of the water to join it, crunching a wing in its grip. If I had once thought the roar of a dragon was unsettling, I had never heard one scream. Nausea and panic flooded my system. Nixy stood horror-struck beside me, neither of us breathing.

"She can't swim," I whispered, rushing forward to brace my hands on the railing, not caring if any of the pirates or selkies saw me. "Oh gods, Brenna can't swim."

Mairin had turned, using her dagger to slash at the tentacle, though it did no good. The dragon's legs were being crushed—twisted in the sea monster's grip. Hyše screamed and roared and clawed to get away as Mairin finally gave up, and I watched as she jumped free from the creature, contorting her body into a more graceful dive.

When she came up for air, I was about to yell for her to find Brenna, to save her, but Nixy put a hand over my mouth.

"She hit the water too hard when she fell. There's no way she survived it. Don't reveal us."

Tugging me back as a sob ripped free from my lungs, he motioned toward a few crates for us to hide behind when I heard a rift. I barely caught sight of Fiona's curly mane of hair as she tussled with a selkie. Tetty waited on the other side of the rift, holding out a hand with terror written across their features as Fiona dove toward the rift, rolling through it with not one, but two selkies attached to her as it closed.

"What do we do?"

Nixy grabbed my upper arm, shoving me behind the crates. "You fucking hide, Venia. Hanwen's ass, I don't even—gods," he continued muttering to himself, clearly at a loss.

I folded my arms around my legs, tucking them up into my chin. Brenna was dead, and I wasn't sure Mairin would survive it either. Though she was a merrow and had fallen with grace, the creature might have still wanted her, and I nearly sobbed at the thought of that beast curling a tentacle around her, dragging her beneath the waves.

Then a song began. A haunting melody which spoke of grey-misted coasts and lovers lost at sea. And though I saw no one, the taunting draw of it brought me to my feet.

CHAPTER 58

Emmeline

"Inside!" I screamed, using my divinity to shoot another blast of white fire at the creature as it flew off, careening wildly as it attempted to put out the flames surrounding its wings. The foul beast had dropped Nana on the porch, and as we came upon her, Dewalt grabbed her by the shoulders while Nor and I managed her legs, carrying her inside. She tried to cough, but the sound was far too wet.

"I—I don't know—" I stammered, backing away from her bed inside the dormitory, looking upon her twisted frame in horror. In order for my divinity to work, her spine would need to be set.

"The women and children," Nor murmured. "That thing will be back. You have to get them out of here," she said. I nodded, swallowing hard. "Go gather them. I'll—I'll do what I can while I—" My lip trembled. The small woman on the bed moaned and attempted to cough once more, blood gurgling onto her lips. She was turning blue as her breaths grew more laborious, and her heart was racing because of it.

"Go to her," Dewalt said, voice low. "I'll help gather the women."

"I need your help to set her spine," I said, pleading.

"No," Nana groaned. "Don't want that." I rushed toward the side of her bed and grabbed her hand.

"Can you feel that?" I asked.

"Can't feel anything," she replied. The scent of urine filled the air. Her breathing grew more haggard, and I slid my hand into her shirt above her breastbone, pouring my healing into her. It felt as if she were injured high on her back; I couldn't heal her completely without setting her spine, but I could help.

"No," she snapped. "Do not make it take...long," she said, struggling to speak around her slowing breaths. "Let it...be quick."

"Let me heal you, please. Dewalt, come here," I begged.

I heard his footsteps behind me, but Nana's eyes darted to his, a warning on her face.

"Save those...babies."

"Nana, please."

"Like you and...Lucia. It's been nice...to remember."

A soft knock came behind us, and Nor's apologetic face stared back at me from the doorway.

"Everyone's almost ready. Do you want to open the rift in here?" She glanced at Nana.

"No," Dewalt said, voice lower than normal. "They don't need to see this. I'll sit with her."

"I'll stay too," Nor added. And I nodded, looking down at the woman who I'd only just been able to reconnect with, and knew by the time I returned she would probably be gone. She tried to nod toward the door.

"Save them," she whispered.

I breathed deep before squeezing her hand, knowing in my heart she couldn't feel it. I only stood there for a moment before walking down the hall to where over a dozen faces stared at me, fear thick in the air. Opening a rift into my chambers in the palace, I directed them to stay there, uncertain of where the safest place would be. It only took me a few moments, but by the time I returned, Dewalt was gone, and Nor shook her head, eyes wide and bright, and I knew Nana had slipped out of this life.

"She—she said something about your mother."

Unable to think about Nana's final words, I latched onto something else. "Where did Dewalt go?" I asked, voice raw.

"Theo. He was outside. He ran to get him."

"Oh gods," I said, covering my hand with my mouth. "We left him out there." A loud screeching noise resounded outside, and I drew my fire into my hands as I slammed out the door. "Stay here!" I shouted as Nor made to follow.

Running out front, I turned, finding nothing—then I caught a glimpse of massive wings flapping behind the building. Hearing Dewalt's shout and Theo's scream, I ran for them, opening a rift behind the evil beast and directing my fire at its wings. Letting the rift close in front of me, I started to open a new one to attack it from another angle.

There was a sharp pain in my shoulder blade, and I sucked in a breath before spinning, reaching for my dagger with one hand as I drew fire into the other. I'd thought I was being attacked from behind, but when I found nothing, I shook out my limbs and opened the new rift and hit the attacker with another divine burst of flame.

Dewalt stood in front of Theo, brandishing an old rake at the creature while Theo scrambled backward.

"A sword, Theo. Get him a sword," I ordered, preparing myself as the vile monster lurched back screaming, its massive wings flapping wildly. Instead of extinguishing the flames, the beast only succeeded in lighting the stable on fire. The evil thing leered forward, clawed arms slashing across Dewalt's chest. I attempted to use Rain's divinity, dragging roots upward from the ground to wrap up the creature's legs as Dewalt stumbled back. Reddened stripes of torn skin showed through his ripped shirt, and he scrambled for the sword Theo brought, both men's hands shaking.

I wrapped the beast's leg in a thorny branch, and its screams turned frantic. Between the fire destroying its wings and its inability to move, it panicked, shrieking in a language I didn't know.

A hawk's screech tore through the sky, and a second later, a large mouse dropped to the ground in front of me. My jaw fell open in shock when I recognized Aedwyn in his shifted form, and relief tore through me as he ran up my leg. I plucked him from my pants and cradled his tiny body in my hands. How he had come back to us, how he and his sister, Aerfen, had escaped, I couldn't know. But gods, I was thankful. Grateful Declan had been lying about Aerfen's death to hurt Rain. All these months, we'd been using spies to keep an eye out for Aedwyn and had heard nothing. But now they'd finally come home.

Theo ran toward the dormitory, panic and self-preservation rightfully coming over him. Dewalt staggered toward the beast stuck in the tangle of roots, ready to stab it in the chest.

"Sorry, in my shirt you go," I said, hurrying to protect the shifter as another cursed nightmare soared into view, dipping low in a scream with claws outstretched. I put Aedwyn in my breast pocket just as I pulled more divine fire into my hands, about to attack the newcomer, when another loud sound came from above us.

My dragon.

Irses had come to help. I knew now he was more connected to me than I had ever thought he could be. His giant maw tore a wing from the new creature, and it fell, spinning to the ground. Theo jumped back just in time, turning toward the stable once more as the newest assailant thrashed about.

Ryo startled me, diving from behind me in a roar, not quite as ferocious as Irses but no less intimidating, and tore into the newly grounded horror. Within a few moments, both creatures were dead thanks to the two dragons and Dewalt. My friend dropped his blade in disgust as shadows and a muddy liquid poured from the beast's chest. It fell backward beside the stable, long limbs drawing up as it died, causing chills to creep up my spine. Ryo dragged the other monstrosity toward the copse of trees, settling down to gnaw on it before I reprimanded him. Disgusting.

I staggered toward the stable, pulling water from the creek nearby to extinguish the flames. My attempts were much more messy than Rain's, and I soaked Dewalt in the process. He shot a glare at me but said nothing. I still needed my husband to teach me how to control that aspect of his divinity.

Panicked, I reached down the bond, feeling for Rain, and the anger and rage and worry I felt knocked me back a step. I needed to get to him and Elora. If we were being attacked, I was sure the whole city would be in trouble as well. I did what I could to tell him I was alright, gently tickling those precious threads, when an aching pain ran through my legs. A sharp spear of hurt in my breast a moment later had me wrenching the mouse out of my pocket and gently setting him on the ground, where he began to shift.

"Was that necessary?" I shouted at the mouse before turning to address my loyal beasts. "You two," I directed the dragons. "Get the others and hunt down those monsters."

Ryo was in the sky within a moment, but Irses turned doleful eyes on me. And gods, with the tilt of his head and that vivid green, I was reminded so strongly of Rain. "We'll be alright. Go. There's more of these out there. Do as you're told," I said, and if a dragon could give attitude, I swore, Irses sassed me more than Elora did. He did what I asked though, taking off into the sky as I stumbled over to Dewalt and Theo. My legs ached, and I needed to sit down for a moment before rifting into the capital.

"Aedwyn is back. Aerfen too," I told Dewalt, nodding toward the shifting mouse, as I placed a hand on his sticky chest. He winced and unbuttoned his shirt so I could treat the wounds easier. It took far longer to heal him than it ought to have, and I worried they would fester. Those claws had looked foul.

"Rainier said Aerfen was dead," he grumbled, itching at his healed chest.

"Declan must have lied."

When I finished with Dewalt, I sat down on the ground, rubbing my legs and pouring my own divinity into them. Perhaps I'd pulled a muscle. A moment later, Aedwyn walked over, naked. His face was gaunt, cheeks hollowed and eyes dull.

"There's clothing in the stable. I'll get you some," Dewalt said.

"That won't be necessary. I won't be in this form for long." He tilted his head, looking at me curiously. His light brown hair was sheared short, and he had a full beard—copper in color. Dewalt shrugged, going into the stable anyway to get his own replacement shirt.

"We've been looking for you. I'm so glad—"

A woman stepped out from the sparse gathering of trees beside the stable between the beast corpses. I hadn't seen Aerfen before, always in her hawk form, but judging by the resemblance and her nudity, it had to have been her. When I moved to stand though, the pain in my legs increased, and it moved up my torso, compressing. I couldn't breathe. I leaned back roughly against the wall, gasping for breath, but nothing happened. The shifters looked at me with curiosity while Theo knelt at my side.

"Emma? Are you alright? Do you need some water?"

The pain increased over my body, squeezing tight. I thrashed against the pressure, gulping for air, but I couldn't get any. It felt like drowning, but there was no water. As Theo moved to sit in front of me, I watched as Aerfen pulled something out of her mouth. A tiny black orb. Shining, she held it out in her outstretched palm to her brother.

I was clawing at my throat as a memory surfaced in my mind. My hand reaching in the dark, Keeva standing over me, my bones breaking, me tugging on her hair. Slowing her heart and killing her. The memory I'd used to form Hyše. The memory I felt slip away from my grasp, I watched dissipate, and by the time it was gone, I couldn't remember the woman at all.

But I knew Hyše was dead.

Just as I could finally take a deep breath, the cold air biting, I found the shifters watching me carefully as Aedwyn placed something on the ground—the black orb his sister had handed him, and it was smoking. I didn't understand.

And I didn't have time to understand as the twins ran, and the ball exploded, throwing both me and Theo through the stable wall.

The heavy sound of fists smacking into flesh woke me, and I winced as the setting sun shone directly into my eyes.

"You fucking traitor!" Dewalt yelled, and I dragged a hand over my face, grimacing as I found tiny sharp objects embedded in my skin. I was dizzy, so it took me a moment to gather my bearings and realize my divinity was abnormal. It was faint, buzzing frantically but barely there. A whisper of the power I should have had. It was simultaneously both relieving and terrifying.

"You left me!" Aedwyn shouted, voice a shrill sound as it echoed in the clearing.

My back felt as if it were on fire, and I sat up before looking down at my legs. My breeches were torn, and I could see tiny black fragments of something digging into my flesh, red dots of blood painting my skin. When I went to tug a larger piece out, still no bigger than my smallest nail, I nearly retched when I realized it was obsidian. I was covered in it. Tiny daggers of obstruction stifled my divinity. It was choked, but what little I did have was trying to heal me. Using all of my concentration, I stopped it, afraid my skin would close over the fragmented cursed rock. Instead, I focused on the back of my skull, where I'd slammed into the stable wall. I needed to get my wits about me.

Everything felt as if it were spinning, and it took me a moment to focus on the figures blurring in front of me. Dewalt had Aedwyn pinned to the ground, and his fists were flying into him, beating the shifter into submission. Aedwyn was unarmed, still naked, and he covered his face with his hands. But it was no use against the righteous assault.

"Your Majesty, Emmeline, are you alright?" Nor was at my side, and in my haze I wondered how long she had been there. How long had I been out? Clearly, the blast had drawn her outside even though I'd told her to stay put. I felt heat at the back of my skull, and I was grateful for what small bit of my divinity remained as it worked to heal me.

Dewalt panted, sitting up with his hands in his hair. Aedwyn lay still on the ground, but I saw the shallow rise of his chest. I wouldn't have cared if it never moved again.

"You can stand, can't you?" The novice asked me, looking down at my bleeding legs. "Those creatures will be back; we need to get out of here." She tugged at me, trying to pull me up.

"Hold on, Nor," I said, watching as Dewalt stood, dragging Aedwyn toward us. I wondered if the only reason the shifter survived was because Dewalt's sword sat beneath the debris from the stable.

"Where is his sister?" I called, and Dewalt scanned the surrounding area before shaking his head. I couldn't see her, and the small net my divinity would allow me to cast only let me feel four other heartbeats nearby, though one was— "Theo?" Rising to my knees, I frantically searched for the boy. I'd been so dazed I hadn't even realized he had been hurt. But when I finally found him, my breath caught in my chest.

He was lying closer to the center of the stable, immobile. His chest movements were shallow, and though I'd barely heard it with my divinity, his heart was sluggish. Blood leaked from his nose and ear, and his auburn hair was far more red than it ought to have been. He clearly had a devastating head wound, and I needed to get to him.

"Nor, help me—

The novice fisted my hair and pulled as I screamed. Grabbing onto her hands, I held on as she dragged me backwards out of the rubble into the clearing.

"What the fuck, Nor?" Dewalt shouted, shock not even beginning to describe what both of us seemed to feel. "Let her go!" Though I couldn't see him, I heard the thud of Dewalt dropping Aedwyn.

"We don't have time for you to heal the boy. He's waiting for us."

"What?" I groaned, attempting to stand. Bent over with her hand firmly in my hair made it difficult. I reached for my dagger but was instead met with an empty thigh, the belt I wore having ripped with my pants.

"Fuck, fuck, fuck," she muttered. "He's going to kill me."

"Nor, let her the fuck go!" Dewalt shouted as his footsteps thundered closer.

Though she held me in her grasp, clearly with the intention to take me to Declan, a part of me felt bad when I drew the tiniest flame—the best I could muster—and I placed my palm on her leg. I thought of her other burns, knowing what had been done to her at her father's hand and what he clearly was making her do, as I twisted away when she dropped my hair. She screeched, reaching for the burnt skin, and I forcibly shoved her away from me.

"Hands on your head and don't move," Dewalt barked at the woman, and she listened, panic and regret flooding her features. "What is this?" he said, voice softening as he stepped closer to her. "Gods, I was fucking right all along?" He shifted uncomfortably, and I wondered just how far things had gone between the two of them.

"I'm sorry," she sobbed, looking at him with pleading eyes.

Confident he had the matter in hand, I started back for the stable to heal Theo. Though I didn't want to use my divinity until I got to him, the obsidian fragments still tempering it far too much, I worried he might already be dead. But I spotted movement out of the corner of my eye, and I turned to face the dormitory, not understanding what I saw.

A person was crawling down the back steps of the porch, and I heard a muffled scream from behind the gag she wore as panicked hazel eyes met mine and she tumbled down the stairs.

Nor.

I whipped around to scream to Dewalt, to warn him, to stop what was about to happen, but I was too late.

He'd let her put her arms down, wasn't treating her as a threat as he questioned her, so when she reached behind her to pull my dagger from her waistband, he wasn't prepared. He told her to stop, relying on the coercion he no longer had access to. My scream echoed through the clearing as I ran toward them and Dewalt fell to his knees, my dagger embedded firmly in his chest. She used her foot on him as leverage to pull the dagger free, turning to brandish it toward me as he collapsed.

"You have to come with me," she bellowed.

I wasn't thinking, my instincts and training from the man who lay dying beside me rushing in. Heart racing, everything else fell to the wayside—my throbbing head, the tiny pricks of pain from the obsidian. All of it. Kicking her hand, my dagger flew free, and she cursed.

She dove toward me, but I jumped back, causing her to stumble. And in that moment of weakness, I struck, grabbing her by the forearm and twisting.

"Fuck!" she screamed as she curved the rest of her arm to ease the pain.

"Who the fuck are you?" I screamed as I kicked behind her knee, and she fell to the ground. Shifted to look like Nor, it had to be a dynamic shifter. My head was aching, and I grew dizzy as I pushed her down. I didn't dare waste any of my divinity though, knowing I would be lucky to use it to keep death away from either of the two men who lay bleeding out. Face flattened to the earth, I dug my knee between her shoulder blades to keep her from moving even though she beat and scratched at me the best she could. Her movements grew lethargic, and she stopped fighting me.

"Just kill me already," she cried, and I grabbed her hair at the nape of her neck just as it changed color, turning her to the side so I could see her face. "He's going to kill me either way," she panted. I watched as her hair turned from Nor's dark brown waves to Aerfen's plain brown hair and once more to shorter auburn hair, and that was when I realized.

"You're the fucking shifter. From Darkhold," I spat. "I watched him kill you."

"No, but Declan made me wish he had."

Dewalt groaned, and I glanced over at my friend. He had the wherewithal to put a hand to the wound, doing his best to stop the bleeding. But I could already tell he was growing weaker, and it wouldn't be enough. The real Nor stumbled over, carrying Dewalt's sword in bound hands as tears ran down her face. She handed it to me, and I took it, unsure of what I wanted to do with it.

"Put pressure on his chest," I directed Nor, and I stood, pressing my foot to the center of the shifter's back as I rose.

"It wasn't you," Dewalt mumbled, voice trailing off as Nor knelt beside him.

"I'm sorry," the shifter begged, body writhing. "He made me do it!"

"May the gods forgive you then," I said, as I plunged the blade through the back of her neck.

CHAPTER 59

Elora

I watched in horror as Cyran fell from the sky. He lurched forward, plummeting face-first toward his death. There was nothing anyone could do as a silent scream ripped from his lips. Time slowed down while he fell, and I couldn't look away. Moments of soft silence came back to me, tender quiet in one another's company. I'd had a lot of time to think about what Cyran meant to me, and what I stood to lose if I never let him back into my life. My heart had dropped the moment he said he was leaving, and I had planned to do everything in my power to get him to stay. And then hell had broken loose.

What if I never got to speak to him again?

Cy wasn't what I thought I could have ever wanted. He was soft behind his sarcasm, quite unlike the heroes in my stories. He could barely wield a sword because he'd never been taught. I didn't think he'd done a moment of manual labor in his life. And he demanded nothing of me. He'd always tried to make the best of the situation when I was in Evenmoor, and he'd looked out for the good of the world by doing what he did to me. Cyran was good, despite all the things which should have made him evil. Even if he'd done something tremendously bad to me, I didn't want him to be alone. Perhaps it was naive to think that way. But now, as I watched him dropping to the ground, I wished I'd been kinder to him and allowed his good intentions to count for more when it came to my forgiveness.

Even as he continued to fall, Rainier's shout pulled my attention away from the plummeting prince to the two men scuffling on the ground. Had my scream caused this? Had it distracted Rainier enough that Declan could take him by surprise? Was it my fault?

A shriek tore through the air, followed by a gleeful cackle as the itzki caught Cyran before launching back into the sky. Playing with him. I was able to relax for a second—only a moment—and hope washed over me once more. Cyran was still in danger, but the moment of clarity I'd experienced during his fall only made me know with that much more certainty I wouldn't let him go after we defeated Declan.

Shaking out my tightened limbs, I focused on Rainier and that evil man, not knowing what to do. If I used my divine fire, it would hit both men, and I didn't want to hurt Rainier. He had used his organic divinity to manipulate the ground, pulling Declan down, but he only used his shadows to pull himself out or to wrench Rainier off of him. They tussled in that way for a while, and I used my fire when I could. Rainier landed a punch, and it appeared as if he were about to have the upper hand as he straddled Declan. I knew he said my mother needed her divine fire, but when I saw him cup his hand to wield it, I breathed a sigh of relief.

Declan's shadows plucked Rainier off him just before he could use the fire, tossing him forcefully to the ground. I didn't understand how much I could hate the power coming from Declan when I didn't hate it when Mama or Cy used it. I'd never seen Rainier use the shadows, but something told me I wouldn't hate it from him either. They were fun and playful when they used them, but the ones Declan created were made of malice and destruction.

Rainier groaned, holding his head from where he slammed into the ground as I pulled my own fire into my hands, sending a wave of heat and light toward Declan. He dismissed my assault all too easily, letting his shadows absorb it and turning it into wicked black flames.

He made a show of checking a pocket watch and looking to the skies as he smothered my fire once more. Rainier clambered to his feet, and I wondered what had taken him so long. Was he not able to heal himself? Was Mama alright?

"Afraid to use her divinity, Rainy? She must be having quite a rough go of it right now if you can feel her using it."

After a blessed week of warmer temperatures, it had grown cold once more—blustering winds chilled the air and tiny snowflakes fell intermittently. Though it was frigid, I'd grown sweaty, brow damp as I used my divinity to the best of my ability. I hadn't come into my full power yet, so, though I was far more gifted than many other conduits my age because I was blessed at birth, I was going to run out—and soon.

Rainier was hurting, and I could tell as his wind barely moved Declan's shadows away before they turned into whips, attempting to wrap around his legs. I did my best to help, dispatching them with my fire, but I could tell we didn't have much more fight left in us. We'd lost the brief upper hand because of me. Because I'd screamed, and it had distracted Rainier. Because he had stopped what he was doing to listen and assess, protecting me.

Shivani had told me what my dead grandfather had said. That love would be his weakness. The man had been talking about Mama, but maybe he was right about love. Rainier had shown in his actions and by listening to me that he loved me, and now it was going to be the reason we lost this fight.

He'd never said it to me either—probably for fear of scaring me off. But if we were going to die, he needed to know I was grateful for his love and returned it.

When one shadow wrapped around Rainier's ankle, pulling him to the ground, I knew we were close to the end. He hurled a boulder at Declan, easily diverted with that evil power. Within the span of a breath, Rainier was being wrapped up in vines of dark divinity, the shadows dragging him closer to their master. Rainier bellowed for me to flee, and Declan's gaze landed on me, a smirk playing on his thin lips. He groaned in frustration, spinning to block the water and rocks Rainier threw at him, and I knew what I had to do.

"Elora, no!" my father cried as I barreled toward Declan at a run, throwing my arms around his neck and holding on as tight as I could.

CHAPTER 60

Emmeline

Tossing the sword to the side, I glanced over to make sure Nor's hands were steady on Dewalt's wound. I hesitated to use any of my divinity, not until I could get the blasted obsidian off of me, but I reached out to listen for both his and Theo's hearts as I started picking tiny shards of stone from my exposed skin. Theo's heart was sluggish but steady while Dewalt's raced far too fast. I closed my eyes, inhaling as I attempted to calm my own.

I didn't know what to do. Theo had a head injury and had been unconscious since it happened. If I didn't heal him soon, I might not be able to at all. And he was only a child—barely eighteen. Gods, it might already be too late; he'd been unconscious for a while. But since his heart felt steady enough, I hesitated to go to him first. Head wounds were always far more taxing on my divinity than anything else, and if I started there, I wouldn't be able to heal Dewalt as well. And his situation was more dire by far. With Dewalt's beat racing the way it was and the chest wound? He'd bleed out in minutes without my intervention. Since regrets stemming from whichever choice I made would accompany me during my life's sleepless nights, I only allowed myself a moment to linger in my indecision.

"Nor, I'm going to switch positions with you, and you need to get this obsidian out of my skin."

The woman nodded, not moving until I was ready to take over for her. Before my hands were even hovering over his chest, the little bit of divinity I could access was already frantic in its need to mend.

"Emma, wait," Dewalt's voice was strained as he spoke to me, clutching my wrist. Short of breath, he forced out an order. "You have to cut my hair."

"What?" I sputtered.

"Thyra told me—it's not braided, but—" he groaned, closing his eyes. "It'll have to do. Before I die, you have to."

"You're not fucking dying," I asserted.

"Emma, please," he said, deep brown eyes searching mine as pain forged a path in the creases on his forehead.

"Let me heal you for a second first, alright?" He closed his eyes, sighing, and I slid my fingertips toward Nor's hands, and we gracefully switched places. "I promise, D. I'll—I'll cut your hair if I think—if it comes to that."

With my divinity only a trickle while Nor started frantically picking at the shards on my exposed thigh, I didn't know if I should try to slow his heart so it wouldn't bleed out so much, or if I should focus on knitting the wound—so I tried to do a bit of both. His breathing only grew more rapid as he struggled to get air into his lungs. I worried one was punctured. In my mind, I urged Nor to hurry but knew she was doing the best she could. The shards of obsidian were far too tiny and too numerous for her to do much.

"Is there a well nearby? Water and some cloth, and you can be rough with it. I can heal myself after."

Nor scrambled to her feet, hesitating for only a second as she twisted her hands together, but she said nothing.

"I thought it was really her—Nor," Dewalt muttered.

"Don't talk," I ordered, focusing my attention on the mess beneath my hands. I was slowing the flow of blood, but the moment I tried to knit the wound from the deepest point outward, the blood would start flowing faster. I could barely do anything. His breathing grew ragged—slower and wetter with each passing second. Trying to send so much divinity through me into Dewalt when I couldn't truly access it was tiresome, and, though I knew the well ran deep, my head was already aching. Would I run out?

"I would've deserved it, you know," he said, pausing for breath. "For kissing her."

"I said stop talking." I sobered though, realizing that if she didn't get back fast enough with water, if I didn't have enough access to my divinity, I might be stopping my friend from saying his last words. "You kissed her?" I asked, attempting to be soothing.

He tilted his head down a bit in confirmation. "Thought her stabbing me was a sign." A gasping breath. "Might still be a sign."

"And what would that sign be?" I asked. Adjusting, I maintained pressure on the wound while moving my body to rest beside his.

"Maybe your sister doesn't approve."

I clicked my tongue, shooting a look at him. "She could be an ass, D. Trust me, I know. But she would have wanted you to be happy."

Dewalt glanced over my shoulder before closing his eyes once more. "Fuck, this hurts. Everywhere." One of his hands slid up to his stomach, and I tried to pour more divinity into his chest, but what I had was barely enough to do anything. Footsteps approached behind me and Nor returned, dumping a bucket of water over my thigh. Down on her knees, she began to scrub at my leg with a gentle touch.

"More forceful than that, Nor." I winced as she obeyed. Blood dripped down onto my hands, and I knew the worst of the embedded rock was stuck in my face and chest, but I didn't know how she could do much there while I held compression on his wound. The change in my divinity was barely noticeable, and it was becoming harder and harder to staunch the blood working to pump freely into the rest of his body. Between that and his panting getting worse, I felt for the bond, praying to the gods Rain would come. Though I didn't know what we would do once he found us, because with Dewalt's lungs compromised and his heart beating too fast as they were, could Rain repair it himself? He was still a bit clumsy with my healing divinity.

I felt Dewalt's body twitch, and I glanced up at his face to find it in a grimace.

"Emma," he whispered, gasping for breath. "Cut my hair."

"No," I said, voice breaking as I blinked back tears. "You're not dying."

"I'm not *not* dying though, am I?" He uttered out between inhales which grew weaker and weaker. His small smile as he looked at me undid me. My face screwed up, and a tear slipped free.

"I'm going to fix you, D. You're going to be alright."

Nor scrubbed harder at my extended leg, and it drew a gasp from me. Even if she could pull every tiny shard out of it, it still wouldn't be enough. Dewalt slid his hand over from where it rested on his stomach, and a light brush of his pointer finger against my arm brought my gaze back to his.

"I will be alright, I know. Just...let me look upon her face." I thought he meant Nor, and based on her stilled movements, she thought he meant that too. But he looked at me with shining eyes, and I realized what he meant. He swallowed and took two gasping breaths. "I'm fucking tired, mouse."

"It's alright, D. I'm going to—it's going to be alright."

I could barely feel them, but I tugged on those golden threads with everything I had.

Dewalt closed his eyes, and I panicked. Every bit of my divinity I could pour into him, I did to the point of pain, and I felt his fingertip brush against me once more. "Cut my hair," he breathed, struggling to speak. "And go save the boy. Let me go."

Dewalt didn't open his eyes again as he fell into unconsciousness. I didn't move my hands, didn't dare stop what I was doing. Barely keeping him alive as it was, I wouldn't listen for Theo's heart, hoping it was as steady as I'd left it.

"I'll do it," Nor whispered, and keeping my hands on the wound, I looked over my shoulder at the novice. Her dark hair hung down in front of her face, and she wouldn't look at me. "I'll cut his hair."

I swallowed and nodded as she rose, walking over to retrieve my dagger. Gently lifting his head to rest in her lap, deft fingertips pulled his hair from beneath his head, carefully bundling it together. He moaned a bit, the jostling of his body causing him pain even in sleep.

"I-I don't know the beliefs of the old gods. Do I just cut it?"

"I'm sure however you do it will be fine," I whispered. I watched as my dagger slipped through the strands, cutting the black silk shorter. "A warrior until the end," I said, my voice breaking.

"Until the end," Nor agreed, and her long fingers brushed tiny circles of comfort on his temples, and she began to cry too—as a small smile lifted his lips.

CHAPTER 61

LAVENIA

It felt as if I were gliding as the song pulled my body toward the center of the ship. A serene peace came over me, reminding me of floating on my back in a lake as a child, sun-drenched and tired. Even the wind had seemed to die down, and my worries over Mairin had calmed. She was a merrow, after all. It didn't matter if she didn't have her pendant—I'd seen her swim. I moved past selkie and pirate alike, all frozen. The selkies let their heads turn as they watched me, but the pirates only moved their eyes, as if the same song was keeping them moored to the deck.

A tentacle pushed Mairin onto the ship in a wet heap. She was on her knees, curls drenched, as she held herself up by her hands, coughing. Though I wasn't nearly as worried about her as I had been only moments ago, I found relief in her presence. She was pale as snow and shaking from the cold, but as her green eyes lifted to mine, I couldn't tell what I saw. Fear? Frustration? I watched with a detached awareness as the tentacle behind her seemed to shrink, wrapping around the railing as it heaved a giant body from the water.

I should have been more concerned, but my heart didn't pound and my skin didn't pebble; the song kept me compliant.

As the body belonging to the tentacles slopped onto the deck, I couldn't believe it had been able to take Hyše from the sky. It had to have shrunk—far too small, it was barely bigger than a pony if you didn't count the tentacles. One large eye watched me from the center of a cylindrical body. The song stopped, and the eye blinked, and I realized the haunting melody had been coming from the creature. At once, my heart started racing, and I tried to scramble away from it—but I slammed into the wet body of a selkie who stood behind me.

"Let go of me!" I shouted, tearing myself away from him. He was far warmer than I expected, especially considering just how gods damned frigid the winter air was. His grip was tight on my upper arms as he turned me to face the creature writhing before us.

"Kneel in her presence," the selkie commanded, accent thick as he knocked out the back of my knees and pushed me down. He joined me on the deck, one strong hand gripping my shoulder while the other grabbed my arm. Nixy was dragged out and thrown down on the ground beside me, but they left Mairin where she'd been dumped. She sat back on her haunches, her clothing clinging to each curve of her body. Panting, she rubbed her hands down her thighs, and I wanted to go to her, mentally urging her to look at me.

But her eyes were on the nightmare which undulated before us, limbs shrinking and twisting, body turning nearly translucent, matching its underbelly. An echoing crack ripped through the air as bones took shape and form, and I watched in terrified fascination as the creature shifted and changed, body contorting into a more human shape. First one graceful leg, then another, a slender arm and a narrow waist—all slowly turning into what I'd quickly realized was the Sea Queen herself.

She sat cross-legged on the deck, naked, skin so pale I could see her veins. Though it was overcast, there was a slight gleam to it. Her hair was the same deep red color as her other form, far darker than Mairin's hair. Her eyes were very round and large, but more noticeable was the fact her irises were pure white. Everything about her was sharp—cheekbones, limbs, brows. Her body was made to cut. She tucked her hair behind her ear, pointed at the tips with a small frill leading to where an earlobe would have been. She didn't move once she settled in place, her hands resting on her knees. Turning those otherworldly eyes first to Mairin before sweeping them back over to me, she smiled, and each serrated tooth was a threat.

"Little Rin, how nice of you to bring me so many gifts," she whispered, speaking slowly, as if she hadn't done it in quite some time. Truth be told, it was likely she hadn't—a myth made flesh. "When I received your message, I was quite surprised by my honorable daughter." She rolled the word around on her tongue, and I wondered how she didn't cut it with those sharp teeth. "Oisí, give her the pendant."

A selkie who had knelt near the queen rose. He shared similar features to Mairin, but his hair was a strawberry blond color, and I wondered if he was one of the hundreds of princes the Sea Queen supposedly had birthed. But I dismissed those thoughts, wondering what the hell was going on. She gave Mairin her pendant so soon when the merrow hadn't even asked her for it. I felt my brow furrow as I attempted to gain Mairin's attention, but she wouldn't spare me a glance as the selkie handed her what looked like a shell on a string.

"You may go now, little one. I have no need for you, especially since you failed in delivering the rogue merrow to me."

"That wasn't the deal," Mairin argued, and I ground my teeth. My heart raced, and my blood heated. What deal was she talking about? "The dragon wasn't part of it either!"

"Oisí?" the queen purred, and the selkie in question hoisted Mairin into his arms, despite her protests, and threw her overboard. I shrieked, jumping to my feet. The selkie who held me lost his grip, and I ran toward the railing.

I watched Mairin as she tread water, shucking off her clothes as her skin turned iridescent, taking on a bluish tint, and her hair darkened. Though looking at her from above, I couldn't see most of the changes, but it was impossible to miss as her legs fused together and grew longer. It was strangely horrifying to see the fins spread from the end of her tail, the skin turning a shade of deep scarlet. She rolled over to float on her back as her tail splashed in the water.

She was breathtaking. Her skin shimmered in the sun, her plump curves somehow catching every angle of the light. She glowed. Her eyes were closed where she floated, her hair drifting out around her. She hadn't been in this form for at least a decade, and it was clear that being in it made her forget all the rest. A small smile tipped up her lips, and though I couldn't see her ears, I wondered if they looked like her mother's.

I wanted to trace them with my teeth.

Two hands gripped me as the evocative melody began once more, and I grew pliant in the selkie's hold as I was turned to face the Sea Queen. Her lips didn't move as the song continued, but it came from her all the same. At her nod, he brought me closer to her and sat me down, arranging my limbs so I was her mirror—legs crossed and hands on my knees. Bumps of cold chill formed on my skin, and the selkie dropped a cloak around my shoulders, putting the hood up to protect me from the wind.

"Hello, sweet Lavenia, Princess of Vesta. My name is Estri, and I am quite sorry about your dragon."

"It's alright," I found myself saying, though the words tasted sour, and I forced out a question. "Why?"

She only blinked at me, those milky irises a little less unsettling than before. She smiled softly, hiding most of her teeth. "My other form often falls prey to baser instincts. It saw something new and shiny, and it wanted it." I felt myself nodding, as if that explanation was enough for her killing Hyše. "These two forms are not ones I am often in. I much prefer my merrow form or selkie form. But it would seem they all have one thing in common. It is just a question of if I can control it or not."

"What do you mean?" I asked.

"A lust for treasure. And this form, this body, has its sight set on a rare one."

She cocked her head to the side as the melody grew more frantic, a beat which rose and fell in tandem with my heart. Her eyes slid down my face to my breasts, and though part of me was appalled, frightened even, my nipples still peaked, and I felt my pulse grow stronger between my legs.

"Quit that," I snapped as I closed my eyes, swallowing as I tried to stop listening.

"My daughter brought you here, knowing I have not once forged any kind of bargain with a conduit in the last three millennia. And she brought something which belongs to me along with her to sweeten it, though the one you call Fiona slipped away before I could give her the hello she deserved."

The song continued in the same way, causing heat I didn't want to spark between my legs. I closed my eyes, hearing her words in my mind again, focusing on them and trying to pick apart what she'd said. Mairin brought me here knowing there was no point in making a deal?

"I'll give you anything your heart desires—an army, a palace made of the finest pearls, whatever you wish."

"In exchange for what?" I asked.

"One night with me before I send you on your way with whatever you need."

"Nothing more?" Surely there had to be something else.

She leaned forward, inhaling deeply. I glimpsed her sharpened teeth as she whispered in another language—and yet I somehow still understood. *"To make you in her image and not gift you with her abilities was quite unkind."*

"What?" I breathed.

"I forget how long she's been gone. Of course, you do not know." She used freezing cold fingertips to tuck one of my braids behind my ear. "Rhia wore her hair loose." She sat back, posture straight as she traced her hand over her body, the rasp of her skin touching told me the texture wasn't as smooth as it looked. The harsh angles of her ribs as her long fingers slid down the ridges drew my attention to the tiniest of scales which glinted enticingly. Letting her words sink in, my tongue slipped out and wet my lips. "One night with me, and I will give you my armies. Come back to me after, and I will give you the world," she whispered.

CHAPTER 62

Dewalt

"Hello there, scoundrel."

I blinked, opening my eyes, finding myself lying in the meadow. Logically, I knew I wasn't really there—I was bleeding out beside the dormitory on the edge of the capital. Either I'd died, or this was my mind's way of easing my suffering as I went. But the voice was one I'd dreamed of so many times, and I smiled. She leaned over me, the sun shining behind her and causing her white hair to sparkle.

"Lu?" I asked, unable to focus on her face.

"You don't look much older."

I sat up and rubbed my eyes. It was her, alright. Long, pin-straight white hair, depthless blue eyes, and a disarming smile. She wore a white dress, just like the ones she'd always been forced to wear. Barefoot, she wiggled her toes in the grass. Gods, she looked young. Though I only looked a few years older than when she died, aging prevented by the bond I'd shared with Ven, I was two decades older than her by now. I'd gotten used to the idea of her looking so young, what with seeing her niece every day, but it still took me by surprise. I supposed in my mind's vision of her, I'd always aged her up along with me. I'd begun to picture her the way she was but a bit older, filling in the gaps with what Emma looked like now.

"Neither do you," I said, giving her a half-smile. Gods, I knew this wasn't real and it couldn't last, but seeing her again was something I'd have given anything for all these years.

"Your hair is so long," she said, awe in her tone as a hand reached toward me. But she pulled away too soon. "You're not supposed to be here," she frowned. "I never *saw* it."

"What do you mean?"

She smiled at me, soft and sad. "I had my first vision when I was fifteen. Most seers know what they are far earlier. Mother knew when she was five. She never told anyone, not even Papa, because she said people treat you differently. I suppose she told him eventually. After..." She rolled her lips in, a nervous habit of hers which made my heart ache. Something I'd forgotten. "My first vision was one of Ravemont—empty. It scared me, and I thought it was a bad dream. The only reason I even told Mama about it was because she *saw* the truth and knew I needed guidance."

She settled onto the ground, hands tucked neatly on her lap. I couldn't believe I was sitting across from her. I could barely process what she'd said. Lucia had been a seer? Her mother?

"The goddess owes me a favor." Her jaw was set, and she had a tightness in her eyes I didn't recognize.

"Which one?" I asked.

Lucia merely smiled at me, unanswering. "This was my favor."

"Speaking to me?"

"Allowing me to release the tether I have on you."

"I'm here now though. You don't have to," I argued, adjusting to sit cross-legged in the grass. In my periphery, I saw my torn shirt, blood and gore beneath it, and I did my best to cover it up. She noticed, nose crinkling in disgust as she eyed my injury. "You were a seer and didn't tell anyone? Not even Emma?" I hesitated for only a second before adding, "Not even me?"

"I *am* a seer. And I told no one because I knew what was going to happen that night."

"What?" I demanded.

"My first vision was Ravemont sitting empty. The second showed me the outcome of this world if I didn't die then. I was sixteen when it happened." She didn't sound sad, but I wanted to pull her into my arms anyway. But something made me feel as if I shouldn't. It wasn't right, and I couldn't understand why. "My third vision happened the winter before I...left."

"The winter we wrote to each other?"

"Yes, when you wrote me and made me fall in love with you." Her blue eyes filled with tears as she took my hands in hers. "I saw two visions that winter. Another of what the world would be like if I didn't die that night. And then one that showed me what it could be if I did."

Revulsion hit me. She'd lived with that knowledge on her own and hadn't told me? Hadn't told anyone?

"Lu...there had to have been some way—"

She laughed, a beautiful tinkling sound I heard in my best dreams. "There was. And each one more selfish than the last. I had no choice but to allow things to happen the way they did."

I studied her. The fine hair on her arms which caught the light. The silk of her hair draped over her shoulder. A soul-shredding smile. Her spark had been snuffed far too soon—and because she let it happen.

"Why didn't you tell me? I would have—I don't know, I would have savored it. Savored us. I would have held on and never let you go."

"That's exactly why I couldn't tell you. Because you wouldn't have let me go," she said, chin trembling.

"You're right." I shook my head and tossed my hair over my shoulder. "Would that have been so bad?"

"Yes," she replied, voice firm. "I've had a long time to think about my decision. I don't regret it."

Though I knew she meant more than staying with me, it hurt to hear her say it would've been bad. That she didn't regret leaving me. I'd spent so many years thinking about what our lives would have been like had she survived. The odds were good it wouldn't have been what either of us counted on; with her betrothal to Rainier, things would have been difficult. But if none of us wanted that, would it have been so hard to stop it? If we'd all figured it out a little bit sooner?

"I loved you so much," she said, her smile breaking my heart in two. "It's funny. I can't remember if I ever told you that."

"You didn't. When I said it to you, gods, you looked so beautiful in that pink dress. But you never said it back."

"I remember now." She released my hands and rubbed her face. "It didn't make it any easier, did it? My refusing to say it back?"

I shook my head and clasped my own hands together, suddenly empty. I heard something behind me, and I glanced over my shoulder, only finding the trees at the edge of the meadow swaying in the breeze.

"I'm sorry I was selfish. I-I didn't want to say it. To make it harder. But I tried to show you," she offered.

"You did. You showed me every day." A realization occurred to me, and I felt sick with dread over it. "The night before, when we—when I—"

When I'd made love to her in the olive grove the night before she died, she'd cried after. Huge, gasping breaths, she sobbed in my arms. The night when I almost took her to Emma, almost woke up her sister to heal her, thinking I'd hurt her. She'd begged me to hold her until the sun rose, and I'd done it, eager to stop her tears. She hadn't been crying in pain. It had been because she knew she was going to die, and she was scared. A choking breath escaped me, and she dipped her head so I couldn't look her in the eyes.

"I knew, and it was the most selfish thing I'd ever done. I didn't have a right to take that from you when you didn't know the truth." She wiped her face and looked away. "You need to go back," she said, voice resolute without a hint of hesitation. "Or else it—I made the choice I did for you, Dewalt."

"Why would you—what? What do you even mean?"

"You were always going to outlive me, in every vision I had. And me dying when I did was a decent outcome for the world—for my sister and Rainier. But it was also the only one where you could be happy again. If I hesitated, if I let it go any longer, you never would have—"

She looked away and bit her lip, tears forming on her lashes, and I felt my own lip quiver.

"Were—are we twin flames? Is that why this has been so gods damned hard? Is that what you mean?"

"Almost," she said with a small smile on her face. A secret. That's what that smile was. Those smiles were the ones she'd reserved only for me. She gave everyone her loud joy, her robust happiness. But she only ever gave me her softness. That smile was just for me.

"Almost?" I asked, eyes wet.

"We might have been, if I hadn't—" She looked away. "Rhia told me after, on my way to, well, where I've been...We might have been twin flames. Or we might not have been. Twin flames aren't what we think they are. They're made. We weren't there yet, but we might have been one day."

I nodded, throat bobbing. I heard a whisper behind me, but I ignored it, only able to focus on the shining light in front of me. Greedily, I soaked up her image.

"That's why I had to leave when I did. I didn't like what you became in the visions I had. The ones where I died anyway. You were never truly happy again. You were cold—cruel, even. I didn't want that for you."

"But that wasn't your choice to make," I replied. "You—you changed my future. My future was supposed to be you, Lu."

She smiled, that same soft smile she let grow into a radiant one.

"No. No, you're wrong. I was always part of your journey, but never where you ended up."

Unbidden, an image of Nor appeared in my mind. The look she'd given me as she tucked her hair behind her ear just hours prior. Flushed and embarrassed because I'd dismissed her. The desire to kiss her was just as potent now as it had been, and the same nausea which roiled in my stomach then, when I had her pinned to that desk, returned in force. I shook my head, feeling guilty for thinking of Nor while I was in Lucia's presence. Something I'd dreamed of for so gods damned long, and I let thoughts of the novice taint it. I did my best to banish those bewitching hazel eyes from my mind.

"What if I stay? What if I don't go back?"

"You don't want that. I know you don't. Your heart—" She shook her head. "Let her finish mending it." It was rare she let me see her sorrow, but she did even as a smile graced her features. "And you are just as important in this—this—upheaval," she said, "as my sister and Rainier. Do not let yourself think otherwise."

"Emma is the Beloved. They share divinity. I'm not—"

"I'd have hoped you would have stopped doing that by now." Her smile had turned into a frown, and she gripped my hands in hers. "Dewalt, you have to believe me. You are far more important than you've ever given yourself credit for. And you deserve to be happy." Leaning forward, she tucked my hair behind my ears as a smile lit up her face. "I like what she's done with it."

Not knowing what she was talking about, I glanced down, finding my hair shorter, barely to my shoulder, and uneven as all hell.

Lucia laughed, sitting back on her heels. "It needs some refinement, but so do you, scoundrel."

"*Stay with me. Please.*" The voice interrupted us, and each bone in my body, every hum of my divinity, wanted me to obey it. A soft melody reached my ears, and my body relaxed incrementally. I found myself lulled by it, closing my eyes, even though I didn't want to stop looking at Lu.

"It is not just her who will make you happy if you let her. You will be more to her than you ever have been to anyone else. Including me." When I opened my eyes, I found her wearing a sad smile as she peered over my shoulder. "Our time is running out, Dewalt."

"It's not fair."

Mischievous eyes met mine. "It never is, but this is the best you're going to get. You never got to say goodbye, and you've been tangled up with me ever since. This is our chance."

Lucia leaned forward, hugging me, and a small golden spot in my heart dimmed and faded as she whispered farewells I'd longed for and secrets she'd kept.

CHAPTER 63

Rainier

Unable to move, useless in all the ways which counted, I watched as that beautiful girl—my flesh and blood—threw herself at the monstrous man trying to kill us both. A blur of white hair and yellow dress mussed by the fire's ash, she collided with him, wrapping delicate arms around his neck. Her hand glowed white, and he jerked away from her touch. My voice grew hoarse from all my shouting as he reacted in shock—giving her a sick version of an embrace as he wrapped one arm around her waist while she clung to him.

Stopping my assault of rock and earth so as not to hurt her, I fought with all of my might against the shadows which had grown taut around me. Declan let out a surprised laugh before throwing her to the ground at his feet. She landed hard on her knees as he used his dark divinity to restrain her.

"Precious," Declan said, laughter in his voice as he lifted his hand to his neck where she'd burned him. "Did you think to burn my head off, little girl?" He froze when we heard the first dragon's roar, and he closed his eyes when the others joined in. "I'd hoped you had kept your beasts in that little hovel in the mountains."

The scream of an itzki made him jump, and as Lux and Shika flew over us, circling, he moved to stand between me and Elora. The coward knew our dragons held fire, and he sought to protect himself. He couldn't know the fire breathers wouldn't have used their flames, not without being commanded to do so. Although, I wasn't sure how they'd react to us being threatened. Either way, Lux circled above, watching. Shika bullied the itzki who held Cyran though, chasing the monster as it soared higher.

"Make her stop!" Elora yelled, head whipping around. Her eyes bulged as she looked into the sky, and I didn't know what to do. I called out in hopes the dragon would hear me, but one of Declan's shadows covered my mouth, muffling me. I began my assault with the earth once more now that Elora was out of the way, but he merely shook his head in annoyance as he batted the bigger rocks away with little effort.

I instinctively reached for the divine fire once more, but without the use of my hands, I couldn't control it properly. The bond had felt off with her ever since Cyran first began to fall, and I didn't know why. Those glimmering strands led to her, as they always did, but it was as if she was fading at the end of it. It filled me with the same dread I'd felt when the masters had taken her. Was she still at the dormitory? Outside whatever wards Declan had drawn? Was that the reason for the bond's state? The solution came to me unbidden, the utilization of my divinity in that way the last fucking thing I ever wanted to do, but I would do it to save us both. I closed my eyes, concentrating on doing to Declan what I'd done to those Folterran soldiers all those years ago. But it wouldn't work, not the way it was supposed to. It resisted my divinity, his blood repellant.

Declan grunted and toed Elora with his boot, knocking her off her knees onto her backside. I growled in warning, though there was nothing I could fucking do, wrapped up as I was. He'd relented a bit though, not holding me as tightly when he split his divinity between Elora and me, so I began wiggling, trying to pull myself free. I continued trying to draw his blood from his body, and he coughed, causing my heart to speed up. But when he lifted his hand to his lips, he flicked away a few drops of black liquid, unfazed.

"I suppose your blood might work," he pondered as his gaze lingered on Elora for far too long. I would rip his head off his fucking shoulders. His shadows loosened even more as he stepped in front of her, facing both of us once more. "If it weren't for those bloody dragons, I'd wait. Though there is that pesky matter of my heir." As far as I knew, he hadn't named an heir from his plethora of children, and he didn't have any with his bonded partner, so I wasn't sure what he spoke of. Unless he meant Cyran. He rubbed at his chin, deep in thought, and I watched as his shadows slid up behind him, dancing like flames. My bonds loosened once more, and I wondered just how distracted he was.

One black plume slithered over his shoulder, and he looked at it in annoyance before flapping his hand at it in dismissal. Elora gasped, spine tightening as the dark divinity surrounding her fell away.

I realized it just as he did.

He lunged for Elora as my surrounding shadows released and surged toward him. We both jumped to our feet, and she turned that dark divinity on him as she stumbled backward into me. I felt a tug on the bond from Em, but I held Elora's arms, bracing her as she tightened the shadows around Declan, groaning with the effort.

"You're a siphon," I breathed, and my jaw fell open a moment before I pressed a kiss to the top of her head. My brilliant daughter had saved us, and nothing could hold back my affection. I almost wrapped my arms around her but knew she needed to focus.

"Not a very good one," she grunted. "I'm trying."

"The shadows are a tool. An extension of you. Use your fist to help guide the power," I instructed as Declan's wailing turned into panicked screams. I heard a shriek above, and Cyran began falling once more as the itzki dropped him, diving toward its master. Shika intercepted the creature though, and I turned my attention on the falling prince as my dragon dove out of sight. "You can do it, Elora," I said. She tensed as Cyran's screams drew close enough for us to hear him. "I've got him. Don't worry. I've got you."

Keeping one hand gripping her upper arm, I used my wind to slow the prince's descent, and his screams died down as I guided him slowly to the ground, where he lay in a crumpled heap.

Elora shook as Declan fought against her shadows, but I pulled her against my chest and put my hands on her shoulders.

"If you need me to get my sword to finish this, I will. This is a lot for you to—"

"No," she gritted out, readjusting her stance. "I want to do it. For you, for Cy, for me."

"Alright, little one," I said, squeezing her shoulders in encouragement. She lifted both arms in front of her, fists clenched and knuckles white. She had far greater control than I did of the shadows as Declan lifted into the air. Writhing and shrieking, he tried to escape his fate, but the sound of his bones popping and cracking wrenched through the air—and then there was silence.

She held him there, fists shaking, until I reached forward, circling her wrists with my hands, and she released her hold. Declan dropped to the ground, shadows vanishing, as her hands fell down to her sides.

"Is he dead?" she whispered, and I used Em's harrowing to know for sure.

"Yes. He's dead."

"Good," she said before flames erupted from her hands, clear in her intent to burn his body.

"Wait!" I cried out just as the itzki fell from above, tumbling out of Shika's grasp as it disintegrated into ash. They were tied to him, just as the dragons were tied to Em. Elora's hands were still out, ready to burn Declan's body with the fire she held in her fingertips, but I approached him and knelt. "Look at this," I said. "Tell me I'm seeing what I think I'm seeing."

His ears had changed, narrowing to sharp points at the top.

"Elven," Elora said on an awe-filled breath. "Did he use magick to hide it?"

I reached out with a fingertip, lifting his lip to confirm the sharpened teeth.

"Boy!" I shouted, turning toward the prince, who sat on the ground with a blank look as he took in the body of his brother. "Oh, gods," I said to myself, realizing that while I'd saved him from death, he was now coming to terms with a life he never would have expected. He was the last of the Umbroth line if Declan had never named an heir, and now, he would shoulder the burden of his kingdom. Prince no more, the boy with tear tracks running down his face and his hands in his hair was the king of Folterra.

"He'll be alright," Elora said, brow wrinkling as she bit her lip. She was as unconvinced by her words as I was.

I stood, crossing my arms as I took in the body before me. "I don't want to burn him. Not until I have someone look at the body. Using that kind of magick to hide it means..." I shook my head. "I want to know more."

She nodded and stepped back, and I used my divinity to enclose his body in stone and earth before burying it in the courtyard. With a wave of my arm, I gestured for the dragons who still circled above, all six waiting for my signal. I didn't yet know how to communicate that I didn't need all six of them at the moment, so I waited as they landed.

"Your meetings with Shivani?" I asked, turning toward the best thing I'd ever done.

"I wanted to master it before I showed you and Mama," she replied, cheeks going pink.

"And my mother let you keep that secret? She didn't want to brag about it?"

"Oh, she does, but I think she feels bad about how she's acted. So, she does her best to make me happy."

Her sheepish smile made me chuckle, and I stepped toward her, wanting to embrace her, but hesitated. Just because I felt a certain way toward her, and I suspected she might return my affection, I didn't want to press my luck. So, I stood there, not even realizing my arm had stretched toward her while the other hung at my side. She eyed me for a moment before she surged toward me. Wrapping her arms around my waist, she buried her face in my chest.

"That was terrifying," she said with a sniffle.

"I know," I soothed, running a hand down her back. "I'm sorry I didn't—my own divinity wasn't a match for his, and I was afraid to use your mother's until it was too late. It shouldn't have come down to you."

"You helped me though, at the end. I only knew I could do it because of you."

As I held her tightly, I felt another tug down the bond, this one desperate, and everything in me tightened. With Declan dead and the itzkim gone too, I didn't know what could be the cause of her urgent need. "We have to go," I said, before tenderly stepping out of Elora's embrace and attempting to open a rift. Even in death, Declan's ward held, and I was further validated in my decision to examine his body. He was far stronger than he had any right to be. When he'd mentioned it, I had assumed he had someone with elf-blood do it, but it had to have been him.

Motioning for the dragons to join us, I laughed as Elora held up her hands, fingertips alight, to prevent Ryo from giving her the wet kiss she anticipated.

"We can't leave him here," she said, nodding past me toward Cyran. He sat motionless, with his hands in his lap and his head down.

"I can't ride with both of you," I replied, equally uncertain about what to do.

"I'll ride Ryo, you take Cy." She paused, blinking rapidly as she eyed me. "I knew you'd catch him. I knew you wouldn't let him fall. Just like you won't let me fall." She hesitated a moment, before rushing out, "I-I love you...Pa. No, that's not right," she mumbled, rubbing her face with one hand in an irritated manner. I held my breath as I waited for her to continue, my heart aching with affection. "I don't—I don't know what to call you anymore. Rainier doesn't feel like enough, but Pa or Papa are wrong. What should I call you?"

"Anything you want," I said, tears in my eyes. "It doesn't matter. You can call me Snoots for all I care." Her eyes lit up, mischief taking root at the idea. Fear for Em's safety was the only thing holding me back from tugging my daughter into my arms, but what she'd given me was a gift. "And I love you too, Elora. Until my last breath," I said. Her eyes watered as she nodded. I treasured the moment, unable to stop smiling even as I boosted the children onto the dragons who waited for us before climbing behind Cyran onto Shika.

The boy shook as we launched into the sky, flying east with the setting sun at our back. Fear and chill and shock probably warred within him, but he didn't speak. I wasn't sure when he would, but I didn't pressure him. When I saw smoke coming from the direction of the dormitory, I tried to stay calm. I knew she'd used her fire, and I could feel her down the bond—however faint. I knew she was alright though. She had to be.

It was hard to see below me between the smoke billowing from the stable and Shika's shadows which never quite left her, but I could make out a few people in the middle of the clearing; and I knew one of them was Em as her head lifted to the skies.

"Oh, fuck."

The body of the man she leaned over was my best friend, and, gods, if he was dead, I didn't know what I would do. Coaxing Shika to obey, I cursed Declan for his gods forsaken wards.

Once Ryo and Shika both landed, I slid down, not even bothering to help Cyran, and ran toward where Em and Nor sat with a bloody Dewalt. Using her divinity, I listened for his heart, and breathed a sigh of relief when I heard it, no matter how slowly it beat. Dewalt's eyes were closed, and I'd never seen him so pale. Nor had her hands on either side of his head where she held it in her lap, and I noticed the hair she'd cut on the ground beside him. She was singing softly, a tear rolling down her cheek.

There was a pang in my chest at the sight. Seeing my closest friend lying slack on the ground made me want to vomit. The man I'd grown up with, who had supported me through all my shit, and who I'd dragged with me my entire life. The man who was so vibrant—now pale and lifeless. My divinity rumbled the earth, despite my attempt to control it.

"Help me, Rain!" Emma shouted, and I knelt beside her.

"Can you not heal him? What can I do?" I said, and she turned her head to look at me, tears running down over mangled skin. "What the fuck happened?" I said, gently grasping her by the chin to look at her.

"Obsidian. Rain, come on, slide your hand under mine. Now," she begged, and I obeyed. The divinity hummed inside me, eager to mend. "From the inside out, so we—so we don't lose him. Start with his heart." Closing my eyes, I felt her hands press over mine, her divinity guiding us both. She'd had years to know what she was doing, and I'd barely mended scraped knees. Nor's shaking breath beside me, where she held my best friend's head in her lap, distracted me, and I did my best to block out all the other sounds.

I lifted my head at the sound of footsteps, and Elora's feet came into view. She gasped as she saw Dewalt on the ground. "Mama? I—I know Dewalt is hurt, I just...Theo is hurt too. He's—he's not really breathing." When Em said nothing, Elora spoke louder. "Mama! What about Theo?"

"I don't know if we can save them both, honey. His—Theo's head is where he's hurt, and you know how hard those injuries are for me. I had to choose, and Dewalt was closer—*is* closer to dying."

Elora stared at her mother for a moment before whipping around and stalking toward the smoking remains of the stable.

"I can do this, Em, if you want to go to the boy."

"No. You can't do this. Not yet. Feel the flow of blood? We need to slow it. Can you feel where it's rushing?" Em asked, voice resolute. "Mend the muscle," she instructed, and though I'd never seen what a human heart looked like, I imagined the exposed muscle I'd seen before on injured soldiers, my own injuries, and thought of the wound mending itself.

"We all can hate me later for my choices," she whispered. "I had to make a decision."

I knew Em would have done her best, choosing what would be most likely to save both of them.

"Oh, good," she said, voice thick, as she noticed the blood slowing. "Thank the gods. I-I think his lung caved in, so if any air escaped it, just—make sure all the air is in his lungs and nowhere else. If you can even feel that."

I nodded, noticing a small pocket of air, perhaps around his heart, and I used my own divinity to move it toward where I thought his lung was. Our two distinct gifts meshed together to help my friend, and Em let out a sob as his heartbeat grew steady.

"Now his lung," she said, sliding our hands downward.

"Don't I need to finish with the hole here?" I asked, eyeing the blood still trickling out of his wound.

"Not as important yet. Need him to get more air."

We continued mending and repairing Dewalt's chest, and Nor's breathing calmed as his own breaths deepened.

"Is he going to wake up?" the novice asked, and I looked over at Em. Every instinct told me to stop what I was doing, to pluck the tiny pieces of offensive rock from her face, to swipe away the blood speckling her chest.

"I don't know," my wife replied. "You're almost done. Move back up and seal the wound," she commanded. She stood, calling for Elora, who refused to move from Theo's side.

"Cyran, are you alright?" I heard Em ask as the boy in question wandered over, hands in his pockets and eyes on the ground.

"My brother is dead, so I ought to be. But so is my sister," he said, and Em didn't hesitate before folding him into an embrace. He bent toward her, allowing her to stroke his hair as she whispered soothing words to him. Injured as she was, I wanted her to take care of herself, but seeing her give her healing love to the child felt right.

She sat on the ground, cross-legged, and pulled Cyran down with her. "Help me so I can help Theo?" she asked, and the boy began to pluck the tiny shards of rock from her face, his elegant hands moving tenderly to help her. "Every single thing you're going to feel is normal, and for these first few days and weeks, you're going to feel them to their fullest extent," she began, quietly for privacy, so I did my best not to listen to her comfort him as I finished mending Dewalt's chest.

A few moments later, once the wound was healed and I sat back to look at my handiwork, she asked me if I was finished.

"I think so. His heart—it all feels right."

She nodded. "Everything sound right?" she asked, and I nodded, realizing she was still saving her divinity. She rose, though Cyran had barely removed any rocks from her skin. But as she turned toward the stable and I joined her, we saw Elora collapse over Theo, sobs shaking her body. And when I listened for the boy's heart, I found nothing.

"His heart stopped. Should I try to do what you did with—"

"We can try, but what I did with Elora—that wasn't me."

When I opened the rift into the stable, Emma bent to place a soothing hand on our daughter's back, and she shrugged it off. I knelt beside the boy and put my hands on his head where the blood had pooled on the ground, but my divinity didn't respond. No humming desire to fix rippled through me, and I glanced over at Em as she knelt beside Elora.

"Nothing to heal?"

"No." I shook my head as Em's lip quivered, and she traced a hand down Elora's back, and this time, our girl bowed into her touch.

An hour later, I had lured Em into the empty bathtub at the estate to gently finish picking pieces of rock out of her face and chest. She focused on her leg while I took care of the rest, and we quietly told each other about the events which had brought us here. The circumstances which led to us burying two bodies within the copse of trees beside the dormitory. What had caused Emma to say goodbye to yet another parental figure, and Elora to cry over the grave of her friend.

I'd rifted the rest of us back to the estate, and the only reason Emma sat calmly for me was so she'd have free access to her divinity once more; we planned to set out to the capital to heal anyone injured in the attack. Dewalt was still sleeping, and Cyran and I had struggled to get him into a bed. His lean body was far heavier than expected. Nor wanted to stay with him and had already retrieved supplies to cleanse his skin of blood.

Watching a bead of Em's own blood trickle down her face caused a surge of anger to flood through me. I was kicking myself for not expecting some sort of surprise attack like this from Declan. All the preparation I'd done, all the soldiers I'd sent to both Lamera and Nara's Cove, had been useless when he created those wicked winged creatures. And the dragons Em had made had clearly given him the idea.

I'd been particularly shocked by the revelation that Nor was Declan's child, and Em had been just as stricken by our siphon surprise. Her instinct was immediately to hide it, to forbid Elora from telling anyone. But after taking a moment to relax with me, she realized because of how she'd handled things with Elora in the past, she had to let it be our daughter's decision. Agency over her own life was something we both desired for Elora, and, despite the inclination to protect her, to hide her away, if Emma took that choice away from her again the damage would be irreparable.

"Do you feel any different?" I asked.

Though neither of us said it in so many words, Declan's fixation with wanting Em's blood made us wonder what kind of favor he had planned to seek from the gods. Why would he need a favor when he could just kill her? What did he want? If he was dead, was this all over? Cyran would rule Folterra, and we'd have an alliance with them for the first time since the failed one over five centuries before.

"No. I feel the same. I am just...full of dread. Did Rhia ever bless him? Was he even the Accursed?" When I shook my head, not having an answer for her, she threw a fistful of bloody rocks she'd collected over the side of the bathtub, cursing. "Is this going to be our lives forever? Zealots who think they are or want to be the Accursed, trying to take what we have? What we will build together?"

"Maybe," I said, wincing sympathetically as I had to dig out an especially deep shard of obsidian from her jaw. "But such is the case of any monarch. There will always be a threat to the Crown."

"Your Majesties!" A voice called out from the hallway as Sterling rapped on the door to our suite. "Come immediately. It is most urgent!"

"Dewalt," Emma gasped, already leaping to her feet. She'd been sitting in her underwear and an unbuttoned shirt, and by the time she got out of the bathtub, I had her robe ready.

"What is it?" I asked as we barreled through the door. I heard my mother's voice shouting from the entryway, and I loosened a breath. I hadn't once thought about her after I left her in the street outside the cafe, and my chest grew tight with thoughts of self-loathing.

"Gods, I'm going to kill her," Emma muttered. "I thought something was wrong with—"

She stopped speaking the moment my mother came into view in the entryway. Gown ripped, hair disheveled, and smelling faintly of ash, she came forward with shaking hands as she handed me a scroll.

"Warric died in my arms after delivering this. H-he didn't even have a chance to shift," she said, lip trembling. I'd never seen her so full of emotion, and I hurried to unroll the scroll in my hands. "Zaph. The—the note in your book. The one Larke wrote to a friend? I couldn't place it, not until now. The Supreme's true name is Zaphus."

I blinked at her, not quite comprehending what she'd said. I read the scroll not once, but twice, and I clenched my fist. The Supreme was the one who obsessed over the prophecy—wanting a favor from the gods. Someone stomped down the stairs behind me, and Em gasped. Within a moment she threw herself at Dewalt and pressed her hand to his shirtless chest, smiling as she felt his heartbeat. I used her harrowing to listen for the sound myself, taking solace in the one good thing to come from these past moments.

"Lucia knew everything—all of it. And gods, do I have some shit to tell you," my friend said, eyes aflame, as he looked at me over Em's head. Nor stood at the top of the steps behind him, tears in her eyes, holding a tight fistful of Dewalt's shorn hair to her chest. I wondered if harsh words from him had put the tears in her eyes because it wasn't joyous relief I saw there.

"What?" Em said, pulling away from the arm our friend had circled around her.

"You better do it quick, because Nereza marches from Lamera with twenty thousand soldiers. They slaughtered the thousand men Raj left behind."

Everyone stilled.

"The Supreme?" Em asked.

"He marches with her."

ACKNOWLEDGMENTS

Phew, this one was a tough one.

Between learning how to author and market, making connections with all new readers, not having a kitchen for over six months, and 60,000 words worth of rewrites back in the spring? This has been difficult. The story has turned darker, our characters have gone through it, and I was struggling to get this book out to you guys on time. BUT what a dang problem to have?! READERS I didn't want to disappoint?!

So firstly, thank YOU! Thank you for reading Between Wrath and Mercy. Thank you for giving me the confidence to keep writing this series and telling Em and Rain's story. Thank you for loving these characters almost as much as I do. Without you guys, I wouldn't be able to keep doing this.

Next I'd like to thank my editor Abby Mann and my alpha reader Heather Nix for saving me from writing some really stupid shit on accident. Thankfully no bathtubs were harmed in the making of book 2. You guys can thank Abby for Nor singing at the end, by the way.

And of course, I couldn't have done it without my beta readers: Priscilla, Laura, Amber, and Emily. And I can't even begin to explain how grateful I am for Ruthie and her guidance in this process. Can't forget my group chat who kept me sane, who helped me toss ideas around, and the FaRoFeb discord for all the guidance a baby author needs. Then there's my influencers who let me send my book to them. Janessa, Bailey, and Nicki – you three *especially* really have no idea how much you changed my life by taking a chance on me and posting about my little (big) self-published book. And my lovely ARC readers? The list goes on. This book wouldn't be anything without everyone who has cheered me on and loved my story. I appreciate every single one of you.

And Nick, thank you for listening to my endless requests of "say something sexy" and replying with something stupid but actually really dishing out the sexy quotes when I least expect it. (Yes, some of Rain's quotes were not actually written by a woman. I KNOW! Blasphemy!) Anyway, you're pretty alright. Let's keep forgetting our anniversary together for forever. Love you.

Some Extra Information

That cool tooth paternity thing with Shivani, Rain, and Elora? That's real! Ask me how I know, haha! My mom still has a baby tooth—no adult tooth ever grew in! I had the same situation in the SAME SPOT as my mom, but mine had to be pulled when I was younger. My son had a slight difference in that one of his baby teeth just never came in, and his dentist told us it was hereditary! He might be missing that molar too when it eventually comes in. Anyway, if you'd like to learn more, look up congenitally missing teeth!

When it came to Dewalt and Thyra's hairstyles, it is clear that Thyra teaches her culture to Dewalt, who was interested in her worshiping of the old gods. Thyra is heavily inspired by the Vikings. (Or rather the fictional versions we see on television which have taken quite a bit of creative liberties.) That being said, ritualistic hair styles are prevalent in many different cultures, and I was inspired by multiple different cultures and traditions. I find it fascinating how important hair is and has been all over the world. Here are some really interesting links to take a look at:

https://rudilewis.com/the-ceremony-of-hair/
https://www.vox.com/ad/15453466/chelsey-luger

About the Author

Jess Wisecup was born and raised in Ohio. Growing up, Jess loved to read and dove headfirst into any fantasy world she could get her hands on. She is a stay-at-home mother who has lived all over the country the past six years, and currently resides in coastal Virginia. Her husband, two kids, and two giant dogs keep her busy. If she isn't busy writing, she's busy reading and drinking iced coffee.

To learn more about Jess or her books, visit her at https://beacons.ai/jesswisecup for all social media and website links, or scan the QR code below with your mobile device.

Make sure to PREORDER Book THREE in the DIVINE BETWEEN SERIES

Made in the USA
Middletown, DE
07 April 2023

28223596R00352